THE FAULKNER READER

Soldier's Pay

Sartoris

Mosquitoes

The Sound and the Fury

As I Lay Dying   **Books by William Faulkner**

Sanctuary

These Thirteen (Short Stories)

Light in August

A Green Bough (Poems)

Doctor Martino and Other Stories

Pylon

Absalom, Absalom!

The Unvanquished

The Wild Palms

The Hamlet

Go Down, Moses

Intruder in the Dust

Knight's Gambit

Collected Stories

Requiem for a Nun

THE FAULKNER READER

Selections from the works of

WILLIAM FAULKNER

RANDOM
HOUSE
NEW YORK

v

Contents

Contents

Foreword

MY GRANDFATHER had a moderate though reasonably diffuse and catholic library; I realize now that I got most of my early education in it. It was a little limited in its fiction content, since his taste was for simple straightforward romantic excitement like Scott or Dumas. But there was a heterogeneous scattering of other volumes, chosen apparently at random and by my grandmother, since the flyleaves bore her name and the dates in the 1880's and '90's of that time when even in a town as big as Memphis, Tennessee, ladies stopped in their carriages in the street in front of the stores and shops, and clerks and even proprietors came out to receive their commands— that time when women did most of the book-buying and the reading too, naming their children Byron and Clarissa and St. Elmo and Lothair after the romantic and tragic heroes and heroines and the even more romantic creators of them.

One of these books was by a Pole, Sienkiewicz—a story of the time of King John Sobieski, when the Poles, almost single-handed, kept the Turks from overrunning Central Europe. This one, like all books of that period, at least the ones my grandfather owned, had a preface, a foreword. I never read any of them; I was too eager to get on to what the people themselves were doing and anguishing and triumphing over. But I did read the foreword in this one, the first one I ever took time to read; I don't know why now. It went something like this:

This book was written at the expense of considerable effort, to uplift men's hearts, and I thought: *What a nice thing to have thought to say.* But no more than that. I didn't even think, *Maybe some day I will write a book too and what a shame I didn't think of that first so I could put it on the front page of mine.* Because I hadn't thought of writing books then. The future didn't extend that far. This was 1915 and '16; I had seen an aeroplane and my mind was filled with names: Ball, and Immelman and Boelcke, and Guynemer and Bishop, and I was waiting, biding, until I would be old enough or free enough or anyway could get to France and become glorious and beribboned too.

Then that had passed. It was 1923 and I wrote a book and discovered that my doom, fate, was to keep on writing books: not for any exterior or ulterior purpose: just writing the books for the sake of writing the books; obviously, since the publisher considered them worth the financial risk of being printed, someone would read them. But that was unimportant too as measured against the need to get them written, though naturally one hopes that who read them would find them true and honest and even perhaps moving. Because one was too busy writing the books during the time while the demon which drove him still considered him worthy of, deserving of, the anguish of being driven, while the blood and glands and flesh still remained strong and potent, the heart and the imagination still remained undulled to follies and lusts and heroisms of men and women; still writing the books because they had to be written after the blood and glands began to slow and cool a little and the heart began to tell him, *You don't know the answer either and you will never find it,* but still writing the books because the demon was still kind; only a little more severe and unpitying: until suddenly one day he saw that that old half-forgotten Pole had had the answer all the time.

To uplift man's heart; the same for all of us: for the ones who are trying to be artists, the ones who are trying to write simple entertainment, the ones who write to shock, and the ones who are simply escaping themselves and their own private anguishes.

Some of us don't know that this is what we are writing for. Some of us will know it and deny it, lest we be accused and self-convicted and condemned of sentimentality, which people nowadays for some reason are ashamed to be tainted with; some of us seem to have curious ideas of just where the heart is located, confusing it with other and baser glands and organs and activities. But we all write for this one purpose.

This does not mean that we are trying to change man, improve him, though this is the hope—maybe even the intention—of some of us. On the contrary, in its last analysis, this hope and desire to uplift man's heart is completely selfish, completely personal. He would lift up man's heart for his own benefit because in that way he can say No to death. He is saying No to death for himself by means of the hearts which he has hoped to uplift, or even by means of the mere base glands which he has disturbed to that extent where they can say No to death on their own account by knowing, realizing, having been told and believing it: *At least we are not vegetables because the hearts and glands capable of partaking in this excitement are not those of vegetables, and will, must, endure.*

So he who, from the isolation of cold impersonal print, can engender this excitement, himself partakes of the immortality which he has engendered. Some day he will be no more, which will not matter then, because isolated and itself invulnerable in the cold print remains that which is capable of engendering still the old deathless excitement in hearts and glands whose owners and custodians are generations from even the air he breathed and anguished in; if it was capable once, he knows that it will be capable and potent still long after there remains of him only a dead and fading name.

New York
November, 1953

THE FAULKNER READER

William Faulkner's Speech of Acceptance upon the award of the Nobel Prize for Literature,

delivered in Stockholm on the tenth of December,
nineteen hundred fifty

I FEEL THAT THIS AWARD WAS NOT MADE TO ME AS A MAN, BUT TO MY work—a life's work in the agony and sweat of the human spirit, not for glory and least of all for profit, but to create out of the materials of the human spirit something which did not exist before. So this award is only mine in trust. It will not be difficult to find a dedication for the money part of it commensurate with the purpose and significance of its origin. But I would like to do the same with the acclaim too, by using this moment as a pinnacle from which I might be listened to by the young men and women already dedicated to the same anguish and travail, among whom is already that one who will some day stand here where I am standing.

Our tragedy today is a general and universal physical fear so long sustained by now that we can even bear it. There are no longer problems of the spirit. There is only the question: When will I be blown up? Because of this, the young man or woman writing to-day has forgotten the problems of the human heart in conflict with itself which alone can make good writing because only that is worth writing about, worth the agony and the sweat.

He must learn them again. He must teach himself that the basest of all things is to be afraid; and, teaching himself that, forget it for-ever, leaving no room in his workshop for anything but the old veri-ties and truths of the heart, the old universal truths lacking which any story is ephemeral and doomed—love and honor and pity and pride and compassion and sacrifice. Until he does so, he labors under a curse. He writes not of love but of lust, of defeats in which nobody loses anything of value, of victories without hope and, worst of all, without pity or compassion. His griefs grieve on no universal bones, leaving no scars. He writes not of the heart but of the glands.

Until he relearns these things, he will write as though he stood among and watched the end of man. I decline to accept the end of man. It is easy enough to say that man is immortal simply because he will endure: that when the last ding-dong of doom has clanged and faded from the last worthless rock hanging tideless in the last red and dying evening, that even then there will still be one more sound: that of his puny inexhaustible voice, still talking. I refuse to accept this. I believe that man will not merely endure: he will prevail. He is immortal, not because he alone among creatures has an inexhaustible voice, but because he has a soul, a spirit capable of compassion and sacrifice and endurance. The poet's, the writer's, duty is to write about these things. It is his privilege to help man endure by lifting his heart, by reminding him of the courage and honor and hope and pride and compassion and pity and sacrifice which have been the glory of his past. The poet's voice need not merely be the record of man, it can be one of the props, the pillars to help him endure and prevail.

The Sound and the Fury

Through the fence, between the curling flower spaces, I could see them hitting. They were coming toward where the flag was and I went along the fence. Luster was hunting in the grass by the flower tree. They took the flag out, and they were hitting. Then they put the flag back and they went to the table, and he hit and the other hit. Then they went on, and I went along the fence. Luster came away from the flower tree and we went along the fence and they stopped and we stopped and I looked through the fence while Luster was hunting in the grass.

"Here, caddie." He hit. They went away across the pasture. I held to the fence and watched them going away.

"Listen at you, now." Luster said. "Aint you something, thirty-three years old, going on that way. After I done went all the way to town to buy you that cake. Hush up that moaning. Aint you going to help me find that quarter so I can go to the show tonight."

They were hitting little, across the pasture. I went along the fence to where the flag was. It flapped on the bright grass and the trees.

"Come on." Luster said. "We done looked there. They aint no more coming right now. Lets go down to the branch and find that quarter before them niggers finds it."

It was red, flapping on the pasture. Then there was a bird slanting and tilting on it. Luster threw. The flag flapped on the bright grass and the trees. I held to the fence.

"Shut up that moaning." Luster said. "I cant make them come if they aint coming, can I. If you dont hush up, mammy aint going

5

to have no birthday for you. If you dont hush, you know what I going to do. I going to eat that cake all up. Eat them candles, too. Eat all them thirty-three candles. Come on, let's go down to the branch. I got to find my quarter. Maybe we can find one of they balls. Here. Here they is. Way over yonder. See." He came to the fence and pointed his arm. "See them. They aint coming back here no more. Come on."

We went along the fence and came to the garden fence, where our shadows were. My shadow was higher than Luster's on the fence. We came to the broken place and went through it.

"Wait a minute." Luster said. "You snagged on that nail again. Cant you never crawl through here without snagging on that nail."

Caddy uncaught me and we crawled through. Uncle Maury said to not let anybody see us, so we better stoop over, Caddy said. Stoop over, Benjy. Like this, see. We stooped over and crossed the garden, where the flowers rasped and rattled against us. The ground was hard. We climbed the fence, where the pigs were grunting and snuffing. I expect they're sorry because one of them got killed today, Caddy said. The ground was hard, churned and knotted.

Keep your hands in your pockets, Caddy said. Or they'll get froze. You don't want your hands froze on Christmas, do you.

"It's too cold out there." Versh said. "You dont want to go out doors."

"What is it now." Mother said.

"He want to go out doors." Versh said.

"Let him go." Uncle Maury said.

"It's too cold." Mother said. "He'd better stay in. Benjamin. Stop that, now."

"It wont hurt him." Uncle Maury said.

"You, Benjamin." Mother said. "If you dont be good, you'll have to go to the kitchen."

"Mammy say keep him out the kitchen today." Versh said. "She say she got all that cooking to get done."

"Let him go, Caroline." Uncle Maury said. "You'll worry yourself sick over him."

"I know it." Mother said. "It's a judgment on me. I sometimes wonder."

"I know, I know." Uncle Maury said. "You must keep your strength up. I'll make you a toddy."

"It just upsets me that much more." Mother said. "Dont you know it does."

"You'll feel better." Uncle Maury said. "Wrap him up good, boy, and take him out for a while."

Uncle Maury went away. Versh went away.

"Please hush." Mother said. "We're trying to get you out as fast as we can. I dont want you to get sick."

Versh put my overshoes and overcoat on and we took my cap and went out. Uncle Maury was putting the bottle away in the sideboard in the dining-room.

"Keep him out about half an hour, boy." Uncle Maury said. "Keep him in the yard, now."

"Yes, sir." Versh said. "We dont never let him get off the place."

We went out doors. The sun was cold and bright.

"Where you heading for." Versh said. "You dont think you going to town, does you." We went through the rattling leaves. The gate was cold. "You better keep them hands in your pockets." Versh said, "You get them froze onto that gate, then what you do. Whyn't you wait for them in the house." He put my hands into my pockets. I could hear him rattling in the leaves. I could smell the cold. The gate was cold.

"Here some hickeynuts. Whooey. Git up that tree. Look here at this squirl, Benjy."

I couldn't feel the gate at all, but I could smell the bright cold.

"You better put them hands back in your pockets."

Caddy was walking. Then she was running, her booksatchel swinging and jouncing behind her.

"Hello, Benjy." Caddy said. She opened the gate and came in and stooped down. Caddy smelled like leaves. "Did you come to meet me." she said. "Did you come to meet Caddy. What did you let him get his hands so cold for, Versh."

"I told him to keep them in his pockets." Versh said. "Holding onto that ahun gate."

"Did you come to meet Caddy." she said, rubbing my hands. "What is it. What are you trying to tell Caddy." Caddy smelled like trees and like when she says we were asleep.

What are you moaning about, Luster said. You can watch them again when we get to the branch. Here. Here's you a jimson weed. He gave me the flower. We went through the fence, into the lot.

"What is it." Caddy said. "What are you trying to tell Caddy. Did they send him out, Versh."

"Couldn't keep him in." Versh said. "He kept on until they let him go and he come right straight down here, looking through the gate."

"What is it." Caddy said. "Did you think it would be Christmas when I came home from school. Is that what you thought. Christmas is the day after tomorrow. Santy Claus, Benjy. Santy Claus. Come on, let's run to the house and get warm." She took my hand and we ran through the bright rustling leaves. We ran up the steps and out of the bright cold, into the dark cold. Uncle Maury was putting the bottle back in the sideboard. He called Caddy. Caddy said,

"Take him in to the fire, Versh. Go with Versh." she said. "I'll come in a minute."

We went to the fire. Mother said,

"Is he cold, Versh."

"Nome." Versh said.

"Take his overcoat and overshoes off." Mother said. "How many times do I have to tell you not to bring him into the house with his overshoes on."

"Yessum." Versh said. "Hold still, now." He took my overshoes off and unbuttoned my coat. Caddy said,

"Wait, Versh. Cant he go out again, Mother. I want him to go with me."

"You'd better leave him here." Uncle Maury said. "He's been out enough today."

"I think you'd both better stay in." Mother said. "It's getting colder, Dilsey says."

"Oh, Mother." Caddy said.

"Nonsense." Uncle Maury said. "She's been in school all day. She needs the fresh air. Run along, Candace."

"Let him go, Mother." Caddy said. "Please. You know he'll cry."

"Then why did you mention it before him." Mother said. "Why did you come in here. To give him some excuse to worry me again. You've been out enough today. I think you'd better sit down here and play with him."

"Let them go, Caroline." Uncle Maury said. "A little cold wont hurt them. Remember, you've got to keep your strength up."

"I know." Mother said. "Nobody knows how I dread Christmas.

Nobody knows. I am not one of those women who can stand things. I wish for Jason's and the children's sakes I was stronger."

"You must do the best you can and not let them worry you." Uncle Maury said. "Run along, you two. But dont stay out long, now. Your mother will worry."

"Yes, sir." Caddy said. "Come on, Benjy. We're going out doors again." She buttoned my coat and we went toward the door.

"Are you going to take that baby out without his overshoes." Mother said. "Do you want to make him sick, with the house full of company."

"I forgot." Caddy said. "I thought he had them on."

We went back. "You must think." Mother said. *Hold still now* Versh said. He put my overshoes on. "Someday I'll be gone, and you'll have to think for him." *Now stomp* Versh said. "Come here and kiss Mother, Benjamin."

Caddy took me to Mother's chair and Mother took my face in her hands and then she held me against her.

"My poor baby." she said. She let me go. "You and Versh take good care of him, honey."

"Yessum." Caddy said. We went out. Caddy said,

"You needn't go, Versh. I'll keep him for a while."

"All right." Versh said. "I aint going out in that cold for no fun." He went on and we stopped in the hall and Caddy knelt and put her arms around me and her cold bright face against mine. She smelled like trees.

"You're not a poor baby. Are you. You've got your Caddy. Haven't you got your Caddy.

Cant you shut up that moaning and slobbering, Luster said. Aint you shamed of yourself, making all this racket. We passed the carriage house, where the carriage was. It had a new wheel.

"Git in, now, and set still until your maw come." Dilsey said. She shoved me into the carriage. T. P. held the reins. "'Clare I don't see how come Jason wont get a new surrey." Dilsey said. "This thing going to fall to pieces under you all someday. Look at them wheels."

Mother came out, pulling her veil down. She had some flowers.

"Where's Roskus." she said.

"Roskus cant lift his arms, today." Dilsey said. "T. P. can drive all right."

"I'm afraid to." Mother said. "It seems to me you all could furnish me with a driver for the carriage once a week. It's little enough I ask, Lord knows."

"You know just as well as me that Roskus got the rheumatism too bad to do more than he have to, Miss Cahline." Dilsey said. "You come on and get in, now. T. P. can drive you just as good as Roskus."

"I'm afraid to." Mother said. "With the baby."

Dilsey went up the steps. "You calling that thing a baby," she said. She took Mother's arm. "A man big as T. P. Come on, now, if you going."

"I'm afraid to." Mother said. They came down the steps and Dilsey helped Mother in. "Perhaps it'll be the best thing, for all of us." Mother said.

"Aint you shamed, talking that way." Dilsey said. "Dont you know it'll take more than a eighteen year old nigger to make Queenie run away. She older than him and Benjy put together. And dont you start no projecking with Queenie, you hear me, T. P. If you dont drive to suit Miss Cahline, I going to put Roskus on you. He aint too tied up to do that."

"Yessum." T. P. said.

"I just know something will happen." Mother said. "Stop, Benjamin."

"Give him a flower to hold." Dilsey said, "That what he wanting." She reached her hand in.

"No, no." Mother said. "You'll have them all scattered."

"You hold them." Dilsey said. "I'll get him one out." She gave me a flower and her hand went away.

"Go on now, 'fore Quentin see you and have to go too." Dilsey said.

"Where is she." Mother said.

"She down to the house playing with Luster." Dilsey said. "Go on, T. P. Drive that surrey like Roskus told you, now."

"Yessum." T. P. said. "Hum up, Queenie."

"Quentin." Mother said. "Dont let"

"Course I is." Dilsey said.

The carriage jolted and crunched on the drive. "I'm afraid to go and leave Quentin." Mother said. "I'd better not go. T. P." We went through the gate, where it didnt jolt anymore. T. P. hit Queenie with the whip.

"You, T. P." Mother said.

"Got to get her going." T. P. said. "Keep her wake up till we get back to the barn."

"Turn around." Mother said. "I'm afraid to go and leave Quentin."

"Cant turn here." T. P. said. Then it was broader.

"Cant you turn here." Mother said.

"All right." T. P. said. We began to turn.

"You, T. P." Mother said, clutching me.

"I got to turn around somehow." T. P. said. "Whoa, Queenie." We stopped.

"You'll turn us over." Mother said.

"What you want to do, then." T. P. said.

"I'm afraid for you to try to turn around." Mother said.

"Get up, Queenie." T. P. said. We went on.

"I just know Dilsey will let something happen to Quentin while I'm gone." Mother said. "We must hurry back."

"Hum up, there." T. P. said. He hit Queenie with the whip.

"You, T. P." Mother said, clutching me. I could hear Queenie's feet and the bright shapes went smooth and steady on both sides, the shadows of them flowing across Queenie's back. They went on like the bright tops of wheels. Then those on one side stopped at the tall white post where the soldier was. But on the other side they went on smooth and steady, but a little slower.

"What do you want." Jason said. He had his hands in his pockets and a pencil behind his ear.

"We're going to the cemetery." Mother said.

"All right." Jason said. "I dont aim to stop you, do I. Was that all you wanted with me, just to tell me that."

"I know you wont come." Mother said. "I'd feel safer if you would."

"Safe from what." Jason said. "Father and Quentin cant hurt you."

Mother put her handkerchief under her veil. "Stop it, Mother." Jason said. "Do you want to get that damn loony to bawling in the middle of the square. Drive on, T. P."

"Hum up, Queenie." T. P. said.

"It's a judgment on me." Mother said. "But I'll be gone too, soon."

"Here." Jason said.

"Whoa." T. P. said. Jason said,

"Uncle Maury's drawing on you for fifty. What do you want to do about it."

"Why ask me." Mother said. "I dont have any say so. I try not to worry you and Dilsey. I'll be gone soon, and then you"

"Go on, T. P." Jason said.

"Hum up, Queenie." T. P. said. The shapes flowed on. The ones on the other side began again, bright and fast and smooth, like when Caddy says we are going to sleep.

Cry baby, Luster said. Aint you shamed. We went through the barn. The stalls were all open. You aint got no spotted pony to ride now, Luster said. The floor was dry and dusty. The roof was falling. The slanting holes were full of spinning yellow. What do you want to go that way for. You want to get your head knocked off with one of them balls.

"Keep your hands in your pockets." Caddy said, "Or they'll be froze. You dont want your hands froze on Christmas, do you."

We went around the barn. The big cow and the little one were standing in the door, and we could hear Prince and Queenie and Fancy stomping inside the barn. "If it wasn't so cold, we'd ride Fancy." Caddy said, "But it's too cold to hold on today." Then we could see the branch, where the smoke was blowing. "That's where they are killing the pig." Caddy said. "We can come back by there and see them." We went down the hill.

"You want to carry the letter." Caddy said. "You can carry it." She took the letter out of her pocket and put it in mine. "It's a Christmas present." Caddy said. "Uncle Maury is going to surprise Mrs Patterson with it. We got to give it to her without letting anybody see it. Keep your hands in your pockets good, now." We came to the branch.

"It's froze." Caddy said, "Look." She broke the top of the water and held a piece of it against my face. "Ice. That means how cold it is." She helped me across and we went up the hill. "We cant even tell Mother and Father. You know what I think it is. I think it's a surprise for Mother and Father and Mr Patterson both, because Mr Patterson sent you some candy. Do you remember when Mr Patterson sent you some candy last summer."

There was a fence. The vine was dry, and the wind rattled in it.

"Only I dont see why Uncle Maury didn't send Versh." Caddy said. "Versh wont tell." Mrs Patterson was looking out the window.

"You wait here." Caddy said. "Wait right here, now. I'll be back in
a minute. Give me the letter." She took the letter out of my pocket.
"Keep your hands in your pockets." She climbed the fence with
the letter in her hand and went through the brown, rattling flowers.
Mrs Patterson came to the door and opened it and stood there.

*Mr Patterson was chopping in the green flowers. He stopped
chopping and looked at me. Mrs Patterson came across the garden,
running. When I saw her eyes I began to cry. You idiot, Mrs Patterson said, I told him never to send you alone again. Give it to
me. Quick. Mr Patterson came fast, with the hoe. Mrs Patterson
leaned across the fence, reaching her hand. She was trying to
climb the fence. Give it to me, she said, Give it to me. Mr Patterson
climbed the fence. He took the letter. Mrs Patterson's dress was
caught on the fence. I saw her eyes again and I ran down the hill.*

"They aint nothing over yonder but houses." Luster said. "We
going down to the branch."

They were washing down at the branch. One of them was singing. I could smell the clothes flapping, and the smoke blowing
across the branch.

"You stay down here." Luster said. "You aint got no business up
yonder. Them folks hit you, sho."

"What he want to do."

"He dont know what he want to do." Luster said. "He think he
want to go up yonder where they knocking that ball. You sit down
here and play with your jimson weed. Look at them chillen playing
in the branch, if you got to look at something. How come you cant
behave yourself like folks." I sat down on the bank, where they
were washing, and the smoke blowing blue.

"Is you all seen anything of a quarter down here." Luster said.

"What quarter."

"The one I had here this morning." Luster said. "I lost it somewhere. It fell through this here hole in my pocket. If I dont find
it I cant go to the show tonight."

"Where'd you get a quarter, boy. Find it in white folks' pocket
while they aint looking."

"Got it at the getting place." Luster said. "Plenty more where
that one come from. Only I got to find that one. Is you all found it
yet."

"I aint studying no quarter. I got my own business to tend to."

"Come on here." Luster said. "Help me look for it."

"He wouldn't know a quarter if he was to see it, would he."

"He can help look just the same." Luster said. "You all going to the show tonight."

"Dont talk to me about no show. Time I get done over this here tub I be too tired to lift my hand to do nothing."

"I bet you be there." Luster said. "I bet you was there last night. I bet you all be right there when that tent open."

"Be enough niggers there without me. Was last night."

"Nigger's money good as white folks, I reckon."

"White folks gives nigger money because know first white man comes along with a band going to get it all back, so nigger can go to work for some more."

"Aint nobody going make you go to that show."

"Aint yet. Aint thought of it, I reckon."

"What you got against white folks."

"Aint got nothing against them. I goes my way and lets white folks go theirs. I aint studying that show."

"Got a man in it can play a tune on a saw. Play it like a banjo."

"You go last night." Luster said. "I going tonight. If I can find where I lost that quarter."

"You going take him with you, I reckon."

"Me." Luster said. "You reckon I be found anywhere with him, time he start bellering."

"What does you do when he start bellering."

"I whips him." Luster said. He sat down and rolled up his overalls. They played in the branch.

"You all found any balls yet." Luster said.

"Aint you talking biggity. I bet you better not let your grandmammy hear you talking like that."

Luster got into the branch, where they were playing. He hunted in the water, along the bank.

"I had it when we was down here this morning." Luster said.

"Where 'bouts you lose it."

"Right out this here hole in my pocket." Luster said. They hunted in the branch. Then they all stood up quick and stopped, then they splashed and fought in the branch. Luster got it and they squatted in the water, looking up the hill through the bushes.

"Where is they." Luster said.

"Aint in sight yet."

Luster put it in his pocket. They came down the hill.

"Did a ball come down here."

"It ought to be in the water. Didn't any of you boys see it or hear it."

"Aint heard nothing come down here." Luster said. "Heard something hit that tree up yonder. Dont know which way it went."

They looked in the branch.

"Hell. Look along the branch. It came down here. I saw it."

They looked along the branch. Then they went back up the hill.

"Have you got that ball." the boy said.

"What I want with it." Luster said. "I aint seen no ball."

The boy got in the water. He went on. He turned and looked at Luster again. He went on down the branch.

The man said "Caddie" up the hill. The boy got out of the water and went up the hill.

"Now, just listen at you." Luster said. "Hush up."

"What he moaning about now."

"Lawd knows." Luster said. "He just starts like that. He been at it all morning. Cause it his birthday, I reckon."

"How old he."

"He thirty-three." Luster said. "Thirty-three this morning."

"You mean, he been three years old thirty years."

"I going by what mammy say." Luster said. "I dont know. We going to have thirty-three candles on a cake, anyway. Little cake. Wont hardly hold them. Hush up. Come on back here." He came and caught my arm. "You old loony." he said. "You want me to whip you."

"I bet you will."

"I is done it. Hush, now." Luster said. "Aint I told you you cant go up there. They'll knock your head clean off with one of them balls. Come on, here." He pulled me back. "Sit down." I sat down and he took off my shoes and rolled up my trousers. "Now, git in that water and play and see can you stop that slobbering and moaning."

I hushed and got in the water *and Roskus came and said to come to supper and Caddy said,*

It's not supper time yet. I'm not going.

She was wet. We were playing in the branch and Caddy squatted down and got her dress wet and Versh said,

"Your mommer going to whip you for getting your dress wet."

"She's not going to do any such thing." Caddy said.

"How do you know." Quentin said.

"That's all right how I know." Caddy said. "How do you know."

"She said she was." Quentin said. "Besides, I'm older than you."

"I'm seven years old." Caddy said, "I guess I know."

"I'm older than that." Quentin said. "I go to school. Dont I, Versh."

"I'm going to school next year." Caddy said, "When it comes. Aint I, Versh."

"You know she whip you when you get your dress wet." Versh said.

"It's not wet." Caddy said. She stood up in the water and looked at her dress. "I'll take it off." she said. "Then it'll dry."

"I bet you wont." Quentin said.

"I bet I will." Caddy said.

"I bet you better not." Quentin said.

Caddy came to Versh and me and turned her back.

"Unbutton it, Versh." she said.

"Dont you do it, Versh." Quentin said.

"Taint none of my dress." Versh said.

"You unbutton it, Versh." Caddy said, "Or I'll tell Dilsey what you did yesterday." So Versh unbuttoned it.

"You just take your dress off." Quentin said. Caddy took her dress off and threw it on the bank. Then she didn't have on anything but her bodice and drawers, and Quentin slapped her and she slipped and fell down in the water. When she got up she began to splash water on Quentin, and Quentin splashed water on Caddy. Some of it splashed on Versh and me and Versh picked me up and put me on the bank. He said he was going to tell on Caddy and Quentin, and then Quentin and Caddy began to splash water at Versh. He got behind a bush.

"I'm going to tell mammy on you all." Versh said.

Quentin climbed up on the bank and tried to catch Versh, but Versh ran away and Quentin couldn't. When Quentin came back Versh stopped and hollered that he was going to tell. Caddy told him that if he wouldn't tell, they'd let him come back. So Versh said he wouldn't, and they let him.

"Now I guess you're satisfied." Quentin said, "We'll both get whipped now."

"I dont care." Caddy said. "I'll run away."

"Yes you will." Quentin said.

"I'll run away and never come back." Caddy said. I began to cry. Caddy turned around and said "Hush." So I hushed. Then they played in the branch. Jason was playing too. He was by himself further down the branch. Versh came around the bush and lifted me down into the water again. Caddy was all wet and muddy behind, and I started to cry and she came and squatted in the water.

"Hush now." she said. "I'm not going to run away." So I hushed. Caddy smelled like trees in the rain.

What is the matter with you, Luster said. Cant you get done with that moaning and play in the branch like folks.

Whyn't you take him on home. Didn't they told you not to take him off the place.

He still think they own this pasture, Luster said. Cant nobody see down here from the house, noways.

We can. And folks dont like to look at a loony. Taint no luck in it.

Roskus came and said to come to supper and Caddy said it wasn't supper time yet.

"Yes tis." Roskus said. "Dilsey say for you all to come on to the house. Bring them on, Versh." He went up the hill, where the cow was lowing.

"Maybe we'll be dry by the time we get to the house." Quentin said.

"It was all your fault." Caddy said. "I hope we do get whipped." She put her dress on and Versh buttoned it.

"They wont know you got wet." Versh said. "It dont show on you. Less me and Jason tells."

"Are you going to tell, Jason." Caddy said.

"Tell on who." Jason said.

"He wont tell." Quentin said. "Will you, Jason."

"I bet he does tell." Caddy said. "He'll tell Damuddy."

"He cant tell her." Quentin said. "She's sick. If we walk slow it'll be too dark for them to see."

"I dont care whether they see or not." Caddy said. "I'm going to tell, myself. You carry him up the hill, Versh."

"Jason wont tell." Quentin said. "You remember that bow and arrow I made you, Jason."

"It's broke now." Jason said.

"Let him tell." Caddy said. "I dont give a cuss. Carry Maury up the hill, Versh." Versh squatted and I got on his back.

See you all at the show tonight, Luster said. *Come on, here. We got to find that quarter.*

"If we go slow, it'll be dark when we get there." Quentin said.

"I'm not going slow." Caddy said. We went up the hill, but Quentin didn't come. He was down at the branch when we got to where we could smell the pigs. They were grunting and snuffing in the trough in the corner. Jason came behind us, with his hands in his pockets. Roskus was milking the cow in the barn door.

The cows came jumping out of the barn.

"Go on." T. P. said. "Holler again. I going to holler myself. Whooey." Quentin kicked T. P. again. He kicked T. P. into the trough where the pigs ate and T. P. lay there. "Hot dog." T. P. said, "Didn't he get me then. You see that white man kick me that time. Whooey."

I wasn't crying, but I couldn't stop. I wasn't crying, but the ground wasn't still, and then I was crying. The ground kept sloping up and the cows ran up the hill. T. P. tried to get up. He fell down again and the cows ran down the hill. Quentin held my arm and we went toward the barn. Then the barn wasn't there and we had to wait until it came back. I didn't see it come back. It came behind us and Quentin set me down in the trough where the cows ate. I held on to it. It was going away too, and I held to it. The cows ran down the hill again, across the door. I couldn't stop. Quentin and T. P. came up the hill, fighting. T. P. was falling down the hill and Quentin dragged him up the hill. Quentin hit T. P. I couldn't stop.

"Stand up." Quentin said, "You stay right here. Dont you go away until I get back."

"Me and Benjy going back to the wedding." T. P. said. "Whooey."

Quentin hit T. P. again. Then he began to thump T. P. against the wall. T. P. was laughing. Every time Quentin thumped him against the wall he tried to say Whooey, but he couldn't say it for laughing. I quit crying, but I couldn't stop. T. P. fell on me and the barn door went away. It went down the hill and T. P. was fighting by himself and he fell down again. He was still laughing, and I couldn't stop, and I tried to get up and I fell down, and I couldn't stop. Versh said,

"You sho done it now. I'll declare if you aint. Shut up that yelling."

T. P. was still laughing. He flopped on the door and laughed.

"Whooey." he said, "Me and Benjy going back to the wedding. Sassprilluh." T. P. said.

"Hush." Versh said. "Where you get it."

"Out the cellar." T. P. said. "Whooey."

"Hush up." Versh said, "Where'bouts in the cellar."

"Anywhere." T. P. said. He laughed some more. "Moren a hundred bottles left. Moren a million. Look out, nigger, I going to holler."

Quentin said, "Lift him up."

Versh lifted me up.

"Drink this, Benjy." Quentin said. The glass was hot. "Hush, now." Quentin said. "Drink it."

"Sassprilluh." T. P. said. "Lemme drink it, Mr Quentin."

"You shut your mouth." Versh said, "Mr Quentin wear you out."

"Hold him, Versh." Quentin said.

They held me. It was hot on my chin and on my shirt. "Drink." Quentin said. They held my head. It was hot inside me, and I began again. It was crying now, and something was happening inside me and I cried more, and they held me until it stopped happening. Then I hushed. It was still going around, and then the shapes began. "Open the crib, Versh." They were going slow. "Spread those empty sacks on the floor." They were going faster, almost fast enough. "Now. Pick up his feet." They went on, smooth and bright. I could hear T. P. laughing. I went on with them, up the bright hill.

At the top of the hill Versh put me down. "Come on here, Quentin." he called, looking back down the hill. Quentin was still standing there by the branch. He was chunking into the shadows where the branch was.

"Let the old skizzard stay there." Caddy said. She took my hand and we went on past the barn and through the gate. There was a frog on the brick walk, squatting in the middle of it. Caddy stepped over it and pulled me on.

"Come on, Maury." she said. It still squatted there until Jason poked at it with his toe.

"He'll make a wart on you." Versh said. The frog hopped away.

"Come on, Maury." Caddy said.

"They got company tonight." Versh said.

"How do you know." Caddy said.

"With all them lights on." Versh said, "Light in every window."

"I reckon we can turn all the lights on without company, if we want to." Caddy said.

"I bet it's company." Versh said. "You all better go in the back and slip upstairs."

"I dont care." Caddy said. "I'll walk right in the parlor where they are."

"I bet your pappy whip you if you do." Versh said.

"I dont care." Caddy said. "I'll walk right in the parlor. I'll walk right in the dining room and eat supper."

"Where you sit." Versh said.

"I'd sit in Damuddy's chair." Caddy said. "She eats in bed."

"I'm hungry." Jason said. He passed us and ran on up the walk. He had his hands in his pockets and he fell down. Versh went and picked him up.

"If you keep them hands out your pockets, you could stay on your feet." Versh said. "You cant never get them out in time to catch yourself, fat as you is."

Father was standing by the kitchen steps.

"Where's Quentin." he said.

"He coming up the walk." Versh said. Quentin was coming slow. His shirt was a white blur.

"Oh." Father said. Light fell down the steps, on him.

"Caddy and Quentin threw water on each other." Jason said.

We waited.

"They did." Father said. Quentin came, and Father said, "You can eat supper in the kitchen tonight." He stopped and took me up, and the light came tumbling down the steps on me too, and I could look down at Caddy and Jason and Quentin and Versh. Father turned toward the steps. "You must be quiet, though." he said.

"Why must we be quiet, Father." Caddy said. "Have we got company."

"Yes." Father said.

"I told you they was company." Versh said.

"You did not." Caddy said, "I was the one that said there was. I said I would"

"Hush." Father said. They hushed and Father opened the door and we crossed the back porch and went in to the kitchen. Dilsey was there, and Father put me in the chair and closed the apron down and pushed it to the table, where supper was. It was steaming up.

"You mind Dilsey, now." Father said. "Dont let them make any more noise than they can help, Dilsey."

"Yes, sir." Dilsey said. Father went away.

"Remember to mind Dilsey, now." he said behind us. I leaned my face over where the supper was. It steamed up on my face.

"Let them mind me tonight, Father." Caddy said.

"I wont." Jason said. "I'm going to mind Dilsey."

"You'll have to, if Father says so." Caddy said. "Let them mind me, Father."

"I wont." Jason said, "I wont mind you."

"Hush." Father said. "You all mind Caddy, then. When they are done, bring them up the back stairs, Dilsey."

"Yes, sir." Dilsey said.

"There." Caddy said, "Now I guess you'll mind me."

"You all hush, now." Dilsey said. "You got to be quiet tonight."

"Why do we have to be quiet tonight." Caddy whispered.

"Never you mind." Dilsey said, "You'll know in the Lawd's own time." She brought my bowl. The steam from it came and tickled my face. "Come here, Versh." Dilsey said.

"When is the Lawd's own time, Dilsey." Caddy said.

"It's Sunday." Quentin said. "Dont you know anything."

"Shhhhhh." Dilsey said. "Didn't Mr Jason say for you all to be quiet. Eat your supper, now. Here, Versh. Git his spoon." Versh's hand came with the spoon, into the bowl. The spoon came up to my mouth. The steam tickled into my mouth. Then we quit eating and we looked at each other and we were quiet, and then we heard it again and I began to cry.

"What was that." Caddy said. She put her hand on my hand.

"That was Mother." Quentin said. The spoon came up and I ate, then I cried again.

"Hush." Caddy said. But I didn't hush and she came and put her arms around me. Dilsey went and closed both the doors and then we couldn't hear it.

"Hush, now." Caddy said. I hushed and ate. Quentin wasn't eating, but Jason was.

"That was Mother." Quentin said. He got up.

"You set right down." Dilsey said. "They got company in there, and you in them muddy clothes. You set down too, Caddy, and get done eating."

"She was crying." Quentin said.

"It was somebody singing." Caddy said. "Wasn't it, Dilsey."

"You all eat your supper, now, like Mr Jason said." Dilsey said. "You'll know in the Lawd's own time." Caddy went back to her chair.

"I told you it was a party." she said.

Versh said, "He done et all that."

"Bring his bowl here." Dilsey said. The bowl went away.

"Dilsey." Caddy said, "Quentin's not eating his supper. Hasn't he got to mind me."

"Eat your supper, Quentin." Dilsey said, "You all got to get done and get out of my kitchen."

"I dont want any more supper." Quentin said.

"You've got to eat if I say you have." Caddy said. "Hasn't he, Dilsey."

The bowl steamed up to my face, and Versh's hand dipped the spoon in it and the steam tickled into my mouth.

"I dont want any more." Quentin said. "How can they have a party when Damuddy's sick."

"They'll have it down stairs." Caddy said. "She can come to the landing and see it. That's what I'm going to do when I get my nightie on."

"Mother was crying." Quentin said. "Wasn't she crying, Dilsey."

"Dont you come pestering at me, boy." Dilsey said. "I got to get supper for all them folks soon as you all get done eating."

After a while even Jason was through eating, and he began to cry.

"Now you got to tune up." Dilsey said.

"He does it every night since Damuddy was sick and he cant sleep with her." Caddy said. "Cry baby."

"I'm going to tell on you." Jason said.

He was crying. "You've already told." Caddy said. "There's not anything else you can tell, now."

"You all needs to go to bed." Dilsey said. She came and lifted me down and wiped my face and hands with a warm cloth. "Versh, can you get them up the back stairs quiet. You, Jason, shut up that crying."

"It's too early to go to bed now." Caddy said. "We dont ever have to go to bed this early."

"You is tonight." Dilsey said. "Your pa say for you to come right on up stairs when you et supper. You heard him."

"He said to mind me." Caddy said.

"I'm not going to mind you." Jason said.

"You have to." Caddy said. "Come on, now. You have to do like I say."

"Make them be quiet, Versh." Dilsey said. "You all going to be quiet, aint you."

"What do we have to be so quiet for, tonight." Caddy said.

"Your mommer aint feeling well." Dilsey said. "You all go on with Versh, now."

"I told you Mother was crying." Quentin said. Versh took me up and opened the door onto the back porch. We went out and Versh closed the door back. I could smell Versh and feel him. "You all be quiet, now. We're not going up stairs yet. Mr Jason said for you to come right up stairs. He said to mind me. I'm not going to mind you. But he said for all of us to. Didn't he, Quentin." I could feel Versh's head. I could hear us. "Didn't he, Versh. Yes, that's right. Then I say for us to go out doors a while. Come on." Versh opened the door and we went out.

We went down the steps.

"I expect we'd better go down to Versh's house, so we'll be quiet." Caddy said. Versh put me down and Caddy took my hand and we went down the brick walk.

"Come on." Caddy said, "That frog's gone. He's hopped way over to the garden, by now. Maybe we'll see another one." Roskus came with the milk buckets. He went on. Quentin wasn't coming with us. He was sitting on the kitchen steps. We went down to Versh's house. I liked to smell Versh's house. *There was a fire in it and T. P. squatting in his shirt tail in front of it, chunking it into a blaze.*

Then I got up and T. P. dressed me and we went to the kitchen and ate. Dilsey was singing and I began to cry and she stopped.

"Keep him away from the house, now." Dilsey said.

"We cant go that way." T. P. said.

We played in the branch.

"We cant go around yonder." T. P. said. "Dont you know mammy say we cant."

Dilsey was singing in the kitchen and I began to cry.

"Hush." T. P. said. "Come on. Lets go down to the barn."

Roskus was milking at the barn. He was milking with one hand, and groaning. Some birds sat on the barn door and watched him. One of them came down and ate with the cows. I watched Roskus milk while T. P. was feeding Queenie and Prince. The calf was in the pig pen. It nuzzled at the wire, bawling.

"T. P." Roskus said. T. P. said Sir, in the barn. Fancy held her head over the door, because T. P. hadn't fed her yet. "Git done there." Roskus said. "You got to do this milking. I cant use my right hand no more."

T. P. came and milked.

"Whyn't you get the doctor." T. P. said.

"Doctor cant do no good." Roskus said. "Not on this place."

"What wrong with this place." T. P. said.

"Taint no luck on this place." Roskus said. "Turn that calf in if you done."

Taint no luck on this place, Roskus said. The fire rose and fell behind him and Versh, sliding on his and Versh's face. Dilsey finished putting me to bed. The bed smelled like T. P. I liked it.

"What you know about it." Dilsey said. "What trance you been in."

"Dont need no trance." Roskus said. "Aint the sign of it laying right there on that bed. Aint the sign of it been here for folks to see fifteen years now."

"Spose it is." Dilsey said. "It aint hurt none of you and yourn, is it. Versh working and Frony married off your hands and T. P. getting big enough to take your place when rheumatism finish getting you."

"They been two, now." Roskus said. "Going to be one more. I seen the sign, and you is too."

"I heard a squinch owl that night." T. P. said. "Dan wouldn't come and get his supper, neither. Wouldn't come no closer than the barn. Begun howling right after dark. Versh heard him."

"Going to be more than one more." Dilsey said. "Show me the man what aint going to die, bless Jesus."

"Dying aint all." Roskus said.

"I knows what you thinking." Dilsey said. "And they aint going to be no luck in saying that name, lessen you going to set up with him while he cries."

"'They aint no luck on this place." Roskus said. "I seen it at first but when they changed his name I knowed it."

"Hush your mouth." Dilsey said. She pulled the covers up. It smelled like T. P. "You all shut up now, till he get to sleep."

"I seen the sign." Roskus said.

"Sign T. P. got to do all your work for you." Dilsey said. *Take him and Quentin down to the house and let them play with Luster, where Frony can watch them, T. P., and go and help your pa.*

We finished eating. T. P. took Quentin up and we went down to T. P.'s house. Luster was playing in the dirt. T. P. put Quentin down and she played in the dirt too. Luster had some spools and he and Quentin fought and Quentin had the spools. Luster cried and Frony came and gave Luster a tin can to play with, and then I had the spools and.Quentin fought me and I cried.

"Hush." Frony said, "Aint you shamed of yourself. Taking a baby's play pretty." She took the spools from me and gave them back to Quentin.

"Hush, now." Frony said, "Hush, I tell you."

"Hush up." Frony said. "You needs whipping, that's what you needs." She took Luster and Quentin up. "Come on here." she said. We went to the barn. T. P. was milking the cow. Roskus was sitting on the box.

"What's the matter with him now." Roskus said.

"You have to keep him down here." Frony said. "He fighting these babies again. Taking they play things. Stay here with T. P. now, and see can you hush a while."

"Clean that udder good now." Roskus said. "You milked that young cow dry last winter. If you milk this one dry, they aint going to be no more milk."

Dilsey was singing.

"Not around yonder." T. P. said. "Dont you know mammy say you cant go around there."

They were singing.

"Come on." T. P. said. "Lets go play with Quentin and Luster. Come on."

Quentin and Luster were playing in the dirt in front of T. P.'s house. There was a fire in the house, rising and falling, with Roskus sitting black against it.

"That's three, thank the Lawd." Roskus said. "I told you two years ago. They aint no luck on this place."

"Whyn't you get out, then." Dilsey said. She was undressing me. "Your bad luck talk got them Memphis notions into Versh. That ought to satisfy you."

"If that all the bad luck Versh have." Roskus said.

Frony came in.

"You all done." Dilsey said.

"T. P. finishing up." Frony said. "Miss Cahline want you to put Quentin to bed."

"I'm coming just as fast as I can." Dilsey said. "She ought to know by this time I aint got no wings."

"That's what I tell you." Roskus said. "They aint no luck going be on no place where one of they own chillens' name aint never spoke."

"Hush." Dilsey said. "Do you want to get him started"

"Raising a child not to know its own mammy's name." Roskus said.

"Dont you bother your head about her." Dilsey said. "I raised all of them and I reckon I can raise one more. Hush now. Let him get to sleep if he will."

"Saying a name." Frony said. "He dont know nobody's name."

"You just say it and see if he dont." Dilsey said. "You say it to him while he sleeping and I bet he hear you."

"He know lot more than folks thinks." Roskus said. "He knowed they time was coming, like that pointer done. He could tell you when hisn coming, if he could talk. Or yours. Or mine."

"You take Luster outen that bed, mammy." Frony said. "That boy conjure him."

"Hush your mouth." Dilsey said, "Aint you got no better sense than that. What you want to listen to Roskus for, anyway. Get in, Benjy."

Dilsey pushed me and I got in the bed, where Luster already was. He was asleep. Dilsey took a long piece of wood and laid it between Luster and me. "Stay on your side now." Dilsey said. "Luster little, and you don't want to hurt him."

You can't go yet, T. P. said. Wait.

We looked around the corner of the house and watched the carriages go away.

"Now." T. P. said. He took Quentin up and we ran down to the corner of the fence and watched them pass. "There he go," T. P.

said. "See that one with the glass in it. Look at him. He laying in there. See him."

Come on, Luster said, I going to take this here ball down home, where I wont lose it. Naw, sir, you cant have it. If them men sees you with it, they'll say you stole it. Hush up, now. You cant have it. What business you got with it. You cant play no ball.

Frony and T. P. were playing in the dirt by the door. T. P. had lightning bugs in a bottle.

"How did you all get back out." Frony said.

"We've got company." Caddy said. "Father said for us to mind me tonight. I expect you and T. P. will have to mind me too."

"I'm not going to mind you." Jason said. "Frony and T. P. dont have to either."

"They will if I say so." Caddy said. "Maybe I wont say for them to."

"T. P. dont mind nobody." Frony said. "Is they started the funeral yet."

"What's a funeral." Jason said.

"Didn't mammy tell you not to tell them." Versh said.

"Where they moans." Frony said. "They moaned two days on Sis Beulah Clay."

They moaned at Dilsey's house. Dilsey was moaning. When Dilsey moaned Luster said, Hush, and we hushed, and then I began to cry and Blue howled under the kitchen steps. Then Dilsey stopped and we stopped.

"Oh." Caddy said, "That's niggers. White folks dont have funerals."

"Mammy said us not to tell them, Frony." Versh said.

"Tell them what." Caddy said.

Dilsey moaned, and when it got to the place I began to cry and Blue howled under the steps. Luster, Frony, said in the window, Take them down to the barn. I cant get no cooking done with all that racket. That hound too. Get them outen here.

I aint going down there, Luster said. I might meet pappy down there. I seen him last night, waving his arms in the barn.

"I like to know why not." Frony said. "White folks dies too. Your grandmammy dead as any nigger can get, I reckon."

"Dogs are dead." Caddy said, "And when Nancy fell in the ditch and Roskus shot her and the buzzards came and undressed her."

The bones rounded out of the ditch, where the dark vines were
in the black ditch, into the moonlight, like some of the shapes had
stopped. Then they all stopped and it was dark, and when I
stopped to start again I could hear Mother, and feet walking fast
away, and I could smell it. Then the room came, but my eyes went
shut. I didn't stop. I could smell it. T. P. unpinned the bed clothes.

"Hush." he said, "Shhhhhhh."

But I could smell it. T. P. pulled me up and he put on my
clothes fast.

"Hush, Benjy." he said. "We going down to our house. You want
to go down to our house, where Frony is. Hush. Shhhhh."

He laced my shoes and put my cap on and we went out. There
was a light in the hall. Across the hall we could hear Mother.

"Shhhhhh, Benjy." T. P. said, "We'll be out in a minute."

A door opened and I could smell it more than ever, and a head
came out. It wasn't Father. Father was sick there.

"Can you take him out of the house."

"That's where we going." T. P. said. Dilsey came up the stairs.

"Hush." she said, "Hush. Take him down home, T. P. Frony fixing
him a bed. You all look after him, now. Hush, Benjy. Go on with
T. P."

She went where we could hear Mother.

"Better keep him there." It wasn't Father. He shut the door, but
I could still smell it.

We went down stairs. The stairs went down into the dark and
T. P. took my hand, and we went out the door, out of the dark.
Dan was sitting in the back yard, howling.

"He smell it." T. P. said. "Is that the way you found it out."

We went down the steps, where our shadows were.

"I forgot your coat." T. P. said. "You ought to had it. But I aint
going back."

Dan howled.

"Hush now." T. P. said. Our shadows moved, but Dan's shadow
didn't move except to howl when he did.

"I cant take you down home, bellering like you is." T. P. said.
"You was bad enough before you got that bullfrog voice. Come on."

We went along the brick walk, with our shadows. The pig pen
smelled like pigs. The cow stood in the lot, chewing at us. Dan
howled.

"You going to wake the whole town up." T. P. said. "Cant you hush."

We saw Fancy, eating by the branch. The moon shone on the water when we got there.

"Naw, sir." T. P. said, "This too close. We cant stop here. Come on. Now, just look at you. Got your whole leg wet. Come on, here." Dan howled.

The ditch came up out of the buzzing grass. The bones rounded out of the black vines.

"Now." T. P. said. "Beller your head off if you want to. You got the whole night and a twenty acre pasture to bellcr in."

T. P. lay down in the ditch and I sat down, watching the bones where the buzzards ate Nancy, flapping black and slow and heavy out of the ditch.

I had it when we was down here before, Luster said. I showed it to you. Didn't you see it. I took it out of my pocket right here and showed it to you.

"Do you think buzzards are going to undress Damuddy." Caddy said. "You're crazy."

"You're a skizzard." Jason said. He began to cry.

"You're a knobnot." Caddy said. Jason cried. His hands were in his pockets.

"Jason going to be rich man." Versh said. "He holding his money all the time."

Jason cried.

"Now you've got him started." Caddy said. "Hush up, Jason. How can buzzards get in where Damuddy is. Father wouldn't let them. Would you let a buzzard undress you. Hush up, now."

Jason hushed. "Frony said it was a funeral." he said.

"Well it's not." Caddy said. "It's a party. Frony dont know anything about it. He wants your lightning bugs, T. P. Let him hold it a while."

T. P. gave me the bottle of lightning bugs.

"I bet if we go around to the parlor window we can see something." Caddy said. "Then you'll believe me."

"I already knows." Frony said. "I dont need to see."

"You better hush your mouth, Frony." Versh said. "Mammy going whip you."

"What is it." Caddy said.

"I knows what I knows." Frony said.

"Come on." Caddy said, "Let's go around to the front."

We started to go.

"T. P. wants his lightning bugs." Frony said.

"Let him hold it a while longer, T. P." Caddy said. "We'll bring it back."

"You all never caught them." Frony said.

"If I say you and T. P. can come too, will you let him hold it." Caddy said.

"Aint nobody said me and T. P. got to mind you." Frony said.

"If I say you dont have to, will you let him hold it." Caddy said.

"All right." Frony said. "Let him hold it, T. P. We going to watch them moaning."

"They aint moaning." Caddy said. "I tell you it's a party. Are they moaning, Versh."

"We aint going to know what they doing, standing here." Versh said.

"Come on." Caddy said. "Frony and T. P. dont have to mind me. But the rest of us do. You better carry him, Versh. It's getting dark."

Versh took me up and we went on around the kitchen.

When we looked around the corner we could see the lights coming up the drive. T. P. went back to the cellar door and opened it.

You know what's down there, T. P. said. Soda water. I seen Mr Jason come up with both hands full of them. Wait here a minute.

T. P. went and looked in the kitchen door. Dilsey said, What are you peeping in here for. Where's Benjy.

He out here, T. P. said.

Go on and watch him, Dilsey said. Keep him out the house now.

Yessum, T. P. said. Is they started yet.

You go on and keep that boy out of sight, Dilsey said. I got all I can tend to.

A snake crawled out from under the house. Jason said he wasn't afraid of snakes and Caddy said he was but she wasn't and Versh said they both were and Caddy said to be quiet, like Father said.

You aint got to start bellering now, T. P. said. You want some this sassprilluh.

It tickled my nose and eyes.

If you aint going to drink it, let me get to it, T. P. said. All right, here tis. We better get another bottle while nobody bothering us. You be quiet, now.

We stopped under the tree by the parlor window. Versh set me down in the wet grass. It was cold. There were lights in all the windows.

"That's where Damuddy is." Caddy said. "She's sick every day now. When she gets well we're going to have a picnic."

"I knows what I knows." Frony said.

The trees were buzzing, and the grass.

"The one next to it is where we have the measles." Caddy said. "Where do you and T. P. have the measles, Frony."

"Has them just wherever we is, I reckon." Frony said.

"They haven't started yet." Caddy said.

They getting ready to start, T. P. said. You stand right here now while I get that box so we can see in the window. Here, les finish drinking this here sassprilluh. It make me feel just like a squinch owl inside.

We drank the sassprilluh and T. P. pushed the bottle through the lattice, under the house, and went away. I could hear them in the parlor and I clawed my hands against the wall. T. P. dragged the box. He fell down, and he began to laugh. He lay there, laughing into the grass. He got up and dragged the box under the window, trying not to laugh.

"I skeered I going to holler." T. P. said. "Git on the box and see is they started."

"They haven't started because the band hasn't come yet." Caddy said.

"They aint going to have no band." Frony said.

"How do you know." Caddy said.

"I knows what I knows." Frony said.

"You dont know anything." Caddy said. She went to the tree. "Push me up, Versh."

"Your paw told you to stay out that tree." Versh said.

"That was a long time ago." Caddy said. "I expect he's forgotten about it. Besides, he said to mind me tonight. Didn't he say to mind me tonight."

"I'm not going to mind you." Jason said. "Frony and T. P. are not going to either."

"Push me up, Versh." Caddy said.

"All right." Versh said. "You the one going to get whipped. I aint." He went and pushed Caddy up into the tree to the first limb. We watched the muddy bottom of her drawers. Then we couldn't see her. We could hear the tree thrashing.

"Mr Jason said if you break that tree he whip you." Versh said.

"I'm going to tell on her too." Jason said.

The tree quit thrashing. We looked up into the still branches.

"What you seeing." Frony whispered.

I saw them. Then I saw Caddy, with flowers in her hair, and a long veil like shining wind. Caddy Caddy

"Hush." T. P. said, "They going to hear you. Get down quick." He pulled me. Caddy. I clawed my hands against the wall Caddy. T. P. pulled me.

"Hush." he said. "Hush. Come on here quick." He pulled me on. Caddy "Hush up, Benjy. You want them to hear you. Come on, les drink some more sassprilluh, then we can come back if you hush. We better get one more bottle or we both be hollering. We can say Dan drunk it. Mr Quentin always saying he so smart, we can say he sassprilluh dog, too."

The moonlight came down the cellar stairs. We drank some more sassprilluh.

"You know what I wish." T. P. said. "I wish a bear would walk in that cellar door. You know what I do. I walk right up to him and spit in he eye. Gimme that bottle to stop my mouth before I holler."

T. P. fell down. He began to laugh, and the cellar door and the moonlight jumped away and something hit me.

"Hush up." T. P. said, trying not to laugh, "Lawd, they'll all hear us. Get up." T. P. said, "Get up, Benjy, quick." He was thrashing about and laughing and I tried to get up. The cellar steps ran up the hill in the moonlight and T. P. fell up the hill, into the moonlight, and I ran against the fence and T. P. ran behind me saying "Hush up hush up" Then he fell into the flowers, laughing, and I ran into the box. But when I tried to climb onto it it jumped away and hit me on the back of the head and my throat made a sound. It made the sound again and I stopped trying to get up, and it made the sound again and I began to cry. But my throat kept on making the sound while T. P. was pulling me. It kept on making it and I couldn't tell if I was crying or not, and T. P. fell down on top of me, laughing, and it kept on making the sound and Quentin kicked T. P. and Cad put her arms around me, and her shining veil, and I couldn't smell trees anymore and I began to cry.

Benjy, Caddy said Benjy. She put her arms around me again, but I went away. "What is it, Benjy." she said. "Is it this hat." She took her hat off and came again, and I went away.

"Benjy." she said, "What is it, Benjy. What has Caddy done."

"He dont like that prissy dress." Jason said. "You think you're grown up, dont you. You think you're better than anybody else, dont you. Prissy."

"You shut your mouth." Caddy said, "You dirty little beast. Benjy."

"Just because you are fourteen, you think you're grown up, dont you." Jason said. "You think you're something. Dont you."

"Hush, Benjy." Caddy said. "You'll disturb Mother. Hush."

But I didn't hush, and when she went away I followed, and she stopped on the stairs and waited and I stopped too.

"What is it, Benjy." Caddy said, "Tell Caddy. She'll do it. Try."

"Candace." Mother said.

"Yessum." Caddy said.

"Why are you teasing him." Mother said. "Bring him here."

We went to Mother's room, where she was lying with the sickness on a cloth on her head.

"What is the matter now." Mother said. "Benjamin."

"Benjy." Caddy said. She came again, but I went away.

"You must have done something to him." Mother said. "Why wont you let him alone, so I can have some peace. Give him the box and please go on and let him alone."

Caddy got the box and set it on the floor and opened it. It was full of stars. When I was still, they were still. When I moved, they glinted and sparkled. I hushed.

Then I heard Caddy walking and I began again.

"Benjamin." Mother said, "Come here." I went to the door. "You, Benjamin." Mother said.

"What is it now." Father said, "Where are you going."

"Take him downstairs and get someone to watch him, Jason." Mother said. "You know I'm ill, yet you"

Father shut the door behind us.

"T. P." he said.

"Sir." T. P. said downstairs.

"Benjy's coming down." Father said. "Go with T. P."

I went to the bathroom door. I could hear the water.

"Benjy." T. P. said downstairs.

I could hear the water. I listened to it.

"Benjy." T. P. said downstairs.

I listened to the water.

I couldn't hear the water, and Caddy opened the door.

"Why, Benjy." she said. She looked at me and I went and she put her arms around me. "Did you find Caddy again." she said. "Did you think Caddy had run away." Caddy smelled like trees.

We went to Caddy's room. She sat down at the mirror. She stopped her hands and looked at me.

"Why, Benjy. What is it." she said. "You mustn't cry. Caddy's not going away. See here." she said. She took up the bottle and took the stopper out and held it to my nose. "Sweet. Smell. Good."

I went away and I didn't hush, and she held the bottle in her hand, looking at me.

"Oh." she said. She put the bottle down and came and put her arms around me. "So that was it. And you were trying to tell Caddy and you couldn't tell her. You wanted to, but you couldn't, could you. Of course Caddy wont. Of course Caddy wont. Just wait till I dress."

Caddy dressed and took up the bottle again and we went down to the kitchen.

"Dilsey." Caddy said, "Benjy's got a present for you." She stooped down and put the bottle in my hand. "Hold it out to Dilsey, now." Caddy held my hand out and Dilsey took the bottle.

"Well I'll declare." Dilsey said, "If my baby aint give Dilsey a bottle of perfume. Just look here, Roskus."

Caddy smelled like trees. "We dont like perfume ourselves." Caddy said.

She smelled like trees.

"Come on, now." Dilsey said, "You too big to sleep with folks. You a big boy now. Thirteen years old. Big enough to sleep by yourself in Uncle Maury's room." Dilsey said.

Uncle Maury was sick. His eye was sick, and his mouth. Versh took his supper up to him on the tray.

"Maury says he's going to shoot the scoundrel." Father said. "I told him he'd better not mention it to Patterson before hand." He drank.

"Jason." Mother said.

"Shoot who, Father." Quentin said. "What's Uncle Maury going to shoot him for."

"Because he couldn't take a little joke." Father said.

"Jason." Mother said, "How can you. You'd sit right there and see Maury shot down in ambush, and laugh."

"Then Maury'd better stay out of ambush." Father said.

"Shoot who, Father." Quentin said, "Who's Uncle Maury going to shoot."

"Nobody." Father said. "I dont own a pistol."

Mother began to cry. "If you begrudge Maury your food, why aren't you man enough to say so to his face. To ridicule him before the children, behind his back."

"Of course I dont." Father said, "I admire Maury. He is invaluable to my own sense of racial superiority. I wouldn't swap Maury for a matched team. And do you know why, Quentin."

"No, sir." Quentin said.

"*Et ego in arcadia* I have forgotten the latin for hay." Father said. "There, there." he said, "I was just joking." He drank and set the glass down and went and put his hand on Mother's shoulder.

"It's no joke." Mother said. "My people are every bit as well born as yours. Just because Maury's health is bad."

"Of course." Father said. "Bad health is the primary reason for all life. Created by disease, within putrefaction, into decay. Versh."

"Sir." Versh said behind my chair.

"Take the decanter and fill it."

"And tell Dilsey to come and take Benjamin up to bed." Mother said.

"You a big boy." Dilsey said, "Caddy tired sleeping with you. Hush now, so you can go to sleep." The room went away, but I didn't hush, and the room came back and Dilsey came and sat on the bed, looking at me.

"Aint you going to be a good boy and hush." Dilsey said. "You aint, is you. See can you wait a minute, then."

She went away. There wasn't anything in the door. Then Caddy was in it.

"Hush." Caddy said. "I'm coming."

I hushed and Dilsey turned back the spread and Caddy got in between the spread and the blanket. She didn't take off her bathrobe.

"Now." she said, "Here I am." Dilsey came with a blanket and spread it over her and tucked it around her.

"He be gone in a minute." Dilsey said. "I leave the light on in your room."

"All right." Caddy said. She snuggled her head beside mine on the pillow. "Goodnight, Dilsey."

"Goodnight, honey." Dilsey said. The room went black. *Caddy smelled like trees.*

We looked up into the tree where she was.

"What she seeing, Versh." Frony whispered.

"Shhhhhhh." Caddy said in the tree. Dilsey said,

"You come on here." She came around the corner of the house. "Whyn't you all go on up stairs, like your paw said, stead of slipping out behind my back. Where's Caddy and Quentin."

"I told her not to climb up that tree." Jason said. "I'm going to tell on her."

"Who in what tree." Dilsey said. She came and looked up into the tree. "Caddy." Dilsey said. The branches began to shake again.

"You, Satan." Dilsey said. "Come down from there."

"Hush." Caddy said, "Dont you know Father said to be quiet." Her legs came in sight and Dilsey reached up and lifted her out of the tree.

"Aint you got any better sense than to let them come around here." Dilsey said.

"I couldn't do nothing with her." Versh said.

"What you all doing here." Dilsey said. "Who told you to come up to the house."

"She did." Frony said. "She told us to come."

"Who told you you got to do what she say." Dilsey said. "Get on home, now." Frony and T. P. went on. We couldn't see them when they were still going away.

"Out here in the middle of the night." Dilsey said. She took me up and we went to the kitchen.

"Slipping out behind my back." Dilsey said. "When you knowed it's past your bedtime."

"Shhhh, Dilsey." Caddy said. "Dont talk so loud. We've got to be quiet."

"You hush your mouth and get quiet, then," Dilsey said. "Where's Quentin."

"Quentin's mad because he had to mind me tonight." Caddy said. "He's still got T. P.'s bottle of lightning bugs."

"I reckon T. P. can get along without it." Dilsey said. "You go and find Quentin, Versh. Roskus say he seen him going towards the barn." Versh went on. We couldn't see him.

"They're not doing anything in there." Caddy said. "Just sitting in chairs and looking."

"They dont need no help from you all to do that." Dilsey said. We went around the kitchen.

Where you want to go now, Luster said. You going back to watch them knocking ball again. We done looked for it over there. Here. Wait a minute. You wait right here while I go back and get that ball. I done thought of something.

The kitchen was dark. The trees were black on the sky. Dan came waddling out from under the steps and chewed my ankle. I went around the kitchen, where the moon was. Dan came scuffling along, into the moon.

"Benjy." T. P. said in the house.

The flower tree by the parlor window wasn't dark, but the thick trees were. The grass was buzzing in the moonlight where my shadow walked on the grass.

"You, Benjy." T. P. said in the house. "Where you hiding. You slipping off. I knows it."

Luster came back. Wait, he said. Here. Dont go over there. Miss Quentin and her beau in the swing yonder. You come on this way. Come back here, Benjy.

It was dark under the trees. Dan wouldn't come. He stayed in the moonlight. Then I could see the swing and I began to cry.

Come away from there, Benjy, Luster said. You know Miss Quentin going to get mad.

It was two now, and then one in the swing. Caddy came fast, white in the darkness.

"Benjy," she said. "How did you slip out. Where's Versh."

She put her arms around me and I hushed and held to her dress and tried to pull her away.

"Why, Benjy." she said. "What is it. T. P." she called.

The one in the swing got up and came, and I cried and pulled Caddy's dress.

"Benjy." Caddy said. "It's just Charlie. Dont you know Charlie."

"Where's his nigger." Charlie said. "What do they let him run around loose for."

"Hush, Benjy." Caddy said. "Go away, Charlie. He doesn't like you." Charlie went away and I hushed. I pulled at Caddy's dress.

"Why, Benjy." Caddy said. "Aren't you going to let me stay here and talk to Charlie awhile."

"Call that nigger." Charlie said. He came back. I cried louder and pulled at Caddy's dress.

"Go away, Charlie." Caddy said. Charlie came and put his hands on Caddy and I cried more. I cried loud.

"No, no." Caddy said. "No. No."

"He cant talk." Charlie said. "Caddy."

"Are you crazy." Caddy said. She began to breathe fast. "He can see. Dont. Dont." Caddy fought. They both breathed fast. "Please. Please." Caddy whispered.

"Send him away." Charlie said.

"I will." Caddy said. "Let me go."

"Will you send him away." Charlie said.

"Yes." Caddy said. "Let me go." Charlie went away. "Hush." Caddy said. "He's gone." I hushed. I could hear her and feel her chest going.

"I'll have to take him to the house." she said. She took my hand. "I'm coming." she whispered.

"Wait." Charlie said. "Call the nigger."

"No." Caddy said. "I'll come back. Come on, Benjy."

"Caddy." Charlie whispered, loud. We went on. "You better come back. Are you coming back." Caddy and I were running. "Caddy." Charlie said. We ran out into the moonlight, toward the kitchen. "Caddy." Charlie said.

Caddy and I ran. We ran up the kitchen steps, onto the porch, and Caddy knelt down in the dark and held me. I could hear her and feel her chest. "I wont." she said. "I wont anymore, ever. Benjy. Benjy." Then she was crying, and I cried, and we held each other. "Hush." she said. "Hush. I wont anymore." So I hushed and Caddy got up and we went into the kitchen and turned the light on and Caddy took the kitchen soap and washed her mouth at the sink, hard. Caddy smelled like trees.

I kept a telling you to stay away from there, Luster said. They sat up in the swing, quick. Quentin had her hands on her hair. He had a red tie.

*You old crazy loon, Quentin said. I'm going to tell Dilsey about
the way you let him follow everywhere I go. I'm going to make her
whip you good.*

"I couldn't stop him." Luster said. "Come on here, Benjy."

"Yes you could." Quentin said. "You didn't try. You were both
snooping around after me. Did Grandmother send you all out here
to spy on me." She jumped out of the swing. "If you dont take him
right away this minute and keep him away, I'm going to make
Jason whip you."

"I cant do nothing with him." Luster said. "You try it if you think
you can."

"Shut your mouth." Quentin said. "Are you going to get him
away."

"Ah, let him stay." he said. He had a red tie. The sun was red
on it. "Look here, Jack." He struck a match and put it in his mouth.
Then he took the match out of his mouth. It was still burning.
"Want to try it." he said. I went over there. "Open your mouth." he
said. I opened my mouth. Quentin hit the match with her hand
and it went away.

"Goddamn you." Quentin said. "Do you want to get him started.
Dont you know he'll beller all day. I'm going to tell Dilsey on you."
She went away running.

"Here, kid." he said. "Hey. Come on back. I aint going to fool
with him."

Quentin ran on to the house. She went around the kitchen.

"You played hell then, Jack." he said. "Aint you."

"He cant tell what you saying." Luster said. "He deef and
dumb."

"Is." he said. "How long's he been that way."

"Been that way thirty-three years today." Luster said. "Born
loony. Is you one of them show folks."

"Why." he said.

"I dont ricklick seeing you around here before." Luster said.

"Well, what about it." he said.

"Nothing." Luster said. "I going tonight."

He looked at me.

"You aint the one can play a tune on that saw, is you." Luster
said.

"It'll cost you a quarter to find that out." he said. He looked at

me. "Why dont they lock him up." he said. "What'd you bring
him out here for."

"You aint talking to me." Luster said. "I cant do nothing with
him. I just come over here looking for a quarter I lost so I can go
to the show tonight. Look like now I ain't going to get to go." Luster looked on the ground. "You aint got no extra quarter, is you."
Luster said.

"No." he said. "I aint."

"I reckon I just have to find that other one, then." Luster said.
He put his hand in his pocket. "You dont want to buy no golf ball
neither, does you." Luster said.

"What kind of ball." he said.

"Golf ball." Luster said. "I dont want but a quarter."

"What for." he said. "What do I want with it."

"I didn't think you did." Luster said. "Come on here, mulehead."
he said. "Come on here and watch them knocking that ball. Here.
Here something you can play with along with that jimson weed."
Luster picked it up and gave it to me. It was bright.

"Where'd you get that." he said. His tie was red in the sun, walking.

"Found it under this here bush." Luster said. "I thought for a
minute it was that quarter I lost."

He came and took it.

"Hush." Luster said. "He going to give it back when he done
looking at it."

"Agnes Mabel Becky." he said. He looked toward the house.

"Hush." Luster said. "He fixing to give it back."

He gave it to me and I hushed.

"Who come to see her last night." he said.

"I dont know." Luster said. "They comes every night she can
climb down that tree. I dont keep no track of them."

"Damn if one of them didn't leave a track." he said. He looked
at the house. Then he went and lay down in the swing. "Go away."
he said. "Dont bother me."

"Come on here." Luster said. "You done played hell now. Time
Miss Quentin get done telling on you."

We went to the fence and looked through the curling flower
spaces. Luster hunted in the grass.

"I had it right here." he said. I saw the flag flapping, and the sun
slanting on the broad grass.

"They'll be some along soon." Luster said. "There some now, but they going away. Come on and help me look for it."

We went along the fence.

"Hush." Luster said. "How can I make them come over here, if they aint coming. Wait. They'll be some in a minute. Look yonder. Here they come."

I went along the fence, to the gate, where the girls passed with their booksatchels. "You, Benjy." Luster said. "Come back here."

You cant do no good looking through the gate, T. P. said. Miss Caddy done gone long ways away. Done got married and left you. You cant do no good, holding to the gate and crying. She cant hear you.

What is it he wants, T. P. Mother said. Cant you play with him and keep him quiet.

He wants to go down yonder and look through the gate, T. P. said.

Well, he cannot do it, Mother said. It's raining. You will just have to play with him and keep him quiet. You, Benjamin.

Aint nothing going to quiet him, T. P. said. He think if he down to the gate, Miss Caddy come back.

Nonsense, Mother said.

I could hear them talking. I went out the door and I couldn't hear them, and I went down to the gate, where the girls passed with their booksatchels. They looked at me, walking fast, with their heads turned. I tried to say, but they went on, and I went along the fence, trying to say, and they went faster. Then they were running and I came to the corner of the fence and I couldn't go any further, and I held to the fence, looking after them and trying to say.

"You, Benjy." T. P. said. "What you doing, slipping out. Dont you know Dilsey whip you."

"You cant do no good, moaning and slobbering through the fence." T. P. said. "You done skeered them chillen. Look at them, walking on the other side of the street."

How did he get out, Father said. Did you leave the gate un-latched when you came in, Jason.

Of course not, Jason said. Dont you know I've got better sense than to do that. Do you think I wanted anything like this to happen. This family is bad enough, God knows. I could have told you, all the time. I reckon you'll send him to Jackson, now. If Mrs Burgess dont shoot him first.

Hush, Father said.

I could have told you, all the time, Jason said.

It was open when I touched it, and I held to it in the twilight. I wasn't crying, and I tried to stop, watching the girls coming along in the twilight. I wasn't crying.

"There he is."

They stopped.

"He cant get out. He wont hurt anybody, anyway. Come on."

"I'm scared to. I'm scared. I'm going to cross the street."

"He cant get out."

I wasn't crying.

"Don't be a 'fraid cat. Come on."

They came on in the twilight. I wasn't crying, and I held to the gate. They came slow.

"I'm scared."

"He wont hurt you. I pass here every day. He just runs along the fence."

They came on. I opened the gate and they stopped, turning. I was trying to say, and I caught her, trying to say, and she screamed and I was trying to say and trying and the bright shapes began to stop and I tried to get out. I tried to get it off of my face, but the bright shapes were going again. They were going up the hill to where it fell away and I tried to cry. But when I breathed in, I couldn't breathe out again to cry, and I tried to keep from falling off the hill and I fell off the hill into the bright, whirling shapes.

Here, loony, Luster said. Here come some. Hush your slobbering and moaning, now.

They came to the flag. He took it out and they hit, then he put the flag back.

"Mister." Luster said.

He looked around. "What." he said.

"Want to buy a golf ball." Luster said.

"Let's see it." he said. He came to the fence and Luster reached the ball through.

"Where'd you get it." he said.

"Found it." Luster said.

"I know that." he said. "Where. In somebody's golf bag."

"I found it laying over here in the yard." Luster said. "I'll take a quarter for it."

"What makes you think it's yours." he said.

"I found it." Luster said.

"Then find yourself another one." he said. He put it in his pocket and went away.

"I got to go to that show tonight." Luster said.

"That so." he said. He went to the table. "Fore, caddie." he said. He hit.

"I'll declare." Luster said. "You fusses when you dont see them and you fusses when you does. Why cant you hush. Dont you reckon folks gets tired of listening to you all the time. Here. You dropped your jimson weed." He picked it up and gave it back to me. "You needs a new one. You 'bout wore that one out." We stood at the fence and watched them.

"That white man hard to get along with." Luster said. "You see him take my ball." They went on. We went on along the fence. We came to the garden and we couldn't go any further. I held to the fence and looked through the flower spaces. They went away.

"Now you aint got nothing to moan about." Luster said. "Hush up. I the one got something to moan over, you aint. Here. Whyn't you hold on to that weed. You be bellering about it next." He gave me the flower. "Where you heading now."

Our shadows were on the grass. They got to the trees before we did. Mine got there first. Then we got there, and then the shadows were gone. There was a flower in the bottle. I put the other flower in it.

"Aint you a grown man, now." Luster said. "Playing with two weeds in a bottle. You know what they going to do with you when Miss Cahline die. They going to send you to Jackson, where you belong. Mr Jason say so. Where you can hold the bars all day long with the rest of the loonies and slobber. How you like that."

Luster knocked the flowers over with his hand. "That's what they'll do to you at Jackson when you starts bellering."

I tried to pick up the flowers. Luster picked them up, and they went away. I began to cry.

"Beller." Luster said. "Beller. You want something to beller about. All right, then. Caddy." he whispered. "Caddy. Beller now. Caddy."

"Luster." Dilsey said from the kitchen.

The flowers came back.

"Hush." Luster said. "Here they is. Look. It's fixed back just like it was at first. Hush, now."

"You, Luster." Dilsey said.

"Yessum." Luster said. "We coming. You done played hell. Get up." He jerked my arm and I got up. We went out of the trees. Our shadows were gone.

"Hush." Luster said. "Look at all them folks watching you. Hush."

"You bring him on here." Dilsey said. She came down the steps. "What you done to him now." she said.

"Aint done nothing to him." Luster said. "He just started bellering."

"Yes you is." Dilsey said. "You done something to him. Where you been."

"Over yonder under them cedars." Luster said.

"Getting Quentin all riled up." Dilsey said. "Why can't you keep him away from her. Dont you know she dont like him where she at."

"Got as much time for him as I is." Luster said. "He aint none of my uncle."

"Dont you sass me, nigger boy." Dilsey said.

"I aint done nothing to him." Luster said. "He was playing there, and all of a sudden he started bellering."

"Is you been projecking with his graveyard." Dilsey said.

"I aint touched his graveyard." Luster said.

"Dont lie to me, boy." Dilsey said. We went up the steps and into the kitchen. Dilsey opened the firedoor and drew a chair up in front of it and I sat down. I hushed.

What you want to get her started for, Dilsey said. Whyn't you keep him out of there.

He was just looking at the fire, Caddy said. Mother was telling him his new name. We didn't mean to get her started.

I knows you didn't, Dilsey said. Him at one end of the house and her at the other. You let my things alone, now. Dont you touch nothing till I get back.

"Aint you shamed of yourself." Dilsey said. "Teasing him." She set the cake on the table.

"I aint been teasing him." Luster said. "He was playing with that bottle full of dogfennel and all of a sudden he started up bellering. You heard him."

"You aint done nothing to his flowers." Dilsey said.

"I aint touched his graveyard." Luster said. "What I want with his truck. I was just hunting for that quarter."

"You lost it, did you." Dilsey said. She lit the candles on the cake. Some of them were little ones. Some were big ones cut into little pieces. "I told you to go put it away. Now I reckon you want me to get you another one from Frony."

"I got to go to that show, Benjy or no Benjy." Luster said. "I aint going to follow him around day and night both."

"You going to do just what he want you to, nigger boy." Dilsey said. "You hear me."

"Aint I always done it." Luster said. "Dont I always does what he wants. Dont I, Benjy."

"Then you keep it up." Dilsey said. "Bringing him in here, bawling and getting her started too. You all go ahead and eat this cake, now, before Jason come. I dont want him jumping on me about a cake I bought with my own money. Me baking a cake here, with him counting every egg that comes into this kitchen. See can you let him alone now, less you dont want to go to that show tonight."

Dilsey went away.

"You cant blow out no candles." Luster said. "Watch me blow them out." He leaned down and puffed his face. The candles went away. I began to cry. "Hush." Luster said. "Here. Look at the fire whiles I cuts this cake."

I could hear the clock, and I could hear Caddy standing behind me, and I could hear the roof. It's still raining, Caddy said. I hate rain. I hate everything. And then her head came into my lap and she was crying, holding me, and I began to cry. Then I looked at the fire again and the bright, smooth shapes went again. I could hear the clock and the roof and Caddy.

I ate some cake. Luster's hand came and took another piece. I could hear him eating. I looked at the fire.

A long piece of wire came across my shoulder. It went to the door, and then the fire went away. I began to cry.

"What you howling for now." Luster said. "Look there." The fire was there. I hushed. "Cant you set and look at the fire and be quiet like mammy told you." Luster said. "You ought to be ashamed of yourself. Here. Here's you some more cake."

"What you done to him now." Dilsey said. "Cant you never let him alone."

"I was just trying to get him to hush up and not sturb Miss Cahline." Luster said. "Something got him started again."

"And I know what that something name." Dilsey said. "I'm going to get Versh to take a stick to you when he comes home. You just trying yourself. You been doing it all day. Did you take him down to the branch."

"Nome." Luster said. "We been right here in this yard all day, like you said."

His hand came for another piece of cake. Dilsey hit his hand. "Reach it again, and I chop it right off with this here butcher knife." Dilsey said. "I bet he aint had one piece of it."

"Yes he is." Luster said. "He already had twice as much as me. Ask him if he aint."

"Reach hit one more time." Dilsey said. "Just reach it."

That's right, Dilsey said. I reckon it'll be my time to cry next. Reckon Maury going to let me cry on him a while, too.

His name's Benjy now, Caddy said.

How come it is, Dilsey said. He aint wore out the name he was born with yet, is he.

Benjamin came out of the bible, Caddy said. It's a better name for him than Maury was.

How come it is, Dilsey said.

Mother says it is, Caddy said.

Huh, Dilsey said. Name aint going to help him. Hurt him, neither. Folks dont have no luck, changing names. My name been Dilsey since fore I could remember and it be Dilsey when they's long forgot me.

How will they know it's Dilsey, when it's long forgot, Dilsey, Caddy said.

It'll be in the Book, honey, Dilsey said. Writ out.

Can you read it, Caddy said.

Wont have to, Dilsey said. They'll read it for me. All I got to do is say Ise here.

The long wire came across my shoulder, and the fire went away. I began to cry.

Dilsey and Luster fought.

"I seen you." Dilsey said. "Oho, I seen you." She dragged Luster

out of the corner, shaking him. "Wasn't nothing bothering him, was
they. You just wait till your pappy come home. I wish I was young
like I use to be, I'd tear them years right off your head. I good
mind to lock you up in that cellar and not let you go to that show
tonight, I sho is."

"Ow, mammy." Luster said. "Ow, mammy."

I put my hand out to where the fire had been.

"Catch him." Dilsey said. "Catch him back."

My hand jerked back and I put it in my mouth and Dilsey
caught me. I could still hear the clock between my voice. Dilsey
reached back and hit Luster on the head. My voice was going loud
every time.

"Get that soda." Dilsey said. She took my hand out of my mouth.
My voice went louder then and my hand tried to go back to my
mouth, but Dilsey held it. My voice went loud. She sprinkled soda
on my hand.

"Look in the pantry and tear a piece off of that rag hanging on
the nail." she said. "Hush, now. You dont want to make your ma
sick again, does you. Here, look at the fire. Dilsey make your hand
stop hurting in just a minute. Look at the fire." She opened the
fire door. I looked at the fire, but my hand didn't stop and I didn't
stop. My hand was trying to go to my mouth but Dilsey held it.
She wrapped the cloth around it. Mother said,

"What is it now. Cant I even be sick in peace. Do I have to get
up out of bed to come down to him, with two grown negroes to
take care of him."

"He all right now." Dilsey said. "He going to quit. He just burnt
his hand a little."

"With two grown negroes, you must bring him into the house,
bawling." Mother said. "You got him started on purpose, because
you know I'm sick." She came and stood by me. "Hush." she said.
"Right this minute. Did you give him this cake."

"I bought it." Dilsey said. "It never come out of Jason's pantry. I
fixed him some birthday."

"Do you want to poison him with that cheap store cake." Mother
said. "Is that what you are trying to do. Am I never to have one
minute's peace."

"You go on back up stairs and lay down." Dilsey said. "It'll quit
smarting him in a minute now, and he'll hush. Come on, now."

"And leave him down here for you all to do something else to."
Mother said. "How can I lie there, with him bawling down here.
Benjamin. Hush this minute."

"They aint nowhere else to take him." Dilsey said. "We aint got
the room we use to have. He cant stay out in the yard, crying where
all the neighbors can see him."

"I know, I know." Mother said. "It's all my fault. I'll be gone
soon, and you and Jason will both get along better." She began to
cry.

"You hush that, now." Dilsey said. "You'll get yourself down
again. You come on back up stairs. Luster going to take him to the
liberry and play with him till I get his supper done."

Dilsey and Mother went out.

"Hush up." Luster said. "You hush up. You want me to burn your
other hand for you. You aint hurt. Hush up."

"Here." Dilsey said. "Stop crying, now." She gave me the slipper,
and I hushed. "Take him to the library." she said. "And if I hear
him again, I going to whip you myself."

We went to the library. Luster turned on the light. The windows
went black, and the dark tall place on the wall came and I went
and touched it. It was like a door, only it wasn't a door.

The fire came behind me and I went to the fire and sat on the
floor, holding the slipper. The fire went higher. It went onto the
cushion in Mother's chair.

"Hush up." Luster said. "Cant you never get done for a while.
Here I done built you a fire, and you wont even look at it."

Your name is Benjy. Caddy said. Do you hear. Benjy. Benjy.

Dont tell him that, Mother said. Bring him here.

Caddy lifted me under the arms.

Get up, Mau—— I mean Benjy, she said.

*Dont try to carry him, Mother said. Cant you lead him over here.
Is that too much for you to think of.*

I can carry him, Caddy said. "Let me carry him up, Dilsey."

"Go on, Minute." Dilsey said. "You aint big enough to tote a flea.
You go on and be quiet, like Mr Jason said."

There was a light at the top of the stairs. Father was there, in his
shirt sleeves. The way he looked said Hush. Caddy whispered,
"Is Mother sick."

*Versh set me down and we went into Mother's room. There was a
fire. It was rising and falling on the walls. There was another fire*

in the mirror. I could smell the sickness. It was a cloth folded on Mother's head. Her hair was on the pillow. The fire didn't reach it, but it shone on her hand, where her rings were jumping.

"Come and tell Mother goodnight." Caddy said. We went to the bed. The fire went out of the mirror. Father got up from the bed and lifted me up and Mother put her hand on my head.

"What time is it." Mother said. Her eyes were closed.

"Ten minutes to seven." Father said.

"It's too early for him to go to bed." Mother said. "He'll wake up at daybreak, and I simply cannot bear another day like today."

"There, there." Father said. He touched Mother's face.

"I know I'm nothing but a burden to you." Mother said. "But I'll be gone soon. Then you will be rid of my bothering."

"Hush." Father said. "I'll take him downstairs awhile." He took me up. "Come on, old fellow. Let's go downstairs awhile. We'll have to be quiet while Quentin is studying, now."

Caddy went and leaned her face over the bed and Mother's hand came into the firelight. Her rings jumped on Caddy's back.

Mother's sick, Father said. Dilsey will put you to bed. Where's Quentin.

Versh getting him, Dilsey said.

Father stood and watched us go past. We could hear Mother in her room. Caddy said "Hush." Jason was still climbing the stairs. He had his hands in his pockets.

"You all must be good tonight." Father said. "And be quiet, so you wont disturb Mother."

"We'll be quiet." Caddy said. "You must be quiet now, Jason." she said. We tiptoed.

We could hear the roof. I could see the fire in the mirror too. Caddy lifted me again.

"Come on, now." she said. "Then you can come back to the fire. Hush, now."

"Candace." Mother said.

"Hush, Benjy." Caddy said. "Mother wants you a minute. Like a good boy. Then you can come back, Benjy."

Caddy let me down, and I hushed.

"Let him stay here, Mother. When he's through looking at the fire, then you can tell him."

"Candace." Mother said. Caddy stooped and lifted me. We staggered. "Candace." Mother said.

"Hush." Caddy said. "You can still see it. Hush."

"Bring him here." Mother said. "He's too big for you to carry. You must stop trying. You'll injure your back. All of our women have prided themselves on their carriage. Do you want to look like a washer-woman."

"He's not too heavy." Caddy said. "I can carry him."

"Well, I dont want him carried, then." Mother said. "A five year old child. No, no. Not in my lap. Let him stand up."

"If you'll hold him, he'll stop." Caddy said. "Hush." she said. "You can go right back. Here. Here's your cushion. See."

"Dont, Candace." Mother said.

"Let him look at it and he'll be quiet." Caddy said. "Hold up just a minute while I slip it out. There, Benjy. Look."

I looked at it and hushed.

"You humour him too much." Mother said. "You and your father both. You dont realise that I am the one who has to pay for it. Damuddy spoiled Jason that way and it took him two years to outgrow it, and I am not strong enough to go through the same thing with Benjamin."

"You dont need to bother with him." Caddy said. "I like to take care of him. Dont I, Benjy."

"Candace." Mother said. "I told you not to call him that. It was bad enough when your father insisted on calling you by that silly nickname, and I will not have him called by one. Nicknames are vulgar. Only common people use them. Benjamin." she said.

"Look at me." Mother said.

"Benjamin." she said. She took my face in her hands and turned it to hers.

"Benjamin." she said. "Take that cushion away, Candace."

"He'll cry." Caddy said.

"Take that cushion away, like I told you." Mother said. "He must learn to mind."

The cushion went away.

"Hush, Benjy." Caddy said.

"You go over there and sit down." Mother said. "Benjamin." She held my face to hers.

"Stop that." she said. "Stop it."

But I didn't stop and Mother caught me in her arms and began to cry, and I cried. Then the cushion came back and Caddy held it above Mother's head. She drew Mother back in the chair and Mother lay crying against the red and yellow cushion.

"Hush, Mother." Caddy said. "You go upstairs and lay down, so you can be sick. I'll go get Dilsey." She led me to the fire and I looked at the bright, smooth shapes. I could hear the fire and the roof.

Father took me up. He smelled like rain.

"Well, Benjy." he said. "Have you been a good boy today."

Caddy and Jason were fighting in the mirror.

"You, Caddy." Father said.

They fought. Jason began to cry.

"Caddy." Father said. Jason was crying. He wasn't fighting any more, but we could see Caddy fighting in the mirror and Father put me down and went into the mirror and fought too. He lifted Caddy up. She fought. Jason lay on the floor, crying. He had the scissors in his hand. Father held Caddy.

"He cut up all Benjy's dolls." Caddy said. "I'll slit his gizzle."

"Candace." Father said.

"I will." Caddy said. "I will." She fought. Father held her. She kicked at Jason. He rolled into the corner, out of the mirror. Father brought Caddy to the fire. They were all out of the mirror. Only the fire was in it. Like the fire was in a door.

"Stop that." Father said. "Do you want to make Mother sick in her room."

Caddy stopped. "He cut up all the dolls Mau—Benjy and I made." Caddy said. "He did it just for meanness."

"I didn't." Jason said. He was sitting up, crying. "I didn't know they were his. I just thought they were some old papers."

"You couldn't help but know." Caddy said. "You did it just."

"Hush." Father said. "Jason." he said.

"I'll make you some more tomorrow." Caddy said. "We'll make a lot of them. Here, you can look at the cushion, too."

Jason came in.

I kept telling you to hush, Luster said.

What's the matter now, Jason said.

"He just trying hisself." Luster said. "That the way he been going on all day."

"Why dont you let him alone, then." Jason said. "If you cant keep him quiet, you'll have to take him out to the kitchen. The rest of us cant shut ourselves up in a room like Mother does."

"Mammy say keep him out the kitchen till she get supper." Luster said.

"Then play with him and keep him quiet." Jason said. "Do I have to work all day and then come home to a mad house." He opened the paper and read it.

You can look at the fire and the mirror and the cushion too, Caddy said. You wont have to wait until supper to look at the cushion, now. We could hear the roof. We could hear Jason too, crying loud beyond the wall.

Dilsey said, "You come, Jason. You letting him alone, is you."

"Yessum." Luster said.

"Where Quentin." Dilsey said. "Supper near bout ready."

"I dont know'm." Luster said. "I aint seen her."

Dilsey went away. "Quentin." she said in the hall. "Quentin. Supper ready."

We could hear the roof. Quentin smelled like rain, too.

What did Jason do, he said.

He cut up all Benjy's dolls, Caddy said.

Mother said to not call him Benjy, Quentin said. He sat on the rug by us. I wish it wouldn't rain, he said. You cant do anything.

You've been in a fight, Caddy said. Haven't you.

It wasn't much, Quentin said.

You can tell it, Caddy said. Father'll see it.

I dont care, Quentin said. I wish it wouldn't rain.

Quentin said, "Didn't Dilsey say supper was ready."

"Yessum." Luster said. Jason looked at Quentin. Then he read the paper again. Quentin came in. "She say it bout ready." Luster said. Quentin jumped down in Mother's chair. Luster said,

"Mr Jason."

"What." Jason said.

"Let me have two bits." Luster said.

"What for." Jason said.

"To go to the show tonight." Luster said.

"I thought Dilsey was going to get a quarter from Frony for you." Jason said.

"She did." Luster said. "I lost it. Me and Benjy hunted all day for that quarter. You can ask him."

"Then borrow one from him." Jason said. "I have to work for mine." He read the paper. Quentin looked at the fire. The fire was in her eyes and on her mouth. Her mouth was red.

"I tried to keep him away from there." Luster said.

"Shut your mouth." Quentin said. Jason looked at her.

"What did I tell you I was going to do if I saw you with that show fellow again." he said. Quentin looked at the fire. "Did you hear me." Jason said.

"I heard you." Quentin said. "Why dont you do it, then."

"Dont you worry." Jason said.

"I'm not." Quentin said. Jason read the paper again.

I could hear the roof. Father leaned forward and looked at Quentin.

Hello, he said. Who won.

"Nobody." Quentin said. "They stopped us. Teachers."

"Who was it." Father said. "Will you tell."

"It was all right." Quentin said. "He was as big as me."

"That's good." Father said. "Can you tell what it was about."

"It wasn't anything." Quentin said. "He said he would put a frog in her desk and she wouldn't dare to whip him."

"Oh." Father said. "She. And then what."

"Yes, sir." Quentin said. "And then I kind of hit him."

We could hear the roof and the fire, and a snuffling outside the door.

"Where was he going to get a frog in November." Father said.

"I dont know, sir." Quentin said.

We could hear them.

"Jason." Father said. We could hear Jason.

"Jason." Father said. "Come in here and stop that."

We could hear the roof and the fire and Jason.

"Stop that, now." Father said. "Do you want me to whip you again." Father lifted Jason up into the chair by him. Jason snuffled. We could hear the fire and the roof. Jason snuffled a little louder.

"One more time." Father said. We could hear the fire and the roof.

Dilsey said, All right. You all can come on to supper.

Versh smelled like rain. He smelled like a dog, too. We could hear the fire and the roof.

We could hear Caddy walking fast. Father and Mother looked at the door. Caddy passed it, walking fast. She didn't look. She walked fast.

"Candace." Mother said. Caddy stopped walking.

"Yes, Mother." she said.

"Hush, Caroline." Father said.

"Come here." Mother said.

"Hush, Caroline." Father said. "Let her alone."

Caddy came to the door and stood there, looking at Father and Mother. Her eyes flew at me, and away. I began to cry. It went loud and I got up. Caddy came in and stood with her back to the wall, looking at me. I went toward her, crying, and she shrank against the wall and I saw her eyes and I cried louder and pulled at her dress. She put her hands out but I pulled at her dress. Her eyes ran.

Versh said, Your name Benjamin now. You know how come your name Benjamin now. They making a bluegum out of you. Mammy say in old time your granpa changed nigger's name, and he turn preacher, and when they look at him, he bluegum too. Didn't use to be bluegum, neither. And when family woman look him in the eye in the full of the moon, chile born bluegum. And one evening, when they was about a dozen them bluegum chillen running round the place, he never come home. Possum hunters found him in the woods, et clean. And you know who et him. Them bluegum chillen did.

We were in the hall. Caddy was still looking at me. Her hand was against her mouth and I saw her eyes and I cried. We went up the stairs. She stopped again, against the wall, looking at me and I cried and she went on and I came on, crying, and she shrank against the wall, looking at me. She opened the door to her room, but I pulled at her dress and we went to the bathroom and she stood against the door, looking at me. Then she put her arm across her face and I pushed at her, crying.

What are you doing to him, Jason said. Why cant you let him alone.

I aint touching him, Luster said. He been doing this way all day long. He needs whipping.

He needs to be sent to Jackson, Quentin said. How can anybody live in a house like this.

If you dont like it, young lady, you'd better get out, Jason said.

I'm going to, Quentin said. Dont you worry.

Versh said, "You move back some, so I can dry my legs off." He shoved me back a little. "Dont you start bellering, now. You can still see it. That's all you have to do. You aint had to be out in the rain like I is. You's born lucky and dont know it." He lay on his back before the fire.

"You know how come your name Benjamin now." Versh said. "Your mamma too proud for you. What mammy say."

"You be still there and let me dry my legs off." Versh said. "Or you know what I'll do. I'll skin your rinktum."

We could hear the fire and the roof and Versh.

Versh got up quick and jerked his legs back. Father said, "All right, Versh."

"I'll feed him tonight." Caddy said. "Sometimes he cries when Versh feeds him."

"Take this tray up," Dilsey said. "And hurry back and feed Benjy."

"Dont you want Caddy to feed you." Caddy said.

Has he got to keep that old dirty slipper on the table, Quentin said. Why dont you feed him in the kitchen. It's like eating with a pig.

If you dont like the way we eat, you'd better not come to the table, Jason said.

Steam came off of Roskus. He was sitting in front of the stove. The oven door was open and Roskus had his feet in it. Steam came off the bowl. Caddy put the spoon into my mouth easy. There was a black spot on the inside of the bowl.

Now, now, Dilsey said. He aint going to bother you no more.

It got down below the mark. Then the bowl was empty. It went away. "He's hungry tonight." Caddy said. The bowl came back. I couldn't see the spot. Then I could. "He's starved, tonight." Caddy said. "Look how much he's eaten."

Yes he will, Quentin said. You all send him out to spy on me. I hate this house. I'm going to run away.

Roskus said, "It going to rain all night."

You've been running a long time, not to 've got any further off than mealtime, Jason said.

See if I dont, Quentin said.

"Then I dont know what I going to do." Dilsey said. "It caught me in the hip so bad now I cant scarcely move. Climbing them stairs all evening."

Oh, I wouldn't be surprised, Jason said. I wouldn't be surprised at anything you'd do.

Quentin threw her napkin on the table.

Hush your mouth, Jason, Dilsey said. *She went and put her arm around Quentin. Sit down, honey,* Dilsey said. *He ought to be shamed of hisself, throwing what aint your fault up to you.*

"She sulling again, is she." Roskus said.

"Hush your mouth." Dilsey said.

Quentin pushed Dilsey away. She looked at Jason. Her mouth was red. She picked up her glass of water and swung her arm back, looking at Jason. Dilsey caught her arm. They fought. The glass broke on the table, and the water ran into the table. Quentin was running.

"Mother's sick again." Caddy said.

"Sho she is." Dilsey said. "Weather like this make anybody sick. When you going to get done eating, boy."

Goddamn you, Quentin said. *Goddamn you. We could hear her running on the stairs. We went to the library.*

Caddy gave me the cushion, and I could look at the cushion and the mirror and the fire.

"We must be quiet while Quentin's studying." Father said. "What are you doing, Jason."

"Nothing." Jason said.

"Suppose you come over here to do it, then." Father said.

Jason came out of the corner.

"What are you chewing." Father said.

"Nothing." Jason said.

"He's chewing paper again." Caddy said.

"Come here, Jason." Father said.

Jason threw into the fire. It hissed, uncurled, turning black. Then it was gray. Then it was gone. Caddy and Father and Jason were in Mother's chair. Jason's eyes were puffed shut and his mouth moved, like tasting. Caddy's head was on Father's shoulder. Her hair was like fire, and little points of fire were in her eyes, and I went and Father lifted me into the chair too, and Caddy held me. She smelled like trees.

She smelled like trees. In the corner it was dark, but I could see the window. I squatted there, holding the slipper. I couldn't see it, but my hands saw it, and I could hear it getting night, and my hands saw the slipper but I couldn't see myself, but my hands could see the slipper and I squatted there, hearing it getting dark.

Here you is, Luster said. *Look what I got. He showed it to me. You know where I got it. Miss Quentin gave it to me. I knowed they*

*couldn't keep me out. What you doing, off in here. I thought you
done slipped back out doors. Aint you done enough moaning and
slobbering today, without hiding off in this here empty room, mumbling and taking on. Come on here to bed, so I can get up there
before it starts. I cant fool with you all night tonight. Just let them
horns toot the first toot and I done gone.*

We didn't go to our room.

"This is where we have the measles." Caddy said. "Why do we
have to sleep in here tonight."

"What you care where you sleep." Dilsey said. She shut the
door and sat down and began to undress me. Jason began to cry.
"Hush." Dilsey said.

"I want to sleep with Damuddy." Jason said.

"She's sick." Caddy said. "You can sleep with her when she gets
well. Cant he, Dilsey."

"Hush, now." Dilsey said. Jason hushed.

"Our nighties are here, and everything." Caddy said. "It's like
moving."

"And you better get into them." Dilsey said. "You be unbutton-
ing Jason."

Caddy unbuttoned Jason. He began to cry.

"You want to get whipped." Dilsey said. Jason hushed.

Quentin, Mother said in the hall.

*What, Quentin said beyond the wall. We heard Mother lock the
door. She looked in our door and came in and stooped over the
bed and kissed me on the forehead.*

*When you get him to bed, go and ask Dilsey if she objects to my
having a hot water bottle, Mother said. Tell her that if she does,
I'll try to get along without it. Tell her I just want to know.*

Yessum, Luster said. Come on. Get your pants off.

Quentin and Versh came in. Quentin had his face turned away.
"What are you crying for." Caddy said.

"Hush." Dilsey said. "You all get undressed, now. You can go on
home, Versh."

*I got undressed and I looked at myself, and I began to cry.
Hush, Luster said. Looking for them aint going to do no good.
They're gone. You keep on like this, and we aint going have you
no more birthday. He put my gown on. I hushed, and then Luster
stopped, his head toward the window. Then he went to the window
and looked out. He came back and took my arm. Here she come,*

he said. Be quiet, now. We went to the window and looked out.
It came out of Quentin's window and climbed across into the tree.
We watched the tree shaking. The shaking went down the tree, then
it came out and we watched it go away across the grass. Then we
couldn't see it. Come on, Luster said. There now. Hear them
horns. You get in that bed while my foots behaves.

There were two beds. Quentin got in the other one. He turned his
face to the wall. Dilsey put Jason in with him. Caddy took her dress
off.

"Just look at your drawers." Dilsey said. "You better be glad your
ma aint seen you."

"I already told on her." Jason said.

"I bound you would." Dilsey said.

"And see what you got by it." Caddy said. "Tattletale."

"What did I get by it." Jason said.

"Whyn't you get your nightie on." Dilsey said. She went and
helped Caddy take off her bodice and drawers. "Just look at you."
Dilsey said. She wadded the drawers and scrubbed Caddy behind
with them. "It done soaked clean through onto you." she said. "But
you wont get no bath this night. Here." She put Caddy's nightie
on her and Caddy climbed into the bed and Dilsey went to the
door and stood with her hand on the light. "You all be quiet now,
you hear." she said.

"All right." Caddy said. "Mother's not coming in tonight." she
said. "So we still have to mind me."

"Yes." Dilsey said. "Go to sleep, now."

"Mother's sick." Caddy said. "She and Damuddy are both sick."

"Hush." Dilsey said. "You go to sleep."

The room went black, except the door. Then the door went
black. Caddy said, "Hush, Maury," putting her hand on me. So I
stayed hushed. We could hear us. We could hear the dark.

It went away, and Father looked at us. He looked at Quentin and
Jason, then he came and kissed Caddy and put his hand on my
head.

"Is Mother very sick." Caddy said.

"No." Father said. "Are you going to take good care of Maury."

"Yes." Caddy said.

Father went to the door and looked at us again. Then the dark
came back, and he stood black in the door, and then the door
turned black again. Caddy held me and I could hear us all, and

the darkness, and something I could smell. And then I could see the windows, where the trees were buzzing. Then the dark began to go in smooth, bright shapes, like it always does, even when Caddy says that I have been asleep.

JUNE 2, 1910

When the shadow of the sash appeared on the curtains it was between seven and eight oclock and then I was in time again, hearing the watch. It was Grandfather's and when Father gave it to me he said, Quentin, I give you the mausoleum of all hope and desire; it's rather excrutiating-ly apt that you will use it to gain the reducto absurdum of all human experience which can fit your individual needs no better than it fitted his or his father's. I give it to you not that you may remember time, but that you might forget it now and then for a moment and not spend all your breath trying to conquer it. Because no battle is ever won he said. They are not even fought. The field only reveals to man his own folly and despair, and victory is an illusion of philosophers and fools.

It was propped against the collar box and I lay listening to it. Hearing it, that is. I dont suppose anybody ever deliberately listens to a watch or a clock. You dont have to. You can be oblivious to the sound for a long while, then in a second of ticking it can create in the mind unbroken the long diminishing parade of time you didn't hear. Like Father said down the long and lonely light-rays you might see Jesus walking, like. And the good Saint Francis that said Little Sister Death, that never had a sister.

Through the wall I heard Shreve's bed-springs and then his slippers on the floor hishing. I got up and went to the dresser and slid my hand along it and touched the watch and turned it face-down and went back to bed. But the shadow of the sash was still there and I had learned to tell almost to the minute, so I'd have to turn my back to it, feeling the eyes animals used to have in the back of their heads when it was on top, itching. It's always the idle habits you acquire which you will regret. Father said that. That Christ was not crucified: he was worn away by a minute clicking of little wheels. That had no sister.

And so as soon as I knew I couldn't see it, I began to wonder what time it was. Father said that constant speculation regarding the position of mechanical hands on an arbitrary dial which is a symptom of mind-function. Excrement Father said like sweating. And I saying All right. Wonder. Go on and wonder.

If it had been cloudy I could have looked at the window, thinking what he said about idle habits. Thinking it would be nice for them down at New London if the weather held up like this. Why shouldn't it? The mouth of brides, the voice that breathed *She ran right out of the mirror, out of the banked scent. Roses. Roses. Mr and Mrs Jason Richmond Compson announce the marriage of.* Roses. Not virgins like dogwood, milkweed. I said I have committed incest, Father I said. Roses. Cunning and serene. If you attend Harvard one year, but dont see the boat race, there should be a refund. Let Jason have it. Give Jason a year at Harvard.

Shreve stood in the door, putting his collar on, his glasses glinting rosily, as though he had washed them with his face. "You taking a cut this morning?"

"Is it that late?"

He looked at his watch. "Bell in two minutes."

"I didn't know it was that late." He was still looking at the watch, his mouth shaping. "I'll have to hustle. I cant stand another cut. The dean told me last week—" He put the watch back into his pocket. Then I quit talking.

"You'd better slip on your pants and run," he said. He went out. I got up and moved about, listening to him through the wall. He entered the sitting room, toward the door.

"Aren't you ready yet?"

"Not yet. Run along. I'll make it."

He went out. The door closed. His feet went down the corridor. Then I could hear the watch again. I quit moving around and went to the window and drew the curtains aside and watched them running for chapel, the same ones fighting the same heaving coatsleeves, the same books and flapping collars flushing past like debris on a flood, and Spoade. Calling Shreve my husband. Ah let him alone, Shreve said, if he's got better sense than to chase after the little dirty sluts, whose business. In the South you are ashamed of being a virgin. Boys. Men. They lie about it. Because it means less to women, Father said. He said it was men invented virginity not women. Father said it's like death: only a state in which the others are left and I said, But to believe it doesn't matter and he said, That's what's so sad about anything: not only virginity, and I said, Why couldn't it have been me and not her who is unvirgin and he said, That's why that's sad too; nothing is even worth the changing of it, and Shreve said if he's got better sense than to chase after the little dirty sluts and I said Did you ever have a sister? Did you? Did you?

Spoade was in the middle of them like a terrapin in a street full of scuttering dead leaves, his collar about his ears, moving at his customary unhurried walk. He was from South Carolina, a senior. It was his club's boast that he never ran for chapel and had never got there on time and had never been absent in four years and had never made either chapel or first lecture with a shirt on his back and socks on his feet. About ten oclock he'd come in Thompson's, get two cups of coffee, sit down and take his socks out of his pocket and remove his shoes and put them on while the coffee cooled. About noon you'd see him with a shirt and collar on, like anybody else. The others passed him running, but he never increased his pace at all. After a while the quad was empty.

A sparrow slanted across the sunlight, onto the window ledge, and cocked his head at me. His eye was round and bright. First he'd watch me with one eye, then flick! and it would be the other one, his throat pumping faster than any pulse. The hour began to strike. The sparrow quit swapping eyes and watched me steadily with the same one until the chimes ceased, as if he were listening too. Then he flicked off the ledge and was gone.

It was a while before the last stroke ceased vibrating. It stayed in the air, more felt than heard, for a long time. Like all the bells that ever rang still ringing in the long dying light-rays and Jesus and Saint Francis talking about his sister. Because if it were just to hell; if that were all of it. Finished. If things just finished themselves. Nobody else there but her and me. If we could just have done something so dreadful that they would have fled hell except us. *I have committed incest I said Father it was I it was not Dalton Ames* And when he put Dalton Ames. Dalton Ames. Dalton Ames. When he put the pistol in my hand I didn't. That's why I didn't. He would be there and she would and I would. Dalton Ames. Dalton Ames. Dalton Ames. If we could have just done something so dreadful and Father said That's sad too, people cannot do anything that dreadful they cannot do anything very dreadful at all they cannot even remember tomorrow what seemed dreadful today and I said, You can shirk all things and he said, Ah can you. And I will look down and see my murmuring bones and the deep water like wind, like a roof of wind, and after a long time they cannot distinguish even bones upon the lonely and inviolate sand. Until on the Day when He says Rise only the flatiron would come floating up. It's not when you realise that nothing can help you—religion, pride, anything—it's when you realise that you dont need any aid. Dalton Ames. Dalton Ames. Dalton Ames. If I could have been his mother lying with open body lifted laughing, holding his father with my hand refraining, seeing, watching him die before he lived. *One minute she was standing in the door*

I went to the dresser and took up the watch, with the face still down. I tapped the crystal on the corner of the dresser and caught the fragments of glass in my hand and put them into the ashtray and twisted the hands off and put them in the tray. The watch ticked on. I turned the face up, the blank dial with little wheels clicking and clicking behind it, not knowing any better. Jesus walking on Galilee and Washington not telling lies. Father brought back a watch-charm from the Saint Louis Fair to Jason: a tiny opera glass into which you squinted with one eye and saw a skyscraper, a ferris wheel all spidery, Niagara Falls on a pinhead. There was a red smear on the dial. When I saw it my thumb began to smart. I put the watch down and went into Shreve's room and got the iodine and painted the cut. I cleaned the rest of the glass out of the rim with the towel.

I laid out two suits of underwear, with socks, shirts, collars and ties, and packed my trunk. I put in everything except my new suit and an old one and two pairs of shoes and two hats, and my books. I carried the books into the sitting-room and stacked them on the table, the ones I had brought from home and the ones *Father said it used to be a gentleman was known by his books; nowadays he is known by the ones he has not returned* and locked the trunk and addressed it. The quarter hour sounded. I stopped and listened to it until the chimes ceased.

I bathed and shaved. The water made my finger smart a little, so I painted it again. I put on my new suit and put my watch on and packed the other suit and the accessories and my razor and brushes in my hand bag, and wrapped the trunk key into a sheet of paper and put it in an envelope and addressed it to Father, and wrote the two notes and sealed them.

The shadow hadn't quite cleared the stoop. I stopped inside the door, watching the shadow move. It moved almost perceptibly, creeping back inside the door, driving the shadow back into the door. *Only she was running already when I heard it. In the mirror she was running before I knew what it was. That quick, her train caught up over her arm she ran out of the mirror like a cloud, her veil swirling in long glints her heels brittle and fast clutching her dress onto her shoulder with the other hand, running out of the mirror the smells roses roses the voice that breathed o'er Eden. Then she was across the porch I couldn't hear her heels then in the moonlight like a cloud, the floating shadow of the veil running across the grass, into the bellowing. She ran out of her dress, clutching her bridal, running into the bellowing where T. P. in the dew Whooey Sassprilluh Benjy under the box bellowing. Father had a V-shaped silver cuirass on his running chest*

Shreve said, "Well, you didn't. . . . Is it a wedding or a wake?"

"I couldn't make it," I said.

"Not with all that primping. What's the matter? You think this was Sunday?"

"I reckon the police wont get me for wearing my new suit one time," I said.

"I was thinking about the Square students. Have you got too proud to attend classes too?"

"I'm going to eat first." The shadow on the stoop was gone. I stepped into sunlight, finding my shadow again. I walked down the steps just ahead of it. The half hour went. Then the chimes ceased and died away.

Deacon wasn't at the postoffice either. I stamped the two envelopes and mailed the one to Father and put Shreve's in my inside pocket, and then I remembered where I had last seen the Deacon. It was on Decoration Day, in a G. A. R. uniform, in the middle of the parade. If you waited long enough on any corner you would see him in whatever parade came along. The one before was on Columbus' or Garibaldi's or somebody's birthday. He was in the Street Sweeper's section, in a stovepipe hat, carrying a two inch Italian flag, smoking a cigar among the brooms and scoops. But the last time was the G. A. R. one, because Shreve said:

"There now. Just look at what your grandpa did to that poor old nigger."

"Yes," I said, "Now he can spend day after day marching in parades. If it hadn't been for my grandfather, he'd have to work like whitefolks."

I didn't see him anywhere. But I never knew even a working nigger that you could find when you wanted him, let alone one that lived off the fat of the land. A car came along. I went over to town and went to Parker's and had a good breakfast. While I was eating I heard a clock strike the hour. But then I suppose it takes at least one hour to lose time in, who has been longer than history getting into the mechanical progression of it.

When I finished breakfast I bought a cigar. The girl said a fifty cent one was the best, so I took one and lit it and went out to the street. I stood there and took a couple of puffs, then I held it in my hand and went on toward the corner. I passed a jeweller's window, but I looked away in time. At the corner two bootblacks caught me, one on either side, shrill and raucous, like blackbirds. I gave the cigar to one of them, and the other one a nickel. Then they let me alone. The one with the cigar was trying to sell it to the other for the nickel.

There was a clock, high up in the sun, and I thought about how, when you dont want to do a thing, your body will try to trick you into doing it, sort of unawares. I could feel the muscles in the back of my neck, and then I could hear my watch ticking away in my pocket and after a while I had all the other sounds shut away, leaving only the watch in my pocket. I turned back up the street, to the window. He was working at the table behind the window. He was going bald. There was a glass in his eye—a metal tube screwed into his face. I went in.

The place was full of ticking, like crickets in September grass, and I could hear a big clock on the wall above his head. He looked up, his eye big and blurred and rushing beyond the glass. I took mine out and handed it to him.

"I broke my watch."

He flipped it over in his hand. "I should say you have. You must have stepped on it."

"Yes, sir. I knocked it off the dresser and stepped on it in the dark. It's still running though."

He pried the back open and squinted into it. "Seems to be all right. I cant tell until I go over it, though. I'll go into it this afternoon."

"I'll bring it back later," I said. "Would you mind telling me if any of those watches in the window are right?"

He held my watch on his palm and looked up at me with his blurred rushing eye.

"I made a bet with a fellow," I said, "And I forgot my glasses this morning."

"Why, all right," he said. He laid the watch down and half rose on his stool and looked over the barrier. Then he glanced up at the wall. "It's twen—"

"Dont tell me," I said, "please sir. Just tell me if any of them are right."

He looked at me again. He sat back on the stool and pushed the glass up onto his forehead. It left a red circle around his eye and when it was gone his whole face looked naked. "What're you celebrating today?" he said. "That boat race aint until next week, is it?"

"No, sir. This is just a private celebration. Birthday. Are any of them right?"

"No. But they haven't been regulated and set yet. If you're thinking of buying one of them—"

"No, sir. I dont need a watch. We have a clock in our sitting room. I'll have this one fixed when I do." I reached my hand.

"Better leave it now."

"I'll bring it back later." He gave me the watch. I put it in my pocket. I couldn't hear it now, above all the others. "I'm much obliged to you. I hope I haven't taken up your time."

"That's all right. Bring it in when you are ready. And you better put off this celebration until after we win that boat race."

"Yes, sir. I reckon I had."

I went out, shutting the door upon the ticking. I looked back into the window. He was watching me across the barrier. There were about a dozen watches in the window, a dozen different hours and each with the same assertive and contradictory assurance that mine had, without any hands at all. Contradicting one another. I could hear mine, ticking away inside my pocket, even though nobody could see it, even though it could tell nothing if anyone could.

And so I told myself to take that one. Because Father said clocks slay time. He said time is dead as long as it is being clicked off by little wheels; only when the clock stops does time come to life. The hands were extended, slightly off the horizontal at a faint angle, like a gull tilting into the wind. Holding all I used to be sorry about like the new moon holding water, niggers say. The jeweller was working again, bent over his bench, the tube tunnelled into his face. His hair was parted in the center. The part ran up into the bald spot, like a drained marsh in December.

I saw the hardware store from across the street. I didn't know you bought flatirons by the pound.

The clerk said, "These weigh ten pounds." Only they were bigger than I thought. So I got two six-pound little ones, because they would look like a pair of shoes wrapped up. They felt heavy enough together, but I thought again how Father had said about the reducto absurdum of human experience, thinking how the only opportunity I seemed to have for the application of Harvard. Maybe by next year; thinking maybe it takes two years in school to learn to do that properly.

But they felt heavy enough in the air. A street car came. I got on. I didn't see the placard on the front. It was full, mostly prosperous looking people reading newspapers. The only vacant seat was beside a nigger. He wore a derby and shined shoes and he was holding a dead cigar stub. I used to think that a Southerner had to be always conscious of niggers. I thought that Northerners would expect him to. When I first came East I kept thinking You've got to remember to think of them as coloured people not niggers, and if it hadn't happened that I wasn't thrown with many of them, I'd have wasted a lot of time and trouble before I learned that the best way to take all people, black or white, is to take them for what they think they are, then leave them alone. That was when I realised that a nigger is not a person so much as a form of behaviour; a sort of obverse reflection of the white people he lives among. But I thought at first that I ought to miss having a lot of them around me because I thought that Northerners thought I did, but I didn't know that I really had missed Roskus and Dilsey and them until that morning in Virginia. The train was stopped when I waked and I raised the shade and looked out. The car was blocking a road crossing, where two white fences came down a hill and then sprayed outward and downward like part of the skeleton of a horn, and there was a nigger on a mule in the middle of the stiff ruts, waiting for the train to move. How long he had been there I didn't know, but he sat straddle of the mule, his head wrapped in a piece of blanket, as if they had been built there with the fence and the road, or with the hill, carved out of the hill itself, like a sign put there saying You are home again. He didn't have a saddle and his feet dangled almost to the ground. The mule looked like a rabbit. I raised the window.

"Hey, Uncle," I said, "Is this the way?"

"Suh?" He looked at me, then he loosened the blanket and lifted it away from his ear.

"Christmas gift!" I said.

"Sho comin, boss. You done caught me, aint you?"

"I'll let you off this time." I dragged my pants out of the little hammock and got a quarter out. "But look out next time. I'll be coming back through here two days after New Year, and look out then." I threw the quarter out the window. "Buy yourself some Santy Claus."

"Yes, suh," he said. He got down and picked up the quarter and rubbed it on his leg. "Thanky, young marster. Thanky." Then the train began to move. I leaned out the window, into the cold air, looking back. He stood there beside the gaunt rabbit of a mule, the two of them shabby and motionless and unimpatient. The train swung around the curve, the engine puffing with short, heavy blasts, and they passed smoothly from sight that way, with that quality about them of shabby and timeless patience, of static serenity: that blending of childlike and ready incompetence and paradoxical reliability that tends and protects them it loves out of all reason and robs them steadily and evades responsibility and obligations by means too barefaced to be called subterfuge even and is taken in theft or evasion with only that frank and spontaneous admiration for the victor which a gentleman feels for anyone who beats him in a fair contest, and withal a fond and unflagging tolerance for whitefolks' vagaries like that of a grandparent for unpredictable and troublesome children, which I had forgotten. And all that day, while the train wound through rushing gaps and along ledges where movement was only a labouring sound of the exhaust and groaning wheels and the eternal mountains stood fading into the thick sky, I thought of home, of the bleak station and the mud and the niggers and country folks thronging slowly about the square, with toy monkeys and wagons and candy in sacks and roman candles sticking out, and my insides would move like they used to do in school when the bell rang.

I wouldn't begin counting until the clock struck three. Then I would begin, counting to sixty and folding down one finger and thinking of the other fourteen fingers waiting to be folded down, or thirteen or twelve or eight or seven, until all of a sudden I'd realise silence and the unwinking minds, and I'd say "Ma'am?" "Your name is Quentin, isn't it?" Miss Laura said. Then more silence and the cruel unwinking minds and hands jerking into the silence. "Tell Quentin who discovered the Mississippi River, Henry." "DeSoto." Then the minds would go away, and after a while I'd be afraid I had gotten behind and I'd count fast and fold down another finger, then I'd be afraid I was going too fast and I'd slow up, then I'd get afraid and count fast again. So I never could come out even with the bell, and the released surging of feet moving already, feeling earth in the scuffed floor, and the day like a pane of glass struck a light, sharp blow, and my insides would move, sitting still. *Moving sitting still. One minute she was standing in the door. Benjy. Bellowing. Benjamin the child of mine old age bellowing. Caddy! Caddy!*

I'm going to run away. He began to cry she went and touched him. Hush. I'm not going to. Hush. He hushed. Dilsey.

He smell what you tell him when he want to. Dont have to listen nor talk.

Can he smell that new name they give him? Can he smell bad luck?

What he want to worry about luck for? Luck cant do him no hurt.

What they change his name for then if aint trying to help his luck?

The street car stopped, started, stopped again. Below the window I watched the crowns of people's heads passing beneath new straw hats not yet unbleached. There were women in the car now, with market baskets, and men in work-clothes were beginning to outnumber the shined shoes and collars.

The nigger touched my knee. "Pardon me," he said. I swung my legs out and let him pass. We were going beside a blank wall, the sound clattering back into the car, at the women with market baskets on their knees and a man in a stained hat with a pipe stuck in the band. I could smell water, and in a break in the wall I saw a glint of water and two masts, and a gull motionless in midair, like on an invisible wire between the masts, and I raised my hand and through my coat touched the letters I had written. When the car stopped I got off.

The bridge was open to let a schooner through. She was in tow, the tug nudging along under her quarter, trailing smoke, but the ship herself was like she was moving without visible means. A man naked to the waist was coiling down a line on the fo'c's'le head. His body was burned the colour of leaf tobacco. Another man in a straw hat without any crown was at the wheel. The ship went through the bridge, moving under bare poles like a ghost in broad day, with three gulls hovering above the stern like toys on invisible wires.

When it closed I crossed to the other side and leaned on the rail above the boathouses. The float was empty and the doors were closed. The crew just pulled in the late afternoon now, resting up before. The shadow of the bridge, the tiers of railing, my shadow leaning flat upon the water, so easily had I tricked it that it would not quit me. At least fifty feet it was, and if I only had something to blot it into the water, holding it until it was drowned, the shadow of the package like two shoes wrapped up lying on the water. Niggers say a drowned man's shadow was watching for him in the water all the time. It twinkled and glinted, like breathing, the float slow like breathing too, and debris half submerged, healing out to the sea and the caverns and the grottoes of the sea. The displacement of water is equal to the something of something. Reducto absurdum of all human experience, and two six-pound flatirons weigh more than one tailor's goose. What a sinful waste Dilsey would say. Benjy knew it when Damuddy died. He cried. *He smell hit. He smell hit.*

The tug came back downstream, the water shearing in long rolling cylinders, rocking the float at last with the echo of passage, the float lurching onto the rolling cylinder with a plopping sound and a long jarring noise as the door rolled back and two men emerged, carrying a shell. They set it in the water and a moment later Bland came out, with the sculls. He wore flannels, a grey jacket and a stiff straw hat. Either he or his mother had read somewhere that Oxford students pulled in flannels and stiff hats, so early one March they bought Gerald a one pair shell and in his flannels and stiff hat he went on the river. The folks at the boathouses threatened to call a policeman, but he went anyway. His mother came down in a hired auto, in a fur suit like an arctic explorer's, and saw him off in a twenty-five mile wind and a steady drove of ice floes like dirty sheep. Ever since then I have believed that God is not only a gentleman and a sport; He is a Kentuckian too. When he sailed away she made a detour and came down to the river again and drove along parallel with him, the car in low gear. They said you couldn't have told they'd ever seen one another before, like a King and Queen, not even looking at one another, just moving side by side across Massachusetts on parallel courses like a couple of planets.

He got in and pulled away. He pulled pretty well now. He ought to. They said his mother tried to make him give rowing up and do something else the rest of his class couldn't or wouldn't do, but for once he was stubborn. If you could call it stubbornness, sitting in his attitudes of princely boredom, with his curly yellow hair and his violet eyes and his eyelashes and his New York clothes, while his mamma was telling us about Gerald's horses and Gerald's niggers and Gerald's women. Husbands and fathers in Kentucky must have been awful glad when she carried Gerald off to Cambridge. She had an apartment over in town, and Gerald had one there too, besides his rooms in college. She approved of Gerald associating with me because I at least revealed a blundering sense of noblesse oblige by getting myself born below Mason and Dixon, and a few others whose geography met the requirements (minimum) Forgave, at least. Or condoned. But since she met Spoade coming out of chapel one He said she couldn't be a lady no lady would be out at that hour of the night she never had been able to forgive him for having five names, including that of a present English ducal house. I'm sure she solaced herself by being convinced that some misfit Maingault or Mortemar had got mixed up with the lodge-keeper's daughter. Which was quite probable, whether she invented it or not. Spoade was the world's champion sitter-a-round, no holds barred and gouging discretionary.

The shell was a speck now, the oars catching the sun in spaced glints, as if the hull were winking itself along. *Did you ever have a sister? No but they're all bitches. Did you ever have a sister? One minute she was. Bitches. Not bitch one minute she stood in the door* Dalton Ames. Dalton Ames. Dalton Shirts. I thought all the time they were khaki, army issue khaki, until I saw they were of heavy Chinese silk or finest flannel because they made his face so brown his eyes so blue. Dalton Ames. It just missed gentility. Theatrical fixture. Just papier-mache, then touch. Oh. Asbestos. Not quite bronze. *But wont see him at the house.*

Caddy's a woman too, remember. She must do things for women's reasons, too.

Why wont you bring him to the house, Caddy? Why must you do like nigger women do in the pasture the ditches the dark woods not hidden furious in the dark woods.

And after a while I had been hearing my watch for some time and I could feel the letters crackle through my coat, against the railing, and I leaned on the railing, watching my shadow, how I had tricked it. I moved along the rail, but my suit was dark too and I could wipe my hands, watching my shadow, how I had tricked it. I walked it into the shadow of the quai. Then I went east.

Harvard my Harvard boy Harvard harvard That pimple-faced infant she met at the field-meet with coloured ribbons. Skulking along the fence trying to whistle her out like a puppy. Because they couldn't cajole him into the diningroom Mother believed he had some sort of spell he was going to cast on her when he got her alone. Yet any blackguard *He was lying beside the box under the window bellowing* that could drive up in a limousine with a flower in his buttonhole. *Harvard. Quentin this is Herbert. My Harvard boy. Herbert will be a big brother has already promised Jason a position in the bank.*

Hearty, celluloid like a drummer. Face full of teeth white but not smiling. *I've heard of him up there.* All teeth but not smiling. *You going to drive?*

Get in Quentin.

You going to drive.

It's her car aren't you proud of your little sister owns first auto in town Herbert his present. Louis has been giving her lessons every morning didn't you get my letter Mr and Mrs Jason Richmond Compson announce the marriage of their daughter Candace to Mr Sydney Herbert Head on the twenty-fifth of April one thousand nine hundred and ten at Jefferson Mississippi. At home after the first of August number Something Something Avenue South Bend Indiana. Shreve said Aren't you even going to open it? *Three days. Times. Mr and Mrs Jason Richmond Compson* Young Lochinvar rode out of the west a little too soon, didn't he?

I'm from the south. You're funny, aren't you.

O yes I knew it was somewhere in the country.

You're funny, aren't you. You ought to join the circus.

I did. That's how I ruined my eyes watering the elephant's fleas.

Three times These country girls. You cant even tell about them,
can you. Well, anyway Byron never had his wish, thank God. *But
not hit a man in glasses.* Aren't you even going to open it? *It lay
on the table a candle burning at each corner upon the envelope
tied in a soiled pink garter two artificial flowers. Not hit a man in
glasses.*

Country people poor things they never saw an auto before lots
of them honk the horn Candace so *She wouldn't look at me* they'll
get out of the way *wouldn't look at me* your father wouldn't like
it if you were to injure one of them I'll declare your father will
simply have to get an auto now I'm almost sorry you brought it
down Herbert I've enjoyed it so much of course there's the carriage
but so often when I'd like to go out Mr Compson has the darkies
doing something it would be worth my head to interrupt he insists
that Roskus is at my call all the time but I know what that means
I know how often people make promises just to satisfy their con-
sciences are you going to treat my little baby girl that way Herbert
but I know you wont Herbert has spoiled us all to death Quentin
did I write you that he is going to take Jason into his bank when
Jason finishes high school Jason will make a splendid banker he
is the only one of my children with any practical sense you can
thank me for that he takes after my people the others are all Compson *Jason furnished the flour. They made kites on the back porch
and sold them for a nickel a piece, he and the Patterson boy. Jason
was treasurer.*

There was no nigger in this street car, and the hats unbleached
as yet flowing past under the window. Going to Harvard. We have
sold Benjy's *He lay on the ground under the window, bellowing.
We have sold Benjy's pasture so that Quentin may go to Harvard*
a brother to you Your little brother.

You should have a car it's done you no end of good dont you
think so Quentin I call him Quentin at once you see I have heard
so much about him from Candace.

Why shouldn't you I want my boys to be more than friends yes
Candace and Quentin more than friends *Father I have committed*
what a pity you had no brother or sister *No sister no sister had no
sister* Dont ask Quentin he and Mr Compson both feel a little insulted when I am strong enough to come down to the table I am
going on nerve now I'll pay for it after it's all over and you have

taken my little daughter away from me *My little sister had no. If I could say Mother. Mother*

Unless I do what I am tempted to and take you instead I dont think Mr Compson could overtake the car.

Ah Herbert Candace do you hear that *She wouldn't look at me soft stubborn jaw-angle not back-looking* You needn't be jealous though it's just an old woman he's flattering a grown married daughter I cant believe it.

Nonsense you look like a girl you are lots younger than Candace colour in your cheeks like a girl *A face reproachful tearful an odour of camphor and of tears a voice weeping steadily and softly beyond the twilit door the twilight-coloured smell of honeysuckle. Bringing empty trunks down the attic stairs they sounded like coffins French Lick. Found not death at the salt lick*

Hats not unbleached and not hats. In three years I can not wear a hat. I could not. Was. Will there be hats then since I was not and not Harvard then. Where the best of thought Father said clings like dead ivy vines upon old dead brick. Not Harvard then. Not to me, anyway. Again. Sadder than was. Again. Saddest of all. Again.

Spoade had a shirt on; then it must be. When I can see my shadow again if not careful that I tricked into the water shall tread again upon my impervious shadow. But no sister. I wouldn't have done it. *I wont have my daughter spied on* I wouldn't have.

How can I control any of them when you have always taught them to have no respect for me and my wishes I know you look down on my people but is that any reason for teaching my children my own children I suffered for to have no respect Trampling my shadow's bones into the concrete with hard heels and then I was hearing the watch, and I touched the letters through my coat.

I will not have my daughter spied on by you or Quentin or anybody no matter what you think she has done

At least you agree there is reason for having her watched

I wouldn't have I wouldn't have. *I know you wouldn't I didn't mean to speak so sharply but women have no respect for each other for themselves*

But why did she The chimes began as I stepped on my shadow, but it was the quarter hour. The Deacon wasn't in sight anywhere. *think I would have could have*

She didn't mean that that's the way women do things its because she loves Caddy

The street lamps would go down the hill then rise toward town I walked upon the belly of my shadow. I could extend my hand beyond it. *feeling Father behind me beyond the rasping darkness of summer and August the street lamps* Father and I protect women from one another from themselves our women *Women are like that they dont acquire knowledge of people we are for that they are just born with a practical fertility of suspicion that makes a crop every so often and usually right they have an affinity for evil for supplying whatever the evil lacks in itself for drawing it about them instinctively as you do bedclothing in slumber fertilising the mind for it until the evil has served its purpose whether it ever existed or no* He was coming along between a couple of freshmen. He hadn't quite recovered from the parade, for he gave me a salute, a very superior-officerish kind.

"I want to see you a minute," I said, stopping.

"See me? All right. See you again, fellows," he said, stopping and turning back; "glad to have chatted with you." That was the Deacon, all over. Talk about your natural psychologists. They said he hadn't missed a train at the beginning of school in forty years, and that he could pick out a Southerner with one glance. He never missed, and once he had heard you speak, he could name your state. He had a regular uniform he met trains in, a sort of Uncle Tom's cabin outfit, patches and all.

"Yes, suh. Right dis way, young marster, hyer we is," taking your bags. "Hyer, boy, come hyer and git dese grips." Whereupon a moving mountain of luggage would edge up, revealing a white boy of about fifteen, and the Deacon would hang another bag on him somehow and drive him off. "Now, den, dont you drap hit. Yes, suh, young marster, jes give de old nigger yo room number, and hit'll be done got cold dar when you arrives."

From then on until he had you completely subjugated he was always in or out of your room, ubiquitous and garrulous, though his manner gradually moved northward as his raiment improved, until at last when he had bled you until you began to learn better he was calling you Quentin or whatever, and when you saw him next he'd be wearing a cast-off Brooks suit and a hat with a Princeton club I forget which band that someone had given him and which he was pleasantly and unshakably convinced was a part of

Abe Lincoln's military sash. Someone spread the story years ago, when he first appeared around college from wherever he came from, that he was a graduate of the divinity school. And when he came to understand what it meant he was so taken with it that he began to retail the story himself, until at last he must come to believe he really had. Anyway he related long pointless anecdotes of his undergraduate days, speaking familiarly of dead and departed professors by their first names, usually incorrect ones. But he had been guide mentor and friend to unnumbered crops of innocent and lonely freshmen, and I suppose that with all his petty chicanery and hypocrisy he stank no higher in heaven's nostrils than any other.

"Haven't seen you in three-four days," he said, staring at me from his still military aura. "You been sick?"

"No. I've been all right. Working, I reckon. I've seen you, though."

"Yes?"

"In the parade the other day."

"Oh, that. Yes, I was there. I dont care nothing about that sort of thing, you understand, but the boys likes to have me with them, the vet'runs does. Ladies wants all the old vet'runs to turn out, you know. So I has to oblige them."

"And on that Wop holiday too," I said. "You were obliging the W. C. T. U. then, I reckon."

"That? I was doing that for my son-in-law. He aims to get a job on the city forces. Street cleaner. I tells him all he wants is a broom to sleep on. You saw me, did you?"

"Both times. Yes."

"I mean, in uniform. How'd I look?"

"You looked fine. You looked better than any of them. They ought to make you a general, Deacon."

He touched my arm, lightly, his hand that worn, gentle quality of niggers' hands. "Listen. This aint for outside talking. I dont mind telling you because you and me's the same folks, come long and short." He leaned a little to me, speaking rapidly, his eyes not looking at me. "I've got strings out, right now. Wait till next year. Just wait. Then see where I'm marching. I wont need to tell you how I'm fixing it; I say, just wait and see, my boy." He looked at me now and clapped me lightly on the shoulder and rocked back on his heels, nodding at me. "Yes, sir. I didnt turn Democrat three years ago for nothing. My son-in-law on the city; me—Yes, sir. If just turning Democrat'll make that son of a bitch go to work. . . . And me: just you stand on that corner yonder a year from two days ago, and see."

"I hope so. You deserve it, Deacon. And while I think about it—" I took the letter from my pocket. "Take this around to my room tomorrow and give it to Shreve. He'll have something for you. But not till tomorrow, mind."

He took the letter and examined it. "It's sealed up."

"Yes. And it's written inside, Not good until tomorrow."

"H'm," he said. He looked at the envelope, his mouth pursed. "Something for me, you say?"

"Yes. A present I'm making you."

He was looking at me now, the envelope white in his black hand, in the sun. His eyes were soft and irisless and brown, and suddenly I saw Roskus watching me from behind all his whitefolks' claptrap of uniform and politics and Harvard manner, diffident, secret, inarticulate and sad. "You aint playing a joke on the old nigger, is you?"

"You know I'm not. Did any Southerner ever play a joke on you?"

"You're right. They're fine folks. But you cant live with them."

"Did you ever try?" I said. But Roskus was gone. Once more he was that self he had long since taught himself to wear in the world's eye, pompous, spurious, not quite gross.

"I'll confer to your wishes, my boy."

"Not until tomorrow, remember."

"Sure," he said; "understood, my boy. Well—"

"I hope—" I said. He looked down at me, benignant, profound. Suddenly I held out my hand and we shook, he gravely, from the pompous height of his municipal and military dream. "You're a good fellow, Deacon. I hope. . . . You've helped a lot of young fellows, here and there."

"I've tried to treat all folks right," he said. "I draw no petty social lines. A man to me is a man, wherever I find him."

"I hope you'll always find as many friends as you've made."

"Young fellows. I get along with them. They dont forget me, neither," he said, waving the envelope. He put it into his pocket and buttoned his coat. "Yes, sir," he said, "I've had good friends."

The chimes began again, the half hour. I stood in the belly of

my shadow and listened to the strokes spaced and tranquil along
the sunlight, among the thin, still little leaves. Spaced and peaceful
and serene, with that quality of autumn always in bells even in the
month of brides. *Lying on the ground under the window bellowing*
He took one look at her and knew. Out of the mouths of babes.
The street lamps The chimes ceased. I went back to the postoffice, treading my shadow into pavement. *go down the hill then
they rise toward town like lanterns hung one above another on a
wall.* Father said because she loves Caddy she loves people through
their shortcomings. Uncle Maury straddling his legs before the fire
must remove one hand long enough to drink Christmas. Jason ran
on, his hands in his pockets fell down and lay there like a trussed
fowl until Versh set him up. *Whyn't you keep them hands outen
your pockets when you running you could stand up then* Rolling
his head in the cradle rolling it flat across the back. Caddy told
Jason Versh said that the reason Uncle Maury didn't work was that
he used to roll his head in the cradle when he was little.

Shreve was coming up the walk, shambling, fatly earnest, his
glasses glinting beneath the running leaves like little pools.

"I gave Deacon a note for some things. I may not be in this afternoon, so dont you let him have anything until tomorrow, will you?"

"All right." He looked at me. "Say, what're you doing today,
anyhow? All dressed up and mooning around like the prologue to
a suttee. Did you go to Psychology this morning?"

"I'm not doing anything. Not until tomorrow, now."

"What's that you got there?"

"Nothing. Pair of shoes I had half-soled. Not until tomorrow, you
hear?"

"Sure. All right. Oh, by the way, did you get a letter off the
table this morning?"

"No."

"It's there. From Semiramis. Chauffeur brought it before ten
o'clock."

"All right. I'll get it. Wonder what she wants now."

"Another band recital, I guess. Tumpty ta ta Gerald blah. 'A
little louder on the drum, Quentin.' God, I'm glad I'm not a gentleman." He went on, nursing a book, a little shapeless, fatly intent.
The street lamps do you think so because one of our forefathers
was a governor and three were generals and Mother's weren't

any live man is better than any dead man but no live or dead

man is very much better than any other live or dead man *Done in
Mother's mind though. Finished. Finished. Then we were all poisoned* you are confusing sin and morality women dont do that your
Mother is thinking of morality whether it be sin or not has not
occurred to her

Jason I must go away you keep the others I'll take Jason and go
where nobody knows us so he'll have a chance to grow up and forget all this the others dont love me they have never loved anything
with that streak of Compson selfishness and false pride Jason was
the only one my heart went out to without dread

nonsense Jason is all right I was thinking that as soon as you feel
better you and Caddy might go up to French Lick

and leave Jason here with nobody but you and the darkies

she will forget him then all the talk will die away *found not
death at the salt licks*

maybe I could find a husband for her *not death at the salt licks*

The car came up and stopped. The bells were still ringing the
half hour. I got on and it went on again, blotting the half hour.
No: the three quarters. Then it would be ten minutes anyway. To
leave Harvard *your Mother's dream for sold Benjy's pasture for*
what have I done to have been given children like these Benjamin was punishment enough and now for her to have no more
regard for me her own mother I've suffered for her dreamed and
planned and sacrificed I went down into the valley yet never since
she opened her eyes has she given me one unselfish thought at times
I look at her I wonder if she can be my child except Jason he has
never given me one moment's sorrow since I first held him in my
arms I knew then that he was to be my joy and my salvation I
thought that Benjamin was punishment enough for any sins I have
committed I thought he was my punishment for putting aside my
pride and marrying a man who held himself above me I dont complain I loved him above all of them because of it because my duty
though Jason pulling at my heart all the while but I see now that I
have not suffered enough I see now that I must pay for your sins
as well as mine what have you done what sins have your high and
mighty people visited upon me but you'll take up for them you always have found excuses for your own blood only Jason can do
wrong because he is more Bascomb than Compson while your own
daughter my little daughter my baby girl she is she is no better
than that when I was a girl I was unfortunate I was only a Bas-

comb I was taught that there is no halfway ground that a woman is either a lady or not but I never dreamed when I held her in my arms that any daughter of mine could let herself dont you know I can look at her eyes and tell you may think she'd tell you but she doesn't tell things she is secretive you dont know her I know things she's done that I'd die before I'd have you know that's it go on criticise Jason accuse me of setting him to watch her as if it were a crime while your own daughter can I know you dont love him that you wish to believe faults against him you never have yes ridicule him as you always have Maury you cannot hurt me any more than your children already have and then I'll be gone and Jason with no one to love him shield him from this I look at him every day dreading to see this Compson blood beginning to show in him at last with his sister slipping out to see what do you call it then have you ever laid eyes on him will you even let me try to find out who he is it's not for myself I couldn't bear to see him it's for your sake to protect you but who can fight against bad blood you wont let me try we are to sit back with our hands folded while she not only drags your name in the dirt but corrupts the very air your children breathe Jason you must let me go away I cannot stand it let me have Jason and you keep the others they're not my flesh and blood like he is strangers nothing of mine and I am afraid of them I can take Jason and go where we are not known I'll go down on my knees and pray for the absolution of my sins that he may escape this curse try to forget that the others ever were

If that was the three quarters, not over ten minutes now. One car had just left, and people were already waiting for the next one. I asked, but he didn't know whether another one would leave before noon or not because you'd think that interurbans. So the first one was another trolley. I got on. You can feel noon. I wonder if even miners in the bowels of the earth. That's why whistles: because people that sweat, and if just far enough from sweat you wont hear whistles and in eight minutes you should be that far from sweat in Boston. Father said a man is the sum of his misfortunes. One day you'd think misfortune would get tired, but then time is your misfortune Father said. A gull on an invisible wire attached through space dragged. You carry the symbol of your frustration into eternity. Then the wings are bigger Father said only who can play a harp.

I could hear my watch whenever the car stopped, but not often they were already eating *Who would play a* Eating the business of eating inside of you space to space and time confused Stomach saying noon brain saying eat oclock All right I wonder what time it is what of it. People were getting out. The trolley didn't stop so often now, emptied by eating.

Then it was past. I got off and stood in my shadow and after a while a car came along and I got on and went back to the interurban station. There was a car ready to leave, and I found a seat next the window and it started and I watched it sort of frazzle out into slack tide flats, and then trees. Now and then I saw the river and I thought how nice it would be for them down at New London if the weather and Gerald's shell going solemnly up the glinting forenoon and I wondered what the old woman would be wanting now, sending me a note before ten oclock in the morning. What picture of Gerald I to be one of the *Dalton Ames oh asbestos Quentin has shot* background. Something with girls in it. Women do have *always his voice above the gabble voice* that breathed an affinity for evil, for believing that no woman is to be trusted, but that some men are too innocent to protect themselves. Plain girls. Remote cousins and family friends whom mere acquaintanceship invested with a sort of blood obligation noblesse oblige. And she sitting there telling us before their faces what a shame it was that Gerald should have all the family looks because a man didn't need it, was better off without it but without it a girl was simply lost. Telling us about Gerald's women in a *Quentin has shot Herbert he shot his voice through the floor of Caddy's room* tone of smug approbation. "When he was seventeen I said to him one day 'What a shame that you should have a mouth like that it should be on a girls face' and can you imagine *the curtains leaning in on the twilight upon the odour of the apple tree her head against the twilight her arms behind her head kimono-winged the voice that breathed o'er eden clothes upon the bed by the nose seen above the apple* what he said? just seventeen, mind. 'Mother' he said 'it often is.'" And him sitting there in attitudes regal watching two or three of them through his eyelashes. They gushed like swallows swooping his eyelashes. Shreve said he always had *Are you going to look after Benjy and Father*

The less you say about Benjy and Father the better when have you ever considered them Caddy

Promise

*You needn't worry about them you're getting out in good shape
Promise I'm sick you'll have to promise* wondered who invented
that joke but then he always had considered Mrs Bland a remark-
ably preserved woman he said she was grooming Gerald to seduce
a duchess sometime. She called Shreve that fat Canadian youth
twice she arranged a new room-mate for me without consulting me
at all, once for me to move out, once for

He opened the door in the twilight. His face looked like a pump-
kin pie.

"Well, I'll say a fond farewell. Cruel fate may part us, but I will
never love another. Never."

"What are you talking about?"

"I'm talking about cruel fate in eight yards of apricot silk and
more metal pound for pound that a galley slave and the sole owner
and proprietor of the unchallenged peripatetic john of the late
Confederacy." Then he told me how she had gone to the proctor
to have him moved out and how the proctor had revealed enough
low stubbornness to insist on consulting Shreve first. Then she
suggested that he send for Shreve right off and do it, and he
wouldnt do that, so after that she was hardly civil to Shreve. "I
make it a point never to speak harshly of females," Shreve said,
"but that woman has got more ways like a bitch than any lady in
these sovereign states and dominions." and now Letter on the table
by hand, command orchid scented coloured If she knew I had
passed almost beneath the window knowing it there without My
dear Madam I have not yet had an opportunity of receiving your
communication but I beg in advance to be excused today or yesterday and tomorrow or when As I remember that the next one is to
be how Gerald throws his nigger downstairs and how the nigger
plead to be allowed to matriculate in the divinity school to be near
marster marse gerald and How he ran all the way to the station beside the carriage with tears in his eyes when marse gerald rid away
I will wait until the day for the one about the sawmill husband
came to the kitchen door with a shotgun Gerald went down and
bit the gun in two and handed it back and wiped his hands on a
silk handkerchief threw the handkerchief in the stove I've only
heard that one twice

shot him through the I saw you come in here so I watched my
chance and came along thought we might get acquainted have a
cigar

Thanks I dont smoke

No things must have changed up there since my day mind if I light up

Help yourself

Thanks I've heard a lot I guess your mother wont mind if I put the match behind the screen will she a lot about you Candace talked about you all the time up there at the Licks I got pretty jealous I says to myself who is this Quentin anyway I must see what this animal looks like because I was hit pretty hard see soon as I saw the little girl I dont mind telling you it never occurred to me it was her brother she kept talking about she couldnt have talked about you any more if you'd been the only man in the world husband wouldnt have been in it you wont change your mind and have a smoke

I dont smoke

In that case I wont insist even though it is a pretty fair weed cost me twenty-five bucks a hundred wholesale friend in Havana yes I guess there are lots of changes up there I keep promising myself a visit but I never get around to it been hitting the ball now for ten years I cant get away from the bank during school fellow's habits change things that seem important to an undergraduate you know tell me about things up there

I'm not going to tell Father and Mother if that's what you are getting at

Not going to tell not going to oh that that's what you are talking about is it you understand that I dont give a damn whether you tell or not understand that a thing like that unfortunate but no police crime I wasn't the first or the last I was just unlucky you might have been luckier

You lie

Keep your shirt on I'm not trying to make you tell anything you dont want to meant no offense of course a young fellow like you would consider a thing of that sort a lot more serious than you will in five years

I dont know but one way to consider cheating I dont think I'm likely to learn different at Harvard

We're better than a play you must have made the Dramat well you're right no need to tell them we'll let bygones be bygones eh no reason why you and I should let a little thing like that come between us I like you Quentin I like your appearance you dont look

like these other hicks I'm glad we're going to hit off like this I've
promised your mother to do something for Jason but I would like
to give you a hand too Jason would be just as well off here but
there's no future in a hole like this for a young fellow like you

Thanks you'd better stick to Jason he'd suit you better than I
would

I'm sorry about that business but a kid like I was then I never
had a mother like yours to teach me the finer points it would just
hurt her unnecessarily to know it yes you're right no need to that
includes Candace of course

I said Mother and Father

Look here take a look at me how long do you think you'd last
with me

I wont have to last long if you learned to fight up at school too
try and see how long I would

You damned little what do you think you're getting at

Try and see

My God the cigar what would your mother say if she found a
blister on her mantel just in time too look here Quentin we're about
to do something we'll both regret I like you liked you as soon as I
saw you I says he must be a damned good fellow whoever he is
or Candace wouldnt be so keen on him listen I've been out in the
world now for ten years things dont matter so much then you'll
find that out let's you and I get together on this thing sons of old
Harvard and all I guess I wouldnt know the place now best place
for a young fellow in the world I'm going to send my sons there
give them a better chance than I had wait dont go yet let's discuss
this thing a young man gets these ideas and I'm all for them does
him good while he's in school forms his character good for tradition
the school but when he gets out into the world he'll have to get his
the best way he can because he'll find that everybody else is doing
the same thing and be damned to here let's shake hands and let
bygones be bygones for your mother's sake remember her health
come on give me your hand here look at it it's just out of convent
look not a blemish not even been creased yet see here

To hell with your money

No no come on I belong to the family now see I know how it is
with a young fellow he has lots of private affairs it's always pretty
hard to get the old man to stump up for I know havent I been
there and not so long ago either but now I'm getting married and

all specially up there come on dont be a fool listen when we get a chance for a real talk I want to tell you about a little widow over in town

I've heard that too keep your damned money

Call it a loan then just shut your eyes a minute and you'll be fifty

Keep your hands off of me you'd better get that cigar off the mantel

Tell and be damned then see what it gets you if you were not a damned fool you'd have seen that I've got them too tight for any half-baked Galahad of a brother your mother's told me about your sort with your head swelled up come in oh come in dear Quentin and I were just getting acquainted talking about Harvard did you want me cant stay away from the old man can she

Go out a minute Herbert I want to talk to Quentin

Come in come in let's all have a gabfest and get acquainted I was just telling Quentin

Go on Herbert go out a while

Well all right then I suppose you and bubber do want to see one another once more eh

You'd better take that cigar off the mantel

Right as usual my boy then I'll toddle along let them order you around while they can Quentin after day after tomorrow it'll be pretty please to the old man wont it dear give us a kiss honey

Oh stop that save that for day after tomorrow

I'll want interest then dont let Quentin do anything he cant finish oh by the way did I tell Quentin the story about the man's parrot and what happened to it a sad story remind me of that think of it yourself ta-ta see you in the funnypaper

Well

Well

What are you up to now

Nothing

You're meddling in my business again didn't you get enough of that last summer

Caddy you've got fever *You're sick how are you sick*

I'm just sick. I cant ask.

Shot his voice through the

Not that blackguard Caddy

Now and then the river glinted beyond things in sort of swooping glints, across noon and after. Well after now, though we had passed where he was still pulling upstream majestical in the face of god gods. Better. Gods. God would be canaille too in Boston Massachusetts. Or maybe just not a husband. The wet oars winking him along in bright winks and female palms. Adulant. Adulant if not a husband he'd ignore God. *That blackguard, Caddy* The river glinted away beyond a swooping curve.

I'm sick you'll have to promise

Sick how are you sick

I'm just sick I cant ask anybody yet promise you will

If they need any looking after it's because of you how are you sick Under the window we could hear the car leaving for the station, the 8:10 train. To bring back cousins. Heads. Increasing himself head by head but not barbers. Manicure girls. We had a blood horse once. In the stable yes, but under leather a cur. *Quentin has shot all of their voices through the floor of Caddy's room*

The car stopped. I got off, into the middle of my shadow. A road crossed the track. There was a wooden marquee with an old man eating something out of a paper bag, and then the car was out of hearing too. The road went into the trees, where it would be shady, but June foliage in New England not much thicker than April at home in Mississippi. I could see a smoke stack. I turned my back to it, tramping my shadow into the dust. *There was something terrible in me sometimes at night I could see it grinning at me I could see it through them grinning at me through their faces it's gone now and I'm sick*

Caddy

Dont touch me just promise

If you're sick you cant

Yes I can after that it'll be all right it wont matter dont let them send him to Jackson promise

I promise Caddy Caddy

Dont touch me dont touch me

What does it look like Caddy

What

That that grins at you that thing through them

I could still see the smoke stack. That's where the water would be, heading out to the sea and the peaceful grottoes. Tumbling peacefully they would, and when He said Rise only the flatirons. When Versh and I hunted all day we wouldn't take any lunch, and at twelve oclock I'd get hungry. I'd stay hungry until about one, then all of a sudden I'd even forget that I wasn't hungry anymore. *The street lamps go down the hill then heard the car go down the hill. The chair-arm flat cool smooth under my forehead shaping the chair the apple tree leaning on my hair above the eden clothes by the nose seen* You've got fever I felt it yesterday it's like being near a stove.

Dont touch me.

Caddy you cant do it if you are sick. That blackguard.

I've got to marry somebody. *Then they told me the bone would have to be broken again*

At last I couldn't see the smoke stack. The road went beside a wall. Trees leaned over the wall, sprayed with sunlight. The stone was cool. Walking near it you could feel the coolness. Only our country was not like this country. There was something about just walking through it. A kind of still and violent fecundity that satisfied ever bread-hunger like. Flowing around you, not brooding and nursing every niggard stone. Like it were put to makeshift for enough green to go around among the trees and even the blue of distance not that rich chimaera. *told me the bone would have to be broken again and inside me it began to say Ah Ah Ah and I began to sweat. What do I care I know what a broken leg is all it is it wont be anything I'll just have to stay in the house a little longer that's all and my jaw-muscles getting numb and my mouth saying Wait Wait just a minute through the sweat ah ah ah behind my teeth and Father damn that horse damn that horse. Wait it's my fault. He came along the fence every morning with a basket toward the kitchen dragging a stick along the fence every morning I dragged myself to the window cast and all and laid for him with a piece of coal Dilsey said you goin to ruin yoself aint you got no mo sense than that not fo days since you bruck hit. Wait I'll get used to it in a minute wait just a minute I'll get*

Even sound seemed to fail in this air, like the air was worn out with carrying sounds so long. A dog's voice carries further than a train, in the darkness anyway. And some people's. Niggers. Louis Hatcher never even used his horn carrying it and that old lantern. I said, "Louis, when was the last time you cleaned that lantern?"

"I cleant hit a little while back. You member when all dat flood-watter wash dem folks away up yonder? I cleant hit dat ve'y day,

Old woman and me settin fore de fire dat night and she say 'Louis, whut you gwine do ef dat flood git out dis fur?' and I say 'Dat's a fack. I reckon I had better clean dat lantun up.' So I cleant hit dat night."

"That flood was way up in Pennsylvania," I said. "It couldn't even have got down this far."

"Dat's whut you says," Louis said. "Watter kin git des ez high en wet in Jefferson ez hit kin in Pennsylvaney, I reckon. Hit's de folks dat says de high watter cant git dis fur dat comes floatin out on de ridge-pole, too."

"Did you and Martha get out that night?"

"We done jest that. I cleant dat lantun and me and her sot de balance of de night on top o dat knoll back de graveyard. En ef I'd a knowed of aihy one higher, we'd a been on hit instead."

"And you haven't cleaned that lantern since then."

"Whut I want to clean hit when dey aint no need?"

"You mean, until another flood comes along?"

"Hit kep us outen dat un."

"Oh, come on, Uncle Louis," I said.

"Yes, suh. You do you way en I do mine. Ef all I got to do to keep outen de high watter is to clean dis yere lantun, I wont quoil wid no man."

"Unc' Louis wouldn't ketch nothin wid a light he could see by," Versh said.

"I wuz huntin possums in dis country when dey was still drowndin nits in yo pappy's head wid coal oil, boy," Louis said. "Ketchin um, too."

"Dat's de troof," Versh said. "I reckon Unc' Louis done caught mo possums than aihy man in dis country."

"Yes, suh," Louis said, "I got plenty light fer possums to see, all right. I aint heard non o dem complainin. Hush, now. Dar he. Whooey. Hum awn, dawg." And we'd sit in the dry leaves that whispered a little with the slow respiration of our waiting and with the slow breathing of the earth and the windless October, the rank smell of the lantern fouling the brittle air, listening to the dogs and to the echo of Louis' voice dying away. He never raised it, yet on a still night we have heard it from our front porch. When he called the dogs in he sounded just like the horn he carried slung on his shoulder and never used, but clearer, mellower, as though his voice were a part of darkness and silence, coiling out of it, coiling into it again. WhoOoooo. WhoOoooo. WhoOooooooooooooooooo. *Got to marry somebody*

Have there been very many Caddy
I dont know too many will you look after Benjy and Father
You dont know whose it is then does he know
Dont touch me will you look after Benjy and Father

I began to feel the water before I came to the bridge. The bridge was of grey stone, lichened, dappled with slow moisture where the fungus crept. Beneath it the water was clear and still in the shadow, whispering and clucking about the stone in fading swirls of spinning sky. *Caddy that*

I've got to marry somebody Versh told me about a man mutilated himself. He went into the woods and did it with a razor, sitting in a ditch. A broken razor, flinging them backward over his shoulder the same motion complete the jerked skein of blood backward not looping. But that's not it. It's not not having them. It's never to have had them then I could say O That That's Chinese I dont know Chinese. And Father said it's because you are a virgin: dont you see? Women are never virgins. Purity is a negative state and therefore contrary to nature. It's nature is hurting you not Caddy and I said That's just words and he said So is virginity and I said you dont know. You cant know and he said Yes. On the instant when we come to realise that tragedy is second-hand.

Where the shadow of the bridge fell I could see down for a long way, but not as far as the bottom. When you leave a leaf in water a long time after awhile the tissue will be gone and the delicate fibers waving slow as the motion of sleep. They dont touch one another, no matter how knotted up they once were, no matter how close they lay once to the bones. And maybe when He says Rise the eyes will come floating up too, out of the deep quiet and the sleep, to look on glory. And after awhile the flatirons would come floating up. I hid them under the end of the bridge and went back and leaned on the rail.

I could not see the bottom, but I could see a long way into the motion of the water before the eye gave out, and then I saw a shadow hanging like a fat arrow stemming into the current. Mayflies skimmed in and out of the shadow of the bridge just above the surface. *If it could just be a hell beyond that: the clean flame*

*the two of us more than dead. Then you will have only me then
only me then the two of us amid the pointing and the horror beyond the clean flame* The arrow increased without motion, then in
a quick swirl the trout lipped a fly beneath the surface with that
sort of gigantic delicacy of an elephant picking up a peanut. The
fading vortex drifted away downstream and then I saw the arrow
again, nose into the current, wavering delicately to the motion of
the water above which the Mayflies slanted and poised. *Only you
and me then amid the pointing and the horror walled by the clean
flame*

The trout hung, delicate and motionless among the wavering
shadows. Three boys with fishing poles came onto the bridge and
we leaned on the rail and looked down at the trout. They knew the
fish. He was a neighbourhood character.

"They've been trying to catch that trout for twenty-five years.
There's a store in Boston offers a twenty-five dollar fishing rod to
anybody that can catch him."

"Why dont you all catch him, then? Wouldnt you like to have
a twenty-five dollar fishing rod?"

"Yes," they said. They leaned on the rail, looking down at the
trout. "I sure would," one said.

"I wouldnt take the rod," the second said. "I'd take the money
instead."

"Maybe they wouldnt do that," the first said. "I bet he'd make
you take the rod."

"Then I'd sell it."

"You couldnt get twenty-five dollars for it."

"I'd take what I could get, then. I can catch just as many fish
with this pole as I could with a twenty-five dollar one." Then they
talked about what they would do with twenty-five dollars. They all
talked at once, their voices insistent and contradictory and impatient, making of unreality a possibility, then a probability, then
an incontrovertible fact, as people will when their desires become
words.

"I'd buy a horse and wagon," the second said.

"Yes you would," the others said.

"I would. I know where I can buy one for twenty-five dollars.
I know the man."

"Who is it?"

"That's all right who it is. I can buy it for twenty-five dollars."

"Yah," the others said, "He dont know any such thing. He's just talking."

"Do you think so?" the boy said. They continued to jeer at him, but he said nothing more. He leaned on the rail, looking down at the trout which he had already spent, and suddenly the acrimony, the conflict, was gone from their voices, as if to them too it was as though he had captured the fish and bought his horse and wagon, they too partaking of that adult trait of being convinced of anything by an assumption of silent superiority. I suppose that people, using themselves and each other so much by words, are at least consistent in attributing wisdom to a still tongue, and for a while I could feel the other two seeking swiftly for some means by which to cope with him, to rob him of his horse and wagon.

"You couldnt get twenty-five dollars for that pole," the first said. "I bet anything you couldnt."

"He hasnt caught that trout yet," the third said suddenly, then they both cried:

"Yah, wha'd I tell you? What's the man's name? I dare you to tell. There aint any such man."

"Ah, shut up," the second said. "Look, Here he comes again." They leaned on the rail, motionless, identical, their poles slanting slenderly in the sunlight, also identical. The trout rose without haste, a shadow in faint wavering increase; again the little vortex faded slowly downstream. "Gee," the first one murmured.

"We dont try to catch him anymore," he said. "We just watch Boston folks that come out and try."

"Is he the only fish in this pool?"

"Yes. He ran all the others out. The best place to fish around here is down at the Eddy."

"No it aint," the second said. "It's better at Bigelow's Mill two to one." Then they argued for a while about which was the best fishing and then left off all of a sudden to watch the trout rise again and the broken swirl of water suck down a little of the sky. I asked how far it was to the nearest town. They told me.

"But the closest car line is that way," the second said, pointing back down the road. "Where are you going?"

"Nowhere. Just walking."

"You from the college?"

"Yes. Are there any factories in that town?"

"Factories?" They looked at me.

"No," the second said. "Not there." They looked at my clothes. "You looking for work?"

"How about Bigelow's Mill?" the third said. "That's a factory."

"Factory my eye. He means a sure enough factory."

"One with a whistle," I said. "I havent heard any one oclock whistles yet."

"Oh," the second said. "There's a clock in the Unitarian steeple. You can find out the time from that. Havent you got a watch on that chain?"

"I broke it this morning." I showed them my watch. They examined it gravely.

"It's still running," the second said. "What does a watch like that cost?"

"It was a present," I said. "My father gave it to me when I graduated from high school."

"Are you a Canadian?" the third said. He had red hair.

"Canadian?"

"He dont talk like them," the second said. "I've heard them talk. He talks like they do in minstrel shows."

"Say," the third said, "aint you afraid he'll hit you?"

"Hit me?"

"You said he talks like a coloured man."

"Ah, dry up," the second said. "You can see the steeple when you get over that hill there."

I thanked them. "I hope you have good luck. Only dont catch that old fellow down there. He deserves to be let alone."

"Cant anybody catch that fish," the first said. They leaned on the rail, looking down into the water, the three poles like three slanting threads of yellow fire in the sun. I walked upon my shadow, tramping it into the dappled shade of trees again. The road curved, mounting away from the water. It crossed the hill, then descended winding, carrying the eye, the mind on ahead beneath a still green tunnel, and the square cupola above the trees and the round eye of the clock but far enough. I sat down at the roadside. The grass was ankle deep, myriad. The shadows on the road were as still as if they had been put there with a stencil, with slanting pencils of sunlight. But it was only a train, and after a while it died away beyond the trees, the long sound, and then I could hear my watch and the train dying away, as though it were running through another month or another summer somewhere, rushing away under the poised gull and all things rushing. Except Gerald. He would be sort of grand too, pulling in lonely state across the noon, rowing himself right out of noon, up the long bright air like an apotheosis, mounting into a drowsing infinity where only he and the gull, the one terrifically motionless, the other in a steady and measured pull and recover that partook of inertia itself, the world punily beneath their shadows on the sun. Caddy that blackguard that blackguard Caddy

Their voices came over the hill, and the three slender poles like balanced threads of running fire. They looked at me passing, not slowing.

"Well," I said, "I dont see him."

"We didnt try to catch him," the first said. "You cant catch that fish."

"There's the clock," the second said, pointing. "You can tell the time when you get a little closer."

"Yes," I said, "All right." I got up. "You all going to town?"

"We're going to the Eddy for chub," the first said.

"You cant catch anything at the Eddy," the second said.

"I guess you want to go to the mill, with a lot of fellows splashing and scaring all the fish away."

"You cant catch any fish at the Eddy."

"We wont catch none nowhere if we dont go on," the third said.

"I dont see why you keep on talking about the Eddy," the second said. "You cant catch anything there."

"You dont have to go," the first said. "You're not tied to me."

"Let's go to the mill and go swimming," the third said.

"I'm going to the Eddy and fish," the first said. "You can do as you please."

"Say, how long has it been since you heard of anybody catching a fish at the Eddy?" the second said to the third.

"Let's go to the mill and go swimming," the third said. The cupola sank slowly beyond the trees, with the round face of the clock far enough yet. We went on in the dappled shade. We came to an orchard, pink and white. It was full of bees; already we could hear them.

"Let's go to the mill and go swimming," the third said. A lane turned off beside the orchard. The third boy slowed and halted. The first went on, flecks of sunlight slipping along the pole across

his shoulder and down the back of his shirt. "Come on," the third
said. The second boy stopped too. *Why must you marry somebody
Caddy*

Do you want me to say it do you think that if I say it it wont be
"Let's go up to the mill," he said. "Come on."

The first boy went on. His bare feet made no sound, falling softer
than leaves in the thin dust. In the orchard the bees sounded like
a wind getting up, a sound caught by a spell just under crescendo
and sustained. The lane went along the wall, arched over, shattered with bloom, dissolving into trees. Sunlight slanted into it,
sparse and eager. Yellow butterflies flickered along the shade like
flecks of sun.

"What do you want to go to the Eddy for?" the second boy said.
"You can fish at the mill if you want to."

"Ah, let him go," the third said. They looked after the first boy.
Sunlight slid patchily across his walking shoulders, glinting along
the pole like yellow ants.

"Kenny," the second said. *Say it to Father will you I will am
my fathers Progenitive I invented him created I him Say it to him
it will not be for he will say I was not and then you and I since
philoprogenitive*

"Ah, come on," the boy said, "They're already in." They looked
after the first boy. "Yah," they said suddenly, "go on then, mamma's
boy. If he goes swimming he'll get his head wet and then he'll get
a licking." They turned into the lane and went on, the yellow butterflies slanting about them along the shade.

*it is because there is nothing else I believe there is something else
but there may not be and then I You will find that even injustice
is scarcely worthy of what you believe yourself to be* He paid me
no attention, his jaw set in profile, his face turned a little away beneath his broken hat.

"Why dont you go swimming with them?" I said. *that blackguard
Caddy*

Were you trying to pick a fight with him were you

*A liar and a scoundrel Caddy was dropped from his club for
cheating at cards got sent to Coventry caught cheating at midterm
exams and expelled*

Well what about it I'm not going to play cards with

"Do you like fishing better than swimming?" I said. The sound
of the bees diminished, sustained yet, as though instead of sinking

into silence, silence merely increased between us, as water rises. The road curved again and became a street between shady lawns with white houses. *Caddy that blackguard can you think of Benjy and Father and do it not of me*

What else can I think about what else have I thought about The boy turned from the street. He climbed a picket fence without looking back and crossed the lawn to a tree and laid the pole down and climbed into the fork of the tree and sat there, his back to the road and the dappled sun motionless at last upon his white shirt. *Else have I thought about I cant even cry I died last year I told you I had but I didnt know then what I meant I didnt know what I was saying* Some days in late August at home are like this, the air thin and eager like this, with something in it sad and nostalgic and familiar. Man the sum of his climatic experiences Father said. Man the sum of what have you. A problem in impure properties carried tediously to an unvarying nil: stalemate of dust and desire. *But now I know I'm dead I tell you*

Then why must you listen we can go away you and Benjy and me where nobody knows us where The buggy was drawn by a white horse, his feet clopping in the thin dust; spidery wheels chattering thin and dry, moving uphill beneath a rippling shawl of leaves. Elm. No: ellum. Ellum.

On what on your school money the money they sold the pasture for so you could go to Harvard dont you see you've got to finish now if you dont finish he'll have nothing

Sold the pasture His white shirt was motionless in the fork, in the flickering shade. The wheels were spidery. Beneath the sag of the buggy the hooves neatly rapid like the motions of a lady doing embroidery, diminishing without progress like a figure on a treadmill being drawn rapidly offstage. The street turned again. I could see the white cupola, the round stupid assertion of the clock. *Sold the pasture*

Father will be dead in a year they say if he doesnt stop drinking and he wont stop he cant stop since I since last summer and then they'll send Benjy to Jackson I cant cry I cant even cry one minute she was standing in the door the next minute he was pulling at her dress and bellowing his voice hammered back and forth between the walls in waves and she shrinking against the wall getting smaller and smaller with her white face her eyes like thumbs dug into it until he pushed her out of the room his voice hammering

back and forth as though its own momentum would not let it stop as
though there were no place for it in silence bellowing

When you opened the door a bell tinkled, but just once, high and clear and small in the neat obscurity above the door, as though it were gauged and tempered to make that single clear small sound so as not to wear the bell out nor to require the expenditure of too much silence in restoring it when the door opened upon the recent warm scent of baking; a little dirty child with eyes like a toy bear's and two patent-leather pig-tails.

"Hello, sister." Her face was like a cup of milk dashed with coffee in the sweet warm emptiness. "Anybody here?"

But she merely watched me until a door opened and the lady came. Above the counter where the ranks of crisp shapes behind the glass her neat grey face her hair tight and sparse from her neat grey skull, spectacles in neat grey rims riding approaching like something on a wire, like a cash box in a store. She looked like a librarian. Something among dusty shelves of ordered certitudes long divorced from reality, desiccating peacefully, as if a breath of that air which sees injustice done

"Two of these, please, ma'am."

From under the counter she produced a square cut from a newspaper and laid it on the counter and lifted the two buns out. The little girl watched them with still and unwinking eyes like two currants floating motionless in a cup of weak coffee Land of the kike home of the wop. Watching the bread, the neat grey hands, a broad gold band on the left forefinger, knuckled there by a blue knuckle.

"Do you do your own baking, ma'am?"

"Sir?" she said. Like that. Sir? Like on the stage Sir? "Five cents. Was there anything else?"

"No, ma'am. Not for me. This lady wants something." She was not tall enough to see over the case, so she went to the end of the counter and looked at the little girl

"Did you bring her in here?"

"No, ma'am. She was here when I came."

"You little wretch," she said. She came out around the counter, but she didnt touch the little girl. "Have you got anything in your pockets?"

"She hasnt got any pockets," I said. "She wasnt doing anything. She was standing here, waiting for you."

"Why didnt the bell ring, then?" She glared at me. She just

needed a bunch of switches, a blackboard behind her 2 x 2 e 5. "She'll hide it under her dress and a body'd never know it. You, child. How'd you get in here?"

The little girl said nothing. She looked at the woman, then she gave me a flying black glance and looked at the woman again, "Them foreigners," the woman said. "How'd she get in without the bell ringing?"

"She came in when I opened the door," I said. "It rang once for both of us. She couldnt reach anything from here, anyway. Besides, I dont think she would. Would you, sister?" The little girl looked at me, secretive, contemplative. "What do you want? bread?"

She extended her fist. It uncurled upon a nickel, moist and dirty, moist dirt ridged into her flesh. The coin was damp and warm. I could smell it, faintly metallic.

"Have you got a five cent loaf, please, ma'am?"

From beneath the counter she produced a square cut from a newspaper sheet and laid it on the counter and wrapped a loaf into it. I laid the coin and another one on the counter. "And another one of those buns, please, ma'am."

She took another bun from the case. "Give me that parcel," she said. I gave it to her and she unwrapped it and put the third bun in and wrapped it and took the coins and found two coppers in her apron and gave them to me. I handed them to the little girl. Her fingers closed about them, damp and hot, like worms.

"You going to give her that bun?" the woman said.

"Yessum," I said. "I expect your cooking smells as good to her as it does to me."

I took up the two packages and gave the bread to the little girl, the woman all iron-grey behind the counter, watching us with cold certitude. "You wait a minute," she said. She went to the rear. The door opened again and closed. The little girl watched me, holding the bread against her dirty-dress.

"What's your name?" I said. She quit looking at me, but she was still motionless. She didnt even seem to breathe. The woman returned. She had a funny looking thing in her hand. She carried it sort of like it might have been a dead pet rat.

"Here," she said. The child looked at her. "Take it," the woman said, jabbing it at the little girl. "It just looks peculiar. I calculate you wont know the difference when you eat it. Here. I cant stand here all day." The child took it, still watching her. The woman rubbed her hands on her apron. "I got to have that bell fixed," she said. She went to the door and jerked it open. The little bell tinkled once, faint and clear and invisible. We moved toward the door and the woman's peering back.

"Thank you for the cake," I said.

"Them foreigners," she said, staring up into the obscurity where the bell tinkled. "Take my advice and stay clear of them, young man."

"Yessum," I said. "Come on, sister." We went out. "Thank you, ma'am."

She swung the door to, then jerked it open again, making the bell give forth its single small note. "Foreigners," she said, peering up at the bell.

We went on. "Well," I said. "How about some ice cream?" She was eating the gnarled cake. "Do you like ice cream?" She gave me a black still look, chewing. "Come on."

We came to the drugstore and had some ice cream. She wouldnt put the loaf down. "Why not put it down so you can eat better?" I said, offering to take it. But she held to it, chewing the ice cream like it was taffy. The bitten cake lay on the table. She ate the ice cream steadily, then she fell to on the cake again, looking about at the showcases. I finished mine and we went out.

"Which way do you live?" I said.

A buggy, the one with the horse it was. Only Doc Peabody is fat. Three hundred pounds. You ride with him on the uphill side, holding on. Children. Walking easier than holding uphill. *Seen the doctor yet have you seen Caddy*

I dont have to I cant ask now afterward it will be all right it wont matter

Because women so delicate so mysterious Father said. Delicate equilibrium of periodical filth between two moons balanced. Moons he said full and yellow as harvest moons her hips thighs. Outside outside of them always but. Yellow. Feetsoles with walking like. Then know that some man that all those mysterious and imperious concealed. With all that inside of them shapes an outward suavity waiting for a touch to. Liquid putrefaction like drowned things floating like pale rubber flabbily filled getting the odour of honeysuckle all mixed up.

"You'd better take your bread on home, hadnt you?"

She looked at me. She chewed quietly and steadily; at regular intervals a small distension passed smoothly down her throat. I opened my package and gave her one of the buns. "Goodbye," I said.

I went on. Then I looked back. She was behind me. "Do you live down this way?" She said nothing. She walked beside me, under my elbow sort of, eating. We went on. It was quiet, hardly anyone about *getting the odour of honeysuckle all mixed She would have told me not to let me sit there on the steps hearing her door twilight slamming hearing Benjy still crying Supper she would have to come down then getting honeysuckle all mixed up in it* We reached the corner.

"Well, I've got to go down this way," I said, "Goodbye." She stopped too. She swallowed the last of the cake, then she began on the bun, watching me across it. "Goodbye," I said. I turned into the street and went on, but I went to the next corner before I stopped.

"Which way do you live?" I said. "This way?" I pointed down the street. She just looked at me. "Do you live over that way? I bet you live close to the station, where the trains are. Dont you?" She just looked at me, serene and secret and chewing. The street was empty both ways, with quiet lawns and houses neat among the trees, but no one at all except back there. We turned and went back. Two men sat in chairs in front of a store.

"Do you all know this little girl? She sort of took up with me and I cant find where she lives."

They quit looking at me and looked at her.

"Must be one of them new Italian families," one said. He wore a rusty frock coat. "I've seen her before. What's your name, little girl?" She looked at them blackly for awhile, her jaws moving steadily. She swallowed without ceasing to chew.

"Maybe she cant speak English," the other said.

"They sent her after bread," I said. "She must be able to speak something."

"What's your pa's name?" the first said. "Pete? Joe? name John huh?" She took another bite from the bun.

"What must I do with her?" I said. "She just follows me. I've got to get back to Boston."

"You from the college?"

"Yes, sir. And I've got to get on back."

"You might go up the street and turn her over to Anse. He'll be up at the livery stable. The marshal."

"I reckon that's what I'll have to do," I said. "I've got to do something with her. Much obliged. Come on, sister."

We went up the street, on the shady side, where the shadow of the broken façade blotted slowly across the road. We came to the livery stable. The marshal wasnt there. A man sitting in a chair tilted in the broad low door, where a dark cool breeze smelling of ammonia blew among the ranked stalls, said to look at the post-office. He didn't know her either.

"Them furriners. I cant tell one from another. You might take her across the tracks where they live, and maybe somebody'll claim her."

We went to the postoffice. It was back down the street. The man in the frock coat was opening a newspaper.

"Anse just drove out of town," he said. "I guess you'd better go down past the station and walk past them houses by the river. Somebody there'll know her."

"I guess I'll have to," I said. "Come on, sister." She pushed the last piece of the bun into her mouth and swallowed it. "Want another?" I said. She looked at me, chewing, her eyes black and unwinking and friendly. I took the other two buns out and gave her one and bit into the other. I asked a man where the station was and he showed me. "Come on, sister."

We reached the station and crossed the tracks, where the river was. A bridge crossed it, and a street of jumbled frame houses followed the river, backed onto it. A shabby street, but with an air heterogeneous and vivid too. In the center of an untrimmed plot enclosed by a fence of gaping and broken pickets stood an ancient lopsided surrey and a weathered house from an upper window of which hung a garment of vivid pink.

"Does that look like your house?" I said. She looked at me over the bun. "This one?" I said, pointing. She just chewed, but it seemed to me that I discerned something affirmative, acquiescent even if it wasn't eager, in her air. "This one?" I said. "Come on, then." I entered the broken gate. I looked back at her. "Here?" I said. "This look like your house?"

She nodded her head rapidly, looking at me, gnawing into the damp halfmoon of the bread. We went on. A walk of broken random flags, speared by fresh coarse blades of grass, led to the broken

stoop. There was no movement about the house at all, and the pink
garment hanging in no wind from the upper window. There was
a bell pull with a porcelain knob, attached to about six feet of wire
when I stopped pulling and knocked. The little girl had the crust
edgeways in her chewing mouth.

A woman opened the door. She looked at me, then she spoke
rapidly to the little girl in Italian, with a rising inflection, then a
pause, interrogatory. She spoke to her again, the little girl looking
at her across the end of the crust, pushing it into her mouth with a
dirty hand.

"She says she lives here," I said. "I met her down town. Is this
your bread?"

"No spika," the woman said. She spoke to the little girl again.
The little girl just looked at her.

"No live here?" I said. I pointed to the girl, then at her, then at
the door. The woman shook her head. She spoke rapidly. She
came to the edge of the porch and pointed down the road, speaking.

I nodded violently too. "You come show?" I said. I took her arm,
waving my other hand toward the road. She spoke swiftly, pointing. "You come show," I said, trying to lead her down the steps.

"Si, si," she said, holding back, showing me whatever it was. I
nodded again.

"Thanks. Thanks. Thanks." I went down the steps and walked
toward the gate, not running, but pretty fast. I reached the gate
and stopped and looked at her for a while. The crust was gone now,
and she looked at me with her black, friendly stare. The woman
stood on the stoop, watching us.

"Come on, then," I said. "We'll have to find the right one sooner
or later."

She moved along just under my elbow. We went on. The houses
all seemed empty. Not a soul in sight. A sort of breathlessness that
empty houses have. Yet they couldnt all be empty. All the different
rooms, if you could just slice the walls away all of a sudden
Madam, your daughter, if you please. No. Madam, for God's sake,
your daughter. She moved along just under my elbow, her shiny
tight pigtails, and then the last house played out and the road
curved out of sight beyond a wall, following the river. The woman
was emerging from the broken gate, with a shawl over her head
and clutched under her chin. The road curved on, empty. I found

a coin and gave it to the little girl. A quarter. "Goodbye, sister,"
I said. Then I ran.

I ran fast, not looking back. Just before the road curved away I
looked back. She stood in the road, a small figure clasping the loaf
of bread to her filthy little dress, her eyes still and black and unwinking. I ran on.

A lane turned from the road. I entered it and after a while I
slowed to a fast walk. The lane went between back premises—
unpainted houses with more of those gay and startling coloured
garments on lines, a barn broken-backed, decaying quietly among
rank orchard trees, unpruned and weedchoked, pink and white and
murmurous with sunlight and with bees. I looked back. The entrance to the lane was empty. I slowed still more, my shadow pacing me, dragging its head through the weeds that hid the fence.

The lane went back to a barred gate, became defunctive in grass,
a mere path scarred quietly into new grass. I climbed the gate into
a woodlot and crossed it and came to another wall and followed
that one, my shadow behind me now. There were vines and
creepers where at home would be honeysuckle. Coming and coming especially in the dusk when it rained, getting honeysuckle all
mixed up in it as though it were not enough without that, not unbearable enough. *What did you let him for kiss kiss*

*I didn't let him I made him watching me getting mad What do
you think of that? Red print of my hand coming up through her
face like turning a light on under your hand her eyes going bright*

*It's not for kissing I slapped you. Girl's elbows at fifteen Father
said you swallow like you had a fishbone in your throat what's the
matter with you and Caddy across the table not to look at me. It's
for letting it be some darn town squirt I slapped you you will will
you now I guess you say calf rope. My red hand coming up out of
her face. What do you think of that scouring her head into the.
Grass sticks crisscrossed into the flesh tingling scouring her head.
Say calf rope say it*

I didnt kiss a dirty girl like Natalie anyway The wall went into
shadow, and then my shadow, I had tricked it again. I had forgot
about the river curving along the road. I climbed the wall. And
then she watched me jump down, holding the loaf against her
dress.

I stood in the weeds and we looked at one another for a while.
"Why didnt you tell me you lived out this way, sister?" The loaf

was wearing slowly out of the paper; already it needed a new one. "Well, come on then and show me the house." *not a dirty girl like Natalie. It was raining we could hear it on the roof, sighing through the high sweet emptiness of the barn.*

There? touching her

Not there

There? not raining hard but we couldnt hear anything but the roof and as if it was my blood or her blood

She pushed me down the ladder and ran off and left me Caddy did

Was it there it hurt you when Caddy did ran off was it there

Oh She walked just under my elbow, the top of her patent leather head, the loaf fraying out of the newspaper.

"If you dont get home pretty soon you're going to wear that loaf out. And then what'll your mamma say?" *I bet I can lift you up*

You cant I'm too heavy

Did Caddy go away did she go to the house you cant see the barn from our house did you ever try to see the barn from

It was her fault she pushed me she ran away

I can lift you up see how I can

oh her blood or my blood Oh We went on in the thin dust, our feet silent as rubber in the thin dust where pencils of sun slanted in the trees. And I could feel water again running swift and peaceful in the secret shade.

"You live a long way, dont you. You're mighty smart to go this far to town by yourself." *It's like dancing sitting down did you ever dance sitting down? We could hear the rain, a rat in the crib, the empty barn vacant with horses. How do you hold to dance do you hold like this*

Oh

I used to hold like this you thought I wasnt strong enough didn't you

Oh Oh Oh Oh

I hold to use like this I mean did you hear what I said I said oh oh oh oh

The road went on, still and empty, the sun slanting more and more. Her stiff little pigtails were bound at the tips with bits of crimson cloth. A corner of the wrapping flapped a little as she walked, the nose of the loaf naked. I stopped.

"Look here. Do you live down this road? We havent passed a house in a mile, almost."

She looked at me, black and secret and friendly.

"Where do you live, sister? Dont you live back there in town?"

There was a bird somewhere in the woods, beyond the broken and infrequent slanting of sunlight.

"Your papa's going to be worried about you. Dont you reckon you'll get a whipping for not coming straight home with that bread?"

The bird whistled again, invisible, a sound meaningless and profound, inflexionless, ceasing as though cut off with the blow of a knife, and again, and that sense of water swift and peaceful above secret places, felt, not seen not heard.

"Oh, hell, sister." About half the paper hung limp. "That's not doing any good now." I tore it off and dropped it beside the road. "Come on. We'll have to go back to town. We'll go back along the river."

We left the road. Among the moss little pale flowers grew, and the sense of water mute and unseen. *I hold to use like this I mean I use to hold She stood in the door looking at us her hands on her hips*

You pushed me it was your fault it hurt me too

We were dancing sitting down I bet Caddy cant dance sitting down

Stop that stop that

I was just brushing the trash off the back of your dress

You keep your nasty old hands off of me it was your fault you pushed me down I'm mad at you

I dont care she looked at us stay mad she went away We began to hear the shouts, the splashings; I saw a brown body gleam for an instant.

Stay mad. My shirt was getting wet and my hair. Across the roof hearing the roof loud now I could see Natalie going through the garden among the rain. Get wet I hope you catch pneumonia go on home Cowface. I jumped hard as I could into the hogwallow and mud yellowed up to my waist stinking I kept on plunging until I fell down and rolled over in it "Hear them in swimming, sister? I wouldn't mind doing that myself." If I had time. When I have time. I could hear my watch. *mud was warmer than the rain it*

*smelled awful. She had her back turned I went around in front
of her. You know what I was doing? She turned her back I went
around in front of her the rain creeping into the mud flatting her
bodice through her dress it smelled horrible. I was hugging her
that's what I was doing. She turned her back I went around in
front of her. I was hugging her I tell you.*

I dont give a damn what you were doing

*You dont you dont I'll make you I'll make you give a damn. She
hit my hands away I smeared mud on her with the other hand I
couldn't feel the wet smacking of her hand I wiped mud from my
legs smeared it on her wet hard turning body hearing her fingers
going into my face but I couldn't feel it even when the rain began
to taste sweet on my lips*

They saw us from the water first, heads and shoulders. They
yelled and one rose squatting and sprang among them. They
looked like beavers, the water lipping about their chins, yelling.

"Take that girl away! What did you want to bring a girl here
for? Go on away!"

"She wont hurt you. We just want to watch you for a while."

They squatted in the water. Their heads drew into a clump,
watching us, then they broke and rushed toward us, hurling water
with their hands. We moved quick.

"Look out, boys; she wont hurt you."

"Go on away, Harvard!" It was the second boy, the one that
thought the horse and wagon back there at the bridge. "Splash
them, fellows!"

"Let's get out and throw them in," another said. "I aint afraid of
any girl."

"Splash them! Splash them!" They rushed toward us, hurling
water. We moved back. "Go on away!" they yelled. "Go on away!"

We went away. They huddled just under the bank, their slick
heads in a row against the bright water. We went on. "That's not
for us, is it." The sun slanted through to the moss here and there,
leveller. "Poor kid, you're just a girl." Little flowers grew among the
moss, littler than I had ever seen. "You're just a girl. Poor kid."
There was a path, curving along beside the water. Then the water
was still again, dark and still and swift. "Nothing but a girl. Poor
sister." *We lay in the wet grass panting the rain like cold shot on
my back. Do you care now do you do you*

My Lord we sure are in a mess get up. Where the rain touched

*my forehead it began to smart my hand came red away streaking
off pink in the rain. Does it hurt*

Of course it does what do you reckon

*I tried to scratch your eyes out my Lord we sure do stink we bet-
ter try to wash it off in the branch* "There's town again, sister.
You'll have to go home now. I've got to get back to school. Look
how late it's getting. You'll go home now, wont you?" But she just
looked at me with her black, secret, friendly gaze, the half-naked
loaf clutched to her breast. "It's wet. I thought we jumped back
in time." I took my handkerchief and tried to wipe the loaf, but
the crust began to come off, so I stopped. "We'll just have to let it
dry itself. Hold it like this." She held it like that. It looked kind of
like rats had been eating it now. *and the water building and building up the squatting back the sloughed mud stinking surfaceward
pocking the pattering surface like grease on a hot stove. I told you
I'd make you*

I dont give a goddam what you do

Then we heard the running and we stopped and looked back
and saw him coming up the path running, the level shadows flicking upon his legs.

"He's in a hurry. We'd—" then I saw another man, an oldish man
running heavily, clutching a stick, and a boy naked from the waist
up, clutching his pants as he ran.

"There's Julio," the little girl said, and then I saw his Italian face
and his eyes as he sprang upon me. We went down. His hands were
jabbing at my face and he was saying something and trying to bite
me, I reckon, and then they hauled him off and held him heaving
and thrashing and yelling and they held his arms and he tried to
kick me until they dragged him back. The little girl was howling,
holding the loaf in both arms. The half-naked boy was darting and
jumping up and down, clutching his trousers and someone pulled
me up in time to see another stark naked figure come around the
tranquil bend in the path running and change direction in midstride and leap into the woods, a couple of garments rigid as boards
behind it. Julio still struggled. The man who had pulled me up said,
"Whoa, now. We got you." He wore a vest but no coat. Upon it
was a metal shield. In his other hand he clutched a knotted,
polished stick.

"You're Anse, aren't you?" I said. "I was looking for you. What's
the matter?"

"I warn you that anything you say will be used against you," he said. "You're under arrest."

"I killa heem," Julio said. He struggled. Two men held him. The little girl howled steadily, holding the bread. "You steala my seester," Julio said. "Let go, meesters."

"Steal his sister?" I said. "Why, I've been—"

"Shet up," Anse said. "You can tell that to Squire."

"Steal his sister?" I said. Julio broke from the men and sprang at me again, but the marshal met him and they struggled until the other two pinioned his arms again. Anse released him, panting.

"You durn furriner," he said, "I've got a good mind to take you up too, for assault and battery." He turned to me again. "Will you come peaceable, or do I handcuff you?"

"I'll come peaceable," I said. "Anything, just so I can find someone—do something with—Stole his sister," I said. "Stole his—"

"I've warned you," Anse said, "He aims to charge you with meditated criminal assault. Here, you, make that gal shut up that noise."

"Oh," I said. Then I began to laugh. Two more boys with plastered heads and round eyes came out of the bushes, buttoning shirts that had already dampened onto their shoulders and arms, and I tried to stop the laughter, but I couldnt.

"Watch him, Anse, he's crazy, I believe."

"I'll h-have to qu-quit," I said, "It'll stop in a mu-minute. The other time it said ah ah ah," I said, laughing. "Let me sit down a while." I sat down, they watching me, and the little girl with her streaked face and the gnawed looking loaf, and the water swift and peaceful below the path. After a while the laughter ran out. But my throat wouldnt quit trying to laugh, like retching after your stomach is empty.

"Whoa, now," Anse said. "Get a grip on yourself."

"Yes," I said, tightening my throat. There was another yellow butterfly, like one of the sunflecks had come loose. After a while I didnt have to hold my throat so tight. I got up. "I'm ready. Which way?"

We followed the path, the two others watching Julio and the little girl and the boys somewhere in the rear. The path went along the river to the bridge. We crossed it and the tracks, people coming to the doors to look at us and more boys materializing from somewhere until when we turned into the main street we had quite a procession. Before the drugstore stood an auto, a big one, but I didn't recognise them until Mrs Bland said,

"Why, Quentin! Quentin Compson!" Then I saw Gerald, and Spoade in the back seat, sitting on the back of his neck. And Shreve. I didnt know the two girls.

"Quentin Compson!" Mrs Bland said.

"Good afternoon," I said, raising my hat. "I'm under arrest. I'm sorry I didnt get your note. Did Shreve tell you?"

"Under arrest?" Shreve said. "Excuse me," he said. He heaved himself up and climbed over their feet and got out. He had on a pair of my flannel pants, like a glove. I didnt remember forgetting them. I didnt remember how many chins Mrs Bland had, either. The prettiest girl was with Gerald in front, too. They watched me through veils, with a kind of delicate horror. "Who's under arrest?" Shreve said. "What's this, mister?"

"Gerald," Mrs Bland said, "Send these people away. You get in this car, Quentin."

Gerald got out. Spoade hadnt moved.

"What's he done, Cap?" he said. "Robbed a hen house?"

"I warn you," Anse said. "Do you know the prisoner?"

"Know him," Shreve said. "Look here—"

"Then you can come along to the squire's. You're obstructing justice. Come along." He shook my arm.

"Well, good afternoon," I said. "I'm glad to have seen you all. Sorry I couldnt be with you."

"You, Gerald," Mrs Bland said.

"Look here, constable," Gerald said.

"I warn you you're interfering with an officer of the law," Anse said. "If you've anything to say, you can come to the squire's and make cognizance of the prisoner." We went on. Quite a procession now, Anse and I leading. I could hear them telling them what it was, and Spoade asking questions, and then Julio said something violently in Italian and I looked back and saw the little girl standing at the curb looking at me with her friendly, inscrutable regard.

"Git on home," Julio shouted at her, "I beat hell outa you."

We went down the street and turned into a bit of lawn in which, set back from the street, stood a one storey building of brick trimmed with white. We went up the rock path to the door, where Anse halted everyone except us and made them remain outside.

We entered a bare room smelling of stale tobacco. There was a
sheet iron stove in the center of a wooden frame filled with sand,
and a faded map on the wall and the dingy plat of a township. Behind a scarred littered table a man with a fierce roach of iron grey
hair peered at us over steel spectacles.

"Got him, did ye, Anse?" he said.

"Got him, Squire."

He opened a huge dusty book and drew it to him and dipped
a foul pen into an inkwell filled with what looked like coal dust.

"Look here, mister," Shreve said.

"The prisoner's name," the squire said. I told him. He wrote it
slowly into the books, the pen scratching with excruciating deliberation.

"Look here, mister," Shreve said, "We know this fellow. We—"

"Order in the court," Anse said.

"Shut up, bud," Spoade said. "Let him do it his way. He's going
to anyhow."

"Age," the squire said. I told him. He wrote that, his mouth moving as he wrote. "Occupation." I told him. "Harvard student, hey?"
he said. He looked up at me, bowing his neck a little to see over
the spectacles. His eyes were clear and cold, like a goat's. "What are
you up to, coming out here kidnapping children?"

"They're crazy, Squire," Shreve said. "Whoever says this boy's
kidnapping—"

Julio moved violently. "Crazy?" he said. "Dont I catcha heem,
eh? Dont I see weetha my own eyes—"

"You're a liar," Shreve said. "You never—"

"Order, order," Anse said, raising his voice.

"You fellers shet up," the squire said. "If they dont stay quiet,
turn 'em out, Anse." They got quiet. The squire looked at Shreve,
then at Spoade, then at Gerald. "You know this young man?" he
said to Spoade.

"Yes, your honour," Spoade said. "He's just a country boy in
school up there. He dont mean any harm. I think the marshal'll
find it's a mistake. His father's a congregational minister."

"H'm," the squire said. "What was you doing, exactly?" I told
him, he watching me with his cold, pale eyes. "How about it,
Anse?"

"Might have been," Anse said. "Them durn furriners."

"I American," Julio said. "I gotta da pape'."

"Where's the gal?"

"He sent her home," Anse said.

"Was she scared or anything?"

"Not till Julio there jumped on the prisoner. They were just walking along the river path, towards town. Some boys swimming told us which way they went."

"It's a mistake, Squire," Spoade said. "Children and dogs are always taking up with him like that. He cant help it."

"H'm," the squire said. He looked out of the window for a while. We watched him. I could hear Julio scratching himself. The squire looked back.

"Air you satisfied the gal aint took any hurt, you, there?"

"No hurt now," Julio said sullenly.

"You quit work to hunt for her?"

"Sure I quit. I run. I run like hell. Looka here, looka there, then man tella me he seen him giva her she eat. She go weetha."

"H'm," the squire said. "Well, son, I calculate you owe Julio something for taking him away from his work."

"Yes, sir," I said. "How much?"

"Dollar, I calculate."

I gave Julio a dollar.

"Well," Spoade said, "If that's all—I reckon he's discharged, your honour?"

The squire didn't look at him. "How far'd you run him, Anse?"

"Two miles, at least. It was about two hours before we caught him."

"H'm," the squire said. He mused a while. We watched him, his stiff crest, the spectacles riding low on his nose. The yellow shape of the window grew slowly across the floor, reached the wall, climbing. Dust motes whirled and slanted. "Six dollars."

"Six dollars?" Shreve said. "What's that for?"

"Six dollars," the squire said. He looked at Shreve a moment, then at me again.

"Look here," Shreve said.

"Shut up," Spoade said. "Give it to him, bud, and let's get out of here. The ladies are waiting for us. You got six dollars?"

"Yes," I said. I gave him six dollars.

"Case dismissed," he said.

"You get a receipt," Shreve said. "You get a signed receipt for that money."

The squire looked at Shreve mildly. "Case dismissed," he said without raising his voice.

"I'll be damned—" Shreve said.

"Come on here," Spoade said, taking his arm. "Good afternoon, Judge. Much obliged." As we passed out the door Julio's voice rose again, violent, then ceased. Spoade was looking at me, his brown eyes quizzical, a little cold. "Well, bud, I reckon you'll do your girl chasing in Boston after this."

"You damned fool," Shreve said, "What the hell do you mean anyway, straggling off here, fooling with these damn wops?"

"Come on," Spoade said, "They must be getting impatient."

Mrs Bland was talking to them. They were Miss Holmes and Miss Daingerfield and they quit listening to her and looked at me again with that delicate and curious horror, their veils turned back upon their little white noses and their eyes fleeing and mysterious beneath the veils.

"Quentin Compson," Mrs Bland said, "What would your mother say? A young man naturally gets into scrapes, but to be arrested on foot by a country policeman. What did they think he'd done, Gerald?"

"Nothing," Gerald said.

"Nonsense. What was it, you, Spoade?"

"He was trying to kidnap that little dirty girl, but they caught him in time," Spoade said.

"Nonsense," Mrs Bland said, but her voice sort of died away and she stared at me for a moment, and the girls drew their breaths in with a soft concerted sound. "Fiddlesticks," Mrs Bland said briskly, "If that isn't just like these ignorant lowclass Yankees. Get in, Quentin."

Shreve and I sat on two small collapsible seats. Gerald cranked the car and got in and we started.

"Now, Quentin, you tell me what all this foolishness is about," Mrs Bland said. I told them, Shreve hunched and furious on his little seat and Spoade sitting again on the back of his neck beside Miss Daingerfield.

"And the joke is, all the time Quentin had us all fooled," Spoade said. "All the time we thought he was the model youth that anybody could trust a daughter with, until the police showed him up at his nefarious work."

"Hush up, Spoade," Mrs Bland said. We drove down the street and crossed the bridge and passed the house where the pink garment hung in the window. "That's what you get for not reading my note. Why didnt you come and get it? Mr MacKenzie says he told you it was there."

"Yessum. I intended to, but I never went back to the room."

"You'd have let us sit there waiting I dont know how long, if it hadnt been for Mr MacKenzie. When he said you hadnt come back, that left an extra place, so we asked him to come. We're very glad to have you anyway, Mr MacKenzie." Shreve said nothing. His arms were folded and he glared straight ahead past Gerald's cap. It was a cap for motoring in England. Mrs Bland said so. We passed that house, and three others, and another yard where the little girl stood by the gate. She didnt have the bread now, and her face looked like it had been streaked with coal dust. I waved my hand, but she made no reply, only her head turned slowly as the car passed, following us with her unwinking gaze. Then we ran beside the wall, our shadows running along the wall, and after a while we passed a piece of torn newspaper lying beside the road and I began to laugh again. I could feel it in my throat and I looked off into the trees where the afternoon slanted, thinking of afternoon and of the bird and the boys in swimming. But still I couldnt stop it and then I knew that if I tried too hard to stop it I'd be crying and I thought about how I'd thought about I could not be a virgin, with so many of them walking along in the shadows and whispering with their soft girlvoices lingering in the shadowy places and the words coming out and perfume and eyes you could feel not see, but if it was that simple to do it wouldnt be anything and if it wasnt anything, what was I and then Mrs Bland said, "Quentin? Is he sick, Mr MacKenzie?" and then Shreve's fat hand touched my knee and Spoade began talking and I quit trying to stop it.

"If that hamper is in his way, Mr MacKenzie, move it over on your side. I brought a hamper of wine because I think young gentlemen should drink wine, although my father, Gerald's grandfather" *ever do that Have you ever done that In the grey darkness a little light her hands locked about*

"They do, when they can get it," Spoade said. "Hey, Shreve?" *her knees her face looking at the sky the smell of honeysuckle upon her face and throat*

"Beer, too," Shreve said. His hand touched my knee again. I moved my knee again. *like a thin wash of lilac coloured paint talking about him bringing*

"You're not a gentleman," Spoade said. *him between us until the shape of her blurred not with dark*

"No. I'm Canadian," Shreve said. *talking about him the oar blades winking him along winking the Cap made for motoring in England and all time rushing beneath and they two blurred within the other forever more he had been in the army had killed men*

"I adore Canada," Miss Daingerfield said. "I think it's marvellous."

"Did you ever drink perfume?" Spoade said. *with one hand he could lift her to his shoulder and run with her running Running*

"No," Shreve said. *running the beast with two backs and she blurred in the winking oars running the swine of Euboeleus running coupled within how many Caddy*

"Neither did I," Spoade said. *I dont know too many there was something terrible in me terrible in me Father I have committed Have you ever done that We didnt we didnt do that did we do that*

"and Gerald's grandfather always picked his own mint before breakfast, while the dew was still on it. He wouldnt even let old Wilkie touch it do you remember Gerald but always gathered it himself and made his own julep. He was as crotchety about his julep as an old maid, measuring everything by a recipe in his head. There was only one man he ever gave that recipe to; that was" *we did how can you not know if it youll just wait I'll tell you how it was it was a crime we did a terrible crime it cannot be hid you think it can but wait Poor Quentin youve never done that have you and I'll tell you how it was I'll tell Father then itll have to be because you love Father then we'll have to go away amid the pointing and the horror the clean flame I'll make you say we did I'm stronger than you I'll make you know we did you thought it was them but it was me listen I fooled you all the time it was me you thought I was in the house where that damn honeysuckle trying not to think the swing the cedars the secret surges the breathing locked drinking the wild breath the yes Yes Yes yes* "never be got to drink wine himself, but he always said that a hamper what book did you read that in the one where Geralds rowing suit of wine was a necessary part of any gentlemen's picnic basket" *did you love them Caddy did you love them When they touched me I died*

one minute she was standing there the next he was yelling and pulling at her dress they went into the hall and up the stairs yelling and shoving at her up the stairs to the bathroom door and stopped her back against the door and her arm across her face yelling and trying to shove her into the bathroom when she came in to supper T. P. was feeding him he started again just whimpering at first until she touched him then he yelled she stood there her eyes like cornered rats then I was running in the grey darkness it smelled of rain and all flower scents the damp warm air released and crickets sawing away in the grass pacing me with a small travelling island of silence Fancy watched me across the fence blotchy like a quilt on a line I thought damn that nigger he forgot to feed her again I ran down the hill in that vacuum of crickets like a breath travelling across a mirror she was lying in the water her head on the sand spit the water flowing about her hips there was a little more light in the water her skirt half saturated flopped along her flanks to the waters motion in heavy ripples going nowhere renewed themselves of their own movement I stood on the bank I could smell the honeysuckle on the water gap the air seemed to drizzle with honeysuckle and with the rasping of crickets a substance you could feel on the flesh

is Benjy still crying

I dont know yes I dont know

poor Benjy

I sat down on the bank the grass was damp a little then I found my shoes wet

get out of that water are you crazy

but she didnt move her face was a white blur framed out of the blur of the sand by her hair

get out now

she sat up then she rose her skirt flopped against her draining she climbed the bank her clothes flopping sat down

why dont you wring it out do you want to catch cold

yes

the water sucked and gurgled across the sand spit and on in the dark among the willows across the shallow the water rippled like a piece of cloth holding still a little light as water does he's crossed all the oceans all around the world

then she talked about him clasping her wet knees her face tilted back in the grey light the smell of honeysuckle there was a light in mothers room and in Benjys where T. P. was putting him to bed

do you love him

her hand came out I didnt move it fumbled down my arm and she held my hand flat against her chest her heart thudding

no no

did he make you then he made you do it let him he was stronger than you and he tomorrow Ill kill him I swear I will father neednt know until afterward and then you and I nobody need ever know we can take my school money we can cancel my matriculation Caddy you hate him dont you dont you

she held my hand against her chest her heart thudding I turned and caught her arm

Caddy you hate him dont you

she moved my hand up against her throat her heart was hammering there

poor Quentin

her face looked at the sky it was low so low that all smells and sounds of night seemed to have been crowded down like under a slack tent especially the honeysuckle it had got into my breathing it was on her face and throat like paint her blood pounded against my hand I was leaning on my other arm it began to jerk and jump and I had to pant to get any air at all out of that thick grey honeysuckle

yes I hate him I would die for him I've already died for him I die for him over and over again everytime this goes

when I lifted my hand I could still feel crisscrossed twigs and grass burning into the palm

poor Quentin

she leaned back on her arms her hands locked about her knees

youve never done that have you

what done what

that what I have what I did

yes yes lots of times with lots of girls

then I was crying her hand touched me again and I was crying against her damp blouse then she lying on her back looking past my head into the sky I could see a rim of white under her irises I opened my knife

do you remember the day damuddy died when you sat down
in the water in your drawers
　　yes
　　I held the point of the knife at her throat
　　it wont take but a second just a second then I can do mine I can
do mine then
　　all right can you do yours by yourself
　　yes the blades long enough Benjys in bed by now
　　yes
　　it wont take but a second Ill try not to hurt
　　all right
　　will you close your eyes
　　no like this youll have to push it harder
　　touch your hand to it
　　but she didnt move her eyes were wide open looking past my
head at the sky
　　Caddy do you remember how Dilsey fussed at you because your
drawers were muddy
　　dont cry
　　Im not crying Caddy
　　push it are you going to
　　do you want me to
　　yes push it
　　touch your hand to it
　　dont cry poor Quentin
　　but I couldnt stop she held my head against her damp hard
breast I could hear her heart going firm and slow now not hammering and the water gurgling among the willows in the dark and
waves of honeysuckle coming up the air my arm and shoulder were
twisted under me
　　what is it what are you doing
　　her muscles gathered I sat up
　　its my knife I dropped it
　　she sat up
　　what time is it
　　I dont know
　　she rose to her feet I fumbled along the ground
　　Im going let it go
　　I could feel her standing there I could smell her damp clothes
feeling her there

its right here somewhere

let it go you can find it tomorrow come on

wait a minute I'll find it

are you afraid to

here it is it was right here all the time

was it come on

I got up and followed we went up the hill the crickets hushing
before us

its funny how you can sit down and drop something and have
to hunt all around for it

the grey it was grey with dew slanting up into the grey sky then
the trees beyond

damn that honeysuckle I wish it would stop

you used to like it

we crossed the crest and went on toward the trees she walked
into me she gave over a little the ditch was a black scar on the grey
grass she walked into me again she looked at me and gave over we
reached the ditch

lets go this way

what for

lets see if you can still see Nancys bones I havent thought to look
in a long time have you

it was matted with vines and briers dark

they were right here you cant tell whether you see them or not
can you

stop Quentin

come on

the ditch narrowed closed she turned toward the trees

stop Quentin

Caddy

I got in front of her again

Caddy

stop it

I held her

Im stronger than you

she was motionless hard unyielding but still

I wont fight stop youd better stop

Caddy dont Caddy

it wont do any good dont you know it wont let me go

the honeysuckle drizzled and drizzled I could hear the crickets

watching us in a circle she moved back went around me on toward
the trees

you go on back to the house you neednt come

I went on

why dont you go on back to the house

damn that honeysuckle

we reached the fence she crawled through I crawled through
when I rose from stooping he was coming out of the trees into the
grey toward us coming toward us tall and flat and still even moving like he was still she went to him

this is Quentin Im wet Im wet all over you dont have to if you
dont want to

their shadows one shadow her head rose it was above his on the
sky higher their two heads

you dont have to if you dont want to

then not two heads the darkness smelled of rain of damp grass
and leaves the grey light drizzling like rain the honeysuckle coming up in damp waves I could see her face a blur against his shoulder he held her in one arm like she was no bigger than a child he
extended his hand

glad to know you

we shook hands then we stood there her shadow high against his
shadow one shadow

whatre you going to do Quentin

walk a while I think Ill go through the woods to the road and
come back through town

I turned away going

goodnight

Quentin

I stopped

what do you want

in the woods the tree frogs were going smelling rain in the air
they sounded like toy music boxes that were hard to turn and the
honeysuckle

come here

what do you want

come here Quentin

I went back she touched my shoulder leaning down her shadow
the blur of her face leaning down from his high shadow I drew
back

look out

you go on home

Im not sleepy Im going to take a walk

wait for me at the branch

Im going for a walk

Ill be there soon wait for me you wait

no Im going through the woods

I didnt look back the tree frogs didnt pay me any mind the grey light like moss in the trees drizzling but still it wouldnt rain after a while I turned went back to the edge of the woods as soon as I got there I began to smell honeysuckle again I could see the lights on the courthouse clock and the glare of town the square on the sky and the dark willows along the branch and the light in mothers windows the light still on in Benjys room and I stooped through the fence and went across the pasture running I ran in the grey grass among the crickets the honeysuckle getting stronger and stronger and the smell of water then I could see the water the colour of grey honeysuckle I lay down on the bank with my face close to the ground so I couldnt smell the honeysuckle I couldnt smell it then and I lay there feeling the earth going through my clothes listening to the water and after a while I wasnt breathing so hard and I lay there thinking that if I didnt move my face I wouldnt have to breathe hard and smell it and then I wasnt thinking about anything at all she came along the bank and stopped I didnt move

its late you go on home

what

you go on home its late

all right

her clothes rustled I didnt move they stopped rustling

are you going in like I told you

I didnt hear anything

Caddy

yes I will if you want me to I will

I sat up she was sitting on the ground her hands clasped about her knee

go on to the house like I told you

yes Ill do anything you want me to anything yes

she didnt even look at me I caught her shoulder and shook her hard you shut up

I shook her

you shut up you shut up

yes

she lifted her face then I saw she wasnt even looking at me at all I could see that white rim

get up

I pulled her she was limp I lifted her to her feet

go on now

was Benjy still crying when you left

go on

we crossed the branch the roof came in sight then the window upstairs

hes asleep now

I had to stop and fasten the gate she went on in the grey light the smell of rain and still it wouldnt rain and honeysuckle beginning to come from the garden fence beginning she went into the shadow I could hear her feet then

Caddy

I stopped at the steps I couldnt hear her feet

Caddy

I heard her feet then my hand touched her not warm not cool just still her clothes a little damp still

do you love him now

not breathing except slow like far away breathing

Caddy do you love him now

I dont know

outside the grey light the shadows of things like dead things in stagnant water

I wish you were dead

do you you coming in now

are you thinking about him now

I dont know

tell me what youre thinking about tell me

stop stop Quentin

you shut up you shut up you hear me you shut up are you going to shut up

all right I will stop we'll make too much noise

Ill kill you do you hear

lets go out to the swing theyll hear you here

Im not crying do you say Im crying

no hush now we'll wake Benjy up

you go on into the house go on now

I am dont cry Im bad anyway you cant help it

theres a curse on us its not our fault is it our fault

hush come on and go to bed now

you cant make me theres a curse on us

finally I saw him he was just going into the barbershop he looked
out I went on and waited

Ive been looking for you two or three days

you wanted to see me

Im going to see you

he rolled the cigarette quickly with about two motions he struck
the match with his thumb

we cant talk here suppose I meet you somewhere

Ill come to your room are you at the hotel

no thats not so good you know that bridge over the creek in
there back of

yes all right

at one oclock right

yes

I turned away

Im obliged to you

look

I stopped looked back

she all right

he looked like he was made out of bronze his khaki shirt

she need me for anything now

I'll be there at one

she heard me tell T. P. to saddle Prince at one oclock she kept
watching me not eating much she came too

what are you going to do

nothing cant I go for a ride if I want to

youre going to do something what is it

none of your business whore whore

T. P. had Prince at the side door

I wont want him Im going to walk

I went down the drive and out the gate I turned into the lane
then I ran before I reached the bridge I saw him leaning on the rail
the horse was hitched in the woods he looked over his shoulder

then he turned his back he didnt look up until I came onto the
bridge and stopped he had a piece of bark in his hands breaking
pieces from it and dropping them over the rail into the water

I came to tell you to leave town

he broke a piece of bark deliberately dropped it carefully into
the water watched it float away

I said you must leave town

he looked at me

did she send you to me

I say you must go not my father not anybody I say it

listen save this for a while I want to know if shes all right have
they been bothering her up there

thats something you dont need to trouble yourself about

then I heard myself saying Ill give you until sundown to leave
town

he broke a piece of bark and dropped it into the water then he
laid the bark on the rail and rolled a cigarette with those two swift
motions spun the match over the rail

what will you do if I dont leave

Ill kill you dont think that just because I look like a kid to you

the smoke flowed in two jets from his nostrils across his face

how old are you

I began to shake my hands were on the rail I thought if I hid
them hed know why

Ill give you until tonight

listen buddy whats your name Benjys the natural isnt he you
are

Quentin

my mouth said it I didnt say it at all

Ill give you till sundown

Quentin

he raked the cigarette ash carefully off against the rail he did it
slowly and carefully like sharpening a pencil my hands had quit
shaking

listen no good taking it so hard its not your fault kid it would
have been some other fellow

did you ever have a sister did you

no but theyre all bitches

I hit him my open hand beat the impulse to shut it to his face
his hand moved as fast as mine the cigarette went over the rail I

swung with the other hand he caught it too before the cigarette
reached the water he held both my wrists in the same hand his
other hand flicked to his armpit under his coat behind him the sun
slanted and a bird singing somewhere beyond the sun we looked
at one another while the bird singing he turned my hands loose

look here

he took the bark from the rail and dropped it into the water it
bobbed up the current took it floated away his hand lay on the rail
holding the pistol loosely we waited

you cant hit it now

no

it floated on it was quite still in the woods I heard the bird again
and the water afterward the pistol came up he didnt aim at all the
bark disappeared then pieces of it floated up spreading he hit two
more of them pieces of bark no bigger than silver dollars

thats enough I guess

he swung the cylinder out and blew into the barrel a thin wisp
of smoke dissolved he reloaded the three chambers shut the cylinder he handed it to me butt first

what for I wont try to beat that

youll need it from what you said Im giving you this one because
youve seen what itll do

to hell with your gun

I hit him I was still trying to hit him long after he was holding
my wrists but I still tried then it was like I was looking at him
through a piece of coloured glass I could hear my blood and then I
could see the sky again and branches against it and the sun slanting through them and he holding me on my feet

did you hit me

I couldnt hear

what

yes how do you feel

all right let go

he let me go I leaned against the rail

do you feel all right

let me alone Im all right

can you make it home all right

go on let me alone

youd better not try to walk take my horse

no you go on

you can hang the reins on the pommel and turn him loose he'll go back to the stable

let me alone you go on and let me alone

I leaned on the rail looking at the water I heard him untie the horse and ride off and after a while I couldnt hear anything but the water and then the bird again I left the bridge and sat down with my back against a tree and leaned my head against the tree and shut my eyes a patch of sun came through and fell across my eyes and I moved a little further around the tree I heard the bird again and the water and then everything sort of rolled away and I didnt feel anything at all I felt almost good after all those days and the nights with honeysuckle coming up out of the darkness into my room where I was trying to sleep even when after a while I knew that he hadnt hit me that he had lied about that for her sake too and that I had just passed out like a girl but even that didnt matter anymore and I sat there against the tree with little flecks of sunlight brushing across my face like yellow leaves on a twig listening to the water and not thinking about anything at all even when I heard the horse coming fast I sat there with my eyes closed and heard its feet bunch scuttering the hissing sand and feet running and her hard running hands

fool fool are you hurt

I opened my eyes her hands running on my face

I didnt know which way until I heard the pistol I didnt know where I didnt think he and you running off slipping I didnt think he would have

she held my face between her hands bumping my head against the tree

stop stop that

I caught her wrists

quit that quit it

I knew he wouldnt I knew he wouldnt

she tried to bump my head against the tree

I told him never to speak to me again I told him

she tried to break her wrists free

let me go

stop it I'm stronger than you stop it now

let me go Ive got to catch him and ask his let me go Quentin please let me go let me go

all at once she quit her wrists went lax

yes I can tell him I can make him believe anytime I can make him

Caddy

she hadnt hitched Prince he was liable to strike out for home if the notion took him

anytime he will believe me

do you love him Caddy

do I what

she looked at me then everything emptied out of her eyes and they looked like the eyes in the statues blank and unseeing and serene

put your hand against my throat

she took my hand and held it flat against her throat

now say his name

Dalton Ames

I felt the first surge of blood there it surged in strong accelerating beats

say it again

her face looked off into the trees where the sun slanted and where the bird

say it again

Dalton Ames

her blood surged steadily beating and beating against my hand

It kept on running for a long time, but my face felt cold and sort of dead, and my eye, and the cut place on my finger was smarting again. I could hear Shreve working the pump, then he came back with the basin and a round blob of twilight wobbling in it, with a yellow edge like a fading ballon, then my reflection. I tried to see my face in it.

"Has it stopped?" Shreve said. "Give me the rag." He tried to take it from my hand.

"Look out," I said, "I can do it. Yes, it's about stopped now." I dipped the rag again, breaking the balloon. The rag stained the water. "I wish I had a clean one."

"You need a piece of beefsteak for that eye," Shreve said. "Damn if you wont have a shiner tomorrow. The son of a bitch," he said.

"Did I hurt him any?" I wrung out the handkerchief and tried to clean the blood off of my vest.

"You cant get that off," Shreve said. "You'll have to send it to the cleaner's. Come on, hold it on your eye, why dont you."

"I can get some of it off," I said. But I wasn't doing much good. "What sort of shape is my collar in?"

"I dont know," Shreve said. "Hold it against your eye. Here."

"Look out," I said. "I can do it. Did I hurt him any?"

"You may have hit him. I may have looked away just then or blinked or something. He boxed the hell out of you. He boxed you all over the place. What did you want to fight him with your fists for? You goddamn fool. How do you feel?"

"I feel fine," I said. "I wonder if I can get something to clean my vest."

"Oh, forget your damn clothes. Does your eye hurt?"

"I feel fine," I said. Everything was sort of violet and still, the sky green paling into gold beyond the gable of the house and a plume of smoke rising from the chimney without any wind. I heard the pump again. A man was filling a pail, watching us across his pumping shoulder. A woman crossed the door, but she didnt look out. I could hear a cow lowing somewhere.

"Come on," Shreve said, "Let your clothes alone and put that rag on your eye. I'll send your suit out first thing tomorrow."

"All right. I'm sorry I didn't bleed on him a little, at least."

"Son of a bitch," Shreve said. Spoade came out of the house, talking to the woman I reckon, and crossed the yard. He looked at me with his cold, quizzical eyes.

"Well, bud," he said, looking at me, "I'll be damned if you dont go to a lot of trouble to have your fun. Kidnapping, then fighting. What do you do on your holidays? burn houses?"

"I'm all right," I said. "What did Mrs Bland say?"

"She's giving Gerald hell for bloodying you up. She'll give you hell for letting him, when she sees you. She dont object to the fighting, it's the blood that annoys her. I think you lost caste with her a little by not holding your blood better. How do you feel?"

"Sure," Shreve said, "If you cant be a Bland, the next best thing is to commit adultery with one or get drunk and fight him, as the case may be."

"Quite right," Spoade said. "But I didnt know Quentin was drunk."

"He wasnt," Shreve said. "Do you have to be drunk to want to hit that son of a bitch?"

"Well, I think I'd have to be pretty drunk to try it, after seeing how Quentin came out. Where'd he learn to box?"

"He's been going to Mike's every day, over in town," I said.

"He has?" Spoade said. "Did you know that when you hit him?"

"I dont know," I said. "I guess so. Yes."

"Wet it again," Shreve said. "Want some fresh water?"

"This is all right," I said. I dipped the cloth again and held it to my eye. "Wish I had something to clean my vest." Spoade was still watching me.

"Say," he said, "What did you hit him for? What was it he said?"

"I dont know. I dont know why I did."

"The first I knew was when you jumped up all of a sudden and said, 'Did you ever have a sister? did you?' and when he said No, you hit him. I noticed you kept on looking at him, but you didnt seem to be paying any attention to what anybody was saying until you jumped up and asked him if he had any sisters."

"Ah, he was blowing off as usual," Shreve said, "about his women. You know: like he does, before girls, so they dont know exactly what he's saying. All his damn innuendo and lying and a lot of stuff that dont make sense even. Telling us about some wench that he made a date with to meet at a dance hall in Atlantic City and stood her up and went to the hotel and went to bed and how he lay there being sorry for her waiting on the pier for him, without him there to give her what she wanted. Talking about the body's beauty and the sorry ends thereof and how tough women have it, without anything else they can do except lie on their backs. Leda lurking in the bushes, whimpering and moaning for the swan, see. The son of a bitch. I'd hit him myself. Only I'd grabbed up her damn hamper of wine and done it if it had been me."

"Oh," Spoade said, "the champion of dames. Bud, you excite not only admiration, but horror." He looked at me, cold and quizzical. "Good God," he said.

"I'm sorry I hit him," I said. "Do I look too bad to go back and get it over with?"

"Apologies, hell," Shreve said, "Let them go to hell. We're going to town."

"He ought to go back so they'll know he fights like a gentleman," Spoade said. "Gets licked like one, I mean."

"Like this?" Shreve said, "With his clothes all over blood?"

"Why, all right," Spoade said, "You know best."

"He cant go around in his undershirt," Shreve said, "He's not a senior yet. Come on, let's go to town."

"You neednt come," I said. "You go on back to the picnic."

"Hell with them," Shreve said. "Come on here."

"What'll I tell them?" Spoade said. "Tell them you and Quentin had a fight too?"

"Tell them nothing," Shreve said. "Tell her her option expired at sunset. Come on, Quentin. I'll ask that woman where the nearest interurban—"

"No," I said, "I'm not going back to town."

Shreve stopped, looking at me. Turning, his glasses looked like small yellow moons.

"What are you going to do?"

"I'm not going back to town yet. You go on back to the picnic. Tell them I wouldnt come back because my clothes were spoiled."

"Look here," he said, "What are you up to?"

"Nothing. I'm all right. You and Spoade go on back. I'll see you tomorrow." I went on across the yard, toward the road.

"Do you know where the station is?" Shreve said.

"I'll find it. I'll see you all tomorrow. Tell Mrs Bland I'm sorry I spoiled her party." They stood watching me. I went around the house. A rock path went down to the road. Roses grew on both sides of the path. I went through the gate, onto the road. It dropped downhill, toward the woods, and I could make out the auto beside the road. I went up the hill. The light increased as I mounted, and before I reached the top I heard a car. It sounded far away across the twilight and I stopped and listened to it. I couldnt make out the auto any longer, but Shreve was standing in the road before the house, looking up the hill. Behind him the yellow light lay like a wash of paint on the roof of the house. I lifted my hand and went on over the hill, listening to the car. Then the house was gone and I stopped in the green and yellow light and heard the car growing louder and louder, until just as it began to die away it ceased all together. I waited until I heard it start again. Then I went on.

As I descended the light dwindled slowly, yet at the same time without altering its quality, as if I and not light were changing, decreasing, though even when the road ran into trees you could have read a newspaper. Pretty soon I came to a lane. I turned into it. It was closer and darker than the road, but when it came out at the trolley stop—another wooden marquee—the light was still unchanged. After the lane it seemed brighter, as though I had walked through night in the lane and come out into morning again. Pretty soon the car came. I got on it, they turning to look at my eye, and found a seat on the left side.

The lights were on in the car, so while we ran between trees I couldnt see anything except my own face and a woman across the aisle with a hat sitting right on top of her head, with a broken feather in it, but when we ran out of the trees I could see the twilight again, that quality of light as if time really had stopped for a while, with the sun hanging just under the horizon, and then we passed the marquee where the old man had been eating out of the sack, and the road going on under the twilight, into twilight and the sense of water peaceful and swift beyond. Then the car went on, the draught building steadily up in the open door until it was drawing steadily through the car with the odour of summer and darkness except honeysuckle. Honeysuckle was the saddest odour of all, I think. I remember lots of them. Wistaria was one. On the rainy days when Mother wasnt feeling quite bad enough to stay away from the windows we used to play under it. When Mother stayed in bed Dilsey would put old clothes on us and let us go out in the rain because she said rain never hurt young folks. But if Mother was up we always began by playing on the porch until she said we were making too much noise, then we went out and played under the wistaria frame.

This was where I saw the river for the last time this morning, about here. I could feel water beyond the twilight, smell. When it bloomed in the spring and it rained the smell was everywhere you didnt notice it so much at other times but when it rained the smell began to come into the house at twilight either it would rain more at twilight or there was something in the light itself but it always smelled strongest then until I would lie in bed thinking when will it stop when will it stop. The draft in the door smelled of water, a damp steady breath. Sometimes I could put myself to sleep saying that over and over until after the honeysuckle got all mixed up in it the whole thing came to symbolise night and unrest I seemed to be lying neither asleep nor awake looking down a long corridor of grey halflight where all stable things had become shadowy paradoxical all I had done shadows all I had felt suffered taking visible form antic and perverse mocking without relevance inherent themselves with the denial of the significance they should have affirmed thinking I was I was not who was not was not who.

I could smell the curves of the river beyond the dusk and I saw the last light supine and tranquil upon tideflats like pieces of broken mirror, then beyond them lights began in the pale clear air, trembling a little like butterflies hovering a long way off. Benjamin the child of. How he used to sit before that mirror. Refuge unfailing in which conflict tempered silenced reconciled. Benjamin the child of mine old age held hostage into Egypt. O Benjamin. Dilsey said it was because Mother was too proud for him. They come into white people's lives like that in sudden sharp black trickles that isolate white facts for an instant in unarguable truth like under a microscope; the rest of the time just voices that laugh when you see nothing to laugh at, tears when no reason for tears. They will bet on the odd or even number of mourners at a funeral. A brothel full of them in Memphis went into a religious trance ran naked into the street. It took three policemen to subdue one of them. Yes Jesus O good man Jesus O that good man.

The car stopped. I got out, with them looking at my eye. When the trolley came it was full. I stopped on the back platform.

"Seats up front," the conductor said. I looked into the car. There were no seats on the left side.

"I'm not going far," I said. "I'll just stand here."

We crossed the river. The bridge, that is, arching slow and high into space, between silence and nothingness where lights—yellow and red and green—trembled in the clear air, repeating themselves.

"Better go up front and get a seat," the conductor said.

"I get off pretty soon," I said. "A couple of blocks."

I got off before we reached the postoffice. They'd all be sitting around somewhere by now though, and then I was hearing my watch and I began to listen for the chimes and I touched Shreve's letter through my coat, the bitten shadows of the elms flowing upon my hand. And then as I turned into the quad the chimes did begin and I went on while the notes came up like ripples on a pool and passed me and went on, saying Quarter to what? All right. Quarter to what.

Our windows were dark. The entrance was empty. I walked close to the left wall when I entered, but it was empty: just the stairs curving up into shadows echoes of feet in the sad generations like light dust upon the shadows, my feet waking them like dust, lightly to settle again.

I could see the letter before I turned the light on, propped against

a book on the table so I would see it. Calling him my husband.
And then Spoade said they were going somewhere, would not be
back until late, and Mrs Bland would need another cavalier. But I
would have seen him and he cannot get another car for an hour
because after six oclock. I took out my watch and listened to it
clicking away, not knowing it couldnt even lie. Then I laid it face
upon the table and took Mrs Bland's letter and tore it across and
dropped the pieces into the waste basket and took off my coat,
vest, collar, tie and shirt. The tie was spoiled too, but then niggers.
Maybe a pattern of blood he could call that the one Christ was
wearing. I found the gasoline in Shreve's room and spread the vest
on the table, where it would be flat, and opened the gasoline.

*the first car in town a girl Girl that's what Jason couldn't bear
smell of gasoline making him sick then got madder than ever because a girl Girl had no sister but Benjamin Benjamin the child of*
my sorrowful if I'd just had a mother so I could say Mother Mother
It took a lot of gasoline, and then I couldnt tell if it was still the
stain or just the gasoline. It had started the cut to smarting again
so when I went to wash I hung the vest on a chair and lowered
the light cord so that the bulb would be drying the splotch. I
washed my face and hands, but even then I could smell it within
the soap stinging, constricting the nostrils a little. Then I opened
the bag and took the shirt and collar and tie out and put the
bloody ones in and closed the bag, and dressed. While I was
brushing my hair the half hour went. But there was until the three
quarters anyway, except suppose *seeing on the rushing darkness*
only his own face no broken feather unless two of them but not
two like that going to Boston the same night then my face his face
for an instant across the crashing when out of darkness two lighted
windows in rigid fleeing crash gone his face and mine just I see
saw did I see not goodbye the marquee empty of eating the road
empty in darkness in silence the bridge arching into silence dark-
ness sleep the water peaceful and swift not goodbye
I turned out the light and went into my bedroom, out of the
gasoline but I could still smell it. I stood at the window the curtains
moved slow out of the darkness touching my face like someone
breathing asleep, breathing slow into the darkness again, leaving
the touch. *After they had gone up stairs Mother lay back in her*
chair, the camphor handkerchief to her mouth. Father hadn't
moved he still sat beside her holding her hand the bellowing ham-

mering away like no place for it in silence When I was little there
was a picture in one of our books, a dark place into which a single
weak ray of light came slanting upon two faces lifted out of the
shadow. *You know what I'd do if I were King?* she never was a
queen or a fairy she was always a king or a giant or a general *I'd
break that place open and drag them out and I'd whip them good*
It was torn out, jagged out. I was glad. I'd have to turn back to it
until the dungeon was Mother herself she and Father upward into
weak light holding hands and us lost somewhere below even them
without even a ray of light. Then the honeysuckle got into it. As
soon as I turned off the light and tried to go to sleep it would begin
to come into the room in waves building and building up until I
would have to pant to get any air at all out of it until I would have
to get up and feel my way like when I was a little boy *hands can
see touching in the mind shaping unseen door Door now nothing
hands can see* My nose could see gasoline, the vest on the table,
the door. The corridor was still empty of all the feet in sad generations seeking water. *yet the eyes unseeing clenched like teeth not
disbelieving doubting even the absence of pain shin ankle knee
the long invisible flowing of the stair-railing where a misstep in the
darkness filled with sleeping Mother Father Caddy Jason Maury
door I am not afraid only Mother Father Caddy Jason Maury getting so far ahead sleeping I will sleep fast when I door Door door*
It was empty too, the pipes, the porcelain, the stained quiet walls,
the throne of contemplation. I had forgotten the glass, but I could
*hands can see cooling fingers invisible swan-throat where less than
Moses rod the glass touch tentative not to drumming lean cool
throat drumming cooling the metal the glass full overfull cooling
the glass the fingers flushing sleep leaving the taste of dampened
sleep in the long silence of the throat* I returned up the corridor,
waking the lost feet in whispering battalions in the silence, into the
gasoline, the watch telling its furious lie on the dark table. Then
the curtains breathing out of the dark upon my face, leaving the
breathing upon my face. A quarter hour yet. And then I'll not be.
The peacefullest words. Peacefullest words. *Non fui. Sum. Fui.
Non sum.* Somewhere I heard bells once. Mississippi or Massachusetts. I was. I am not. Massachusetts or Mississippi. Shreve has a
bottle in his trunk. *Aren't you even going to open it* Mr and Mrs
Jason Richmond Compson announce the *Three times. Days. Aren't
you even going to open it* marriage of their daughter Candace *that*

liquor teaches you to confuse the means with the end. I am. Drink.
I was not. Let us sell Benjy's pasture so that Quentin may go to
Harvard and I may knock my bones together and together. I will
be dead in. Was it one year Caddy said. Shreve has a bottle in his
trunk. Sir I will not need Shreve's I have sold Benjy's pasture and
I can be dead in Harvard Caddy said in the caverns and the grottoes of the sea tumbling peacefully to the wavering tides because
Harvard is such a fine sound forty acres is no high price for a fine
sound. A fine dead sound we will swap Benjy's pasture for a fine
dead sound. It will last him a long time because he cannot hear it
unless he can smell it *as soon as she came in the door he began to
cry* I thought all the time it was just one of those town squirts that
Father was always teasing her about until. I didnt notice him any
more than any other stranger drummer or what thought they were
army shirts until all of a sudden I knew he wasn't thinking of me at
all as a potential source of harm, but was thinking of her when he
looked at me was looking at me through her like through a piece
of coloured glass *why must you meddle with me dont you know it
wont do any good I thought you'd have left that for Mother and
Jason*
    did Mother set Jason to spy on you I wouldnt have.
*Women only use other people's codes of honour it's because she
loves Caddy* staying downstairs even when she was sick so Father
couldnt kid Uncle Maury before Jason Father said Uncle Maury
was too poor a classicist to risk the blind immortal boy in person he
should have chosen Jason because Jason would have made only the
same kind of blunder Uncle Maury himself would have made not
one to get him a black eye the Patterson boy was smaller than Jason
too they sold the kites for a nickel apiece until the trouble over
finances Jason got a new partner still smaller one small enough anyway because T. P. said Jason still treasurer but Father said why
should Uncle Maury work if he father could support five or six niggers that did nothing at all but sit with their feet in the oven he certainly could board and lodge Uncle Maury now and then and lend
him a little money who kept his Father's belief in the celestial derivation of his own species at such a fine heat then Mother would
cry and say that Father believed his people were better than hers
that he was ridiculing Uncle Maury to teach us the same thing she
couldnt see that Father was teaching us that all men are just ac-
cumulations dolls stuffed with sawdust swept up from the trash

heaps where all previous dolls had been thrown away the sawdust flowing from what wound in what side that not for me died not. It used to be I thought of death as a man something like Grandfather a friend of his a kind of private and particular friend like we used to think of Grandfather's desk not to touch it not even to talk loud in the room where it was I always thought of them as being together somewhere all the time waiting for old Colonel Sartoris to come down and sit with them waiting on a high place beyond cedar trees Colonel Sartoris was on a still higher place looking out across at something and they were waiting for him to get done looking at it and come down Grandfather wore his uniform and we could hear the murmur of their voices from beyond the cedars they were always talking and Grandfather was always right.

The three quarters began. The first note sounded, measured and tranquil, serenely peremptory, emptying the unhurried silence for the next one and that's it if people could only change one another forever that way merge like a flame swirling up for an instant then blown cleanly out along the cool eternal dark instead of lying there trying not to think of the swing until all cedars came to have that vivid dead smell of perfume that Benjy hated so. Just by imagining the clump it seemed to me that I could hear whispers secret surges smell the beating of hot blood under wild unsecret flesh watching against red eyelids the swine untethered in pairs rushing coupled into the sea and he we must just stay awake and see evil done for a little while its not always and i it doesnt have to be even that long for a man of courage and he do you consider that courage and i yes sir dont you and he every man is the arbiter of his own virtues whether or not you consider it courageous is of more importance than the act itself than any act otherwise you could not be in earnest and i you dont believe i am serious and he i think you are too serious to give me any cause for alarm you wouldnt have felt driven to the expedient of telling me you have committed incest otherwise and i i wasnt lying i wasnt lying and he you wanted to sublimate a piece of natural human folly into a horror and then exorcise it with truth and i it was to isolate her out of the loud world so that it would have to flee us of necessity and then the sound of it would be as though it had never been and he did you try to make her do it and i i was afraid to i was afraid she might and then it wouldnt have done any good but if i could tell you we did it would have been so and then the others wouldnt be so and then the world

would roar away and he and now this other you are not lying now
either but you are still blind to what is in yourself to that part of
general truth the sequence of natural events and their causes which
shadows every mans brow even benjys you are not thinking of fin-
itude you are contemplating an apotheosis in which a temporary
state of mind will become symmetrical above the flesh and aware
both of itself and of the flesh it will not quite discard you will not
even be dead and i temporary and he you cannot bear to think that
someday it will no longer hurt you like this now were getting at
it you seem to regard it merely as an experience that will whiten
your hair overnight so to speak without altering your appearance
at all you wont do it under these conditions it will be a gamble and
the strange thing is that man who is conceived by accident and
whose every breath is a fresh cast with dice already loaded against
him will not face that final main which he knows before hand he
has assuredly to face without essaying expedients ranging all the
way from violence to petty chicanery that would not deceive a
child until someday in very disgust he risks everything on a single
blind turn of a card no man ever does that under the first fury of
despair or remorse or bereavement he does it only when he has
realised that even the despair or remorse or bereavement is not
particularly important to the dark diceman and i temporary and
he it is hard believing to think that a love or a sorrow is a bond
purchased without design and which matures willynilly and is recalled without warning to be replaced by whatever issue the gods
happen to be floating at the time no you will not do that until you
come to believe that even she was not quite worth despair perhaps
and i i will never do that nobody knows what i know and he i think
youd better go on up to cambridge right away you might go up
into maine for a month you can afford it if you are careful it might
be a good thing watching pennies has healed more scars than jesus
and i suppose i realise what you believe i will realise up there next
week or next month and he then you will remember that for you
to go to harvard has been your mothers dream since you were born
and no compson has ever disappointed a lady and i temporary it
will be better for me for all of us and he every man is the arbiter
of his own virtues but let no man prescribe for another mans wellbeing and i temporary and he was the saddest word of all there is
nothing else in the world its not despair until time its not even time
until it was

The last note sounded. At last it stopped vibrating and the darkness was still again. I entered the sitting room and turned on the light. I put my vest on. The gasoline was faint now, barely noticeable, and in the mirror the stain didnt show. Not like my eye did, anyway. I put on my coat. Shreve's letter crackled through the cloth and I took it out and examined the address, and put it in my side pocket. Then I carried the watch into Shreve's room and put it in his drawer and went to my room and got a fresh handkerchief and went to the door and put my hand on the light switch. Then I remembered I hadnt brushed my teeth, so I had to open the bag again. I found my toothbrush and got some of Shreve's paste and went out and brushed my teeth. I squeezed the brush as dry as I could and put it back in the bag and shut it, and went to the door again. Before I snapped the light out I looked around to see if there was anything else, then I saw that I had forgotten my hat. I'd have to go by the postoffice and I'd be sure to meet some of them, and they'd think I was a Harvard Square student making like he was a senior. I had forgotten to brush it too, but Shreve had a brush, so I didnt have to open the bag any more.

APRIL 6, 1928

Once a bitch always a bitch, what I say. I says you're lucky if her playing out of school is all that worries you. I says she ought to be down there in that kitchen right now, instead of up there in her room, gobbing paint on her face and waiting for six niggers that cant even stand up out of a chair unless they've got a pan full of bread and meat to balance them, to fix breakfast for her. And Mother says,

"But to have the school authorities think that I have no control over her, that I cant—"

"Well," I says, "You cant, can you? You never have tried to do anything with her," I says, "How do you expect to begin this late, when she's seventeen years old?"

She thought about that for a while.

"But to have them think that . . . I didn't even know she had a report card. She told me last fall that they had quit using them this year. And now for Professor Junkin to call me on the telephone and tell me if she's absent one more time, she will have to leave

school. How does she do it? Where does she go? You're down town
all day; you ought to see her if she stays on the streets."

"Yes," I says, "If she stayed on the streets. I dont reckon she'd
be playing out of school just to do something she could do in
public," I says.

"What do you mean?" she says.

"I dont mean anything," I says. "I just answered your question."
Then she begun to cry again, talking about how her own flesh
and blood rose up to curse her

"You asked me," I says.

"I don't mean you," she says. "You are the only one of them
that isn't a reproach to me."

"Sure," I says, "I never had time to be. I never had time to go
to Harvard like Quentin or drink myself into the ground like
Father. I had to work. But of course if you want me to follow her
around and see what she does, I can quit the store and get a job
where I can work at night. Then I can watch her during the day
and you can use Ben for the night shift."

"I know I'm just a trouble and a burden to you," she says, crying on the pillow.

"I ought to know it," I says. "You've been telling me that for
thirty years. Even Ben ought to know it now. Do you want me
to say anything to her about it?"

"Do you think it will do any good?" she says.

"Not if you come down there interfering just when I get
started," I says. "If you want me to control her, just say so and
keep your hands off. Everytime I try to, you come butting in and
then she gives both of us the laugh."

"Remember she's your own flesh and blood," she says.

"Sure," I says, "that's just what I'm thinking of—flesh. And a
little blood too, if I had my way. When people act like niggers, no
matter who they are the only thing to do is treat them like a
nigger."

"I'm afraid you'll lose your temper with her," she says.

"Well," I says, "You haven't had much luck with your system.
You want me to do anything about it, or not? Say one way or
the other; I've got to get on to work."

"I know you have to slave your life away for us," she says. "You
know if I had my way, you'd have an office of your own to go to,
and hours that became a Bascomb. Because you are a Bascomb,

despite your name. I know that if your father could have foreseen—"

"Well," I says, "I reckon he's entitled to guess wrong now and then, like anybody else, even a Smith or a Jones." She began to cry again.

"To hear you speak bitterly of your dead father," she says.

"All right," I says, "all right. Have it your way. But as I haven't got an office, I'll have to get on to what I have got. Do you want me to say anything to her?"

"I'm afraid you'll lose your temper with her," she says.

"All right," I says, "I wont say anything, then."

"But something must be done," she says. "To have people think I permit her to stay out of school and run about the streets, or that I cant prevent her doing it. . . . Jason, Jason," she says, "How could you. How could you leave me with these burdens."

"Now, now," I says, "You'll make yourself sick. Why dont you either lock her up all day too, or turn her over to me and quit worrying over her?"

"My own flesh and blood," she says, crying. So I says,

"All right. I'll tend to her. Quit crying, now."

"Dont lose your temper," she says. "She's just a child, remember."

"No," I says, "I wont." I went out, closing the door.

"Jason," she says. I didn't answer. I went down the hall. "Jason," she says beyond the door. I went on down stairs. There wasn't anybody in the diningroom, then I heard her in the kitchen. She was trying to make Dilsey let her have another cup of coffee. I went in.

"I reckon that's your school costume, is it?" I says. "Or maybe today's a holiday?"

"Just a half a cup, Dilsey," she says. "Please."

"No, suh," Dilsey says, "I aint gwine do it. You aint got no business wid mo'n one cup, a seventeen year old gal, let lone whut Miss Cahline say. You go on and git dressed for school, so you kin ride to town wid Jason. You fixin to be late again."

"No she's not," I says. "We're going to fix that right now." She looked at me, the cup in her hand. She brushed her hair back from her face, her kimono slipping off her shoulder. "You put that cup down and come in here a minute," I says.

"What for?" she says.

"Come on," I says. "Put that cup in the sink and come in here."

"What you up to now, Jason?" Dilsey says.

"You may think you can run over me like you do your grandmother and everybody else," I says, "But you'll find out different. I'll give you ten seconds to put that cup down like I told you."

She quit looking at me. She looked at Dilsey. "What time is it, Dilsey?" she says. "When it's ten seconds, you whistle. Just a half a cup. Dilsey, pl—"

I grabbed her by the arm. She dropped the cup. It broke on the floor and she jerked back, looking at me, but I held her arm. Dilsey got up from her chair.

"You, Jason," she says.

"You turn me loose," Quentin says, "I'll slap you."

"You will, will you?" I says, "You will will you?" She slapped at me. I caught that hand too and held her like a wildcat. "You will, will you?" I says. "You think you will?"

"You, Jason!" Dilsey says. I dragged her into the diningroom. Her kimono came unfastened, flapping about her; damn near naked. Dilsey came hobbling along. I turned and kicked the door shut in her face.

"You keep out of here," I says.

Quentin was leaning against the table, fastening her kimono. I looked at her.

"Now," I says, "I want to know what you mean, playing out of school and telling your grandmother lies and forging her name on your report and worrying her sick. What do you mean by it?"

She didn't say anything. She was fastening her kimono up under her chin, pulling it tight around her, looking at me. She hadn't got around to painting herself yet and her face looked like she had polished it with a gun rag. I went and grabbed her wrist. "What do you mean?" I says.

"None of your damn business," she says. "You turn me loose."

Dilsey came in the door. "You, Jason," she says.

"You get out of here, like I told you," I says, not even looking back. "I want to know where you go when you play out of school," I says. "You keep off the streets, or I'd see you. Who do you play out with? Are you hiding out in the woods with one of those damn slick-headed jellybeans? Is that where you go?"

"You—you old goddamn!" she says. She fought, but I held her. "You damn old goddamn!" she says.

"I'll show you," I says. "You may can scare an old woman off, but I'll show you who's got hold of you now." I held her with one hand, then she quit fighting and watched me, her eyes getting wide and black.

"What are you going to do?" she says.

"You wait until I get this belt out and I'll show you," I says, pulling my belt out. Then Dilsey grabbed my arm.

"Jason," she says, "You, Jason! Aint you shamed of yourself."

"Dilsey," Quentin says, "Dilsey."

"I aint gwine let him," Dilsey says, "Dont you worry, honey." She held to my arm. Then the belt came out and I jerked loose and flung her away. She stumbled into the table. She was so old she couldn't do any more than move hardly. But that's all right: we need somebody in the kitchen to eat up the grub the young ones cant tote off. She came hobbling between us, trying to hold me again. "Hit me, den," she says, "ef nothin else but hittin somebody wont do you. Hit me," she says.

"You think I wont?" I says.

"I dont put no devilment beyond you," she says. Then I heard Mother on the stairs. I might have known she wasn't going to keep out of it. I let go. She stumbled back against the wall, holding her kimono shut.

"All right," I says, "We'll just put this off a while. But dont think you can run it over me. I'm not an old woman, nor an old half dead nigger, either. You damn little slut," I says.

"Dilsey," she says, "Dilsey, I want my mother."

Dilsey went to her. "Now, now," she says, "He aint gwine so much as lay his hand on you while Ise here." Mother came on down the stairs.

"Jason," she says, "Dilsey."

"Now, now," Dilsey says, "I aint gwine let him tech you." She put her hand on Quentin. She knocked it down.

"You damn old nigger," she says. She ran toward the door.

"Dilsey," Mother says on the stairs. Quentin ran up the stairs, passing her. "Quentin," Mother says, "You, Quentin." Quentin ran on. I could hear her when she reached the top, then in the hall. Then the door slammed.

Mother had stopped. Then she came on. "Dilsey," she says.

"All right," Dilsey says, "Ise comin. You go on and git dat car and wait now," she says, "so you kin cahy her to school."

"Dont you worry," I says. "I'll take her to school and I'm going to see that she stays there. I've started this thing, and I'm going through with it."

"Jason," Mother says on the stairs.

"Go on, now," Dilsey says, going toward the door. "You want to git her started too? Ise comin, Miss Cahline."

I went on out. I could hear them on the steps. "You go on back to bed now," Dilsey was saying, "Don't you know you aint feeling well enough to git up yet? Go on back, now. I'm gwine to see she gits to school in time."

I went on out the back to back the car out, then I had to go all the way round to the front before I found them.

"I thought I told you to put that tire on the back of the car," I says.

"I aint had time," Luster says. "Aint nobody to watch him till mammy git done in de kitchen."

"Yes," I says, "I feed a whole damn kitchen full of niggers to follow around after him, but if I want an automobile tire changed, I have to do it myself."

"I aint had nobody to leave him wid," he says. Then he begun moaning and slobbering.

"Take him on round to the back," I says. "What the hell makes you want to keep him around here where people can see him?" I made them go on, before he got started bellowing good. It's bad enough on Sundays, with that damn field full of people that haven't got a side show and six niggers to feed, knocking a damn oversize mothball around. He's going to keep on running up and down that fence and bellowing every time they come in sight until first thing I know they're going to begin charging me golf dues, then Mother and Dilsey'll have to get a couple of china door knobs and a walking stick and work it out, unless I play at night with a lantern. Then they'd send us all to Jackson, maybe. God knows, they'd hold Old Home week when that happened.

I went on back to the garage. There was the tire, leaning against the wall, but be damned if I was going to put it on. I backed out and turned around. She was standing by the drive. I says,

"I know you haven't got any books: I just want to ask you what you did with them, if it's any of my business. Of course I haven't got any right to ask," I says, "I'm just the one that paid $11.65 for them last September."

"Mother buys my books," she says. "There's not a cent of your money on me. I'd starve first."

"Yes?" I says. "You tell your grandmother that and see what she says. You dont look all the way naked," I says, "even if that stuff on your face does hide more of you than anything else you've got on."

"Do you think your money or hers either paid for a cent of this?" she says.

"Ask your grandmother," I says. "Ask her what became of those checks. You saw her burn one of them, as I remember." She wasn't even listening, with her face all gummed up with paint and her eyes hard as a fice dog's.

"Do you know what I'd do if I thought your money or hers either bought one cent of this?" she says, putting her hand on her dress.

"What would you do?" I says, "Wear a barrel?"

"I'd tear it right off and throw it into the street," she says. "Dont you believe me?"

"Sure you would," I says. "You do it every time."

"See if I wouldn't," she says. She grabbed the neck of her dress in both hands and made like she would tear it.

"You tear that dress," I says, "and I'll give you a whipping right here that you'll remember all your life."

"See if I dont," she says. Then I saw that she really was trying to tear it, to tear it right off of her. By the time I got the car stopped and grabbed her hands there was about a dozen people looking. It made me so mad for a minute it kind of blinded me.

"You do a thing like that again and I'll make you sorry you ever drew breath," I says.

"I'm sorry now," she says. She quit, then her eyes turned kind of funny and I says to myself if you cry here in this car, on the street, I'll whip you. I'll wear you out. Lucky for her she didn't, so I turned her wrists loose and drove on. Luckily we were near an alley, where I could turn into the back street and dodge the square. They were already putting the tent up in Beard's lot. Earl had already given me the two passes for our show windows. She sat there with her face turned away, chewing her lip. "I'm sorry now," she says. "I dont see why I was ever born."

"And I know of at least one other person that dont understand all he knows about that," I says. I stopped in front of the school house. The bell had rung, and the last of them were just going in. "You're on time for once, anyway," I says. "Are you going in there and stay there, or am I coming with you and make you?" She got out and banged the door. "Remember what I say," I says, "I mean it. Let me hear one more time that you are slipping up and down back alleys with one of those damn squirts."

She turned back at that. "I dont slip around," she says. "I dare anybody to know everything I do."

"And they all know it, too," I says. "Everybody in this town knows what you are. But I wont have it anymore, you hear? I dont care what you do, myself," I says, "But I've got a position in this town, and I'm not going to have any member of my family going on like a nigger wench. You hear me?"

"I dont care," she says, "I'm bad and I'm going to hell, and I dont care. I'd rather be in hell than anywhere where you are."

"If I hear one more time that you haven't been to school, you'll wish you were in hell," I says. She turned and ran on across the yard. "One more time, remember," I says. She didn't look back.

I went to the postoffice and got the mail and drove on to the store and parked. Earl looked at me when I came in. I gave him a chance to say something about my being late, but he just said,

"Those cultivators have come. You'd better help Uncle Job put them up."

I went on to the back, where old Job was uncrating them, at the rate of about three bolts to the hour.

"You ought to be working for me," I says. "Every other no-count nigger in town eats in my kitchen."

"I works to suit de man whut pays me Sat'dy night," he says. "When I does dat, it dont leave me a whole lot of time to please other folks." He screwed up a nut. "Aint nobody works much in dis country cep de boll-weevil, noways," he says.

"You'd better be glad you're not a boll-weevil waiting on those cultivators," I says. "You'd work yourself to death before they'd be ready to prevent you."

"Dat's de troof," he says, "Boll-weevil got tough time. Work ev'y day in de week out in de hot sun, rain er shine. Aint got no front porch to set on en watch de wattermilyuns growin and Sat'dy dont mean nothin a-tall to him."

"Saturday wouldn't mean nothing to you, either," I says, "if it depended on me to pay you wages. Get those things out of the crates now and drag them inside."

I opened her letter first and took the check out. Just like a woman. Six days late. Yet they try to make men believe that they're capable of conducting a business. How long would a man that thought the first of the month came on the sixth last in business. And like as not, when they sent the bank statement out, she would want to know why I never deposited my salary until the sixth. Things like that never occur to a woman.

"I had no answer to my letter about Quentin's easter dress. Did it arrive all right? I've had no answer to the last two letters I wrote her, though the check in the second one was cashed with the other check. Is she sick? Let me know at once or I'll come there and see for myself. You promised you would let me know when she needed things. I will expect to hear from you before the 10th. No you'd better wire me at once. You are opening my letters to her. I know that as well as if I were looking at you. You'd better wire me at once about her to this address."

About that time Earl started yelling at Job, so I put them away and went over to try to put some life into him. What this country needs is white labour. Let these damn trifling niggers starve for a couple of years, then they'd see what a soft thing they have.

Along toward ten oclock I went up front. There was a drummer there. It was a couple of minutes to ten, and I invited him up the street to get a coca-cola. We got to talking about crops.

"There's nothing to it," I says, "Cotton is a speculator's crop. They fill the farmer full of hot air and get him to raise a big crop for them to whipsaw on the market, to trim the suckers with. Do you think the farmer gets anything out of it except a red neck and a hump in his back? You think the man that sweats to put it into the ground gets a red cent more than a bare living," I says. "Let him make a big crop and it wont be worth picking; let him make a small crop and he wont have enough to gin. And what for? so a bunch of damn eastern jews, I'm not talking about men of the jewish religion," I says, "I've known some jews that were fine citizens. You might be one yourself," I says.

"No," he says, "I'm an American."

"No offense," I says. "I give every man his due, regardless of religion or anything else. I have nothing against jews as an individual," I says. "It's just the race. You'll admit that they produce nothing. They follow the pioneers into a new country and sell them clothes."

"You're thinking of Armenians," he says, "aren't you. A pioneer wouldn't have any use for new clothes."

"No offense," I says. "I dont hold a man's religion against him."

"Sure," he says, "I'm an American. My folks have some French blood, why I have a nose like this. I'm an American, all right."

"So am I," I says. "Not many of us left. What I'm talking about is the fellows that sit up there in New York and trim the sucker gamblers."

"That's right," he says. "Nothing to gambling, for a poor man. There ought to be a law against it."

"Don't you think I'm right?" I says.

"Yes," he says, "I guess you're right. The farmer catches it coming and going."

"I know I'm right," I says. "It's a sucker game, unless a man gets inside information from somebody that knows what's going on. I happen to be associated with some people who're right there on the ground. They have one of the biggest manipulators in New York for an adviser. Way I do it," I says, "I never risk much at a time. It's the fellow that thinks he knows it all and is trying to make a killing with three dollars that they're laying for. That's why they are in the business."

Then it struck ten. I went up to the telegraph office. It opened up a little, just like they said. I went into the corner and took out the telegram again, just to be sure. While I was looking at it a report came in. It was up two points. They were all buying. I could tell that from what they were saying. Getting aboard. Like they didn't know it could go but one way. Like there was a law or something against doing anything but buying. Well, I reckon those eastern jews have got to live too. But I'll be damned if it hasn't come to a pretty pass when any damn foreigner that cant make a living in the country where God put him, can come to this one and take money right out of an American's pockets. It was up two points more. Four points. But hell, they were right there and knew what was going on. And if I wasn't going to take the advice, what was I paying them ten dollars a month for. I went out, then I remembered and came back and sent the wire. "All well. Q writing today."

"Q?" the operator says.

"Yes," I says, "Q. Cant you spell Q?"

"I just asked to be sure," he says.

"You send it like I wrote it and I'll guarantee you to be sure," I says. "Send it collect."

"What you sending, Jason?" Doc Wright says, looking over my shoulder. "Is that a code message to buy?"

"That's all right about that," I says. "You boys use your own judgment. You know more about it than those New York folks do."

"Well, I ought to," Doc says, "I'd a saved money this year raising it at two cents a pound."

Another report came in. It was down a point.

"Jason's selling," Hopkins says. "Look at his face."

"That's all right about what I'm doing," I says. "You boys follow your own judgment. Those rich New York jews have got to live like everybody else," I says.

I went on back to the store. Earl was busy up front. I went on back to the desk and read Lorraine's letter. "Dear daddy wish you were here. No good parties when daddys out of town I miss my sweet daddy." I reckon she does. Last time I gave her forty dollars. Gave it to her. I never promise a woman anything nor let her know what I'm going to give her. That's the only way to manage them. Always keep them guessing. If you cant think of any other way to surprise them, give them a bust in the jaw.

I tore it up and burned it over the spittoon. I make it a rule never to keep a scrap of paper bearing a woman's hand, and I never write them at all. Lorraine is always after me to write to her but I says anything I forgot to tell you will save till I get to Memphis again but I says I dont mind you writing me now and then in a plain envelope, but if you ever try to call me up on the telephone, Memphis wont hold you I says. I says when I'm up there I'm one of the boys, but I'm not going to have any woman calling me on the telephone. Here I says, giving her the forty dollars. If you ever get drunk and take a notion to call me on the phone, just remember this and count ten before you do it.

"When'll that be?" she says.

"What?" I says.

"When you're coming back," she says.

"I'll let you know," I says. Then she tried to buy a beer, but I wouldn't let her. "Keep your money," I says. "Buy yourself a dress with it." I gave the maid a five, too. After all, like I say money has no value; it's just the way you spend it. It dont belong to anybody, so why try to hoard it. It just belongs to the man that can get it and keep it. There's a man right here in Jefferson made a lot of money selling rotten goods to niggers, lived in a room over the store about the size of a pigpen, and did his own cooking. About four or five years ago he was taken sick. Scared the hell out of him so that when he was up again he joined the church and bought himself a Chinese missionary, five thousand dollars a year. I often think how mad he'll be if he was to die and find out there's not any heaven, when he thinks about that five thousand a year. Like I say, he'd better go on and die now and save money.

When it was burned good I was just about to shove the others into my coat when all of a sudden something told me to open Quentin's before I went home, but about that time Earl started yelling for me up front, so I put them away and went and waited on the damn redneck while he spent fifteen minutes deciding whether he wanted a twenty cent hame string or a thirty-five cent one.

"You'd better take that good one," I says. "How do you fellows ever expect to get ahead, trying to work with cheap equipment?"

"If this one aint any good," he says, "why have you got it on sale?"

"I didn't say it wasn't any good," I says, "I said it's not as good as that other one."

"How do you know it's not," he says. "You ever use airy one of them?"

"Because they dont ask thirty-five cents for it," I says. "That's how I know it's not as good."

He held the twenty cent one in his hands, drawing it through his fingers. "I reckon I'll take this hyer one," he says. I offered to take it and wrap it, but he rolled it up and put it in his overalls. Then he took out a tobacco sack and finally got it untied and shook some coins out. He handed me a quarter. "That fifteen cents will buy me a snack of dinner," he says.

"All right," I says, "You're the doctor. But dont come complaining to me next year when you have to buy a new outfit."

"I aint makin next year's crop yit," he says. Finally I got rid
of him, but every time I took that letter out something would
come up. They were all in town for the show, coming in in droves
to give their money to something that brought nothing to the
town and wouldn't leave anything except what those grafters in
the Mayor's office will split among themselves, and Earl chasing
back and forth like a hen in a coop, saying "Yes, ma'am, Mr Compson will wait on you. Jason, show this lady a churn or a nickel's
worth of screen hooks."

Well, Jason likes work. I says no I never had university advan-
tages because at Harvard they teach you how to go for a swim at
night without knowing how to swim and at Sewanee they dont
even teach you what water is. I says you might send me to the
state University; maybe I'll learn how to stop my clock with a
nose spray and then you can send Ben to the Navy I says or to
the cavalry anyway, they use geldings in the cavalry. Then when
she sent Quentin home for me to feed too I says I guess that's
right too, instead of me having to go way up north for a job they
sent the job down here to me and then Mother begun to cry and I
says it's not that I have any objection to having it here; if it's
any satisfaction to you I'll quit work and nurse it myself and let
you and Dilsey keep the flour barrel full, or Ben. Rent him out to
a sideshow; there must be folks somewhere that would pay a dime
to see him, then she cried more and kept saying my poor afflicted
baby and I says yes he'll be quite a help to you when he gets his
growth not being more than one and a half times as high as me
now and she says she'd be dead soon and then we'd all be better
off and so I says all right, all right, have it your way. It's your
grandchild, which is more than any other grandparents it's got
can say for certain. Only I says it's only a question of time. If you
believe she'll do what she says and not try to see it, you fool
yourself because the first time that was that Mother kept on saying thank God you are not a Compson except in name, because
you are all I have left now, you and Maury, and I says well I
could spare Uncle Maury myself and then they came and said
they were ready to start. Mother stopped crying then. She pulled
her veil down and we went down stairs. Uncle Maury was coming
out of the diningroom, his handkerchief to his mouth. They kind
of made a lane and we went out the door just in time to see Dilsey
driving Ben and T. P. back around the corner. We went down the

steps and got in. Uncle Maury kept saying Poor little sister, poor little sister, talking around his mouth and patting Mother's hand. Talking around whatever it was.

"Have you got your band on?" she says. "Why dont they go on, before Benjamin comes out and makes a spectacle. Poor little boy. He doesn't know. He cant even realise."

"There, there," Uncle Maury says, patting her hand, talking around his mouth. "It's better so. Let him be unaware of bereavement until he has to."

"Other women have their children to support them in times like this," Mother says.

"You have Jason and me," he says.

"It's so terrible to me," she says, "Having the two of them like this, in less than two years."

"There, there," he says. After a while he kind of sneaked his hand to his mouth and dropped them out the window. Then I knew what I had been smelling. Clove stems. I reckon he thought that the least he could do at Father's funeral or maybe the sideboard thought it was still Father and tripped him up when he passed. Like I say, if he had to sell something to send Quentin to Harvard we'd all been a damn sight better off if he'd sold that sideboard and bought himself a one-armed strait jacket with part of the money. I reckon the reason all the Compson gave out before it got to me like Mother says, is that he drank it up. At least I never heard of him offering to sell anything to send me to Harvard.

So he kept on patting her hand and saying "Poor little sister," patting her hand with one of the black gloves that we got the bill for four days later because it was the twenty-sixth because it was the same day one month that Father went up there and got it and brought it home and wouldn't tell anything about where she was or anything and Mother crying and saying "And you didn't even see him? You didn't even try to get him to make any provision for it?" and Father says "No she shall not touch his money not one cent of it" and Mother says "He can be forced to by law. He can prove nothing, unless—Jason Compson," she says, "Were you fool enough to tell—"

"Hush, Caroline," Father says, then he sent me to help Dilsey get that old cradle out of the attic and I says,

"Well, they brought my job home tonight" because all the time we kept hoping they'd get things straightened out and he'd keep her because Mother kept saying she would at least have enough regard for the family not to jeopardize my chance after she and Quentin had had theirs.

"And whar else do she belong?" Dilsey says, "Who else gwine raise her 'cep me? Aint I raised eve'y one of y'all?"

"And a damn fine job you made of it," I says. "Anyway it'll give her something to sure enough worry over now." So we carried the cradle down and Dilsey started to set it up in her old room. Then Mother started sure enough.

"Hush, Miss Cahline," Dilsey says, "You gwine wake her up."

"In there?" Mother says, "To be contaminated by that atmosphere? It'll be hard enough as it is, with the heritage she already has."

"Hush," Father says, "Dont be silly."

"Why aint she gwine sleep in here," Dilsey says, "In the same room whar I put her ma to bed ev'y night of her life since she was big enough to sleep by herself."

"You dont know," Mother says, "To have my own daughter cast off by her husband. Poor little innocent baby," she says, looking at Quentin. "You will never know the suffering you've caused."

"Hush, Caroline," Father says.

"What you want to go on like that fo Jason fer?" Dilsey says.

"I've tried to protect him," Mother says. "I've always tried to protect him from it. At least I can do my best to shield her."

"How sleepin in dis room gwine hurt her, I like to know," Dilsey says.

"I cant help it," Mother says. "I know I'm just a troublesome old woman. But I know that people cannot flout God's laws with impunity."

"Nonsense," Father said. "Fix it in Miss Caroline's room then, Dilsey."

"You can say nonsense," Mother says. "But she must never know. She must never even learn that name. Dilsey, I forbid you ever to speak that name in her hearing. If she could grow up never to know that she had a mother, I would thank God."

"Dont be a fool," Father says.

"I have never interfered with the way you brought them up," Mother says, "But now I cannot stand anymore. We must decide this now, tonight. Either that name is never to be spoken in her hearing, or she must go, or I will go. Take your choice."

"Hush," Father says, "You're just upset. Fix it in here, Dilsey."

"En you's about sick too," Dilsey says. "You looks like a hant. You git in bed and I'll fix you a toddy and see kin you sleep. I bet you aint had a full night's sleep since you lef."

"No," Mother says, "Dont you know what the doctor says? Why must you encourage him to drink? That's what's the matter with him now. Look at me, I suffer too, but I'm not so weak that I must kill myself with whiskey."

"Fiddlesticks," Father says, "What do doctors know? They make their livings advising people to do whatever they are not doing at the time, which is the extent of anyone's knowledge of the degenerate ape. You'll have a minister in to hold my hand next." Then Mother cried, and he went out. Went down stairs, and then I heard the sideboard. I woke up and heard him going down again. Mother had gone to sleep or something, because the house was quiet at last. He was trying to be quiet too, because I couldn't hear him, only the bottom of his nightshirt and his bare legs in front of the sideboard.

Dilsey fixed the cradle and undressed her and put her in it. She never had waked up since he brought her in the house.

"She pretty near too big fer hit," Dilsey says. "Dar now. I gwine spread me a pallet right acrost de hall, so you wont need to git up in de night."

"I wont sleep," Mother says. "You go on home. I wont mind. I'll be happy to give the rest of my life to her, if I can just prevent—"

"Hush, now," Dilsey says. "We gwine take keer of her. En you go on to bed too," she says to me, "You got to go to school tomorrow."

So I went out, then Mother called me back and cried on me awhile.

"You are my only hope," she says. "Every night I thank God for you." While we were waiting there for them to start she says Thank God if he had to be taken too, it is you left me and not Quentin. Thank God you are not a Compson, because all I have left now is you and Maury and I says, Well I could spare Uncle Maury myself. Well, he kept on patting her hand with his black glove, talking away from her. He took them off when his turn with the shovel came. He got up near the first, where they were holding the umbrellas over them, stamping every now and then and trying to kick the mud off their feet and sticking to the shovels so they'd have to knock it off, making a hollow sound when it fell on it, and when I stepped back around the hack I could see him behind a tombstone, taking another one out of a bottle. I thought he never was going to stop because I had on my new suit too, but it happened that there wasn't much mud on the wheels yet, only Mother saw it and says I dont know when you'll ever have another one and Uncle Maury says, "Now, now. Dont you worry at all. You have me to depend on, always."

And we have. Always. The fourth letter was from him but there wasn't any need to open it. I could have written it myself, or recited it to her from memory, adding ten dollars just to be safe. But I had a hunch about that other letter. I just felt that it was about time she was up to some of her tricks again. She got pretty wise after that first time. She found out pretty quick that I was a different breed of cat from Father. When they begun to get it filled up toward the top Mother started crying sure enough, so Uncle Maury got in with her and drove off. He says You can come in with somebody; they'll be glad to give you a lift. I'll have to take your mother on and I thought about saying, Yes you ought to brought two bottles instead of just one only I thought about where we were, so I let them go on. Little they cared how wet I got, because then Mother could have a whale of a time being afraid I was taking pneumonia.

Well, I got to thinking about that and watching them throwing dirt into it, slapping it on anyway like they were making mortar or something or building a fence, and I began to feel sort of funny and so I decided to walk around a while. I thought that if I went toward town they'd catch up and be trying to make me get in one of them, so I went on back toward the nigger graveyard. I got under some cedars, where the rain didn't come much, only dripping now and then, where I could see when they got through and went away. After a while they were all gone and I waited a minute and came out.

I had to follow the path to keep out of the wet grass so I didn't see her until I was pretty near there, standing there in a black cloak, looking at the flowers. I knew who it was right off, before she turned and looked at me and lifted up her veil.

"Hello, Jason," she says, holding out her hand. We shook hands.

"What are you doing here?" I says. "I thought you promised her you wouldn't come back here. I thought you had more sense than that."

"Yes?" she says. She looked at the flowers again. There must have been fifty dollars' worth. Somebody had put one bunch on Quentin's. "You did?" she says.

"I'm not surprised though," I says. "I wouldn't put anything past you. You dont mind anybody. You dont give a damn about anybody."

"Oh," she says, "that job." She looked at the grave. "I'm sorry about that, Jason."

"I bet you are," I says. "You'll talk mighty meek now. But you needn't have come back. There's not anything left. Ask Uncle Maury, if you dont believe me."

"I dont want anything," she says. She looked at the grave. "Why didn't they let me know?" she says. "I just happened to see it in the paper. On the back page. Just happened to."

I didn't say anything. We stood there, looking at the grave, and then I got to thinking about when we were little and one thing and another and I got to feeling funny again, kind of mad or something, thinking about now we'd have Uncle Maury around the house all the time, running things like the way he left me to come home in the rain by myself. I says,

"A fine lot you care, sneaking in here soon as he's dead. But it wont do you any good. Dont think that you can take advantage of this to come sneaking back. If you cant stay on the horse you've got, you'll have to walk," I says. "We dont even know your name at that house," I says. "Do you know that? We don't even know you with him and Quentin," I says. "Do you know that?"

"I know it," she says. "Jason," she says, looking at the grave, "if you'll fix it so I can see her a minute I'll give you fifty dollars."

"You haven't got fifty dollars," I says.

"Will you?" she says, not looking at me.

"Let's see it," I says. "I dont believe you've got fifty dollars."

I could see where her hands were moving under her cloak, then she held her hand out. Damn if it wasn't full of money. I could see two or three yellow ones.

"Does he still give you money?" I says. "How much does he send you?"

"I'll give you a hundred," she says. "Will you?"

"Just a minute," I says, "And just like I say. I wouldn't have her know it for a thousand dollars."

"Yes," she says. "Just like you say do it. Just so I see her a minute. I wont beg or do anything. I'll go right on away."

"Give me the money," I says.

"I'll give it to you afterward," she says.

"Dont you trust me?" I says.

"No," she says. "I know you. I grew up with you."

"You're a fine one to talk about trusting people," I says. "Well," I says, "I got to get on out of the rain. Goodbye." I made to go away.

"Jason," she says. I stopped.

"Yes?" I says. "Hurry up. I'm getting wet."

"All right," she says. "Here." There wasn't anybody in sight. I went back and took the money. She still held to it. "You'll do it?" she says, looking at me from under the veil, "You promise?"

"Let go," I says, "You want somebody to come along and see us?"

She let go. I put the money in my pocket. "You'll do it, Jason?" she says. "I wouldn't ask you, if there was any other way."

"You're damn right there's no other way," I says. "Sure I'll do it. I said I would, didn't I? Only you'll have to do just like I say, now."

"Yes," she says, "I will." So I told her where to be, and went to the livery stable. I hurried and got there just as they were unhitching the hack. I asked if they had paid for it yet and he said No and I said Mrs Compson forgot something and wanted it again, so they let me take it. Mink was driving. I bought him a cigar, so we drove around until it begun to get dark on the back streets where they wouldn't see him. Then Mink said he'd have to take the team on back and so I said I'd buy him another cigar and so we drove into the lane and I went across the yard to the house. I stopped in the hall until I could hear Mother and Uncle Maury upstairs, then I went on back to the kitchen. She and Ben were there with Dilsey. I said Mother wanted her and I took her into the house. I found Uncle Maury's raincoat and put it around her and picked her up and went back to the lane and got in the hack. I told Mink to drive to the depot. He was afraid to pass the stable, so we had to go the back way and I saw her standing on the corner under the light and I told Mink to drive close to the walk and when I said Go on, to give the team a bat. Then I took the

raincoat off of her and held her to the window and Caddy saw
her and sort of jumped forward.

"Hit 'em, Mink!" I says, and Mink gave them a cut and we went
past her like a fire engine. "Now get on that train like you promised," I says. I could see her running after us through the back window. "Hit 'em again," I says," "Let's get on home." When we turned
the corner she was still running.

And so I counted the money again that night and put it away,
and I didn't feel so bad. I says I reckon that'll show you. I reckon
you'll know now that you cant beat me out of a job and get away
with it. It never occurred to me she wouldn't keep her promise
and take that train. But I didn't know much about them then; I
didn't have any more sense than to believe what they said, because
the next morning damn if she didn't walk right into the store, only
she had sense enough to wear the veil and not speak to anybody.
It was Saturday morning, because I was at the store, and she
came right on back to the desk where I was, walking fast.

"Liar," she says, "Liar."

"Are you crazy?" I says. "What do you mean? coming in here
like this?" She started in, but I shut her off. I says, "You already
cost me one job; do you want me to lose this one too? If you've
got anything to say to me, I'll meet you somewhere after dark.
What have you got to say to me?" I says, "Didn't I do everything I
said? I said see her a minute, didn't I? Well, didn't you?" She just
stood there looking at me, shaking like an ague-fit, her hands
clenched and kind of jerking. "I did just what I said I would," I
says, "You're the one that lied. You promised to take that train.
Didn't you Didn't you promise? If you think you can get that
money back, just try it," I says. "If it'd been a thousand dollars,
you'd still owe me after the risk I took. And if I see or hear you're
still in town after number 17 runs," I says, "I'll tell Mother and
Uncle Maury. Then hold your breath until you see her again." She
just stood there, looking at me, twisting her hands together.

"Damn you," she says, "Damn you."

"Sure," I says, "That's all right too. Mind what I say, now. After
number 17, and I tell them."

After she was gone I felt better. I says I reckon you'll think twice
before you deprive me of a job that was promised me. I was a kid
then. I believed folks when they said they'd do things. I've learned
better since. Besides, like I say I guess I dont need any man's help

to get along I can stand on my own feet like I always have. Then all of a sudden I thought of Dilsey and Uncle Maury. I thought how she'd get around Dilsey and that Uncle Maury would do anything for ten dollars. And there I was, couldn't even get away from the store to protect my own Mother. Like she says, if one of you had to be taken, thank God it was you left me I can depend on you and I says well I dont reckon I'll ever get far enough from the store to get out of your reach. Somebody's got to hold on to what little we have left, I reckon.

So as soon as I got home I fixed Dilsey. I told Dilsey she had leprosy and I got the bible and read where a man's flesh rotted off and I told her that if she ever looked at her or Ben or Quentin they'd catch it too. So I thought I had everything all fixed until that day when I came home and found Ben bellowing. Raising hell and nobody could quiet him. Mother said, Well, get him the slipper then. Dilsey made out she didn't hear. Mother said it again and I says I'd go I couldn't stand that damn noise. Like I say I can stand lots of things I dont expect much from them but if I have to work all day long in a damn store damn if I dont think I deserve a little peace and quiet to eat dinner in. So I says I'd go and Dilsey says quick, "Jason!"

Well, like a flash I knew what was up, but just to make sure I went and got the slipper and brought it back, and just like I thought, when he saw it you'd thought we were killing him. So I made Dilsey own up, then I told Mother. We had to take her up to bed then, and after things got quieted down a little I put the fear of God into Dilsey. As much as you can into a nigger, that is. That's the trouble with nigger servants, when they've been with you for a long time they get so full of self importance that they're not worth a damn. Think they run the whole family.

"I like to know whut's de hurt in lettin dat po chile see her own baby," Dilsey says. "If Mr Jason was still here hit ud be different."

"Only Mr Jason's not here," I says. "I know you wont pay me any mind, but I reckon you'll do what Mother says. You keep on worrying her like this until you get her into the graveyard too, then you can fill the whole house full of ragtag and bobtail. But what did you want to let that damn idiot see her for?"

"You's a cold man, Jason, if man you is," she says. "I thank de Lawd I got mo heart dan dat, even ef hit is black."

"At least I'm man enough to keep that flour barrel full," I says.

"And if you do that again, you wont be eating out of it either."

So the next time I told her that if she tried Dilsey again, Mother was going to fire Dilsey and send Ben to Jackson and take Quentin and go away. She looked at me for a while. There wasn't any street light close and I couldn't see her face much. But I could feel her looking at me. When we were little when she'd get mad and couldn't do anything about it her upper lip would begin to jump. Everytime it jumped it would leave a little more of her teeth showing, and all the time she'd be as still as a post, not a muscle moving except her lip jerking higher and higher up her teeth. But she didn't say anything. She just said,

"All right. How much?"

"Well, if one look through a hack window was worth a hundred," I says. So after that she behaved pretty well, only one time she asked to see a statement of the bank account.

"I know they have Mother's indorsement on them," she says, "But I want to see the bank statement. I want to see myself where those checks go."

"That's in Mother's private business," I says. "If you think you have any right to pry into her private affairs I'll tell her you believe those checks are being misappropriated and you want an audit because you dont trust her."

She didn't say anything or move. I could hear her whispering Damn you oh damn you oh damn you.

"Say it out," I says, "I dont reckon it's any secret what you and I think of one another. Maybe you want the money back," I says.

"Listen, Jason," she says, "Dont lie to me now. About her. I wont ask to see anything. If that isn't enough, I'll send more each month. Just promise that she'll—that she—You can do that. Things for her. Be kind to her. Little things that I cant, they wont let. . . . But you wont. You never had a drop of warm blood in you. Listen," she says, "If you'll get Mother to let me have her back, I'll give you a thousand dollars."

"You haven't got a thousand dollars," I says, "I know you're lying now."

"Yes I have. I will have. I can get it."

"And I know how you'll get it," I says, "You'll get it the same way you got her. And when she gets big enough—" Then I thought she really was going to hit at me, and then I didn't know what she was going to do. She acted for a minute like some kind of a toy that's wound up too tight and about to burst all to pieces.

"Oh, I'm crazy," she says, "I'm insane. I can't take her. Keep her. What am I thinking of. Jason," she says, grabbing my arm. Her hands were hot as fever. "You'll have to promise to take care of her, to—She's kin to you; your own flesh and blood. Promise, Jason. You have Father's name: do you think I'd have to ask him twice? once, even?"

"That's so," I says, "He did leave me something. What do you want me to do," I says, "Buy an apron and a gocart? I never got you into this," I says. "I run more risk than you do, because you haven't got anything at stake. So if you expect—"

"No," she says, then she begun to laugh and to try to hold it back all at the same time. "No. I have nothing at stake," she says, making that noise, putting her hands to her mouth, "Nuh-nuh-nothing," she says.

"Here," I says, "Stop that!"

"I'm trying to," she says, holding her hands over her mouth. "Oh God, oh God."

"I'm going away from here," I says, "I cant be seen here. You get on out of town now, you hear?"

"Wait," she says, catching my arm. "I've stopped. I wont again. You promise, Jason?" she says, and me feeling her eyes almost like they were touching my face, "You promise? Mother—that money —if sometimes she needs things—If I send checks for her to you, other ones besides those, you'll give them to her? You won't tell? You'll see that she has things like other girls?"

"Sure," I says, "As long as you behave and do like I tell you."

And so when Earl came up front with his hat on he says, "I'm going to step up to Rogers' and get a snack. We wont have time to go home to dinner, I reckon."

"What's the matter we wont have time?" I says.

"With this show in town and all," he says. "They're going to give an afternoon performance too, and they'll all want to get done trading in time to go to it. So we'd better just run up to Rogers'."

"All right," I says, "It's your stomach. If you want to make a slave of yourself to your business, it's all right with me."

"I reckon you'll never be a slave to any business," he says.

"Not unless it's Jason Compson's business," I says.

So when I went back and opened it the only thing that sur-

prised me was it was a money order not a check. Yes, sir. You
cant trust a one of them. After all the risk I'd taken, risking Mother
finding out about her coming down here once or twice a year
sometimes, and me having to tell Mother lies about it. That's
gratitude for you. And I wouldn't put it past her to try to notify
the postoffice not to let anyone except her cash it. Giving a kid like
that fifty dollars. Why I never saw fifty dollars until I was twenty-
one years old, with all the other boys with the afternoon off and
all day Saturday and me working in a store. Like I say, how can
they expect anybody to control her, with her giving her money
behind our backs. She has the same home you had I says, and the
same raising. I reckon Mother is a better judge of what she needs
than you are, that haven't even got a home. "If you want to give
her money," I says, "You send it to Mother, dont be giving it to
her. If I've got to run this risk every few months, you'll have to do
like I say, or it's out."

And just about the time I got ready to begin on it because if
Earl thought I was going to dash up the street and gobble two bits
worth of indigestion on his account he was bad fooled. I may not
be sitting with my feet on a mahogany desk but I am being paid
for what I do inside this building and if I can manage to live a
civilised life outside of it I'll go where I can. I can stand on my
own feet; I dont need any man's mahogany desk to prop me up.
So just about the time I got ready to start I'd have to drop everything and run to sell some redneck a dime's worth of nails or something, and Earl up there gobbling a sandwich and half way back
already, like as not, and then I found that all the blanks were gone.
I remembered then that I had aimed to get some more, but it was
too late now, and then I looked up and there Quentin came. In the
back door. I heard her asking old Job if I was there. I just had time
to stick them in the drawer and close it.

She came around to the desk. I looked at my watch.

"You been to dinner already?" I says. "It's just twelve; I just
heard it strike. You must have flown home and back."

"I'm not going home to dinner," she says. "Did I get a letter
today?"

"Were you expecting one?" I says. "Have you got a sweetie
that can write?"

"From Mother," she says. "Did I get a letter from Mother?" she
says, looking at me.

"Mother got one from her," I says. "I haven't opened it. You'll have to wait until she opens it. She'll let you see it, I imagine."

"Please, Jason," she says, not paying any attention, "Did I get one?"

"What's the matter?" I says. "I never knew you to be this anxious about anybody. You must expect some money from her."

"She said she—" she says. "Please, Jason," she says, "Did I?"

"You must have been to school today, after all," I says, "Somewhere where they taught you to say please. Wait a minute, while I wait on that customer."

I went and waited on him. When I turned to come back she was out of sight behind the desk. I ran. I ran around the desk and caught her as she jerked her hand out of the drawer. I took the letter away from her, beating her knuckles on the desk until she let go.

"You would, would you?" I says.

"Give it to me," she says, "You've already opened it. Give it to me. Please, Jason. It's mine. I saw the name."

"I'll take a hame string to you," I says. "That's what I'll give you. Going into my papers."

"Is there some money in it?" she says, reaching for it. "She said she would send me some money. She promised she would. Give it to me."

"What do you want with money?" I says.

"She said she would," she says, "Give it to me. Please, Jason. I wont ever ask you anything again, if you'll give it to me this time."

"I'm going to, if you'll give me time," I says. I took the letter and the money order out and gave her the letter. She reached for the money order, not hardly glancing at the letter. "You'll have to sign it first," I says.

"How much is it?" she says.

"Read the letter," I says. "I reckon it'll say."

She read it fast, in about two looks.

"It dont say," she says, looking up. She dropped the letter to the floor. "How much is it?"

"It's ten dollars," I says.

"Ten dollars?" she says, staring at me.

"And you ought to be damn glad to get that," I says, "A kid like you. What are you in such a rush for money all of a sudden for?"

"Ten dollars?" she says, like she was talking in her sleep, "Just ten dollars?" She made a grab at the money order. "You're lying," she says. "Thief!" she says, "Thief!"

"You would, would you?" I says, holding her off.

"Give it to me!" she says, "It's mine. She sent it to me. I will see it. I will."

"You will?" I says, holding her, "How're you going to do it?"

"Just let me see it, Jason," she says, "Please. I wont ask you for anything again."

"Think I'm lying, do you?" I says. "Just for that you wont see it."

"But just ten dollars," she says, "She told me she—she told me—Jason, please please please. I've got to have some money. I've just got to. Give it to me, Jason. I'll do anything if you will."

"Tell me what you've got to have money for," I says.

"I've got to have it," she says. She was looking at me. Then all of a sudden she quit looking at me without moving her eyes at all. I knew she was going to lie. "It's some money I owe," she says. "I've got to pay it. I've got to pay it today."

"Who to?" I says. Her hands were sort of twisting. I could watch her trying to think of a lie to tell. "Have you been charging things at stores again?" I says. "You needn't bother to tell me that. If you can find anybody in this town that'll charge anything to you after what I told them, I'll eat it."

"It's a girl," she says, "It's a girl. I borrowed some money from a girl. I've got to pay it back. Jason, give it to me. Please. I'll do anything. I've got to have it. Mother will pay you. I'll write to her to pay you and that I wont ever ask her for anything again. You can see the letter. Please, Jason. I've got to have it."

"Tell me what you want with it, and I'll see about it," I says. "Tell me." She just stood there, with her hands working against her dress. "All right," I says, "If ten dollars is too little for you, I'll just take it home to Mother, and you know what'll happen to it then. Of course, if you're so rich you dont need ten dollars—"

She stood there, looking at the floor, kind of mumbling to herself. "She said she would send me some money. She said she sends money here and you say she dont send any. She said she's sent a lot of money here. She says it's for me. That it's for me to have some of it. And you say we haven't got any money."

"You know as much about that as I do," I says. "You've seen what happens to those checks."

"Yes," she says, looking at the floor. "Ten dollars," she says, "Ten dollars."

"And you'd better thank your stars it's ten dollars," I says. "Here," I says. I put the money order face down on the desk, holding my hand on it, "Sign it."

"Will you let me see it?" she says. "I just want to look at it. Whatever it says, I wont ask for but ten dollars. You can have the rest. I just want to see it."

"Not after the way you've acted," I says. "You've got to learn one thing, and that is that when I tell you to do something, you've got it to do. You sign your name on that line."

She took the pen, but instead of signing it she just stood there with her head bent and the pen shaking in her hand. Just like her mother. "Oh, God," she says, "oh, God."

"Yes," I says, "That's one thing you'll have to learn if you never learn anything else. Sign it now, and get on out of here."

She signed it. "Where's the money?" she says. I took the order and blotted it and put it in my pocket. Then I gave her the ten dollars.

"Now you go on back to school this afternoon, you hear?" I says. She didn't answer. She crumpled the bill up in her hand like it was a rag or something and went on out the front door just as Earl came in. A customer came in with him and they stopped up front. I gathered up the things and put on my hat and went up front.

"Been much busy?" Earl says.

"Not much," I says. He looked out the door.

"That your car over yonder?" he says. "Better not try to go out home to dinner. We'll likely have another rush just before the show opens. Get you a lunch at Rogers' and put a ticket in the drawer."

"Much obliged," I says. "I can still manage to feed myself, I reckon."

And right there he'd stay, watching that door like a hawk until I came through it again. Well, he'd just have to watch it for a while; I was doing the best I could. The time before I says that's the last one now; you'll have to remember to get some more right away. But who can remember anything in all this hurrah. And now this damn show had to come here the one day I'd have to hunt all over town for a blank check, besides all the other things I had to do to keep the house running, and Earl watching the door like a hawk.

I went to the printing shop and told him I wanted to play a joke on a fellow, but he didn't have anything. Then he told me to have a look in the old opera house, where somebody had stored a lot of papers and junk out of the old Merchants' and Farmers' Bank when it failed, so I dodged up a few more alleys so Earl couldn't see me and finally found old man Simmons and got the key from him and went up there and dug around. At last I found a pad on a Saint Louis bank. And of course she'd pick this one time to look at it close. Well, it would have to do. I couldn't waste any more time now.

I went back to the store. "Forgot some papers Mother wants to go to the bank," I says. I went back to the desk and fixed the check. Trying to hurry and all, I says to myself it's a good thing her eyes are giving out, with that little whore in the house, a Christian for-bearing woman like Mother. I says you know just as well as I do what she's going to grow up into but I says that's your business, if you want to keep her and raise her in your house just because of Father. Then she would begin to cry and say it was her own flesh and blood so I just says All right. Have it your way. I can stand it if you can.

I fixed the letter up again and glued it back and went out.

"Try not to be gone any longer than you can help," Earl says.

"All right," I says. I went to the telegraph office. The smart boys were all there.

"Any of you boys made your million yet?" I says.

"Who can do anything, with a market like that?" Doc says.

"What's it doing?" I says. I went in and looked. It was three points under the opening. "You boys are not going to let a little thing like the cotton market beat you, are you?" I says. "I thought you were too smart for that."

"Smart, hell," Doc says. "It was down twelve points at twelve oclock. Cleaned me out."

"Twelve points?" I says. "Why the hell didn't somebody let me know? Why didn't you let me know?" I says to the operator.

"I take it as it comes in," he says. "I'm not running a bucket shop."

"You're smart, aren't you?" I says. "Seems to me, with the money I spend with you, you could take time to call me up. Or maybe your damn company's in a conspiracy with those damn eastern sharks."

He didn't say anything. He made like he was busy.

"You're getting a little too big for your pants," I says. "First thing you know you'll be working for a living."

"What's the matter with you?" Doc says. "You're still three points to the good."

"Yes," I says, "If I happened to be selling. I haven't mentioned that yet, I think. You boys all cleaned out?"

"I got caught twice," Doc says. "I switched just in time."

"Well," I. O. Snopes says, "I've picked hit; I reckon taint no more than fair fer hit to pick me once in a while."

So I left them buying and selling among themselves at a nickel a point. I found a nigger and sent him for my car and stood on the corner and waited. I couldn't see Earl looking up and down the street, with one eye on the clock, because I couldn't see the door from here. After about a week he got back with it.

"Where the hell have you been?" I says, "Riding around where the wenches could see you?"

"I come straight as I could," he says, "I had to drive clean around the square, wid all dem wagons."

I never found a nigger yet that didn't have an airtight alibi for whatever he did. But just turn one loose in a car and he's bound to show off. I got in and went on around the square. I caught a glimpse of Earl in the door across the square.

I went straight to the kitchen and told Dilsey to hurry up with dinner.

"Quentin aint come yit," she says.

"What of that?" I says. "You'll be telling me next that Luster's not quite ready to eat yet. Quentin knows when meals are served in this house. Hurry up with it, now."

Mother was in her room. I gave her the letter. She opened it and took the check out and sat holding it in her hand. I went and got the shovel from the corner and gave her a match. "Come on," I says, "Get it over with. You'll be crying in a minute."

She took the match, but she didn't strike it. She sat there, looking at the check. Just like I said it would be.

"I hate to do it," she says, "To increase your burden by adding Quentin. . . ."

"I guess we'll get along," I says. "Come on. Get it over with."

But she just sat there, holding the check.

"This one is on a different bank," she says. "They have been on an Indianapolis bank."

"Yes," I says. "Women are allowed to do that too."

"Do what?" she says.

"Keep money in two different banks," I says.

"Oh," she says. She looked at the check a while. "I'm glad to know she's so . . . she has so much . . . God sees that I am doing right," she says.

"Come on," I says, "Finish it. Get the fun over."

"Fun?" she says, "When I think—"

"I thought you were burning this two hundred dollars a month for fun," I says. "Come on, now. Want me to strike the match?"

"I could bring myself to accept them," she says, "For my children's sake. I have no pride."

"You'd never be satisfied," I says, "You know you wouldn't. You've settled that once, let it stay settled. We can get along."

"I leave everything to you," she says. "But sometimes I become afraid that in doing this I am depriving you all of what is rightfully yours. Perhaps I shall be punished for it. If you want me to, I will smother my pride and accept them."

"What would be the good in beginning now, when you've been destroying them for fifteen years?" I says. "If you keep on doing it, you have lost nothing, but if you'd begin to take them now, you'll have lost fifty thousand dollars. We've got along so far, haven't we?" I says. "I haven't seen you in the poorhouse yet."

"Yes," she says, "We Bascombs need nobody's charity. Certainly not that of a fallen woman."

She struck the match and lit the check and put it in the shovel, and then the envelope, and watched them burn.

"You dont know what it is," she says, "Thank God you will never know what a mother feels."

"There are lots of women in this world no better than her," I says.

"But they are not my daughters," she says. "It's not myself," she says, "I'd gladly take her back, sins and all, because she is my flesh and blood. It's for Quentin's sake."

Well, I could have said it wasn't much chance of anybody hurting Quentin much, but like I say I dont expect much but I do want to eat and sleep without a couple of women squabbling and crying in the house.

"And yours," she says. "I know how you feel toward her."

"Let her come back," I says, "far as I'm concerned."

"No," she says. "I owe that to your father's memory."

"When he was trying all the time to persuade you to let her come home when Herbert threw her out?" I says.

"You dont understand," she says. "I know you dont intend to make it more difficult for me. But it's my place to suffer for my children," she says. "I can bear it."

"Seems to me you go to a lot of unnecessary trouble doing it," I says. The paper burned out. I carried it to the grate and put it in. "It just seems a shame to me to burn up good money," I says.

"Let me never see the day when my children will have to accept that, the wages of sin," she says. "I'd rather see even you dead in your coffin first."

"Have it your way," I says. "Are we going to have dinner soon?" I says, "Because if we're not, I'll have to go on back. We're pretty busy today." She got up. "I've told her once," I says. "It seems she's waiting on Quentin or Luster or somebody. Here, I'll call her. Wait." But she went to the head of the stairs and called.

"Quentin aint come yit," Dilsey says.

"Well, I'll have to get on back," I says. "I can get a sandwich down town. I dont want to interfere with Dilsey's arrangements," I says. Well, that got her started again, with Dilsey hobbling and mumbling back and forth, saying,

"All right, all right, Ise puttin hit on fast as I kin."

"I try to please you all," Mother says, "I try to make things as easy for you as I can."

"I'm not complaining, am I?" I says. "Have I said a word except I had to go back to work?"

"I know," she says, "I know you haven't had the chance the others had, that you've had to bury yourself in a little country store. I wanted you to get ahead. I knew your father would never realise that you were the only one who had any business sense, and then when everything else failed I believed that when she married, and Herbert . . . after his promise . . ."

"Well, he was probably lying too," I says. "He may not have even had a bank. And if he had, I dont reckon he'd have to come all the way to Mississippi to get a man for it."

We ate awhile. I could hear Ben in the kitchen, where Luster was feeding him. Like I say, if we've got to feed another mouth and she wont take that money, why not send him down to Jackson. He'll be happier there, with people like him. I says God knows there's little enough room for pride in this family, but it dont take much pride to not like to see a thirty year old man playing around the yard with a nigger boy, running up and down the fence and lowing like a cow whenever they play golf over there. I says if they'd sent him to Jackson at first we'd all be better off today. I says, you've done your duty by him; you've done all anybody can expect of you and more than most folks would do, so why not send him there and get that much benefit out of the taxes we pay. Then she says, "I'll be gone soon. I know I'm just a burden to you" and I says "You've been saying that so long that I'm beginning to believe you" only I says you'd better be sure and not let me know you're gone because I'll sure have him on number seventeen that night and I says I think I know a place where they'll take her too and the name of it's not Milk street and Honey avenue either. Then she begun to cry and I says All right all right I have as much pride about my kinfolks as anybody even if I dont always know where they come from.

We ate for awhile. Mother sent Dilsey to the front to look for Quentin again.

"I keep telling you she's not coming to dinner," I says.

"She knows better than that," Mother says, "She knows I dont permit her to run about the streets and not come home at meal time. Did you look good, Dilsey?"

"Dont let her, then," I says.

"What can I do," she says. "You have all of you flouted me. Always."

"If you wouldn't come interfering, I'd make her mind," I says. "It wouldn't take me but about one day to straighten her out."

"You'd be too brutal with her," she says. "You have your Uncle Maury's temper."

That reminded me of the letter. I took it out and handed it to her. "You wont have to open it," I says. "The bank will let you know how much it is this time."

"It's addressed to you," she says.

"Go on and open it," I says. She opened it and read it and handed it to me.

" 'My dear young nephew,' it says,

'You will be glad to learn that I am now in a position to avail myself of an opportunity regarding which, for reasons which I will make obvious to you, I shall not go into details until I have an opportunity to divulge it to you in a more secure manner. My business experience has taught me to be chary of committing anything of a confidential nature to any more concrete medium than speech, and my extreme precaution in this instance should give you some inkling of its value. Needless to say, I have just completed a most exhaustive examination of all its phases, and I feel no hesitancy in telling you that it is that sort of golden chance that comes but once in a lifetime, and I now see clearly before me that goal toward which I have long and unflaggingly striven: i.e., the ultimate solidification of my affairs by which I may restore to its rightful position that family of which I have the honour to be the sole remaining male descendant; that family in which I have ever included your lady mother and her children.

'As it so happens, I am not quite in a position to avail myself of this opportunity to the uttermost which it warrants, but rather than go out of the family to do so, I am today drawing upon your Mother's bank for the small sum necessary to complement my own initial investment, for which I herewith enclose, as a matter of formality, my note of hand at eight percent per annum. Needless to say, this is merely a formality, to secure your Mother in the event of that circumstance of which man is ever the plaything and sport. For naturally I shall employ this sum as though it were my own and so permit your Mother to avail herself of this opportunity which my exhaustive investigation has shown to be a bonanza—if you will permit the vulgarism—of the first water and purest ray serene.

'This is in confidence, you will understand, from one business man to another; we will harvest our own vineyards, eh? And knowing your Mother's delicate health and that timorousness which such delicately nurtured Southern ladies would naturally feel regarding matters of business, and their charming proneness to divulge unwittingly such matters in conversation, I would suggest that you do not mention it to her at all. On second thought, I advise you not to do so. It might be better to simply restore this sum to the bank at some future date, say, in a lump sum with the other small sums for which I am indebted to her, and say nothing about

it at all. It is our duty to shield her from the crass material world
as much as possible.

'Your affectionate Uncle,

'Maury L. Bascomb.' "

"What do you want to do about it?" I says, flipping it across the
table.

"I know you grudge what I give him," she says.

"It's your money," I says. "If you want to throw it to the birds
even, it's your business."

"He's my own brother," Mother says. "He's the last Bascomb.
When we are gone there wont be any more of them."

"That'll be hard on somebody, I guess," I says. "All right, all
right," I says, "It's your money. Do as you please with it. You want
me to tell the bank to pay it?"

"I know you begrudge him," she says. "I realise the burden on
your shoulders. When I'm gone it will be easier on you."

"I could make it easier right now," I says. "All right, all right, I
wont mention it again. Move all bedlam in here if you want to."

"He's your own brother," she says, "Even if he is afflicted."

"I'll take your bank book," I says. "I'll draw my check today."

"He kept you waiting six days," she says. "Are you sure the business is sound? It seems strange to me that a solvent business cannot pay its employees promptly."

"He's all right," I says, "Safe as a bank. I tell him not to bother
about mine until we get done collecting every month. That's why
it's late sometimes."

"I just couldn't bear to have you lose the little I had to invest for
you," she says. "I've often thought that Earl is not a good business
man. I know he doesn't take you into his confidence to the extent
that your investment in the business should warrant. I'm going to
speak to him."

"No, you let him alone," I says. "It's his business."

"You have a thousand dollars in it."

"You let him alone," I says, "I'm watching things. I have your
power of attorney. It'll be all right."

"You dont know what a comfort you are to me," she says. "You
have always been my pride and joy, but when you came to me of
your own accord and insisted on banking your salary each month

in my name, I thanked God it was you left me if they had to be taken."

"They were all right," I says. "They did the best they could, I reckon."

"When you talk that way I know you are thinking bitterly of your father's memory," she says. "You have a right to, I suppose. But it breaks my heart to hear you."

I got up. "If you've got any crying to do," I says, "you'll have to do it alone, because I've got to get on back. I'll get the bank book."

"I'll get it," she says.

"Keep still," I says, "I'll get it." I went upstairs and got the bank book out of her desk and went back to town. I went to the bank and deposited the check and the money order and the other ten, and stopped at the telegraph office. It was one point above the opening. I had already lost thirteen points, all because she had to come helling in there at twelve, worrying me about that letter.

"What time did that report come in?" I says.

"About an hour ago," he says.

"An hour ago?" I says. "What are we paying you for?" I says, "Weekly reports? How do you expect a man to do anything? The whole damn top could blow off and we'd not know it."

"I dont expect you to do anything," he says. "They changed that law making folks play the cotton market."

"They have," I says. "I hadn't heard. They must have sent the news out over the Western Union."

I went back to the store. Thirteen points. Damn if I believe anybody knows anything about the damn thing except the ones that sit back in those New York offices and watch the country suckers come up and beg them to take their money. Well, a man that just calls shows he has no faith in himself, and like I say if you aren't going to take the advice, what's the use in paying money for it. Besides, these people are right up there on the ground; they know everything that's going on. I could feel the telegram in my pocket. I'd just have to prove that they were using the telegraph company to defraud. That would constitute a bucket shop. And I wouldn't hesitate that long, either. Only be damned if it doesn't look like a company as big and rich as the Western Union could get a market report out on time. Half as quick as they'll get a wire to you saying Your account closed out. But what the hell do they care about the people. They're hand in glove with that New York crowd. Anybody could see that.

When I came in Earl looked at his watch. But he didn't say anything until the customer was gone. Then he says,

"You go home to dinner?"

"I had to go to the dentist," I says because it's not any of his business where I eat but I've got to be in the store with him all the afternoon. And with his jaw running off after all I've stood. You take a little two by four country storekeeper like I say it takes a man with just five hundred dollars to worry about it fifty thousand dollars' worth.

"You might have told me," he says. "I expected you back right away."

"I'll trade you this tooth and give you ten dollars to boot, any time," I says. "Our agreement was an hour for dinner," I says, "and if you dont like the way I do, you know what you can do about it."

"I've known that some time," he says. "If it hadn't been for your mother I'd have done it before now, too. She's a lady I've got a lot of sympathy for, Jason. Too bad some other folks I know cant say as much."

"Then you can keep it," I says. "When we need any sympathy I'll let you know in plenty of time."

"I've protected you about that business a long time, Jason," he says.

"Yes?" I says, letting him go on. Listening to what he would say before I shut him up.

"I believe I know more about where that automobile came from than she does."

"You think so, do you?" I says. "When are you going to spread the news that I stole it from my mother?"

"I dont say anything," he says, "I know you have her power of attorney. And I know she still believes that thousand dollars is in this business."

"All right," I says, "Since you know so much, I'll tell you a little more: go to the bank and ask them whose account I've been depositing a hundred and sixty dollars on the first of every month for twelve years."

"I dont say anything," he says, "I just ask you to be a little more careful after this."

I never said anything more. It doesn't do any good. I've found that when a man gets into a rut the best thing you can do is let him stay there. And when a man gets it in his head that he's got to tell something on you for your own good, good-night. I'm glad I haven't got the sort of conscience I've got to nurse like a sick puppy all the time. If I'd ever be as careful over anything as he is to keep his little shirt tail full of business from making him more than eight percent. I reckon he thinks they'd get him on the usury law if he netted more than eight percent. What the hell chance has a man got, tied down in a town like this and to a business like this. Why I could take his business in one year and fix him so he'd never have to work again, only he'd give it all away to the church or something. If there's one thing gets under my skin, it's a damn hypocrite. A man that thinks anything he dont understand all about must be crooked and that first chance he gets he's morally bound to tell the third party what's none of his business to tell. Like I say if I thought every time a man did something I didn't know all about he was bound to be a crook, I reckon I wouldn't have any trouble finding something back there on those books that you wouldn't see any use for running and telling somebody I thought ought to know about it, when for all I knew they might know a damn sight more about it now than I did, and if they didn't it was damn little of my business anyway and he says, "My books are open to anybody. Anybody that has any claim or believes she has any claim on this business can go back there and welcome."

"Sure, you wont tell," I says, "You couldn't square your conscience with that. You'll just take her back there and let her find it. You wont tell, yourself."

"I'm not trying to meddle in your business," he says. "I know you missed out on some things like Quentin had. But your mother has had a misfortunate life too, and if she was to come in here and ask me why you quit, I'd have to tell her. It aint that thousand dollars. You know that. It's because a man never gets anywhere if fact and his ledgers dont square. And I'm not going to lie to anybody, for myself or anybody else."

"Well, then," I says, "I reckon that conscience of yours is a more valuable clerk than I am; it dont have to go home at noon to eat. Only dont let it interfere with my appetite," I says, because how the hell can I do anything right, with that damn family and her not making any effort to control her nor any of them, like that time when she happened to see one of them kissing Caddy and all next day she went around the house in a black dress and a veil and even Father couldn't get her to say a word except crying and saying her little daughter was dead and Caddy about fifteen then only in three years she'd been wearing haircloth or probably sandpaper at that rate. Do you think I can afford to have her running about the streets with every drummer that comes to town, I says, and them telling the new ones up and down the road where to pick up a hot one when they made Jefferson. I haven't got much pride, I can't afford it with a kitchen full of niggers to feed and robbing the state asylum of its star freshman. Blood, I says, governors and generals. It's a damn good thing we never had any kings and presidents; we'd all be down there at Jackson chasing butterflies. I say it'd be bad enough if it was mine; I'd at least be sure it was a bastard to begin with, and now even the Lord doesn't know that for certain probably.

So after awhile I heard the band start up, and then they begun to clear out. Headed for the show, every one of them. Haggling over a twenty cent hame string to save fifteen cents, so they can give it to a bunch of Yankees that come in and pay maybe ten dollars for the privilege. I went on out to the back.

"Well," I says, "If you dont look out, that bolt will grow into your hand. And then I'm going to take an axe and chop it out. What do you reckon the boll-weevils'll eat if you dont get those cultivators in shape to raise them a crop?" I says, "sage grass?"

"Dem folks sho do play dem horns," he says. "Tell me man in dat show kin play a tune on a handsaw. Pick hit like a banjo."

"Listen," I says. "Do you know how much that show'll spend in this town? About ten dollars," I says. "The ten dollars Buck Turpin has in his pocket right now."

"Whut dey give Mr Buck ten dollars fer?" he says.

"For the privilege of showing here," I says. "You can put the balance of what they'll spend in your eye."

"You mean dey pays ten dollars jest to give dey show here?" he says.

"That's all," I says. "And how much do you reckon . . ."

"Gret day," he says, "You mean to tell me dey chargin um to let um show here? I'd pay ten dollars to see dat man pick dat saw, ef I had to. I figures dat tomorrow mawnin I be still owin um nine dollars and six bits at dat rate."

And then a Yankee will talk your head off about niggers getting ahead. Get them ahead, what I say. Get them so far ahead you cant find one south of Louisville with a blood hound. Because when I told him about how they'd pick up Saturday night and carry off at least a thousand dollars out of the county, he says,

"I dont begrudge um. I kin sho afford my two bits."

"Two bits hell," I says. "That dont begin it. How about the dime or fifteen cents you'll spend for a damn two cent box of candy or something. How about the time you're wasting right now, listening to that band."

"Dat's de troof," he says. "Well, ef I lives twell night hit's gwine to be two bits mo dey takin out of town, dat's sho."

"Then you're a fool," I says.

"Well," he says, "I dont spute dat neither. Ef dat uz a crime, all chain-gangs wouldn't be black."

Well, just about that time I happened to look up the alley and saw her. When I stepped back and looked at my watch I didn't notice at the time who he was because I was looking at the watch. It was just two thirty, forty-five minutes before anybody but me expected her to be out. So when I looked around the door the first thing I saw was the red tie he had on and I was thinking what the hell kind of a man would wear a red tie. But she was sneaking along the alley, watching the door, so I wasn't thinking anything about him until they had gone past. I was wondering if she'd have so little respect for me that she'd not only play out of school when I told her not to but would walk right past the store, daring me not to see her. Only she couldn't see into the door because the sun fell straight into it and it was like trying to see through an automobile searchlight, so I stood there and watched her go on past, with her face painted up like a damn clown's and her hair all gummed and twisted and a dress that if a woman had come out doors even on Gayoso or Beale street when I was a young fellow with no more than that to cover her legs and behind, she'd been thrown in jail. I'll be damned if they dont dress like they were trying to make every man they passed on the street want to reach out and clap his hand on it. And so I was thinking what kind of a damn man would wear a red tie when all of a sudden I knew he was one of those show folks well as if she'd told me. Well, I can stand a lot; if I couldn't, damn if I wouldn't be in a hell of a fix, so when they turned the corner I jumped down and followed. Me, without any hat, in the middle of the afternoon, having to chase up and down back alleys because of my mother's good name. Like I say you cant do anything with a woman like that, if she's got it in her. If it's in her blood, you cant do anything with her. The only thing you can do is to get rid of her, let her go on and live with her own sort.

I went on to the street, but they were out of sight. And there I was, without any hat, looking like I was crazy too. Like a man would naturally think, one of them is crazy and another one drowned himself and the other one was turned out into the street by her husband, what's the reason the rest of them are not crazy too. All the time I could see them watching me like a hawk, waiting for a chance to say Well I'm not surprised I expected it all the time the whole family's crazy. Selling land to send him to Harvard and paying taxes to support a state University all the time that I never saw except twice at a baseball game and not letting her daughter's name be spoken on the place until after a while Father wouldn't even come down town anymore but just sat there all day with the decanter I could see the bottom of his nightshirt and his bare legs and hear the decanter clinking until finally T. P. had to pour it for him and she says You have no respect for your Father's memory and I says I dont know why not it sure is preserved well enough to last only if I'm crazy too God knows what I'll do about it just to look at water makes me sick and I'd just as soon swallow gasoline as a glass of whiskey and Lorraine telling them he may not drink but if you dont believe he's a man I can tell you how to find out she says If I catch you fooling with any of these whores you know what I'll do she says I'll whip her grabbing at her I'll whip her as long as I can find her she says and I says if I dont drink that's my business but have you ever found me short I says I'll buy you enough beer to take a bath in if you want it because I've got every respect for a good honest whore because with Mother's health and the position I try to uphold to have her with no more respect for what I try to do for her than to make her name and my name and my Mother's name a byword in the town.

She had dodged out of sight somewhere. Saw me coming and dodged into another alley, running up and down the alleys with a damn show man in a red tie that everybody would look at and think what kind of a damn man would wear a red tie. Well, the boy kept speaking to me and so I took the telegram without knowing I had taken it. I didn't realise what it was until I was signing for it, and I tore it open without even caring much what it was. I knew all the time what it would be, I reckon. That was the only thing else that could happen, especially holding it up until I had already had the check entered on the pass book.

I don't see how a city no bigger than New York can hold enough people to take the money away from us country suckers. Work like hell all day every day, send them your money and get a little piece of paper back, Your account closed at 20.62. Teasing you along, letting you pile up a little paper profit, then bang! Your account closed at 20.62. And if that wasn't enough, paying ten dollars a month to somebody to tell you how to lose it fast, that either dont know anything about it or is in cahoots with the telegraph company. Well, I'm done with them. They've sucked me in for the last time. Any fool except a fellow that hasn't got any more sense than to take a jew's word for anything could tell the market was going up all the time, with the whole damn delta about to be flooded again and the cotton washed right out of the ground like it was last year. Let it wash a man's crop out of the ground year after year, and them up there in Washington spending fifty thousand dollars a day keeping an army in Nicaragua or some place. Of course it'll overflow again, and then cotton'll be worth thirty cents a pound. Well, I just want to hit them one time and get my money back. I don't want a killing; only these small town gamblers are out for that, I just want my money back that these damn jews have gotten with all their guaranteed inside dope. Then I'm through; they can kiss my foot for every other red cent of mine they get.

I went back to the store. It was half past three almost. Damn little time to do anything in, but then I am used to that. I never had to go to Harvard to learn that. The band had quit playing. Got them all inside now, and they wouldn't have to waste any more wind. Earl says,

"He found you, did he? He was in here with it a while ago. I thought you were out back somewhere."

"Yes," I says, "I got it. They couldn't keep it away from me all afternoon. The town's too small. I've got to go out home a minute," I says. "You can dock me if it'll make you feel any better."

"Go ahead," he says, "I can handle it now. No bad news, I hope."

"You'll have to go to the telegraph office and find that out," I says. "They'll have time to tell you. I haven't."

"I just asked," he says. "Your mother knows she can depend on me."

"She'll appreciate it," I says. "I wont be gone any longer than I have to."

"Take your time," he says. "I can handle it now. You go ahead."

I got the car and went home. Once this morning, twice at noon, and now again, with her and having to chase all over town and having to beg them to let me eat a little of the food I am paying for. Sometimes I think what's the use of anything. With the precedent I've been set I must be crazy to keep on. And now I reckon I'll get home just in time to take a nice long drive after a basket of tomatoes or something and then have to go back to town smelling like a camphor factory so my head wont explode right on my shoulders. I keep telling her there's not a damn thing in that aspirin except flour and water for imaginary invalids. I says you dont know what a headache is. I says you think I'd fool with that damn car at all if it depended on me. I says I can get along without one I've learned to get along without lots of things but if you want to risk yourself in that old wornout surrey with a halfgrown nigger boy all right because I says God looks after Ben's kind, God knows He ought to do something for him but if you think I'm going to trust a thousand dollars' worth of delicate machinery to a halfgrown nigger or a grown one either, you'd better buy him one yourself because I says you like to ride in the car and you know you do.

Dilsey said Mother was in the house. I went on into the hall and listened, but I didn't hear anything. I went up stairs, but just as I passed her door she called me.

"I just wanted to know who it was," she says. "I'm here alone so much that I hear every sound."

"You dont have to stay here," I says. "You could spend the whole day visiting like other women, if you wanted to." She came to the door.

"I thought maybe you were sick," she says. "Having to hurry through your dinner like you did."

"Better luck next time," I says. "What do you want?"

"Is anything wrong?" she says.

"What could be?" I says. "Cant I come home in the middle of the afternoon without upsetting the whole house?"

"Have you seen Quentin?" she says.

"She's in school," I says.

"It's after three," she says. "I heard the clock strike at least a half an hour ago. She ought to be home by now."

"Ought she?" I says. "When have you ever seen her before dark?"

"She ought to be home," she says. "When I was a girl . . ."

"You had somebody to make you behave yourself," I says. "She hasn't."

"I can't do anything with her," she says. "I've tried and I've tried."

"And you wont let me, for some reason," I says, "So you ought to be satisfied." I went on to my room. I turned the key easy and stood there until the knob turned. Then she says,

"Jason."

"What," I says.

"I just thought something was wrong."

"Not in here," I says. "You've come to the wrong place."

"I dont mean to worry you," she says.

"I'm glad to hear that," I says. "I wasn't sure. I thought I might have been mistaken. Do you want anything?"

After awhile she says, "No. Not anything." Then she went away. I took the box down and counted out the money and hid the box again and unlocked the door and went out. I thought about the camphor, but it would be too late now, anyway. And I'd just have one more round trip. She was at her door, waiting.

"You want anything from town?" I says.

"No," she says. "I dont mean to meddle in your affairs. But I dont know what I'd do if anything happened to you, Jason."

"I'm all right," I says. "Just a headache."

"I wish you'd take some aspirin," she says. "I know you're not going to stop using the car."

"What's the car got to do with it?" I says. "How can a car give a man a headache?"

"You know gasoline always made you sick," she says. "Ever since you were a child. I wish you'd take some aspirin."

"Keep on wishing it," I says. "It wont hurt you."

I got in the car and started back to town. I had just turned onto the street when I saw a ford coming helling toward me. All of a sudden it stopped. I could hear the wheels sliding and it slewed around and backed and whirled and just as I was thinking what the hell they were up to, I saw that red tie. Then I recognised her face looking back through the window. It whirled into the alley. I saw it turn again, but when I got to the back street it was just disappearing, running like hell.

I saw red. When I recognised that red tie, after all I had told her,

I forgot about everything. I never thought about my head even until I came to the first forks and had to stop. Yet we spend money and spend money on roads and damn if it isn't like trying to drive over a sheet of corrugated iron roofing. I'd like to know how a man could be expected to keep up with even a wheelbarrow. I think too much of my car; I'm not going to hammer it to pieces like it was a ford. Chances were they had stolen it, anyway, so why should they give a damn. Like I say blood always tells. If you've got blood like that in you, you'll do anything. I says whatever claim you believe she has on you has already been discharged; I says from now on you have only yourself to blame because you know what any sensible person would do. I says if I've got to spend half my time being a damn detective, at least I'll go where I can get paid for it.

So I had to stop there at the forks. Then I remembered it. It felt like somebody was inside with a hammer, beating on it. I says I've tried to keep you from being worried by her; I says far as I'm concerned, let her go to hell as fast as she pleases and the sooner the better. I says what else do you expect except every drummer and cheap show that comes to town because even these town jelly-beans give her the go-by now. You dont know what goes on I says, you dont hear the talk that I hear and you can just bet I shut them up too. I says my people owned slaves here when you all were running little shirt tail country stores and farming land no nigger would look at on shares.

If they ever farmed it. It's a good thing the Lord did something for this country; the folks that live on it never have. Friday afternoon, and from right here I could see three miles of land that hadn't even been broken, and every able bodied man in the county in town at that show. I might have been a stranger starving to death, and there wasn't a soul in sight to ask which way to town even. And she trying to get me to take aspirin. I says when I eat bread I'll do it at the table. I says you always talking about how much you give up for us when you could buy ten new dresses a year on the money you spend for those damn patent medicines. It's not something to cure it I need it's just an even break not to have to have them but as long as I have to work ten hours a day to support a kitchen full of niggers in the style they're accustomed to and send them to the show with every other nigger in the county, only he was late already. By the time he got there it would be over.

After awhile he got up to the car and when I finally got it through

his head if two people in a ford had passed him, he said yes. So I
went on, and when I came to where the wagon road turned off I
could see the tire tracks. Ab Russell was in his lot, but I didn't
bother to ask him and I hadn't got out of sight of his barn hardly
when I saw the ford. They had tried to hide it. Done about as well
at it as she did at everything else she did. Like I say it's not that I
object to so much; maybe she cant help that, it's because she hasn't
even got enough consideration for her own family to have any discretion. I'm afraid all the time I'll run into them right in the middle
of the street or under a wagon on the square, like a couple of dogs.

I parked and got out. And now I'd have to go way around and
cross a plowed field, the only one I had seen since I left town, with
every step like somebody was walking along behind me, hitting
me on the head with a club. I kept thinking that when I got across
the field at least I'd have something level to walk on, that wouldn't
jolt me every step, but when I got into the woods it was full of underbrush and I had to twist around through it, and then I came
to a ditch full of briers. I went along it for awhile, but it got thicker
and thicker, and all the time Earl probably telephoning home about
where I was and getting Mother all upset again.

When I finally got through I had had to wind around so much
that I had to stop and figure out just where the car would be. I knew
they wouldn't be far from it, just under the closest bush, so I turned
and worked back toward the road. Then I couldn't tell just how far
I was, so I'd have to stop and listen, and then with my legs not
using so much blood, it all would go into my head like it would
explode any minute, and the sun getting down just to where it
could shine straight into my eyes and my ears ringing so I couldn't
hear anything. I went on, trying to move quiet, then I heard a dog
or something and I knew that when he scented me he'd have to
come helling up, then it would be all off.

I had gotten beggar lice and twigs and stuff all over me, inside
my clothes and shoes and all, and then I happened to look around
and I had my hand right on a bunch of poison oak. The only thing
I couldn't understand was why it was just poison oak and not a
snake or something. So I didn't even bother to move it. I just stood
there until the dog went away. Then I went on.

I didn't have any idea where the car was now. I couldn't think
about anything except my head, and I'd just stand in one place and
sort of wonder if I had really seen a ford even, and I didn't even

care much whether I had or not. Like I say, let her lay out all day and all night with everything in town that wears pants, what do I care. I dont owe anything to anybody that has no more consideration for me, that wouldn't be a damn bit above planting that ford there and making me spend a whole afternoon and Earl taking her back there and showing her the books just because he's too damn virtuous for this world. I says you'll have one hell of a time in heaven, without anybody's business to meddle in only dont you ever let me catch you at it I says, I close my eyes to it because of your grandmother, but just you let me catch you doing it one time on this place, where my mother lives. These damn little slick haired squirts, thinking they are raising so much hell, I'll show them something about hell I says, and you too. I'll make him think that damn red tie is the latch string to hell, if he thinks he can run the woods with my niece.

With the sun and all in my eyes and my blood going so I kept thinking every time my head would go on and burst and get it over with, with briers and things grabbing at me, then I came onto the sand ditch where they had been and I recognised the tree where the car was, and just as I got out of the ditch and started running I heard the car start. It went off fast, blowing the horn. They kept on blowing it, like it was saying Yah. Yah. Yaaahhhhhhhh, going out of sight. I got to the road just in time to see it go out of sight.

By the time I got up to where my car was, they were clean out of sight, the horn still blowing. Well, I never thought anything about it except I was saying Run. Run back to town. Run home and try to convince Mother that I never saw you in that car. Try to make her believe that I dont know who he was. Try to make her believe that I didn't miss ten feet of catching you in that ditch. Try to make her believe you were standing up, too.

It kept on saying Yahhhhh, Yahhhhh, Yaaahhhhhhhhh, getting fainter and fainter. Then it quit, and I could hear a cow lowing up at Russell's barn. And still I never thought. I went up to the door and opened it and raised my foot. I kind of thought then that the car was leaning a little more than the slant of the road would be, but I never found it out until I got in and started off.

Well, I just sat there. It was getting on toward sundown, and town was about five miles. They never even had guts enough to puncture it, to jab a hole in it. They just let the air out. I just stood there for a while, thinking about that kitchen full of niggers and not

one of them had time to lift a tire onto the rack and screw up a
couple of bolts. It was kind of funny because even she couldn't
have seen far enough ahead to take the pump out on purpose, unless she thought about it while he was letting out the air maybe. But
what it probably was, was somebody took it out and gave it to Ben
to play with for a squirt gun because they'd take the whole car to
pieces if he wanted it and Dilsey says, Aint nobody teched yo car.
What we want to fool with hit fer? and I says You're a nigger.
You're lucky, do you know it? I says I'll swap with you any day because it takes a white man not to have anymore sense than to worry
about what a little slut of a girl does.

I walked up to Russell's. He had a pump. That was just an over-
sight on their part, I reckon. Only I still couldn't believe she'd have
had the nerve to. I kept thinking that. I dont know why it is I
cant seem to learn that a woman'll do anything. I kept thinking,
Let's forget for awhile how I feel toward you and how you feel toward me: I just wouldn't do you this way. I wouldn't do you this
way no matter what you had done to me. Because like I say blood
is blood and you cant get around it. It's not playing a joke that any
eight year old boy could have thought of, it's letting your own
uncle be laughed at by a man that would wear a red tie. They
come into town and call us all a bunch of hicks and think it's too
small to hold them. Well he doesn't know just how right he is. And
her too. If that's the way she feels about it, she'd better keep right
on going and a damn good riddance.

I stopped and returned Russell's pump and drove on to town. I
went to the drugstore and got a coca-cola and then I went to the
telegraph office. It had closed at 12.21, forty points down. Forty
times five dollars; buy something with that if you can, and she'll
say, I've got to have it I've just got to and I'll say that's too bad
you'll have to try somebody else, I haven't got any money; I've
been too busy to make any.

I just looked at him.

"I'll tell you some news," I says, "You'll be astonished to learn
that I am interested in the cotton market," I says. "That never occurred to you, did it?"

"I did my best to deliver it," he says. "I tried the store twice and
called up your house, but they didn't know where you were," he
says, digging in the drawer.

"Deliver what?" I says. He handed me a telegram. "What time did this come?" I says.

"About half past three," he says.

"And now it's ten minutes past five," I says.

"I tried to deliver it," he says. "I couldn't find you."

"That's not my fault, is it?" I says. I opened it, just to see what kind of a lie they'd tell me this time. They must be in one hell of a shape if they've got to come all the way to Mississippi to steal ten dollars a month. Sell, it says. The market will be unstable, with a general downward tendency. Do not be alarmed following government report.

"How much would a message like this cost?" I says. He told me.

"They paid it," he says.

"Then I owe them that much," I says. "I already knew this. Send this collect," I says, taking a blank. Buy, I wrote, Market just on point of blowing its head off. Occasional flurries for purpose of hooking a few more country suckers who haven't got in to the telegraph office yet. Do not be alarmed. "Send that collect," I says.

He looked at the message, then he looked at the clock. "Market closed an hour ago," he says.

"Well," I says, "That's not my fault either. I didn't invent it; I just bought a little of it while under the impression that the telegraph company would keep me informed as to what it was doing."

"A report is posted whenever it comes in," he says.

"Yes," I says, "And in Memphis they have it on a blackboard every ten seconds," I says. "I was within sixty-seven miles of there once this afternoon."

He looked at the message. "You want to send this?" he says.

"I still haven't changed my mind," I says. I wrote the other one out and counted the money. "And this one too, if you're sure you can spell b-u-y."

I went back to the store. I could hear the band from down the street. Prohibition's a fine thing. Used to be they'd come in Saturday with just one pair of shoes in the family and him wearing them, and they'd go down to the express office and get his package; now they all go to the show barefooted, with the merchants in the door like a row of tigers or something in a cage, watching them pass. Earl says,

"I hope it wasn't anything serious."

"What?" I says. He looked at his watch. Then he went to the door and looked at the courthouse clock. "You ought to have a dollar watch," I says. "It wont cost you so much to believe it's lying each time."

"What?" he says.

"Nothing," I says. "Hope I haven't inconvenienced you."

"We were not busy much," he says. "They all went to the show. It's all right."

"If it's not all right," I says, "You know what you can do about it."

"I said it was all right," he says.

"I heard you," I says. "And if it's not all right, you know what you can do about it."

"Do you want to quit?" he says.

"It's not my business," I says. "My wishes dont matter. But dont get the idea that you are protecting me by keeping me."

"You'd be a good business man if you'd let yourself, Jason," he says.

"At least I can tend to my own business and let other peoples' alone," I says.

"I dont know why you are trying to make me fire you," he says. "You know you could quit anytime and there wouldn't be any hard feelings between us."

"Maybe that's why I dont quit," I says. "As long as I tend to my job, that's what you are paying me for." I went on to the back and got a drink of water and went on out to the back door. Job had the cultivators all set up at last. It was quiet there, and pretty soon my head got a little easier. I could hear them singing now, and then the band played again. Well, let them get every quarter and dime in the county; it was no skin off my back. I've done what I could; a man that can live as long as I have and not know when to quit is a fool. Especially as it's no business of mine. If it was my own daughter now it would be different, because she wouldn't have time to; she'd have to work some to feed a few invalids and idiots and niggers, because how could I have the face to bring anybody there. I've too much respect for anybody to do that. I'm a man, I can stand it, it's my own flesh and blood and I'd like to see the colour of the man's eyes that would speak disrespectful of any woman that was my friend it's these damn good women that do it I'd like to see the good, church-going woman that's half as square as Lorraine, whore or no whore. Like I say if I was to get married you'd go up like a

balloon and you know it and she says I want you to be happy to
have a family of your own not to slave your life away for us. But
I'll be gone soon and then you can take a wife but you'll never find
a woman who is worthy of you and I says yes I could. You'd get
right up out of your grave you know you would. I says no thank
you I have all the women I can take care of now if I married a
wife she'd probably turn out to be a hophead or something. That's
all we lack in this family, I says.

The sun was down beyond the Methodist church now, and the
pigeons were flying back and forth around the steeple, and when
the band stopped I could hear them cooing. It hadn't been four
months since Christmas, and yet they were almost as thick as ever.
I reckon Parson Walthall was getting a belly full of them now.
You'd have thought we were shooting people, with him making
speeches and even holding onto a man's gun when they came over.
Talking about peace on earth good will toward all and not a sparrow can fall to earth. But what does he care how thick they get,
he hasn't got anything to do; what does he care what time it is. He
pays no taxes, he doesn't have to see his money going every year
to have the courthouse clock cleaned to where it'll run. They had
to pay a man forty-five dollars to clean it. I counted over a hundred
half-hatched pigeons on the ground. You'd think they'd have
sense enough to leave town. It's a good thing I dont have any more
ties than a pigeon, I'll say that.

The band was playing again, a loud fast tune, like they were
breaking up. I reckon they'd be satisfied now. Maybe they'd have
enough music to entertain them while they drove fourteen or fifteen miles home and unharnessed in the dark and fed the stock and
milked. All they'd have to do would be to whistle the music and
tell the jokes to the live stock in the barn, and then they could
count up how much they'd made by not taking the stock to the
show too. They could figure that if a man had five children and
seven mules, he cleared a quarter by taking his family to the show.
Just like that. Earl came back with a couple of packages.

"Here's some more stuff going out," he says. "Where's Uncle Job?"

"Gone to the show, I imagine," I says. "Unless you watched him."

"He doesn't slip off," he says. "I can depend on him."

"Meaning me by that," I says.

He went to the door and looked out, listening.

"That's a good band," he says. "It's about time they were breaking up, I'd say."

"Unless they're going to spend the night there," I says. The swallows had begun, and I could hear the sparrows beginning to swarm in the trees in the courthouse yard. Every once in a while a bunch of them would come swirling around in sight above the roof, then go away. They are as big a nuisance as the pigeons, to my notion. You cant even sit in the courthouse yard for them. First thing you know, bing. Right on your hat. But it would take a millionaire to afford to shoot them at five cents a shot. If they'd just put a little poison out there in the square, they'd get rid of them in a day, because if a merchant cant keep his stock from running around the square, he'd better try to deal in something besides chickens, something that dont eat, like plows or onions. And if a man dont keep his dogs up, he either dont want it or he hasn't any business with one. Like I say if all the businesses in a town are run like country businesses, you're going to have a country town.

"It wont do you any good if they have broke up," I says. "They'll have to hitch up and take out to get home by midnight as it is."

"Well," he says, "They enjoy it. Let them spend a little money on a show now and then. A hill farmer works pretty hard and gets mighty little for it."

"There's no law making them farm in the hills," I says, "Or anywhere else."

"Where would you and me be, if it wasn't for the farmers?" he says.

"I'd be home right now," I says, "Lying down, with an ice pack on my head."

"You have these headaches too often," he says. "Why dont you have your teeth examined good? Did he go over them all this morning?"

"Did who?" I says.

"You said you went to the dentist this morning."

"Do you object to my having the headache on your time?" I says. "Is that it?" They were crossing the alley now, coming up from the show.

"There they come," he says. "I reckon I better get up front." He went on. It's a curious thing how no matter what's wrong with you, a man'll tell you to have your teeth examined and a woman'll tell you to get married. It always takes a man that never made much at any thing to tell you how to run your business, though. Like these college professors without a whole pair of socks to their name, telling you how to make a million in ten years, and a woman that couldn't even get a husband can always tell you how to raise a family.

Old man Job came up with the wagon. After a while he got through wrapping the lines around the whip socket.

"Well," I says, "Was it a good show?"

"I aint been yit," he says. "But I kin be arrested in dat tent to-night, dough."

"Like hell you haven't," I says. "You've been away from here since three oclock. Mr Earl was just back here looking for you."

"I been tendin to my business," he says. "Mr Earl knows whar I been."

"You may can fool him," I says. "I wont tell on you."

"Den he's de onliest man here I'd try to fool," he says. "Whut I want to waste my time foolin a man whut I dont keer whether I sees him Sat'dy night er not? I wont try to fool you," he says. "You too smart fer me. Yes, suh," he says, looking busy as hell, putting five or six little packages into the wagon, "You's too smart fer me. Aint a man in dis town kin keep up wid you fer smartness. You fools a man whut so smart he cant even keep up wid hisself," he says, getting in the wagon and unwrapping the reins.

"Who's that?" I says.

"Dat's Mr Jason Compson," he says. "Git up dar, Dan!"

One of the wheels was just about to come off. I watched to see if he'd get out of the alley before it did. Just turn any vehicle over to a nigger, though. I says that old rattletrap's just an eyesore, yet you'll keep it standing there in the carriage house a hundred years just so that boy can ride to the cemetery once a week. I says he's not the first fellow that'll have to do things he doesn't want to. I'd make him ride in that car like a civilised man or stay at home. What does he know about where he goes or what he goes in, and us keeping a carriage and a horse so he can take a ride on Sunday afternoon.

A lot Job cared whether the wheel came off or not, long as he wouldn't have too far to walk back. Like I say the only place for them is in the field, where they'd have to work from sunup to sundown. They cant stand prosperity or an easy job. Let one stay around white people for a while and he's not worth killing. They get so they can outguess you about work before your very eyes, like Roskus the only mistake he ever made was he got careless one day and died. Shirking and stealing and giving you a little more lip and a little more lip until some day you have to lay them out with a scantling or something. Well, it's Earl's business. But I'd hate to have my business advertised over this town by an old doddering nigger and a wagon that you thought every time it turned a corner it would come all to pieces.

The sun was all high up in the air now, and inside it was beginning to get dark. I went up front. The square was empty. Earl was back closing the safe, and then the clock begun to strike.

"You lock the back door," he says. I went back and locked it and came back. "I suppose you're going to the show tonight," he says. "I gave you those passes yesterday, didn't I?"

"Yes," I said. "You want them back?"

"No, no," he says, "I just forgot whether I gave them to you or not. No sense in wasting them."

He locked the door and said Goodnight and went on. The sparrows were still rattling away in the trees, but the square was empty except for a few cars. There was a ford in front of the drugstore, but I didn't even look at it. I know when I've had enough of anything. I dont mind trying to help her, but I know when I've had enough. I guess I could teach Luster to drive it, then they could chase her all day long if they wanted to, and I could stay home and play with Ben.

I went in and got a couple of cigars. Then I thought I'd have another headache shot for luck, and I stood and talked with them awhile.

"Well," Mac says, "I reckon you've got your money on the Yankees this year."

"What for?" I says.

"The Pennant," he says. "Not anything in the League can beat them."

"Like hell there's not," I says. "They're shot," I says. "You think a team can be that lucky forever?"

"I dont call it luck," Mac says.

"I wouldn't bet on any team that fellow Ruth played on," I says. "Even if I knew it was going to win."

"Yes?" Mac says.

"I can name you a dozen men in either League who're more valuable than he is," I says.

"What have you got against Ruth?" Mac says.

"Nothing," I says. "I haven't got any thing against him. I dont even like to look at his picture." I went on out. The lights were coming on, and people going along the streets toward home. Sometimes the sparrows never got still until full dark. The night they turned on the new lights around the courthouse it waked them up and they were flying around and blundering into the lights all night long. They kept it up two or three nights, then one morning they were all gone. Then after about two months they all came back again.

I drove on home. There were no lights in the house yet, but they'd all be looking out the windows, and Dilsey jawing away in the kitchen like it was her own food she was having to keep hot until I got there. You'd think to hear her that there wasn't but one supper in the world, and that was the one she had to keep back a few minutes on my account. Well at least I could come home one time without finding Ben and that nigger hanging on the gate like a bear and a monkey in the same cage. Just let it come toward sundown and he'd head for the gate like a cow for the barn, hanging onto it and bobbing his head and sort of moaning to himself. That's a hog for punishment for you. If what had happened to him for fooling with open gates had happened to me, I never would want to see another one. I often wondered what he'd be thinking about, down there at the gate, watching the girls going home from school, trying to want something he couldn't even remember he didn't and couldn't want any longer. And what he'd think when they'd be undressing him and he'd happen to take a look at himself and begin to cry like he'd do. But like I say they never did enough of that. I says I know what you need, you need what they did to Ben then you'd behave. And if you dont know what that was I says, ask Dilsey to tell you.

There was a light in Mother's room. I put the car up and went on into the kitchen. Luster and Ben were there.

"Where's Dilsey?" I says. "Putting supper on?"

"She upstairs wid Miss Cahline," Luster says. "Dey been goin hit. Ever since Miss Quentin come home. Mammy up there keepin um fom fightin. Is dat show come, Mr Jason?"

"Yes," I says.

"I thought I heard de band," he says. "Wish I could go," he says. "I could ef I jes had a quarter."

Dilsey came in. "You come, is you?" she says. "Whut you been up to dis evenin? You knows how much work I got to do; whyn't you git here on time?"

"Maybe I went to the show," I says. "Is supper ready?"

"Wish I could go," Luster said. "I could ef I jes had a quarter."

"You aint got no business at no show," Dilsey says. "You go on in de house and set down," she says. "Dont you go up stairs and get um started again, now."

"What's the matter?" I says.

"Quentin come in a while ago and says you been follerin her around all evenin and den Miss Cahline jumped on her. Whyn't you let her alone? Cant you live in de same house wid you own blood niece widout quoilin?"

"I cant quarrel with her," I says, "because I haven't seen her since this morning. What does she say I've done now? made her go to school? That's pretty bad," I says.

"Well, you tend to yo business and let her alone," Dilsey says, "I'll take keer of her ef you'n Miss Cahline'll let me. Go on in dar now and behave yoself twell I git supper on."

"If I jes had a quarter," Luster says, "I could go to dat show."

"En ef you had wings you could fly to heaven," Dilsey says. "I dont want to hear another word about dat show."

"That reminds me," I says, "I've got a couple of tickets they gave me." I took them out of my coat.

"You fixin to use um?" Luster says.

"Not me," I says. "I wouldn't go to it for ten dollars."

"Gimme one of um, Mr Jason," he says.

"I'll sell you one," I says. "How about it?"

"I aint got no money," he says.

"That's too bad," I says. I made to go out.

"Gimme one of um, Mr Jason," he says. "You aint gwine need um bofe."

"Hush yo mouf," Dilsey says, "Dont you know he aint gwine give nothing away?"

"How much you want fer hit?" he says.

"Five cents," I says.

"I aint got dat much," he says.

"How much you got?" I says.

"I aint got nothing," he says.

"All right," I says. I went on.

"Mr Jason," he says.

"Whyn't you hush up?" Dilsey says. "He jes teasin you. He fixin to use dem tickets hisself. Go on, Jason, and let him lone."

"I dont want them," I says. I came back to the stove. "I came in here to burn them up. But if you want to buy one for a nickel?" I says, looking at him and opening the stove lid.

"I aint got dat much," he says.

"All right," I says. I dropped one of them in the stove.

"You, Jason," Dilsey says, "Aint you shamed?"

"Mr Jason," he says, "Please, suh. I'll fix dem tires ev'ry day fer a mont'."

"I need the cash," I says. "You can have it for a nickel."

"Hush, Luster," Dilsey says. She jerked him back. "Go on," she says, "Drop hit in. Go on. Git hit over with."

"You can have it for a nickel," I says.

"Go on," Dilsey says. "He aint got no nickel. Go on. Drop hit in."

"All right," I says. I dropped it in and Dilsey shut the stove.

"A big growed man like you," she says. "Git on outen my kitchen. Hush," she says to Luster. "Dont you git Benjy started. I'll git you a quarter from Frony tonight and you kin go tomorrow night. Hush up, now."

I went on into the living room. I couldn't hear anything from upstairs. I opened the paper. After awhile Ben and Luster came in. Ben went to the dark place on the wall where the mirror used to be, rubbing his hands on it and slobbering and moaning. Luster begun punching at the fire.

"What're you doing?" I says. "We dont need any fire tonight."

"I trying to keep him quiet," he says. "Hit always cold Easter," he says.

"Only this is not Easter," I says. "Let it alone."

He put the poker back and got the cushion out of Mother's chair and gave it to Ben, and he hunkered down in front of the fireplace and got quiet.

I read the paper. There hadn't been a sound from upstairs when Dilsey came in and sent Ben and Luster on to the kitchen and said supper was ready.

"All right," I says. She went out. I sat there, reading the paper. After a while I heard Dilsey looking in at the door.

"Whyn't you come on and eat?" she says.

"I'm waiting for supper," I says.

"Hit's on the table," she says. "I done told you."

"Is it?" I says. "Excuse me. I didn't hear anybody come down."

"They aint comin," she says. "You come on and eat, so I can take something up to them."

"Are they sick?" I says. "What did the doctor say it was? Not Smallpox, I hope."

"Come on here, Jason," she says, "So I kin git done."

"All right," I says, raising the paper again. "I'm waiting for supper now."

I could feel her watching me at the door. I read the paper.

"Whut you want to ack like this fer?" she says. "When you knows how much bother I has anyway."

"If Mother is any sicker than she was when she came down to dinner, all right," I says. "But as long as I am buying food for people younger than I am, they'll have to come down to the table to eat it. Let me know when supper's ready," I says, reading the paper again. I heard her climbing the stairs, dragging her feet and grunting and groaning like they were straight up and three feet apart. I heard her at Mother's door, then I heard her calling Quentin, like the door was locked, then she went back to Mother's room and then Mother went and talked to Quentin. Then they came down stairs. I read the paper.

Dilsey came back to the door. "Come on," she says, "fo you kin think up some mo devilment. You just tryin yoself tonight."

I went to the diningroom. Quentin was sitting with her head bent. She had painted her face again. Her nose looked like a porcelain insulator.

"I'm glad you feel well enough to come down," I says to Mother.

"It's little enough I can do for you, to come to the table," she says. "No matter how I feel. I realise that when a man works all day he likes to be surrounded by his family at the supper table. I want to please you. I only wish you and Quentin got along better. It would be easier for me."

"We get along all right," I says. "I dont mind her staying locked up in her room all day if she wants to. But I cant have all this whoop-de-do and sulking at mealtimes. I know that's a lot to ask her, but I'm that way in my own house. Your house, I meant to say."

"It's yours," Mother says, "You are the head of it now."

Quentin hadn't looked up. I helped the plates and she begun to eat.

"Did you get a good piece of meat?" I says. "If you didn't, I'll try to find you a better one."

She didn't say anything.

"I say, did you get a good piece of meat?" I says.

"What?" she says. "Yes. It's all right."

"Will you have some more rice?" I says.

"No," she says.

"Better let me give you some more," I says.

"I dont want any more," she says.

"Not at all," I says, "You're welcome."

"Is your headache gone?" Mother says.

"Headache?" I says.

"I was afraid you were developing one," she says. "When you came in this afternoon."

"Oh," I says. "No, it didn't show up. We stayed so busy this afternoon I forgot about it."

"Was that why you were late?" Mother says. I could see Quentin listening. I looked at her. Her knife and fork were still going, but I caught her looking at me, then she looked at her plate again. I says,

"No. I loaned my car to a fellow about three o'clock and I had to wait until he got back with it." I ate for a while.

"Who was it?" Mother says.

"It was one of those show men," I says. "It seems his sister's husband was out riding with some town woman, and he was chasing them."

Quentin sat perfectly still, chewing.

"You ought not to lend your car to people like that," Mother says. "You are too generous with it. That's why I never call on you for it if I can help it."

"I was beginning to think that myself, for awhile," I says. "But he got back, all right. He says he found what he was looking for."

"Who was the woman?" Mother says.

"I'll tell you later," I says. "I dont like to talk about such things before Quentin."

Quentin had quit eating. Every once in a while she'd take a

drink of water, then she'd sit there crumbling a biscuit up, her face bent over her plate.

"Yes," Mother says, "I suppose women who stay shut up like I do have no idea what goes on in this town."

"Yes," I says, "They dont."

"My life has been so different from that," Mother says. "Thank God I dont know about such wickedness. I dont even want to know about it. I'm not like most people."

I didn't say any more. Quentin sat there, crumbling the biscuit until I quit eating, then she says,

"Can I go now?" without looking at anybody.

"What?" I says. "Sure, you can go. Were you waiting on us?"

She looked at me. She had crumbled all the biscuit, but her hands still went on like they were crumbling it yet and her eyes looked like they were cornered or something and then she started biting her mouth like it ought to have poisoned her, with all that red lead.

"Grandmother," she says, "Grandmother—"

"Did you want something else to eat?" I says.

"Why does he treat me like this, Grandmother?" she says. "I never hurt him."

"I want you all to get along with one another," Mother says, "You are all that's left now, and I do want you all to get along better."

"It's his fault," she says, "He wont let me alone, and I have to. If he doesn't want me here, why wont he let me go back to—"

"That's enough," I says, "Not another word."

"Then why wont he let me alone?" she says. "He—he just—"

"He is the nearest thing to a father you've ever had," Mother says. "It's his bread you and I eat. It's only right that he should expect obedience from you."

"It's his fault," she says. She jumped up. "He makes me do it. If he would just—" she looked at us, her eyes cornered, kind of jerking her arms against her sides.

"If I would just what?" I says.

"Whatever I do, it's your fault," she says. "If I'm bad, it's because I had to be. You made me. I wish I was dead. I wish we were all dead." Then she ran. We heard her run up the stairs. Then a door slammed.

"That's the first sensible thing she ever said," I says.

"She didn't go to school today," Mother says.

"How do you know?" I says. "Were you down town?"

"I just know," she says. "I wish you could be kinder to her."

"If I did that I'd have to arrange to see her more than once a day," I says. "You'll have to make her come to the table every meal. Then I could give her an extra piece of meat every time."

"There are little things you could do," she says.

"Like not paying any attention when you ask me to see that she goes to school?" I says.

"She didn't go to school today," she says. "I just know she didn't. She says she went for a car ride with one of the boys this afternoon and you followed her."

"How could I," I says, "When somebody had my car all afternoon? Whether or not she was in school today is already past," I says, "If you've got to worry about it, worry about next Monday."

"I wanted you and she to get along with one another," she says. "But she has inherited all of the headstrong traits. Quentin's too. I thought at the time, with the heritage she would already have, to give her that name, too. Sometimes I think she is the judgment of Caddy and Quentin upon me."

"Good Lord," I says, "You've got a fine mind. No wonder you kept yourself sick all the time."

"What?" she says. "I dont understand."

"I hope not," I says. "A good woman misses a lot she's better off without knowing."

"They were both that way," she says, "They would make interest with your father against me when I tried to correct them. He was always saying they didn't need controlling, that they already knew what cleanliness and honesty were, which was all that anyone could hope to be taught. And now I hope he's satisfied."

"You've got Ben to depend on," I says, "Cheer up."

"They deliberately shut me out of their lives," she says, "It was always her and Quentin. They were always conspiring against me. Against you too, though you were too young to realise it. They always looked on you and me as outsiders, like they did your Uncle Maury. I always told your father that they were allowed too much freedom, to be together too much. When Quentin started to school we had to let her go the next year, so she could be with him. She couldn't bear for any of you to do anything she couldn't. It was vanity in her, vanity and false pride. And then when her troubles began I knew that Quentin would feel that he had to do something just as bad. But I didn't believe that he would have been so selfish as to—I didn't dream that he—"

"Maybe he knew it was going to be a girl," I says, "And that one more of them would be more than he could stand."

"He could have controlled her," she says. "He seemed to be the only person she had any consideration for. But that is a part of the judgment too, I suppose."

"Yes," I says, "Too bad it wasn't me instead of him. You'd be a lot better off."

"You say things like that to hurt me," she says. "I deserve it though. When they began to sell the land to send Quentin to Harvard I told your father that he must make an equal provision for you. Then when Herbert offered to take you into the bank I said, Jason is provided for now, and when all the expense began to pile up and I was forced to sell our furniture and the rest of the pasture, I wrote her at once because I said she will realise that she and Quentin have had their share and part of Jason's too and that it depends on her now to compensate him. I said she will do that out of respect for her father. I believed that, then. But I'm just a poor old woman; I was raised to believe that people would deny themselves for their own flesh and blood. It's my fault. You were right to reproach me."

"Do you think I need any man's help to stand on my feet?" I says, "Let alone a woman that cant name the father of her own child."

"Jason," she says.

"All right," I says. "I didn't mean that. Of course not."

"If I believed that were possible, after all my suffering."

"Of course it's not," I says. "I didn't mean it."

"I hope that at least is spared me," she says.

"Sure it is," I says, "She's too much like both of them to doubt that."

"I couldn't bear that," she says.

"Then quit thinking about it," I says. "Has she been worrying you any more about getting out at night?"

"No. I made her realise that it was for her own good and that she'd thank me for it some day. She takes her books with her and studies after I lock the door. I see the light on as late as eleven oclock some nights."

"How do you know she's studying?" I says.

"I don't know what else she'd do in there alone," she says. "She never did read any."

"No," I says, "You wouldn't know. And you can thank your stars for that," I says. Only what would be the use in saying it aloud. It would just have her crying on me again.

I heard her go up stairs. Then she called Quentin and Quentin says What? through the door. "Goodnight," Mother says. Then I heard the key in the lock, and Mother went back to her room.

When I finished my cigar and went up, the light was still on. I could see the empty keyhole, but I couldn't hear a sound. She studied quiet. Maybe she learned that in school. I told Mother goodnight and went on to my room and got the box out and counted it again. I could hear the Great American Gelding snoring away like a planing mill. I read somewhere they'd fix men that way to give them women's voices. But maybe he didn't know what they'd done to him. I dont reckon he even knew what he had been trying to do, or why Mr Burgess knocked him out with the fence picket. And if they'd just sent him on to Jackson while he was under the ether, he'd never have known the difference. But that would have been too simple for a Compson to think of. Not half complex enough. Having to wait to do it at all until he broke out and tried to run a little girl down on the street with her own father looking at him. Well, like I say they never started soon enough with their cutting, and they quit too quick. I know at least two more that needed something like that, and one of them not over a mile away, either. But then I dont reckon even that would do any good. Like I say once a bitch always a bitch. And just let me have twenty-four hours without any damn New York jew to advise me what it's going to do. I dont want to make a killing; save that to suck in the smart gamblers with. I just want an even chance to get my money back. And once I've done that they can bring all Beale Street and all bedlam in here and two of them can sleep in my bed and another one can have my place at the table too.

APRIL 8, 1928

The day dawned bleak and chill. A moving wall of grey light out of the northeast which, instead of dissolving into moisture, seemed to disintegrate into minute and venomous particles, like dust that, when Dilsey opened the door of the cabin and emerged,

needled laterally into her flesh, precipitating not so much a moisture as a substance partaking of the quality of thin, not quite con-
gealed oil. She wore a stiff black straw hat perched upon her turban,
and a maroon velvet cape with a border of mangy and anonymous
fur above a dress of purple silk, and she stood in the door for awhile
with her myriad and sunken face lifted to the weather, and one
gaunt hand flac-soled as the belly of a fish, then she moved the cape
aside and examined the bosom of her gown.

The gown fell gauntly from her shoulders, across her fallen
breasts, then tightened upon her paunch and fell again, ballooning
a little above the nether garments which she would remove layer
by layer as the spring accomplished and the warm days, in colour
regal and moribund. She had been a big woman once but now her
skeleton rose, draped loosely in unpadded skin that tightened again
upon a paunch almost dropsical, as though muscle and tissue had
been courage or fortitude which the days or the years had consumed
until only the indomitable skeleton was left rising like a ruin or a
landmark above the somnolent and impervious guts, and above that
the collapsed face that gave the impression of the bones themselves being outside the flesh, lifted into the driving day with an
expression at once fatalistic and of a child's astonished disappointment, until she turned and entered the house again and closed the
door.

The earth immediately about the door was bare. It had a patina,
as though from the soles of bare feet in generations, like old silver
or the walls of Mexican houses which have been plastered by hand.
Beside the house, shading it in summer, stood three mulberry trees,
the fledged leaves that would later be broad and placid as the palms
of hands streaming flatly undulant upon the driving air. A pair of
jaybirds came up from nowhere, whirled up on the blast like gaudy
scraps of cloth or paper and lodged in the mulberries, where they
swung in raucous tilt and recover, screaming into the wind that
ripped their harsh cries onward and away like scraps of paper or
of cloth in turn. Then three more joined them and they swung and
tilted in the wrung branches for a time, screaming. The door of
the cabin opened and Dilsey emerged once more, this time in a
man's felt hat and an army overcoat, beneath the frayed skirts of
which her blue gingham dress fell in uneven balloonings, streaming
too about her as she crossed the yard and mounted the steps to the
kitchen door.

A moment later she emerged. carrying an open umbrella now, which she slanted ahead into the wind, and crossed to the woodpile and laid the umbrella down, still open. Immediately she caught at it and arrested it and held to it for a while, looking about her. Then she closed it and laid it down and stacked stovewood into her crooked arm, against her breast, and picked up the umbrella and got it open at last and returned to the steps and held the wood precariously balanced while she contrived to close the umbrella, which she propped in the corner just within the door. She dumped the wood into the box behind the stove. Then she removed the overcoat and hat and took a soiled apron down from the wall and put it on and built a fire in the stove. While she was doing so, rattling the grate bars and clattering the lids, Mrs Compson began to call her from the head of the stairs.

She wore a dressing gown of quilted black satin, holding it close under her chin. In the other hand she held a red rubber hot water bottle and she stood at the head of the back stairway, calling "Dilsey" at steady and inflectionless intervals into the quiet stairwell that descended into complete darkness, then opened again where a grey window fell across it. "Dilsey," she called, without inflection or emphasis or haste, as though she were not listening for a reply at all. "Dilsey."

Dilsey answered and ceased clattering the stove, but before she could cross the kitchen Mrs Compson called her again, and before she crossed the diningroom and brought her head into relief against the grey splash of the window, still again.

"All right," Dilsey said, "All right, here I is. I'll fill hit soon ez I git some hot water." She gathered up her skirts and mounted the stairs, wholly blotting the grey light. "Put hit down dar en g'awn back to bed."

"I couldn't understand what was the matter," Mrs Compson said. "I've been lying awake for an hour at least, without hearing a sound from the kitchen."

"You put hit down and g'awn back to bed," Dilsey said. She toiled painfully up the steps, shapeless, breathing heavily. "I'll have de fire gwine in a minute, en de water hot in two mo."

"I've been lying there for an hour, at least," Mrs Compson said. "I thought maybe you were waiting for me to come down and start the fire."

Dilsey reached the top of the stairs and took the water bottle. "I'll fix hit in a minute," she said. "Luster oversep dis mawnin, up half de night at dat show. I gwine build de fire myself. Go on now, so you wont wake de others twell I ready."

"If you permit Luster to do things that interfere with his work, you'll have to suffer for it yourself," Mrs Compson said. "Jason wont like this if he hears about it. You know he wont."

"Twusn't none of Jason's money he went on," Dilsey said. "Dat's one thing sho." She went on down the stairs. Mrs Compson returned to her room. As she got into bed again she could hear Dilsey yet descending the stairs with a sort of painful and terrific slowness that would have become maddening had it not presently ceased beyond the flapping diminishment of the pantry door.

She entered the kitchen and built up the fire and began to prepare breakfast. In the midst of this she ceased and went to the window and looked out toward her cabin, then she went to the door and opened it and shouted into the driving weather.

"Luster!" she shouted, standing to listen, tilting her face from the wind, "You, Luster?" She listened, then as she prepared to shout again Luster appeared around the corner of the kitchen.

"Ma'am?" he said innocently, so innocently that Dilsey looked down at him, for a moment motionless with something more than mere surprise.

"Whar you at?" she said.

"Nowhere," he said. "Jes in de cellar."

"Whut you doin in de cellar?" she said. "Dont stand dar in de rain, fool," she said.

"Aint doin nothin," he said. He came up the steps.

"Dont you dare come in dis do widout a armful of wood," she said. "Here I done had to tote yo wood en build yo fire bofe. Didn't I tole you not to leave dis place last night befo dat woodbox wus full to de top?"

"I did," Luster said, "I filled hit."

"Whar hit gone to, den?"

"I dont know'm. I aint teched hit."

"Well, you git hit full up now," she said. "And git on up den en see bout Benjy."

She shut the door. Luster went to the woodpile. The five jaybirds whirled over the house, screaming, and into the mulberries again. He watched them. He picked up a rock and threw it. "Whoo," he said, "Git on back to hell, whar you belong at. 'Taint Monday yit."

He loaded himself mountainously with stovewood. He could not see over it, and he staggered to the steps and up them and blundered crashing against the door, shedding billets. Then Dilsey came and opened the door for him and he blundered across the kitchen. "You, Luster!" she shouted, but he had already hurled the wood into the box with a thunderous crash. "H'h!" he said.

"Is you tryin to wake up de whole house?" Dilsey said. She hit him on the back of his head with the flat of her hand. "Go on up dar and git Benjy dressed, now."

"Yessum," he said. He went toward the outer door.

"Whar you gwine?" Dilsey said.

"I thought I better go round de house en in by de front, so I wont wake up Miss Cahline en dem."

"You go on up dem backstairs like I tole you en git Benjy's clothes on him," Dilsey said. "Go on, now."

"Yessum," Luster said. He returned and left by the diningroom door. After awhile it ceased to flap. Dilsey prepared to make biscuit. As she ground the sifter steadily above the breadboard, she sang, to herself at first, something without particular tune or words, repetitive, mournful and plaintive, austere, as she ground a faint, steady snowing of flour onto the breadboard. The stove had begun to heat the room and to fill it with murmurous minors of the fire, and presently she was singing louder, as if her voice too had been thawed out by the growing warmth, and then Mrs Compson called her name again from within the house. Dilsey raised her face as if her eyes could and did penetrate the walls and ceiling and saw the old woman in her quilted dressing gown at the head of the stairs, calling her name with machinelike regularity.

"Oh, Lawd," Dilsey said. She set the sifter down and swept up the hem of her apron and wiped her hands and caught up the bottle from the chair on which she had laid it and gathered her apron about the handle of the kettle which was now jetting faintly. "Jes a minute," she called, "De water jes dis minute got hot."

It was not the bottle which Mrs Compson wanted, however, and clutching it by the neck like a dead hen Dilsey went to the foot of the stairs and looked upward.

"Aint Luster up dar wid him?" she said.

"Luster hasn't been in the house. I've been lying here listening for him. I knew he would be late, but I did hope he'd come in time to keep Benjamin from disturbing Jason on Jason's one day in the week to sleep in the morning."

"I dont see how you expect anybody to sleep, wid you standin in de hall, holl'in at folks fum de crack of dawn," Dilsey said. She began to mount the stairs, toiling heavily. "I sont dat boy up dar half hour ago."

Mrs Compson watched her, holding the dressing gown under her chin. "What are you going to do?" she said.

"Gwine git Benjy dressed en bring him down to de kitchen, whar he wont wake Jason en Quentin," Dilsey said.

"Haven't you started breakfast yet?"

"I'll tend to dat too," Dilsey said. "You better git back in bed twell Luster make yo fire. Hit cold dis mawnin."

"I know it," Mrs Compson said. "My feet are like ice. They were so cold they waked me up." She watched Dilsey mount the stairs. It took her a long while. "You know how it frets Jason when breakfast is late," Mrs Compson said.

"I cant do but one thing at a time," Dilsey said. "You git on back to bed, fo I has you on my hands dis mawnin too."

"If you're going to drop everything to dress Benjamin, I'd better come down and get breakfast. You know as well as I do how Jason acts when it's late."

"En who gwine eat yo messin?" Dilsey said. "Tell me dat. Go on now," she said, toiling upward. Mrs Compson stood watching her as she mounted, steadying herself against the wall with one hand, holding her skirts up with the other.

"Are you going to wake him up just to dress him?" she said.

Dilsey stopped. With her foot lifted to the next step she stood there, her hand against the wall and the grey splash of the window behind her, motionless and shapeless she loomed.

"He aint awake den?" she said.

"He wasn't when I looked in," Mrs Compson said. "But it's past his time. He never does sleep after half past seven. You know he doesn't."

Dilsey said nothing. She made no further move, but though she could not see her save as a blobby shape without depth, Mrs Compson knew that she had lowered her face a little and that she stood now like a cow in the rain, as she held the empty water bottle by its neck.

"You're not the one who has to bear it," Mrs Compson said. "It's not your responsibility. You can go away. You dont have to bear the brunt of it day in and day out. You owe nothing to them, to Mr Compson's memory. I know you have never had any tenderness for Jason. You've never tried to conceal it."

Dilsey said nothing. She turned slowly and descended, lowering her body from step to step, as a small child does, her hand against the wall. "You go on and let him alone," she said. "Dont go in dar no mo, now. I'll send Luster up soon as I find him. Let him alone, now."

She returned to the kitchen. She looked into the stove, then she drew her apron over her head and donned the overcoat and opened the outer door and looked up and down the yard. The weather drove upon her flesh, harsh and minute, but the scene was empty of all else that moved. She descended the steps, gingerly, as if for silence, and went around the corner of the kitchen. As she did so Luster emerged quickly and innocently from the cellar door.

Dilsey stopped. "Whut you up to?" she said.

"Nothin," Luster said, "Mr Jason say fer me to find out what dat water leak in de cellar fum."

"En when wus hit he say fer you to do dat?" Dilsey said. "Last New Year's day, wasn't hit?"

"I thought I jes be lookin whiles dey sleep," Luster said. Dilsey went to the cellar door. He stood aside and she peered down into the obscurity odorous of dank earth and mould and rubber.

"Huh," Dilsey said. She looked at Luster again. He met her gaze blandly, innocent and open. "I dont know whut you up to, but you aint got no business doin hit. You jes tryin me too dis mawnin cause de others is, aint you? You git on up dar en see to Benjy, you hear?"

"Yessum," Luster said. He went on toward the kitchen steps, swiftly.

"Here," Dilsey said, "You git me another armful of wood while I got you."

"Yessum," he said. He passed her on the steps and went to the woodpile. When he blundered again at the door a moment later, again invisible and blind within and beyond his wooden avatar,

Dilsey opened the door and guided him across the kitchen with a firm hand.

"Jes thow hit at dat box again," she said, "Jes thow hit."

"I got to," Luster said, panting, "I cant put hit down no other way."

"Den you stand dar en hold hit a while," Dilsey said. She unloaded him a stick at a time. "Whut got into you dis mawnin? Here I sont you fer wood en you aint never brought mo'n six sticks at a time to save yo life twell today. Whut you fixin to ax me kin you do now? Aint dat show lef town yit?"

"Yessum. Hit done gone."

She put the last stick into the box. "Now you go on up dar wid Benjy, like I tole you befo," she said. "And I dont want nobody else yellin down dem stairs at me twell I rings de bell. You hear me."

"Yessum," Luster said. He vanished through the swing door. Dilsey put some more wood in the stove and returned to the breadboard. Presently she began to sing again.

The room grew warmer. Soon Dilsey's skin had taken on a rich, lustrous quality as compared with that as of a faint dusting of wood ashes which both it and Luster's had worn, as she moved about the kitchen, gathering about her the raw materials of food, coordinating the meal. On the wall above a cupboard, invisible save at night, by lamp light and even then evincing an enigmatic profundity because it had but one hand, a cabinet clock ticked, then with a preliminary sound as if it had cleared its throat, struck five times.

"Eight oclock," Dilsey said. She ceased and tilted her head upward, listening. But there was no sound save the clock and the fire. She opened the oven and looked at the pan of bread, then stooping she paused while someone descended the stairs. She heard the feet cross the diningroom, then the swing door opened and Luster entered, followed by a big man who appeared to have been shaped of some substance whose particles would not or did not cohere to one another or to the frame which supported it. His skin was dead looking and hairless; dropsical too, he moved with a shambling gait like a trained bear. His hair was pale and fine. It had been brushed smoothly down upon his brow like that of children in daguerreotypes. His eyes were clear, of the pale sweet blue of cornflowers, his thick mouth hung open, drooling a little.

"Is he cold?" Dilsey said. She wiped her hands on her apron and touched his hand.

"Ef he aint, I is," Luster said. "Always cold Easter. Aint never seen hit fail. Miss Cahline say ef you aint got time to fix her hot water bottle to never mind about hit."

"Oh, Lawd," Dilsey said. She drew a chair into the corner between the woodbox and the stove. The man went obediently and sat in it. "Look in de dinin room and see whar I laid dat bottle down," Dilsey said. Luster fetched the bottle from the diningroom and Dilsey filled it and gave it to him. "Hurry up, now," she said. "See ef Jason wake now. Tell em hit's all ready."

Luster went out. Ben sat beside the stove. He sat loosely, utterly motionless save for his head, which made a continual bobbing sort of movement as he watched Dilsey with his sweet vague gaze as she moved about. Luster returned.

"He up," he said, "Miss Cahline say put hit on de table." He came to the stove and spread his hands palm down above the firebox. "He up, too," He said, "Gwine hit wid bofe feet dis mawnin."

"Whut's de matter now?" Dilsey said. "Git away fum dar. How kin I do anything wid you standin over de stove?"

"I cold," Luster said.

"You ought to thought about dat whiles you wus down dar in dat cellar," Dilsey said. "Whut de matter wid Jason?"

"Sayin me en Benjy broke dat winder in his room."

"Is dey one broke?" Dilsey said.

"Dat's whut he sayin," Luster said. "Say I broke hit."

"How could you, when he keep hit locked all day en night?"

"Say I broke hit chunkin rocks at hit," Luster said.

"En did you?"

"Nome," Luster said.

"Dont lie to me, boy," Dilsey said.

"I never done hit," Luster said. "Ask Benjy ef I did. I aint stud'in dat winder."

"Who could a broke hit, den?" Dilsey said. "He jes tryin hisself, to wake Quentin up," she said, taking the pan of biscuits out of the stove.

"Reckin so," Luster said. "Dese is funny folks. Glad I aint none of em."

"Aint none of who?" Dilsey said. "Lemme tell you somethin, nigger boy, you got jes es much Compson devilment in you es any of em. Is you right sho you never broke dat window?"

"Whut I want to break hit fur?"

"Whut you do any of you devilment fur?" Dilsey said. "Watch him now, so he cant burn his hand again twell I git de table set."

She went to the diningroom, where they heard her moving about, then she returned and set a plate at the kitchen table and set food there. Ben watched her, slobbering, making a faint, eager sound.

"All right, honey," she said, "Here yo breakfast. Bring his chair, Luster." Luster moved the chair up and Ben sat down, whimpering and slobbering. Dilsey tied a cloth about his neck and wiped his mouth with the end of it. "And see kin you kep fum messin up his clothes one time," she said, handing Luster a spoon.

Ben ceased whimpering. He watched the spoon as it rose to his mouth. It was as if even eagerness were muscle-bound in him too, and hunger itself inarticulate, not knowing it is hunger. Luster fed him with skill and detachment. Now and then his attention would return long enough to enable him to feint the spoon and cause Ben to close his mouth upon the empty air, but it was apparent that Luster's mind was elsewhere. His other hand lay on the back of the chair and upon that dead surface it moved tentatively, delicately, as if he were picking an inaudible tune out of the dead void, and once he even forgot to tease Ben with the spoon while his fingers teased out of the slain wood a soundless and involved arpeggio until Ben recalled him by whimpering again.

In the diningroom Dilsey moved back and forth. Presently she rang a small clear bell, then in the kitchen Luster heard Mrs Compson and Jason descending, and Jason's voice, and he rolled his eyes whitely with listening.

"Sure, I know they didn't break it," Jason said. "Sure, I know that. Maybe the change of weather broke it."

"I dont see how it could have," Mrs Compson said. "Your room stays locked all day long, just as you leave it when you go to town. None of us ever go in there except Sunday, to clean it. I dont want you to think that I would go where I'm not wanted, or that I would permit anyone else to."

"I never said you broke it, did I?" Jason said.

"I dont want to go in your room," Mrs Compson said. "I respect anybody's private affairs. I wouldn't put my foot over the threshold, even if I had a key."

"Yes," Jason said, "I know your keys wont fit. That's why I had the lock changed. What I want to know is, how that window got broken."

"Luster say he didn't do hit," Dilsey said.

"I knew that without asking him," Jason said. "Where's Quentin?" he said.

"Where she is ev'y Sunday mawnin," Dilsey said. "Whut got into you de last few days, anyhow?"

"Well, we're going to change all that," Jason said. "Go up and tell her breakfast is ready."

"You leave her alone now, Jason," Dilsey said. "She gits up fer breakfast ev'y week mawnin, en Cahline lets her stay in bed ev'y Sunday. You knows dat."

"I cant keep a kitchen full of niggers to wait on her pleasure, much as I'd like to," Jason said. "Go and tell her to come down to breakfast."

"Aint nobody have to wait on her," Dilsey said. "I puts her breakfast in de warmer en she—"

"Did you hear me?" Jason said.

"I hears you," Dilsey said. "All I been hearin, when you in de house. Ef hit aint Quentin er yo maw, hit's Luster en Benjy. Whut you let him go on dat way fer, Miss Cahline?"

"You'd better do as he says," Mrs Compson said, "He's head of the house now. It's his right to require us to respect his wishes. I try to do it, and if I can, you can too."

"Taint no sense in him bein so bad tempered he got to make Quentin git up jes to suit him," Dilsey said. "Maybe you think she broke dat window."

"She would, if she happened to think of it," Jason said. "You go and do what I told you."

"En I wouldn't blame her none ef she did," Dilsey said, going toward the stairs. "Wid you naggin at her all de blessed time yo in de house."

"Hush, Dilsey," Mrs Compson said, "It's neither your place nor mine to tell Jason what to do. Sometimes I think he is wrong, but I try to obey his wishes for you alls' sakes. If I'm strong enough to come to the table, Quentin can too."

Dilsey went out. They heard her mounting the stairs. They heard her a long while on the stairs.

"You've got a prize set of servants," Jason said. He helped his mother and himself to food. "Did you ever have one that was worth killing? You must have had some before I was big enough to remember."

"I have to humour them," Mrs Compson said. "I have to depend on them so completely. It's not as if I were strong. I wish I were. I wish I could do all the house work myself. I could at least take that much off your shoulders."

"And a fine pigsty we'd live in, too," Jason said. "Hurry up, Dilsey," he shouted.

"I know you blame me," Mrs Compson said, "for letting them off to go to church today."

"Go where?" Jason said. "Hasn't that damn show left yet?"

"To church," Mrs Compson said. "The darkies are having a special Easter service. I promised Dilsey two weeks ago that they could get off."

"Which means we'll eat cold dinner," Jason said, "or none at all."

"I know it's my fault," Mrs Compson said. "I know you blame me."

"For what?" Jason said. "You never resurrected Christ, did you?"

They heard Dilsey mount the final stair, then her slow feet overhead.

"Quentin," she said. When she called the first time Jason laid his knife and fork down and he and his mother appeared to wait across the table from one another, in identical attitudes; the one cold and shrewd, with close-thatched brown hair curled into two stubborn hooks, one on either side of his forehead like a bartender in caricature, and hazel eyes with black-ringed irises like marbles, the other cold and querulous, with perfectly white hair and eyes pouched and baffled and so dark as to appear to be all pupil or all iris.

"Quentin," Dilsey said, "Git up, honey. Dey waitin breakfast on you."

"I cant understand how that window got broken," Mrs Compson said. "Are you sure it was done yesterday? It could have been like that a long time, with the warm weather. The upper sash, behind the shade like that."

"I've told you for the last time that it happened yesterday," Jason said. "Dont you reckon I know the room I live in? Do you reckon I could have lived in it a week with a hole in the window you could stick your hand—" his voice ceased, ebbed, left him staring at his mother with eyes that for an instant were quite empty of anything. It was as though his eyes were holding their breath, while his mother looked at him, her face flaccid and querulous, interminable, clairvoyant yet obtuse. As they sat so Dilsey said,

"Quentin. Dont play wid me, honey. Come on to breakfast, honey. Dey waitin fer you."

"I cant understand it," Mrs Compson said, "It's just as if somebody had tried to break into the house—" Jason sprang up. His chair crashed over backward. "What—" Mrs Compson said, staring at him as he ran past her and went jumping up the stairs, where he met Dilsey. His face was now in shadow, and Dilsey said,

"She sullin. Yo ma aint unlocked—" But Jason ran on past her and along the corridor to a door. He didn't call. He grasped the knob and tried it, then he stood with the knob in his hand and his head bent a little, as if he were listening to something much further away than the dimensioned room beyond the door, and which he already heard. His attitude was that of one who goes through the motions of listening in order to deceive himself as to what he already hears. Behind him Mrs Compson mounted the stairs, calling his name. Then she saw Dilsey and she quit calling him and began to call Dilsey instead.

"I told you she aint unlocked dat do' yit," Dilsey said.

When she spoke he turned and ran toward her, but his voice was quiet, matter of fact. "She carry the key with her?" he said. "Has she got it now, I mean, or will she have—"

"Dilsey," Mrs Compson said on the stairs.

"Is which?" Dilsey said. "Whyn't you let—"

"The key," Jason said, "To that room. Does she carry it with her all the time. Mother." Then he saw Mrs Compson and he went down the stairs and met her. "Give me the key," he said. He fell to pawing at the pockets of the rusty black dressing sacque she wore. She resisted.

"Jason," she said, "Jason! Are you and Dilsey trying to put me to bed again?" she said, trying to fend him off, "Cant you even let me have Sunday in peace?"

"The key," Jason said, pawing at her, "Give it here." He looked back at the door, as if he expected it to fly open before he could get back to it with the key he did not have.

"You, Dilsey!" Mrs Compson said, clutching her sacque about her.

"Give me the key, you old fool!" Jason cried suddenly. From her pocket he tugged a huge bunch of rusted keys on an iron ring like a mediaeval jailer's and ran back up the hall with the two women behind him.

"You, Jason!" Mrs Compson said. "He will never find the right one," she said, "You know I never let anyone take my keys, Dilsey," she said. She began to wail.

"Hush," Dilsey said, "He aint gwine do nothin to her. I aint gwine let him."

"But on Sunday morning, in my own house," Mrs Compson said, "When I've tried so hard to raise them Christians. Let me find the right key, Jason," she said. She put her hand on his arm. Then she began to struggle with him, but he flung her aside with a motion of his elbow and looked around at her for a moment, his eyes cold and harried, then he turned to the door again and the unwieldy keys.

"Hush," Dilsey said, "You, Jason!"

"Something terrible has happened," Mrs Compson said, wailing again, "I know it has. You, Jason," she said, grasping at him again. "He wont even let me find the key to a room in my own house!"

"Now, now," Dilsey said, "Whut kin happen? I right here. I aint gwine let him hurt her. Quentin," she said, raising her voice, "Dont you be skeered, honey, I'se right here."

The door opened, swung inward. He stood in it for a moment, hiding the room, then he stepped aside. "Go in," he said in a thick, light voice. They went in. It was not a girl's room. It was not anybody's room, and the faint scent of cheap cosmetics and the few feminine objects and other evidences of crude and hopeless efforts to feminize it but added to its anonymity, giving it that dead and stereotyped transience of rooms in assignation houses. The bed had not been disturbed. On the floor lay a soiled undergarment of cheap silk a little too pink; from a half open bureau drawer dangled a single stocking. The window was open. A pear tree grew there, close against the house. It was in bloom and the branches scraped and rasped against the house and the myriad air, driving in the window, brought into the room the forlorn scent of the blossoms.

"Dar now," Dilsey said, "Didn't I told you she all right?"

"All right?" Mrs Compson said. Dilsey followed her into the room and touched her.

"You come on and lay down, now," she said. "I find her in ten minutes."

Mrs Compson shook her off. "Find the note," she said. "Quentin left a note when he did it."

"All right," Dilsey said, "I'll find hit. You come on to yo room, now."

"I knew the minute they named her Quentin this would happen," Mrs Compson said. She went to the bureau and began to turn over the scattered objects there—scent bottles, a box of powder, a chewed pencil, a pair of scissors with one broken blade lying upon a darned scarf dusted with powder and stained with rouge. "Find the note," she said.

"I is," Dilsey said. "You come on, now. Me and Jason'll find hit. You come on to yo room."

"Jason," Mrs Compson said, "Where is he?" She went to the door. Dilsey followed her on down the hall, to another door. It was closed. "Jason," she called through the door. There was no answer. She tried the knob, then she called him again. But there was still no answer, for he was hurling things backward out of the closet: garments, shoes, a suitcase. Then he emerged carrying a sawn section of tongue-and-groove planking and laid it down and entered the closet again and emerged with a metal box. He set it on the bed and stood looking at the broken lock while he dug a key ring from his pocket and selected a key, and for a time longer he stood with the selected key in his hand, looking at the broken lock, then he put the keys back in his pocket and carefully tilted the contents of the box out upon the bed. Still carefully he sorted the papers, taking them up one at a time and shaking them. Then he upended the box and shook it too and slowly replaced the papers and stood again, looking at the broken lock, with the box in his hands and his head bent. Outside the window he heard some jaybirds swirl shrieking past, and away, their cries whipping away along the wind, and an automobile passed somewhere and died away also. His mother spoke his name again beyond the door, but he didn't move. He heard Dilsey lead her away up the hall, and then a door closed. Then he replaced the box in the closet and flung the garments back into it and went down stairs to the telephone. While he stood there with the receiver to his ear, waiting, Dilsey came down the stairs. She looked at him, without stopping, and went on.

The wire opened. "This is Jason Compson," he said, his voice so harsh and thick that he had to repeat himself. "Jason Compson," he said, controlling his voice. "Have a car ready, with a deputy, if you cant go, in ten minutes. I'll be there—What?—Robbery. My house.

I know who it—Robbery, I say. Have a car ready—What? Aren't you a paid law enforcement—Yes, I'll be there in five minutes. Have that car ready to leave at once. If you dont, I'll report it to the governor."

He clapped the receiver back and crossed the diningroom, where the scarce-broken meal now lay cold on the table, and entered the kitchen. Dilsey was filling the hot water bottle. Ben sat, tranquil and empty. Beside him Luster looked like a fice dog, brightly watchful. He was eating something. Jason went on across the kitchen.

"Aint you going to eat no breakfast?" Dilsey said. He paid her no attention. "Go and eat yo breakfast, Jason." He went on. The outer door banged behind him. Luster rose and went to the window and looked out.

"Whoo," he said, "What happenin up dar? He been beatin' Miss Quentin?"

"You hush yo mouf," Dilsey said. "You git Benjy started now en I beat yo head off. You keep him quiet es you kin twell I get back, now." She screwed the cap on the bottle and went out. They heard her go up the stairs, then they heard Jason pass the house in his car. Then there was no sound in the kitchen save the simmering murmur of the kettle and the clock.

"You know whut I bet?" Luster said. "I bet he beat her. I bet he knock her in de head en now he gone fer de doctor. Dat's whut I bet." The clock tick-tocked, solemn and profound. It might have been the dry pulse of the decaying house itself; after a while it whirred and cleared its throat and struck six times. Ben looked up at it, then he looked at the bullet-like silhouette of Luster's head in the window and he begun to bob his head again, drooling. He whimpered.

"Hush up, loony," Luster said without turning. "Look like we aint gwine git to go to no church today." But Ben sat in the chair, his big soft hands dangling between his knees, moaning faintly. Suddenly he wept, a slow bellowing sound, meaningless and sustained. "Hush," Luster said. He turned and lifted his hand. "You want me to whup you?" But Ben looked at him, bellowing slowly with each expiration. Luster came and shook him. "You hush dis minute!" he shouted. "Here," he said. He hauled Ben out of the chair and dragged the chair around facing the stove and opened the door to the firebox and shoved Ben into the chair. They looked like a tug nudging at a clumsy tanker in a narrow dock. Ben sat down again facing the rosy door. He hushed. Then they heard the clock again, and Dilsey slow on the stairs. When she entered he began to whimper again. Then he lifted his voice.

"Whut you done to him?" Dilsey said. "Why cant you let him lone dis mawnin, of all times?"

"I aint doin nothin to him," Luster said. "Mr Jason skeered him, dat's whut hit is. He aint kilt Miss Quentin, is he?"

"Hush, Benjy," Dilsey said. He hushed. She went to the window and looked out. "Is it quit rainin?" she said.

"Yessum," Luster said. "Quit long time ago."

"Den ya'll go out do's a while," she said. "I jes got Miss Cahline quiet now."

"Is we gwine to church?" Luster said.

"I let you know bout dat when de time come. You keep him away fum de house twell I calls you."

"Kin we go to de pastuh?" Luster said.

"All right. Only you keep him away fum de house. I done stood all I kin."

"Yessum," Luster said. "Whar Mr Jason gone, mammy?"

"Dat's some mo of yo business, aint it?" Dilsey said. She began to clear the table. "Hush, Benjy. Luster gwine take you out to play."

"Whut he done to Miss Quentin, mammy?" Luster said.

"Aint done nothin to her. You all git on outen here."

"I bet she aint here," Luster said.

Dilsey looked at him. "How you know she aint here?"

"Me and Benjy seed her clamb out de window last night. Didn't us, Benjy?"

"You did?" Dilsey said, looking at him.

"We sees her doin hit ev'y night," Luster said, "Clamb right down dat pear tree."

"Dont you lie to me, nigger boy," Dilsey said.

"I aint lyin. Ask Benjy ef I is."

"Whyn't you say somethin about it, den?"

" 'Twarn't none o my business," Luster said. "I aint gwine git mixed up in white folks' business. Come on here, Benjy, les go out do's."

They went out. Dilsey stood for awhile at the table, then she went and cleared the breakfast things from the diningroom and ate her breakfast and cleaned up the kitchen. Then she removed her

apron and hung it up and went to the foot of the stairs and listened
for a moment. There was no sound. She donned the overcoat and
the hat and went across to her cabin.

The rain had stopped. The air now drove out of the southeast,
broken overhead into blue patches. Upon the crest of a hill beyond
the trees and roofs and spires of town sunlight lay like a pale scrap
of cloth, was blotted away. Upon the air a bell came, then as if at
a signal, other bells took up the sound and repeated it.

The cabin door opened and Dilsey emerged, again in the maroon
cape and the purple gown, and wearing soiled white elbow-length
gloves and minus her headcloth now. She came into the yard and
called Luster. She waited awhile, then she went to the house and
around it to the cellar door, moving close to the wall, and looked
into the door. Ben sat on the steps. Before him Luster squatted on
the damp floor. He held a saw in his left hand, the blade sprung a
little by pressure of his hand, and he was in the act of striking the
blade with the worn wooden mallet with which she had been making beaten biscuit for more than thirty years. The saw gave forth a
single sluggish twang that ceased with lifeless alacrity, leaving the
blade in a thin clean curve between Luster's hand and the floor.
Still, inscrutable, it bellied.

"Dat's de way he done hit," Luster said. "I jes aint foun de right
thing to hit it wid."

"Dat's whut you doin, is it?" Dilsey said. "Bring me dat mallet,"
she said.

"I aint hurt hit," Luster said.

"Bring hit here," Dilsey said. "Put dat saw whar you got hit
first."

He put the saw away and brought the mallet to her. Then Ben
wailed again, hopeless and prolonged. It was nothing. Just sound.
It might have been all time and injustice and sorrow become
vocal for an instant by a conjunction of planets.

"Listen at him," Luster said, "He been gwine on dat way ev'y
since you sont us outen de house. I dont know whut got in to him
dis mawnin."

"Bring him here," Dilsey said.

"Come on, Benjy," Luster said. He went back down the steps and
took Ben's arm. He came obediently, wailing, that slow hoarse
sound that ships make, that seems to begin before the sound itself
has started, seems to cease before the sound itself has stopped.

"Run and git his cap," Dilsey said. "Dont make no noise Miss Cahline kin hear. Hurry, now. We already late."

"She gwine hear him anyhow, ef you dont stop him." Luster said.

"He stop when we git off de place," Dilsey said. "He smellin hit. Dat's whut hit is."

"Smell whut, mammy?" Luster said.

"You go git dat cap," Dilsey said. Luster went on. They stood in the cellar door, Ben one step below her. The sky was broken now into scudding patches that dragged their swift shadows up out of the shabby garden, over the broken fence and across the yard. Dilsey stroked Ben's head, slowly and steadily, smoothing the bang upon his brow. He wailed quietly, unhurriedly. "Hush," Dilsey said, "Hush, now. We be gone in a minute. Hush, now." He wailed quietly and steadily.

Luster returned, wearing a stiff new straw hat with a coloured band and carrying a cloth cap. The hat seemed to isolate Luster's skull, in the beholder's eye as a spotlight would, in all its individual planes and angles. So peculiarly individual was its shape that at first glance the hat appeared to be on the head of someone standing immediately behind Luster. Dilsey looked at the hat.

"Whyn't you wear yo old hat?" she said.

"Couldn't find hit," Luster said.

"I bet you couldn't. I bet you fixed hit last night so you couldn't find hit. You fixin to ruin dat un."

"Aw, mammy," Luster said, "Hit aint gwine rain."

"How you know? You go git dat old hat en put dat new un away."

"Aw, mammy."

"Den you go git de umbreller."

"Aw, mammy."

"Take yo choice," Dilsey said. "Git yo old hat, er de umbreller. I dont keer which."

Luster went to the cabin. Ben wailed quietly.

"Come on," Dilsey said, "Dey kin ketch up wid us. We gwine to hear de singin." They went around the house, toward the gate. "Hush," Dilsey said from time to time as they went down the drive. They reached the gate. Dilsey opened it. Luster was coming down the drive behind them, carrying the umbrella. A woman was with him. "Here dey come," Dilsey said. They passed out the gate. "Now, den," she said. Ben ceased. Luster and his mother overtook them. Frony wore a dress of bright blue silk and a flowered hat. She was a thin woman, with a flat, pleasant face.

"You got six weeks' work right dar on yo back," Dilsey said. "Whut you gwine do ef hit rain?"

"Git wet, I reckon," Frony said. "I aint never stopped no rain yit."

"Mammy always talkin bout hit gwine rain," Luster said.

"Ef I dont worry bout y'all, I dont know who is," Dilsey said. "Come on, we already late."

"Rev'un Shegog gwine preach today," Frony said.

"Is?" Dilsey said. "Who him?"

"He fum Saint Looey," Frony said. "Dat big preacher."

"Huh," Dilsey said, "Whut dey needs is a man kin put de fear of God into dese here triflin young niggers."

"Rev'un Shegog gwine preach today," Frony said. "So dey tells."

They went on along the street. Along its quiet length white people in bright clumps moved churchward, under the windy bells, walking now and then in the random and tentative sun. The wind was gusty, out of the southeast, chill and raw after the warm days.

"I wish you wouldn't keep on bringin him to church, mammy," Frony said. "Folks talkin."

"Whut folks?" Dilsey said.

"I hears em," Frony said.

"And I knows whut kind of folks," Dilsey said, "Trash white folks. Dat's who it is. Thinks he aint good enough fer white church, but nigger church aint good enough fer him."

"Dey talks, jes de same," Frony said.

"Den you send um to me," Dilsey said. "Tell um de good Lawd dont keer whether he smart er not. Dont nobody but white trash keer dat."

A street turned off at right angles, descending, and became a dirt road. On either hand the land dropped more sharply; a broad flat dotted with small cabins whose weathered roofs were on a level with the crown of the road. They were set in small grassless plots littered with broken things, bricks, planks, crockery, things of a once utilitarian value. What growth there was consisted of rank weeds and the trees were mulberries and locusts and sycamores— trees that partook also of the foul desiccation which surrounded the houses; trees whose very burgeoning seemed to be the sad and stubborn remnant of September, as if even spring had passed them by, leaving them to feed upon the rich and unmistakable smell of negroes in which they grew.

From the doors negroes spoke to them as they passed, to Dilsey usually:

"Sis' Gibson! How you dis mawnin?"

"I'm well. Is you well?"

"I'm right well, I thank you."

They emerged from the cabins and struggled up the shading levee to the road—men in staid, hard brown or black, with gold watch chains and now and then a stick; young men in cheap violent blues or stripes and swaggering hats; women a little stiffly sibilant, and children in garments bought second hand of white people, who looked at Ben with the covertness of nocturnal animals:

"I bet you wont go up en tech him."

"How come I wont?"

"I bet you wont. I bet you skeered to."

"He wont hurt folks. He des a loony."

"How come a loony wont hurt folks?"

"Dat un wont. I teched him."

"I bet you wont now."

"Case Miss Dilsey lookin."

"You wont no ways."

"He dont hurt folks. He des a loony."

And steadily the older people speaking to Dilsey, though, unless they were quite old, Dilsey permitted Frony to respond.

"Mammy aint feelin well dis mawnin."

"Dat's too bad. But Rev'un Shegog'll cure dat. He'll give her de comfort en de unburdenin."

The road rose again, to a scene like a painted backdrop. Notched into a cut of red clay crowned with oaks the road appeared to stop short off, like a cut ribbon. Beside it a weathered church lifted its crazy steeple like a painted church, and the whole scene was as flat and without perspective as a painted cardboard set upon the ultimate edge of the flat earth, against the windy sunlight of space and April and a midmorning filled with bells. Toward the church they thronged with slow sabbath deliberation. The women and children went on in, the men stopped outside and talked in quiet groups until the bell ceased ringing. Then they too entered.

The church had been decorated, with sparse flowers from kitchen gardens and hedgerows, and with streamers of coloured crepe paper. Above the pulpit hung a battered Christmas bell, the accordion sort that collapses. The pulpit was empty, though the choir was already in place, fanning themselves although it was not warm.

Most of the women were gathered on one side of the room. They were talking. Then the bell struck one time and they dispersed to their seats and the congregation sat for an instant, expectant. The bell struck again one time. The choir rose and began to sing and the congregation turned its head as one, as six small children—four girls with tight pigtails bound with small scraps of cloth like butterflies, and two boys with close napped heads,—entered and marched up the aisle, strung together in a harness of white ribbons and flowers, and followed by two men in single file. The second man was huge, of a light coffee colour, imposing in a frock coat and white tie. His head was magisterial and profound, his neck rolled above his collar in rich folds. But he was familiar to them, and so the heads were still reverted when he had passed, and it was not until the choir ceased singing that they realised that the visiting clergyman had already entered, and when they saw the man who had preceded their minister enter the pulpit still ahead of him an indescribable sound went up, a sigh, a sound of astonishment and disappointment.

The visitor was undersized, in a shabby alpaca coat. He had a wizened black face like a small, aged monkey. And all the while that the choir sang again and while the six children rose and sang in thin, frightened, tuneless whispers, they watched the insignificant looking man sitting dwarfed and countrified by the minister's imposing bulk, with something like consternation. They were still looking at him with consternation and unbelief when the minister rose and introduced him in rich, rolling tones whose very unction served to increase the visitor's insignificance.

"En dey brung dat all de way fum Saint Looey," Frony whispered.

"I've knowed de Lawd to use cuiser tools dan dat," Dilsey said. "Hush, now," she said to Ben, "Dey fixin to sing again in a minute."

When the visitor rose to speak he sounded like a white man. His voice was level and cold. It sounded too big to have come from him and they listened at first through curiosity, as they would have to a monkey talking. They began to watch him as they would a man on a tight rope. They even forgot his insignificant appearance in the virtuosity with which he ran and poised and swooped upon the cold inflectionless wire of his voice, so that at last, when with a sort of swooping glide he came to rest again beside the reading desk with one arm resting upon it at shoulder height and his monkey body as reft of all motion as a mummy or an emptied vessel, the congregation sighed as if it waked from a collective dream and moved a little in its seats. Behind the pulpit the choir fanned steadily. Dilsey whispered, "Hush, now. Dey fixin to sing in a minute."

Then a voice said, "Brethren."

The preacher had not moved. His arm lay yet across the desk, and he still held that pose while the voice died in sonorous echoes between the walls. It was as different as day and dark from his former tone, with a sad, timbrous quality like an alto horn, sinking into their hearts and speaking there again when it had ceased in fading and cumulate echoes.

"Brethren and sisteren," it said again. The preacher removed his arm and he began to walk back and forth before the desk, his hands clasped behind him, a meagre figure, hunched over upon itself like that of one long immured in striving with the implacable earth, "I got the recollection and the blood of the Lamb!" He tramped steadily back and forth beneath the twisted paper and the Christmas bell, hunched, his hands clasped behind him. He was like a worn small rock whelmed by the successive waves of his voice. With his body he seemed to feed the voice that, succubus like, had fleshed its teeth in him. And the congregation seemed to watch with its own eyes while the voice consumed him, until he was nothing and they were nothing and there was not even a voice but instead their hearts were speaking to one another in chanting measures beyond the need for words, so that when he came to rest against the reading desk, his monkey face lifted and his whole attitude that of a serene, tortured crucifix that transcended its shabbiness and insignificance and made it of no moment, a long moaning expulsion of breath rose from them, and a woman's single soprano: "Yes, Jesus!"

As the scudding day passed overhead the dingy windows glowed and faded in ghostly retrograde. A car passed along the road outside, labouring in the sand, died away. Dilsey sat bolt upright, her hand on Ben's knee. Two tears slid down her fallen cheeks, in and out of the myriad coruscations of immolation and abnegation and time.

"Brethren," the minister said in a harsh whisper, without moving.

"Yes, Jesus!" The woman's voice said, hushed yet.

"Breddren en sistuhn!" His voice rang again, with the horns. He removed his arm and stood erect and raised his hands. "I got de ricklickshun en de blood of de Lamb!" They did not mark just when his intonation, his pronunciation, became negroid, they just sat swaying a little in their seats as the voice took them into itself.

"When de long, cold—Oh, I tells you, breddren, when de long, cold—I sees de light en I sees de word, po sinner! Dey passed away in Egypt, de swingin chariots; de generations passed away. Wus a rich man: whar he now, O breddren? Was a po man: whar he now, O sistuhn? Oh I tells you, ef you aint got de milk en de dew of de old salvation when de long, cold years rolls away!"

"Yes, Jesus!"

"I tells you, breddren, en I tells you, sistuhn, dey'll come a time. Po sinner saying Let me lay down wid de Lawd, lemme lay down my load. Den whut Jesus gwine say, O breddren? O sistuhn? Is you got de ricklickshun en de Blood of de Lamb? Case I aint gwine load down heaven!"

He fumbled in his coat and took out a handkerchief and mopped his face. A low concerted sound rose from the congregation: "Mm-mmmmmmmmmmmmm!" The woman's voice said, "Yes, Jesus! Jesus!"

"Breddren! Look at dem little chillen settin dar. Jesus wus like dat once. He mammy suffered de glory en de pangs. Sometime maybe she helt him at de nightfall, whilst de angels singin him to sleep; maybe she look out de do' en see de Roman po-lice passin." He tramped back and forth, mopping his face. "Listen, breddren! I sees de day. Ma'y settin in de do' wid Jesus on her lap, de little Jesus. Like dem chillen dar, de little Jesus. I hears de angels singin de peaceful songs en de glory; I sees de closin eyes; sees Mary jump up, sees de sojer face: We gwine to kill! We gwine to kill! We gwine to kill yo little Jesus! I hears de weepin en de lamentation of de po mammy widout de salvation en de word of God!"

"Mmmmmmmmmmmmmmmmmm! Jesus! Little Jesus!" and another voice, rising:

"I sees, O Jesus! Oh I sees!" and still another, without words, like bubbles rising in water.

"I sees hit, breddren! I sees hit! Sees de blastin, blindin sight! I sees Calvary, wid de sacred trees, sees de thief en de murderer en de least of dese; I hears de boasting en de braggin: Ef you be

Jesus, lif up yo tree en walk! I hears de wailin of women en de evenin lamentations; I hears de weepin en de cryin en de turntaway face of God: dey done kilt Jesus; dey done kilt my Son!"

"Mmmmmmmmmmmmmm. Jesus! I sees, O Jesus!"

"O blind sinner! Breddren, I tells you; sistuhn, I says to you, when de Lawd did turn His mighty face, say, Aint gwine overload heaven! I can see de widowed God shet His do'; I sees de whelmin flood roll between; I sees de darkness en de death everlastin upon de generations. Den, lo! Breddren! Yes, breddren! Whut I see? Whut I see, O sinner? I sees de resurrection en de light; sees de meek Jesus sayin Dey kilt Me dat ye shall live again; I died dat dem whut sees en believes shall never die. Breddren, O breddren! I sees de doom crack en hears de golden horns shoutin down de glory, en de arisen dead whut got de blood en de ricklickshun of de Lamb!"

In the midst of the voices and the hands Ben sat, rapt in his sweet blue gaze. Dilsey sat bolt upright beside, crying rigidly and quietly in the annealment and the blood of the remembered Lamb.

As they walked through the bright noon, up the sandy road with the dispersing congregation talking easily again group to group, she continued to weep, unmindful of the talk.

"He sho a preacher, mon! He didn't look like much at first, but hush!"

"He seed de power en de glory."

"Yes, suh. He seed hit. Face to face he seed hit."

Dilsey made no sound, her face did not quiver as the tears took their sunken and devious courses, walking with her head up, making no effort to dry them away even.

"Whyn't you quit dat, mammy?" Frony said. "Wid all dese people lookin. We be passin white folks soon."

"I've seed de first en de last," Dilsey said. "Never you mind me."

"First en last whut?" Frony said.

"Never you mind," Dilsey said. "I seed de beginnin, en now I sees de endin."

Before they reached the street, though, she stopped and lifted her skirt and dried her eyes on the hem of her topmost underskirt. Then they went on. Ben shambled along beside Dilsey, watching Luster who anticked along ahead, the umbrella in his hand and his new straw hat slanted viciously in the sunlight, like a big foolish dog watching a small clever one. They reached the gate and entered. Immediately Ben began to whimper again, and for a while all of them looked up the drive at the square, paintless house with its rotting portico.

"Whut's gwine on up dar today?" Frony said. "Something is."

"Nothin," Dilsey said. "You tend to yo business en let de white folks tend to deir'n."

"Somethin is," Frony said. "I heard him first thing dis mawnin. 'Taint none of my business, dough."

"En I knows whut, too," Luster said.

"You knows mo dan you got any use fer," Dilsey said. "Aint you jes heard Frony say hit aint none of yo business? You take Benjy on to de back and keep him quiet twell I put dinner on."

"I knows whar Miss Quentin is," Luster said.

"Den jes keep hit," Dilsey said. "Soon es Quentin need any of yo egvice, I'll let you know. Y'all g'awn en play in de back, now."

"You know whut gwine happen soon es dey start playin dat ball over yonder," Luster said.

"Dey wont start fer awhile yit. By dat time T. P. be here to take him ridin. Here, you gimme dat new hat."

Luster gave her the hat and he and Ben went on across the back yard. Ben was still whimpering, though not loud. Dilsey and Frony went to the cabin. After a while Dilsey emerged, again in the faded calico dress, and went to the kitchen. The fire had died down. There was no sound in the house. She put on the apron and went up stairs. There was no sound anywhere. Quentin's room was as they had left it. She entered and picked up the undergarment and put the stocking back in the drawer and closed it. Mrs Compson's door was closed. Dilsey stood beside it for a moment, listening. Then she opened it and entered, entered a pervading reek of camphor. The shades were drawn, the room in halflight, and the bed, so that at first she thought Mrs Compson was asleep and was about to close the door when the other spoke.

"Well?" she said, "What is it?"

"Hit's me," Dilsey said. "You want anything?"

Mrs Compson didn't answer. After awhile, without moving her head at all, she said: "Where's Jason?"

"He aint come back yit," Dilsey said. "Whut you want?"

Mrs Compson said nothing. Like so many cold, weak people, when faced at last by the incontrovertible disaster she exhumed from somewhere a sort of fortitude, strength. In her case it was an unshakable conviction regarding the yet unplumbed event. "Well," she said presently, "Did you find it?"

"Find whut? Whut you talkin about?"

"The note. At least she would have enough consideration to leave a note. Even Quentin did that."

"Whut you talkin about?" Dilsey said, "Dont you know she all right? I bet she be walkin right in dis do' befo dark."

"Fiddlesticks," Mrs Compson said, "It's in the blood. Like uncle, like niece. Or mother. I dont know which would be worse. I dont seem to care."

"Whut you keep on talkin that way fur?" Dilsey said. "Whut she want to do anything like that fur?"

"I dont know. What reason did Quentin have? Under God's heaven what reason did he have? It cant be simply to flout and hurt me. Whoever God is, He would not permit that. I'm a lady. You might not believe that from my offspring, but I am."

"You des wait en see," Dilsey said. "She be here by night, right dar in her bed." Mrs Compson said nothing. The camphor-soaked cloth lay upon her brow. The black robe lay across the foot of the bed. Dilsey stood with her hand on the door knob.

"Well," Mrs Compson said. "What do you want? Are you going to fix some dinner for Jason and Benjamin, or not?"

"Jason aint come yit," Dilsey said. "I gwine fix somethin. You sho you dont want nothin? Yo bottle still hot enough?"

"You might hand me my Bible."

"I give hit to you dis mawnin, befo I left."

"You laid it on the edge of the bed. How long did you expect it to stay there?"

Dilsey crossed to the bed and groped among the shadows beneath the edge of it and found the Bible, face down. She smoothed the bent pages and laid the book on the bed again. Mrs Compson didn't open her eyes. Her hair and the pillow were the same color, beneath the wimple of the medicated cloth she looked like an old nun praying. "Dont put it there again," she said, without opening her eyes. "That's where you put it before. Do you want me to have to get out of bed to pick it up?"

Dilsey reached the book across her and laid it on the broad side of the bed. "You cant see to read, noways," she said. "You want me to raise de shade a little?"

"No. Let them alone. Go on and fix Jason something to eat."

Dilsey went out. She closed the door and returned to the
kitchen. The stove was almost cold. While she stood there the clock
above the cupboard struck ten times. "One oclock," she said aloud,
"Jason aint comin home. Ise seed de first en de last," she said, looking at the cold stove, "I seed de first en de last." She set out some
cold food on a table. As she moved back and forth she sang a hymn.
She sang the first two lines over and over to the complete tune.
She arranged the meal and went to the door and called Luster, and
after a time Luster and Ben entered. Ben was still moaning a little,
as to himself.

"He aint never quit," Luster said.

"Y'all come on en eat," Dilsey said. "Jason aint coming to dinner."
They sat down at the table. Ben could manage solid food pretty
well for himself, though even now, with cold food before him, Dilsey tied a cloth about his neck. He and Luster ate. Dilsey moved
about the kitchen, singing the two lines of the hymn which she
remembered. "Y'all kin g'awn en eat," she said, "Jason aint comin
home."

He was twenty miles away at that time. When he left the house
he drove rapidly to town, overreaching the slow sabbath groups
and the peremptory bells along the broken air. He crossed the
empty square and turned into a narrow street that was abruptly
quieter even yet, and stopped before a frame house and went up
the flower-bordered walk to the porch.

Beyond the screen door people were talking. As he lifted his
hand to knock he heard steps, so he withheld his hand until a big
man in black broadcloth trousers and a stiff-bosomed white shirt
without collar opened the door. He had vigorous untidy iron-grey
hair and his grey eyes were round and shiny like a little boy's. He
took Jason's hand and drew him into the house, still shaking it.

"Come right in," he said, "Come right in."

"You ready to go now?" Jason said.

"Walk right in," the other said, propelling him by the elbow into
a room where a man and a woman sat. "You know Myrtle's husband, don't you? Jason Compson, Vernon."

"Yes," Jason said. He did not even look at the man, and as the
sheriff drew a chair across the room the man said,

"We'll go out so you can talk. Come on, Myrtle."

"No, no," the sheriff said, "You folks keep your seat. I reckon it
aint that serious, Jason? Have a seat."

"I'll tell you as we go along," Jason said. "Get your hat and coat."

"We'll go out," the man said, rising.

"Keep your seat," the sheriff said. "Me and Jason will go out on the porch."

"You get your hat and coat," Jason said. "They've already got a twelve hour start." The sheriff led the way back to the porch. A man and a woman passing spoke to him. He responded with a hearty florid gesture. Bells were still ringing, from the direction of the section known as Nigger Hollow. "Get your hat, Sheriff," Jason said. The sheriff drew up two chairs.

"Have a seat and tell me what the trouble is."

"I told you over the phone," Jason said, standing. "I did that to save time. Am I going to have to go to law to compel you to do your sworn duty?"

"You sit down and tell me about it," the sheriff said. "I'll take care of you all right."

"Care, hell," Jason said. "Is this what you call taking care of me?"

"You're the one that's holding us up," the sheriff said. "You sit down and tell me about it."

Jason told him, his sense of injury and impotence feeding upon its own sound, so that after a time he forgot his haste in the violent cumulation of his self justification and his outrage. The sheriff watched him steadily with his cold shiny eyes.

"But you dont know they done it," he said. "You just think so."

"Dont know?" Jason said. "When I spent two damn days chasing her through alleys, trying to keep her away from him, after I told her what I'd do to her if I ever caught her with him, and you say I dont know that that little b——"

"Now, then," the sheriff said, "That'll do. That's enough of that." He looked out across the street, his hands in his pockets.

"And when I come to you, a commissioned officer of the law," Jason said.

"That show's in Mottson this week," the sheriff said.

"Yes," Jason said, "And if I could find a law officer that gave a solitary damn about protecting the people that elected him to office, I'd be there too by now." He repeated his story, harshly recapitulant, seeming to get an actual pleasure out of his outrage and impotence. The sheriff did not appear to be listening at all.

"Jason," he said, "What were you doing with three thousand dollars hid in the house?"

"What?" Jason said. "That's my business where I keep my money. Your business is to help me get it back."

"Did your mother know you had that much on the place?"

"Look here," Jason said, "My house has been robbed. I know who did it and I know where they are. I come to you as the commissioned officer of the law, and I ask you once more, are you going to make any effort to recover my property, or not?"

"What do you aim to do with that girl, if you catch them?"

"Nothing," Jason said, "Not anything. I wouldn't lay my hand on her. The bitch that cost me a job, the one chance I ever had to get ahead, that killed my father and is shortening my mother's life every day and made my name a laughing stock in the town. I wont do anything to her," he said. "Not anything."

"You drove that girl into running off, Jason," the sheriff said.

"How I conduct my family is no business of yours," Jason said. "Are you going to help me or not?"

"You drove her away from home," the sheriff said. "And I have some suspicions about who that money belongs to that I dont reckon I'll ever know for certain."

Jason stood, slowly wringing the brim of his hat in his hands. He said quietly: "You're not going to make any effort to catch them for me?"

"That's not any of my business, Jason. If you had any actual proof, I'd have to act. But without that I dont figger it's any of my business."

"That's your answer, is it?" Jason said. "Think well, now."

"That's it, Jason."

"All right," Jason said. He put his hat on. "You'll regret this. I wont be helpless. This is not Russia, where just because he wears a little metal badge, a man is immune to law." He went down the steps and got in his car and started the engine. The sheriff watched him drive away, turn, and rush past the house toward town.

The bells were ringing again, high in the scudding sunlight in bright disorderly tatters of sound. He stopped at a filling station and had his tires examined and the tank filled.

"Gwine on a trip, is you?" the negro asked him. He didn't answer. "Look like hit gwine fair off, after all," the negro said.

"Fair off, hell," Jason said, "It'll be raining like hell by twelve oclock." He looked at the sky, thinking about rain, about the slick clay roads, himself stalled somewhere miles from town. He thought about it with a sort of triumph, of the fact that he was going to miss dinner, that by starting now and so serving his compulsion of haste, he would be at the greatest possible distance from both towns when noon came. It seemed to him that, in this, circumstance was giving him a break, so he said to the negro:

"What the hell are you doing? Has somebody paid you to keep this car standing here as long as you can?"

"Dis here ti' aint got no air a-tall in hit," the negro said.

"Then get the hell away from there and let me have that tube," Jason said.

"Hit up now," the negro said, rising. "You kin ride now."

Jason got in and started the engine and drove off. He went into second gear, the engine spluttering and gasping, and he raced the engine, jamming the throttle down and snapping the choker in and out savagely. "It's goin to rain," he said, "Get me half way there, and rain like hell." And he drove on out of the bells and out of town, thinking of himself slogging through the mud, hunting a team. "And every damn one of them will be at church." He thought how he'd find a church at last and take a team and of the owner coming out, shouting at him and of himself striking the man down. "I'm Jason Compson. See if you can stop me. See if you can elect a man to office that can stop me," he said, thinking of himself entering the courthouse with a file of soldiers and dragging the sheriff out. "Thinks he can sit with his hands folded and see me lose my job. I'll show him about jobs." Of his niece he did not think at all, nor the arbitrary valuation of the money. Neither of them had had entity or individuality for him for ten years; together they merely symbolized the job in the bank of which he had been deprived before he ever got it.

The air brightened, the running shadow patches were not the obverse, and it seemed to him that the fact that the day was clearing was another cunning stroke on the part of the foe, the fresh battle toward which he was carrying ancient wounds. From time to time he passed churches, unpainted frame buildings with sheet iron steeples, surrounded by tethered teams and shabby motorcars, and it seemed to him that each of them was a picket-post where the rear guards of Circumstance peeped fleetingly back at him. "And damn You, too," he said, "See if You can stop me," thinking of himself, his file of soldiers with the manacled sheriff in the rear, dragging Omnipotence down from His throne, if necessary; of the embattled legions of both hell and heaven through which he tore his way and put his hands at last on his fleeing niece.

The wind was out of the southeast. It blew steadily upon his cheek. It seemed that he could feel the prolonged blow of it sinking through his skull, and suddenly with an old premonition he clapped the brakes on and stopped and sat perfectly still. Then he lifted his hand to his neck and began to curse, and sat there, cursing in a harsh whisper. When it was necessary for him to drive for any length of time he fortified himself with a handkerchief soaked in camphor, which he would tie about his throat when clear of town, thus inhaling the fumes, and he got out and lifted the seat cushion on the chance that there might be a forgotten one there. He looked beneath both seats and stood again for a while, cursing, seeing himself mocked by his own triumphing. He closed his eyes, leaning on the door. He could return and get the forgotten camphor, or he could go on. In either case, his head would be splitting, but at home he could be sure of finding camphor on Sunday, while if he went on he could not be sure. But if he went back, he would be an hour and a half later in reaching Mottson. "Maybe I can drive slow," he said. "Maybe I can drive slow, thinking of something else—"

He got in and started. "I'll think of something else," he said, so he thought about Lorraine. He imagined himself in bed with her, only he was just lying beside her, pleading with her to help him, then he thought of the money again, and that he had been outwitted by a woman, a girl. If he could just believe it was the man who had robbed him. But to have been robbed of that which was to have compensated him for the lost job, which he had acquired through so much effort and risk, by the very symbol of the lost job itself, and worst of all, by a bitch of a girl. He drove on, shielding his face from the steady wind with the corner of his coat.

He could see the opposed forces of his destiny and his will drawing swiftly together now, toward a junction that would be irrevocable; he became cunning. I cant make a blunder, he told himself. There would be just one right thing, without alternatives: he must do that. He believed that both of them would know him on sight, while he'd have to trust to seeing her first, unless the man still wore the red tie. And the fact that he must depend on that red tie seemed to be the sum of the impending disaster; he could almost smell it, feel it above the throbbing of his head.

He crested the final hill. Smoke lay in the valley, and roofs, a spire or two above trees. He drove down the hill and into the town, slowing, telling himself again of the need for caution, to find where the tent was located first. He could not see very well now, and he knew that it was the disaster which kept telling him to go directly and get something for his head. At a filling station they told him that the tent was not up yet, but that the show cars were on a siding at the station. He drove there.

Two gaudily painted pullman cars stood on the track. He reconnoitred them before he got out. He was trying to breathe shallowly, so that the blood would not beat so in his skull. He got out and went along the station wall, watching the cars. A few garments hung out of the windows, limp and crinkled, as though they had been recently laundered. On the earth beside the steps of one sat three canvas chairs. But he saw no sign of life at all until a man in a dirty apron came to the door and emptied a pan of dishwater with a broad gesture, the sunlight glinting on the metal belly of the pan, then entered the car again.

Now I'll have to take him by surprise, before he can warn them, he thought. It never occurred to him that they might not be there, in the car. That they should not be there, that the whole result should not hinge on whether he saw them first or they saw him first, would be opposed to all nature and contrary to the whole rhythm of events. And more than that: he must see them first, get the money back, then what they did would be of no importance to him, while otherwise the whole world would know that he, Jason Compson, had been robbed by Quentin, his niece, a bitch.

He reconnoitred again. Then he went to the car and mounted the steps, swiftly and quietly, and paused at the door. The galley was dark, rank with stale food. The man was a white blur, singing in a cracked, shaky tenor. An old man, he thought, and not as big as I am. He entered the car as the man looked up.

"Hey?" the man said, stopping his song.

"Where are they?" Jason said. "Quick, now. In the sleeping car?"

"Where's who?" the man said.

"Dont lie to me," Jason said. He blundered on in the cluttered obscurity.

"What's that?" the other said, "Who you calling a liar?" And when Jason grasped his shoulder he exclaimed, "Look out, fellow!"

"Dont lie," Jason said, "Where are they?"

"Why, you bastard," the man said. His arm was frail and thin in Jason's grasp. He tried to wrench free, then he turned and fell to scrabbling on the littered table behind him.

"Come on," Jason said, "Where are they?"

"I'll tell you where they are," the man shrieked, "Lemme find my butcher knife."

"Here," Jason said, trying to hold the other, "I'm just asking you a question."

"You bastard," the other shrieked, scrabbling at the table. Jason tried to grasp him in both arms, trying to prison the puny fury of him. The man's body felt so old, so frail, yet so fatally single-purposed that for the first time Jason saw clear and unshadowed the disaster toward which he rushed.

"Quit it!" he said, "Here! Here! I'll get out. Give me time, and I'll get out."

"Call me a liar," the other wailed, "Lemme go. Lemme go just one minute. I'll show you."

Jason glared wildly about, holding the other. Outside it was now bright and sunny, swift and bright and empty, and he thought of the people soon to be going quietly home to Sunday dinner, decorously festive, and of himself trying to hold the fatal, furious little old man whom he dared not release long enough to turn his back and run.

"Will you quit long enough for me to get out?" he said, "Will you?" But the other still struggled, and Jason freed one hand and struck him on the head. A clumsy, hurried blow, and not hard, but the other slumped immediately and slid clattering among pans and buckets to the floor. Jason stood above him, panting, listening. Then he turned and ran from the car. At the door he restrained himself and descended more slowly and stood there again. His breath made a hah hah hah sound and he stood there trying to repress it, darting his gaze this way and that, when at a scuffling sound behind him he turned in time to see the little old man leaping awkwardly and furiously from the vestibule, a rusty hatchet high in his hand.

He grasped at the hatchet, feeling no shock but knowing that he was falling, thinking So this is how it'll end, and he believed that he was about to die and when something crashed against the back of his head he thought How did he hit me there? Only maybe he hit me a long time ago, he thought, And I just now felt it, and he thought Hurry. Hurry. Get it over with, and then a furious desire not to die seized him and he struggled, hearing the old man wailing and cursing in his cracked voice.

He still struggled when they hauled him to his feet, but they held him and he ceased.

"Am I bleeding much?" he said, "The back of my head. Am I bleeding?" He was still saying that while he felt himself being propelled rapidly away, heard the old man's thin furious voice dying away behind him. "Look at my head," he said, "Wait, I—"

"Wait, hell," the man who held him said, "That damn little wasp'll kill you. Keep going. You aint hurt."

"He hit me," Jason said. "Am I bleeding?"

"Keep going," the other said. He led Jason on around the corner of the station, to the empty platform where an express truck stood, where grass grew rigidly in a plot bordered with rigid flowers and a sign in electric lights: Keep your eye on Mottson, the gap filled by an eye with an electric pupil. The man released him.

"Now," he said, "You get on out of here and stay out. What were you trying to do? Commit suicide?"

"I was looking for two people," Jason said. "I just asked him where they were."

"Who you looking for?"

"It's a girl," Jason said. "And a man. He had on a red tie in Jefferson yesterday. With this show. They robbed me."

"Oh," the man said. "You're the one, are you. Well, they aint here."

"I reckon so," Jason said. He leaned against the wall and put his hand to the back of his head and looked at his palm. "I thought I was bleeding," he said. "I thought he hit me with that hatchet."

"You hit your head on the rail," the man said. "You better go on. They aint here."

"Yes. He said they were not here. I thought he was lying."

"Do you think I'm lying?" the man said.

"No," Jason said. "I know they're not here."

"I told him to get the hell out of there, both of them," the man said. "I wont have nothing like that in my show. I run a respectable show, with a respectable troupe."

"Yes," Jason said. "You dont know where they went?"

"No. And I dont want to know. No member of my show can pull a stunt like that. You her—brother?"

"No," Jason said. "It dont matter. I just wanted to see them. You sure he didn't hit me? No blood, I mean."

"There would have been blood if I hadn't got there when I did. You stay away from here, now. That little bastard'll kill you. That your car yonder?"

"Yes."

"Well, you get in it and go back to Jefferson. If you find them, it wont be in my show. I run a respectable show. You say they robbed you?"

"No," Jason said, "It dont make any difference." He went to the car and got in. What is it I must do? he thought. Then he remembered. He started the engine and drove slowly up the street until he found a drugstore. The door was locked. He stood for a while with his hand on the knob and his head bent a little. Then he turned away and when a man came along after a while he asked if there was a drugstore open anywhere, but there was not. Then he asked when the northbound train ran, and the man told him at two thirty. He crossed the pavement and got in the car again and sat there. After a while two negro lads passed. He called to them.

"Can either of you boys drive a car?"

"Yes, suh."

"What'll you charge to drive me to Jefferson right away?"

They looked at one another, murmuring.

"I'll pay a dollar," Jason said.

They murmured again. "Couldn't go fer dat," one said.

"What will you go for?"

"Kin you go?" one said.

"I cant git off," the other said. "Whyn't you drive him up dar? You aint got nothin to do."

"Yes I is."

"Whut you got to do?"

They murmured again, laughing.

"I'll give you two dollars," Jason said. "Either of you."

"I cant git away neither," the first said.

"All right," Jason said. "Go on."

He sat there for sometime. He heard a clock strike the half hour, then people began to pass, in Sunday and Easter clothes. Some looked at him as they passed, at the man sitting quietly behind the wheel of a small car, with his invisible life ravelled out about him like a worn-out sock. After a while a negro in overalls came up.

"Is you de one wants to go to Jefferson?" he said.

"Yes," Jason said. "What'll you charge me?"

"Fo dollars."

"Give you two."

"Cant go fer no less'n fo." The man in the car sat quietly. He wasn't even looking at him. The negro said, "You want me er not?"

"All right," Jason said, "Get in."

He moved over and the negro took the wheel. Jason closed his eyes. I can get something for it at Jefferson, he told himself, easing himself to the jolting, I can get something there. They drove on, along the streets where people were turning peacefully into houses and Sunday dinners, and on out of town. He thought that. He wasn't thinking of home, where Ben and Luster were eating cold dinner at the kitchen table. Something—the absence of disaster, threat, in any constant evil—permitted him to forget Jefferson as any place which he had ever seen before, where his life must resume itself.

When Ben and Luster were done Dilsey sent them outdoors. "And see kin you keep let him alone twell fo oclock. T. P. be here den."

"Yessum," Luster said. They went out. Dilsey ate her dinner and cleared up the kitchen. Then she went to the foot of the stairs and listened, but there was no sound. She returned through the kitchen and out the outer door and stopped on the steps. Ben and Luster were not in sight, but while she stood there she heard another sluggish twang from the direction of the cellar door and she went to the door and looked down upon a repetition of the morning's scene.

"He done it jes dat way," Luster said. He contemplated the motionless saw with a kind of hopeful dejection. "I aint got de right thing to hit it wid yit," he said.

"En you aint gwine find hit down here, neither," Dilsey said. "You take him on out in de sun. You bofe get pneumonia down here on dis wet flo."

She waited and watched them cross the yard toward a clump of cedar trees near the fence. Then she went on to her cabin.

"Now, dont you git started," Luster said, "I had enough trouble wid you today." There was a hammock made of barrel staves slatted into woven wires. Luster lay down in the swing, but Ben went on vaguely and purposelessly. He began to whimper again. "Hush, now," Luster said, "I fixin to whup you." He lay back in the swing. Ben had stopped moving, but Luster could hear him whimpering. "Is you gwine hush, er aint you?" Luster said. He got up and followed and came upon Ben squatting before a small mound of earth. At either end of it an empty bottle of blue glass that once contained poison was fixed in the ground. In one was a withered stalk of jimson weed. Ben squatted before it, moaning, a slow, inarticulate sound. Still moaning he sought vaguely about and found a twig and put it in the other bottle. "Whyn't you hush?" Luster said, "You want me to give you somethin' to sho nough moan about? Sposin I does dis." He knelt and swept the bottle suddenly up and behind him. Ben ceased moaning. He squatted, looking at the small depression where the bottle had sat, then as he drew his lungs full Luster brought the bottle back into view. "Hush!" he hissed, "Dont you dast to beller! Dont you. Dar hit is. See? Here. You fixin to start ef you stays here. Come on, les go see ef dey started knockin ball yit." He took Ben's arm and drew him up and they went to the fence and stood side by side there, peering between the matted honeysuckle not yet in bloom.

"Dar," Luster said, "Dar come some. See um?"

They watched the foursome play onto the green and out, and move to the tee and drive. Ben watched, whimpering, slobbering. When the foursome went on he followed along the fence, bobbing and moaning. One said.

"Here, caddie. Bring the bag."

"Hush, Benjy," Luster said, but Ben went on at his shambling trot, clinging to the fence, wailing in his hoarse, hopeless voice. The man played and went on, Ben keeping pace with him until the fence turned at right angles, and he clung to the fence, watching the people move on and away.

"Will you hush now?" Luster said. "Will you hush now?" He shook Ben's arm. Ben clung to the fence, wailing steadily and hoarsely. "Aint you gwine stop?" Luster said, "Or is you?" Ben gazed through the fence. "All right, den," Luster said, "You want somethin to beller about?" He looked over his shoulder, toward the house. Then he whispered: "Caddy! Beller now. Caddy! Caddy! Caddy!"

A moment later, in the slow intervals of Ben's voice, Luster heard Dilsey calling. He took Ben by the arm and they crossed the yard toward her.

"I tole you he warn't gwine stay quiet," Luster said.

"You vilyun!" Dilsey said, "Whut you done to him?"

"I aint done nothin. I tole you when dem folks start playin, he git started up."

"You come on here," Dilsey said. "Hush, Benjy. Hush, now." But he wouldn't hush. They crossed the yard quickly and went to the cabin and entered. "Run git dat shoe," Dilsey said. "Dont you sturb Miss Cahline, now. Ef she say anything, tell her I got him. Go on, now; you kin sho do dat right, I reckon." Luster went out. Dilsey led Ben to the bed and drew him down beside her and she held him, rocking back and forth, wiping his drooling mouth upon the hem of her skirt. "Hush, now," she said, stroking his head, "Hush. Dilsey got you." But he bellowed slowly, abjectly, without tears; the grave hopeless sound of all voiceless misery under the sun. Luster returned, carrying a white satin slipper. It was yellow now, and cracked and soiled, and when they placed it into Ben's hand he hushed for a while. But he still whimpered, and soon he lifted his voice again.

"You reckon you kin find T. P.?" Dilsey said.

"He say yistiddy he gwine out to St John's today. Say he be back at fo."

Dilsey rocked back and forth, stroking Ben's head.

"Dis long time, O Jesus," she said, "Dis long time."

"I kin drive dat surrey, mammy," Luster said.

"You kill bofe y'all," Dilsey said. "You do hit fer devilment. I knows you got plenty sense to. But I cant trust you. Hush, now," she said. "Hush. Hush."

"Nome I wont," Luster said. "I drives wid T. P." Dilsey rocked back and forth, holding Ben. "Miss Cahline say ef you cant quiet him, she gwine git up en come down en do hit."

"Hush, honey," Dilsey said, stroking Ben's head. "Luster, honey," she said, "Will you think about yo ole mammy en drive dat surrey right?"

"Yessum," Luster said. "I drive hit jes like T. P."

Dilsey stroked Ben's head, rocking back and forth. "I does de bes I kin," she said, "Lawd knows dat. Go git it, den," she said, rising. Luster scuttled out. Ben held the slipper, crying. "Hush, now.

Luster gone to git de surrey en take you to de graveyard. We aint gwine risk gitting yo cap," she said. She went to a closet contrived of a calico curtain hung across a corner of the room and got the felt hat she had worn. "We's down to worse'n dis, ef folks jes knowed," she said. "You's de Lawd's chile, anyway. En I be His'n too, fo long, praise Jesus. Here." She put the hat on his head and buttoned his coat. He wailed steadily. She took the slipper from him and put it away and they went out. Luster came up, with an ancient white horse in a battered and lopsided surrey.

"You gwine be careful, Luster?" she said.

"Yessum," Luster said. She helped Ben into the back seat. He had ceased crying, but now he began to whimper again.

"Hit's his flower," Luster said. "Wait, I'll git him one."

"You set right dar," Dilsey said. She went and took the cheekstrap. "Now, hurry en git him one." Luster ran around the house, toward the garden. He came back with a single narcissus.

"Dat un broke," Dilsey said, "Whyn't you git him a good un?"

"Hit de onliest one I could find," Luster said. "Y'all took all of um Friday to dec'rate de church. Wait, I'll fix hit." So while Dilsey held the horse Luster put a splint on the flower stalk with a twig and two bits of string and gave it to Ben. Then he mounted and took the reins. Dilsey still held the bridle.

"You knows de way now?" she said, "Up de street, round de square, to de graveyard, den straight back home."

"Yessum," Luster said, "Hum up, Queenie."

"You gwine be careful, now?"

"Yessum." Dilsey released the bridle.

"Hum up, Queenie," Luster said.

"Here," Dilsey said, "You han me dat whup."

"Aw, mammy," Luster said.

"Give hit here," Dilsey said, approaching the wheel. Luster gave it to her reluctantly.

"I wont never git Queenie started now."

"Never you mind about dat," Dilsey said. "Queenie know mo bout whar she gwine dan you does. All you got to do is set dar en hold dem reins. You knows de way, now?"

"Yessum. Same way T. P. goes ev'y Sunday."

"Den you do de same thing dis Sunday."

"Cose I is. Aint I drove fer T. P. mo'n a hund'ed times?"

"Den do hit again," Dilsey said. "G'awn, now. En ef you hurts

Benjy, nigger boy, I dont know whut I do. You bound fer de chain gang, but I'll send you dar fo even chain gang ready fer you."

"Yessum," Luster said. "Hum up, Queenie."

He flapped the lines on Queenie's broad back and the surrey lurched into motion.

"You, Luster!" Dilsey said.

"Hum up, dar!" Luster said. He flapped the lines again. With subterranean rumblings Queenie jogged slowly down the drive and turned into the street, where Luster exhorted her into a gait resembling a prolonged and suspended fall in a forward direction. Ben quit whimpering. He sat in the middle of the seat, holding the repaired flower upright in his fist, his eyes serene and ineffable. Directly before him Luster's bullet head turned backward continually until the house passed from view, then he pulled to the side of the street and while Ben watched him he descended and broke a switch from a hedge. Queenie lowered her head and fell to cropping the grass until Luster mounted and hauled her head up and harried her into motion again, then he squared his elbows and with the switch and the reins held high he assumed a swaggering attitude out of all proportion to the sedate clopping of Queenie's hooves and the organlike basso of her internal accompaniment. Motors passed them, and pedestrians; once a group of half grown negroes:

"Dar Luster. Whar you gwine, Luster? To de boneyard?"

"Hi," Luster said, "Aint de same boneyard y'all headed fer. Hum up, elefump."

They approached the square, where the Confederate soldier gazed with empty eyes beneath his marble hand into wind and weather. Luster took still another notch in himself and gave the impervious Queenie a cut with the switch, casting his glance about the square. "Dar Mr Jason's car," he said then he spied another group of negroes. "Les show dem niggers how quality does, Benjy," he said, "Whut you say?" He looked back. Ben sat, holding the flower in his fist, his gaze empty and untroubled. Luster hit Queenie again and swung her to the left at the monument.

For an instant Ben sat in an utter hiatus. Then he bellowed. Bellow on bellow, his voice mounted, with scarce interval for breath. There was more than astonishment in it, it was horror; shock; agony eyeless, tongueless; just sound, and Luster's eyes back-rolling for a white instant. "Gret God," he said, "Hush! Hush! Gret God!"

He whirled again and struck Queenie with the switch. It broke and he cast it away and with Ben's voice mounting toward its unbelievable crescendo Luster caught up the end of the reins and leaned forward as Jason came jumping across the square and onto the step.

With a backhanded blow he hurled Luster aside and caught the reins and sawed Queenie about and doubled the reins back and slashed her across the hips. He cut her again and again, into a plunging gallop, while Ben's hoarse agony roared about them, and swung her about to the right of the monument. Then he struck Luster over the head with his fist.

"Dont you know any better than to take him to the left?" he said. He reached back and struck Ben, breaking the flower stalk again. "Shut up!" he said, "Shut up!" He jerked Queenie back and jumped down. "Get to hell on home with him. If you ever cross that gate with him again, I'll kill you!"

"Yes, suh!" Luster said. He took the reins and hit Queenie with the end of them. "Git up! Git up, dar! Benjy, fer God's sake!"

Ben's voice roared and roared. Queenie moved again, her feet began to clop-clop steadily again, and at once Ben hushed. Luster looked quickly back over his shoulder, then he drove on. The broken flower drooped over Ben's fist and his eyes were empty and blue and serene again as cornice and façade flowed smoothly once more from left to right; post and tree, window and doorway, and signboard, each in its ordered place.

APPENDIX

COMPSON 1699—1945

IKKEMOTUBBE. A DISPOSSESSED AMERICAN KING. CALLED "L'HOMME" (and sometimes "de l'homme") by his fosterbrother, a Chevalier of France, who had he not been born too late could have been among the brightest in that glittering galaxy of knightly blackguards who were Napoleon's marshals, who thus translated the Chickasaw title meaning "The Man"; which translation Ikkemotubbe, himself a man of wit and imagination as well as a shrewd judge of character, including his own, carried one step further and anglicised it to "Doom." Who granted out of his vast lost domain a solid square

mile of virgin North Mississippi dirt as truly angled as the four corners of a cardtable top (forested then because these were the old
days before 1883 when the stars fell and Jefferson Mississippi was
one long rambling onestorey mudchinked log building housing the
Chickasaw Agent and his tradingpost store) to the grandson of a
Scottish refugee who had lost his own birthright by casting his lot
with a king who himself had been dispossessed. This in partial return for the right to proceed in peace, by whatever means he and
his people saw fit, afoot or ahorse provided they were Chickasaw
horses, to the wild western land presently to be called Oklahoma:
not knowing then about the oil.

JACKSON. A Great White Father with a sword. (An old duellist,
a brawling lean fierce mangy durable imperishable old lion who set
the wellbeing of the nation above the White House and the health
of his new political party above either and above them all set not
his wife's honor but the principle that honor must be defended
whether it was or not because defended it was whether or not.)
Who patented sealed and countersigned the grant with his own
hand in his gold tepee in Wassi Town, not knowing about the oil
either: so that one day the homeless descendants of the dispossessed
would ride supine with drink and splendidly comatose above the
dusty allotted harborage of their bones in speciallybuilt scarlet-
painted hearses and fire-engines.

These were Compsons:

QUENTIN MACLACHAN. Son of a Glasgow printer, orphaned and
raised by his mother's people in the Perth highlands. Fled to Carolina from Culloden Moor with a claymore and the tartan he wore
by day and slept under by night, and little else. At eighty, having
fought once against an English king and lost, he would not make
that mistake twice and so fled again one night in 1779, with his infant grandson and the tartan (the claymore had vanished, along
with his son, the grandson's father, from one of Tarleton's regiments
on a Georgia battlefield about a year ago) into Kentucky, where a
neighbor named Boon or Boone had already established a settlement.

CHARLES STUART. Attained and proscribed by name and grade in
his British regiment. Left for dead in a Georgia swamp by his own

retreating army and then by the advancing American one, both of which were wrong. He still had the claymore even when on his homemade wooden leg he finally overtook his father and son four years later at Harrodsburg, Kentucky, just in time to bury the father and enter upon a long period of being a split personality while still trying to be the schoolteacher which he believed he wanted to be, until he gave up at last and became the gambler he actually was and which no Compson seemed to realize they all were provided the gambit was desperate and the odds long enough. Succeeded at last in risking not only his neck but the security of his family and the very integrity of the name he would leave behind him, by joining the confederation headed by an acquaintance named Wilkinson (a man of considerable talent and influence and intellect and power) in a plot to secede the whole Mississippi Valley from the United States and join it to Spain. Fled in his turn when the bubble burst (as anyone except a Compson schoolteacher should have known it would), himself unique in being the only one of the plotters who had to flee the country: this not from the vengeance and retribution of the government which he had attempted to dismember, but from the furious revulsion of his late confederates now frantic for their own safety. He was not expelled from the United States, he talked himself countryless, his expulsion due not to the treason but to his having been so vocal and vociferant in the conduct of it, burning each bridge vocally behind him before he had even reached the place to build the next one: so that it was no provost marshal nor even a civic agency but his late coplotters themselves who put afoot the movement to evict him from Kentucky and the United States and, if they had caught him, probably from the world too. Fled by night, running true to family tradition, with his son and the old claymore and the tartan.

JASON LYCURGUS. Who, driven perhaps by the compulsion of the flamboyant name given him by the sardonic embittered woodenlegged indomitable father who perhaps still believed with his heart that what he wanted to be was a classicist schoolteacher, rode up the Natchez Trace one day in 1811 with a pair of fine pistols and one meagre saddlebag on a small lightwaisted but stronghocked mare which could do the first two furlongs in definitely under the halfminute and the next two in not appreciably more, though that was all. But it was enough: who reached the Chickasaw Agency at

Okatoba (which in 1860 was still called Old Jefferson) and went
no further. Who within six months was the Agent's clerk and within
twelve his partner, officially still the clerk though actually half-
owner of what was now a considerable store stocked with the
mare's winnings in races against the horses of Ikkemotubbe's young
men which he, Compson, was always careful to limit to a quarter
or at most three furlongs; and in the next year it was Ikkemotubbe
who owned the little mare and Compson owned the solid square
mile of land which someday would be almost in the center of the
town of Jefferson, forested then and still forested twenty years later
though rather a park than a forest by that time, with its slave-quar-
ters and stables and kitchengardens and the formal lawns and
promenades and pavilions laid out by the same architect who built
the columned porticoed house furnished by steamboat from France
and New Orleans, and still the square intact mile in 1840 (with not
only the little white village called Jefferson beginning to enclose it
but an entire white county about to surround it because in a few
years now Ikkemotubbe's descendants and people would be gone,
those remaining living not as warriors and hunters but as white men
—as shiftless farmers or, here and there, the masters of what they
too called plantations and the owners of shiftless slaves, a little dirt-
ier than the white man, a litte lazier, a little crueller—until at last
even the wild blood itself would have vanished, to be seen only occasionally in the noseshape of a Negro on a cottonwagon or a white
sawmill hand or trapper or locomotive fireman), known as the
Compson Domain then, since now it was fit to breed princes, states-
men and generals and bishops, to avenge the dispossessed Compsons from Culloden and Carolina and Kentucky, then known as the
Governor's house because sure enough in time it did produce or at
least spawn a governor—Quentin MacLachan again, after the Culloden grandfather—and still known as the Old Governor's even
after it had spawned (1861) a general—(called so by predeter-
mined accord and agreement by the whole town and county, as
though they knew even then and beforehand that the old governor
was the last Compson who would not fail at everything he touched
save longevity or suicide)—the Brigadier Jason Lycurgus II who
failed at Shiloh in '62 and failed again though not so badly at
Resaca in '64, who put the first mortgage on the still intact square
mile to a New England carpetbagger in '66, after the old town had
been burned by the Federal General Smith and the new little town,

in time to be populated mainly by the descendants not of Compsons but of Snopeses, had begun to encroach and then nibble at
and into it as the failed brigadier spent the next forty years selling
fragments of it off to keep up the mortgage on the remainder: until
one day in 1900 he died quietly on an army cot in the hunting and
fishing camp in the Tallahatchie River bottom where he passed
most of the end of his days.

And even the old governor was forgotten now; what was left of
the old square mile was now known merely as the Compson place
—the weedchoked traces of the old ruined lawns and promenades,
the house which had needed painting too long already, the scaling
columns of the portico where Jason III (bred for a lawyer and indeed he kept an office upstairs above the Square, where entombed
in dusty filingcases some of the oldest names in the county—Holston and Sutpen, Grenier and Beauchamp and Coldfield—faded
year by year among the bottomless labyrinths of chancery: and who
knows what dream in the perennial heart of his father, now completing the third of his three avatars—the one as son of a brilliant
and gallant statesman, the second as battleleader of brave and gallant men, the third as a sort of privileged pseudo-Daniel Boone-
Robinson Crusoe, who had not returned to juvenility because actually he had never left it—that that lawyer's office might again be
the anteroom to the governor's mansion and the old splendor) sat
all day long with a decanter of whiskey and a litter of dogeared
Horaces and Livys and Catulluses, composing (it was said) caustic
and satiric eulogies on both his dead and his living fellowtownsmen,
who sold the last of the property, except that fragment containing
the house and the kitchengarden and the collapsing stables and one
servant's cabin in which Dilsey's family lived, to a golfclub for the
ready money with which his daughter Candace could have her fine
wedding in April and his son Quentin could finish one year at
Harvard and commit suicide in the following June of 1910; already
known as the Old Compson place even while Compsons were still
living in it on that spring dusk in 1928 when the old governor's
doomed lost nameless seventeen-year-old greatgreatgranddaughter
robbed her last remaining sane male relative (her uncle Jason IV)
of his secret hoard of money and climbed down a rainpipe and ran
off with a pitchman in a travelling streetshow, and still known as
the Old Compson place long after all traces of Compsons were gone
from it: after the widowed mother died and Jason IV, no longer

needing to fear Dilsey now, committed his idiot brother, Benjamin, to the State Asylum in Jackson and sold the house to a country- man who operated it as a boardinghouse for juries and horse- and muletraders, and still known as the Old Compson place even after the boardinghouse (and presently the golfcourse too) had vanished and the old square mile was even intact again in row after row of small crowded jerrybuilt individuallyowned demiurban bungalows.

And these:

QUENTIN III. Who loved not his sister's body but some concept of Compson honor precariously and (he knew well) only temporarily supported by the minute fragile membrane of her maidenhead as a miniature replica of all the whole vast globy earth may be poised on the nose of a trained seal. Who loved not the idea of the incest which he would not commit, but some presbyterian concept of its eternal punishment: he, not God, could by that means cast himself and his sister both into hell, where he could guard her forever and keep her forevermore intact amid the eternal fires. But who loved death above all, who loved only death, loved and lived in a deliber- ate and almost perverted anticipation of death as a lover loves and deliberately refrains from the waiting willing friendly tender in- credible body of his beloved, until he can no longer bear not the refraining but the restraint and so flings, hurls himself, relinquish- ing, drowning. Committed suicide in Cambridge Massachusetts, June 1910, two months after his sister's wedding, waiting first to complete the current academic year and so get the full value of his paid-in-advance tuition, not because he had his old Culloden and Carolina and Kentucky grandfathers in him but because the re- maining piece of the old Compson mile which had been sold to pay for his sister's wedding and his year at Harvard had been the one thing, excepting that same sister and the sight of an open fire, which his youngest brother, born an idiot, had loved.

CANDACE (CADDY). Doomed and knew it, accepted the doom without either seeking or fleeing it. Loved her brother despite him, loved not only him but loved in him that bitter prophet and inflex- ible corruptless judge of what he considered the family's honor and its doom, as he thought he loved but really hated in her what he considered the frail doomed vessel of its pride and the foul instru- ment of its disgrace; not only this, she loved him not only in spite of but because of the fact that he himself was incapable of love, accepting the fact that he must value above all not her but the virginity of which she was custodian and on which she placed no value whatever: the frail physical stricture which to her was no more than a hangnail would have been. Knew the brother loved death best of all and was not jealous, would (and perhaps in the calculation and deliberation of her marriage did) have handed him the hypothetical hemlock. Was two months pregnant with another man's child which regardless of what its sex would be she had already named Quentin after the brother whom they both (she and the brother) knew was already the same as dead, when she married (1910) an extremely eligible young Indianian she and her mother had met while vacationing at French Lick the summer before. Divorced by him 1911. Married 1920 to a minor movingpicture magnate, Hollywood California. Divorced by mutual agreement, Mexico 1925. Vanished in Paris with the German occupation, 1940, still beautiful and probably still wealthy too since she did not look within fifteen years of her actual fortyeight, and was not heard of again. Except there was a woman in Jefferson, the county librarian, a mousesized and -colored woman who had never married, who had passed through the city schools in the same class with Candace Compson and then spent the rest of her life trying to keep *Forever Amber* in its orderly overlapping avatars and *Jurgen* and *Tom Jones* out of the hands of the highschool juniors and seniors who could reach them down without even having to tiptoe from the back shelves where she herself would have to stand on a box to hide them. One day in 1943, after a week of a distraction bordering on disintegration almost, during which those entering the library would find her always in the act of hurriedly closing her desk drawer and turning the key in it (so that the matrons, wives of the bankers and doctors and lawyers, some of whom had also been in that old highschool class, who came and went in the afternoons with the copies of the *Forever Ambers* and the volumes of Thorne Smith carefully wrapped from view in sheets of Memphis and Jackson newspapers, believed she was on the verge of illness or perhaps even loss of mind) she closed and locked the library in the middle of the afternoon and with her handbag clasped tightly under her arm and two feverish spots of determination in her ordinarily colorless cheeks, she entered the farmers' supply store where Jason IV had started as a clerk and where he now owned his own business as a buyer of

and dealer in cotton, striding on through that gloomy cavern which
only men ever entered—a cavern cluttered and walled and stalag-
mitehung with plows and discs and loops of tracechain and
singletrees and mulecollars and sidemeat and cheap shoes and
horseliniment and flour and molasses, gloomy because the goods it
contained were not shown but hidden rather since those who supplied Mississippi farmers or at least Negro Mississippi farmers for
a share of the crop did not wish, until that crop was made and its
value approximately computable, to show them what they could
learn to want but only to supply them on specific demand with
what they could not help but need—and strode on back to Jason's
particular domain in the rear: a railed enclosure cluttered with
shelves and pigeonholes bearing spiked dust-and-lintgathering gin
receipts and ledgers and cottonsamples and rank with the blended
smell of cheese and kerosene and harnessoil and the tremendous
iron stove against which chewed tobacco had been spat for almost
a hundred years, and up to the long high sloping counter behind
which Jason stood and, not looking again at the overalled men who
had quietly stopped talking and even chewing when she entered,
with a kind of fainting desperation she opened the handbag and
fumbled something out of it and laid it open on the counter and
stood trembling and breathing rapidly while Jason looked down at
it—a picture, a photograph in color clipped obviously from a slick
magazine—a picture filled with luxury and money and sunlight—a
Cannebière backdrop of mountains and palms and cypresses and
the sea, an open powerful expensive chromiumtrimmed sports car,
the woman's face hatless between a rich scarf and a seal coat, ageless and beautiful, cold serene and damned; beside her a handsome
lean man of middleage in the ribbons and tabs of a German staff-
general—and the mousesized mousecolored spinster trembling and
aghast at her own temerity, staring across it at the childless bachelor in whom ended that long line of men who had had something
in them of decency and pride even after they had begun to fail at
the integrity and the pride had become mostly vanity and selfpity:
from the expatriate who had to flee his native land with little else
except his life yet who still refused to accept defeat, through the
man who gambled his life and his good name twice and lost twice
and declined to accept that either, and the one who with only a
clever small quarterhorse for tool avenged his dispossessed father
and grandfather and gained a principality, and the brilliant and

gallant governor and the general who though he failed at leading in battle brave and gallant men at least risked his own life too in the failing, to the cultured dipsomaniac who sold the last of his patrimony not to buy drink but to give one of his descendants at least the best chance in life he could think of.

'It's Caddy!' the librarian whispered. 'We must save her!'

'It's Cad, all right,' Jason said. Then he began to laugh. He stood there laughing above the picture, above the cold beautiful face now creased and dogeared from its week's sojourn in the desk drawer and the handbag. And the librarian knew why he was laughing, who had not called him anything but Mr Compson for thirty-two years now, ever since the day in 1911 when Candace, cast off by her husband, had brought her infant daughter home and left the child and departed by the next train, to return no more, and not only the Negro cook, Dilsey, but the librarian too divined by simple instinct that Jason was somehow using the child's life and its illegitimacy both to blackmail the mother not only into staying away from Jefferson for the rest of her life but into appointing him sole unchallengeable trustee of the money she would send for the child's maintenance, and had refused to speak to him at all since that day in 1928 when the daughter climbed down the rainpipe and ran away with the pitchman.

'Jason!' she cried. 'We must save her! Jason! Jason!'——and still crying it even when he took up the picture between thumb and finger and threw it back across the counter toward her.

'That Candace?' he said. 'Dont make me laugh. This bitch aint thirty yet. The other one's fifty now.'

And the library was still locked all the next day too when at three o'clock in the afternoon, footsore and spent yet still unflagging and still clasping the handbag tightly under her arm, she turned into a neat small yard in the Negro residence section of Memphis and mounted the steps of the neat small house and rang the bell and the door opened and a black woman of about her own age looked quietly out at her. 'It's Frony, isn't it?' the librarian said. 'Dont you remember me——Melissa Meek, from Jefferson——'

'Yes,' the Negress said. 'Come in. You want to see Mama.' And she entered the room, the neat yet cluttered bedroom of an old Negro, rank with the smell of old people, old women, old Negroes, where the old woman herself sat in a rocker beside the hearth where even though it was June a fire smoldered—a big woman once, in faded clean calico and an immaculate turban wound round her head above the bleared and now apparently almost sightless eyes—and put the dogeared clipping into the black hands which, like the women of her race, were still as supple and delicately shaped as they had been when she was thirty or twenty or even seventeen.

'It's Caddy!' the librarian said. 'It is! Dilsey! Dilsey!'

'What did he say?' the old Negress said. And the librarian knew whom she meant by 'he', nor did the librarian marvel, not only that the old Negress would know that she (the librarian) would know whom she meant by the 'he', but that the old Negress would know at once that she had already shown the picture to Jason.

'Dont you know what he said?' she cried. 'When he realised she was in danger, he said it was her, even if I hadn't even had a picture to show him. But as soon as he realised that somebody, anybody, even just me, wanted to save her, would try to save her, he said it wasn't. But it is! Look at it!'

'Look at my eyes,' the old Negress said. 'How can I see that picture?'

'Call Frony!' the librarian cried. 'She will know her!' But already the old Negress was folding the clipping carefully back into its old creases, handing it back.

'My eyes aint any good anymore,' she said. 'I cant see it.'

And that was all. At six oclock she fought her way through the crowded bus terminal, the bag clutched under one arm and the return half of her roundtrip ticket in the other hand, and was swept out onto the roaring platform on the diurnal tide of a few middle-aged civilians but mostly soldiers and sailors enroute either to leave or to death and the homeless young women, their companions, who for two years now had lived from day to day in pullmans and hotels when they were lucky and in daycoaches and busses and stations and lobbies and public restrooms when not, pausing only long enough to drop their foals in charity wards or policestations and then move on again, and fought her way into the bus, smaller than any other there so that her feet touched the floor only occasionally until a shape (a man in khaki; she couldn't see him at all because she was already crying) rose and picked her up bodily and set her into a seat next the window, where still crying quietly she could look out upon the fleeing city as it streaked past and then was behind and presently now she would be home again, safe in Jefferson where life lived too with all its incomprehensible passion and tur-

moil and grief and fury and despair, but here at six oclock you
could close the covers on it and even the weightless hand of a child
could put it back among its unfeatured kindred on the quiet eternal
shelves and turn the key upon it for the whole and dreamless night.
Yes she thought, crying quietly *that was it she didn't want to see it
know whether it was Caddy or not because she knows Caddy
doesn't want to be saved hasn't anything anymore worth being
saved for nothing worth being lost that she can lose*

JASON IV. The first sane Compson since before Culloden and (a
childless bachelor) hence the last. Logical rational contained and
even a philosopher in the old stoic tradition: thinking nothing whatever of God one way or the other and simply considering the police
and so fearing and respecting only the Negro woman, his sworn
enemy since his birth and his mortal one since that day in 1911
when she too divined by simple clairvoyance that he was somehow
using his infant niece's illegitimacy to blackmail its mother, who
cooked the food he ate. Who not only fended off and held his own
with Compsons but competed and held his own with the Snopeses
who took over the little town following the turn of the century as
the Compsons and Sartorises and their ilk faded from it (no
Snopes, but Jason Compson himself who as soon as his mother died
—the niece had already climbed down the rainpipe and vanished
so Dilsey no longer had either of these clubs to hold over him—
committed his idiot younger brother to the state and vacated the
old house, first chopping up the vast oncesplendid rooms into what
he called apartments and selling the whole thing to a countryman
who opened a boardinghouse in it), though this was not difficult
since to him all the rest of the town and the world and the human
race too except himself were Compsons, inexplicable yet quite pre-
dictable in that they were in no sense whatever to be trusted. Who,
all the money from the sale of the pasture having gone for his sister's wedding and his brother's course at Harvard, used his own
niggard savings out of his meagre wages as a storeclerk to send himself to a Memphis school where he learned to class and grade
cotton, and so established his own business with which, following
his dipsomaniac father's death, he assumed the entire burden of the
rotting family in the rotting house, supporting his idiot brother because of their mother, sacrificing what pleasures might have been
the right and just due and even the necessity of a thirty-year-old

bachelor, so that his mother's life might continue as nearly as possible to what it had been; this not because he loved her but (a sane man always) simply because he was afraid of the Negro cook whom he could not even force to leave, even when he tried to stop paying her weekly wages; and who despite all this, still managed to save almost three thousand dollars ($2840.50 as he reported it on the night his niece stole it in niggard and agonised dimes and quarters and halfdollars, which hoard he kept in no bank because to him a banker too was just one more Compson, but hid in a locked bureau drawer in his bedroom whose bed he made and changed himself since he kept the bedroom door locked all the time save when he was passing through it. Who, following a fumbling abortive attempt by his idiot brother on a passing female child, had himself appointed the idiot's guardian without letting their mother know and so was able to have the creature castrated before the mother even knew it was out of the house, and who following the mother's death in 1933 was able to free himself forever not only from the idiot brother and the house but from the Negro woman too, moving into a pair of offices up a flight of stairs above the supplystore containing his cotton ledgers and samples, which he had converted into a bedroom-kitchen-bath, in and out of which on weekends there would be seen a big plain friendly brazenhaired pleasantfaced woman no longer very young, in round picture hats and (in its season) an imitation fur coat, the two of them, the middleaged cottonbuyer and the woman whom the town called, simply, his friend from Memphis, seen at the local picture show on Saturday night and on Sunday morning mounting the apartment stairs with paper bags from the grocer's containing loaves and eggs and oranges and cans of soup, domestic, uxorious, connubial, until the late afternoon bus carried her back to Memphis. He was emancipated now. He was free. 'In 1865,' he would say, 'Abe Lincoln freed the niggers from the Compsons. In 1933, Jason Compson freed the Compsons from the niggers.'

BENJAMIN. Born Maury, after his mother's only brother: a handsome flashing swaggering workless bachelor who borrowed money from almost anyone, even Dilsey although she was a Negro, explaining to her as he withdrew his hand from his pocket that she was not only in his eyes the same as a member of his sister's family, she would be considered a born lady anywhere in any eyes. Who, when at last even his mother realised what he was and insisted weeping that his name must be changed, was rechristened Benjamin by his brother Quentin (Benjamin, our lastborn, sold into Egypt). Who loved three things: the pasture which was sold to pay for Candace's wedding and to send Quentin to Harvard, his sister Candace, firelight. Who lost none of them because he could not remember his sister but only the loss of her, and firelight was the same bright shape as going to sleep, and the pasture was even better sold than before because now he and TP could not only follow timeless along the fence the motions which it did not even matter to him were humanbeings swinging golfsticks, TP could lead them to clumps of grass or weeds where there would appear suddenly in TP's hand small white spherules which competed with and even conquered what he did not even know was gravity and all the immutable laws when released from the hand toward plank floor or smokehouse wall or concrete sidewalk. Gelded 1913. Committed to the State Asylum, Jackson 1933. Lost nothing then either because, as with his sister, he remembered not the pasture but only its loss, and firelight was still the same bright shape of sleep.

QUENTIN. The last. Candace's daughter. Fatherless nine months before her birth, nameless at birth and already doomed to be unwed from the instant the dividing egg determined its sex. Who at seventeen, on the one thousand eight hundred ninetyfifth anniversary of the day before the resurrection of Our Lord, swung herself by a rainpipe from the window of the room in which her uncle had locked her at noon, to the locked window of his own locked and empty bedroom and broke a pane and entered the window and with the uncle's firepoker burst open the locked bureau drawer and took the money (it was not $2840.50 either, it was almost seven thousand dollars and this was Jason's rage, the red unbearable fury which on that night and at intervals recurring with little or no diminishment for the next five years, made him seriously believe would at some unwarned instant destroy him, kill him as instantaneously dead as a bullet or a lightningbolt: that although he had been robbed not of a mere petty three thousand dollars but of almost seven thousand he couldn't even tell anybody; because he had been robbed of seven thousand dollars instead of just three he could not only never receive justification—he did not want sympathy— from other men unlucky enough to have one bitch for a sister and another for a niece, he couldn't even go to the police; because he had lost four thousand dollars which did not belong to him he couldn't even recover the three thousand which did since those first four thousand dollars were not only the legal property of his niece as a part of the money supplied for her support and maintenance by her mother over the last sixteen years, they did not exist at all, having been officially recorded as expended and consumed in the annual reports he submitted to the district Chancellor, as required of him as guardian and trustee by his bondsmen: so that he had been robbed not only of his thievings but his savings too, and by his own victim; he had been robbed not only of the four thousand dollars which he had risked jail to acquire but of the three thousand which he had hoarded at the price of sacrifice and denial, almost a nickel and a dime at a time, over a period of almost twenty years: and this not only by his own victim but by a child who did it at one blow, without premeditation or plan, not even knowing or even caring how much she would find when she broke the drawer open; and now he couldn't even go to the police for help: he who had considered the police always, never given them any trouble, had paid the taxes for years which supported them in parasitic and sadistic idleness; not only that, he didn't dare pursue the girl himself because he might catch her and she would talk, so that his only recourse was a vain dream which kept him tossing and sweating on nights two and three and even four years after the event, when he should have forgotten about it: of catching her without warning, springing on her out of the dark, before she had spent all the money, and murder her before she had time to open her mouth) and climbed down the same rainpipe in the dusk and ran away with the pitchman who was already under sentence for bigamy. And so vanished; whatever occupation overtook her would have arrived in no chromium Mercedes; whatever snapshot would have contained no general of staff.

And that was all. These others were not Compsons. They were black:

т. р. Who wore on Memphis's Beale Street the fine bright cheap intransigent clothes manufactured specifically for him by the owners of Chicago and New York sweatshops.

FRONY. Who married a pullman porter and went to St Louis to

live and later moved back to Memphis to make a home for her
mother since Dilsey refused to go further than that.

LUSTER. A man, aged 14. Who was not only capable of the complete care and security of an idiot twice his age and three times his
size, but could keep him entertained.

DILSEY.
They endured.

The Bear

– 1 –

THERE WAS A MAN AND A DOG TOO THIS TIME. TWO BEASTS, COUNT-ing Old Ben, the bear, and two men, counting Boon Hogganbeck, in whom some of the same blood ran which ran in Sam Fathers, even though Boon's was a plebeian strain of it and only Sam and Old Ben and the mongrel Lion were taintless and incorruptible.

He was sixteen. For six years now he had been a man's hunter. For six years now he had heard the best of all talking. It was of the wilderness, the big woods, bigger and older than any recorded document:—of white man fatuous enough to believe he had bought any fragment of it, of Indian ruthless enough to pretend that any fragment of it had been his to convey; bigger than Major de Spain and the scrap he pretended to, knowing better; older than old Thomas Sutpen of whom Major de Spain had had it and who knew better; older even than old Ikkemotubbe, the Chickasaw chief, of whom old Sutpen had had it and who knew better in his turn. It was of the men, not white nor black nor red but men, hunters, with the will and hardihood to endure and the humility and skill to sur-vive, and the dogs and the bear and deer juxtaposed and reliefed against it, ordered and compelled by and within the wilderness in the ancient and unremitting contest according to the ancient and immitigable rules which voided all regrets and brooked no quar-ter;—the best game of all, the best of all breathing and forever the best of all listening, the voices quiet and weighty and deliberate for retrospection and recollection and exactitude among the concrete trophies—the racked guns and the heads and skins—in the libraries of town houses or the offices of plantation houses or (and best of all) in the camps themselves where the intact and still-warm meat yet hung, the men who had slain it sitting before the burning logs on hearths when there were houses and hearths or about the smoky blazing of piled wood in front of stretched tarpaulins when there were not. There was always a bottle present, so that it would seem to him that those fine fierce instants of heart and brain and courage and wiliness and speed were concentrated and distilled into that brown liquor which not women, not boys and children, but only hunters drank, drinking not of the blood they spilled but some condensation of the wild immortal spirit, drinking it moderately, humbly even, not with the pagan's base and baseless hope of acquiring thereby the virtues of cunning and strength and speed but in salute to them. Thus it seemed to him on this December morning not only natural but actually fitting that this should have begun with whisky.

He realised later that it had begun long before that. It had already begun on that day when he first wrote his age in two ciphers and his cousin McCaslin brought him for the first time to the camp, the big woods, to earn for himself from the wilderness the name and state of hunter provided he in his turn were humble and enduring enough. He had already inherited then, without ever having seen it, the big old bear with one trap-ruined foot that in an area almost a hundred miles square had earned for himself a name, a definite designation like a living man:—the long legend of corncribs broken down and rifled, of shoats and grown pigs and even calves carried bodily into the woods and devoured and traps and deadfalls overthrown and dogs mangled and slain and shotgun and even rifle shots delivered at point-blank range yet with no more effect than so many peas blown through a tube by a child—a corridor of wreckage and destruction beginning back before the boy was born, through which sped, not fast but rather with the ruthless and irresistible deliberation of a locomotive, the shaggy tremendous shape. It ran in his knowledge before he ever saw it. It loomed and towered in his dreams before he even saw the unaxed woods where it left its crooked print, shaggy, tremendous, red-eyed, not malevolent but just big, too big for the dogs which tried to bay it, for the horses which tried to ride it down, for the men and the bullets they fired into it; too big for the very country which was its constricting scope. It was as if the boy had already divined what his senses and intellect had not encompassed yet: that doomed wilderness whose edges were being constantly and punily gnawed at by men with plows and axes who feared it because it was wilderness, men myriad and nameless even to one another in the land where the old bear had earned a name, and through which ran not even a mortal beast but an anachronism indomitable and invincible out of an old dead time, a phantom, epitome and apotheosis of the old wild life which the little puny humans swarmed and hacked at in a fury of abhorrence and fear like pygmies about the ankles of a drowsing elephant;—the old bear, solitary, indomitable, and alone; widowered childless and absolved of mortality—old Priam reft of his old wife and outlived all his sons.

Still a child, with three years then two years then one year yet before he too could make one of them, each November he would watch the wagon containing the dogs and the bedding and food and guns and his cousin McCaslin and Tennie's Jim and Sam Fathers too until Sam moved to the camp to live, depart for the Big Bottom, the big woods. To him, they were going not to hunt bear and deer but to keep yearly rendezvous with the bear which they did not even intend to kill. Two weeks later they would return, with no trophy, no skin. He had not expected it. He had not even feared that it might be in the wagon this time with the other skins and heads. He did not even tell himself that in three years or two years or one year more he would be present and that it might even be his gun. He believed that only after he had served his apprenticeship in the woods which would prove him worthy to be a hunter, would he even be permitted to distinguish the crooked print, and that even then for two November weeks he would merely make another minor one, along with his cousin and Major de Spain and General Compson and Walter Ewell and Boon and the dogs which feared to bay it and the shotguns and rifles which failed even to bleed it, in the yearly pageant-rite of the old bear's furious immortality.

His day came at last. In the surrey with his cousin and Major de Spain and General Compson he saw the wilderness through a slow drizzle of November rain just above the ice point as it seemed to him later he always saw it or at least always remembered it—the tall and endless wall of dense November woods under the dissolving afternoon and the year's death, sombre, impenetrable (he could not even discern yet how, at what point they could possibly hope to enter it even though he knew that Sam Fathers was waiting there with the wagon), the surrey moving through the skeleton stalks of cotton and corn in the last of open country, the last trace of man's puny gnawing at the immemorial flank, until, dwarfed by that perspective into an almost ridiculous diminishment, the surrey itself seemed to have ceased to move (this too to be completed later, years later, after he had grown to a man and had seen the sea) as a solitary small boat hangs in lonely immobility, merely tossing up and down, in the infinite waste of the ocean while the water and then the apparently impenetrable land which it nears without appreciable progress, swings slowly and opens the widening inlet which is the anchorage. He entered it. Sam was waiting, wrapped in a quilt on the wagon seat behind the patient and steaming mules. He entered his novitiate to the true wilderness with Sam beside him as he had begun his apprenticeship in miniature to manhood after the rabbits and such with Sam beside him, the two of them wrapped in the damp, warm Negro-rank quilt while the wilderness closed behind his entrance as it had opened momentarily to accept him, opening before his advancement as it closed behind his progress, no fixed path the wagon followed but a channel nonexistent ten yards ahead of it and ceasing to exist ten yards after it had passed, the wagon progressing not by its own volition but by attrition of their intact yet fluid circumambience, drowsing, earless, almost lightless.

It seemed to him that at the age of ten he was witnessing his own birth. It was not even strange to him. He had experienced it all before, and not merely in dreams. He saw the camp—a paintless six-room bungalow set on piles above the spring high-water—and he knew already how it was going to look. He helped in the rapid orderly disorder of their establishment in it and even his motions were familiar to him, foreknown. Then for two weeks he ate the coarse, rapid food—the shapeless sour bread, the wild strange meat, venison and bear and turkey and coon which he had never tasted before—which men ate, cooked by men who were hunters first and cooks afterward; he slept in harsh sheetless blankets as hunters slept. Each morning the gray of dawn found him and Sam Fathers on the stand, the crossing, which had been allotted him. It was the poorest one, the most barren. He had expected that; he had not dared yet to hope even to himself that he would even hear the running dogs this first time. But he did hear them. It was on the third morning—a murmur, sourceless, almost indistinguishable, yet he knew what it was although he had never before heard that many dogs running at once, the murmur swelling into separate and distinct voices until he could call the five dogs which his cousin owned from among the others. "Now," Sam said, "slant your gun up a little and draw back the hammers and then stand still."

But it was not for him, not yet. The humility was there; he had learned that. And he could learn the patience. He was only ten, only one week. The instant had passed. It seemed to him that he could actually see the deer, the buck, smoke-colored, elongated with speed, vanished, the woods, the gray solitude still ringing even when the voices of the dogs had died away; from far away across the sombre woods and the gray half-liquid morning there came two shots. "Now let your hammers down," Sam said.

He did so. "You knew it too," he said.

"Yes," Sam said. "I want you to learn how to do when you didn't shoot. It's after the chance for the bear or the deer has done already come and gone that men and dogs get killed."

"Anyway, it wasn't him," the boy said. "It wasn't even a bear. It was just a deer."

"Yes," Sam said, "it was just a deer."

Then one morning, it was in the second week, he heard the dogs again. This time before Sam even spoke he readied the too-long, too-heavy, man-size gun as Sam had taught him, even though this time he knew the dogs and the deer were coming less close than ever, hardly within hearing even. They didn't sound like any running dogs he had ever heard before even. Then he found that Sam, who had taught him first of all to cock the gun and take position where he could see best in all directions and then never to move again, had himself moved up beside him. "There," he said. "Listen." The boy listened, to no ringing chorus strong and fast on a free scent but a moiling yapping an octave too high and with something more than indecision and even abjectness in it which he could not yet recognise, reluctant, not even moving very fast, taking a long time to pass out of hearing, leaving even then in the air that echo of thin and almost human hysteria, abject, almost humanly grieving, with this time nothing ahead of it, no sense of a fleeing unseen smoke-colored shape. He could hear Sam breathing at his shoulder. He saw the arched curve of the old man's inhaling nostrils.

"It's Old Ben!" he cried, whispering.

Sam didn't move save for the slow gradual turning of his head as the voices faded on and the faint steady rapid arch and collapse of his nostrils. "Hah," he said. "Not even running. Walking."

"But up here!" the boy cried. "Way up here!"

"He do it every year," Sam said. "Once. Ash and Boon say he comes up here to run the other little bears away. Tell them to get to hell out of here and stay out until the hunters are gone. Maybe." The boy no longer heard anything at all, yet still Sam's head con-

tinued to turn gradually and steadily until the back of it was toward him. Then it turned back and looked down at him—the same
face, grave, familiar, expressionless until it smiled, the same old
man's eyes from which as he watched there faded slowly a quality
darkly and fiercely lambent, passionate and proud. "He dont care
no more for bears than he does for dogs or men neither. He come
to see who's here, who's new in camp this year, whether he can
shoot or not, can stay or not. Whether we got the dog yet that can
bay and hold him until a man gets there with a gun. Because he's
the head bear. He's the man." It faded, was gone; again they were
the eyes as he had known them all his life. "He'll let them follow
him to the river. Then he'll send them home. We might as well go
too; see how they look when they get back to camp."

The dogs were there first, ten of them huddled back under the
kitchen, himself and Sam squatting to peer back into the obscurity
where they crouched, quiet, the eyes rolling and luminous, vanishing, and no sound, only that effluvium which the boy could not
quite place yet, of something more than dog, stronger than dog and
not just animal, just beast even. Because there had been nothing in
front of the abject and painful yapping except the solitude, the
wilderness, so that when the eleventh hound got back about mid-
afternoon and he and Tennie's Jim held the passive and still trembling bitch while Sam daubed her tattered ear and raked shoulder
with turpentine and axle-grease, it was still no living creature but
only the wilderness which, leaning for a moment, had patted lightly
once her temerity. "Just like a man," Sam said. "Just like folks. Put
off as long as she could having to be brave, knowing all the time
that sooner or later she would have to be brave once so she could
keep on calling herself a dog, and knowing beforehand what was
going to happen when she done it."

He did not know just when Sam left. He only knew that he was
gone. For the next three mornings he rose and ate breakfast and
Sam was not waiting for him. He went to his stand alone; he found
it without help now and stood on it as Sam had taught him. On the
third morning he heard the dogs again, running strong and free on
a true scent again, and he readied the gun as he had learned to do
and heard the hunt sweep past on since he was not ready yet, had
not deserved other yet in just one short period of two weeks as
compared to all the long life which he had already dedicated to the
wilderness with patience and humility; he heard the shot again,

one shot, the single clapping report of Walter Ewell's rifle. By now
he could not only find his stand and then return to camp without guidance, by using the compass his cousin had given him he
reached Walter waiting beside the buck and the moiling of dogs
over the cast entrails before any of the others except Major de
Spain and Tennie's Jim on the horses, even before Uncle Ash arrived with the one-eyed wagon-mule which did not mind the smell
of blood or even, so they said, of bear.

It was not Uncle Ash on the mule. It was Sam, returned. And
Sam was waiting when he finished his dinner and, himself on the
one-eyed mule and Sam on the other one of the wagon team, they
rode for more than three hours through the rapid shortening sunless afternoon, following no path, no trail even that he could discern, into a section of country he had never seen before. Then he
understood why Sam had made him ride the one-eyed mule which
would not spook at the smell of blood, of wild animals. The other
one, the sound one, stopped short and tried to whirl and bolt even
as Sam got down, jerking and wrenching at the rein while Sam
held it, coaxing it forward with his voice since he did not dare risk
hitching it, drawing it forward while the boy dismounted from the
marred one which would stand. Then, standing beside Sam in the
thick great gloom of ancient woods and the winter's dying afternoon, he looked quietly down at the rotted log scored and gutted
with claw-marks and, in the wet earth beside it, the print of the
enormous warped two-toed foot. Now he knew what he had heard
in the hounds' voices in the woods that morning and what he had
smelled when he peered under the kitchen where they huddled. It
was in him too, a little different because they were brute beasts
and he was not, but only a little different—an eagerness, passive;
an abjectness, a sense of his own fragility and impotence against
the timeless woods, yet without doubt or dread; a flavor like brass
in the sudden run of saliva in his mouth, a hard sharp constriction
either in his brain or his stomach, he could not tell which and it
did not matter; he knew only that for the first time he realised that
the bear which had run in his listening and loomed in his dreams
since before he could remember and which therefore must have
existed in the listening and the dreams of his cousin and Major de
Spain and even old General Compson before they began to remember in their turn, was a mortal animal and that they had departed
for the camp each November with no actual intention of slaying it,

not because it could not be slain but because so far they had no
actual hope of being able to. "It will be tomorrow," he said.

"You mean we will try tomorrow," Sam said. "We aint got the
dog yet."

"We've got eleven," he said. "They ran him Monday."

"And you heard them," Sam said. "Saw them too. We aint got the
dog yet. It wont take but one. But he aint there. Maybe he aint
nowhere. The only other way will be for him to run by accident
over somebody that had a gun and knowed how to shoot it."

"That wouldn't be me," the boy said. "It would be Walter or
Major or——"

"It might," Sam said. "You watch close tomorrow. Because he's
smart. That's how come he has lived this long. If he gets hemmed
up and has got to pick out somebody to run over, he will pick out
you."

"How?" he said. "How will he know. . . ." He ceased. "You mean
he already knows me, that I aint never been to the big bottom before, aint had time to find out yet whether I . . ." He ceased again,
staring at Sam; he said humbly, not even amazed: "It was me he
was watching. I dont reckon he did need to come but once."

"You watch tomorrow," Sam said. "I reckon we better start back.
It'll be long after dark now before we get to camp."

The next morning they started three hours earlier than they had
ever done. Even Uncle Ash went, the cook, who called himself by
profession a camp cook and who did little else save cook for Major
de Spain's hunting and camping parties, yet who had been marked
by the wilderness from simple juxtaposition to it until he responded
as they all did, even the boy who until two weeks ago had never
even seen the wilderness, to a hound's ripped ear and shoulder and
the print of a crooked foot in a patch of wet earth. They rode. It
was too far to walk: the boy and Sam and Uncle Ash in the wagon
with the dogs, his cousin and Major de Spain and General Compson and Boon and Walter and Tennie's Jim riding double on the
horses; again the first gray light found him, as on that first morning
two weeks ago, on the stand where Sam had placed and left him.
With the gun which was too big for him, the breech-loader which
did not even belong to him but to Major de Spain and which he
had fired only once, at a stump on the first day to learn the recoil
and how to reload it with the paper shells, he stood against a big
gum tree beside a little bayou whose black still water crept without

motion out of a cane-brake, across a small clearing and into the
cane again, where, invisible, a bird, the big woodpecker called
Lord-to-God by Negroes, clattered at a dead trunk. It was a stand
like any other stand, dissimilar only in incidentals to the one where
he had stood each morning for two weeks; a territory new to him
yet no less familiar than that other one which after two weeks he
had come to believe he knew a little—the same solitude, the same
loneliness through which frail and timorous man had merely passed
without altering it, leaving no mark nor scar, which looked exactly
as it must have looked when the first ancestor of Sam Fathers'
Chickasaw predecessors crept into it and looked about him, club or
stone axe or bone arrow drawn and ready, different only because,
squatting at the edge of the kitchen, he had smelled the dogs huddled and cringing beneath it and saw the raked ear and side of the
bitch that, as Sam had said, had to be brave once in order to keep
on calling herself a dog, and saw yesterday in the earth beside the
gutted log, the print of the living foot. He heard no dogs at all. He
never did certainly hear them. He only heard the drumming of the
woodpecker stop short off, and knew that the bear was looking at
him. He never saw it. He did not know whether it was facing him
from the cane or behind him. He did not move, holding the useless
gun which he knew now he would never fire at it, now or ever, tasting in his saliva that taint of brass which he had smelled in the
huddled dogs when he peered under the kitchen.

Then it was gone. As abruptly as it had stopped, the woodpecker's dry hammering set up again, and after a while he believed
he even heard the dogs—a murmur, scarce a sound even, which he
had probably been hearing for a time, perhaps a minute or two, before he remarked it, drifting into hearing and then out again, dying
away. They came nowhere near him. If it was dogs he heard, he
could not have sworn to it; if it was a bear they ran, it was another
bear. It was Sam himself who emerged from the cane and crossed
the bayou, the injured bitch following at heel as a bird dog is
taught to walk. She came and crouched against his leg, trembling.
"I didn't see him," he said. "I didn't, Sam."

"I know it," Sam said. "He done the looking. You didn't hear him
neither, did you?"

"No," the boy said. "I——"

"He's smart," Sam said. "Too smart." Again the boy saw in his
eyes that quality of dark and brooding lambence as Sam looked

down at the bitch trembling faintly and steadily against the boy's leg. From her raked shoulder a few drops of fresh blood clung like bright berries. "Too big. We aint got the dog yet. But maybe some day."

Because there would be a next time, after and after. He was only ten. It seemed to him that he could see them, the two of them, shadowy in the limbo from which time emerged and became time: the old bear absolved of mortality and himself who shared a little of it. Because he recognised now what he had smelled in the huddled dogs and tasted in his own saliva, recognised fear as a boy, a youth, recognises the existence of love and passion and experience which is his heritage but not yet his patrimony, from entering by chance the presence or perhaps even merely the bedroom of a woman who has loved and been loved by many men. *So I will have to see him,* he thought, without dread or even hope. *I will have to look at him.* So it was in June of the next summer. They were at the camp again, celebrating Major de Spain's and General Compson's birthdays. Although the one had been born in September and the other in the depth of winter and almost thirty years earlier, each June the two of them and McCaslin and Boon and Walter Ewell (and the boy too from now on) spent two weeks at the camp, fishing and shooting squirrels and turkey and running coons and wildcats with the dogs at night. That is, Boon and the Negroes (and the boy too now) fished and shot squirrels and ran the coons and cats, because the proven hunters, not only Major de Spain and old General Compson (who spent those two weeks sitting in a rocking chair before a tremendous iron pot of Brunswick stew, stirring and tasting, with Uncle Ash to quarrel with about how he was making it and Tennie's Jim to pour whisky into the tin dipper from which he drank it) but even McCaslin and Walter Ewell who were still young enough, scorned such other than shooting the wild gobblers with pistols for wagers or to test their marksmanship.

That is, his cousin McCaslin and the others thought he was hunting squirrels. Until the third evening he believed that Sam Fathers thought so too. Each morning he would leave the camp right after breakfast. He had his own gun now, a new breech-loader, a Christmas gift; he would own and shoot it for almost seventy years, through two new pairs of barrels and locks and one new stock, until all that remained of the original gun was the silver-inlaid trigger-guard with his and McCaslin's engraved names and the date in 1878. He found the tree beside the little bayou where he had stood that morning. Using the compass he ranged from that point; he was teaching himself to be better than a fair woodsman without even knowing he was doing it. On the third day he even found the gutted log where he had first seen the print. It was almost completely crumbled now, healing with unbelievable speed, a passionate and almost visible relinquishment, back into the earth from which the tree had grown. He ranged the summer woods now, green with gloom, if anything actually dimmer than they had been in November's gray dissolution, where even at noon the sun fell only in windless dappling upon the earth which never completely dried and which crawled with snakes—moccasins and watersnakes and rattlers, themselves the color of the dappled gloom so that he would not always see them until they moved; returning to camp later and later and later, first day, second day, passing in the twilight of the third evening the little log pen enclosing the log barn where Sam was putting up the stock for the night. "You aint looked right yet," Sam said.

He stopped. For a moment he didn't answer. Then he said peacefully, in a peaceful rushing burst, as when a boy's miniature dam in a little brook gives way: "All right. Yes. But how? I went to the bayou. I even found that log again. I——"

"I reckon that was all right. Likely he's been watching you. You never saw his foot?"

"I . . ." the boy said. "I didn't . . . I never thought . . ."

"It's the gun," Sam said. He stood beside the fence, motionless, the old man, son of a Negro slave and a Chickasaw chief, in the battered and faded overalls and the frayed five-cent straw hat which had been the badge of the Negro's slavery and was now the regalia of his freedom. The camp—the clearing, the house, the barn and its tiny lot with which Major de Spain in his turn had scratched punily and evanescently at the wilderness—faded in the dusk, back into the immemorial darkness of the woods. *The gun,* the boy thought. *The gun.* "You will have to choose," Sam said.

He left the next morning before light, without breakfast, long before Uncle Ash would wake in his quilts on the kitchen floor and start the fire. He had only the compass and a stick for the snakes. He could go almost a mile before he would need to see the compass. He sat on a log, the invisible compass in his hand, while the secret night-sounds which had ceased at his movements, scurried again and then fell still for good and the owls ceased and gave over to the waking day birds and there was light in the gray wet woods and he could see the compass. He went fast yet still quietly, becoming steadily better and better as a woodsman without yet having time to realise it; he jumped a doe and a fawn, walked them out of the bed, close enough to see them—the crash of undergrowth, the white scut, the fawn scudding along behind her, faster than he had known it could have run. He was hunting right, upwind, as Sam had taught him, but that didn't matter now. He had left the gun; by his own will and relinquishment he had accepted not a gambit, not a choice, but a condition in which not only the bear's heretofore inviolable anonymity but all the ancient rules and balances of hunter and hunted had been abrogated. He would not even be afraid, not even in the moment when the fear would take him completely: blood, skin, bowels, bones, memory from the long time before it even became his memory—all save that thin clear quenchless lucidity which alone differed him from this bear and from all the other bears and bucks he would follow during almost seventy years, to which Sam had said: "Be scared. You cant help that. But dont be afraid. Aint nothing in the woods going to hurt you if you dont corner it or it dont smell that you are afraid. A bear or a deer has got to be scared of a coward the same as a brave man has got to be."

By noon he was far beyond the crossing on the little bayou, farther into the new and alien country than he had ever been, travelling now not only by the compass but by the old, heavy, biscuit-thick silver watch which had been his father's. He had left the camp nine hours ago; nine hours from now, dark would already have been an hour old. He stopped, for the first time since he had risen from the log when he could see the compass face at last, and looked about, mopping his sweating face on his sleeve. He had already relinquished, of his will, because of his need, in humility and peace and without regret, yet apparently that had not been enough, the leaving of the gun was not enough. He stood for a moment—a child, alien and lost in the green and soaring gloom of the markless wilderness. Then he relinquished completely to it. It was the watch and the compass. He was still tainted. He removed the linked chain of the one and the looped thong of the other from his over-

alls and hung them on a bush and leaned the stick beside them and
entered it.

When he realised he was lost, he did as Sam had coached and
drilled him: made a cast to cross his backtrack. He had not been
going very fast for the last two or three hours, and he had gone
even less fast since he left the compass and watch on the bush. So
he went slower still now, since the tree could not be very far; in
fact, he found it before he really expected to and turned and went
to it. But there was no bush beneath it, no compass nor watch, so
he did next as Sam had coached and drilled him: made this next
circle in the opposite direction and much larger, so that the pattern
of the two of them would bisect his track somewhere, but crossing
no trace nor mark anywhere of his feet or any feet, and now he was
going faster though still not panicked, his heart beating a little
more rapidly but strong and steady enough, and this time it was
not even the tree because there was a down log beside it which he
had never seen before and beyond the log a little swamp, a seepage
of moisture somewhere between earth and water, and he did what
Sam had coached and drilled him as the next and the last, seeing as
he sat down on the log the crooked print, the warped indentation
in the wet ground which while he looked at it continued to fill with
water until it was level full and the water began to overflow and
the sides of the print began to dissolve away. Even as he looked up
he saw the next one, and, moving, the one beyond it; moving, not
hurrying, running, but merely keeping pace with them as they appeared before him as though they were being shaped out of thin
air just one constant pace short of where he would lose them forever and be lost forever himself, tireless, eager, without doubt or
dread, panting a little above the strong rapid little hammer of his
heart, emerging suddenly into a little glade and the wilderness coa-
lesced. It rushed, soundless, and solidified—the tree, the bush, the
compass and the watch glinting where a ray of sunlight touched
them. Then he saw the bear. It did not emerge, appear: it was just
there, immobile, fixed in the green and windless noon's hot dappling, not as big as he had dreamed it but as big as he had expected, bigger, dimensionless against the dappled obscurity, looking
at him. Then it moved. It crossed the glade without haste, walking
for an instant into the sun's full glare and out of it, and stopped
again and looked back at him across one shoulder. Then it was

gone. It didn't walk into the woods. It faded, sank back into the wilderness without motion as he had watched a fish, a huge old bass, sink back into the dark depths of its pool and vanish without even any movement of its fins.

– 2 –

So he should have hated and feared Lion. He was thirteen then. He had killed his buck and Sam Fathers had marked his face with the hot blood, and in the next November he killed a bear. But before that accolade he had become as competent in the woods as many grown men with the same experience. By now he was a better woodsman than most grown men with more. There was no territory within twenty-five miles of the camp that he did not know— bayou, ridge, landmark trees and path; he could have led anyone direct to any spot in it and brought him back. He knew game trails that even Sam Fathers had never seen; in the third fall he found a buck's bedding-place by himself and unbeknown to his cousin he borrowed Walter Ewell's rifle and lay in wait for the buck at dawn and killed it when it walked back to the bed as Sam had told him how the old Chickasaw fathers did.

By now he knew the old bear's footprint better than he did his own, and not only the crooked one. He could see any one of the three sound prints and distinguish it at once from any other, and not only because of its size. There were other bears within that fifty miles which left tracks almost as large, or at least so near that the one would have appeared larger only by juxtaposition. It was more than that. If Sam Fathers had been his mentor and the backyard rabbits and squirrels his kindergarten, then the wilderness the old bear ran was his college and the old male bear itself, so long unwifed and childless as to have become its own ungendered progenitor, was his alma mater.

He could find the crooked print now whenever he wished, ten miles or five miles or sometimes closer than that, to the camp. Twice while on stand during the next three years he heard the dogs strike its trail and once even jump it by chance, the voices high, abject, almost human in their hysteria. Once, still-hunting with Walter Ewell's rifle, he saw it cross a long corridor of down timber where a tornado had passed. It rushed through rather than across the tangle of trunks and branches as a locomotive would, faster than he had ever believed it could have moved, almost as fast as a

deer even because the deer would have spent most of that distance
in the air; he realised then why it would take a dog not only of ab-
normal courage but size and speed too ever to bring it to bay. He
had a little dog at home, a mongrel, of the sort called fyce by
Negroes, a ratter, itself not much bigger than a rat and possessing
that sort of courage which had long since stopped being bravery
and had become foolhardiness. He brought it with him one June
and, timing them as if they were meeting an appointment with another human being, himself carrying the fyce with a sack over its
head and Sam Fathers with a brace of the hounds on a rope leash,
they lay downwind of the trail and actually ambushed the bear.
They were so close that it turned at bay although he realised later
this might have been from surprise and amazement at the shrill
and frantic uproar of the fyce. It turned at bay against the trunk of
a big cypress, on its hind feet; it seemed to the boy that it would
never stop rising, taller and taller, and even the two hounds seemed
to have taken a kind of desperate and despairing courage from the
fyce. Then he realised that the fyce was actually not going to stop.
He flung the gun down and ran. When he overtook and grasped
the shrill, frantically pinwheeling little dog, it seemed to him that
he was directly under the bear. He could smell it, strong and hot
and rank. Sprawling, he looked up where it loomed and towered
over him like a thunderclap. It was quite familiar, until he remembered: this was the way he had used to dream about it.

Then it was gone. He didn't see it go. He knelt, holding the frantic fyce with both hands, hearing the abased wailing of the two
hounds drawing further and further away, until Sam came up, carrying the gun. He laid it quietly down beside the boy and stood
looking down at him. "You've done seed him twice now, with a gun
in your hands," he said. "This time you couldn't have missed him."

The boy rose. He still held the fyce. Even in his arms it continued to yap frantically, surging and straining toward the fading
sound of the hounds like a collection of live-wire springs. The boy
was panting a little. "Neither could you," he said. "You had the gun.
Why didn't you shoot him?"

Sam didn't seem to have heard. He put out his hand and touched
the little dog in the boy's arms which still yapped and strained even
though the two hounds were out of hearing now. "He's done gone,"
Sam said. "You can slack off and rest now, until next time." He
stroked the little dog until it began to grow quiet under his hand.

"You's almost the one we wants," he said. "You just aint big enough. We aint got that one yet. He will need to be just a little bigger than smart, and a little braver than either." He withdrew his hand from the fyce's head and stood looking into the woods where the bear and the hounds had vanished. "Somebody is going to, some day."

"I know it," the boy said. "That's why it must be one of us. So it wont be until the last day. When even he dont want it to last any longer."

So he should have hated and feared Lion. It was in the fourth summer, the fourth time he had made one in the celebration of Major de Spain's and General Compson's birthday. In the early spring Major de Spain's mare had foaled a horse colt. One evening when Sam brought the horses and mules up to stable them for the night, the colt was missing and it was all he could do to get the frantic mare into the lot. He had thought at first to let the mare lead him back to where she had become separated from the foal. But she would not do it. She would not even feint toward any particular part of the woods or even in any particular direction. She merely ran, as if she couldn't see, still frantic with terror. She whirled and ran at Sam once, as if to attack him in some ultimate desperation, as if she could not for the moment realise that he was a man and a long-familiar one. He got her into the lot at last. It was too dark by that time to back-track her, to unravel the erratic course she had doubtless pursued.

He came to the house and told Major de Spain. It was an animal, of course, a big one, and the colt was dead now, wherever it was. They all knew that. "It's a panther," General Compson said at once. "The same one. That doe and fawn last March." Sam had sent Major de Spain word of it when Boon Hogganbeck came to the camp on a routine visit to see how the stock had wintered—the doe's throat torn out, and the beast had run down the helpless fawn and killed it too.

"Sam never did say that was a panther," Major de Spain said. Sam said nothing now, standing behind Major de Spain where they sat at supper, inscrutable, as if he were just waiting for them to stop talking so he could go home. He didn't even seem to be looking at anything. "A panther might jump a doe, and he wouldn't have much trouble catching the fawn afterward. But no panther would have jumped that colt with the dam right there with it. It was Old Ben," Major de Spain said. "I'm disappointed in him. He has broken the rules. I didn't think he would have done that. He has killed mine and McCaslin's dogs, but that was all right. We gambled the dogs against him; we gave each other warning. But now he has come into my house and destroyed my property, out of season too. He broke the rules. It was Old Ben, Sam." Still Sam said nothing, standing there until Major de Spain should stop talking. "We'll back-track her tomorrow and see," Major de Spain said.

Sam departed. He would not live in the camp; he had built himself a little hut something like Joe Baker's, only stouter, tighter, on the bayou a quarter-mile away, and a stout log crib where he stored a little corn for the shoat he raised each year. The next morning he was waiting when they waked. He had already found the colt. They did not even wait for breakfast. It was not far, not five hundred yards from the stable—the three-months' colt lying on its side, its throat torn out and the entrails and one ham partly eaten. It lay not as if it had been dropped but as if it had been struck and hurled, and no cat-mark, no claw-mark where a panther would have gripped it while finding its throat. They read the tracks where the frantic mare had circled and at last rushed in with that same ultimate desperation with which she had whirled on Sam Fathers yesterday evening, and the long tracks of dead and terrified running and those of the beast which had not even rushed at her when she advanced but had merely walked three or four paces toward her until she broke, and General Compson said, "Good God, what a wolf!"

Still Sam said nothing. The boy watched him while the men knelt, measuring the tracks. There was something in Sam's face now. It was neither exultation nor joy nor hope. Later, a man, the boy realised what it had been, and that Sam had known all the time what had made the tracks and what had torn the throat out of the doe in the spring and killed the fawn. It had been foreknowledge in Sam's face that morning. *And he was glad, he told himself. He was old. He had no children, no people, none of his blood anywhere above earth that he would ever meet again. And even if he were to, he could not have touched it, spoken to it, because for seventy years now he had had to be a Negro. It was almost over now and he was glad.*

They returned to camp and had breakfast and came back with guns and the hounds. Afterward the boy realised that they also should have known then what killed the colt as well as Sam

Fathers did. But that was neither the first nor the last time he had
seen men rationalise from and even act upon their misconceptions.
After Boon, standing astride the colt, had whipped the dogs away
from it with his belt, they snuffed at the tracks. One of them, a
young dog hound without judgment yet, bayed once, and they ran
for a few feet on what seemed to be a trail. Then they stopped,
looking back at the men, eager enough, not baffled, merely questioning, as if they were asking "Now what?" Then they rushed back
to the colt, where Boon, still astride it, slashed at them with the
belt.

"I never knew a trail to get cold that quick," General Compson
said.

"Maybe a single wolf big enough to kill a colt with the dam right
there beside it dont leave scent," Major de Spain said.

"Maybe it was a hant," Walter Ewell said. He looked at Tennie's
Jim. "Hah, Jim?"

Because the hounds would not run it, Major de Spain had Sam
hunt out and find the tracks a hundred yards farther on and they
put the dogs on it again and again the young one bayed and not
one of them realised then that the hound was not baying like a dog
striking game but was merely bellowing like a country dog whose
yard has been invaded. General Compson spoke to the boy and
Boon and Tennie's Jim: to the squirrel hunters. "You boys keep the
dogs with you this morning. He's probably hanging around somewhere, waiting to get his breakfast off the colt. You might strike
him."

But they did not. The boy remembered how Sam stood watching
them as they went into the woods with the leashed hounds—the
Indian face in which he had never seen anything until it smiled, except that faint arching of the nostrils on that first morning when
the hounds had found Old Ben. They took the hounds with them
on the next day, though when they reached the place where they
hoped to strike a fresh trail, the carcass of the colt was gone. Then
on the third morning Sam was waiting again, this time until they
had finished breakfast. He said, "Come." He led them to his house,
his little hut, to the corn-crib beyond it. He had removed the corn
and had made a deadfall of the door, baiting it with the colt's carcass; peering between the logs, they saw an animal almost the
color of a gun or pistol barrel, what little time they had to examine
its color or shape. It was not crouched nor even standing. It was in

motion, in the air, coming toward them—a heavy body crashing
with tremendous force against the door so that the thick door
jumped and clattered in its frame, the animal, whatever it was,
hurling itself against the door again seemingly before it could have
touched the floor and got a new purchase to spring from. "Come
away," Sam said, "fore he break his neck." Even when they retreated the heavy and measured crashes continued, the stout door
jumping and clattering each time, and still no sound from the beast
itself—no snarl, no cry.

"What in hell's name is it?" Major de Spain said.

"It's a dog," Sam said, his nostrils arching and collapsing faintly
and steadily and that faint, fierce milkiness in his eyes again as on
that first morning when the hounds had struck the old bear. "It's
the dog."

"*The* dog?" Major de Spain said.

"That's gonter hold Old Ben."

"Dog the devil," Major de Spain said. "I'd rather have Old Ben
himself in my pack than that brute. Shoot him."

"No," Sam said.

"You'll never tame him. How do you ever expect to make an
animal like that afraid of you?"

"I dont want him tame," Sam said; again the boy watched his
nostrils and the fierce milky light in his eyes. "But I almost rather
he be tame than scared, of me or any man or any thing. But he
wont be neither, of nothing."

"Then what are you going to do with it?"

"You can watch," Sam said.

Each morning through the second week they would go to Sam's
crib. He had removed a few shingles from the roof and had put a
rope on the colt's carcass and had drawn it out when the trap fell.
Each morning they would watch him lower a pail of water into
the crib while the dog hurled itself tirelessly against the door and
dropped back and leaped again. It never made any sound and
there was nothing frenzied in the act but only a cold and grim indomitable determination. Toward the end of the week it stopped
jumping at the door. Yet it had not weakened appreciably and it
was not as if it had rationalised the fact that the door was not going to give. It was as if for that time it simply disdained to jump
any longer. It was not down. None of them had ever seen it down.
It stood, and they could see it now—part mastiff, something of

Airedale and something of a dozen other strains probably, better than thirty inches at the shoulders and weighing as they guessed almost ninety pounds, with cold yellow eyes and a tremendous chest and over all that strange color like a blued gun-barrel.

Then the two weeks were up. They prepared to break camp. The boy begged to remain and his cousin let him. He moved into the little hut with Sam Fathers. Each morning he watched Sam lower the pail of water into the crib. By the end of that week the dog was down. It would rise and half stagger, half crawl to the water and drink and collapse again. One morning it could not even reach the water, could not raise its forequarters even from the floor. Sam took a short stick and prepared to enter the crib. "Wait," the boy said. "Let me get the gun——"

"No," Sam said. "He cant move now." Nor could it. It lay on its side while Sam touched it, its head and the gaunted body, the dog lying motionless, the yellow eyes open. They were not fierce and there was nothing of petty malevolence in them, but a cold and almost impersonal malignance like some natural force. It was not even looking at Sam nor at the boy peering at it between the logs.

Sam began to feed it again. The first time he had to raise its head so it could lap the broth. That night he left a bowl of broth containing lumps of meat where the dog could reach it. The next morning the bowl was empty and the dog was lying on its belly, its head up, the cold yellow eyes watching the door as Sam entered, no change whatever in the cold yellow eyes and still no sound from it even when it sprang, its aim and co-ordination still bad from weakness so that Sam had time to strike it down with the stick and leap from the crib and slam the door as the dog, still without having had time to get its feet under it to jump again seemingly, hurled itself against the door as if the two weeks of starving had never been.

At noon that day someone came whooping through the woods from the direction of the camp. It was Boon. He came and looked for a while between the logs, at the tremendous dog lying again on its belly, its head up, the yellow eyes blinking sleepily at nothing: the indomitable and unbroken spirit. "What we better do," Boon said, "is to let that son of a bitch go and catch Old Ben and run him on the dog." He turned to the boy his weather-reddened and beetling face. "Get your traps together. Cass says for you to come on home. You been in here fooling with that horse-eating varmint long enough."

Boon had a borrowed mule at the camp; the buggy was waiting at the edge of the bottom. He was at home that night. He told McCaslin about it. "Sam's going to starve him again until he can go in and touch him. Then he will feed him again. Then he will starve him again, if he has to."

"But why?" McCaslin said. "What for? Even Sam will never tame that brute."

"We dont want him tame. We want him like he is. We just want him to find out at last that the only way he can get out of that crib and stay out of it is to do what Sam or somebody tells him to do. He's the dog that's going to stop Old Ben and hold him. We've already named him. His name is Lion."

Then November came at last. They returned to the camp. With General Compson and Major de Spain and his cousin and Walter and Boon he stood in the yard among the guns and bedding and boxes of food and watched Sam Fathers and Lion come up the lane from the lot—the Indian, the old man in battered overalls and rubber boots and a worn sheepskin coat and a hat which had belonged to the boy's father; the tremendous dog pacing gravely beside him. The hounds rushed out to meet them and stopped, except the young one which still had but little of judgment. It ran up to Lion, fawning. Lion didn't snap at it. He didn't even pause. He struck it rolling and yelping for five or six feet with a blow of one paw as a bear would have done and came on into the yard and stood, blinking sleepily at nothing, looking at no one, while Boon said, "Jesus. Jesus.—Will he let me touch him?"

"You can touch him," Sam said. "He dont care. He dont care about nothing or nobody."

The boy watched that too. He watched it for the next two years from that moment when Boon touched Lion's head and then knelt beside him, feeling the bones and muscles, the power. It was as if Lion were a woman—or perhaps Boon was the woman. That was more like it—the big, grave, sleepy-seeming dog which, as Sam Fathers said, cared about no man and no thing; and the violent, insensitive, hard-faced man with his touch of remote Indian blood and the mind almost of a child. He watched Boon take over Lion's feeding from Sam and Uncle Ash both. He would see Boon squat-

ting in the cold rain beside the kitchen while Lion ate. Because
Lion neither slept nor ate with the other dogs though none of them
knew where he did sleep until in the second November, thinking
until then that Lion slept in his kennel beside Sam Fathers' hut,
when the boy's cousin McCaslin said something about it to Sam by
sheer chance and Sam told him. And that night the boy and Major
de Spain and McCaslin with a lamp entered the back room where
Boon slept—the little, tight, airless room rank with the smell of
Boon's unwashed body and his wet hunting-clothes—where Boon,
snoring on his back, choked and waked and Lion raised his head
beside him and looked back at them from his cold, slumbrous yellow eyes.

"Damn it, Boon," McCaslin said. "Get that dog out of here. He's
got to run Old Ben tomorrow morning. How in hell do you expect
him to smell anything fainter than a skunk after breathing you all
night?"

"The way I smell aint hurt my nose none that I ever noticed,"
Boon said.

"It wouldn't matter if it had," Major de Spain said. "We're not
depending on you to trail a bear. Put him outside. Put him under
the house with the other dogs."

Boon began to get up. "He'll kill the first one that happens to
yawn or sneeze in his face or touches him."

"I reckon not," Major de Spain said. "None of them are going to
risk yawning in his face or touching him either, even asleep. Put
him outside. I want his nose right tomorrow. Old Ben fooled him
last year. I dont think he will do it again."

Boon put on his shoes without lacing them; in his long soiled
underwear, his hair still tousled from sleep, he and Lion went out.
The others returned to the front room and the poker game where
McCaslin's and Major de Spain's hands waited for them on the table. After a while McCaslin said, "Do you want me to go back and
look again?"

"No," Major de Spain said. "I call," he said to Walter Ewell. He
spoke to McCaslin again. "If you do, dont tell me. I am beginning
to see the first sign of my increasing age: I dont like to know that
my orders have been disobeyed, even when I knew when I gave
them that they would be.—A small pair," he said to Walter Ewell.

"How small?" Walter said.

"Very small," Major de Spain said.

And the boy, lying beneath his piled quilts and blankets waiting for sleep, knew likewise that Lion was already back in Boon's bed, for the rest of that night and the next one and during all the nights of the next November and the next one. He thought then: *I wonder what Sam thinks. He could have Lion with him, even if Boon is a white man. He could ask Major or McCaslin either. And more than that. It was Sam's hand that touched Lion first and Lion knows it.* Then he became a man and he knew that too. It had been all right. That was the way it should have been. Sam was the chief, the prince; Boon, the plebeian, was his huntsman. Boon should have nursed the dogs.

On the first morning that Lion led the pack after Old Ben, seven strangers appeared in the camp. They were swampers: gaunt, malaria-ridden men appearing from nowhere, who ran trap-lines for coons or perhaps farmed little patches of cotton and corn along the edge of the bottom, in clothes but little better than Sam Fathers' and nowhere near as good as Tennie's Jim's, with worn shotguns and rifles, already squatting patiently in the cold drizzle in the side yard when day broke. They had a spokesman; afterward Sam Fathers told Major de Spain how all during the past summer and fall they had drifted into the camp singly or in pairs and threes, to look quietly at Lion for a while and then go away: "Mawnin, Major. We heerd you was aimin to put that ere blue dawg on that old two-toed bear this mawnin. We figgered we'd come up and watch, if you dont mind. We wont do no shooting, lessen he runs over us."

"You are welcome," Major de Spain said. "You are welcome to shoot. He's more your bear than ours."

"I reckon that aint no lie. I done fed him enough cawn to have a sheer in him. Not to mention a shoat three years ago."

"I reckon I got a sheer too," another said. "Only it aint in the bear." Major de Spain looked at him. He was chewing tobacco. He spat. "Hit was a heifer calf. Nice un too. Last year. When I finally found her, I reckon she looked about like that colt of yourn looked last June."

"Oh," Major de Spain said. "Be welcome. If you see game in front of my dogs, shoot it."

Nobody shot Old Ben that day. No man saw him. The dogs jumped him within a hundred yards of the glade where the boy had seen him that day in the summer of his eleventh year. The boy was less than a quarter-mile away. He heard the jump but he could distinguish no voice among the dogs that he did not know and therefore would be Lion's, and he thought, believed, that Lion was not among them. Even the fact that they were going much faster than he had ever heard them run behind Old Ben before and that the high thin note of hysteria was missing now from their voices was not enough to disabuse him. He didn't comprehend until that night, when Sam told him that Lion would never cry on a trail. "He gonter growl when he catches Old Ben's throat," Sam said. "But he aint gonter never holler, no more than he ever done when he was jumping at that two-inch door. It's that blue dog in him. What you call it?"

"Airedale," the boy said.

Lion was there; the jump was just too close to the river. When Boon returned with Lion about eleven that night, he swore that Lion had stopped Old Ben once but that the hounds would not go in and Old Ben broke away and took to the river and swam for miles down it and he and Lion went down one bank for about ten miles and crossed and came up the other but it had begun to get dark before they struck any trail where Old Ben had come up out of the water, unless he was still in the water when he passed the ford where they crossed. Then he fell to cursing the hounds and ate the supper Uncle Ash had saved for him and went off to bed and after a while the boy opened the door of the little stale room thunderous with snoring and the great grave dog raised its head from Boon's pillow and blinked at him for a moment and lowered its head again.

When the next November came and the last day, the day on which it was now becoming traditional to save for Old Ben, there were more than a dozen strangers waiting. They were not all swampers this time. Some of them were townsmen, from other county seats like Jefferson, who had heard about Lion and Old Ben and had come to watch the great blue dog keep his yearly rendezvous with the old two-toed bear. Some of them didn't even have guns and the hunting-clothes and boots they wore had been on a store shelf yesterday.

This time Lion jumped Old Ben more than five miles from the river and bayed and held him and this time the hounds went in, in a sort of desperate emulation. The boy heard them; he was that near. He heard Boon whooping; he heard the two shots when General Compson delivered both barrels, one containing five buckshot, the other a single ball, into the bear from as close as he could force his almost unmanageable horse. He heard the dogs when the bear broke free again. He was running now; panting, stumbling, his lungs bursting, he reached the place where General Compson had fired and where Old Ben had killed two of the hounds. He saw the blood from General Compson's shots, but he could go no further. He stopped, leaning against a tree for his breathing to ease and his heart to slow, hearing the sound of the dogs as it faded on and died away.

In camp that night—they had as guests five of the still terrified strangers in new hunting coats and boots who had been lost all day until Sam Fathers went out and got them—he heard the rest of it: how Lion had stopped and held the bear again but only the one-eyed mule which did not mind the smell of wild blood would approach and Boon was riding the mule and Boon had never been known to hit anything. He shot at the bear five times with his pump gun, touching nothing, and Old Ben killed another hound and broke free once more and reached the river and was gone. Again Boon and Lion hunted as far down one bank as they dared. Too far; they crossed in the first of dusk and dark overtook them within a mile. And this time Lion found the broken trail, the blood perhaps, in the darkness where Old Ben had come up out of the water, but Boon had him on a rope, luckily, and he got down from the mule and fought Lion hand-to-hand until he got him back to camp. This time Boon didn't even curse. He stood in the door, muddy, spent, his huge gargoyle's face tragic and still amazed. "I missed him," he said. "I was in twenty-five feet of him and I missed him five times."

"But we have drawn blood," Major de Spain said. "General Compson drew blood. We have never done that before."

"But I missed him," Boon said. "I missed him five times. With Lion looking right at me."

"Never mind," Major de Spain said. "It was a damned fine race. And we drew blood. Next year we'll let General Compson or Walter ride Katie, and we'll get him."

Then McCaslin said, "Where is Lion, Boon?"

"I left him at Sam's," Boon said. He was already turning away. "I aint fit to sleep with him."

So he should have hated and feared Lion. Yet he did not. It

seemed to him that there was a fatality in it. It seemed to him that something, he didn't know what, was beginning; had already begun. It was like the last act on a set stage. It was the beginning of the end of something, he didn't know what except that he would not grieve. He would be humble and proud that he had been found worthy to be a part of it too or even just to see it too.

– 3 –

It was December. It was the coldest December he had ever remembered. They had been in camp four days over two weeks, waiting for the weather to soften so that Lion and Old Ben could run their yearly race. Then they would break camp and go home. Because of these unforeseen additional days which they had had to pass waiting on the weather, with nothing to do but play poker, the whisky had given out and he and Boon were being sent to Memphis with a suitcase and a note from Major de Spain to Mr Semmes, the distiller, to get more. That is, Major de Spain and McCaslin were sending Boon to get the whisky and sending him to see that Boon got back with it or most of it or at least some of it.

Tennie's Jim waked him at three. He dressed rapidly, shivering, not so much from the cold because a fresh fire already boomed and roared on the hearth, but in that dead winter hour when the blood and the heart are slow and sleep is incomplete. He crossed the gap between house and kitchen, the gap of iron earth beneath the brilliant and rigid night where dawn would not begin for three hours yet, tasting, tongue palate and to the very bottom of his lungs the searing dark, and entered the kitchen, the lamplit warmth where the stove glowed, fogging the windows, and where Boon already sat at the table at breakfast, hunched over his plate, almost in his plate, his working jaws blue with stubble and his face innocent of water and his coarse, horse-mane hair innocent of comb—the quarter Indian, grandson of a Chickasaw squaw, who on occasion resented with his hard and furious fists the intimation of one single drop of alien blood and on others, usually after whisky, affirmed with the same fists and the same fury that his father had been the full-blood Chickasaw and even a chief and that even his mother had been only half white. He was four inches over six feet; he had the mind of a child, the heart of a horse, and little hard shoe-button eyes without depth or meanness or generosity or viciousness or gentleness or anything else, in the ugliest face the boy had ever

seen. It looked like somebody had found a walnut a little larger
than a football and with a machinist's hammer had shaped features
into it and then painted it, mostly red; not Indian red but a fine
bright ruddy color which whisky might have had something to do
with but which was mostly just happy and violent out-of-doors, the
wrinkles in it not the residue of the forty years it had survived but
from squinting into the sun or into the gloom of cane-brakes where
game had run, baked into it by the camp fires before which he had
lain trying to sleep on the cold November or December ground
while waiting for daylight so he could rise and hunt again, as
though time were merely something he walked through as he did
through air, aging him no more than air did. He was brave, faith-
ful, improvident and unreliable; he had neither profession job nor
trade and owned one vice and one virtue: whisky, and that absolute and unquestioning fidelity to Major de Spain and the boy's
cousin McCaslin. "Sometimes I'd call them both virtues," Major de
Spain said once. "Or both vices," McCaslin said.

He ate his breakfast, hearing the dogs under the kitchen, wakened by the smell of frying meat or perhaps by the feet overhead.
He heard Lion once, short and peremptory, as the best hunter in
any camp has only to speak once to all save the fools, and none
other of Major de Spain's and McCaslin's dogs were Lion's equal in
size and strength and perhaps even in courage, but they were not
fools; Old Ben had killed the last fool among them last year.

Tennie's Jim came in as they finished. The wagon was outside.
Ash decided he would drive them over to the log-line where they
would flag the outbound log-train and let Tennie's Jim wash the
dishes. The boy knew why. It would not be the first time he had
listened to old Ash badgering Boon.

It was cold. The wagon wheels banged and clattered on the
frozen ground; the sky was fixed and brilliant. He was not shivering,
he was shaking, slow and steady and hard, the food he had just
eaten still warm and solid inside him while his outside shook slow
and steady around it as though his stomach floated loose. "They
wont run this morning," he said. "No dog will have any nose today."

"Cep Lion," Ash said. "Lion dont need no nose. All he need is a
bear." He had wrapped his feet in towsacks and he had a quilt
from his pallet bed on the kitchen floor drawn over his head and
wrapped around him until in the thin brilliant starlight he looked

like nothing at all that the boy had ever seen before. "He run
a bear through a thousand-acre ice-house. Catch him too. Them
other dogs dont matter because they aint going to keep up with
Lion nohow, long as he got a bear in front of him."

"What's wrong with the other dogs?" Boon said. "What the hell
do you know about it anyway? This is the first time you've had
your tail out of that kitchen since we got here except to chop a little wood."

"Aint nothing wrong with them," Ash said. "And long as it's left
up to them, aint nothing going to be. I just wish I had knowed all
my life how to take care of my health good as them hounds knows."

"Well, they aint going to run this morning," Boon said. His voice
was harsh and positive. "Major promised they wouldn't until me
and Ike get back."

"Weather gonter break today. Gonter soft up. Rain by night."
Then Ash laughed, chuckled, somewhere inside the quilt which
concealed even his face. "Hum up here, mules!" he said, jerking the
reins so that the mules leaped forward and snatched the lurching
and banging wagon for several feet before they slowed again into
their quick, short-paced, rapid plodding. "Sides, I like to know why
Major need to wait on you. It's Lion he aiming to use. I aint never
heard tell of you bringing no bear nor no other kind of meat into
this camp."

Now Boon's going to curse Ash or maybe even hit him, the boy
thought. But Boon never did, never had; the boy knew he never
would even though four years ago Boon had shot five times with a
borrowed pistol at a Negro on the street in Jefferson, with the same
result as when he had shot five times at Old Ben last fall. "By God,"
Boon said, "he aint going to put Lion or no other dog on nothing
until I get back tonight. Because he promised me. Whip up them
mules and keep them whipped up. Do you want me to freeze to
death?"

They reached the log-line and built a fire. After a while the log-
train came up out of the woods under the paling east and Boon
flagged it. Then in the warm caboose the boy slept again while
Boon and the conductor and brakeman talked about Lion and Old
Ben as people later would talk about Sullivan and Kilrain and, later
still, about Dempsey and Tunney. Dozing, swaying as the springless caboose lurched and clattered, he would hear them still talking, about the shoats and calves Old Ben had killed and the cribs

he had rifled and the traps and deadfalls he had wrecked and the lead he probably carried under his hide—Old Ben, the two-toed bear in a land where bears with trap-ruined feet had been called Two-Toe or Three-Toe or Cripple-Foot for fifty years, only Old Ben was an extra bear (the head bear, General Compson called him) and so had earned a name such as a human man could have worn and not been sorry.

They reached Hoke's at sunup. They emerged from the warm caboose in their hunting clothes, the muddy boots and stained khaki and Boon's blue unshaven jowls. But that was all right. Hoke's was a sawmill and commissary and two stores and a loading-chute on a sidetrack from the main line, and all the men in it wore boots and khaki too. Presently the Memphis train came. Boon bought three packages of popcorn-and-molasses and a bottle of beer from the news butch and the boy went to sleep again to the sound of his chewing.

But in Memphis it was not all right. It was as if the high buildings and the hard pavements, the fine carriages and the horse cars and the men in starched collars and neckties made their boots and khaki look a little rougher and a little muddier and made Boon's beard look worse and more unshaven and his face look more and more like he should never have brought it out of the woods at all or at least out of reach of Major de Spain or McCaslin or someone who knew it and could have said, "Dont be afraid. He wont hurt you." He walked through the station, on the slick floor, his face moving as he worked the popcorn out of his teeth with his tongue, his legs spraddled and stiff in the hips as if he were walking on buttered glass, and that blue stubble on his face like the filings from a new gun-barrel. They passed the first saloon. Even through the closed doors the boy could seem to smell the sawdust and the reek of old drink. Boon began to cough. He coughed for something less than a minute. "Damn this cold," he said. "I'd sure like to know where I got it."

"Back there in the station," the boy said.

Boon had started to cough again. He stopped. He looked at the boy. "What?" he said.

"You never had it when we left camp nor on the train either." Boon looked at him, blinking. Then he stopped blinking. He didn't cough again. He said quietly:

"Lend me a dollar. Come on. You've got it. If you ever had one, you've still got it. I dont mean you are tight with your money because you aint. You just dont never seem to ever think of nothing you want. When I was sixteen a dollar bill melted off of me before I even had time to read the name of the bank that issued it." He said quietly: "Let me have a dollar, Ike."

"You promised Major. You promised McCaslin. Not till we get back to camp."

"All right," Boon said in that quiet and patient voice. "What can I do on just one dollar? You aint going to lend me another."

"You're damn right I aint," the boy said, his voice quiet too, cold with rage which was not at Boon, remembering: Boon snoring in a hard chair in the kitchen so he could watch the clock and wake him and McCaslin and drive them the seventeen miles in to Jefferson to catch the train to Memphis; the wild, never-bridled Texas paint pony which he had persuaded McCaslin to let him buy and which he and Boon had bought at auction for four dollars and seventy-five cents and fetched home wired between two gentle old mares with pieces of barbed wire and which had never even seen shelled corn before and didn't even know what it was unless the grains were bugs maybe and at last (he was ten and Boon had been ten all his life) Boon said the pony was gentled and with a towsack over its head and four Negroes to hold it they backed it into an old two-wheeled cart and hooked up the gear and he and Boon got up and Boon said, "All right, boys. Let him go" and one of the Negroes—it was Tennie's Jim—snatched the towsack off and leaped for his life and they lost the first wheel against a post of the open gate only at that moment Boon caught him by the scruff of the neck and flung him into the roadside ditch so he only saw the rest of it in fragments: the other wheel as it slammed through the side gate and crossed the back yard and leaped up onto the gallery and scraps of the cart here and there along the road and Boon vanishing rapidly on his stomach in the leaping and spurting dust and still holding the reins until they broke too and two days later they finally caught the pony seven miles away still wearing the hames and the headstall of the bridle around its neck like a duchess with two necklaces at one time. He gave Boon the dollar.

"All right," Boon said. "Come on in out of the cold."

"I aint cold," he said.

"You can have some lemonade."

"I dont want any lemonade."

The door closed behind him. The sun was well up now. It was a brilliant day, though Ash had said it would rain before night. Already it was warmer; they could run tomorrow. He felt the old lift of the heart, as pristine as ever, as on the first day; he would never lose it, no matter how old in hunting and pursuit: the best, the best of all breathing, the humility and the pride. He must stop thinking about it. Already it seemed to him that he was running, back to the station, to the tracks themselves: the first train going south; he must stop thinking about it. The street was busy. He watched the big Norman draft horses, the Percherons; the trim carriages from which the men in the fine overcoats and the ladies rosy in furs descended and entered the station. (They were still next door to it but one.) Twenty years ago his father had ridden into Memphis as a member of Colonel Sartoris' horse in Forrest's command, up Main street and (the tale told) into the lobby of the Gayoso Hotel where the Yankee officers sat in the leather chairs spitting into the tall bright cuspidors and then out again, scot-free——

The door opened behind him. Boon was wiping his mouth on the back of his hand. "All right," he said. "Let's go tend to it and get the hell out of here."

They went and had the suitcase packed. He never knew where or when Boon got the other bottle. Doubtless Mr Semmes gave it to him. When they reached Hoke's again at sundown, it was empty. They could get a return train to Hoke's in two hours; they went straight back to the station as Major de Spain and then McCaslin had told Boon to do and then ordered him to do and had sent the boy along to see that he did. Boon took the first drink from his bottle in the washroom. A man in a uniform cap came to tell him he couldn't drink there and looked at Boon's face once and said nothing. The next time he was pouring into his water glass beneath the edge of a table in the restaurant when the manager (she was a woman) did tell him he couldn't drink there and he went back to the washroom. He had been telling the Negro waiter and all the other people in the restaurant who couldn't help but hear him and who had never heard of Lion and didn't want to, about Lion and Old Ben. Then he happened to think of the zoo. He had found out that there was another train to Hoke's at three oclock and so they would spend the time at the zoo and take the three oclock train until he came back from the washroom for the third time. Then they would take the first train back to camp, get Lion and come back to the zoo where, he said, the bears were fed on ice cream and lady fingers and he would match Lion against them all.

So they missed the first train, the one they were supposed to take, but he got Boon onto the three oclock train and they were all right again, with Boon not even going to the washroom now but drinking in the aisle and talking about Lion and the men he buttonholed no more daring to tell Boon he couldn't drink there than the man in the station had dared.

When they reached Hoke's at sundown, Boon was asleep. The boy waked him at last and got him and the suitcase off the train and he even persuaded him to eat some supper at the sawmill commissary. So he was all right when they got in the caboose of the log-train to go back into the woods, with the sun going down red and the sky already overcast and the ground would not freeze tonight. It was the boy who slept now, sitting behind the ruby stove while the springless caboose jumped and clattered and Boon and the brakeman and the conductor talked about Lion and Old Ben because they knew what Boon was talking about because this was home. "Overcast and already thawing," Boon said. "Lion will get him tomorrow."

It would have to be Lion, or somebody. It would not be Boon. He had never hit anything bigger than a squirrel that anybody ever knew, except the Negro woman that day when he was shooting at the Negro man. He was a big Negro and not ten feet away but Boon shot five times with the pistol he had borrowed from Major de Spain's Negro coachman and the Negro he was shooting at outed with a dollar-and-a-half mail-order pistol and would have burned Boon down with it only it never went off, it just went snicksnicksnicksnicksnick five times and Boon still blasting away and he broke a plate-glass window that cost McCaslin forty-five dollars and hit a Negro woman who happened to be passing in the leg only Major de Spain paid for that; he and McCaslin cut cards, the plate-glass window against the Negro woman's leg. And the first day on stand this year, the first morning in camp, the buck ran right over Boon; he heard Boon's old pump gun go whow. whow. whow. whow. whow. and then his voice: "God damn, here he comes! Head him! Head him!" and when he got there the buck's tracks and the five exploded shells were not twenty paces apart.

There were five guests in camp that night, from Jefferson: Mr Bayard Sartoris and his son and General Compson's son and two others. And the next morning he looked out the window, into the gray thin drizzle of daybreak which Ash had predicted, and there they were, standing and squatting beneath the thin rain, almost two dozen of them who had fed Old Ben corn and shoats and even calves for ten years, in their worn hats and hunting coats and overalls which any town Negro would have thrown away or burned and only the rubber boots strong and sound, and the worn and blueless guns and some even without guns. While they ate breakfast a dozen more arrived, mounted and on foot: loggers from the camp thirteen miles below and sawmill men from Hoke's and the only gun among them that one which the log-train conductor carried: so that when they went into the woods this morning Major de Spain led a party almost as strong, excepting that some of them were not armed, as some he had led in the last darkening days of '64 and '65. The little yard would not hold them. They overflowed it, into the lane where Major de Spain sat his mare while Ash in his dirty apron thrust the greasy cartridges into his carbine and passed it up to him and the great grave blue dog stood at his stirrup not as a dog stands but as a horse stands, blinking his sleepy topaz eyes at nothing, deaf even to the yelling of the hounds which Boon and Tennie's Jim held on leash.

"We'll put General Compson on Katie this morning," Major de Spain said. "He drew blood last year; if he'd had a mule then that would have stood, he would have——"

"No," General Compson said. "I'm too old to go helling through the woods on a mule or a horse or anything else any more. Besides, I had my chance last year and missed it. I'm going on a stand this morning. I'm going to let that boy ride Katie."

"No, wait," McCaslin said. "Ike's got the rest of his life to hunt bears in. Let somebody else——"

"No," General Compson said. "I want Ike to ride Katie. He's already a better woodsman than you or me either and in another ten years he'll be as good as Walter."

At first he couldn't believe it, not until Major de Spain spoke to him. Then he was up, on the one-eyed mule which would not spook at wild blood, looking down at the dog motionless at Major de Spain's stirrup, looking in the gray streaming light bigger than a calf, bigger than he knew it actually was—the big head, the chest almost as big as his own, the blue hide beneath which the muscles flinched or quivered to no touch since the heart which drove blood to them loved no man and no thing, standing as a horse stands yet different from a horse which infers only weight and speed while Lion inferred not only courage and all else that went to make up the will and desire to pursue and kill, but endurance, the will and desire to endure beyond all imaginable limits of flesh in order to overtake and slay. Then the dog looked at him. It moved its head and looked at him across the trivial uproar of the hounds, out of the yellow eyes as depthless as Boon's, as free as Boon's of meanness or generosity or gentleness or viciousness. They were just cold and sleepy. Then it blinked, and he knew it was not looking at him and never had been, without even bothering to turn its head away.

That morning he heard the first cry. Lion had already vanished while Sam and Tennie's Jim were putting saddles on the mule and horse which had drawn the wagon and he watched the hounds as they crossed and cast, snuffing and whimpering, until they too disappeared. Then he and Major de Spain and Sam and Tennie's Jim rode after them and heard the first cry out of the wet and thawing woods not two hundred yards ahead, high, with that abject, almost human quality he had come to know, and the other hounds joining in until the gloomed woods rang and clamored. They rode then. It seemed to him that he could actually see the big blue dog boring on, silent, and the bear too: the thick, locomotive-like shape which he had seen that day four years ago crossing the blow-down, crashing on ahead of the dogs faster than he had believed it could have moved, drawing away even from the running mules. He heard a shotgun, once. The woods had opened, they were going fast, the clamor faint and fading on ahead; they passed the man who had fired—a swamper, a pointing arm, a gaunt face, the small black orifice of his yelling studded with rotten teeth.

He heard the changed note in the hounds' uproar and two hundred yards ahead he saw them. The bear had turned. He saw Lion drive in without pausing and saw the bear strike him aside and lunge into the yelling hounds and kill one of them almost in its tracks and whirl and run again. Then they were in a streaming tide of dogs. He heard Major de Spain and Tennie's Jim shouting and the pistol sound of Tennie's Jim's leather thong as he tried to turn them. Then he and Sam Fathers were riding alone. One of the hounds had kept on with Lion though. He recognised its voice. It was the young hound which even a year ago had had no judgment and which, by the lights of the other hounds anyway, still had none. *Maybe that's what courage is,* he thought. "Right," Sam said behind him. "Right. We got to turn him from the river if we can."

Now they were in cane: a brake. He knew the path through it as well as Sam did. They came out of the undergrowth and struck the entrance almost exactly. It would traverse the brake and come out onto a high open ridge above the river. He heard the flat clap of Walter Ewell's rifle, then two more. "No," Sam said. "I can hear the hound. Go on."

They emerged from the narrow roofless tunnel of snapping and hissing cane, still galloping, onto the open ridge below which the thick yellow river, reflectionless in the gray and streaming light, seemed not to move. Now he could hear the hound too. It was not running. The cry was a high frantic yapping and Boon was running along the edge of the bluff, his old gun leaping and jouncing against his back on its sling made of a piece of cotton plowline. He whirled and ran up to them, wild-faced, and flung himself onto the mule behind the boy. "That damn boat!" he cried. "It's on the other side! He went straight across! Lion was too close to him! That little hound too! Lion was so close I couldn't shoot! Go on!" he cried, beating his heels into the mule's flanks. "Go on!"

They plunged down the bank, slipping and sliding in the thawed earth, crashing through the willows and into the water. He felt no shock, no cold, he on one side of the swimming mule, grasping the pommel with one hand and holding his gun above the water with the other, Boon opposite him. Sam was behind them somewhere, and then the river, the water about them, was full of dogs. They swam faster than the mules; they were scrabbling up the bank before the mules touched bottom. Major de Spain was whooping from the bank they had just left and, looking back, he saw Tennie's Jim and the horse as they went into the water.

Now the woods ahead of them and the rain-heavy air were one uproar. It rang and clamored; it echoed and broke against the bank behind them and reformed and clamored and rang until it seemed to the boy that all the hounds which had ever bayed game in this land were yelling down at him. He got his leg over the mule as it came up out of the water. Boon didn't try to mount again. He grasped one stirrup as they went up the bank and crashed through the undergrowth which fringed the bluff and saw the bear, on its hind feet, its back against a tree while the bellowing hounds swirled around it and once more Lion drove in, leaping clear of the ground.

This time the bear didn't strike him down. It caught the dog in both arms, almost loverlike, and they both went down. He was off the mule now. He drew back both hammers of the gun but he could see nothing but moiling spotted houndbodies until the bear surged up again. Boon was yelling something, he could not tell what; he could see Lion still clinging to the bear's throat and he saw the bear, half erect, strike one of the hounds with one paw and hurl it five or six feet and then, rising and rising as though it would never stop, stand erect again and begin to rake at Lion's belly with its forepaws. Then Boon was running. The boy saw the gleam of the blade in his hand and watched him leap among the hounds, hurdling them, kicking them aside as he ran, and fling himself astride the bear as he had hurled himself onto the mule, his legs locked around the bear's belly, his left arm under the bear's throat where Lion clung, and the glint of the knife as it rose and fell.

It fell just once. For an instant they almost resembled a piece of statuary: the clinging dog, the bear, the man astride its back, working and probing the buried blade. Then they went down, pulled over backward by Boon's weight, Boon underneath. It was the bear's back which reappeared first but at once Boon was astride it again. He had never released the knife and again the boy saw the almost infinitesimal movement of his arm and shoulder as he probed and sought; then the bear surged erect, raising with it the man and the dog too, and turned and still carrying the man and the dog it took two or three steps toward the woods on its hind feet as a man would have walked and crashed down. It didn't collapse, crumple. It fell all of a piece, as a tree falls, so that all three of them, man dog and bear, seemed to bounce once.

He and Tennie's Jim ran forward. Boon was kneeling at the bear's head. His left ear was shredded, his left coat sleeve was completely gone, his right boot had been ripped from knee to instep; the bright blood thinned in the thin rain down his leg and hand and arm and down the side of his face which was no longer wild but was quite calm. Together they prized Lion's jaws from the bear's throat. "Easy, goddamn it," Boon said. "Cant you see his guts are all out of him?" He began to remove his coat. He spoke to Tennie's

Jim in that calm voice: "Bring the boat up. It's about a hundred yards down the bank there. I saw it." Tennie's Jim rose and went away. Then, and he could not remember if it had been a call or an exclamation from Tennie's Jim or if he had glanced up by chance, he saw Tennie's Jim stooping and saw Sam Fathers lying motionless on his face in the trampled mud.

The mule had not thrown him. He remembered that Sam was down too even before Boon began to run. There was no mark on him whatever and when he and Boon turned him over, his eyes were open and he said something in that tongue which he and Joe Baker had used to speak together. But he couldn't move. Tennie's Jim brought the skiff up; they could hear him shouting to Major de Spain across the river. Boon wrapped Lion in his hunting coat and carried him down to the skiff and they carried Sam down and returned and hitched the bear to the one-eyed mule's saddle-bow with Tennie's Jim's leash-thong and dragged him down to the skiff and got him into it and left Tennie's Jim to swim the horse and the two mules back across. Major de Spain caught the bow of the skiff as Boon jumped out and past him before it touched the bank. He looked at Old Ben and said quietly: "Well." Then he walked into the water and leaned down and touched Sam and Sam looked up at him and said something in that old tongue he and Joe Baker spoke. "You dont know what happened?" Major de Spain said.

"No, sir," the boy said. "It wasn't the mule. It wasn't anything. He was off the mule when Boon ran in on the bear. Then we looked up and he was lying on the ground." Boon was shouting at Tennie's Jim, still in the middle of the river.

"Come on, goddamn it!" he said. "Bring me that mule!"

"What do you want with a mule?" Major de Spain said.

Boon didn't even look at him. "I'm going to Hoke's to get the doctor," he said in that calm voice, his face quite calm beneath the steady thinning of the bright blood.

"You need a doctor yourself," Major de Spain said. "Tennie's Jim——"

"Damn that," Boon said. He turned on Major de Spain. His face was still calm, only his voice was a pitch higher. "Cant you see his goddamn guts are all out of him?"

"Boon!" Major de Spain said. They looked at one another. Boon was a good head taller than Major de Spain; even the boy was taller now than Major de Spain.

"I've got to get the doctor," Boon said. "His goddamn guts——"

"All right," Major de Spain said. Tennie's Jim came up out of the water. The horse and the sound mule had already scented Old Ben; they surged and plunged all the way up to the top of the bluff, dragging Tennie's Jim with them, before he could stop them and tie them and come back. Major de Spain unlooped the leather thong of his compass from his buttonhole and gave it to Tennie's Jim. "Go straight to Hoke's," he said. "Bring Doctor Crawford back with you. Tell him there are two men to be looked at. Take my mare. Can you find the road from here?"

"Yes, sir," Tennie's Jim said.

"All right," Major de Spain said. "Go on." He turned to the boy. "Take the mules and the horse and go back and get the wagon. We'll go on down the river in the boat to Coon bridge. Meet us there. Can you find it again?"

"Yes, sir," the boy said.

"All right. Get started."

He went back to the wagon. He realised then how far they had run. It was already afternoon when he put the mules into the traces and tied the horse's lead-rope to the tail-gate. He reached Coon bridge at dusk. The skiff was already there. Before he could see it and almost before he could see the water he had to leap from the tilting wagon, still holding the reins, and work around to where he could grasp the bit and then the ear of the plunging sound mule and dig his heels and hold it until Boon came up the bank. The rope of the led horse had already snapped and it had already disappeared up the road toward camp. They turned the wagon around and took the mules out and he led the sound mule a hundred yards up the road and tied it. Boon had already brought Lion up to the wagon and Sam was sitting up in the skiff now and when they raised him he tried to walk, up the bank and to the wagon and he tried to climb into the wagon but Boon did not wait; he picked Sam up bodily and set him on the seat. Then they hitched Old Ben to the one-eyed mule's saddle again and dragged him up the bank and set two skid-poles into the open tail-gate and got him into the wagon and he went and got the sound mule and Boon fought it into the traces, striking it across its hard hollow-sounding face until it came into position and stood trembling. Then the rain came down, as though it had held off all day waiting on them.

They returned to camp through it, through the streaming and

sightless dark, hearing long before they saw any light the horn and the spaced shots to guide them. When they came to Sam's dark little hut he tried to stand up. He spoke again in the tongue of the old fathers; then he said clearly: "Let me out. Let me out."

"He hasn't got any fire," Major said. "Go on!" he said sharply.

But Sam was struggling now, trying to stand up. "Let me out, master," he said. "Let me go home."

So he stopped the wagon and Boon got down and lifted Sam out. He did not wait to let Sam try to walk this time. He carried him into the hut and Major de Spain got light on a paper spill from the buried embers on the hearth and lit the lamp and Boon put Sam on his bunk and drew off his boots and Major de Spain covered him and the boy was not there, he was holding the mules, the sound one which was trying again to bolt since when the wagon stopped Old Ben's scent drifted forward again along the streaming blackness of air, but Sam's eyes were probably open again on that profound look which saw further than them or the hut, further than the death of a bear and the dying of a dog. Then they went on, toward the long wailing of the horn and the shots which seemed each to linger intact somewhere in the thick streaming air until the next spaced report joined and blended with it, to the lighted house, the bright streaming windows, the quiet faces as Boon entered, bloody and quite calm, carrying the bundled coat. He laid Lion, blood coat and all, on his stale sheetless pallet bed which not even Ash, as deft in the house as a woman, could ever make smooth.

The sawmill doctor from Hoke's was already there. Boon would not let the doctor touch him until he had seen to Lion. He wouldn't risk giving Lion chloroform. He put the entrails back and sewed him up without it while Major de Spain held his head and Boon his feet. But he never tried to move. He lay there, the yellow eyes open upon nothing while the quiet men in the new hunting clothes and in the old ones crowded into the little airless room rank with the smell of Boon's body and garments, and watched. Then the doctor cleaned and disinfected Boon's face and arm and leg and bandaged them and, the boy in front with a lantern and the doctor and McCaslin and Major de Spain and General Compson following, they went to Sam Fathers' hut. Tennie's Jim had built up the fire; he squatted before it, dozing. Sam had not moved since Boon had put him in the bunk and Major de

Spain had covered him with the blankets, yet he opened his eyes
and looked from one to another of the faces and when McCaslin
touched his shoulder and said, "Sam. The doctor wants to look at
you," he even drew his hands out of the blanket and began to fum-
ble at his shirt buttons until McCaslin said, "Wait. We'll do it."
They undressed him. He lay there—the copper-brown, almost hairless body, the old man's body, the old man, the wild man not even
one generation from the woods, childless, kinless, peopleless—motionless, his eyes open but no longer looking at any of them, while
the doctor examined him and drew the blankets up and put the
stethoscope back into his bag and snapped the bag and only the
boy knew that Sam too was going to die.

"Exhaustion," the doctor said. "Shock maybe. A man his age
swimming rivers in December. He'll be all right. Just make him
stay in bed for a day or two. Will there be somebody here with
him?"

"There will be somebody here," Major de Spain said.

They went back to the house, to the rank little room where Boon
still sat on the pallet bed with Lion's head under his hand while
the men, the ones who had hunted behind Lion and the ones who
had never seen him before today, came quietly in to look at him
and went away. Then it was dawn and they all went out into the
yard to look at Old Ben, with his eyes open too and his lips snarled
back from his worn teeth and his mutilated foot and the little hard
lumps under his skin which were the old bullets (there were fifty-
two of them, buckshot rifle and ball) and the single almost invisible slit under his left shoulder where Boon's blade had finally
found his life. Then Ash began to beat on the bottom of the dishpan with a heavy spoon to call them to breakfast and it was the
first time he could remember hearing no sound from the dogs under the kitchen while they were eating. It was as if the old bear,
even dead there in the yard, was a more potent terror still than
they could face without Lion between them.

The rain had stopped during the night. By midmorning the thin
sun appeared, rapidly burning away mist and cloud, warming the
air and the earth; it would be one of those windless Mississippi December days which are a sort of Indian summer's Indian summer.
They moved Lion out to the front gallery, into the sun. It was
Boon's idea. "Goddamn it," he said, "he never did want to stay in
the house until I made him. You know that." He took a crowbar

and loosened the floor boards under his pallet bed so it could be raised, mattress and all, without disturbing Lion's position, and they carried him out to the gallery and put him down facing the woods.

Then he and the doctor and McCaslin and Major de Spain went to Sam's hut. This time Sam didn't open his eyes and his breathing was so quiet, so peaceful that they could hardly see that he breathed. The doctor didn't even take out his stethoscope nor even touch him. "He's all right," the doctor said. "He didn't even catch cold. He just quit."

"Quit?" McCaslin said.

"Yes. Old people do that sometimes. Then they get a good night's sleep or maybe it's just a drink of whisky, and they change their minds."

They returned to the house. And then they began to arrive—the swamp-dwellers, the gaunt men who ran trap-lines and lived on quinine and coons and river water, the farmers of little corn- and cotton-patches along the bottom's edge whose fields and cribs and pig-pens the old bear had rifled, the loggers from the camp and the sawmill men from Hoke's and the town men from further away than that, whose hounds the old bear had slain and traps and deadfalls he had wrecked and whose lead he carried. They came up mounted and on foot and in wagons, to enter the yard and look at him and then go on to the front where Lion lay, filling the little yard and overflowing it until there were almost a hundred of them squatting and standing in the warm and drowsing sunlight, talking quietly of hunting, of the game and the dogs which ran it, of hounds and bear and deer and men of yesterday vanished from the earth, while from time to time the great blue dog would open his eyes, not as if he were listening to them but as though to look at the woods for a moment before closing his eyes again, to remember the woods or to see that they were still there. He died at sundown.

Major de Spain broke camp that night. They carried Lion into the woods, or Boon carried him that is, wrapped in a quilt from his bed, just as he had refused to let anyone else touch Lion yesterday until the doctor got there; Boon carrying Lion, and the boy and General Compson and Walter and still almost fifty of them following with lanterns and lighted pine-knots—men from Hoke's and even further, who would have to ride out of the bottom in the dark, and swampers and trappers who would have to walk even, scattering toward the little hidden huts where they lived. And Boon would let nobody else dig the grave either and lay Lion in it and cover him and then General Compson stood at the head of it while the blaze and smoke of the pine-knots streamed away among the winter branches and spoke as he would have spoken over a man. Then they returned to camp. Major de Spain and McCaslin and Ash had rolled and tied all the bedding. The mules were hitched to the wagon and pointed out of the bottom and the wagon was already loaded and the stove in the kitchen was cold and the table was set with scraps of cold food and bread and only the coffee was hot when the boy ran into the kitchen where Major de Spain and McCaslin had already eaten. "What?" he cried. "What? I'm not going."

"Yes," McCaslin said, "we're going out tonight. Major wants to get on back home."

"No!" he said. "I'm going to stay."

"You've got to be back in school Monday. You've already missed a week more than I intended. It will take you from now until Monday to catch up. Sam's all right. You heard Doctor Crawford. I'm going to leave Boon and Tennie's Jim both to stay with him until he feels like getting up."

He was panting. The others had come in. He looked rapidly and almost frantically around at the other faces. Boon had a fresh bottle. He upended it and started the cork by striking the bottom of the bottle with the heel of his hand and drew the cork with his teeth and spat it out and drank. "You're damn right you're going back to school," Boon said. "Or I'll burn the tail off of you myself if Cass dont, whether you are sixteen or sixty. Where in hell do you expect to get without education? Where would Cass be? Where in hell would I be if I hadn't never went to school?"

He looked at McCaslin again. He could feel his breath coming shorter and shorter and shallower and shallower, as if there were not enough air in the kitchen for that many to breathe. "This is just Thursday. I'll come home Sunday night on one of the horses. I'll come home Sunday, then. I'll make up the time I lost studying Sunday night. McCaslin," he said, without even despair.

"No, I tell you," McCaslin said. "Sit down here and eat your supper. We're going out to——"

"Hold up, Cass," General Compson said. The boy did not know General Compson had moved until he put his hand on his shoulder. "What is it, bud?" he said.

"I've got to stay," he said. "I've got to."

"All right," General Compson said. "You can stay. If missing an extra week of school is going to throw you so far behind you'll have to sweat to find out what some hired pedagogue put between the covers of a book, you better quit altogether.—And you shut up, Cass," he said, though McCaslin had not spoken. "You've got one foot straddled into a farm and the other foot straddled into a bank; you aint even got a good hand-hold where this boy was already an old man long before you damned Sartorises and Edmondses invented farms and banks to keep yourselves from having to find out what this boy was born knowing and fearing too maybe but without being afraid, that could go ten miles on a compass because he wanted to look at a bear none of us had ever got near enough to put a bullet in and looked at the bear and came the ten miles back on the compass in the dark; maybe by God that's the why and the wherefore of farms and banks.—I reckon you still aint going to tell what it is?"

But still he could not. "I've got to stay," he said.

"All right," General Compson said. "There's plenty of grub left. And you'll come home Sunday, like you promised McCaslin? Not Sunday night: Sunday."

"Yes, sir," he said.

"All right," General Compson said. "Sit down and eat, boys," he said. "Let's get started. It's going to be cold before we get home."

They ate. The wagon was already loaded and ready to depart; all they had to do was to get into it. Boon would drive them out to the road, to the farmer's stable where the surrey had been left. He stood beside the wagon, in silhouette on the sky, turbaned like a Paythan and taller than any there, the bottle tilted. Then he flung the bottle from his lips without even lowering it, spinning and glinting in the faint starlight, empty. "Them that's going," he said, "get in the goddamn wagon. Them that aint, get out of the goddamn way." The others got in. Boon mounted to the seat beside General Compson and the wagon moved, on into the obscurity until the boy could no longer see it, even the moving density of it amid the greater night. But he could still hear it, for a long while:

the slow, deliberate banging of the wooden frame as it lurched from rut to rut. And he could hear Boon even when he could no longer hear the wagon. He was singing, harsh, tuneless, loud.

That was Thursday. On Saturday morning Tennie's Jim left on McCaslin's woods-horse which had not been out of the bottom one time now in six years, and late that afternoon rode through the gate on the spent horse and on to the commissary where McCaslin was rationing the tenants and the wage-hands for the coming week, and this time McCaslin forestalled any necessity or risk of having to wait while Major de Spain's surrey was being horsed and harnessed. He took their own, and with Tennie's Jim already asleep in the back seat he drove in to Jefferson and waited while Major de Spain changed to boots and put on his overcoat, and they drove the thirty miles in the dark of that night and at daybreak on Sunday morning they swapped to the waiting mare and mule and as the sun rose they rode out of the jungle and onto the low ridge where they had buried Lion: the low mound of unannealed earth where Boon's spade-marks still showed and beyond the grave the platform of freshly cut saplings bound between four posts and the blanket-wrapped bundle upon the platform and Boon and the boy squatting between the platform and the grave until Boon, the bandage removed, ripped, from his head so that the long scoriations of Old Ben's claws resembled crusted tar in the sunlight, sprang up and threw down upon them with the old gun with which he had never been known to hit anything although McCaslin was already off the mule, kicked both feet free of the irons and vaulted down before the mule had stopped, walking toward Boon.

"Stand back," Boon said. "By God, you wont touch him. Stand back, McCaslin." Still McCaslin came on, fast yet without haste.

"Cass!" Major de Spain said. Then he said "Boon! You, Boon!" and he was down too and the boy rose too, quickly, and still McCaslin came on not fast but steady and walked up to the grave and reached his hand steadily out, quickly yet still not fast, and took hold the gun by the middle so that he and Boon faced one another across Lion's grave, both holding the gun, Boon's spent indomitable amazed and frantic face almost a head higher than McCaslin's beneath the black scoriations of beast's claws and then Boon's chest began to heave as though there were not enough air in all the woods, in all the wilderness, for all of them, for him and anyone else, even for him alone.

"Turn it loose, Boon," McCaslin said.

"You damn little spindling—" Boon said. "Dont you know I can take it away from you? Dont you know I can tie it around your neck like a damn cravat?"

"Yes," McCaslin said. "Turn it loose, Boon."

"This is the way he wanted it. He told us. He told us exactly how to do it. And by God you aint going to move him. So we did it like he said, and I been sitting here ever since to keep the damn wildcats and varmints away from him and by God—." Then McCaslin had the gun, down-slanted while he pumped the slide, the five shells snicking out of it so fast that the last one was almost out before the first one touched the ground and McCaslin dropped the gun behind him without once having taken his eyes from Boon's.

"Did you kill him, Boon?" he said. Then Boon moved. He turned, he moved like he was still drunk and then for a moment blind too, one hand out as he blundered toward the big tree and seemed to stop walking before he reached the tree so that he plunged, fell toward it, flinging up both hands and catching himself against the tree and turning until his back was against it, backing with the tree's trunk his wild spent scoriated face and the tremendous heave and collapse of his chest, McCaslin following, facing him again, never once having moved his eyes from Boon's eyes. "Did you kill him, Boon?"

"No!" Boon said. "No!"

"Tell the truth," McCaslin said. "I would have done it if he had asked me to." Then the boy moved. He was between them, facing McCaslin; the water felt as if it had burst and sprung not from his eyes alone but from his whole face, like sweat.

"Leave him alone!" he cried. "Goddamn it! Leave him alone!"

— 4 —

then he was twenty-one. He could say it, himself and his cousin juxtaposed not against the wilderness but against the tamed land which was to have been his heritage, the land which old Carothers McCaslin his grandfather had bought with white man's money from the wild men whose grandfathers without guns hunted it, and tamed and ordered or believed he had tamed and ordered it for the reason that the human beings he held in bondage and in the power of life and death had removed the forest from it and in their

sweat scratched the surface of it to a depth of perhaps fourteen
inches in order to grow something out of it which had not been
there before and which could be translated back into the money he
who believed he had bought it had had to pay to get it and hold it
and a reasonable profit too: and for which reason old Carothers
McCaslin, knowing better, could raise his children, his descendants
and heirs, to believe the land was his to hold and bequeath since
the strong and ruthless man has a cynical foreknowledge of his
own vanity and pride and strength and a contempt for all his get:
just as, knowing better, Major de Spain and his fragment of that
wilderness which was bigger and older than any recorded deed:
just as, knowing better, old Thomas Sutpen, from whom Major de
Spain had had his fragment for money: just as Ikkemotubbe, the
Chickasaw chief, from whom Thomas Sutpen had had the fragment
for money or rum or whatever it was, knew in his turn that not
even a fragment of it had been his to relinquish or sell

not against the wilderness but against the land, not in pursuit
and lust but in relinquishment, and in the commissary as it should
have been, not the heart perhaps but certainly the solar-plexus
of the repudiated and relinquished: the square, galleried, wooden
building squatting like a portent above the fields whose laborers it
still held in thrall '65 or no and placarded over with advertise-
ments for snuff and cures for chills and salves and potions manufactured and sold by white men to bleach the pigment and
straighten the hair of Negroes that they might resemble the very
race which for two hundred years had held them in bondage and
from which for another hundred years not even a bloody civil war
would have set them completely free

himself and his cousin amid the old smells of cheese and salt
meat and kerosene and harness, the ranked shelves of tobacco and
overalls and bottled medicine and thread and plow-bolts, the barrels and kegs of flour and meal and molasses and nails, the wall
pegs dependant with plowlines and plow-collars and hames and
trace-chains, and the desk and the shelf above it on which rested
the ledgers in which McCaslin recorded the slow outward trickle of
food and supplies and equipment which returned each fall as cotton made and ginned and sold (two threads frail as truth and impalpable as equators yet cable-strong to bind for life them who
made the cotton to the land their sweat fell on), and the older ledg-

ers clumsy and archaic in size and shape, on the yellowed pages of
which were recorded in the faded hand of his father Theophilus
and his uncle Amodeus during the two decades before the Civil
War, the manumission in title at least of Carothers McCaslin's
slaves:

'Relinquish,' McCaslin said. 'Relinquish. You, the direct male descendant of him who saw the opportunity and took it, bought the
land, took the land, got the land no matter how, held it to bequeath, no matter how, out of the old grant, the first patent, when
it was a wilderness of wild beasts and wilder men, and cleared it,
translated it into something to bequeath to his children, worthy of
bequeathment for his descendants' ease and security and pride and
to perpetuate his name and accomplishments. Not only the male
descendant but the only and last descendant in the male line and
in the third generation, while I am not only four generations from
old Carothers, I derived through a woman and the very McCaslin in my name is mine only by sufferance and courtesy and my
grandmother's pride in what that man accomplished whose legacy
and monument you think you can repudiate.' and he

'I cant repudiate it. It was never mine to repudiate. It was never
Father's and Uncle Buddy's to bequeath me to repudiate because
it was never Grandfather's to bequeath them to bequeath me to
repudiate because it was never old Ikkemotubbe's to sell to Grandfather for bequeathment and repudiation. Because it was never
Ikkemotubbe's fathers' fathers' to bequeath Ikkemotubbe to sell to
Grandfather or any man because on the instant when Ikkemotubbe discovered, realised, that he could sell it for money, on that
instant it ceased ever to have been his forever, father to father to
father, and the man who bought it bought nothing.'

'Bought nothing?' and he

'Bought nothing. Because He told in the Book how He created
the earth, made it and looked at it and said it was all right, and
then He made man. He made the earth first and peopled it with
dumb creatures, and then He created man to be His overseer on
the earth and to hold suzerainty over the earth and the animals on
it in His name, not to hold for himself and his descendants inviolable title forever, generation after generation, to the oblongs and
squares of the earth, but to hold the earth mutual and intact in the
communal anonymity of brotherhood, and all the fee He asked

was pity and humility and sufferance and endurance and the sweat
of his face for bread. And I know what you are going to say,' he
said: 'That nevertheless Grandfather—' and McCaslin
   '—did own it. And not the first. Not alone and not the first since,
as your Authority states, man was dispossessed of Eden. Nor yet
the second and still not alone, on down through the tedious and
shabby chronicle of His chosen sprung from Abraham, and of the
sons of them who dispossessed Abraham, and of the five hundred
years during which half the known world and all it contained was
chattel to one city as this plantation and all the life it contained
was chattel and revokeless thrall to this commissary store and
those ledgers yonder during your grandfather's life, and the next
thousand years while men fought over the fragments of that collapse until at last even the fragments were exhausted and men
snarled over the gnawed bones of the old world's worthless evening until an accidental egg discovered to them a new hemisphere.
So let me say it: That nevertheless and notwithstanding old
Carothers did own it. Bought it, got it, no matter; kept it, held it,
no matter; bequeathed it: else why do you stand here relinquishing
and repudiating? Held it, kept it for fifty years until you could
repudiate it, while He—this Arbiter, this Architect, this Umpire—
condoned—or did He? looked down and saw—or did He? Or at
least did nothing: saw, and could not, or did not see; saw, and
would not, or perhaps He would not see—perverse, impotent, or
blind: which?' and he
   'Dispossessed.' and McCaslin
   'What?' and he
   'Dispossessed. Not impotent: He didn't condone; not blind, because He watched it. And let me say it. Dispossessed of Eden. Dispossessed of Canaan, and those who dispossessed him dispossessed
him dispossessed, and the five hundred years of absentee landlords
in the Roman bagnios, and the thousand years of wild men from
the northern woods who dispossessed them and devoured their
ravished substance ravished in turn again and then snarled in what
you call the old world's worthless twilight over the old world's
gnawed bones, blasphemous in His name until He used a simple
egg to discover to them a new world where a nation of people
could be founded in humility and pity and sufferance and pride
of one to another. And Grandfather did own the land nevertheless and notwithstanding because He permitted it, not impotent and

not condoning and not blind because He ordered and watched it. He saw the land already accursed even as Ikkemotubbe and Ikkemotubbe's father old Issetibbeha and old Issetibbeha's fathers too held it, already tainted even before any white man owned it by what Grandfather and his kind, his fathers, had brought into the new land which He had vouchsafed them out of pity and sufferance, on condition of pity and humility and sufferance and endurance, from that old world's corrupt and worthless twilight as though in the sailfuls of the old world's tainted wind which drove the ships—' and McCaslin

'Ah.'

'—and no hope for the land anywhere so long as Ikkemotubbe and Ikkemotubbe's descendants held it in unbroken succession. Maybe He saw that only by voiding the land for a time of Ikkemotubbe's blood and substituting for it another blood, could He accomplish His purpose. Maybe He knew already what that other blood would be, maybe it was more than justice that only the white man's blood was available and capable to raise the white man's curse, more than vengeance when—' and McCaslin

'Ah.'

'—when He used the blood which had brought in the evil to destroy the evil as doctors use fever to burn up fever, poison to slay poison. Maybe He chose Grandfather out of all of them He might have picked. Maybe He knew that Grandfather himself would not serve His purpose because Grandfather was born too soon too, but that Grandfather would have descendants, the right descendants; maybe He had foreseen already the descendants Grandfather would have, maybe He saw already in Grandfather the seed progenitive of the three generations He saw it would take to set at least some of His lowly people free—' and McCaslin

'The sons of Ham. You who quote the Book: the sons of Ham.' and he

'There are some things He said in the Book, and some things reported of Him that He did not say. And I know what you will say now: That if truth is one thing to me and another thing to you, how will we choose which is truth? You dont need to choose. The heart already knows. He didn't have His Book written to be read by what must elect and choose, but by the heart, not by the wise of the earth because maybe they dont need it or maybe the wise no longer have any heart, but by the doomed and lowly of the earth who have nothing else to read with but the heart. Because the men who wrote His Book for Him were writing about truth and there is only one truth and it covers all things that touch the heart.' and McCaslin

'So these men who transcribed His Book for Him were sometime liars.' and he

'Yes. Because they were human men. They were trying to write down the heart's truth out of the heart's driving complexity, for all the complex and troubled hearts which would beat after them. What they were trying to tell, what He wanted said, was too simple. Those for whom they transcribed His words could not have believed them. It had to be expounded in the everyday terms which they were familiar with and could comprehend, not only those who listened but those who told it too, because if they who were that near to Him as to have been elected from among all who breathed and spoke language to transcribe and relay His words, could comprehend truth only through the complexity of passion and lust and hate and fear which drives the heart, what distance back to truth must they traverse whom truth could only reach by word-of-mouth?' and McCaslin

'I might answer that, since you have taken to proving your points and disproving mine by the same text, I dont know. But I dont say that, because you have answered yourself: No time at all if, as you say, the heart knows truth, the infallible and unerring heart. And perhaps you are right, since although you admitted three generations from old Carothers to you, there were not three. There were not even completely two. Uncle Buck and Uncle Buddy. And they not the first and not alone. A thousand other Bucks and Buddies in less than two generations and sometimes less than one in this land which so you claim God created and man himself cursed and tainted. Not to mention 1865.' and he

'Yes. More men than Father and Uncle Buddy,' not even glancing toward the shelf above the desk, nor did McCaslin. They did not need to. To him it was as though the ledgers in their scarred cracked leather bindings were being lifted down one by one in their fading sequence and spread open on the desk or perhaps upon some apocryphal Bench or even Altar or perhaps before the Throne Itself for a last perusal and contemplation and refreshment of the Allknowledgeable before the yellowed pages and the brown thin ink in which was recorded the injustice and a little at least of

its amelioration and restitution faded back forever into the anonymous communal original dust

the yellowed pages scrawled in fading ink by the hand first of
his grandfather and then of his father and uncle, bachelors up to
and past fifty and then sixty, the one who ran the plantation and
the farming of it and the other who did the housework and the
cooking and continued to do it even after his twin married and the
boy himself was born

the two brothers who as soon as their father was buried moved
out of the tremendously-conceived, the almost barnlike edifice
which he had not even completed, into a one-room log cabin which
the two of them built themselves and added other rooms to while
they lived in it, refusing to allow any slave to touch any timber of
it other than the actual raising into place the logs which two men
alone could not handle, and domiciled all the slaves in the big
house some of the windows of which were still merely boarded up
with odds and ends of plank or with the skins of bear and deer
nailed over the empty frames: each sundown the brother who su-
perintended the farming would parade the Negroes as a first sergeant dismisses a company, and herd them willynilly, man woman
and child, without question protest or recourse, into the tremendous abortive edifice scarcely yet out of embryo, as if even old
Carothers McCaslin had paused aghast at the concrete indication
of his own vanity's boundless conceiving: he would call his men-
tal roll and herd them in and with a hand-wrought nail as long as a
flenching-knife and suspended from a short deer-hide thong attached to the door-jamb for that purpose, he would nail to the door
of that house which lacked half its windows and had no hinged
back door at all, so that presently and for fifty years afterward,
when the boy himself was big to hear and remember it, there was
in the land a sort of folk-tale: of the countryside all night long
full of skulking McCaslin slaves dodging the moonlit roads and
the Patrol-riders to visit other plantations, and of the unspoken
gentlemen's agreement between the two white men and the two
dozen black ones that, after the white man had counted them and
driven the home-made nail into the front door at sundown, neither
of the white men would go around behind the house and look at
the back door, provided that all the Negroes were behind the front
one when the brother who drove it drew out the nail again at daybreak

the twins who were identical even in their handwriting, unless
you had specimens side by side to compare, and even when both
hands appeared on the same page (as often happened, as if, long
since past any oral intercourse, they had used the diurnally advancing pages to conduct the unavoidable business of the compulsion
which had traversed all the waste wilderness of North Mississippi
in 1830 and '40 and singled them out to drive) they both looked as
though they had been written by the same perfectly normal ten-
year-old boy, even to the spelling, except that the spelling did not
improve as one by one the slaves which Carothers McCaslin had
inherited and purchased— Roscius and Phoebe and Thucydides
and Eunice and their descendants, and Sam Fathers and his
mother for both of whom he had swapped an underbred trotting
gelding to old Ikkemotubbe, the Chickasaw chief from whom he
had likewise bought the land, and Tennie Beauchamp whom the
twin Amodeus had won from a neighbor in a poker-game, and the
anomaly calling itself Percival Brownlee which the twin Theophilus
had purchased, neither he nor his brother ever knew why apparently, from Bedford Forrest while he was still only a slave-dealer
and not yet a general (It was a single page, not long and covering
less than a year, not seven months in fact, begun in the hand which
the boy had learned to distinguish as that of his father:

> *Percavil Brownly 26yr Old. cleark @ Bookepper. bought from
> N.B.Forest at Cold Water 3 Mar 1856 $265. dolars*

and beneath that, in the same hand:

> *5 mar 1856 No bookepper any way Cant read. Can write his
> Name but I already put that down My self Says he can Plough
> but dont look like it to Me. sent to Feild to day Mar 5 1856*

and the same hand:

> *6 Mar 1856 Cant plough either Says he aims to be a Precher so
> may be he can lead live stock to Crick to Drink*

and this time it was the other, the hand which he now recognised as
his uncle's when he could see them both on the same page:

> *Mar 23th 1856 Cant do that either Except one at a Time Get
> shut of him*

then the first again:

24 Mar 1856 Who in hell would buy him

then the second:

19th of Apr 1856 Nobody You put yourself out of Market at Cold Water two months ago I never said sell him Free him

the first:

22 Apr 1856 Ill get it out of him

the second:

Jun 13th 1856 How $1 per yr 265$ 265 yrs Wholl sign his Free paper

then the first again:

1 Oct 1856 Mule josephine Broke Leg @ shot Wrong stall wrong niger wrong everything $100. dolars

and the same:

2 Oct 1856 Freed Debit McCaslin @ McCaslin $265. dolars

then the second again:

Oct 3rd Debit Theophilus McCaslin Niger 265$ Mule 100$ 365$ He hasnt gone yet Father should be here

then the first:

3 Oct 1856 Son of a bitch wont leave What would father done

the second:

29th of Oct 1856 Renamed him

the first:

31 Oct 1856 Renamed him what

the second:

Chrstms 1856 Spintrius

) took substance and even a sort of shadowy life with their passions and complexities too as page followed page and year year; all there, not only the general and condoned injustice and its slow amortization but the specific tragedy which had not been condoned and could never be amortized, the new page and the new ledger, the hand which he could now recognise at first glance as his father's:

> *Father dide Lucius Quintus Carothers McCaslin, Callina 1772*
> *Missippy 1837. Dide and burid 27 June 1837*
> *Roskus. rased by Granfather in Callina Dont know how old.*
> *Freed 27 June 1837 Dont want to leave. Dide and Burid 12 Jan*
> *1841*
> *Fibby Roskus Wife. bought by granfather in Callina says Fifty*
> *Freed 27 June 1837 Dont want to leave. Dide and burd 1 Aug*
> *1849*
> *Thucydus Roskus @ Fibby Son born in Callina 1779. Refused*
> *10acre peace fathers Will 28 June 1837 Refused Cash offer $200.*
> *dolars from A.@ T. McCaslin 28 Jun 1837 Wants to stay and*
> *work it out*

and beneath this and covering the next five pages and almost that many years, the slow, day-by-day accruement of the wages allowed him and the food and clothing—the molasses and meat and meal, the cheap durable shirts and jeans and shoes and now and then a coat against rain and cold—charged against the slowly yet steadily mounting sum of balance (and it would seem to the boy that he could actually see the black man, the slave whom his white owner had forever manumitted by the very act from which the black man could never be free so long as memory lasted, entering the commissary, asking permission perhaps of the white man's son to see the ledger-page which he could not even read, not even asking for the white man's word, which he would have had to accept for the reason that there was absolutely no way under the sun for him to test it, as to how the account stood, how much longer before he could go and never return, even if only as far as Jefferson seventeen miles away) on to the double pen-stroke closing the final entry:

> *3 Nov 1841 By Cash to Thucydus McCaslin $200. dolars Set Up*
> *blaksmith in J. Dec 1841 Dide and burid in J. 17 feb 1854*
> *Eunice Bought by Father in New Orleans 1807 $650. dolars.*
> *Marrid to Thucydus 1809 Drownd in Crick Cristmas Day 1832*

and then the other hand appeared, the first time he had seen it in the ledger to distinguish it as his uncle's, the cook and housekeeper whom even McCaslin, who had known him and the boy's father for sixteen years before the boy was born, remembered as sitting all day

long in the rocking chair from which he cooked the food, before the
kitchen fire on which he cooked it:

> *June 21th 1833 Drownd herself*

and the first:

> *23 Jun 1833 Who in hell ever heard of a niger drownding him
> self*

and the second, unhurried, with a complete finality; the two identical entries might have been made with a rubber stamp save for the
date:

> *Aug 13th 1833 Drownd herself*

and he thought *But why? But why?* He was sixteen then. It was
neither the first time he had been alone in the commissary nor the
first time he had taken down the old ledgers familiar on their shelf
above the desk ever since he could remember. As a child and even
after nine and ten and eleven, when he had learned to read, he
would look up at the scarred and cracked backs and ends but with
no particular desire to open them, and though he intended to examine them someday because he realised that they probably contained a chronological and much more comprehensive though
doubtless tedious record than he would ever get from any other
source, not alone of his own flesh and blood but of all his people,
not only the whites but the black one too, who were as much a
part of his ancestry as his white progenitors, and of the land
which they had all held and used in common and fed from and on
and would continue to use in common without regard to color or
titular ownership, it would only be on some idle day when he was
old and perhaps even bored a little since what the old books contained would be after all these years fixed immutably, finished,
unalterable, harmless. Then he was sixteen. He knew what he was
going to find before he found it. He got the commissary key from
McCaslin's room after midnight while McCaslin was asleep and
with the commissary door shut and locked behind him and the forgotten lantern stinking anew the rank dead icy air, he leaned above
the yellowed page and thought not Why drowned herself, but
thinking what he believed his father had thought when he found
his brother's first comment: Why did Uncle Buddy think she had
drowned herself? finding, beginning to find on the next succeeding

page what he knew he would find, only this was still not it because
he already knew this:

> *Tomasina called Tomy Daughter of Thucydus @ Eunice Born*
> *1810 dide in Child bed June 1833 and Burd. Yr stars fell*

nor the next:

> *Turl Son of Thucydus @ Eunice Tomy born Jun 1833 yr stars*
> *fell Fathers will*

and nothing more, no tedious recording filling this page of wages
day by day and food and clothing charged against them, no entry
of his death and burial because he had outlived his white half-
brothers and the books which McCaslin kept did not include obituaries: just *Fathers will* and he had seen that too: old Carothers'
bold cramped hand far less legible than his sons' even and not
much better in spelling, who while capitalising almost every noun
and verb, made no effort to punctuate or construct whatever, just
as he made no effort either to explain or obfuscate the thousand-
dollar legacy to the son of an unmarried slave-girl, to be paid only
at the child's coming-of-age, bearing the consequence of the act
of which there was still no definite incontrovertible proof that he
acknowledged, not out of his own substance but penalising his sons
with it, charging them a cash forfeit on the accident of their own
paternity; not even a bribe for silence toward his own fame since
his fame would suffer only after he was no longer present to defend it, flinging almost contemptuously, as he might a cast-off hat
or pair of shoes, the thousand dollars which could have had no
more reality to him under those conditions than it would have to
the Negro, the slave who would not even see it until he came of
age, twenty-one years too late to begin to learn what money was.
So I reckon that was cheaper than saying My son to a nigger he
thought. *Even if My son wasn't but just two words. But there must
have been love* he thought. *Some sort of love. Even what he would
have called love: not just an afternoon's or a night's spittoon.* There
was the old man, old, within five years of his life's end, long a widower and, since his sons were not only bachelors but were approaching middleage, lonely in the house and doubtless even bored
since his plantation was established now and functioning and there
was enough money now, too much of it probably for a man whose
vices even apparently remained below his means; there was the

girl, husbandless and young, only twenty-three when the child was born: perhaps he had sent for her at first out of loneliness, to have a young voice and movement in the house, summoned her, bade her mother send her each morning to sweep the floors and make the beds and the mother acquiescing since that was probably already understood, already planned: the only child of a couple who were not field hands and who held themselves something above the other slaves not alone for that reason but because the husband and his father and mother too had been inherited by the white man from his father, and the white man himself had travelled three hundred miles and better to New Orleans in a day when men travelled by horseback or steamboat, and bought the girl's mother as a wife for

and that was all. The old frail pages seemed to turn of their own accord even while he thought *His own daughter His own daughter. No No Not even him* back to that one where the white man (not even a widower then) who never went anywhere any more than his sons in their time ever did and who did not need another slave, had gone all the way to New Orleans and bought one. And Tomey's Terrel was still alive when the boy was ten years old and he knew from his own observation and memory that there had already been some white in Tomey's Terrel's blood before his father gave him the rest of it; and looking down at the yellowed page spread beneath the yellow glow of the lantern smoking and stinking in that rank chill midnight room fifty years later, he seemed to see her actually walking into the icy creek on that Christmas day six months before her daughter's and her lover's (*Her first lover's* he thought. *Her first*) child was born, solitary, inflexible, griefless, ceremonial, in formal and succinct repudiation of grief and despair who had already had to repudiate belief and hope

that was all. He would never need look at the ledgers again nor did he; the yellowed pages in their fading and implacable succession were as much a part of his consciousness and would remain so forever, as the fact of his own nativity:

Tennie Beauchamp 21yrs Won by Amodeus McCaslin from Hubert Beauchamp Esqre Possible Strait against three Treys in sigt Not called 1851 Marrid to Tomys Turl 1859

and no date of freedom because her freedom, as well as that of her first surviving child, derived not from Buck and Buddy McCaslin

in the commissary but from a stranger in Washington and no date
of death and burial, not only because McCaslin kept no obituaries
in his books, but because in this year 1883 she was still alive and
would remain so to see a grandson by her last surviving child:

Amodeus McCaslin Beauchamp Son of tomys Turl @ Tennie
Beauchamp 1859 dide 1859

then his uncle's hand entire, because his father was now a member
of the cavalry command of that man whose name as a slave-dealer
he could not even spell: and not even a page and not even a full
line:

Dauter Tomes Turl and tenny 1862

and not even a line and not even a sex and no cause given though
the boy could guess it because McCaslin was thirteen then and he
remembered how there was not always enough to eat in more
places than Vicksburg:

Child of tomes Turl and Tenny 1863

and the same hand again and this one lived, as though Tennie's
perseverance and the fading and diluted ghost of old Carothers'
ruthlessness had at last conquered even starvation: and clearer,
fuller, more carefully written and spelled than the boy had yet
seen it, as if the old man, who should have been a woman to begin
with, trying to run what was left of the plantation in his brother's
absence in the intervals of cooking and caring for himself and the
fourteen-year-old orphan, had taken as an omen for renewed hope
the fact that this nameless inheritor of slaves was at least remaining alive long enough to receive a name:

James Thucydus Beauchamp Son of Tomes Turl and Tenny
Beauchamp Born 29th december 1864 and both Well Wanted
to call him Theophilus but Tride Amodeus McCaslin and Cal-
lina McCaslin and both dide so Disswaded Them Born at
Two clock A,m, both Well

but no more, nothing; it would be another two years yet before the
boy, almost a man now, would return from the abortive trip into
Tennessee with the still-intact third of old Carothers' legacy to his
Negro son and his descendants, which as the three surviving children established at last one by one their apparent intention of

surviving, their white half-uncles had increased to a thousand dollars each, conditions permitting, as they came of age, and completed the page himself as far as it would even be completed when that day was long passed beyond which a man born in 1864 (or 1867 either, when he himself saw light) could have expected or himself hoped or even wanted to be still alive; his own hand now, queerly enough resembling neither his father's nor his uncle's nor even McCaslin's, but like that of his grandfather's save for the spelling:

> *Vanished sometime on night of his twenty-first birthday Dec 29 1885. Traced by Isaac McCaslin to Jackson Tenn. and there lost. His third of legacy $1000.00 returned to McCaslin Edmonds Trustee this day Jan 12 1886*

but not yet: that would be two years yet, and now his father's again, whose old commander was now quit of soldiering and slave-trading both; once more in the ledger and then not again and more illegible than ever, almost indecipherable at all from the rheumatism which now crippled him and almost completely innocent now even of any sort of spelling as well as punctuation, as if the four years during which he had followed the sword of the only man ever breathing who ever sold him a Negro, let alone beat him in a trade, had convinced him not only of the vanity of faith and hope but of orthography too:

> *Miss sophonsiba b dtr t t @ t 1869*

but not of belief and will because it was there, written, as McCaslin had told him, with the left hand, but there in the ledger one time more and then not again, for the boy himself was a year old, and when Lucas was born six years later, his father and uncle had been dead inside the same twelve-months almost five years; his own hand again, who was there and saw it, 1886, she was just seventeen, two years younger than himself, and he was in the commissary when McCaslin entered out of the first of dusk and said, 'He wants to marry Fonsiba,' like that: and he looked past McCaslin and saw the man, the stranger, taller than McCaslin and wearing better clothes than McCaslin and most of the other white men the boy knew habitually wore, who entered the room like a white man and stood in it like a white man, as though he had let McCaslin precede him into it not because McCaslin's skin was white but simply because McCaslin lived there and knew the way, and who talked like a white man too, looking at him past McCaslin's shoulder rapidly and keenly once and then no more, without further interest, as a mature and contained white man not impatient but just pressed for time might have looked. 'Marry Fonsiba?' he cried. 'Marry Fonsiba?' and then no more either, just watching and listening while McCaslin and the Negro talked:

'To live in Arkansas, I believe you said.'

'Yes. I have property there. A farm.'

'Property? A farm? You own it?'

'Yes.'

'You dont say Sir, do you?'

'To my elders, yes.'

'I see. You are from the North.'

'Yes. Since a child.'

'Then your father was a slave.'

'Yes. Once.'

'Then how do you own a farm in Arkansas?'

'I have a grant. It was my father's. From the United States. For military service.'

'I see,' McCaslin said. 'The Yankee army.'

'The United States army,' the stranger said; and then himself again, crying it at McCaslin's back:

'Call aunt Tennie! I'll go get her! I'll—' But McCaslin was not even including him; the stranger did not even glance back toward his voice, the two of them speaking to one another again as if he were not even there:

'Since you seem to have it all settled,' McCaslin said, 'why have you bothered to consult my authority at all?'

'I dont,' the stranger said. 'I acknowledge your authority only so far as you admit your responsibility toward her as a female member of the family of which you are the head. I dont ask your permission. I——'

'That will do!' McCaslin said. But the stranger did not falter. It was neither as if he were ignoring McCaslin nor as if he had failed to hear him. It was as though he were making, not at all an excuse and not exactly a justification, but simply a statement which the situation absolutely required and demanded should be made in McCaslin's hearing whether McCaslin listened to it or not. It was as if he were talking to himself, for himself to hear the words spoken aloud. They faced one another, not close yet at slightly less than foils' distance, erect, their voices not raised, not impactive, just succinct:

'—I inform you, notify you in advance as chief of her family. No man of honor could do less. Besides, you have, in your way, according to your lights and upbringing——'

'That's enough, I said,' McCaslin said. 'Be off this place by full dark. Go.' But for another moment the other did not move, contemplating McCaslin with that detached and heatless look, as if he were watching reflected in McCaslin's pupils the tiny image of the figure he was sustaining.

'Yes,' he said. 'After all, this is your house. And in your fashion you have. . . . But no matter. You are right. This is enough.' He turned back toward the door; he paused again but only for a second, already moving while he spoke: 'Be easy. I will be good to her.' Then he was gone.

'But how did she ever know him?' the boy cried. 'I never even heard of him before! And Fonsiba, that's never been off this place except to go to church since she was born——'

'Ha,' McCaslin said. 'Even their parents dont know until too late how seventeen-year-old girls ever met the men who marry them too, if they are lucky.' And the next morning they were both gone, Fonsiba too. McCaslin never saw her again, nor did he, because the woman he found at last five months later was no one he had ever known. He carried a third of the three-thousand-dollar fund in gold in a money-belt, as when he had vainly traced Tennie's Jim into Tennessee a year ago. They—the man—had left an address of some sort with Tennie, and three months later a letter came, written by the man although McCaslin's wife Alice had taught Fonsiba to read and write too a little. But it bore a different postmark from the address the man had left with Tennie, and he travelled by rail as far as he could and then by contracted stage and then by a hired livery rig and then by rail again for a distance: an experienced traveller by now and an experienced bloodhound too and a successful one this time because he would have to be; as the slow interminable empty muddy December miles crawled and crawled and night followed night in hotels, in roadside taverns of rough logs and containing little else but a bar, and in the cabins of strangers and the hay of lonely barns, in none of which he dared undress because of his secret golden girdle like that of a disguised

one of the Magi travelling incognito and not even hope to draw
him but only determination and desperation, he would tell himself: *I will have to find her. I will have to. We have already lost
one of them. I will have to find her this time.* He did. Hunched in
the slow and icy rain, on a spent hired horse splashed to the chest
and higher, he saw it—a single log edifice with a clay chimney
which seemed in process of being flattened by the rain to a nameless and valueless rubble of dissolution in that roadless and even
pathless waste of unfenced fallow and wilderness jungle—no barn,
no stable, not so much as a hen-coop: just a log cabin built by
hand and no clever hand either, a meagre pile of clumsily-cut fire-
wood sufficient for about one day and not even a gaunt hound to
come bellowing out from under the house when he rode up—a
farm only in embryo, perhaps a good farm, maybe even a plantation someday, but not now, not for years yet and only then with
labor, hard and enduring and unflagging work and sacrifice; he
shoved open the crazy kitchen door in its awry frame and entered
an icy gloom where not even a fire for cooking burned and after
another moment saw, crouched into the wall's angle behind a
crude table, the coffee-colored face which he had known all his life
but knew no more, the body which had been born within a hundred yards of the room that he was born in and in which some
of his own blood ran but which was now completely inheritor of
generation after generation to whom an unannounced white man
on a horse was a white man's hired Patroller wearing a pistol sometimes and a blacksnake whip always; he entered the next room,
the only other room the cabin owned, and found, sitting in a rocking chair before the hearth, the man himself, reading—sitting there
in the only chair in the house, before that miserable fire for which
there was not wood sufficient to last twenty-four hours, in the same
ministerial clothing in which he had entered the commissary five
months ago and a pair of gold-framed spectacles which, when he
looked up and then rose to his feet, the boy saw did not even contain lenses, reading a book in the midst of that desolation, that
muddy waste fenceless and even pathless and without even a
walled shed for stock to stand beneath: and over all, permeant,
clinging to the man's very clothing and exuding from his skin itself,
that rank stink of baseless and imbecile delusion, that boundless
rapacity and folly, of the carpet-bagger followers of victorious
armies.

'Dont you see?' he cried. 'Dont you see? This whole land, the whole South, is cursed, and all of us who derive from it, whom it ever suckled, white and black both, lie under the curse? Granted that my people brought the curse onto the land: maybe for that reason their descendants alone can—not resist it, not combat it— maybe just endure and outlast it until the curse is lifted. Then your peoples' turn will come because we have forfeited ours. But not now. Not yet. Dont you see?'

The other stood now, the unfrayed garments still ministerial even if not quite so fine, the book closed upon one finger to keep the place, the lensless spectacles held like a music master's wand in the other workless hand while the owner of it spoke his measured and sonorous imbecility of the boundless folly and the baseless hope: 'You're wrong. The curse you whites brought into this land has been lifted. It has been voided and discharged. We are seeing a new era, an era dedicated, as our founders intended it, to freedom, liberty and equality for all, to which this country will be the new Canaan——'

'Freedom from what? From work? Canaan?' He jerked his arm, comprehensive, almost violent: whereupon it all seemed to stand there about them, intact and complete and visible in the drafty, damp, heatless, Negro-stale Negro-rank sorry room—the empty fields without plow or seed to work them, fenceless against the stock which did not exist within or without the walled stable which likewise was not there. 'What corner of Canaan is this?'

'You are seeing it at a bad time. This is winter. No man farms this time of year.'

'I see. And of course her need for food and clothing will stand still while the land lies fallow.'

'I have a pension,' the other said. He said it as a man might say *I have grace* or *I own a gold mine.* 'I have my father's pension too. It will arrive on the first of the month. What day is this?'

'The eleventh,' he said. 'Twenty days more. And until then?'

'I have a few groceries in the house from my credit account with the merchant in Midnight who banks my pension check for me. I have executed to him a power of attorney to handle it for me as a matter of mutual——'

'I see. And if the groceries dont last the twenty days?'

'I still have one more hog.'

'Where?'

'Outside,' the other said. 'It is customary in this country to allow stock to range free during the winter for food. It comes up from time to time. But no matter if it doesn't; I can probably trace its footprints when the need——'

'Yes!' he cried. 'Because no matter: you still have the pension check. And the man in Midnight will cash it and pay himself out of it for what you have already eaten and if there is any left over, it is yours. And the hog will be eaten by then or you still cant catch it, and then what will you do?'

'It will be almost spring then,' the other said. 'I am planning in the spring——'

'It will be January,' he said. 'And then February. And then more than half of March—' and when he stopped again in the kitchen she had not moved, she did not even seem to breathe or to be alive except her eyes watching him; when he took a step toward her it was still not movement because she could have retreated no further: only the tremendous fathomless ink-colored eyes in the narrow, thin, too thin coffee-colored face watching him without alarm, without recognition, without hope. 'Fonsiba,' he said. 'Fonsiba. Are you all right?'

'I'm free,' she said. Midnight was a tavern, a livery stable, a big store (that would be where the pension check banked itself as a matter of mutual elimination of bother and fret, he thought) and a little one, a saloon and a blacksmith shop. But there was a bank there too. The president (the owner, for all practical purposes) of it was a translated Mississippian who had been one of Forrest's men too: and his body lightened of the golden belt for the first time since he left home eight days ago, with pencil and paper he multiplied three dollars by twelve months and divided it into one thousand dollars; it would stretch that way over almost twenty-eight years and for twenty-eight years at least she would not starve, the banker promising to send the three dollars himself by a trusty messenger on the fifteenth of each month and put it into her actual hand, and he returned home and that was all because in 1874 his father and his uncle were both dead and the old ledgers never again came down from the shelf above the desk to which his father had returned them for the last time that day in 1869. But he could have completed it:

Lucas Quintus Carothers McCaslin Beauchamp. Last surviving son and child of Tomey's Terrel and Tennie Beauchamp. March 17, 1874

except that there was no need: not *Lucius Quintus* @c @c @c, but *Lucas Quintus,* not refusing to be called Lucius, because he simply eliminated that word from the name; not denying, declining the name itself, because he used three quarters of it; but simply taking the name and changing, altering it, making it no longer the white man's but his own, by himself composed, himself selfprogenitive and nominate, by himself ancestored, as, for all the old ledgers recorded to the contrary, old Carothers himself was

and that was all: 1874 the boy; 1888 the man, repudiated denied and free; 1895 and husband but no father, unwidowered but without a wife, and found long since that no man is ever free and probably could not bear it if he were; married then and living in Jefferson in the little new jerrybuilt bungalow which his wife's father had given them: and one morning Lucas stood suddenly in the doorway of the room where he was reading the Memphis paper and he looked at the paper's dateline and thought *It's his birthday. He's twenty-one today* and Lucas said: 'Whar's the rest of that money old Carothers left? I wants it. All of it.'

that was all: and McCaslin

'More men than that one Buck and Buddy to fumble-heed that truth so mazed for them that spoke it and so confused for them that heard yet still there was 1865:' and he

'But not enough. Not enough of even Father and Uncle Buddy to fumble-heed in even three generations not even three generations fathered by Grandfather not even if there had been nowhere beneath His sight any but Grandfather and so He would not even have needed to elect and choose. But He tried and I know what you will say. That having Himself created them He could have known no more of hope than He could have pride and grief but He didn't hope He just waited because He had made them: not just because He had set them alive and in motion but because He had already worried with them so long: worried with them so long because He had seen how in individual cases they were capable of anything any height or depth remembered in mazed incomprehension out of heaven where hell was created too and so He must ad-

mit them or else admit His equal somewhere and so be no longer
God and therefore must accept responsibility for what He Himself
had done in order to live with Himself in His lonely and para-
mount heaven. And He probably knew it was vain but He had created them and knew them capable of all things because He had
shaped them out of the primal Absolute which contained all and
had watched them since in their individual exaltation and baseness
and they themselves not knowing why nor how nor even when:
until at last He saw that they were all Grandfather all of them and
that even from them the elected and chosen the best the very best
He could expect (not hope mind: not hope) would be Bucks and
Buddies and not even enough of them and in the third generation
not even Bucks and Buddies but—' and McCaslin

'Ah:' and he

'Yes. If He could see Father and Uncle Buddy in Grandfather He
must have seen me too. —an Isaac born into a later life than
Abraham's and repudiating immolation: fatherless and therefore
safe declining the altar because maybe this time the exasperated
Hand might not supply the kid—' and McCaslin

'Escape:' and he

'All right. Escape.—Until one day He said what you told Fonsiba's husband that afternoon here in this room: *This will do. This
is enough:* not in exasperation or rage or even just sick to death
as you were sick that day: just *This is enough* and looked about for
one last time, for one time more since He had created them, upon
this land this South for which He had done so much with woods
for game and streams for fish and deep rich soil for seed and lush
springs to sprout it and long summers to mature it and serene falls
to harvest it and short mild winters for men and animals and saw
no hope anywhere and looked beyond it where hope should have
been, where to East North and West lay illimitable that whole
hopeful continent dedicated as a refuge and sanctuary of liberty
and freedom from what you called the old world's worthless evening and saw the rich descendants of slavers, females of both sexes,
to whom the black they shrieked of was another specimen another
example like the Brazilian macaw brought home in a cage by a
traveller, passing resolutions about horror and outrage in warm
and air-proof halls: and the thundering cannonade of politicians
earning votes and the medicine-shows of pulpiteers earning Chau-

tauqua fees, to whom the outrage and the injustice were as much abstractions as Tariff or Silver or Immortality and who employed the very shackles of its servitude and the sorry rags of its regalia as they did the other beer and banners and mottoes redfire and brimstone and sleight-of-hand and musical handsaws: and the whirling wheels which manufactured for a profit the pristine replacements of the shackles and shoddy garments as they wore out and spun the cotton and made the gins which ginned it and the cars and ships which hauled it, and the men who ran the wheels for that profit and established and collected the taxes it was taxed with and the rates for hauling it and the commissions for selling it: and He could have repudiated them since they were his creation now and forever more throughout all their generations until not only that old world from which He had rescued them but this new one too which He had revealed and led them to as a sanctuary and refuge were become the same worthless tideless rock cooling in the last crimson evening except that out of all that empty sound and bootless fury one silence, among that loud and moiling all of them just one simple enough to believe that horror and outrage were first and last simply horror and outrage and was crude enough to act upon that, illiterate and had no words for talking or perhaps was just busy and had no time to, one out of them all who did not bother Him with cajolery and adjuration then pleading then threat and had not even bothered to inform Him in advance what he was about so that a lesser than He might have even missed the simple act of lifting the long ancestral musket down from the deerhorns above the door, whereupon He said *My name is Brown too* and the other *So is mine* and He *Then mine or yours cant be because I am against it* and the other *So am I* and He triumphantly *Then where are you going with that gun?* and the other told him in one sentence one word and He: amazed: Who knew neither hope nor pride nor grief *But your Association, your Committee, your Officers. Where are your Minutes, your Motions, your Parliamentary Procedures?* and the other *I aint against them. They are all right I reckon for them that have the time. I am just against the weak because they are niggers being held in bondage by the strong just because they are white.* So He turned once more to this land which He still intended to save because He had done so much for it—' and McCaslin

'What?' and he

'—to these people He was still committed to because they were his creations—' and McCaslin

'Turned back to us? His face to us?' and he

'—whose wives and daughters at least made soups and jellies for them when they were sick and carried the trays through the mud and the winter too into the stinking cabins and sat in the stinking cabins and kept fires going until crises came and passed but that was not enough: and when they were very sick had them carried into the big house itself into the company room itself maybe and nursed them there which the white man would have done too for any other of his cattle that was sick but at least the man who hired one from a livery wouldn't have and still that was not enough: so that He said and not in grief either Who had made them and so could know no more of grief than He could of pride or hope: *Apparently they can learn nothing save through suffering, remember nothing save when underlined in blood*—' and McCaslin

'Ashby on an afternoon's ride, to call on some remote maiden cousins of his mother or maybe just acquaintances of hers, comes by chance upon a minor engagement of outposts and dismounts and with his crimson-lined cloak for target leads a handful of troops he never saw before against an entrenched position of backwoods-trained riflemen. Lee's battle-order, wrapped maybe about a handful of cigars and doubtless thrown away when the last cigar was smoked, found by a Yankee Intelligence officer on the floor of a saloon behind the Yankee lines after Lee had already divided his forces before Sharpsburg. Jackson on the Plank Road, already rolled up the flank which Hooker believed could not be turned and, waiting only for night to pass to continue the brutal and incessant slogging which would fling that whole wing back into Hooker's lap where he sat on a front gallery in Chancellorsville drinking rum toddies and telegraphing Lincoln that he had defeated Lee, is shot from among a whole covey of minor officers and in the blind night by one of his own patrols, leaving as next by seniority Stuart that gallant man born apparently already horsed and sabred and already knowing all there was to know about war except the slogging and brutal stupidity of it: and that same Stuart off raiding Pennsylvania hen-roosts when Lee should have known of all of Meade just where Hancock was on Cemetery Ridge: and Longstreet too at Gettysburg and that same Longstreet shot out of saddle by his own men in the dark by mistake just as Jackson was. His face to us? His face to us?' and he

'How else have made them fight? Who else but Jacksons and Stuarts and Ashbys and Morgans and Forrests?—the farmers of the central and middle-west, holding land by the acre instead of the tens or maybe even the hundreds, farming it themselves and to no single crop of cotton or tobacco or cane, owning no slaves and needing and wanting none and already looking toward the Pacific coast, not always as long as two generations there and having stopped where they did stop only through the fortuitous mischance that an ox died or a wagon-axle broke. And the New England mechanics who didn't even own land and measured all things by the weight of water and the cost of turning wheels and the narrow fringe of traders and ship-owners still looking backward across the Atlantic and attached to the continent only by their counting-houses. And those who should have had the alertness to see: the wildcat manipulators of mythical wilderness townsites; and the astuteness to rationalise: the bankers who held the mortgages on the land which the first were only waiting to abandon and on the railroads and steamboats to carry them still further west, and on the factories and the wheels and the rented tenements those who ran them lived in; and the leisure and scope to comprehend and fear in time and even anticipate: the Boston-bred (even when not born in Boston) spinster descendants of long lines of similarly-bred and likewise spinster aunts and uncles whose hands knew no callus except that of the indicting pen, to whom the wilderness itself began at the top of tide and who looked, if at anything other than Beacon Hill, only toward heaven—not to mention all the loud rabble of the camp-followers of pioneers: the bellowing of politicians, the mellifluous choiring of self-styled men of God, the—' and McCaslin

'Here, here. Wait a minute:' and he

'Let me talk now. I'm trying to explain to the head of my family something which I have got to do which I dont quite understand myself, not in justification of it but to explain it if I can. I could say I dont know why I must do it but that I do know I have got to because I have got myself to have to live with for the rest of my life and all I want is peace to do it in. But you are the head of my family. More. I knew a long time ago that I would never have to miss my father, even if you are just finding out that you have missed your son.—the drawers of bills and the shavers of notes and the

schoolmasters and the self-ordained to teach and lead and all that
horde of the semi-literate with a white shirt but no change for it,
with one eye on themselves and watching each other with the
other one. Who else could have made them fight: could have struck
them so aghast with fear and dread as to turn shoulder to shoulder
and face one way and even stop talking for a while and even after
two years of it keep them still so wrung with terror that some
among them would seriously propose moving their very capital into
a foreign country lest it be ravaged and pillaged by a people whose
entire white male population would have little more than filled any
one of their larger cities: except Jackson in the Valley and three
separate armies trying to catch him and none of them ever knowing whether they were just retreating from a battle or just running
into one and Stuart riding his whole command entirely around the
biggest single armed force this continent ever saw in order to see
what it looked like from behind and Morgan leading a cavalry
charge against a stranded man-of-war. Who else could have declared a war against a power with ten times the area and a hundred
times the men and a thousand times the resources, except men who
could believe that all necessary to conduct a successful war was not
acumen nor shrewdness nor politics nor diplomacy nor money nor
even integrity and simple arithmetic but just love of land and courage——'

'And an unblemished and gallant ancestry and the ability to ride
a horse,' McCaslin said. 'Dont leave that out.' It was evening now,
the tranquil sunset of October mazy with windless woodsmoke. The
cotton was long since picked and ginned, and all day now the
wagons loaded with gathered corn moved between field and crib,
processional across the enduring land. 'Well, maybe that's what He
wanted. At least, that's what He got.' This time there was no yellowed procession of fading and harmless ledger-pages. This was
chronicled in a harsher book and McCaslin, fourteen and fifteen
and sixteen, had seen it and the boy himself had inherited it as
Noah's grandchildren had inherited the Flood although they had
not been there to see the deluge: that dark corrupt and bloody time
while three separate peoples had tried to adjust not only to one another but to the new land which they had created and inherited too
and must live in for the reason that those who had lost it were no
less free to quit it than those who had gained it were:—those upon
whom freedom and equality had been dumped overnight and with-

out warning or preparation or any training in how to employ it or
even just endure it and who misused it not as children would nor
yet because they had been so long in bondage and then so suddenly freed, but misused it as human beings always misuse freedom,
so that he thought *Apparently there is a wisdom beyond even that
learned through suffering necessary for a man to distinguish between liberty and license;* those who had fought for four years and
lost to preserve a condition under which that franchisement was
anomaly and paradox, not because they were opposed to freedom
as freedom but for the old reasons for which man (not the generals
and politicians but man) has always fought and died in wars: to
preserve a status quo or to establish a better future one to endure
for his children; and lastly, as if that were not enough for bitterness
and hatred and fear, that third race even more alien to the people
whom they resembled in pigment and in whom even the same
blood ran, than to the people whom they did not,—that race three-
fold in one and alien even among themselves save for a single fierce
will for rapine and pillage, composed of the sons of middleaged
Quartermaster lieutenants and Army sutlers and contractors in military blankets and shoes and transport mules, who followed the bat-
tles they themselves had not fought and inherited the conquest
they themselves had not helped to gain, sanctioned and protected
even if not blessed, and left their bones and in another generation would be engaged in a fierce economic competition of small
sloven farms with the black men they were supposed to have freed
and the white descendants of fathers who had owned no slaves
anyway whom they were supposed to have disinherited and in the
third generation would be back once more in the little lost county
seats as barbers and garage mechanics and deputy sheriffs and mill-
and gin-hands and power-plant firemen, leading, first in mufti then
later in an actual formalised regalia of hooded sheets and pass-
words and fiery christian symbols, lynching mobs against the race
their ancestors had come to save: and of all that other nameless
horde of speculators in human misery, manipulators of money and
politics and land, who follow catastrophe and are their own protection as grasshoppers are and need no blessing and sweat no plow
or axe-helve and batten and vanish and leave no bones, just as they
derived apparently from no ancestry, no mortal flesh, no act even
of passion or even of lust: and the Jew who came without protection too since after two thousand years he had got out of the habit

of being or needing it, and solitary, without even the solidarity of
the locusts and in this a sort of courage since he had come thinking not in terms of simple pillage but in terms of his great-grand-
children, seeking yet some place to establish them to endure even
though forever alien: and unblessed: a pariah about the face of the
Western earth which twenty centuries later was still taking revenge
on him for the fairy tale with which he had conquered it. McCaslin
had actually seen it, and the boy even at almost eighty would
never be able to distinguish certainly between what he had seen
and what had been told him: a lightless and gutted and empty land
where women crouched with the huddled children behind locked
doors and men armed in sheets and masks rode the silent roads and
the bodies of white and black both, victims not so much of hate as
of desperation and despair, swung from lonely limbs: and men shot
dead in polling-booths with the still wet pen in one hand and the
unblotted ballot in the other: and a United States marshal in Jefferson who signed his official papers with a crude cross, an ex-slave
called Sickymo, not at all because his ex-owner was a doctor and
apothecary but because, still a slave, he would steal his master's
grain alcohol and dilute it with water and peddle it in pint bottles
from a cache beneath the roots of a big sycamore tree behind the
drug store, who had attained his high office because his half-white
sister was the concubine of the Federal A.P.M.: and this time
McCaslin did not even say Look but merely lifted one hand, not
even pointing, not even specifically toward the shelf of ledgers but
toward the desk, toward the corner where it sat beside the scuffed
patch on the floor where two decades of heavy shoes had stood
while the white man at the desk added and multiplied and sub-
tracted. And again he did not need to look because he had seen this
himself and, twenty-three years after the Surrender and twenty-
four after the Proclamation, was still watching it: the ledgers, new
ones now and filled rapidly, succeeding one another rapidly and
containing more names than old Carothers or even his father and
Uncle Buddy had ever dreamed of; new names and new faces to
go with them, among which the old names and faces that even his
father and uncle would have recognised, were lost, vanished—
Tomey's Terrel dead, and even the tragic and miscast Percival
Brownlee, who couldn't keep books and couldn't farm either, found
his true niche at last, reappeared in 1862 during the boy's father's
absence and had apparently been living on the plantation for at

least a month before his uncle found out about it, conducting im-
promptu revival meetings among Negroes, preaching and leading
the singing also in his high sweet true soprano voice and disappeared again on foot and at top speed, not behind but ahead of a
body of raiding Federal horse and reappeared for the third and
last time in the entourage of a travelling Army paymaster, the two
of them passing through Jefferson in a surrey at the exact moment
when the boy's father (it was 1866) also happened to be crossing
the Square, the surrey and its occupants traversing rapidly that
quiet and bucolic scene and even in that fleeting moment and to
others beside the boy's father giving an illusion of flight and illicit
holiday like a man on an excursion during his wife's absence with
his wife's personal maid, until Brownlee glanced up and saw his
late co-master and gave him one defiant female glance and then
broke again, leaped from the surrey and disappeared this time for
good and it was only by chance that McCaslin, twenty years later,
heard of him again, an old man now and quite fat, as the well-to-do
proprietor of a select New Orleans brothel; and Tennie's Jim gone,
nobody knew where, and Fonsiba in Arkansas with her three dollars each month and the scholar-husband with his lensless spectacles and frock coat and his plans for the spring; and only Lucas
was left, the baby, the last save himself of old Carothers' doomed
and fatal blood which in the male derivation seemed to destroy all
it touched, and even he was repudiating and at least hoping to escape it;—Lucas, the boy of fourteen whose name would not even
appear for six years yet among those rapid pages in the bindings
new and dustless too since McCaslin lifted them down daily now to
write into them the continuation of that record which two hundred
years had not been enough to complete and another hundred
would not be enough to discharge; that chronicle which was a
whole land in miniature, which multiplied and compounded was
the entire South, twenty-three years after surrender and twenty-
four from emancipation—that slow trickle of molasses and meal
and meat, of shoes and straw hats and overalls, of plowlines and
collars and heel-bolts and buckheads and clevises, which returned
each fall as cotton—the two threads frail as truth and impalpable
as equators yet cable-strong to bind for life them who made the
cotton to the land their sweat fell on: and he

'Yes. Binding them for a while yet, a little while yet. Through
and beyond that life and maybe through and beyond the life of

that life's sons and maybe even through and beyond that of the
sons of those sons. But not always, because they will endure. They
will outlast us because they are—' it was not a pause, barely a falter even, possibly appreciable only to himself, as if he couldn't
speak even to McCaslin, even to explain his repudiation, that
which to him too, even in the act of escaping (and maybe this was
the reality and the truth of his need to escape) was heresy: so that
even in escaping he was taking with him more of that evil and
unregenerate old man who could summon, because she was his
property, a human being because she was old enough and female,
to his widower's house and get a child on her and then dismiss her
because she was of an inferior race, and then bequeath a thousand
dollars to the infant because he would be dead then and wouldn't
have to pay it, than even he had feared. 'Yes. He didn't want to.
He had to. Because they will endure. They are better than we are.
Stronger than we are. Their vices are vices aped from white men or
that white men and bondage have taught them: improvidence and
intemperance and evasion—not laziness: evasion: of what white
men had set them to, not for their aggrandisement or even comfort
but his own—' and McCaslin

'All right. Go on: Promiscuity. Violence. Instability and lack of
control. Inability to distinguish between mine and thine—' and he

'How distinguish, when for two hundred years mine did not even
exist for them?' and McCaslin

'All right. Go on. And their virtues—' and he

'Yes. Their own. Endurance—' and McCaslin

'So have mules:' and he

'—and pity and tolerance and forbearance and fidelity and love
of children—' and McCaslin

'So have dogs:' and he

'—whether their own or not or black or not. And more: what
they got not only not from white people but not even despite white
people because they had it already from the old free fathers a
longer time free than us because we have never been free—' and it
was in McCaslin's eyes too, he had only to look at McCaslin's eyes
and it was there, that summer twilight seven years ago, almost a
week after they had returned from the camp before he discovered
that Sam Fathers had told McCaslin: an old bear, fierce and ruthless not just to stay alive but ruthless with the fierce pride of
liberty and freedom, jealous and proud enough of liberty and

freedom to see it threatened not with fear nor even alarm but
almost with joy, seeming deliberately to put it into jeopardy in
order to savor it and keep his old strong bones and flesh supple
and quick to defend and preserve it; an old man, son of a Negro
slave and an Indian king, inheritor on the one hand of the long
chronicle of a people who had learned humility through suffering
and learned pride through the endurance which survived the suffering, and on the other side the chronicle of a people even longer
in the land than the first, yet who now existed there only in the solitary brotherhood of an old and childless Negro's alien blood and
the wild and invincible spirit of an old bear; a boy who wished to
learn humility and pride in order to become skillful and worthy in
the woods but found himself becoming so skillful so fast that he
feared he would never become worthy because he had not learned
humility and pride though he had tried, until one day an old man
who could not have defined either led him as though by the hand
to where an old bear and a little mongrel dog showed him that, by
possessing one thing other, he would possess them both; and a little
dog, nameless and mongrel and many-fathered, grown yet weighing less than six pounds, who couldn't be dangerous because there
was nothing anywhere much smaller, not fierce because that would
have been called just noise, not humble because it was already too
near the ground to genuflect, and not proud because it would not
have been close enough for anyone to discern what was casting
that shadow and which didn't even know it was not going to
heaven since they had already decided it had no immortal soul, so
that all it could be was brave even though they would probably
call that too just noise. *'And you didn't shoot,' McCaslin said. 'How
close were you?'*

*'I dont know,' he said. 'There was a big wood tick just inside his
off hind leg. I saw that. But I didn't have the gun then.'*

*'But you didn't shoot when you had the gun,' McCaslin said.
'Why?' But McCaslin didn't wait, rising and crossing the room,
across the pelt of the bear he had killed two years ago and the bigger one McCaslin had killed before he was born, to the bookcase
beneath the mounted head of his first buck, and returned with the
book and sat down again and opened it. 'Listen,' he said. He read
the five stanzas aloud and closed the book on his finger and looked
up. 'All right,' he said. 'Listen,' and read again, but only one stanza
this time and closed the book and laid it on the table. 'She cannot*

*fade, though thou hast not thy bliss,' McCaslin said: 'Forever wilt
thou love, and she be fair.'*

'He's talking about a girl,' he said.

'He had to talk about something,' McCaslin said. Then he said,
'He was talking about truth. Truth is one. It doesn't change. It covers all things which touch the heart—honor and pride and pity and
justice and courage and love. Do you see now?' He didn't know.
Somehow it had seemed simpler than that, simpler than somebody
talking in a book about a young man and a girl he would never
need to grieve over because he could never approach any nearer
and would never have to get any further away. He had heard
about an old bear and finally got big enough to hunt it and he
hunted it four years and at last met it with a gun in his hands and
he didn't shoot. Because a little dog—But he could have shot long
before the fyce covered the twenty yards to where the bear waited,
and Sam Fathers could have shot at any time during the interminable minute while Old Ben stood on his hind legs over them. . . .
He ceased. McCaslin watched him, still speaking, the voice, the
words as quiet as the twilight itself was: 'Courage and honor and
pride, and pity and love of justice and of liberty. They all touch the
heart, and what the heart holds to becomes truth, as far as we
know truth. Do you see now?' and he could still hear them, intact
in this twilight as in that one seven years ago, no louder still because they did not need to be because they would endure: and he
had only to look at McCaslin's eyes beyond the thin and bitter smiling, the faint lip-lift which would have had to be called smiling;—
his kinsman, his father almost, who had been born too late into the
old time and too soon for the new, the two of them juxtaposed and
alien now to each other against their ravaged patrimony, the dark
and ravaged fatherland still prone and panting from its etherless
operation:

'Habet then.—So this land is, indubitably, of and by itself
cursed:' and he

'Cursed:' and again McCaslin merely lifted one hand, not even
speaking and not even toward the ledgers: so that, as the stereop-
ticon condenses into one instantaneous field the myriad minutia of
its scope, so did that slight and rapid gesture establish in the small
cramped and cluttered twilit room not only the ledgers but the
whole plantation in its mazed and intricate entirety—the land, the
fields and what they represented in terms of cotton ginned and

sold, the men and women whom they fed and clothed and even paid a little cash money at Christmas-time in return for the labor which planted and raised and picked and ginned the cotton, the machinery and mules and gear with which they raised it and their cost and upkeep and replacement—that whole edifice intricate and complex and founded upon injustice and erected by ruthless rapacity and carried on even yet with at times downright savagery not only to the human beings but the valuable animals too, yet solvent and efficient and, more than that: not only still intact but enlarged, increased; brought still intact by McCaslin, himself little more than a child then, through and out of the debacle and chaos of twenty years ago where hardly one in ten survived, and enlarged and increased and would continue so, solvent and efficient and intact and still increasing so long as McCaslin and his McCaslin successors lasted, even though their surnames might not even be Edmonds then: and he: 'Habet too. Because that's it: not the land, but us. Not only the blood, but the name too; not only its color but its designation: Edmonds, white, but, a female line, could have no other but the name his father bore; Beauchamp, the elder line and the male one, but, black, could have had any name he liked and no man would have cared, except the name his father bore who had no name—' and McCaslin

'And since I know too what you know I will say now, once more let me say it: And one other, and in the third generation too, and the male, the eldest, the direct and sole and white and still McCaslin even, father to son to son—' and he

'I am free:' and this time McCaslin did not even gesture, no inference of fading pages, no postulation of the stereoptic whole, but the frail and iron thread strong as truth and impervious as evil and longer than life itself and reaching beyond record and patrimony both to join him with the lusts and passions, the hopes and dreams and griefs, of bones whose names while still fleshed and capable even old Carothers' grandfather had never heard: and he: 'And of that too:' and McCaslin

'Chosen, I suppose (I will concede it) out of all your time by Him as you say Buck and Buddy were from theirs. And it took Him a bear and an old man and four years just for you. And it took you fourteen years to reach that point and about that many, maybe more, for Old Ben, and more than seventy for Sam Fathers. And you are just one. How long then? How long?' and he

'It will be long. I have never said otherwise. But it will be all right because they will endure—' and McCaslin

'And anyway, you will be free.—No, not now nor ever, we from them nor they from us. So I repudiate too. I would deny even if I knew it were true. I would have to. Even you can see that I could do no else. I am what I am; I will be always what I was born and have always been. And more than me. More than me, just as there were more than Buck and Buddy in what you called His first plan which failed:' and he

'And more than me:' and McCaslin

'No. Not even you. Because mark. You said how on that instant when Ikkemotubbe realised that he could sell the land to Grandfather, it ceased forever to have been his. All right; go on: Then it belonged to Sam Fathers, old Ikkemotubbe's son. And who inherited from Sam Fathers, if not you? co-heir perhaps with Boon, if not of his life maybe, at least of his quitting it?' and he

'Yes. Sam Fathers set me free.' And Isaac McCaslin, not yet Uncle Ike, a long time yet before he would be uncle to half a county and still father to none, living in one small cramped fireless rented room in a Jefferson boardinghouse where petit juries were domiciled during court terms and itinerant horse- and mule-traders stayed, with his kit of brand-new carpenter's tools and the shotgun McCaslin had given him with his name engraved in silver and old General Compson's compass (and, when the General died, his silver-mounted horn too) and the iron cot and mattress and the blankets which he would take each fall into the woods for more than sixty years and the bright tin coffee-pot

there had been a legacy, from his Uncle Hubert Beauchamp, his godfather, that bluff burly roaring childlike man from whom Uncle Buddy had won Tomey's Terrel's wife Tennie in the poker-game in 1859—'posible strait against three Treys in sigt Not called'—; no pale sentence or paragraph scrawled in cringing fear of death by a weak and trembling hand as a last desperate sop flung backward at retribution, but a Legacy, a Thing, possessing weight to the hand and bulk to the eye and even audible: a silver cup filled with gold pieces and wrapped in burlap and sealed with his godfather's ring in the hot wax, which (intact still) even before his Uncle Hubert's death and long before his own majority, when it would be his, had become not only a legend but one of the family lares. After his father's and his Uncle Hubert's sister's marriage they moved back into the big house, the tremendous cavern which old Carothers had started and never finished, cleared the remaining Negroes out of it and with his mother's dowry completed it, at least the rest of the windows and doors and moved into it, all of them save Uncle Buddy who declined to leave the cabin he and his twin had built, the move being the bride's notion and more than just a notion and none ever to know if she really wanted to live in the big house or if she knew before hand that Uncle Buddy would refuse to move: and two weeks after his birth in 1867, the first time he and his mother came down stairs, one night and the silver cup sitting on the cleared dining-room table beneath the bright lamp and while his mother and his father and McCaslin and Tennie (his nurse: carrying him)—all of them again but Uncle Buddy—watched, his Uncle Hubert rang one by one into the cup the bright and glinting mintage and wrapped it into the burlap envelope and heated the wax and sealed it and carried it back home with him where he lived alone now without even his sister either to hold him down as McCaslin said or to try to raise him up as Uncle Buddy said, and (dark times then in Mississippi) Uncle Buddy said most of the niggers gone and the ones that didn't go even Hub Beauchamp could not have wanted: but the dogs remained and Uncle Buddy said Beauchamp fiddled while Nero fox-hunted

they would go and see it there; at last his mother would prevail and they would depart in the surrey, once more all save Uncle Buddy and McCaslin to keep Uncle Buddy company until one winter Uncle Buddy began to fail and from then on it was himself, beginning to remember now, and his mother and Tennie and Tomey's Terrel to drive: the twenty-two miles into the next county, the twin gateposts on one of which McCaslin could remember the half-grown boy blowing a fox-horn at breakfast dinner and supper-time and jumping down to open to any passer who happened to hear it but where there were no gates at all now, the shabby and over-grown entrance to what his mother still insisted that people call Warwick because her brother was if truth but triumphed and justice but prevailed the rightful earl of it, the paintless house which outwardly did not change but which on the inside seemed each time larger because he was too little to realise then that there was less and less in it of the fine furnishings, the rosewood and mahogany and walnut which for him had never existed anywhere anyway save in his mother's tearful lamentations and the occasional piece

small enough to be roped somehow onto the rear or the top of the
carriage on their return (And he remembered this, he had seen it:
an instant, a flash, his mother's soprano 'Even my dress! Even my
dress!' loud and outraged in the barren unswept hall; a face young
and female and even lighter in color than Tomey's Terrel's for an
instant in a closing door; a swirl, a glimpse of the silk gown and
the flick and glint of an ear-ring: an apparition rapid and tawdry
and illicit yet somehow even to the child, the infant still almost,
breathless and exciting and evocative: as though, like two limpid
and pellucid streams meeting, the child which he still was had
made serene and absolute and perfect rapport and contact through
that glimpsed nameless illicit hybrid female flesh with the boy
which had existed at that stage of inviolable and immortal adolescence in his uncle for almost sixty years; the dress, the face, the
ear-rings gone in that same aghast flash and his uncle's voice: 'She's
my cook! She's my new cook! I had to have a cook, didn't I?' then
the uncle himself, the face alarmed and aghast too yet still innocently and somehow even indomitably of a boy, they retreating
in their turn now, back to the front gallery, and his uncle again,
pained and still amazed, in a sort of desperate resurgence if not of
courage at least of self-assertion: 'They're free now! They're folks
too just like we are!' and his mother: 'That's why! That's why! My
mother's house! Defiled! Defiled!' and his uncle: 'Damn it, Sibbey,
at least give her time to pack her grip:' then over, finished, the
loud uproar and all, himself and Tennie and he remembered Tennie's inscrutable face at the broken shutterless window of the bare
room which had once been the parlor while they watched, hurrying down the lane at a stumbling trot, the routed compounder of
his uncle's uxory: the back, the nameless face which he had seen
only for a moment, the once-hooped dress ballooning and flapping
below a man's overcoat, the worn heavy carpet-bag jouncing and
banging against her knee, routed and in retreat true enough and in
the empty lane solitary young-looking and forlorn yet withal still
exciting and evocative and wearing still the silken banner captured
inside the very citadel of respectability, and unforgettable.)

the cup, the sealed inscrutable burlap, sitting on the shelf in the
locked closet, Uncle Hubert unlocking the door and lifting it down
and passing it from hand to hand: his mother, his father, McCaslin
and even Tennie, insisting that each take it in turn and heft it for
weight and shake it again to prove the sound, Uncle Hubert him-

self standing spraddled before the cold unswept hearth in which
the very bricks themselves were crumbling into a litter of soot and
dust and mortar and the droppings of chimney-sweeps, still roaring
and still innocent and still indomitable: and for a long time he believed nobody but himself had noticed that his uncle now put the
cup only into his hands, unlocked the door and lifted it down and
put it into his hands and stood over him until he had shaken it obediently until it sounded then took it from him and locked it back
into the closet before anyone else could have offered to touch
it, and even later, when competent not only to remember but to
rationalise, he could not say what it was or even if it had been anything because the parcel was still heavy and still rattled, not even
when, Uncle Buddy dead and his father, at last and after almost
seventy-five years in bed after the sun rose, said: 'Go get that damn
cup. Bring that damn Hub Beauchamp too if you have to:' because
it still rattled though his uncle no longer put it even into his hands
now but carried it himself from one to the other, his mother,
McCaslin, Tennie, shaking it before each in turn, saying: 'Hear it?
Hear it?' his face still innocent, not quite baffled but only amazed
and not very amazed and still indomitable: and, his father and
Uncle Buddy both gone now, one day without reason or any warning the almost completely empty house in which his uncle and Tennie's ancient and quarrelsome great-grandfather (who claimed to
have seen Lafayette and McCaslin said in another ten years would
be remembering God) lived, cooked and slept in one single room,
burst into peaceful conflagration, a tranquil instantaneous sourceless unanimity of combustion, walls floors and roof: at sunup it
stood where his uncle's father had built it sixty years ago, at sundown the four blackened and smokeless chimneys rose from a light
white powder of ashes and a few charred ends of planks which
did not even appear to have been very hot: and out of the last
of evening, the last one of the twenty-two miles, on the old white
mare which was the last of that stable which McCaslin remembered, the two old men riding double up to the sister's door, the
one wearing his fox-horn on its braided deerhide thong and the
other carrying the burlap parcel wrapped in a shirt, the tawny wax-
daubed shapeless lump sitting again and on an almost identical
shelf and his uncle holding the half-opened door now, his hand not
only on the knob but one foot against it and the key waiting in the
other hand, the face urgent and still not baffled but still and even

indomitably not very amazed and himself standing in the half-
opened door looking quietly up at the burlap shape become almost
three times its original height and a good half less than its original thickness and turning away and he would remember not his
mother's look this time nor yet Tennie's inscrutable expression but
McCaslin's dark and aquiline face grave insufferable and bemused:
then one night they waked him and fetched him still half-asleep
into the lamp light, the smell of medicine which was familiar by
now in that room and the smell of something else which he had not
smelled before and knew at once and would never forget, the pillow, the worn and ravaged face from which looked out still the boy
innocent and immortal and amazed and urgent, looking at him and
trying to tell him until McCaslin moved and leaned over the bed
and drew from the top of the nightshirt the big iron key on the
greasy cord which suspended it, the eyes saying Yes Yes Yes now,
and cut the cord and unlocked the closet and brought the parcel
to the bed, the eyes still trying to tell him even when he took the
parcel so that was still not it, the hands still clinging to the parcel
even while relinquishing it, the eyes more urgent than ever trying
to tell him but they never did; and he was ten and his mother was
dead too and McCaslin said, 'You are almost halfway now. You
might as well open it:' and he: 'No. He said twenty-one:' and he
was twenty-one and McCaslin shifted the bright lamp to the center
of the cleared dining-room table and set the parcel beside it and
laid his open knife beside the parcel and stood back with that expression of old grave intolerant and repudiating and he lifted it,
the burlap lump which fifteen years ago had changed its shape
completely overnight, which shaken gave forth a thin weightless
not-quite-musical curiously muffled clatter, the bright knife-blade
hunting amid the mazed intricacy of string, the knobby gouts of
wax bearing his uncle's Beauchamp seal rattling onto the table's
polished top and, standing amid the collapse of burlap folds, the
unstained tin coffee-pot still brand new, the handful of copper
coins and now he knew what had given them the muffled sound: a
collection of minutely-folded scraps of paper sufficient almost for a
rat's nest, of good linen bond, of the crude ruled paper such as Negroes use, of raggedly-torn ledger-pages and the margins of newspapers and once the paper label from a new pair of overalls, all
dated and all signed, beginning with the first one not six months
after they had watched him seal the silver cup into the burlap on

this same table in this same room by the light even of this same lamp almost twenty-one years ago:

I owe my Nephew Isaac Beauchamp McCaslin five (5) pieces Gold which I.O.U. constitutes My note of hand with Interest at 5 percent.

Hubert Fitz-Hubert Beauchamp

at Warwick 27 Nov 1867

and he: 'Anyway he called it Warwick:' once at least, even if no more. But there was more:

Isaac 24 Dec 1867 I.O.U. 2 pieces Gold H.Fh.B. I.O.U. Isaac 1 piece Gold 1 Jan 1868 H.Fh.B.

then five again then three then one then one then a long time and what dream, what dreamed splendid recoup, not of any injury or betrayal of trust because it had been merely a loan: nay, a partnership:

I.O.U. Beauchamp McCaslin or his heirs twenty-five (25) pieces Gold This & All preceeding constituting My notes of hand at twenty (20) percentum compounded annually. This date of 19th January 1873

Beauchamp

no location save that in time and signed by the single not name but word as the old proud earl himself might have scrawled Nevile: and that made forty-three and he could not remember himself of course but the legend had it at fifty, which balanced: one: then one: then one: then one and then the last three and then the last chit, dated after he came to live in the house with them and written in the shaky hand not of a beaten old man because he had never been beaten to know it but of a tired old man maybe and even at that tired only on the outside and still indomitable, the simplicity of the last one the simplicity not of resignation but merely of amazement, like a simple comment or remark, and not very much of that:

One silver cup. Hubert Beauchamp

and McCaslin: 'So you have plenty of coppers anyway. But they are still not old enough yet to be either rarities or heirlooms. So you will have to take the money:' except that he didn't hear McCaslin,

standing quietly beside the table and looking peacefully at the coffee-pot and the pot sitting one night later on the mantel above
what was not even a fireplace in the little cramped icelike room in
Jefferson as McCaslin tossed the folded banknotes onto the bed
and, still standing (there was nowhere to sit save on the bed) did
not even remove his hat and overcoat: and he

'As a loan. From you. This one:' and McCaslin

'You cant. I have no money that I can lend to you. And you will
have to go to the bank and get it next month because I wont bring
it to you:' and he could not hear McCaslin now either, looking
peacefully at McCaslin, his kinsman, his father almost yet no kin
now as, at the last, even fathers and sons are no kin: and he

'It's seventeen miles, horseback and in the cold. We could both
sleep here:' and McCaslin

'Why should I sleep here in my house when you wont sleep yonder in yours?' and gone, and he looking at the bright rustless unstained tin and thinking and not for the first time how much it
takes to compound a man (Isaac McCaslin for instance) and of
the devious intricate choosing yet unerring path that man's (Isaac
McCaslin's for instance) spirit takes among all that mass to make
him at last what he is to be, not only to the astonishment of them
(the ones who sired the McCaslin who sired his father and Uncle
Buddy and their sister, and the ones who sired the Beauchamp who
sired his Uncle Hubert and his Uncle Hubert's sister) who believed
they had shaped him, but to Isaac McCaslin too

as a loan and used it though he would not have had to: Major de
Spain offered him a room in his house as long as he wanted it and
asked nor would ever ask any question, and old General Compson
more than that, to take him into his own room, to sleep in half of
his own bed and more than Major de Spain because he told him
baldly why: 'You sleep with me and before this winter is out, I'll
know the reason. You'll tell me. Because I dont believe you just
quit. It looks like you just quit but I have watched you in the
woods too much and I dont believe you just quit even if it does
look damn like it:' using it as a loan, paid his board and rent for a
month and bought the tools, not simply because he was good with
his hands because he had intended to use his hands and it could
have been with horses, and not in mere static and hopeful emulation of the Nazarene as the young gambler buys a spotted shirt
because the old gambler won in one yesterday, but (without the

arrogance of false humility and without the false humbleness of
pride, who intended to earn his bread, didn't especially want to
earn it but had to earn it and for more than just bread) because if
the Nazarene had found carpentering good for the life and ends
He had assumed and elected to serve, it would be all right too for
Isaac McCaslin even though Isaac McCaslin's ends, although simple enough in their apparent motivation, were and would be always incomprehensible to him, and his life, invincible enough in its
needs, if he could have helped himself, not being the Nazarene, he
would not have chosen it: and paid it back. He had forgotten the
thirty dollars which McCaslin would put into the bank in his name
each month, fetched it in to him and flung it onto the bed that first
one time but no more; he had a partner now or rather he was the
partner: a blasphemous profane clever old dipsomaniac who had
built blockade-runners in Charleston in '62 and '3 and had been a
ship's carpenter since and appeared in Jefferson two years ago nobody knew from where nor why and spent a good part of his time
since recovering from delirium tremens in the jail; they had put a
new roof on the stable of the bank's president and (the old man in
jail again still celebrating that job) he went to the bank to collect
for it and the president said, 'I should borrow from you instead of
paying you:' and it had been seven months now and he remembered for the first time, two-hundred-and-ten dollars, and this was
the first job of any size and when he left the bank the account
stood at two-twenty, two-forty to balance, only twenty dollars
more to go, then it did balance though by then the total had increased to three hundred and thirty and he said, 'I will transfer it
now:' and the president said, 'I cant do that. McCaslin told me not
to. Haven't you got another initial you could use and open another
account?' but that was all right, the coins the silver and the bills as
they accumulated knotted into a handkerchief and the coffee-pot
wrapped in an old shirt as when Tennie's great-grandfather had
fetched it from Warwick eighteen years ago, in the bottom of the
iron-bound trunk which old Carothers had brought from Carolina
and his landlady said, 'Not even a lock! And you dont even lock
your door, not even when you leave!' and himself looking at her as
peacefully as he had looked at McCaslin that first night in this
same room, no kin to him at all yet more than kin as those who
serve you even for pay are your kin and those who injure you are
more than brother or wife

and had the wife now, got the old man out of jail and fetched
him to the rented room and sobered him by superior strength, did
not even remove his own shoes for twenty-four hours, got him up
and got food into him and they built the barn this time from the
ground up and he married her: an only child, a small girl yet curiously bigger than she seemed at first, solider perhaps, with dark
eyes and a passionate heart-shaped face, who had time even on
that farm to watch most of the day while he sawed timbers to the
old man's measurements: and she: 'Papa told me about you. That
farm is really yours, isn't it?' and he

'And McCaslin's:' and she

'Was there a will leaving half of it to him?' and he

'There didn't need to be a will. His grandmother was my father's
sister. We were the same as brothers:' and she

'You are the same as second cousins and that's all you ever will
be. But I dont suppose it matters:' and they were married, they
were married and it was the new country, his heritage too as it was
the heritage of all, out of the earth, beyond the earth yet of the
earth because his too was of the earth's long chronicle, his too because each must share with another in order to come into it and in
the sharing they become one: for that while, one: for that little
while at least, one: indivisible, that while at least irrevocable and
unrecoverable, living in a rented room still but for just a little while
and that room wall-less and topless and floorless in glory for him
to leave each morning and return to at night; her father already
owned the lot in town and furnished the material and he and his
partner would build it, her dowry from one: her wedding-present
from three, she not to know it until the bungalow was finished and
ready to be moved into and he never know who told her, not her
father and not his partner and not even in drink though for a while
he believed that, himself coming home from work and just time to
wash and rest a moment before going down to supper, entering no
rented cubicle since it would still partake of glory even after they
would have grown old and lost it: and he saw her face then, just
before she spoke: 'Sit down:' the two of them sitting on the bed's
edge, not even touching yet, her face strained and terrible, her
voice a passionate and expiring whisper of immeasurable promise:
'I love you. You know I love you. When are we going to move?'
and he

'I didn't—I didn't know—Who told you—' the hot fierce palm

clapped over his mouth, crushing his lips into his teeth, the fierce curve of fingers digging into his cheek and only the palm slacked off enough for him to answer:

'The farm. Our farm. Your farm:' and he

'I—' then the hand again, finger and palm, the whole enveloping weight of her although she still was not touching him save the hand, the voice: 'No! No!' and the fingers themselves seeming to follow through the cheek the impulse to speech as it died in his mouth, then the whisper, the breath again, of love and of incredible promise, the palm slackening again to let him answer:

'When?' and he

'I—' then she was gone, the hand too, standing, her back to him and her head bent, the voice so calm now that for an instant it seemed no voice of hers that he ever remembered: 'Stand up and turn your back and shut your eyes:' and repeated before he understood and stood himself with his eyes shut and heard the bell ring for supper below stairs and the calm voice again: 'Lock the door:' and he did so and leaned his forehead against the cold wood, his eyes closed, hearing his heart and the sound he had begun to hear before he moved until it ceased and the bell rang again below stairs and he knew it was for them this time and he heard the bed and turned and he had never seen her naked before, he had asked her to once, and why: that he wanted to see her naked because he loved her and he wanted to see her looking at him naked because he loved her but after that he never mentioned it again, even turning his face when she put the nightgown on over her dress to undress at night and putting the dress on over the gown to remove it in the morning and she would not let him get into bed beside her until the lamp was out and even in the heat of summer she would draw the sheet up over them both before she would let him turn to her: and the landlady came up the stairs up the hall and rapped on the door and then called their names but she didn't move, lying still on the bed outside the covers, her face turned away on the pillow, listening to nothing, thinking of nothing, not of him anyway he thought then the landlady went away and she said, 'Take off your clothes:' her head still turned away, looking at nothing, thinking of nothing, waiting for nothing, not even him, her hand moving as though with volition and vision of its own, catching his wrist at the exact moment when he paused beside the bed so that he never paused but merely changed the direction of moving, downward

now, the hand drawing him and she moved at last, shifted, a movement one single complete inherent not practiced and one time
older than man, looking at him now, drawing him still downward
with the one hand down and down and he neither saw nor felt it
shift, palm flat against his chest now and holding him away with
the same apparent lack of any effort or any need for strength, and
not looking at him now, she didn't need to, the chaste woman, the
wife, already looked upon all the men who ever rutted and now
her whole body had changed, altered, he had never seen it but
once and now it was not even the one he had seen but composite
of all woman-flesh since man that ever of its own will reclined on
its back and opened, and out of it somewhere, without any movement of lips even, the dying and invincible whisper: 'Promise:' and
he

'Promise?'

'The farm.' He moved. He had moved, the hand shifting from his
chest once more to his wrist, grasping it, the arm still lax and only
the light increasing pressure of the fingers as though arm and hand
were a piece of wire cable with one looped end, only the hand
tightening as he pulled against it. 'No,' he said. 'No:' and she was
not looking at him still but not like the other but still the hand:
'No, I tell you. I wont. I cant. Never:' and still the hand and he
said, for the last time, he tried to speak clearly and he knew it was
still gently and he thought, *She already knows more than I with all
the man-listening in camps where there was nothing to read ever
even heard of. They are born already bored with what a boy ap-
proaches only at fourteen and fifteen with blundering and aghast
trembling:* 'I cant. Not ever. Remember:' and still the steady and invincible hand and he said Yes and he thought, *She is lost. She was
born lost. We were all born lost* then he stopped thinking and even
saying Yes, it was like nothing he had ever dreamed, let alone
heard in mere man-talking until after a no-time he returned and lay
spent on the insatiate immemorial beach and again with a movement one time more older than man she turned and freed herself
and on their wedding night she had cried and he thought she was
crying now at first, into the tossed and wadded pillow, the voice
coming from somewhere between the pillow and the cachinnation:
'And that's all. That's all from me. If this dont get you that son you
talk about, it wont be mine:' lying on her side, her back to the
empty rented room, laughing and laughing

– 5 –

He went back to the camp one more time before the lumber
company moved in and began to cut the timber. Major de Spain
himself never saw it again. But he made them welcome to use the
house and hunt the land whenever they liked, and in the winter
following the last hunt when Sam Fathers and Lion died, General
Compson and Walter Ewell invented a plan to corporate themselves, the old group, into a club and lease the camp and the
hunting privileges of the woods—an invention doubtless of the
somewhat childish old General but actually worthy of Boon Hogganbeck himself. Even the boy, listening, recognised it for the
subterfuge it was: to change the leopard's spots when they could
not alter the leopard, a baseless and illusory hope to which even
McCaslin seemed to subscribe for a while, that once they had persuaded Major de Spain to return to the camp he might revoke himself, which even the boy knew he would not do. And he did not.
The boy never knew what occurred when Major de Spain declined.
He was not present when the subject was broached and McCaslin
never told him. But when June came and the time for the double
birthday celebration there was no mention of it and when November came no one spoke of using Major de Spain's house and he
never knew whether or not Major de Spain knew they were going
on the hunt though without doubt old Ash probably told him: he
and McCaslin and General Compson (and that one was the General's last hunt too) and Walter and Boon and Tennie's Jim and
old Ash loaded two wagons and drove two days and almost forty
miles beyond any country the boy had ever seen before and lived
in tents for the two weeks. And the next spring they heard (not
from Major de Spain) that he had sold the timber-rights to a Memphis lumber company and in June the boy came to town with
McCaslin one Saturday and went to Major de Spain's office—the
big, airy, book-lined second-storey room with windows at one end
opening upon the shabby hinder purlieus of stores and at the other
a door giving onto the railed balcony above the Square, with its
curtained alcove where sat a cedar water-bucket and a sugar-bowl
and spoon and tumbler and a wicker-covered demijohn of whisky,
and the bamboo-and-paper punkah swinging back and forth above
the desk while old Ash in a tilted chair beside the entrance pulled
the cord.

"Of course," Major de Spain said. "Ash will probably like to get off in the woods himself for a while, where he wont have to eat Daisy's cooking. Complain about it, anyway. Are you going to take anybody with you?"

"No sir," he said. "I thought that maybe Boon—" For six months now Boon had been town-marshal at Hoke's; Major de Spain had compounded with the lumber company—or perhaps compromised was closer, since it was the lumber company who had decided that Boon might be better as a town-marshal than head of a logging gang.

"Yes," Major de Spain said. "I'll wire him today. He can meet you at Hoke's. I'll send Ash on by the train and they can take some food in and all you will have to do will be to mount your horse and ride over."

"Yes sir," he said. "Thank you." And he heard his voice again. He didn't know he was going to say it yet he did know, he had known it all the time: "Maybe if you . . ." His voice died. It was stopped, he never knew how because Major de Spain did not speak and it was not until his voice ceased that Major de Spain moved, turned back to the desk and the papers spread on it and even that without moving because he was sitting at the desk with a paper in his hand when the boy entered, the boy standing there looking down at the short plumpish gray-haired man in sober fine broadcloth and an immaculate glazed shirt whom he was used to seeing in boots and muddy corduroy, unshaven, sitting the shaggy powerful long-hocked mare with the worn Winchester carbine across the saddle-bow and the great blue dog standing motionless as bronze at the stirrup, the two of them in that last year and to the boy anyway coming to resemble one another somehow as two people competent for love or for business who have been in love or in business together for a long time sometimes do. Major de Spain did not look up again.

"No. I will be too busy. But good luck to you. If you have it, you might bring me a young squirrel."

"Yes sir," he said. "I will."

He rode his mare, the three-year-old filly he had bred and raised and broken himself. He left home a little after midnight and six hours later, without even having sweated her, he rode into Hoke's, the tiny log-line junction which he had always thought of as Major de Spain's property too although Major de Spain had merely sold

the company (and that many years ago) the land on which the
sidetracks and loading-platforms and the commissary store stood,
and looked about in shocked and grieved amazement even though
he had had forewarning and had believed himself prepared: a new
planing-mill already half completed which would cover two or
three acres and what looked like miles and miles of stacked steel
rails red with the light bright rust of newness and of piled crossties
sharp with creosote, and wire corrals and feeding-troughs for two
hundred mules at least and the tents for the men who drove them;
so that he arranged for the care and stabling of his mare as rapidly
as he could and did not look any more, mounted into the log-train
caboose with his gun and climbed into the cupola and looked no
more save toward the wall of wilderness ahead within which he
would be able to hide himself from it once more anyway.

Then the little locomotive shrieked and began to move: a rapid
churning of exhaust, a lethargic deliberate clashing of slack couplings traveling backward along the train, the exhaust changing to
the deep slow clapping bites of power as the caboose too began to
move and from the cupola he watched the train's head complete
the first and only curve in the entire line's length and vanish into
the wilderness, dragging its length of train behind it so that it resembled a small dingy harmless snake vanishing into weeds, drawing him with it too until soon it ran once more at its maximum
clattering speed between the twin walls of unaxed wilderness as of
old. It had been harmless once. Not five years ago Walter Ewell
had shot a six-point buck from this same moving caboose, and
there was the story of the half-grown bear: the train's first trip in
to the cutting thirty miles away, the bear between the rails, its rear
end elevated like that of a playing puppy while it dug to see what
sort of ants or bugs they might contain or perhaps just to examine
the curious symmetrical squared barkless logs which had appeared
apparently from nowhere in one endless mathematical line overnight, still digging until the driver on the braked engine not fifty
feet away blew the whistle at it, whereupon it broke frantically and
took the first tree it came to: an ash sapling not much bigger than a
man's thigh and climbed as high as it could and clung there, its
head ducked between its arms as a man (a woman perhaps) might
have done while the brakeman threw chunks of ballast at it, and
when the engine returned three hours later with the first load of
outbound logs the bear was halfway down the tree and once more

scrambled back up as high as it could and clung again while the
train passed and was still there when the engine went in again in
the afternoon and still there when it came back out at dusk; and
Boon had been in Hoke's with the wagon after a barrel of flour that
noon when the train-crew told about it and Boon and Ash, both
twenty years younger then, sat under the tree all that night to keep
anybody from shooting it and the next morning Major de Spain
had the log-train held at Hoke's and just before sundown on the
second day, with not only Boon and Ash but Major de Spain and
General Compson and Walter and McCaslin, twelve then, watching, it came down the tree after almost thirty-six hours without
even water and McCaslin told him how for a minute they thought
it was going to stop right there at the barrow-pit where they were
standing and drink, how it looked at the water and paused and
looked at them and at the water again, but did not, gone, running, as bears run, the two sets of feet, front and back, tracking two
separate though parallel courses.

It had been harmless then. They would hear the passing log-train
sometimes from the camp; sometimes, because nobody bothered to
listen for it or not. They would hear it going in, running light and
fast, the light clatter of the trucks, the exhaust of the diminutive
locomotive and its shrill peanut-parcher whistle flung for one petty
moment and absorbed by the brooding and inattentive wilderness
without even an echo. They would hear it going out, loaded, not
quite so fast now yet giving its frantic and toylike illusion of
crawling speed, not whistling now to conserve steam, flinging its
bitten laboring miniature puffing into the immemorial woodsface
with frantic and bootless vainglory, empty and noisy and puerile,
carrying to no destination or purpose sticks which left nowhere
any scar or stump as the child's toy loads and transports and un-
loads its dead sand and rushes back for more, tireless and unceasing
and rapid yet never quite so fast as the Hand which plays with it
moves the toy burden back to load the toy again. But it was different now. It was the same train, engine cars and caboose, even the
same enginemen brakeman and conductor to whom Boon, drunk
then sober then drunk again then fairly sober once more all in the
space of fourteen hours, had bragged that day two years ago about
what they were going to do to Old Ben tomorrow, running with its
same illusion of frantic rapidity between the same twin walls of
impenetrable and impervious woods, passing the old landmarks,

the old game crossings over which he had trailed bucks wounded and not wounded and more than once seen them, anything but wounded, break out of the woods, up and across the embankment which bore the rails and ties then down and into the woods again as the earth-bound supposedly move but crossing as arrows travel, groundless, elongated, three times its actual length and even paler, different in color, as if there were a point between immobility and absolute motion where even mass chemically altered, changing without pain or agony not only in bulk and shape but in color too, approaching the color of wind, yet this time it was as though the train (and not only the train but himself, not only his vision which had seen it and his memory which remembered it but his clothes too, as garments carry back into the clean edgeless blowing of air the lingering effluvium of a sick-room or of death) had brought with it into the doomed wilderness even before the actual axe the shadow and portent of the new mill not even finished yet and the rails and ties which were not even laid; and he knew now what he had known as soon as he saw Hoke's this morning but had not yet thought into words: why Major de Spain had not come back, and that after this time he himself, who had had to see it one time other, would return no more.

Now they were near. He knew it before the engine-driver whistled to warn him. Then he saw Ash and the wagon, the reins without doubt wrapped once more about the brake-lever as within the boy's own memory Major de Spain had been forbidding him for eight years to do, the train slowing, the slackened couplings jolting and clashing again from car to car, the caboose slowing past the wagon as he swung down with his gun, the conductor leaning out above him to signal the engine, the caboose still slowing, creeping, although the engine's exhaust was already slatting in mounting tempo against the unechoing wilderness, the crashing of draw-bars once more travelling backward along the train, the caboose picking up speed at last. Then it was gone. It had not been. He could no longer hear it. The wilderness soared, musing, inattentive, myriad, eternal, green; older than any mill-shed, longer than any spurline. "Mr Boon here yet?" he said.

"He beat me in," Ash said. "Had the wagon loaded and ready for me at Hoke's yistiddy when I got there and setting on the front steps at camp last night when I got in. He already been in the woods since fo daylight this morning. Said he gwine up to the Gum

Tree and for you to hunt up that way and meet him." He knew where that was: a single big sweet-gum just outside the woods, in an old clearing; if you crept up to it very quietly this time of year and then ran suddenly into the clearing, sometimes you caught as many as a dozen squirrels in it, trapped, since there was no other tree near they could jump to. So he didn't get into the wagon at all.

"I will," he said.

"I figured you would," Ash said, "I fotch you a box of shells." He passed the shells down and began to unwrap the lines from the brake-pole.

"How many times up to now do you reckon Major has told you not to do that?" the boy said.

"Do which?" Ash said. Then he said: "And tell Boon Hogganbeck dinner gonter be on the table in a hour and if yawl want any to come on and eat it."

"In an hour?" he said. "It aint nine oclock yet." He drew out his watch and extended it face-toward Ash. "Look." Ash didn't even look at the watch.

"That's town time. You aint in town now. You in the woods."

"Look at the sun then."

"Nemmine the sun too," Ash said. "If you and Boon Hogganbeck want any dinner, you better come on in and get it when I tole you. I aim to get done in that kitchen because I got my wood to chop. And watch your feet. They're crawling."

"I will," he said.

Then he was in the woods, not alone but solitary; the solitude closed about him, green with summer. They did not change, and, timeless, would not, anymore than would the green of summer and the fire and rain of fall and the iron cold and sometimes even snow *the day, the morning when he killed the buck and Sam marked his face with its hot blood, they returned to camp and he remembered old Ash's blinking and disgruntled and even outraged disbelief until at last McCaslin had had to affirm the fact that he had really killed it: and that night Ash sat snarling and unapproachable behind the stove so that Tennie's Jim had to serve the supper and waked them with breakfast already on the table the next morning and it was only half-past one oclock and at last out of Major de Spain's angry cursing and Ash's snarling and sullen rejoinders the fact emerged that Ash not only wanted to go into the woods and shoot a deer also but he intended to and Major de Spain said, 'By*

God, if we dont let him we will probably have to do the cooking
from now on:' and Walter Ewell said, 'Or get up at midnight to
eat what Ash cooks:' and since he had already killed his buck for
this hunt and was not to shoot again unless they needed meat, he
offered his gun to Ash until Major de Spain took command and allotted that gun to Boon for the day and gave Boon's unpredictable
pump gun to Ash, with two buckshot shells but Ash said, 'I got
shells:' and showed them, four: one buck, one of number three shot
for rabbits, two of bird-shot and told one by one their history and
their origin and he remembered not Ash's face alone but Major de
Spain's and Walter's and General Compson's too, and Ash's voice:
'Shoot? In course they'll shoot! Genl Cawmpson guv me this un'—
the buckshot—'right outen the same gun he kilt that big buck with
eight years ago. And this un'—it was the rabbit shell: triumphantly
—'is oldern thisyer boy!' And that morning he loaded the gun himself, reversing the order: the bird-shot, the rabbit, then the buck so
that the buckshot would feed first into the chamber, and himself
without a gun, he and Ash walked beside Major de Spain's and
Tennie's Jim's horses and the dogs (that was the snow) until they
cast and struck, the sweet strong cries ringing away into the muffled falling air and gone almost immediately, as if the constant
and unmurmuring flakes had already buried even the unformed
echoes beneath their myriad and weightless falling, Major de Spain
and Tennie's Jim gone too, whooping on into the woods; and then
it was all right, he knew as plainly as if Ash had told him that Ash
had now hunted his deer and that even his tender years had been
forgiven for having killed one, and they turned back toward home
through the falling snow—that is, Ash said, 'Now whut?' and he
said, 'This way'—himself in front because, although they were less
than a mile from camp, he knew that Ash, who had spent two
weeks of his life in the camp each year for the last twenty, had no
idea whatever where they were, until quite soon the manner in
which Ash carried Boon's gun was making him a good deal more
than just nervous and he made Ash walk in front, striding on, talking now, an old man's garrulous monologue beginning with where
he was at the moment then of the woods and of camping in the
woods and of eating in camps then of eating then of cooking it and
of his wife's cooking then briefly of his old wife and almost at once
and at length of a new light-colored woman who nursed next door
to Major de Spain's and if she didn't watch out who she was switch-

*ing her tail at he would show her how old was an old man or not
if his wife just didn't watch him all the time, the two of them in a
game trail through a dense brake of cane and brier which would
bring them out within a quarter-mile of camp, approaching a big
fallen tree-trunk lying athwart the path and just as Ash, still talking, was about to step over it the bear, the yearling, rose suddenly
beyond the log, sitting up, its forearms against its chest and its
wrists limply arrested as if it had been surprised in the act of covering its face to pray: and after a certain time Ash's gun yawed
jerkily up and he said, 'You haven't got a shell in the barrel yet.
Pump it:' but the gun already snicked and he said, 'Pump it. You
haven't got a shell in the barrel yet:' and Ash pumped the action
and in a certain time the gun steadied again and snicked and he
said, 'Pump it:' and watched the buckshot shell jerk, spinning heavily, into the cane. This is the rabbit shot: he thought and the gun
snicked and he thought: The next is bird-shot: and he didn't have
to say Pump it; he cried, 'Dont shoot! Dont shoot!' but that was already too late too, the light dry vicious snick! before he could
speak and the bear turned and dropped to all-fours and then was
gone and there was only the log, the cane, the velvet and constant
snow and Ash said, 'Now whut?' and he said, 'This way. Come on:'
and began to back away down the path and Ash said, 'I got to
find my shells:' and he said, 'Goddamn it, goddamn it, come on:'
but Ash leaned the gun against the log and returned and stooped
and fumbled among the cane roots until he came back and stooped
and found the shells and they rose and at that moment the gun,
untouched, leaning against the log six feet away and for that while
even forgotten by both of them, roared, bellowed and flamed, and
ceased: and he carried it now, pumped out the last mummified
shell and gave that one also to Ash and, the action still open, himself carried the gun until he stood it in the corner behind Boon's
bed at the camp*

—; summer, and fall, and snow, and wet and saprife spring in
their ordered immortal sequence, the deathless and immemorial
phases of the mother who had shaped him if any had toward the
man he almost was, mother and father both to the old man born of
a Negro slave and a Chickasaw chief who had been his spirit's father if any had, whom he had revered and harkened to and loved
and lost and grieved: and he would marry someday and they too
would own for their brief while that brief unsubstanced glory

which inherently of itself cannot last and hence why glory: and they would, might, carry even the remembrance of it into the time when flesh no longer talks to flesh because memory at least does last: but still the woods would be his mistress and his wife.

He was not going toward the Gum Tree. Actually he was getting farther from it. Time was and not so long ago either when he would not have been allowed here without someone with him, and a little later, when he had begun to learn how much he did not know, he would not have dared be here without someone with him, and later still, beginning to ascertain, even if only dimly, the limits of what he did not know, he could have attempted and carried it through with a compass, not because of any increased belief in himself but because McCaslin and Major de Spain and Walter and General Compson too had taught him at last to believe the compass regardless of what it seemed to state. Now he did not even use the compass but merely the sun and that only subconsciously, yet he could have taken a scaled map and plotted at any time to within a hundred feet of where he actually was; and sure enough, at almost the exact moment when he expected it, the earth began to rise faintly, he passed one of the four concrete markers set down by the lumber company's surveyor to establish the four corners of the plot which Major de Spain had reserved out of the sale, then he stood on the crest of the knoll itself, the four corner-markers all visible now, blanched still even beneath the winter's weathering, lifeless and shockingly alien in that place where dissolution itself was a seething turmoil of ejaculation tumescence conception and birth, and death did not even exist. After two winters' blanketings of leaves and the flood-waters of two springs, there was no trace of the two graves anymore at all. But those who would have come this far to find them would not need headstones but would have found them as Sam Fathers himself had taught him to find such: by bearings on trees: and did, almost the first thrust of the hunting knife finding (but only to see if it was still there) the round tin box manufactured for axle-grease and containing now Old Ben's dried mutilated paw, resting above Lion's bones.

He didn't disturb it. He didn't even look for the other grave where he and McCaslin and Major de Spain and Boon had laid Sam's body, along with his hunting horn and his knife and his tobacco-pipe, that Sunday morning two years ago; he didn't have to. He had stepped over it, perhaps on it. But that was all right.

*He probably knew I was in the woods this morning long before I
got here,* he thought, going on to the tree which had supported one
end of the platform where Sam lay when McCaslin and Major de
Spain found them—the tree, the other axle-grease tin nailed to the
trunk, but weathered, rusted, alien too yet healed already into
the wilderness' concordant generality, raising no tuneless note, and
empty, long since empty of the food and tobacco he had put into
it that day, as empty of that as it would presently be of this which
he drew from his pocket—the twist of tobacco, the new bandanna
handkerchief, the small paper sack of the peppermint candy which
Sam had used to love; that gone too, almost before he had turned
his back, not vanished but merely translated into the myriad life
which printed the dark mold of these secret and sunless places with
delicate fairy tracks, which, breathing and biding and immobile,
watched him from beyond every twig and leaf until he moved,
moving again, walking on; he had not stopped, he had only
paused, quitting the knoll which was no abode of the dead because
there was no death, not Lion and not Sam: not held fast in earth
but free in earth and not in earth but of earth, myriad yet undif-
fused of every myriad part, leaf and twig and particle, air and sun
and rain and dew and night, acorn oak and leaf and acorn again,
dark and dawn and dark and dawn again in their immutable progression and, being myriad, one: and Old Ben too, Old Ben too;
they would give him his paw back even, certainly they would give
him his paw back: then the long challenge and the long chase, no
heart to be driven and outraged, no flesh to be mauled and bled—
Even as he froze himself, he seemed to hear Ash's parting admoni-
tion. He could even hear the voice as he froze, immobile, one foot
just taking his weight, the toe of the other just lifted behind him,
not breathing, feeling again and as always the sharp shocking in-
rush from when Isaac McCaslin long yet was not, and so it was
fear all right but not fright as he looked down at it. It had not
coiled yet and the buzzer had not sounded either, only one thick
rapid contraction, one loop cast sideways as though merely for purchase from which the raised head might start slightly backward,
not in fright either, not in threat quite yet, more than six feet of it,
the head raised higher than his knee and less than his knee's length
away, and old, the once-bright markings of its youth dulled now
to a monotone concordant too with the wilderness it crawled and
lurked: the old one, the ancient and accursed about the earth, fatal

and solitary and he could smell it now: the thin sick smell of rotting cucumbers and something else which had no name, evocative
of all knowledge and an old weariness and of pariah-hood and of
death. At last it moved. Not the head. The elevation of the head
did not change as it began to glide away from him, moving erect
yet off the perpendicular as if the head and that elevated third
were complete and all: an entity walking on two feet and free of all
laws of mass and balance and should have been because even now
he could not quite believe that all that shift and flow of shadow
behind that walking head could have been one snake: going and
then gone; he put the other foot down at last and didn't know it,
standing with one hand raised as Sam had stood that afternoon six
years ago when Sam led him into the wilderness and showed him
and he ceased to be a child, speaking the old tongue which Sam
had spoken that day without premeditation either: "Chief," he
said: "Grandfather."

He couldn't tell when he first began to hear the sound, because
when he became aware of it, it seemed to him that he had been
already hearing it for several seconds—a sound as though someone
were hammering a gun-barrel against a piece of railroad iron, a
sound loud and heavy and not rapid yet with something frenzied
about it, as the hammerer were not only a strong man and an earnest one but a little hysterical too. Yet it couldn't be on the log-line
because, although the track lay in that direction, it was at least
two miles from him and this sound was not three hundred yards
away. But even as he thought that, he realised where the sound
must be coming from: whoever the man was and whatever he was
doing, he was somewhere near the edge of the clearing where the
Gum Tree was and where he was to meet Boon. So far, he had
been hunting as he advanced, moving slowly and quietly and
watching the ground and the trees both. Now he went on, his
gun unloaded and the barrel slanted up and back to facilitate its
passage through brier and undergrowth, approaching as it grew
louder and louder that steady savage somehow queerly hysterical
beating of metal on metal, emerging from the woods, into the old
clearing, with the solitary gum tree directly before him. At first
glance the tree seemed to be alive with frantic squirrels. There appeared to be forty or fifty of them leaping and darting from
branch to branch until the whole tree had become one green maelstrom of mad leaves, while from time to time, singly or in twos

and threes, squirrels would dart down the trunk then whirl without stopping and rush back up again as though sucked violently back by the vacuum of their fellows' frenzied vortex. Then he saw Boon, sitting, his back against the trunk, his head bent, hammering furiously at something on his lap. What he hammered with was the barrel of his dismembered gun, what he hammered at was the breech of it. The rest of the gun lay scattered about him in a half-dozen pieces while he bent over the piece on his lap his scarlet and streaming walnut face, hammering the disjointed barrel against the gun-breech with the frantic abandon of a madman. He didn't even look up to see who it was. Still hammering, he merely shouted back at the boy in a hoarse strangled voice:

"Get out of here! Dont touch them! Dont touch a one of them! They're mine!"

Old Man

Once (IT WAS IN MISSISSIPPI, IN MAY, IN THE FLOOD YEAR 1927)
there were two convicts. One of them was about twenty-five, tall,
lean, flat-stomached, with a sunburned face and Indian-black hair
and pale, china-colored outraged eyes—an outrage directed not at
the men who had foiled his crime, not even at the lawyers and
judges who had sent him here, but at the writers, the uncorporeal
names attached to the stories, the paper novels—the Diamond
Dicks and Jesse Jameses and such—whom he believed had led him
into his present predicament through their own ignorance and gul-
libility regarding the medium in which they dealt and took money
for, in accepting information on which they placed the stamp of
verisimilitude and authenticity (this so much the more criminal
since there was no sworn notarised statement attached and hence
so much the quicker would the information be accepted by one
who expected the same unspoken good faith, demanding, asking,
expecting no certification, which he extended along with the dime
or fifteen cents to pay for it) and retailed for money and which on
actual application proved to be impractical and (to the convict)
criminally false; there would be times when he would halt his mule
and plow in midfurrow (there is no walled penitentiary in Mississippi; it is a cotton plantation which the convicts work under the
rifles and shotguns of guards and trusties) and muse with a kind of
enraged impotence, fumbling among the rubbish left him by his
one and only experience with courts and law, fumbling until the
meaningless and verbose shibboleth took form at last (himself
seeking justice at the same blind fount where he had met justice
and been hurled back and down): Using the mails to defraud: who
felt that he had been defrauded by the third-class mail system not

of crass and stupid money which he did not particularly want anyway, but of liberty and honor and pride.

He was in for fifteen years (he had arrived shortly after his nineteenth birthday) for attempted train robbery. He had laid his plans in advance, he had followed his printed (and false) authority to the letter; he had saved the paper-backs for two years, reading and re-reading them, memorising them, comparing and weighing story and method against story and method, taking the good from each and discarding the dross as his workable plan emerged, keeping his mind open to make the subtle last-minute changes, without haste and without impatience, as the newer pamphlets appeared on their appointed days as a conscientious dressmaker makes the subtle alterations in a court presentation costume as the newer bulletins appear. And then when the day came, he did not even have a chance to go through the coaches and collect the watches and the rings, the brooches and the hidden money-belts, because he had been captured as soon as he entered the express car where the safe and the gold would be. He had shot no one because the pistol which they took away from him was not that kind of a pistol although it was loaded; later he admitted to the District Attorney that he had got it, as well as the dark lantern in which a candle burned and the black handkerchief to wear over the face, by peddling among his pinehill neighbors subscriptions to the *Detectives' Gazette*. So now from time to time (he had ample leisure for it) he mused with that raging impotence, because there was something else he could not tell them at the trial, did not know how to tell them. It was not the money he had wanted. It was not riches, not the crass loot; that would have been merely a bangle to wear upon the breast of his pride like the Olympic runner's amateur medal— a symbol, a badge to show that he too was the best at his chosen gambit in the living and fluid world of his time. So that at times as he trod the richly shearing black earth behind his plow or with a hoe thinned the sprouting cotton and corn or lay on his sullen back in his bunk after supper, he cursed in a harsh steady unrepetitive stream, not at the living men who had put him where he was but at what he did not even know were pen-names, did not even know were not actual men but merely the designations of shades who had written about shades.

The second convict was short and plump. Almost hairless, he was quite white. He looked like something exposed to light by turning over rotting logs or planks and he too carried (though not in his eyes like the first convict) a sense of burning and impotent outrage. So it did not show on him and hence none knew it was there. But then nobody knew very much about him, including the people who had sent him here. His outrage was directed at no printed word but at the paradoxical fact that he had been forced to come here of his own free choice and will. He had been forced to choose between the Mississippi State penal farm and the Federal Penitentiary at Atlanta, and the fact that he, who resembled a hairless and pallid slug, had chosen the out-of-doors and the sunlight was merely another manifestation of the close-guarded and solitary enigma of his character, as something recognisable roils momentarily into view from beneath stagnant and opaque water, then sinks again. None of his fellow prisoners knew what his crime had been, save that he was in for a hundred and ninety-nine years—this incredible and impossible period of punishment or restraint itself carrying a vicious and fabulous quality which indicated that his reason for being here was such that the very men, the paladins and pillars of justice and equity who had sent him here had during that moment become blind apostles not of mere justice but of all human decency, blind instruments not of equity but of all human outrage and vengeance, acting in a savage personal concert, judge, lawyer and jury, which certainly abrogated justice and possibly even law. Possibly only the Federal and State's Attorneys knew what the crime actually was. There had been a woman in it and a stolen automobile transported across a State line, a filling station robbed and the attendant shot to death. There had been a second man in the car at the time and anyone could have looked once at the convict (as the two attorneys did) and known he would not even have had the synthetic courage of alcohol to pull trigger on anyone. But he and the woman and the stolen car had been captured while the second man, doubtless the actual murderer, had escaped, so that, brought to bay at last in the State's Attorney's office, harried, dishevelled and snarling, the two grimly implacable and viciously gleeful attorneys in his front and the now raging woman held by two policemen in the anteroom in his rear, he was given his choice. He could be tried in Federal Court under the Mann Act and for the automobile, that is, by electing to pass through the anteroom where the woman raged he could take his chances on the lesser crime in Federal Court, or by accepting a sen-

tence for manslaughter in the State Court he would be permitted
to quit the room by a back entrance, without having to pass the
woman. He had chosen; he stood at the bar and heard a judge
(who looked down at him as if the District Attorney actually had
turned over a rotten plank with his toe and exposed him) sentence
him to a hundred and ninety-nine years at the State Farm. Thus
(he had ample leisure too; they had tried to teach him to plow and
had failed, they had put him in the blacksmith shop and the foreman trusty himself had asked to have him removed: so that now,
in a long apron like a woman, he cooked and swept and dusted in
the deputy wardens' barracks) he too mused at times with that
sense of impotence and outrage though it did not show on him as
on the first convict since he leaned on no halted broom to do it and
so none knew it was there.

It was this second convict who, toward the end of April, began
to read aloud to the others from the daily newspapers when,
chained ankle to ankle and herded by armed guards, they had
come up from the fields and had eaten supper and were gathered in
the bunkhouse. It was the Memphis newspaper which the deputy
wardens had read at breakfast; the convict read aloud from it to
his companions who could have had but little active interest in
the outside world, some of whom could not have read it for themselves at all and did not even know where the Ohio and Missouri
river basins were, some of whom had never even seen the Mississippi River although for past periods ranging from a few days to
ten and twenty and thirty years (and for future periods ranging
from a few months to life) they had plowed and planted and eaten
and slept beneath the shadow of the levee itself, knowing only that
there was water beyond it from hearsay and because now and then
they heard the whistles of steamboats from beyond it and, during
the last week or so had seen the stacks and pilot houses moving
along the sky sixty feet above their heads.

But they listened, and soon even those who like the taller convict
had probably never before seen more water than a horse pond
would hold knew what thirty feet on a river gauge at Cairo or
Memphis meant and could (and did) talk glibly of sandboils. Perhaps what actually moved them were the accounts of the con-
scripted levee gangs, mixed blacks and whites working in double
shifts against the steadily rising water; stories of men, even though
they were negroes, being forced like themselves to do work for

which they received no other pay than coarse food and a place in a mudfloored tent to sleep on—stories, pictures, which emerged from the shorter convict's reading voice: the mudsplashed white men with the inevitable shotguns, the antlike lines of negroes carrying sandbags, slipping and crawling up the steep face of the revetment to hurl their futile ammunition into the face of a flood and return for more. Or perhaps it was more than this. Perhaps they watched the approach of the disaster with that same amazed and incredulous hope of the slaves—the lions and bears and elephants, the grooms and bathmen and pastrycooks—who watched the mounting flames of Rome from Ahenobarbus' gardens. But listen they did and presently it was May and the wardens' newspaper began to talk in headlines two inches tall—those black staccato slashes of ink which, it would almost seem, even the illiterate should be able to read: *Crest Passes Memphis at Midnight 4000 Homeless in White River Basin Governor Calls out National Guard Martial Law Declared in Following Counties Red Cross Train with President Hoover Leaves Washington Tonight;* then, three evenings later (It had been raining all day—not the vivid brief thunderous downpours of April and May, but the slow steady gray rain of November and December before a cold north wind. The men had not gone to the fields at all during the day, and the very second-hand optimism of the almost twenty-four-hour-old news seemed to contain its own refutation.): *Crest Now Below Memphis 22,000 Refugees Safe at Vicksburg Army Engineers Say Levees Will Hold.*

"I reckon that means it will bust tonight," one convict said.

"Well, maybe this rain will hold on until the water gets here," a second said. They all agreed to this because what they meant, the living unspoken thought among them, was that if the weather cleared, even though the levees broke and the flood moved in upon the Farm itself, they would have to return to the fields and work, which they would have had to do. There was nothing paradoxical in this, although they could not have expressed the reason for it which they instinctively perceived: that the land they farmed and the substance they produced from it belonged neither to them who worked it nor to those who forced them at guns' point to do so, that as far as either—convicts or guards—were concerned, it could have been pebbles they put into the ground and papier-mâché cotton- and corn-sprouts which they thinned. So it was that, what between the sudden wild hoping and the idle day and the evening's headlines, they were sleeping restlessly beneath the sound of the rain on the tin roof when at midnight the sudden glare of the electric bulbs and the guards' voices waked them and they heard the throbbing of the waiting trucks.

"Turn out of there!" the deputy shouted. He was fully dressed— rubber boots, slicker and shotgun. "The levee went out at Mound's Landing an hour ago. Get up out of it!"

WHEN THE BELATED AND STREAMING DAWN BROKE THE TWO CONVICTS, along with twenty others, were in a truck. A trusty drove, two armed guards sat in the cab with him. Inside the high, stall-like topless body the convicts stood, packed like matches in an upright box or like the pencil-shaped ranks of cordite in a shell, shackled by the ankles to a single chain which wove among the motionless feet and swaying legs and a clutter of picks and shovels among which they stood, and was riveted by both ends to the steel body of the truck.

Then and without warning they saw the flood about which the plump convict had been reading and they listening for two weeks or more. The road ran south. It was built on a raised levee, known locally as a dump, about eight feet above the flat surrounding land, bordered on both sides by the barrow pits from which the earth of the levee had been excavated. These barrow pits had held water all winter from the fall rains, not to speak of the rain of yesterday, but now they saw that the pit on either side of the road had vanished and instead there lay a flat still sheet of brown water which extended into the fields beyond the pits, ravelled out into long motionless shreds in the bottom of the plow furrows and gleaming faintly in the gray light like the bars of a prone and enormous grating. And then (the truck was moving at good speed) as they watched quietly (they had not been talking much anyway but now they were all silent and quite grave, shifting and craning as one to look soberly off to the west side of the road) the crests of the furrows vanished too and they now looked at a single perfectly flat and motionless steel-colored sheet in which the telephone poles and the straight hedgerows which marked section lines seemed to be fixed and rigid as though set in concrete.

It was perfectly motionless, perfectly flat. It looked, not inno-

cent, but bland. It looked almost demure. It looked as if you could
walk on it. It looked so still that they did not realise it possessed
motion until they came to the first bridge. There was a ditch under the bridge, a small stream, but ditch and stream were both
invisible now, indicated only by the rows of cypress and bramble
which marked its course. Here they both saw and heard movement
—the slow profound eastward and upstream ("It's running backward," one convict said quietly.) set of the still rigid surface, from
beneath which came a deep faint subaquean rumble which
(though none in the truck could have made the comparison)
sounded like a subway train passing far beneath the street and
which inferred a terrific and secret speed. It was as if the water
itself were in three strata, separate and distinct, the bland and unhurried surface bearing a frothy scum and a miniature flotsam of
twigs and screening as though by vicious calculation the rush and
fury of the flood itself, and beneath this in turn the original stream,
trickle, murmuring along in the opposite direction, following un-
disturbed and unaware its appointed course and serving its Lilliputian end, like a thread of ants between the rails on which an
express train passes, they (the ants) as unaware of the power and
fury as if it were a cyclone crossing Saturn.

Now there was water on both sides of the road and now, as if
once they had become aware of movement in the water the water
seemed to have given over deception and concealment, they
seemed to be able to watch it rising up the flanks of the dump;
trees which a few miles back had stood on tall trunks above
the water now seemed to burst from the surface at the level of the
lower branches like decorative shrubs on barbered lawns. The
truck passed a negro cabin. The water was up to the window
ledges. A woman clutching two children squatted on the ridge-
pole, a man and a halfgrown youth, standing waist-deep, were
hoisting a squealing pig onto the slanting roof of a barn, on the
ridgepole of which sat a row of chickens and a turkey. Near the
barn was a haystack on which a cow stood tied by a rope to
the center pole and bawling steadily; a yelling negro boy on a sad-
dleless mule which he flogged steadily, his legs clutching the mule's
barrel and his body leaned to the drag of a rope attached to a second mule, approached the haystack, splashing and floundering.
The woman on the housetop began to shriek at the passing truck,
her voice carrying faint and melodious across the brown water, be-

coming fainter and fainter as the truck passed and went on, ceasing at last, whether because of distance or because she had stopped screaming those in the truck did not know.

Then the road vanished. There was no perceptible slant to it yet it had slipped abruptly beneath the brown surface with no ripple, no ridgy demarcation, like a flat thin blade slipped obliquely into flesh by a delicate hand, annealed into the water without disturbance, as if it had existed so for years, had been built that way. The truck stopped. The trusty descended from the cab and came back and dragged two shovels from among their feet, the blades clashing against the serpentining of the chain about their ankles. "What is it?" one said. "What are you fixing to do?" The trusty didn't answer. He returned to the cab, from which one of the guards had descended, without his shotgun. He and the trusty, both in hip boots and each carrying a shovel, advanced into the water, gingerly, probing and feeling ahead with the shovel handles. The same convict spoke again. He was a middle-aged man with a wild thatch of iron-gray hair and a slightly mad face. "What the hell are they doing?" he said. Again nobody answered him. The truck moved, on into the water, behind the guard and the trusty, beginning to push ahead of itself a thick slow viscid ridge of chocolate water. Then the gray-haired convict began to scream. "God damn it, unlock the chain!" He began to struggle, thrashing violently about him, striking at the men nearest him until he reached the cab, the roof of which he now hammered on with his fists, screaming. "God damn it, unlock us! Unlock us! Son of a bitch!" he screamed, addressing no one. "They're going to drown us! Unlock the chain!" But for all the answer he got the men within radius of his voice might have been dead. The truck crawled on, the guard and the trusty feeling out the road ahead with the reversed shovels, the second guard at the wheel, the twenty-two convicts packed like sardines into the truck bed and padlocked by the ankles to the body of the truck itself. They crossed another bridge—two delicate and paradoxical iron railings slanting out of the water, travelling parallel to it for a distance, then slanting down into it again with an outrageous quality almost significant yet apparently meaningless like something in a dream not quite nightmare. The truck crawled on.

Along toward noon they came to a town, their destination. The streets were paved; now the wheels of the truck made a sound like tearing silk. Moving faster now, the guard and the trusty in the cab again, the truck even had a slight bone in its teeth, its bow-wave spreading beyond the submerged sidewalks and across the adjacent lawns, lapping against the stoops and porches of houses where people stood among piles of furniture. They passed through the business district; a man in hip boots emerged knee-deep in water from a store, dragging a flat-bottomed skiff containing a steel safe.

At last they reached the railroad. It crossed the street at right angles, cutting the town in two. It was on a dump, a levee, also, eight or ten feet above the town itself; the street ran blankly into it and turned at right angles beside a cotton compress and a loading platform on stilts at the level of a freight car door. On this platform was a khaki army tent and a uniformed National Guard sentry with a rifle and bandolier.

The truck turned and crawled out of the water and up the ramp which cotton wagons used and where trucks and private cars filled with household goods came and unloaded onto the platform. They were unlocked from the chain in the truck and shackled ankle to ankle in pairs they mounted the platform and into an apparently inextricable jumble of beds and trunks, gas and electric stoves, radios and tables and chairs and framed pictures which a chain of negroes under the eye of an unshaven white man in muddy corduroy and hip boots carried piece by piece into the compress, at the door of which another guardsman stood with his rifle, they (the convicts) not stopping here but herded on by the two guards with their shotguns, into the dim and cavernous building where among the piled heterogeneous furniture the ends of cotton bales and the mirrors on dressers and sideboards gleamed with an identical mute and unreflecting concentration of pallid light.

They passed on through, onto the loading platform where the army tent and the first sentry were. They waited here. Nobody told them for what nor why. While the two guards talked with the sentry before the tent the convicts sat in a line along the edge of the platform like buzzards on a fence, their shackled feet dangling above the brown motionless flood out of which the railroad embankment rose, pristine and intact, in a kind of paradoxical denial and repudiation of change and portent, not talking, just looking quietly across the track to where the other half of the amputated town seemed to float, house shrub and tree, ordered and pageant-like and without motion, upon the limitless liquid plain beneath the thick gray sky.

After a while the other four trucks from the Farm arrived. They came up, bunched closely, radiator to tail light, with their four separate sounds of tearing silk and vanished beyond the compress. Presently the ones on the platform heard the feet, the mute clashing of the shackles, the first truckload emerged from the compress, the second, the third; there were more than a hundred of them now in their bed-ticking overalls and jumpers and fifteen or twenty guards with rifles and shotguns. The first lot rose and they mingled, paired, twinned by their clanking and clashing umbilicals; then it began to rain, a slow steady gray drizzle like November instead of May. Yet not one of them made any move toward the open door of the compress. They did not even look toward it, with longing or hope or without it. If they thought at all, they doubtless knew that the available space in it would be needed for furniture, even if it were not already filled. Or perhaps they knew that, even if there were room in it, it would not be for them, not that the guards would wish them to get wet but that the guards would not think about getting them out of the rain. So they just stopped talking and with their jumper collars turned up and shackled in braces like dogs at a field trial they stood, immobile, patient, almost ruminant, their backs turned to the rain as sheep and cattle do.

After another while they became aware that the number of soldiers had increased to a dozen or more, warm and dry beneath rubberised ponchos, there was an officer with a pistol at his belt, then and without making any move toward it, they began to smell food and, turning to look, saw an army field kitchen set up just inside the compress door. But they made no move, they waited until they were herded into line, they inched forward, their heads lowered and patient in the rain, and received each a bowl of stew, a mug of coffee, two slices of bread. They ate this in the rain. They did not sit down because the platform was wet, they squatted on their heels as country men do, hunching forward, trying to shield the bowls and mugs into which nevertheless the rain splashed steadily as into miniature ponds and soaked, invisible and soundless, into the bread.

After they had stood on the platform for three hours, a train came for them. Those nearest the edge saw it, watched it—a passenger coach apparently running under its own power and trailing a cloud of smoke from no visible stack, a cloud which did not rise but instead shifted slowly and heavily aside and lay upon the surface of the aqueous earth with a quality at once weightless and completely spent. It came up and stopped, a single old fashioned open-ended wooden car coupled to the nose of a pushing switch engine considerably smaller. They were herded into it, crowding forward to the other end where there was a small cast iron stove. There was no fire in it, nevertheless they crowded about it—the cold and voiceless lump of iron stained with fading tobacco and hovered about by the ghosts of a thousand Sunday excursions to Memphis or Moorhead and return—the peanuts, the bananas, the soiled garments of infants—huddling, shoving for places near it. "Come on, come on," one of the guards shouted. "Sit down, now." At last three of the guards, laying aside their guns, came among them and broke up the huddle, driving them back and into seats.

There were not enough seats for all. The others stood in the aisle, they stood braced, they heard the air hiss out of the released brakes, the engine whistled four blasts, the car came into motion with a snapping jerk; the platform, the compress fled violently as the train seemed to transpose from immobility to full speed with that same quality of unreality with which it had appeared, running backward now though with the engine in front where before it had moved forward but with the engine behind.

When the railroad in its turn ran beneath the surface of the water, the convicts did not even know it. They felt the train stop, they heard the engine blow a long blast which wailed away unechoed across the waste, wild and forlorn, and they were not even curious; they sat or stood behind the rain-streaming windows as the train crawled on again, feeling its way as the truck had while the brown water swirled between the trucks and among the spokes of the driving wheels and lapped in cloudy steam against the dragging fire-filled belly of the engine; again it blew four short harsh blasts filled with the wild triumph and defiance yet also with repudiation and even farewell, as if the articulated steel itself knew it did not dare stop and would not be able to return. Two hours later in the twilight they saw through the streaming windows a burning plantation house. Juxtaposed to nowhere and neighbored by nothing it stood, a clear steady pyre-like flame rigidly fleeing its own reflection, burning in the dusk above the watery desolation with a quality paradoxical, outrageous and bizarre.

Sometime after dark the train stopped. The convicts did not know where they were. They did not ask. They would no more have thought of asking where they were than they would have asked why and what for. They couldn't even see, since the car was unlighted and the windows fogged on the outside by rain and on the inside by the engendered heat of the packed bodies. All they could see was a milky and sourceless flick and glare of flashlights. They could hear shouts and commands, then the guards inside the car began to shout; they were herded to their feet and toward the exit, the ankle chains clashing and clanking. They descended into a fierce hissing of steam, through ragged wisps of it blowing past the car. Laid-to alongside the train and resembling a train itself was a thick blunt motor launch to which was attached a string of skiffs and flat boats. There were more soldiers; the flashlights played on the rifle barrels and bandolier buckles and flicked and glinted on the ankle chains of the convicts as they stepped gingerly down into knee-deep water and entered the boats; now car and engine both vanished completely in steam as the crew began dumping the fire from the firebox.

After another hour they began to see lights ahead—a faint wavering row of red pin-pricks extending along the horizon and apparently hanging low in the sky. But it took almost another hour to reach them while the convicts squatted in the skiffs, huddled into the soaked garments (they no longer felt the rain any more at all as separate drops) and watched the lights draw nearer and nearer until at last the crest of the levee defined itself; now they could discern a row of army tents stretching along it and people squatting about the fires, the wavering reflections from which, stretching across the water, revealed an involved mass of other skiffs tied against the flank of the levee which now stood high and dark overhead. Flashlights glared and winked along the base, among the tethered skiffs; the launch, silent now, drifted in.

When they reached the top of the levee they could see the long line of khaki tents, interspersed with fires about which people—men, women and children, negro and white—crouched or stood among shapeless bales of clothing, their heads turning, their eyeballs glinting in the firelight as they looked quietly at the striped

garments and the chains; further down the levee, huddled together
too though untethered, was a drove of mules and two or three
cows. Then the taller convict became conscious of another sound.
He did not begin to hear it all at once, he suddenly became aware
that he had been hearing it all the time, a sound so much beyond
all his experience and his powers of assimilation that up to this
point he had been as oblivious of it as an ant or a flea might be of
the sound of the avalanche on which it rides; he had been travelling upon water since early afternoon and for seven years now he
had run his plow and harrow and planter within the very shadow
of the levee on which he now stood, but this profound deep whisper which came from the further side of it he did not at once recognise. He stopped. The line of convicts behind jolted into him
like a line of freight cars stopping, with an iron clashing like cars.
"Get on!" a guard shouted.

"What's that?" the convict said. A negro man squatting before
the nearest fire answered him:

"Dat's him. Dat's de Ole Man."

"The old man?" the convict said.

"Get on! Get on up there!" the guard shouted. They went on;
they passed another huddle of mules, the eyeballs rolling too, the
long morose faces turning into and out of the firelight; they passed
them and reached a section of empty tents, the light pup tents of
a military campaign, made to hold two men. The guards herded the
convicts into them, three brace of shackled men to each tent.

They crawled in on all fours, like dogs into cramped kennels,
and settled down. Presently the tent became warm from their bodies. Then they became quiet and then all of them could hear it,
they lay listening to the bass whisper deep, strong and powerful.
"The old man?" the train-robber convict said.

"Yah," another said. "He dont have to brag."

At dawn the guards waked them by kicking the soles of the projecting feet. Opposite the muddy landing and the huddle of skiffs
an army field kitchen was set up, already they could smell the coffee. But the taller convict at least, even though he had had but one
meal yesterday and that at noon in the rain, did not move at once
toward the food. Instead and for the first time he looked at the
River within whose shadow he had spent the last seven years of his
life but had never seen before; he stood in quiet and amazed
surmise and looked at the rigid steel-colored surface not broken

into waves but merely slightly undulant. It stretched from the levee on which he stood, further than he could see—a slowly and heavily roiling chocolate-frothy expanse broken only by a thin line a mile away as fragile in appearance as a single hair, which after a moment he recognised. *It's another levee,* he thought quietly. *That's what we look like from there. That's what I am standing on looks like from there.* He was prodded from the rear; a guard's voice carried forward: "Go on! Go on! You'll have plenty of time to look at that!"

They received the same stew and coffee and bread as the day before; they squatted again with their bowls and mugs as yesterday, though it was not raining yet. During the night an intact wooden barn had floated up. It now lay jammed by the current against the levee while a crowd of negroes swarmed over it, ripping off the shingles and planks and carrying them up the bank; eating steadily and without haste, the taller convict watched the barn dissolve rapidly down to the very water-line exactly as a dead fly vanished beneath the moiling industry of a swarm of ants.

They finished eating. Then it began to rain again, as upon a signal, while they stood or squatted in their harsh garments which had not dried out during the night but had merely become slightly warmer than the air. Presently they were haled to their feet and told off into two groups, one of which was armed from a stack of mud-clogged picks and shovels nearby, and marched away up the levee. A little later the motor launch with its train of skiffs came up across what was, fifteen feet beneath its keel, probably a cotton field, the skiffs loaded to the gunwales with negroes and a scattering of white people nursing bundles on their laps. When the engine shut off the faint plinking of a guitar came across the water. The skiffs warped in and unloaded; the convicts watched the men and women and children struggle up the muddy slope, carrying heavy towsacks and bundles wrapped in quilts. The sound of the guitar had not ceased and now the convicts saw him—a young, black, lean-hipped man, the guitar slung by a piece of cotton plow line about his neck. He mounted the levee, still picking it. He carried nothing else, no food, no change of clothes, not even a coat.

The taller convict was so busy watching this that he did not hear the guard until the guard stood directly beside him shouting

his name. "Wake up!" the guard shouted. "Can you fellows paddle
a boat?"

"Paddle a boat where?" the taller convict said.

"In the water," the guard said. "Where in hell do you think?"

"I aint going to paddle no boat nowhere out yonder," the tall
convict said, jerking his head toward the invisible river beyond the
levee behind him.

"No, it's on this side," the guard said. He stooped swiftly and
unlocked the chain which joined the tall convict and the plump
hairless one. "It's just down the road a piece." He rose. The two
convicts followed him down to the boats. "Follow them telephone
poles until you come to a filling station. You can tell it, the roof is
still above water. It's on a bayou and you can tell the bayou because the tops of the trees are sticking up. Follow the bayou until
you come to a cypress snag with a woman in it. Pick her up and
then cut straight back west until you come to a cotton house with
a fellow sitting on the ridgepole—" He turned, looking at the two
convicts, who stood perfectly still, looking first at the skiff and
then at the water with intense sobriety. "Well? What are you waiting for?"

"I cant row a boat," the plump convict said.

"Then it's high time you learned," the guard said. "Get in."

The tall convict shoved the other forward. "Get in," he said.
"That water aint going to hurt you. Aint nobody going to make
you take a bath."

As, the plump one in the bow and the other in the stern, they
shoved away from the levee, they saw other pairs being unshackled
and manning the other skiffs. "I wonder how many more of them
fellows are seeing this much water for the first time in their lives
too," the tall convict said. The other did not answer. He knelt in
the bottom of the skiff, pecking gingerly at the water now and then
with his paddle. The very shape of his thick soft back seemed to
wear that expression of wary and tense concern.

Some time after midnight a rescue boat filled to the guard rail
with homeless men and women and children docked at Vicksburg.
It was a steamer, shallow of draft; all day long it had poked up
and down cypress- and gum-choked bayous and across cotton
fields (where at times instead of swimming it waded) gathering its
sorry cargo from the tops of houses and barns and even out of

trees, and now it warped into that mushroom city of the forlorn
and despairing where kerosene flares smoked in the drizzle and
hurriedly strung electrics glared upon the bayonets of martial policemen and the Red Cross brassards of doctors and nurses and
canteen-workers. The bluff overhead was almost solid with tents,
yet still there were more people than shelter for them; they sat or
lay, single and by whole families, under what shelter they could
find or sometimes under the rain itself, in the little death of profound exhaustion while the doctors and the nurses and the soldiers
stepped over and around and among them.

Among the first to disembark was one of the penitentiary deputy
wardens, followed closely by the plump convict and another white
man—a small man with a gaunt unshaven wan face still wearing
an expression of incredulous outrage. The deputy warden seemed
to know exactly where he wished to go. Followed closely by his
two companions he threaded his way swiftly among the piled furniture and the sleeping bodies and stood presently in a fiercely
lighted and hastily established temporary office, almost a military
post of command in fact, where the Warden of the Penitentiary
sat with two army officers wearing majors' leaves. The deputy warden spoke without preamble. "We lost a man," he said. He called
the tall convict's name.

"Lost him?" the Warden said.

"Yah. Drowned." Without turning his head he spoke to the
plump convict. "Tell him," he said.

"He was the one that said he could row a boat," the plump convict said. "I never. I told him myself—" he indicated the deputy
warden with a jerk of his head "—I couldn't. So when we got to the
bayou—"

"What's this?" the Warden said.

"The launch brought word in," the deputy warden said. "Woman
in a cypress snag on the bayou, then this fellow—" he indicated the
third man; the Warden and the two officers looked at the third
man "—on a cottonhouse. Never had room in the launch to pick
them up. Go on."

"So we come to where the bayou was," the plump convict continued in a voice perfectly flat, without any inflection whatever.
"Then the boat got away from him. I dont know what happened.
I was just sitting there because he was so positive he could row a
boat. I never saw any current. Just all of a sudden the boat whirled

clean around and begun to run fast backward like it was hitched to a train and it whirled around again and I happened to look up and there was a limb right over my head and I grabbed it just in time and that boat was snatched out from under me like you'd snatch off a sock and I saw it one time more upside down and that fellow that said he knew all about rowing holding to it with one hand and still holding the paddle in the other—" He ceased. There was no dying fall to his voice, it just ceased and the convict stood looking quietly at a half-full quart of whiskey sitting on the table.

"How do you know he's drowned?" the Warden said to the deputy. "How do you know he didn't just see his chance to escape, and took it?"

"Escape where?" the other said. "The whole Delta's flooded. There's fifteen foot of water for fifty miles, clean back to the hills. And that boat was upside down."

"That fellow's drowned," the plump convict said. "You dont need to worry about him. He's got his pardon; it wont cramp nobody's hand signing it, neither."

"And nobody else saw him?" the Warden said. "What about the woman in the tree?"

"I dont know," the deputy said. "I aint found her yet. I reckon some other boat picked her up. But this is the fellow on the cotton house."

Again the Warden and the two officers looked at the third man, at the gaunt, unshaven wild face in which an old terror, an old blending of fear and impotence and rage still lingered. "He never came for you?" the Warden said. "You never saw him?"

"Never nobody came for me," the refugee said. He began to tremble though at first he spoke quietly enough. "I set there on that sonabitching cottonhouse, expecting hit to go any minute. I saw that launch and them boats come up and they never had no room for me. Full of bastard niggers and one of them setting there playing a guitar but there wasn't no room for me. A guitar!" he cried; now he began to scream, trembling, slavering, his face twitching and jerking. "Room for a bastard nigger guitar but not for me—"

"Steady now," the Warden said. "Steady now."

"Give him a drink," one of the officers said. The Warden poured the drink. The deputy handed it to the refugee, who took the glass in both jerking hands and tried to raise it to his mouth. They watched him for perhaps twenty seconds, then the deputy took the glass from him and held it to his lips while he gulped, though even then a thin trickle ran from each corner of his mouth, into the stubble on his chin.

"So we picked him and—" the deputy called the plump convict's name now "—both up just before dark and come on in. But that other fellow is gone."

"Yes," the Warden said. "Well. Here I haven't lost a prisoner in ten years, and now, like this—I'm sending you back to the Farm tomorrow. Have his family notified, and his discharge papers filled out at once."

"All right," the deputy said. "And listen, chief. He wasn't a bad fellow and maybe he never had no business in that boat. Only he did say he could paddle one. Listen. Suppose I write on his discharge, Drowned while trying to save lives in the great flood of nineteen twenty-seven, and send it down for the Governor to sign it. It will be something nice for his folks to have, to hang on the wall when neighbors come in or something. Maybe they will even give his folks a cash bonus because after all they sent him to the Farm to raise cotton, not to fool around in a boat in a flood."

"All right," the Warden said. "I'll see about it. The main thing is to get his name off the books as dead before some politician tries to collect his food allowance."

"All right," the deputy said. He turned and herded his companions out. In the drizzling darkness again he said to the plump convict: "Well, your partner beat you. He's free. He's done served his time out but you've got a right far piece to go yet."

"Yah," the plump convict said. "Free. He can have it."

As the short convict had testified, the tall one, when he returned to the surface, still retained what the short one called the paddle. He clung to it, not instinctively against the time when he would be back inside he boat and would need it, because for a time he did not believe he would ever regain the skiff or anything else that would support him, but because he did not have time to think about turning it loose. Things had moved too fast for him. He had not been warned, he had felt the first snatching tug of the current, he had seen the skiff begin to spin and his companion vanish violently upward like in a translation out of Isaiah, then he himself was in the water, struggling against the drag of the paddle

which he did not know he still held each time he fought back to
the surface and grasped at the spinning skiff which at one instant
was ten feet away and the next poised above his head as though
about to brain him, until at last he grasped the stern, the drag of
his body becoming a rudder to the skiff, the two of them, man and
boat and with the paddle perpendicular above them like a jackstaff,
vanishing from the view of the short convict (who had vanished
from that of the tall one with the same celerity though in a vertical
direction) like a tableau snatched offstage intact with violent and
incredible speed.

He was now in the channel of a slough, a bayou, in which until
today no current had run probably since the old subterranean outrage which had created the country. There was plenty of current in
it now though; from his trough behind the stern he seemed to see
the trees and sky rushing past with vertiginous speed, looking
down at him between the gouts of cold yellow in lugubrious and
mournful amazement. But they were fixed and secure in something;
he thought of that, he remembered in an instant of despairing rage
the firm earth fixed and founded strong and cemented fast and stable forever by the generations of laborious sweat, somewhere beneath him, beyond the reach of his feet, when, and again without
warning, the stern of the skiff struck him a stunning blow across
the bridge of his nose. The instinct which had caused him to cling
to it now caused him to fling the paddle into the boat in order to
grasp the gunwale with both hands just as the skiff pivoted and
spun away again. With both hands free he now dragged himself
over the stern and lay prone on his face, streaming with blood and
water and panting, not with exhaustion but with that furious rage
which is terror's aftermath.

But he had to get up at once because he believed he had come
much faster (and so farther) than he had. So he rose, out of the
watery scarlet puddle in which he had lain, streaming, the soaked
denim heavy as iron on his limbs, the black hair plastered to
his skull, the blood-infused water streaking his jumper, and dragged
his forearm gingerly and hurriedly across his lower face and
glanced at it then grasped the paddle and began to try to swing the
skiff back upstream. It did not even occur to him that he did not
know where his companion was, in which tree among all which he
had passed or might pass. He did not even speculate on that for the
reason that he knew so incontestably that the other was upstream

from him, and after his recent experience the mere connotation of the term upstream carried a sense of such violence and force and speed that the conception of it as other than a straight line was something which the intelligence, reason, simply refused to harbor, like the notion of a rifle bullet the width of a cotton field.

The bow began to swing back upstream. It turned readily, it out-paced the aghast and outraged instant in which he realised it was swinging far too easily, it had swung on over the arc and lay broad-side to the current and began again that vicious spinning while he sat, his teeth bared in his bloody streaming face while his spent arms flailed the impotent paddle at the water, that innocent-appear-ing medium which at one time had held him in iron-like and shifting convolutions like an anaconda yet which now seemed to offer no more resistance to the thrust of his urge and need than so much air, like air; the boat which had threatened him and at last actually struck him in the face with the shocking violence of a mule's hoof now seemed to poise weightless upon it like a thistle bloom, spinning like a wind vane while he flailed at the water and thought of, envisioned, his companion safe, inactive and at ease in the tree with nothing to do but wait, musing with impotent and terrified fury upon that arbitrariness of human affairs which had abrogated to the one the secure tree and to the other the hysterical and unmanageable boat for the very reason that it knew that he alone of the two of them would make any attempt to return and rescue his companion.

The skiff had paid off and now ran with the current again. It seemed again to spring from immobility into incredible speed, and he thought he must already be miles away from where his compan-ion had quitted him, though actually he had merely described a big circle since getting back into the skiff, and the object (a clump of cypress trees choked by floating logs and debris) which the skiff was now about to strike was the same one it had careened into be-fore when the stern had struck him. He didn't know this because he had not yet ever looked higher than the bow of the boat. He didn't look higher now, he just saw that he was going to strike; he seemed to feel run through the very insentient fabric of the skiff a current of eager gleeful vicious incorrigible wilfulness; and he who had never ceased to flail at the bland treacherous water with what he had believed to be the limit of his strength now from somewhere, some ultimate absolute reserve, produced a final measure of endurance, will to endure which adumbrated mere muscle and nerves, continuing to flail the paddle right up to the instant of striking, completing one last reach thrust and recover out of pure desperate reflex, as a man slipping on ice reaches for his hat and money-pocket, as the skiff struck and hurled him once more flat on his face in the bottom of it.

This time he did not get up at once. He lay flat on his face, slightly spread-eagled and in an attitude almost peaceful, a kind of abject meditation. He would have to get up sometime, he knew that, just as all life consists of having to get up sooner or later and then having to lie down again sooner or later after a while. And he was not exactly exhausted and he was not particularly without hope and he did not especially dread getting up. It merely seemed to him that he had accidentally been caught in a situation in which time and environment, not himself, was mesmerised; he was being toyed with by a current of water going nowhere, beneath a day which would wane toward no evening; when it was done with him it would spew him back into the comparatively safe world he had been snatched violently out of and in the meantime it did not much matter just what he did or did not do. So he lay on his face, now not only feeling but hearing the strong quiet rustling of the current on the underside of the planks, for a while longer. Then he raised his head and this time touched his palm gingerly to his face and looked at the blood again, then he sat up onto his heels and leaning over the gunwale he pinched his nostrils between thumb and finger and expelled a gout of blood and was in the act of wiping his fingers on his thigh when a voice slightly above his line of sight said quietly, "It's taken you a while," and he who up to this moment had had neither reason nor time to raise his eyes higher than the bows looked up and saw, sitting in a tree and looking at him, a woman. She was not ten feet away. She sat on the lowest limb of one of the trees holding the jam he had grounded on, in a calico wrapper and an army private's tunic and a sunbonnet, a woman whom he did not even bother to examine since that first startled glance had been ample to reveal to him all the generations of her life and background, who could have been his sister if he had a sister, his wife if he had not entered the penitentiary at an age scarcely out of adolescence and some years younger than that at which even his prolific and monogamous kind married—a woman who sat clutching the trunk of the tree, her stockingless feet in a pair of man's

unlaced brogans less than a yard from the water, who was very
probably somebody's sister and quite certainly (or certainly should
have been) somebody's wife, though this too he had entered the
penitentiary too young to have had more than mere theoretical female experience to discover yet. "I thought for a minute you wasn't
aiming to come back."

"Come back?"

"After the first time. After you run into this brush pile the first
time and got into the boat and went on." He looked about, touching his face tenderly again; it could very well be the same place
where the boat had hit him in the face.

"Yah," he said. "I'm here now though."

"Could you maybe get the boat a little closer? I taken a right
sharp strain getting up here; maybe I better . . ." He was not listening; he had just discovered that the paddle was gone; this time
when the skiff hurled him forward he had flung the paddle not into
it but beyond it. "It's right there in them brush tops," the woman
said. "You can get it. Here. Catch a holt of this." It was a grapevine.
It had grown up into the tree and the flood had torn the roots
loose. She had taken a turn with it about her upper body; she now
loosed it and swung it out until he could grasp it. Holding to the
end of the vine he warped the skiff around the end of the jam, picking up the paddle, and warped the skiff on beneath the limb and
held it and now he watched her move, gather herself heavily and
carefully to descend—that heaviness which was not painful but just
excruciatingly careful, that profound and almost lethargic awk-
wardness which added nothing to the sum of that first aghast
amazement which had served already for the catafalque of invincible dream since even in durance he had continued (and even
with the old avidity, even though they had caused his downfall) to
consume the impossible pulp-printed fables carefully censored and
as carefully smuggled into the penitentiary; and who to say what
Helen, what living Garbo, he had not dreamed of rescuing from
what craggy pinnacle or dragoned keep when he and his companion embarked in the skiff. He watched her, he made no further effort to help her beyond holding the skiff savagely steady while she
lowered herself from the limb—the entire body, the deformed swell
of belly bulging the calico, suspended by its arms, thinking, *And
this is what I get. This, out of all the female meat that walks, is
what I have to be caught in a runaway boat with.*

"Where's that cottonhouse?" he said.

"Cottonhouse?"

"With that fellow on it. The other one."

"I dont know. It's a right smart of cottonhouses around here. With folks on them too, I reckon." She was examining him. "You're bloody as a hog," she said. "You look like a convict."

"Yah," he said, snarled. "I feel like I done already been hung. Well, I got to pick up my pardner and then find that cottonhouse." He cast off. That is, he released his hold on the vine. That was all he had to do, for even while the bow of the skiff hung high on the log jam and even while he held it by the vine in the comparatively dead water behind the jam, he felt steadily and constantly the whisper, the strong purring power of the water just one inch beyond the frail planks on which he squatted and which, as soon as he released the vine, took charge of the skiff not with one powerful clutch but in a series of touches light, tentative, and catlike; he realised now that he had entertained a sort of foundationless hope that the added weight might make the skiff more controllable. During the first moment or two he had a wild (and still foundationless) belief that it had; he had got the head upstream and managed to hold it so by terrific exertion continued even after he discovered that they were travelling straight enough but stern-first and continued somehow even after the bow began to wear away and swing: the old irresistible movement which he knew well by now, too well to fight against it, so that he let the bow swing on downstream with the hope of utilising the skiff's own momentum to bring it through the full circle and so upstream again, the skiff travelling broadside then bow-first then broadside again, diagonally across the channel, toward the other wall of submerged trees; it began to flee beneath him with terrific speed, they were in an eddy but did not know it; he had no time to draw conclusions or even wonder; he crouched, his teeth bared in his blood-caked and swollen face, his lungs bursting, flailing at the water while the trees stooped hugely down at him. The skiff struck, spun, struck again; the woman half lay in the bow, clutching the gunwales, as if she were trying to crouch behind her own pregnancy; he banged now not at the water but at the living sapblooded wood with the paddle, his desire now not to go anywhere, reach any destination, but just to keep the skiff from beating itself to fragments against the tree trunks. Then something exploded, this time against the back of his head, and stooping trees and dizzy water, the woman's face and all, fled together and vanished in bright soundless flash and glare.

An hour later the skiff came slowly up an old logging road and so out of the bottom, the forest, and into (or onto) a cottonfield —a gray and limitless desolation now free of turmoil, broken only by a thin line of telephone poles like a wading millipede. The woman was now paddling, steadily and deliberately, with that curious lethargic care, while the convict squatted, his head between his knees, trying to stanch the fresh and apparently inexhaustible flow of blood from his nose with handfuls of water. The woman ceased paddling, the skiff drifted on, slowing, while she looked about. "We're done out," she said.

The convict raised his head and also looked about. "Out where?"

"I thought maybe you might know."

"I dont even know where I used to be. Even if I knowed which way was north, I wouldn't know if that was where I wanted to go." He cupped another handful of water to his face and lowered his hand and regarded the resulting crimson marbling on his palm, not with dejection, not with concern, but with a kind of sardonic and vicious bemusement. The woman watched the back of his head.

"We got to get somewhere."

"Dont I know it? A fellow on a cottonhouse. Another in a tree. And now that thing in your lap."

"It wasn't due yet. Maybe it was having to climb that tree quick yesterday, and having to set in it all night. I'm doing the best I can. But we better get somewhere soon."

"Yah," the convict said. "I thought I wanted to get somewhere too and I aint had no luck at it. You pick out a place to get to now and we'll try yours. Gimme that oar." The woman passed him the paddle. The boat was a double-ender; he had only to turn around.

"Which way you fixing to go?" the woman said.

"Never you mind that. You just keep on holding on." He began to paddle, on across the cottonfield. It began to rain again, though not hard at first. "Yah," he said. "Ask the boat. I been in it since breakfast and I aint never knowed, where I aimed to go or where I was going either."

That was about one oclock. Toward the end of the afternoon the skiff (they were in a channel of some sort again, they had been in it for some time; they had got into it before they knew it and too late to get out again, granted there had been any reason to get out,

as, to the convict anyway, there was certainly none and the fact
that their speed had increased again was reason enough to stay in
it) shot out upon a broad expanse of debris-filled water which the
convict recognised as a river and, from its size, the Yazoo River
though it was little enough he had seen of this country which he
had not quitted for so much as one single day in the last seven
years of his life. What he did not know was that it was now running
backward. So as soon as the drift of the skiff indicated the set of the
current, he began to paddle in that direction which he believed to
be downstream, where he knew there were towns—Yazoo City, and
as a last resort, Vicksburg, if his luck was that bad, if not, smaller
towns whose names he did not know but where there would be
people, houses, something, anything he might reach and surrender
his charge to and turn his back on her forever, on all pregnant and
female life forever and return to that monastic existence of shotguns and shackles where he would be secure from it. Now, with the
imminence of habitations, release from her, he did not even hate
her. When he looked upon the swelling and unmanageable body
before him it seemed to him that it was not the woman at all but
rather a separate demanding threatening inert yet living mass of
which both he and she were equally victims; thinking, as he had
been for the last three or four hours, of that minute's—nay, second's—aberration of eye or hand which would suffice to precipitate
her into the water to be dragged down to death by that senseless
millstone which in its turn would not even have to feel agony, he
no longer felt any glow of revenge toward her as its custodian, he
felt sorry for her as he would for the living timber in a barn which
had to be burned to rid itself of vermin.

He paddled on, helping the current, steadily and strongly, with a
calculated husbandry of effort, toward what he believed was downstream, towns, people, something to stand upon, while from time to
time the woman raised herself to bail the accumulated rain from
the skiff. It was raining steadily now though still not hard, still
without passion, the sky, the day itself dissolving without grief; the
skiff moved in a nimbus, an aura of gray gauze which merged almost without demarcation with the roiling spittle-frothed debris-
choked water. Now the day, the light, definitely began to end and
the convict permitted himself an extra notch or two of effort because it suddenly seemed to him that the speed of the skiff had
lessened. This was actually the case though the convict did not know

it. He merely took it as a phenomenon of the increasing obfusca-
tion, or at most as a result of the long day's continuous effort with
no food, complicated by the ebbing and fluxing phases of anxiety
and impotent rage at his absolutely gratuitous predicament. So he
stepped up his stroke a beat or so, not from alarm but on the contrary, since he too had received that lift from the mere presence of
a known stream, a river known by its ineradicable name to generations of men who had been drawn to live beside it as man always
has been drawn to dwell beside water, even before he had a name
for water and fire, drawn to the living water, the course of his
destiny and his actual physical appearance rigidly coerced and
postulated by it. So he was not alarmed. He paddled on, upstream
without knowing it, unaware that all the water which for forty
hours now had been pouring through the levee break to the north
was somewhere ahead of him, on its way back to the River.

It was full dark now. That is, night had completely come, the
gray dissolving sky had vanished, yet as though in perverse ratio
surface visibility had sharpened, as though the light which the rain
of the afternoon had washed out of the air had gathered upon the
water as the rain itself had done, so that the yellow flood spread on
before him now with a quality almost phosphorescent, right up to
the instant where vision ceased. The darkness in fact had its advan-
tages; he could now stop seeing the rain. He and his garments had
been wet for more than twenty-four hours now so he had long since
stopped feeling it, and now that he could no longer see it either it
had in a certain sense ceased for him. Also, he now had to make no
effort even not to see the swell of his passenger's belly. So he was
paddling on, strongly and steadily, not alarmed and not concerned
but just exasperated because he had not yet begun to see any reflection on the clouds which would indicate the city or cities which he
believed he was approaching but which were actually now miles
behind him, when he heard a sound. He did not know what it was
because he had never heard it before and he would never be expected to hear such again since it is not given to every man to hear
such at all and to none to hear it more than once in his life. And he
was not alarmed now either because there was not time, for although the visibility ahead, for all its clarity, did not extend very
far, yet in the next instant to the hearing he was also seeing something such as he had never seen before. This was that the sharp
line where the phosphorescent water met the darkness was now

about ten feet higher than it had been an instant before and that it was curled forward upon itself like a sheet of dough being rolled out for a pudding. It reared, stooping; the crest of it swirled like the mane of a galloping horse and, phosphorescent too, fretted and flickered like fire. And while the woman huddled in the bows, aware or not aware the convict did not know which, he (the convict), his swollen and blood-streaked face gaped in an expression of aghast and incredulous amazement, continued to paddle directly into it. Again he simply had not had time to order his rhythm-hypnotised muscles to cease. He continued to paddle though the skiff had ceased to move forward at all but seemed to be hanging in space while the paddle still reached thrust recovered and reached again; now instead of space the skiff became abruptly surrounded by a welter of fleeing debris—planks, small buildings, the bodies of drowned yet antic animals, entire trees leaping and diving like porpoises above which the skiff seemed to hover in weightless and airy indecision like a bird above a fleeing countryside, undecided where to light or whether to light at all, while the convict squatted in it still going through the motions of paddling, waiting for an opportunity to scream. He never found it. For an instant the skiff seemed to stand erect on its stern and then shoot scrabbling and scrambling up the curling wall of water like a cat, and soared on above the licking crest itself and hung cradled into the high actual air in the limbs of a tree, from which bower of new-leafed boughs and branches the convict, like a bird in its nest and still waiting his chance to scream and still going through the motions of paddling though he no longer even had the paddle now, looked down upon a world turned to furious motion and in incredible retrograde.

Some time about midnight, accompanied by a rolling cannonade of thunder and lightning like a battery going into action, as though some forty hours' constipation of the elements, the firmament itself, were discharging in clapping and glaring salute to the ultimate acquiescence to desperate and furious motion, and still leading its charging welter of dead cows and mules and outhouses and cabins and hencoops, the skiff passed Vicksburg. The convict didn't know it. He wasn't looking high enough above the water; he still squatted, clutching the gunwales and glaring at the yellow turmoil about him out of which entire trees, the sharp gables of houses, the long mournful heads of mules which he fended off with a splintered

length of plank snatched from he knew not where in passing (and
which seemed to glare reproachfully back at him with sightless
eyes, in limber-lipped and incredulous amazement) rolled up and
then down again, the skiff now travelling forward now sideways
now sternward, sometimes in the water, sometimes riding for yards
upon the roofs of houses and trees and even upon the backs of the
mules as though even in death they were not to escape that burden-
bearing doom with which their eunuch race was cursed. But he
didn't see Vicksburg; the skiff, travelling at express speed, was in a
seething gut between soaring and dizzy banks with a glare of light
above them but he did not see it; he saw the flotsam ahead of him
divide violently and begin to climb upon itself, mounting, and he
was sucked through the resulting gap too fast to recognise it as the
trestling of a railroad bridge; for a horrible moment the skiff
seemed to hang in static indecision before the looming flank of a
steamboat as though undecided whether to climb over it or dive
under it, then a hard icy wind filled with the smell and taste and
sense of wet and boundless desolation blew upon him; the skiff
made one long bounding lunge as the convict's native state, in a
final paroxysm, regurgitated him onto the wild bosom of the Father
of Waters.

This is how he told about it seven weeks later, sitting in new bed-
ticking garments, shaved and with his hair cut again, on his bunk
in the barracks:

During the next three or four hours after the thunder and lightning had spent itself the skiff ran in pitch streaming darkness upon
a roiling expanse which, even if he could have seen, apparently had
no boundaries. Wild and invisible, it tossed and heaved about and
beneath the boat, ridged with dirty phosphorescent foam and filled
with a debris of destruction—objects nameless and enormous and
invisible which struck and slashed at the skiff and whirled on. He
did not know he was now upon the River. At that time he would
have refused to believe it, even if he had known. Yesterday he had
known he was in a channel by the regularity of the spacing between the bordering trees. Now, since even by daylight he could
have seen no boundaries, the last place under the sun (or the
streaming sky rather) he would have suspected himself to be
would have been a river; if he had pondered at all about his present whereabouts, about the geography beneath him, he would
merely have taken himself to be travelling at dizzy and inexpli-

cable speed above the largest cottonfield in the world; if he who yesterday had known he was in a river, had accepted that fact in good faith and earnest, then had seen that river turn without warning and rush back upon him with furious and deadly intent like a frenzied stallion in a lane—if he had suspected for one second that the wild and limitless expanse on which he now found himself was a river, consciousness would simply have refused; he would have fainted.

When daylight—a gray and ragged dawn filled with driving scud between icy rain-squalls—came and he could see again, he knew he was in no cottonfield. He knew that the wild water on which the skiff tossed and fled flowed above no soil tamely trod by man, behind the straining and surging buttocks of a mule. That was when it occurred to him that its present condition was no phenomenon of a decade, but that the intervening years during which it consented to bear upon its placid and sleepy bosom the frail mechanicals of man's clumsy contriving was the phenomenon and this the norm and the river was now doing what it liked to do, had waited patiently the ten years in order to do, as a mule will work for you ten years for the privilege of kicking you once. And he also learned something else about fear too, something he had even failed to discover on that other occasion when he was really afraid—that three or four seconds of that night in his youth while he looked down the twice-flashing pistol barrel of the terrified mail clerk before the clerk could be persuaded that his (the convict's) pistol would not shoot: that if you just held on long enough a time would come in fear after which it would no longer be agony at all but merely a kind of horrible outrageous itching, as after you have been burned bad.

He did not have to paddle now, he just steered (who had been without food for twenty-four hours now and without any sleep to speak of for fifty) while the skiff sped on across that boiling desolation where he had long since begun to not dare believe he could possibly be where he could not doubt he was, trying with his fragment of splintered plank merely to keep the skiff intact and afloat among the houses and trees and dead animals (the entire towns, stores, residences, parks and farmyards, which leaped and played about him like fish), not trying to reach any destination, just trying to keep the skiff afloat until he did. He wanted so little. He wanted nothing for himself. He just wanted to get rid of the woman, the belly, and he was trying to do that in the right way, not for himself, but for her. He could have put her back into another tree at any time—

"Or you could have jumped out of the boat and let her and it drown," the plump convict said. "Then they could have given you the ten years for escaping and then hung you for the murder and charged the boat to your folks."

"Yah," the tall convict said.—But he had not done that. He wanted to do it the right way, find somebody, anybody he could surrender her to, something solid he could set her down on and then jump back into the river, if that would please anyone. That was all he wanted—just to come to something, anything. That didn't seem like a great deal to ask. And he couldn't do it. He told how the skiff fled on—

"Didn't you pass nobody?" the plump convict said. "No steamboat, nothing?"

"I dont know," the tall one said.—while he tried merely to keep it afloat, until the darkness thinned and lifted and revealed—

"Darkness?" the plump convict said. "I thought you said it was already daylight."

"Yah," the tall one said. He was rolling a cigarette, pouring the tobacco carefully from a new sack, into the creased paper. "This was another one. They had several while I was gone."—the skiff to be moving still rapidly up a winding corridor bordered by drowned trees which the convict recognised again to be a river running again in the direction that, until two days ago, had been upstream. He was not exactly warned through instinct that this one, like that of two days ago, was in reverse. He would not say that he now believed himself to be in the same river, though he would not have been surprised to find that he did believe this, existing now, as he did and had and apparently was to continue for an unnamed period, in a state in which he was toy and pawn on a vicious and inflammable geography. He merely realised that he was in a river again, with all the subsequent inferences of a comprehensible, even if not familiar, portion of the earth's surface. Now he believed that all he had to do would be to paddle far enough and he would come to something horizontal and above water even if not dry and perhaps even populated; and, if fast enough, in time, and that his only other crying urgency was to refrain from looking at the woman who, as vision, the incontrovertible and apparently inescapable presence of his passenger, returned with dawn, had ceased to be a human being and (you could add twenty-four more hours to the first twenty-four and the first fifty now, even counting the hen. It was dead, drowned, caught by one wing under a shingle on a roof which had rolled momentarily up beside the skiff yesterday and he had eaten some of it raw though the woman would not) had become instead one single inert monstrous sentient womb from which, he now believed, if he could only turn his gaze away and keep it away, would disappear, and if he could only keep his gaze from pausing again at the spot it had occupied, would not return. That's what he was doing this time when he discovered the wave was coming.

He didn't know how he discovered it was coming back. He heard no sound, it was nothing felt nor seen. He did not even believe that finding the skiff to be now in slack water—that is, that the motion of the current which, whether right or wrong, had at least been horizontal, had now stopped that and assumed a vertical direction —was sufficient to warn him. Perhaps it was just an invincible and almost fanatic faith in the inventiveness and innate viciousness of that medium on which his destiny was now cast, apparently forever; a sudden conviction far beyond either horror or surprise that now was none too soon for it to prepare to do whatever it was it intended doing. So he whirled the skiff, spun it on its heel like a running horse, whereupon, reversed, he could not even distinguish the very channel he had come up. He did not know whether he simply could not see it or if it had vanished some time ago and he not aware at the time; whether the river had become lost in a drowned world or if the world had become drowned in one limitless river. So now he could not tell if he were running directly before the wave or quartering across its line of charge; all he could do was keep that sense of swiftly accumulating ferocity behind him and paddle as fast as his spent and now numb muscles could be driven, and try not to look at the woman, to wrench his gaze from her and keep it away until he reached something flat and above water. So, gaunt, hollow-eyed, striving and wrenching almost physically at his eyes as if they were two of those suction-tipped rubber arrows shot from the toy gun of a child, his spent muscles obeying not will now but that attenuation beyond mere exhaustion which, mesmeric, can continue easier than cease, he once more drove the skiff full tilt into something it could not pass and, once more hurled

violently forward onto his hands and knees, crouching, he glared
with his wild swollen face up at the man with the shotgun and said
in a harsh, croaking voice: "Vicksburg? Where's Vicksburg?"

Even when he tried to tell it, even after the seven weeks and he
safe, secure, riveted warranted and doubly guaranteed by the ten
years they had added to his sentence for attempted escape, something of the old hysteric incredulous outrage came back into his
face, his voice, his speech. He never did even get on the other boat.
He told how he clung to a strake (it was a dirty unpainted shanty
boat with a drunken rake of tin stove pipe, it had been moving
when he struck it and apparently it had not even changed course
even though the three people on it must have been watching him
all the while—a second man, barefoot and with matted hair and
beard also at the steering sweep, and then—he did not know how
long—a woman leaning in the door, in a filthy assortment of men's
garments, watching him too with the same cold speculation) being
dragged violently along, trying to state and explain his simple (and
to him at least) reasonable desire and need; telling it, trying to tell
it, he could feel again the old unforgettable affronting like an ague
fit as he watched the abortive tobacco rain steadily and faintly
from between his shaking hands and then the paper itself part with
a thin dry snapping report:

"Burn my clothes?" the convict cried. "Burn them?"

"How in hell do you expect to escape in them billboards?" the
man with the shotgun said. He (the convict) tried to tell it, tried
to explain as he had tried to explain not to the three people on the
boat alone but to the entire circumambience—desolate water and
forlorn trees and sky—not for justification because he needed none
and knew that his hearers, the other convicts, required none from
him, but rather as, on the point of exhaustion, he might have
picked dreamily and incredulously at a suffocation. He told the
man with the gun how he and his partner had been given the boat
and told to pick up a man and a woman, how he had lost his partner and failed to find the man, and now all in the world he wanted
was something flat to leave the woman on until he could find an
officer, a sheriff. He thought of home, the place where he had lived
almost since childhood, his friends of years whose ways he knew
and who knew his ways, the familiar fields where he did work he
had learned to do well and to like, the mules with characters he
knew and respected as he knew and respected the characters of cer-

tain men; he thought of the barracks at night, with screens against
the bugs in summer and good stoves in winter and someone to supply the fuel and the food too; the Sunday ball games and the picture shows—things which, with the exception of the ball games, he
had never known before. But most of all, his own character (Two
years ago they had offered to make a trusty of him. He would no
longer need to plow or feed stock, he would only follow those who
did with a loaded gun, but he declined. "I reckon I'll stick to plowing," he said, absolutely without humor. "I done already tried to
use a gun one time too many.") his good name, his responsibility
not only toward those who were responsible toward him but to
himself, his own honor in the doing of what was asked of him, his
pride in being able to do it, no matter what it was. He thought of
this and listened to the man with the gun talking about escape and
it seemed to him that, hanging there, being dragged violently along
(it was here he said that he first noticed the goats' beards of moss
in the trees, though it could have been there for several days so far
as he knew. It just happened that he first noticed it here.) that he
would simply burst.

"Cant you get it into your head that the last thing I want to do is
run away?" he cried. "You can set there with that gun and watch
me; I give you fair lief. All I want is to put this woman—"

"And I told you she could come aboard," the man with the gun
said in his level voice. "But there aint no room on no boat of mine
for nobody hunting a sheriff in no kind of clothes, let alone a penitentiary suit."

"When he steps aboard, knock him in the head with the gun barrel," the man at the sweep said. "He's drunk."

"He aint coming aboard," the man with the gun said. "He's
crazy."

Then the woman spoke. She didn't move, leaning in the door, in
a pair of faded and patched and filthy overalls like the two men:
"Give them some grub and tell them to get out of here." She
moved, she crossed the deck and looked down at the convict's companion with her cold sullen face. "How much more time have you
got?"

"It wasn't due till next month," the woman in the boat said. "But
I—" The woman in overalls turned to the man with the gun.

"Give them some grub," she said. But the man with the gun was
still looking down at the woman in the boat.

"Come on," he said to the convict. "Put her aboard, and beat it."

"And what'll happen to you," the woman in overalls said, "when you try to turn her over to an officer. When you lay alongside a sheriff and the sheriff asks you who you are?" Still the man with the gun didn't even look at her. He hardly even shifted the gun across his arm as he struck the woman across the face with the back of his other hand, hard. "You son of a bitch," she said. Still the man with the gun did not even look at her.

"Well?" he said to the convict.

"Dont you see I cant?" the convict cried. "Cant you see that?"

Now, he said, he gave up. He was doomed. That is, he knew now that he had been doomed from the very start never to get rid of her, just as the ones who sent him out with the skiff knew that he never would actually give up; when he recognised one of the objects which the woman in overalls was hurling into the skiff to be a can of condensed milk, he believed it to be a presage, gratuitous and irrevocable as a death-notice over the telegraph, that he was not even to find a flat stationary surface in time for the child to be born on it. So he told how he held the skiff alongside the shanty boat while the first tentative toying of the second wave made up beneath him, while the woman in overalls passed back and forth between house and rail, flinging the food—the hunk of salt meat, the ragged and filthy quilt, the scorched lumps of cold bread which she poured into the skiff from a heaped dishpan like so much garbage—while he clung to the strake against the mounting pull of the current, the new wave which for the moment he had forgotten because he was still trying to state the incredible simplicity of his desire and need until the man with the gun (the only one of the three who wore shoes) began to stamp at his hands, he snatching his hands away one at a time to avoid the heavy shoes, then grasping the rail again until the man with the gun kicked at his face, he flinging himself sideways to avoid the shoe and so breaking his hold on the rail, his weight canting the skiff off at a tangent on the increasing current so that it began to leave the shanty boat behind and he paddling again now, violently, as a man hurries toward the precipice for which he knows at last he is doomed, looking back at the other boat, the three faces sullen derisive and grim and rapidly diminishing across the widening water and at last, apoplectic, suffocating with the intolerable fact not that he had been refused but that he had been refused so little, had wanted so little, asked for so little, yet there had been demanded of him in return the one price out of all breath which (they must have known) if he could have paid it, he would not have been where he was, asking what he asked, raising the paddle and shaking it and screaming curses back at them even after the shotgun flashed and the charge went scuttering past along the water to one side.

So he hung there, he said, shaking the paddle and howling, when suddenly he remembered that other wave, the second wall of water full of houses and dead mules building up behind him back in the swamp. So he quit yelling then and went back to paddling. He was not trying to outrun it. He just knew from experience that when it overtook him, he would have to travel in the same direction it was moving in anyway, whether he wanted to or not, and when it did overtake him, he would begin to move too fast to stop, no matter what places he might come to where he could leave the woman, land her in time. Time: that was his itch now, so his only chance was to stay ahead of it as long as he could and hope to reach something before it struck. So he went on, driving the skiff with muscles which had been too tired so long they had quit feeling it, as when a man has had bad luck for so long that he ceases to believe it is even bad, let alone luck. Even when he ate—the scorched lumps the size of baseballs and the weight and durability of cannel coal even after having lain in the skiff's bilge where the shanty boat woman had thrown them—the iron-like lead-heavy objects which no man would have called bread outside of the crusted and scorched pan in which they had cooked—it was with one hand, begrudging even that from the paddle.

He tried to tell that too—that day while the skiff fled on among the bearded trees while every now and then small quiet tentative exploratory feelers would come up from the wave behind and toy for a moment at the skiff, light and curious, then go on with a faint hissing sighing, almost a chuckling, sound, the skiff going on, driving on with nothing to see but trees and water and solitude: until after a while it no longer seemed to him that he was trying to put space and distance behind him or shorten space and distance ahead but that both he and the wave were now hanging suspended simultaneous and unprogressing in pure time, upon a dreamy desolation in which he paddled on not from any hope even to reach anything at all but merely to keep intact what little of distance the length of the skiff provided between himself and the inert and inescapable mass of female meat before him; then night and the skiff rushing on, fast since any speed over anything unknown and invisible is too fast, with nothing before him and behind him the outrageous idea of a volume of moving water toppling forward, its crest frothed and shredded like fangs, and then dawn again (another of those dreamlike alterations day to dark then back to day again with that quality truncated, anachronic and unreal as the waxing and waning of lights in a theatre scene) and the skiff emerging now with the woman no longer supine beneath the shrunken soaked private's coat but sitting bolt upright, gripping the gunwales with both hands, her eyes closed and her lower lip caught between her teeth and he driving the splintered board furiously now, glaring at her out of his wild swollen sleepless face and crying, croaking, "Hold on! For God's sake hold on!"

"I'm trying to," she said. "But hurry! Hurry!" He told it, the unbelievable: hurry, hasten: the man falling from a cliff being told to catch onto something and save himself; the very telling of it emerging shadowy and burlesque, ludicrous, comic and mad, from the ague of unbearable forgetting with a quality more dreamily furious than any fable behind proscenium lights:

He was in a basin now— "A basin?" the plump convict said. "That's what you wash in."

"All right," the tall one said, harshly, above his hands. "I did." With a supreme effort he stilled them long enough to release the two bits of cigarette paper and watched them waft in light fluttering indecision to the floor between his feet, holding his hands motionless even for a moment longer—a basin, a broad peaceful yellow sea which had an abruptly and curiously ordered air, giving him, even at that moment, the impression that it was accustomed to water even if not total submersion; he even remembered the name of it, told to him two or three weeks later by someone: Atchafalaya—

"Louisiana?" the plump convict said. "You mean you were clean out of Mississippi? Hell fire." He stared at the tall one. "Shucks," he said. "That aint but just across from Vicksburg."

"They never named any Vicksburg across from where I was," the tall one said. "It was Baton Rouge they named." And now he began to talk about a town, a little neat white portrait town nestling among enormous very green trees, appearing suddenly in the telling as it probably appeared in actuality, abrupt and airy and miragelike and incredibly serene before him behind a scattering of boats moored to a line of freight cars standing flush to the doors in water. And now he tried to tell that too: how he stood waist-deep in water for a moment looking back and down at the skiff in which the woman half lay, her eyes still closed, her knuckles white on the gunwales and a tiny thread of blood creeping down her chin from her chewed lip, and he looking down at her in a kind of furious desperation.

"How far will I have to walk?" she said.

"I dont know, I tell you!" he cried. "But it's land somewhere yonder! It's land, houses."

"If I try to move, it wont even be born inside a boat," she said. "You'll have to get closer."

"Yes," he cried, wild, desperate, incredulous. "Wait. I'll go and surrender, then they will have—" He didn't finish, wait to finish; he told that too: himself splashing, stumbling, trying to run, sobbing and gasping; now he saw it—another loading platform standing above the yellow flood, the khaki figures on it as before, identical, the same; he said how the intervening days since that first innocent morning telescoped, vanished as if they had never been, the two contiguous succeeding instants (succeeding? simultaneous) and he transported across no intervening space but merely turned in his own footsteps, plunging, splashing, his arms raised, croaking harshly. He heard the startled shout, "There's one of them!", the command, the clash of equipment, the alarmed cry: "There he goes! There he goes!"

"Yes!" he cried, running, plunging, "here I am! Here! Here!" running on, into the first scattered volley, stopping among the bullets, waving his arms, shrieking, "I want to surrender! I want to surrender!" watching not in terror but in amazed and absolutely unbearable outrage as a squatting clump of the khaki figures parted and he saw the machine gun, the blunt thick muzzle slant and drop and probe toward him and he still screaming in his hoarse crow's voice, "I want to surrender! Cant you hear me?" continuing to scream even as he whirled and plunged splashing, ducking, went completely under and heard the bullets going thuck-thuck-thuck on the water above him and he scrabbling still on the bottom, still trying to scream even before he regained his feet and still all submerged save his plunging unmistakable buttocks, the outraged screaming bubbling from his mouth and about his face since he merely wanted to surrender. Then he was comparatively screened, out of range, though not for long. That is (he didn't tell how nor where) there was a moment in which he paused, breathed for a second before running again, the course back to the skiff open for the time being though he could still hear the shouts behind him and now and then a shot, and he panting, sobbing, a long savage tear in the flesh of one hand, got when and how he did not know, and he wasting precious breath, speaking to no one now any more than the scream of the dying rabbit is addressed to any mortal ear but rather an indictment of all breath and its folly and suffer-ing, its infinite capacity for folly and pain, which seems to be its only immortality: "All in the world I want is just to surrender."

He returned to the skiff and got in and took up his splintered plank. And now when he told this, despite the fury of element which climaxed it, it (the telling) became quite simple; he now even creased another cigarette paper between fingers which did not tremble at all and filled the paper from the tobacco sack without spilling a flake, as though he had passed from the machine gun's barrage into a bourne beyond any more amazement: so that the subsequent part of his narrative seemed to reach his listeners as though from beyond a sheet of slightly milky though still transpar-ent glass, as something not heard but seen—a series of shadows, edgeless yet distinct, and smoothly flowing, logical and unfrantic and making no sound: They were in the skiff, in the center of the broad placid trough which had no boundaries and down which the tiny forlorn skiff flew to the irresistible coercion of a current go-ing once more he knew not where, the neat small liveoak-bowered towns unattainable and miragelike and apparently attached to nothing upon the airy and unchanging horizon. He did not believe them, they did not matter, he was doomed; they were less than the figments of smoke or of delirium, and he driving his unceasing pad-dle without destination or even hope now, looking now and then at the woman sitting with her knees drawn up and locked and her entire body one terrific clench while the threads of bloody saliva crept from her teeth-clenched lower lip. He was going nowhere and fleeing from nothing, he merely continued to paddle because he had paddled so long now that he believed if he stopped his muscles would scream in agony. So when it happened he was not surprised. He heard the sound which he knew well (he had heard it but once before, true enough, but no man needed hear it but once) and he had been expecting it; he looked back, still driving the paddle, and saw it, curled, crested with its strawlike flotsam of trees and debris and dead beasts and he glared over his shoulder at it for a full minute out of that attenuation far beyond the point of outragement where even suffering, the capability of being further affronted, had ceased, from which he now contemplated with savage and invulnerable curiosity the further extent to which his now anesthetised nerves could bear, what next could be invented for them to bear, until the wave actually began to rear above his head into its thunderous climax. Then only did he turn his head. His stroke did not falter, it neither slowed nor increased; still paddling with that spent hypnotic steadiness, he saw the swimming deer. He did not know what it was nor that he had altered the skiff's course to follow it, he just watched the swimming head before him as the wave boiled down and the skiff rose bodily in the old familiar fashion on a welter of tossing trees and houses and bridges and fences, he still paddling even while the paddle found no purchase save air and still paddled even as he and the deer shot forward side by side at arm's length, he watching the deer now, watching the deer begin to rise out of the water bodily until it was actually running along upon the surface, rising still, soaring clear of the water altogether, vanishing upward in a dying crescendo of splashings and snapping branches, its damp scut flashing upward, the entire animal vanishing upward as smoke vanishes. And now the skiff struck and canted and he was out of it too, standing knee-deep, springing out and falling to his knees, scrambling up, glaring after the vanished deer. "Land!" he croaked. "Land! Hold on! Just hold on!" He caught the woman beneath the arms, dragging her out of the boat, plunging and panting after the vanished deer. Now earth actually appeared —an acclivity smooth and swift and steep, bizarre, solid and unbelievable; an Indian mound, and he plunging at the muddy slope, slipping back, the woman struggling in his muddy hands.

"Let me down!" she cried. "Let me down!" But he held her, panting, sobbing, and rushed again at the muddy slope; he had almost reached the flat crest with his now violently unmanageable burden when a stick under his foot gathered itself with thick convulsive speed. *It was a snake,* he thought as his feet fled beneath him and with the indubitable last of his strength he half pushed and half flung the woman up the bank as he shot feet first and face down back into that medium upon which he had lived for more days and nights than he could remember and from which he himself had never completely emerged, as if his own failed and spent flesh were attempting to carry out his furious unflagging will for severance at any price, even that of drowning, from the burden with which, unwitting and without choice, he had been doomed. Later it seemed to him that he had carried back beneath the surface with him the sound of the infant's first mewling cry.

WHEN THE WOMAN ASKED HIM IF HE HAD A KNIFE, STANDING THERE in the streaming bedticking garments which had got him shot at, the second time by a machine gun, on the two occasions when he had seen any human life after leaving the levee four days ago, the convict felt exactly as he had in the fleeing skiff when the woman suggested that they had better hurry. He felt the same outrageous affronting of a condition purely moral, the same raging impotence to find any answer to it; so that, standing above her, spent suffocating and inarticulate, it was a full minute before he comprehended that she was now crying, "The can! The can in the boat!" He did not anticipate what she could want with it; he did not even wonder nor stop to ask. He turned running; this time he thought, *It's another moccasin* as the thick body truncated in that awkward reflex which had nothing of alarm in it but only alertness, he not even shifting his stride though he knew his running foot would fall within a yard of the flat head. The bow of the skiff was well up the slope now where the wave had set it and there was another snake just crawling over the stern into it and as he stooped for the bailing can he saw something else swimming toward the mound, he didn't know what—a head, a face at the apex of a vee of ripples. He snatched up the can; by pure juxtaposition of it and water he scooped it full, already turning. He saw the deer again, or another one. That is, he saw a deer—a side glance, the light smoke-colored phantom in a cypress vista then gone, vanished, he not pausing to look after it, galloping back to the woman and kneeling with the can to her lips until she told him better.

It had contained a pint of beans or tomatoes, something, hermetically sealed and opened by four blows of an axe heel, the metal flap turned back, the jagged edges razor-sharp. She told him how, and he used this in lieu of a knife, he removed one of his shoelaces and cut it in two with the sharp tin. Then she wanted warm water

—"If I just had a little hot water," she said in a weak serene voice without particular hope; only when he thought of matches it was again a good deal like when she had asked him if he had a knife, until she fumbled in the pocket of the shrunken tunic (it had a darker double vee on one cuff and a darker blotch on the shoulder where service stripes and a divisional emblem had been ripped off but this meant nothing to him) and produced a match-box contrived by telescoping two shotgun shells. So he drew her back a little from the water and went to hunt wood dry enough to burn, thinking this time, *It's just another snake,* only, he said, he should have thought *ten thousand other snakes:* and now he knew it was not the same deer because he saw three at one time, does or bucks he did not know which since they were all antlerless in May and besides he had never seen one of any kind anywhere before except on a Christmas card; and then the rabbit, drowned, dead anyway, already torn open, the bird, the hawk, standing upon it—the erected crest, the hard vicious patrician nose, the intolerant omnivorous yellow eye—and he kicking at it, kicking it lurching and broadwinged into the actual air.

When he returned with the wood and the dead rabbit, the baby, wrapped in the tunic, lay wedged between two cypress-knees and the woman was not in sight, though while the convict knelt in the mud, blowing and nursing his meagre flame, she came slowly and weakly from the direction of the water. Then, the water heated at last and there produced from some where he was never to know, she herself perhaps never to know until the need comes, no woman perhaps ever to know, only no woman will even wonder, that square of something somewhere between sackcloth and silk—squatting, his own wet garments steaming in the fire's heat, he watched her bathe the child with a savage curiosity and interest that became amazed unbelief, so that at last he stood above them both, looking down at the tiny terra-cotta colored creature resembling nothing, and thought, *And this is all. This is what severed me violently from all I ever knew and did not wish to leave and cast me upon a medium I was born to fear, to fetch up at last in a place I never saw before and where I do not even know where I am.*

Then he returned to the water and refilled the bailing can. It was drawing toward sunset now (or what would have been sunset save for the high prevailing overcast) of this day whose beginning he could not even remember; when he returned to where the fire

burned in the interlaced gloom of the cypresses, even after this
short absence, evening had definitely come, as though darkness too
had taken refuge upon that quarter-acre mound, that earthen Ark
out of Genesis, that dim wet cypress-choked life-teeming con-
stricted desolation in what direction and how far from what and
where he had no more idea than of the day of the month, and had
now with the setting of the sun crept forth again to spread upon
the waters. He stewed the rabbit in sections while the fire burned
redder and redder in the darkness where the shy wild eyes of small
animals—once the tall mild almost plate-sized stare of one of the
deer—glowed and vanished and glowed again, the broth hot and
rank after the four days; he seemed to hear the roar of his own saliva as he watched the woman sip the first canful. Then he drank
too; they ate the other fragments which had been charring and
scorching on willow twigs; it was full night now. "You and him
better sleep in the boat," the convict said. "We want to get an early
start tomorrow." He shoved the bow of the skiff off the land so it
would lie level, he lengthened the painter with a piece of grapevine
and returned to the fire and tied the grapevine about his wrist and
lay down. It was mud he lay upon, but it was solid underneath, it
was earth, it did not move; if you fell upon it you broke your bones
against its incontrovertible passivity sometimes but it did not accept you substanceless and enveloping and suffocating, down and
down and down; it was hard at times to drive a plow through, it
sent you spent, weary, and cursing its light-long insatiable demands
back to your bunk at sunset at times but it did not snatch you violently out of all familiar knowing and sweep you thrall and impotent for days against any returning. *I dont know where I am
and I dont reckon I know the way back to where I want to go,* he
thought. *But at least the boat has stopped long enough to give me
a chance to turn it around.*

He waked at dawn, the light faint, the sky jonquil-colored; the
day would be fine. The fire had burned out; on the opposite side of
the cold ashes lay three snakes motionless and parallel as under-
scoring, and in the swiftly making light others seemed to materi-
alise: earth which an instant before had been mere earth broke up
into motionless coils and loops, branches which a moment before
had been mere branches now become immobile ophidian fes-
toons even as the convict stood thinking about food, about something hot before they started. But he decided against this, against

wasting this much time, since there still remained in the skiff quite a few of the rocklike objects which the shanty woman had flung into it, besides (thinking this) no matter how fast nor successfully he hunted, he would never be able to lay up enough food to get them back to where they wanted to go. So he returned to the skiff, paying himself back to it by his vine-spliced painter, back to the water on which a low mist thick as cotton batting (though apparently not very tall, deep) lay, into which the stern of the skiff was already beginning to disappear although it lay with its prow almost touching the mound. The woman waked, stirred. "We fixing to start now?" she said.

"Yah," the convict said. "You aint aiming to have another one this morning, are you?" He got in and shoved the skiff clear of the land, which immediately began to dissolve into the mist. "Hand me the oar," he said over his shoulder, not turning yet.

"The oar?"

He turned his head. "The oar. You're laying on it." But she was not, and for an instant during which the mound, the island continued to fade slowly into the mist which seemed to enclose the skiff in weightless and impalpable wool like a precious or fragile bauble or jewel, the convict squatted not in dismay but in that frantic and astonished outrage of a man who, having just escaped a falling safe, is struck by the following two-ounce paper weight which was sitting on it: this the more unbearable because he knew that never in his life had he less time to give way to it. He did not hesitate. Grasping the grapevine end he sprang into the water, vanishing in the violent action of climbing and reappeared still climbing and (who had never learned to swim) plunged and threshed on toward the almost-vanished mound, moving through the water then upon it as the deer had done yesterday and scrabbled up the muddy slope and lay gasping and panting, still clutching the grapevine end.

Now the first thing he did was to choose what he believed to be the most suitable tree (for an instant in which he knew he was insane he thought of trying to saw it down with the flange of the bailing can) and build a fire against the butt of it. Then he went to seek food. He spent the next six days seeking it while the tree burned through and fell and burned through again at the proper length and he nursing little constant cunning flames along the flanks of the log to make it paddle-shaped, nursing them at night too while the woman and baby (it was eating, nursing now, he turning his back or even returning into the woods each time she prepared to open the faded tunic) slept in the skiff. He learned to watch for stooping hawks and so found more rabbits and twice possums; they ate some drowned fish which gave them both a rash and then a violent flux and one snake which the woman thought was turtle and which did them no harm, and one night it rained and he got up and dragged brush, shaking the snakes (he no longer thought, *It aint nothing but another moccasin,* he just stepped aside for them as they, when there was time, telescoped sullenly aside for him) out of it with the old former feeling of personal invulnerability and built a shelter and the rain stopped at once and did not recommence and the woman went back to the skiff.

Then one night—the slow tedious charring log was almost a paddle now—one night and he was in bed, in his bed in the bunkhouse and it was cold, he was trying to pull the covers up only his mule wouldn't let him, prodding and bumping heavily at him, trying to get into the narrow bed with him and now the bed was cold too and wet and he was trying to get out of it only the mule would not let him, holding him by his belt in its teeth, jerking and bumping him back into the cold wet bed and, leaning, gave him a long swipe across the face with its cold limber musculated tongue and he waked to no fire, no coal even beneath where the almost-finished paddle had been charring and something else prolonged and coldly limber passed swiftly across his body where he lay in four inches of water while the nose of the skiff alternately tugged at the grapevine tied about his waist and bumped and shoved him back into the water again. Then something else came up and began to nudge at his ankle (the log, the oar, it was) even as he groped frantically for the skiff, hearing the swift rustling going to and fro inside the hull as the woman began to thrash about and scream. "Rats!" she cried. "It's full of rats!"

"Lay still!" he cried. "It's just snakes. Cant you hold still long enough for me to find the boat?" Then he found it, he got into it with the unfinished paddle; again the thick muscular body convulsed under his foot; it did not strike; he would not have cared, glaring astern where he could see a little—the faint outer luminosity of the open water. He poled toward it, thrusting aside the snake-looped branches, the bottom of the skiff resounding faintly to thick solid plops, the woman shrieking steadily. Then the skiff was clear of the trees, the mound, and now he could feel the bodies whipping about his ankles and hear the rasp of them as they went over the gunwale. He drew the log in and scooped it forward along the bottom of the boat and up and out; against the pallid water he could see three more of them in lashing convolutions before they vanished. "Shut up!" he cried. "Hush! I wish I was a snake so I could get out too!"

When once more the pale and heatless wafer disc of the early sun stared down at the skiff (whether they were moving or not the convict did not know) in its nimbus of fine cotton batting, the convict was hearing again that sound which he had heard twice before and would never forget—that sound of deliberate and irresistible and monstrously disturbed water. But this time he could not tell from what direction it came. It seemed to be everywhere, waxing and fading; it was like a phantom behind the mist, at one instant miles away, the next on the point of overwhelming the skiff within the next second; suddenly, in the instant he would believe (his whole weary body would spring and scream) that he was about to drive the skiff point-blank into it and with the unfinished paddle of the color and texture of sooty bricks, like something gnawed out of an old chimney by beavers and weighing twenty-five pounds, he would whirl the skiff frantically and find the sound dead ahead of him again. Then something bellowed tremendously above his head, he heard human voices, a bell jangled and the sound ceased and the mist vanished as when you draw your hand across a frosted pane, and the skiff now lay upon a sunny glitter of brown water flank to flank with, and about thirty yards away from, a steamboat. The decks were crowded and packed with men women and children sitting or standing beside and among a homely conglomeration of hurried furniture, who looked mournfully and silently down into the skiff while the convict and the man with a megaphone in the pilot house talked to each other in alternate puny shouts and roars above the chuffing of the reversed engines:

"What in hell are you trying to do? Commit suicide?"

"Which is the way to Vicksburg?"

"Vicksburg? Vicksburg? Lay alongside and come aboard."

"Will you take the boat too?"

"Boat? Boat?" Now the megaphone cursed, the roaring waves of blasphemy and biological supposition empty cavernous and bodiless in turn, as if the water, the air, the mist had spoken it, roaring the words then taking them back to itself and no harm done, no scar, no insult left anywhere. "If I took aboard every floating sardine can you sonabitchin mushrats want me to I wouldn't even have room forrard for a leadsman. Come aboard! Do you expect me to hang here on stern engines till hell freezes?"

"I aint coming without the boat," the convict said. Now another voice spoke, so calm and mild and sensible that for a moment it sounded more foreign and out of place than even the megaphone's bellowing and bodiless profanity:

"Where is it you are trying to go?"

"I aint trying," the convict said. "I'm going. Parchman." The man who had spoken last turned and appeared to converse with a third man in the pilot house. Then he looked down at the skiff again.

"Carnarvon?"

"What?" the convict said. "Parchman?"

"All right. We're going that way. We'll put you off where you can get home. Come aboard."

"The boat too?"

"Yes, yes. Come along. We're burning coal just to talk to you." So the convict came alongside then and watched them help the woman and baby over the rail and he came aboard himself, though he still held to the end of the vine-spliced painter until the skiff was hoisted onto the boiler deck. "My God," the man, the gentle one, said, "is that what you have been using for a paddle?"

"Yah," the convict said. "I lost the plank."

"The plank," the mild man (the convict told how he seemed to whisper it), "the plank. Well. Come along and get something to eat. Your boat is all right now."

"I reckon I'll wait here," the convict said. Because now, he told them, he began to notice for the first time that the other people, the other refugees who crowded the deck, who had gathered in a quiet circle about the upturned skiff on which he and the woman sat, the grapevine painter wrapped several times about his wrist and clutched in his hand, staring at him and the woman with queer hot mournful intensity, were not white people—

"You mean niggers?" the plump convict said.

"No. Not Americans."

"Not Americans? You was clean out of *America* even?"

"I don't know," the tall one said. "They called it Atchafalaya."—

Because after a while he said, "What?" to the man and the man did
it again, gobble-gobble—

"Gobble-gobble?" the plump convict said.

"That's the way they talked," the tall one said. "Gobble-gobble,
whang, caw-caw-to-to."—And he sat there and watched them gobbling at one another and then looking at him again, then they fell
back and the mild man (he wore a Red Cross brassard) entered,
followed by a waiter with a tray of food. The mild man carried
two glasses of whiskey.

"Drink this," the mild man said. "This will warm you." The
woman took hers and drank it but the convict told how he looked
at his and thought, *I aint tasted whiskey in seven years.* He had not
tasted it but once before that; it was at the still itself back in a pine
hollow; he was seventeen, he had gone there with four companions, two of whom were grown men, one of twenty-two or -three,
the other about forty; he remembered it. That is, he remembered
perhaps a third of that evening—a fierce turmoil in the hell-colored
firelight, the shock and shock of blows about his head (and likewise of his own fists on other hard bone), then the waking to a
splitting and blinding sun in a place, a cowshed, he had never seen
before and which later turned out to be twenty miles from his
home. He said he thought of this and he looked about at the faces
watching him and he said,

"I reckon not."

"Come, come," the mild man said. "Drink it."

"I dont want it."

"Nonsense," the mild man said. "I'm a doctor. Here. Then you
can eat." So he took the glass and even then he hesitated but
again the mild man said, "Come along, down with it; you're still
holding us up," in that voice still calm and sensible but a little
sharp too—the voice of a man who could keep calm and affable because he wasn't used to being crossed—and he drank the whiskey
and even in the second between the sweet full fire in his belly and
when it began to happen he was trying to say, "I tried to tell you!
I tried to!" But it was too late now in the pallid sun-glare of the
tenth day of terror and hopelessness and despair and impotence
and rage and outrage and it was himself and the mule, his mule
(they had let him name it—John Henry) which no man save he
had plowed for five years now and whose ways and habits he
knew and respected and who knew his ways and habits so well that

each of them could anticipate the other's very movements and intentions; it was himself and the mule, the little gobbling faces flying before them, the familiar hard skull-bones shocking against his fists, his voice shouting, "Come on, John Henry! Plow them down! Gobble them down, boy!" even as the bright hot red wave turned back, meeting it joyously, happily, lifted, poised, then hurling through space, triumphant and yelling, then again the old shocking blow at the back of his head: he lay on the deck, flat on his back and pinned arm and leg and cold sober again, his nostrils gushing again, the mild man stooping over him with behind the thin rimless glasses the coldest eyes the convict had ever seen—eyes which the convict said were not looking at him but at the gushing blood with nothing in the world in them but complete impersonal interest.

"Good man," the mild man said. "Plenty of life in the old carcass yet, eh? Plenty of good red blood too. Anyone ever suggest to you that you were hemophilic?" ("What?" the plump convict said. "Hemophilic? You know what that means?" The tall convict had his cigarette going now, his body jackknifed backward into the coffinlike space between the upper and lower bunks, lean, clean, motionless, the blue smoke wreathing across his lean dark aquiline shaven face. "That's a calf that's a bull and a cow at the same time."

"No, it aint," a third convict said. "It's a calf or a colt that aint neither one."

"Hell fire," the plump one said. "He's got to be one or the other to keep from drounding." He had never ceased to look at the tall one in the bunk; now he spoke to him again: "You let him call you that?") The tall one had done so. He did not answer the doctor (this was where he stopped thinking of him as the mild man) at all. He could not move either, though he felt fine, he felt better than he had in ten days. So they helped him to his feet and steadied him over and lowered him onto the upturned skiff beside the woman, where he sat bent forward, elbows on knees in the immemorial attitude, watching his own bright crimson staining the mud-trodden deck, until the doctor's clean clipped hand appeared under his nose with a phial.

"Smell," the doctor said. "Deep." The convict inhaled, the sharp ammoniac sensation burned up his nostrils and into his throat. "Again," the doctor said. The convict inhaled obediently. This time he choked and spat a gout of blood, his nose now had no more feeling than a toenail, other than it felt about the size of a ten-inch shovel, and as cold.

"I ask you to excuse me," he said. "I never meant—"

"Why?" the doctor said. "You put up as pretty a scrap against forty or fifty men as I ever saw. You lasted a good two seconds. Now you can eat something. Or do you think that will send you haywire again?"

They both ate, sitting on the skiff, the gobbling faces no longer watching them now, the convict gnawing slowly and painfully at the thick sandwich, hunched, his face laid sideways to the food and parallel to the earth as a dog chews; the steamboat went on. At noon there were bowls of hot soup and bread and more coffee; they ate this too, sitting side by side on the skiff, the grapevine still wrapped about the convict's wrist. The baby waked and nursed and slept again and they talked quietly:

"Was it Parchman he said he was going to take us?"

"That's where I told him I wanted to go."

"It never sounded exactly like Parchman to me. It sounded like he said something else." The convict had thought that too. He had been thinking about that fairly soberly ever since they boarded the steamboat and soberly indeed ever since he had remarked the nature of the other passengers, those men and women definitely a little shorter than he and with skin a little different in pigmentation from any sunburn, even though the eyes were sometimes blue or gray, who talked to one another in a tongue he had never heard before and who apparently did not understand his own, people the like of whom he had never seen about Parchman nor anywhere else and whom he did not believe were going there or beyond there either. But after his hill-billy country fashion and kind he would not ask, because to his raising asking information was asking a favor and you did not ask favors of strangers; if they offered them perhaps you accepted and you expressed gratitude almost tediously recapitulant, but you did not ask. So he would watch and wait, as he had done before, and do or try to do to the best of his ability what the best of his judgment dictated.

So he waited, and in midafternoon the steamboat chuffed and thrust through a willow-choked gorge and emerged from it, and now the convict knew it was the River. He could believe it now—the tremendous reach, yellow and sleepy in the afternoon—("Because it's too big," he told them soberly. "Aint no flood in the world big enough to make it do more than stand a little higher so it can look back and see just where the flea is, just exactly where to scratch. It's the little ones, the little piddling creeks that run backward one day and forward the next and come busting down on a man full of dead mules and hen houses.")—and the steamboat moving up this now (*like a ant crossing a plate,* the convict thought, sitting beside the woman on the upturned skiff, the baby nursing again, apparently looking too out across the water where, a mile away on either hand, the twin lines of levee resembled parallel unbroken floating thread) and then it was nearing sunset and he began to hear, to notice, the voices of the doctor and of the man who had first bawled at him through the megaphone now bawling again from the pilot house overhead:

"Stop? Stop? Am I running a street car?"

"Stop for the novelty then," the doctor's pleasant voice said. "I dont know how many trips back and forth you have made in yonder nor how many of what you call mushrats you have fetched out. But this is the first time you ever had two people—no, three— who not only knew the name of some place they wished to go to but were actually trying to go there." So the convict waited while the sun slanted more and more and the steamboat-ant crawled steadily on across its vacant and gigantic plate turning more and more to copper. But he did not ask, he just waited. *Maybe it was Carrollton he said,* he thought. *It began with a C.* But he did not believe that either. He did not know where he was, but he did know that this was not anywhere near the Carrollton he remembered from that day seven years ago when, shackled wrist to wrist with the deputy sheriff, he had passed through it on the train— the slow spaced repeated shattering banging of trucks where two railroads crossed, a random scattering of white houses tranquil among trees on green hills lush with summer, a pointing spire, the finger of the hand of God. But there was no river there. *And you aint never close to this river without knowing it,* he thought. *I dont care who you are nor where you have been all your life.* Then the head of the steamboat began to swing across the stream, its shadow swinging too, travelling long before it across the water, toward the vacant ridge of willow-massed earth empty of all life. There was nothing there at all, the convict could not even see either earth or water beyond it; it was as though the steamboat were about to crash slowly through the thin low frail willow barrier and embark into space, or lacking this, slow and back and fill and disembark him into space, granted it was about to disembark him, granted this was that place which was not near Parchman and was not Carrollton either, even though it did begin with C. Then he turned his head and saw the doctor stooping over the woman, pushing the baby's eyelid up with his forefinger, peering at it.

"Who else was there when he came?" the doctor said.

"Nobody," the convict said.

"Did it all yourselves, eh?"

"Yes," the convict said. Now the doctor stood up and looked at the convict.

"This is Carnarvon," he said.

"Carnarvon?" the convict said. "That aint—" Then he stopped, ceased. And now he told about that—the intent eyes as dispassionate as ice behind the rimless glasses, the clipped quick-tempered face that was not accustomed to being crossed or lied to either. ("Yes," the plump convict said. "That's what I was aiming to ask. Them clothes. Anybody would know them. How if this doctor was as smart as you claim he was—"

"I had slept in them for ten nights, mostly in the mud," the tall one said. "I had been rowing since midnight with that sapling oar I had tried to burn out that I never had time to scrape the soot off. But it's being scared and worried and then scared and then worried again in clothes for days and days and days that changes the way they look. I dont mean just your pants." He did not laugh. "Your face too. That doctor knowed."

"All right," the plump one said. "Go on.")

"I know it," the doctor said. "I discovered that while you were lying on the deck yonder sobering up again. Now dont lie to me. I dont like lying. This boat is going to New Orleans."

"No," the convict said immediately, quietly, with absolute finality. He could hear them again—the thuck-thuck-thuck on the water where an instant before he had been. But he was not thinking of the bullets. He had forgotten them, forgiven them. He was thinking of himself crouching, sobbing, panting before running again— the voice, the indictment, the cry of final and irrevocable repudiation of the old primal faithless Manipulator of all the lust and folly and injustice: *All in the world I wanted was just to surrender;* thinking of it, remembering it but without heat now, without passion now and briefer than an epitaph: *No. I tried that once. They shot at me.*

"So you dont want to go to New Orleans. And you didn't exactly plan to go to Carnarvon. But you will take Carnarvon in preference to New Orleans." The convict said nothing. The doctor looked at him, the magnified pupils like the heads of two bridge nails. "What were you in for? Hit him harder than you thought, eh?"

"No. I tried to rob a train."

"Say that again." The convict said it again. "Well? Go on. You dont say that in the year 1927 and just stop, man." So the convict told it, dispassionately too—about the magazines, the pistol which would not shoot, the mask and the dark lantern in which no draft had been arranged to keep the candle burning so that it died almost with the match but even then left the metal too hot to carry, won with subscriptions. *Only it aint my eyes or my mouth either he's watching,* he thought. *It's like he is watching the way my hair grows on my head.* "I see," the doctor said. "But something went wrong. But you've had plenty of time to think about it since. To decide what was wrong, what you failed to do."

"Yes," the convict said. "I've thought about it a right smart since."

"So next time you are not going to make that mistake."

"I don't know," the convict said. "There aint going to be a next time."

"Why? If you know what you did wrong, they wont catch you next time."

The convict looked at the doctor steadily. They looked at each other steadily; the two sets of eyes were not so different after all. "I reckon I see what you mean," the convict said presently. "I was eighteen then. I'm twenty-five now."

"Oh," the doctor said. Now (the convict tried to tell it) the doctor did not move, he just simply quit looking at the convict. He produced a pack of cheap cigarettes from his coat. "Smoke?" he said.

"I wouldn't care for none," the convict said.

"Quite," the doctor said in that affable clipped voice. He put the cigarettes away. "There has been conferred upon my race (the Medical race) also the power to bind and to loose, if not by Jehovah perhaps, certainly by the American Medical Association—on which incidentally, in this day of Our Lord, I would put my

money, at any odds, at any amount, at any time. I dont know just
how far out of bounds I am on this specific occasion but I think
we'll put it to the touch." He cupped his hands to his mouth, toward the pilot house overhead. "Captain!" he shouted. "We'll put
these three passengers ashore here." He turned to the convict
again. "Yes," he said, "I think I shall let your native State lick its
own vomit. Here." Again his hand emerged from his pocket, this
time with a bill in it.

"No," the convict said.

"Come, come; I dont like to be disputed either."

"No," the convict said. "I aint got any way to pay it back."

"Did I ask you to pay it back?"

"No," the convict said. "I never asked to borrow it either."

So once more he stood on dry land, who had already been toyed
with twice by that risible and concentrated power of water, once
more than should have fallen to the lot of any one man, any one
lifetime, yet for whom there was reserved still another unbelievable recapitulation, he and the woman standing on the empty
levee, the sleeping child wrapped in the faded tunic and the grapevine painter still wrapped about the convict's wrist, watching the
steamboat back away and turn and once more crawl onward up
the platter-like reach of vacant water burnished more and more to
copper, its trailing smoke roiling in slow copper-edged gouts, thinning out along the water, fading, stinking away across the vast
serene desolation, the boat growing smaller and smaller until it did
not seem to crawl at all but to hang stationary in the airy substanceless sunset, dissolving into nothing like a pellet of floating
mud.

Then he turned and for the first time looked about him, behind
him, recoiling, not through fear but through pure reflex and not
physically but the soul, the spirit, that profound sober alert atten-
tiveness of the hillman who will not ask anything of strangers, not
even information, thinking quietly, *No. This aint Carrollton neither.* Because he now looked down the almost perpendicular land-
ward slope of the levee through sixty feet of absolute space, upon
a surface, a terrain flat as a waffle and of the color of a waffle or
perhaps of the summer coat of a claybank horse and possessing
that same piled density of a rug or peltry, spreading away without
undulation yet with that curious appearance of imponderable solidity like fluid, broken here and there by thick humps of arsenical

green which nevertheless still seemed to possess no height and by
writhen veins of the color of ink which he began to suspect to be
actual water but with judgment reserved, with judgment still reserved even when presently he was walking in it. That's what he
said, told: So they went on. He didn't tell how he got the skiff singlehanded up the revetment and across the crown and down the
opposite sixty foot drop, he just said he went on, in a swirling
cloud of mosquitoes like hot cinders, thrusting and plunging
through the saw-edged grass which grew taller than his head and
which whipped back at his arms and face like limber knives,
dragging by the vine-spliced painter the skiff in which the woman
sat, slogging and stumbling knee-deep in something less of earth
than water, along one of those black winding channels less of water than earth: and then (he was in the skiff too now, paddling
with the charred log, what footing there had been having given
away beneath him without warning thirty minutes ago, leaving
only the air-filled bubble of his jumper-back ballooning lightly on
the twilit water until he rose to the surface and scrambled into the
skiff) the house, the cabin a little larger than a horse-box, of cypress boards and an iron roof, rising on ten-foot stilts slender as
spiders' legs, like a shabby and death-stricken (and probably poi-
sonous) wading creature which had got that far into that flat
waste and died with nothing nowhere in reach or sight to lie down
upon, a pirogue tied to the foot of a crude ladder, a man standing
in the open door holding a lantern (it was that dark now) above
his head, gobbling down at them.

He told it—of the next eight or nine or ten days, he did not remember which, while the four of them—himself and the woman
and baby and the little wiry man with rotting teeth and soft wild
bright eyes like a rat or a chipmunk, whose language neither of
them could understand—lived in the room and a half. He did not
tell it that way, just as he apparently did not consider it worth the
breath to tell how he had got the hundred-and-sixty-pound skiff
singlehanded up and across and down the sixty-foot levee. He just
said, "After a while we come to a house and we stayed there eight
or nine days then they blew up the levee with dynamite so we had
to leave." That was all. But he remembered it, but quietly now,
with the cigar now, the good one the Warden had given him
(though not lighted yet) in his peaceful and steadfast hand, remembering that first morning when he waked on the thin pallet

beside his host (the woman and baby had the one bed) with the
fierce sun already latticed through the warped rough planking of
the wall, and stood on the rickety porch looking out upon that
flat fecund waste neither earth nor water, where even the senses
doubted which was which, which rich and massy air and which
mazy and impalpable vegetation, and thought quietly, *He must do
something here to eat and live. But I dont know what. And until I
can go on again, until I can find where I am and how to pass that
town without them seeing me I will have to help him do it so we
can eat and live too, and I dont know what.* And he had a change
of clothing too, almost at once on that first morning, not telling any
more than he had about the skiff and the levee how he had begged
borrowed or bought from the man whom he had not laid eyes on
twelve hours ago and with whom on the day he saw him for the
last time he still could exchange no word, the pair of dungaree
pants which even the Cajan had discarded as no longer wearable,
filthy, buttonless, the legs slashed and frayed into fringe like that
on an 1890 hammock, in which he stood naked from the waist up
and holding out to her the mud-caked and soot-stained jumper and
overall when the woman waked on that first morning in the crude
bunk nailed into one corner and filled with dried grass, saying,
"Wash them. Good. I want all them stains out. All of them."

"But the jumper," she said. "Aint he got ere old shirt too? That
sun and them mosquitoes—" But he did not even answer, and she
said no more either, though when he and the Cajan returned at
dark the garments were clean, stained a little still with the old mud
and soot, but clean, resembling again what they were supposed to
resemble as (his arms and back already a fiery red which would
be blisters by tomorrow) he spread the garments out and examined them and then rolled them up carefully in a six-months-old
New Orleans paper and thrust the bundle behind a rafter, where
it remained while day followed day and the blisters on his back
broke and suppurated and he would sit with his face expressionless
as a wooden mask beneath the sweat while the Cajan doped his
back with something on a filthy rag from a filthy saucer, she still
saying nothing since she too doubtless knew what his reason was,
not from that rapport of the wedded conferred upon her by the
two weeks during which they had jointly suffered all the crises
emotional social economic and even moral which do not always occur even in the ordinary fifty married years (the old married: you

have seen them, the electroplate reproductions, the thousand identical coupled faces with only a collarless stud or a fichu out of Louisa Alcott to denote the sex, looking in pairs like the winning braces of dogs after a field trial, out from among the packed columns of disaster and alarm and baseless assurance and hope and incredible insensitivity and insulation from tomorrow propped by a thousand morning sugar bowls or coffee urns; or singly, rocking on porches or sitting in the sun beneath the tobacco-stained porticoes of a thousand county courthouses, as though with the death of the other having inherited a sort of rejuvenescence, immortality; relict, they take a new lease on breath and seem to live forever, as though that flesh which the old ceremony or ritual had morally purified and made legally one had actually become so with long tedious habit and he or she who entered the ground first took all of it with him or her, leaving only the old permanent enduring bone, free and trameless)—not because of this but because she too had stemmed at some point from the same dim hill-bred Abraham.

So the bundle remained behind the rafter and day followed day while he and his partner (he was in partnership now with his host, hunting alligators on shares, on the halvers he called it—"Halvers?" the plump convict said. "How could you make a business agreement with a man you claim you couldn't even talk to?"

"I never had to talk to him," the tall one said. "Money aint got but one language.") departed at dawn each day, at first together in the pirogue but later singly, the one in the pirogue and the other in the skiff, the one with the battered and pitted rifle, the other with the knife and a piece of knotted rope and a lightwood club the size and weight and shape of a Thuringian mace, stalking their pleistocene nightmares up and down the secret inky channels which writhed the flat brass-colored land. He remembered that too: that first morning when turning in the sunrise from the rickety platform he saw the hide nailed drying to the wall and stopped dead, looking at it quietly, thinking quietly and soberly, So *that's it. That's what he does in order to eat and live,* knowing it was a hide, a skin, but from what animal, by association, ratiocination or even memory of any picture out of his dead youth, he did not know but knowing that it was the reason, the explanation, for the little lost spider-legged house (which had already begun to die, to rot from the legs upward almost before the roof was nailed on) set in that teeming and myriad desolation, enclosed and lost within the furi-

ous embrace of flowing mare earth and stallion sun, divining
through pure rapport of kind for kind, hill-billy and bayou-rat, the
two one and identical because of the same grudged dispensation
and niggard fate of hard and unceasing travail not to gain future
security, a balance in the bank or even in a buried soda can for
slothful and easy old age, but just permission to endure and endure to buy air to feel and sun to drink for each's little while, thinking (the convict), *Well, anyway I am going to find out what it is
sooner than I expected to,* and did so, re-entered the house where
the woman was just waking in the one sorry built-in straw-filled
bunk which the Cajan had surrendered to her, and ate the breakfast (the rice, a semi-liquid mess violent with pepper and mostly
fish considerably high, the chicory-thickened coffee) and, shirtless,
followed the little scuttling bobbing bright-eyed rotten-toothed
man down the crude ladder and into the pirogue. He had never
seen a pirogue either and he believed that it would not remain
upright—not that it was light and precariously balanced with its
open side upward but that there was inherent in the wood, the
very log, some dynamic and unsleeping natural law, almost will,
which its present position outraged and violated—yet accepting
this too as he had the fact that that hide had belonged to something larger than any calf or hog and that anything which looked
like that on the outside would be more than likely to have teeth
and claws too, accepting this, squatting in the pirogue, clutching
both gunwales, rigidly immobile as though he had an egg filled
with nitroglycerin in his mouth and scarcely breathing, thinking,
*If that's it, then I can do it too and even if he cant tell me how I
reckon I can watch him and find out.* And he did this too, he remembered it, quietly even yet, thinking, *I thought that was how
to do it and I reckon I would still think that even if I had it to do
again now for the first time*—the brazen day already fierce upon his
naked back, the crooked channel like a voluted thread of ink, the
pirogue moving steadily to the paddle which both entered and left
the water without a sound; then the sudden cessation of the paddle
behind him and the fierce hissing gobble of the Cajan at his back
and he squatting bate-breathed and with that intense immobility
of complete sobriety of a blind man listening while the frail
wooden shell stole on at the dying apex of its own parted water.
Afterward he remembered the rifle too—the rust-pitted single-shot
weapon with a clumsily wired stock and a muzzle you could have

driven a whiskey cork into, which the Cajan had brought into the boat—but not now; now he just squatted, crouched, immobile, breathing with infinitesimal care, his sober unceasing gaze going here and there constantly as he thought, *What? What? I not only dont know what I am looking for, I dont even know where to look for it.* Then he felt the motion of the pirogue as the Cajan moved and then the tense gobbling hissing actually, hot rapid and repressed, against his neck and ear, and glancing downward saw projecting between his own arm and body from behind the Cajan's hand holding the knife, and glaring up again saw the flat thick spit of mud which as he looked at it divided and became a thick mud-colored log which in turn seemed, still immobile, to leap suddenly against his retinae in three—no, four—dimensions: volume, solidity, shape, and another: not fear but pure and intense speculation and he looking at the scaled motionless shape, thinking not, *It looks dangerous* but *It looks big*, thinking, *Well, maybe a mule standing in a lot looks big to a man that never walked up to one with a halter before*, thinking, *Only if he could just tell me what to do it would save time*, the pirogue drawing nearer now, creeping now, with no ripple now even and it seemed to him that he could even hear his companion's held breath and he taking the knife from the other's hand now and not even thinking this since it was too fast, a flash; it was not a surrender, not a resignation, it was too calm, it was a part of him, he had drunk it with his mother's milk and lived with it all his life: *After all a man cant only do what he has to do, with what he has to do it with, with what he has learned, to the best of his judgment. And I reckon a hog is still a hog, no matter what it looks like. So here goes,* sitting still for an instant longer until the bow of the pirogue grounded lighter than the falling of a leaf and stepped out of it and paused just for one instant while the words *It does look big* stood for just a second, unemphatic and trivial, somewhere where some fragment of his attention could see them and vanished, and stooped straddling, the knife driving even as he grasped the near foreleg, this all in the same instant when the lashing tail struck him a terrific blow upon the back. But the knife was home, he knew that even on his back in the mud, the weight of the thrashing beast longwise upon him, its ridged back clutched to his stomach, his arm about its throat, the hissing head clamped against his jaw, the furious tail lashing and flailing, the knife in his other hand probing for the life and finding

it, the hot fierce gush: and now sitting beside the profound up-
bellied carcass, his head again between his knees in the old attitude
while his own blood freshened the other which drenched him,
thinking, *It's my durn nose again.*

So he sat there, his head, his streaming face, bowed between his
knees in an attitude not of dejection but profoundly bemused,
contemplative, while the shrill voice of the Cajan seemed to buzz
at him from an enormous distance; after a time he even looked up
at the antic wiry figure bouncing hysterically about him, the face
wild and grimacing, the voice gobbling and high; while the convict, holding his face carefully slanted so the blood would run free,
looked at him with the cold intentness of a curator or custodian
paused before one of his own glass cases, the Cajan threw up the
rifle, cried "Boom-boom-boom!" flung it down and in pantomime
re-enacted the recent scene then whirled his hands again, crying
"Magnifique! Magnifique! Cent d'argent! mille d'argent! Tout l'argent sous le ciel de Dieu!" But the convict was already looking
down again, cupping the coffee-colored water to his face, watching
the constant bright carmine marble it, thinking, *It's a little late to
be telling me that now,* and not even thinking this long because
presently they were in the pirogue again, the convict squatting
again with that unbreathing rigidity as though he were trying by
holding his breath to decrease his very weight, the bloody skin in
the bows before him and he looking at it, thinking, *And I cant
even ask him how much my half will be.*

But this not for long either, because as he was to tell the plump
convict later, money has but one language. He remembered that
too (they were at home now, the skin spread on the platform,
where for the woman's benefit now the Cajan once more went
through the pantomime—the gun which was not used, the hand-to-
hand battle; for the second time the invisible alligator was slain
amid cries, the victor rose and found this time that not even the
woman was watching him. She was looking at the once more swollen and inflamed face of the convict. "You mean it kicked you right
in the face?" she said.

"Nah," the convict said harshly, savagely. "It never had to. I
done seem to got to where if that boy was to shoot me in the tail
with a bean blower my nose would bleed.")—remembered that
too but he did not try to tell it. Perhaps he could not have—how
two people who could not even talk to one another made an agree-

ment which both not only understood but which each knew the
other would hold true and protect (perhaps for this reason) better
than any written and witnessed contract. They even discussed and
agreed somehow that they should hunt separately, each in his own
vessel, to double the chances of finding prey. But this was easy:
the convict could almost understand the words in which the Cajan
said, "You do not need me and the rifle; we will only hinder you,
be in your way." And more than this, they even agreed about the
second rifle: that there was someone, it did not matter who—
friend, neighbor, perhaps one in business in that line—from whom
they could rent a second rifle; in their two patois, the one bastard
English, the other bastard French—the one volatile, with his wild
bright eyes and his voluble mouth full of stumps of teeth, the other
sober, almost grim, swollen-faced and with his naked back blistered and scoriated like so much beef—they discussed this, squatting on either side of the pegged-out hide like two members of a
corporation facing each other across a mahogany board table, and
decided against it, the convict deciding: "I reckon not," he said.
"I reckon if I had knowed enough to wait to start out with a gun, I
still would. But since I done already started out without one, I dont
reckon I'll change." Because it was a question of the money in
terms of time, days. (Strange to say, that was the one thing which
the Cajan could not tell him: how much the half would be. But
the convict knew it was half.) He had so little of them. He would
have to move on soon, thinking (the convict), *All this durn foolishness will stop soon and I can get on back,* and then suddenly he
found that he was thinking, *Will have to get on back,* and he became quite still and looked about at the rich strange desert which
surrounded him, in which he was temporarily lost in peace and
hope and into which the last seven years had sunk like so many
trivial pebbles into a pool, leaving no ripple, and he thought quietly, with a kind of bemused amazement, *Yes. I reckon I had done
forgot how good making money was. Being let to make it.*

So he used no gun, his the knotted rope and the Thuringian
mace, and each morning he and the Cajan took their separate ways
in the two boats to comb and creep the secret channels about the
lost land from (or out of) which now and then still other pint-sized
dark men appeared gobbling, abruptly and as though by magic
from nowhere, in other hollowed logs, to follow quietly and watch
him at his single combats—men named Tine and Toto and Theule,

who were not much larger than and looked a good deal like the muskrats which the Cajan (the host did this too, supplied the kitchen too, he expressed this too like the rifle business, in his own tongue, the convict comprehending this too as though it had been English: "Do not concern yourself about food, O Hercules. Catch alligators; I will supply the pot.") took now and then from traps as you take a shoat pig at need from a pen, and varied the eternal rice and fish (the convict did tell this: how at night, in the cabin, the door and one sashless window battened against mosquitoes—a form, a ritual, as empty as crossing the fingers or knocking on wood—sitting beside the bug-swirled lantern on the plank table in a temperature close to blood heat he would look down at the swimming segment of meat on his sweating plate and think, *It must be Theule. He was the fat one.*)—day following day, unemphatic and identical, each like the one before and the one which would follow while his theoretical half of a sum to be reckoned in pennies, dollars, or tens of dollars he did not know, mounted—the mornings when he set forth to find waiting for him like the *matador* his *aficianados* the small clump of constant and deferential pirogues, the hard noons when ringed half about by little motionless shells he fought his solitary combats, the evenings, the return, the pirogues departing one by one into inlets and passages which during the first few days he could not even distinguish, then the platform in the twilight where before the static woman and the usually nursing infant and the one or two bloody hides of the day's take the Cajan would perform his ritualistic victorious pantomime before the two growing rows of knifemarks in one of the boards of the wall; then the nights when, the woman and child in the single bunk and the Cajan already snoring on the pallet and the reeking lantern set close, he (the convict) would sit on his naked heels, sweating steadily, his face worn and calm, immersed and indomitable, his bowed back raw and savage as beef beneath the suppurant old blisters and the fierce welts of tails, and scrape and chip at the charred sapling which was almost a paddle now, pausing now and then to raise his head while the cloud of mosquitoes about it whined and whirled, to stare at the wall before him until after a while the crude boards themselves must have dissolved away and let his blank unseeing gaze go on and on unhampered, through the rich oblivious darkness, beyond it even perhaps, even perhaps beyond the seven wasted years during which, so he had just realised, he had been permitted to toil but not to work. Then he would retire himself, he would take a last look at the rolled bundle behind the rafter and blow out the lantern and lie down as he was beside his snoring partner, to lie sweating (on his stomach, he could not bear the touch of anything to his back) in the whining ovenlike darkness filled with the forlorn bellowing of alligators, thinking not, *They never gave me time to learn* but *I had forgot how good it is to work.*

Then on the tenth day it happened. It happened for the third time. At first he refused to believe it, not that he felt that now he had served out and discharged his apprenticeship to mischance, had with the birth of the child reached and crossed the crest of his Golgotha and would now be, possibly not permitted so much as ignored, to descend the opposite slope free-wheeling. That was not his feeling at all. What he declined to accept was the fact that a power, a force such as that which had been consistent enough to concentrate upon him with deadly undeviation for weeks, should with all the wealth of cosmic violence and disaster to draw from, have been so barren of invention and imagination, so lacking in pride of artistry and craftsmanship, as to repeat itself twice. Once he had accepted, twice he even forgave, but three times he simply declined to believe, particularly when he was at last persuaded to realise that this third time was to be instigated not by the blind potency of volume and motion but by human direction and hands: that now the cosmic joker, foiled twice, had stooped in its vindictive concentration to the employing of dynamite.

He did not tell that. Doubtless he did not know himself how it happened, what was happening. But he doubtless remembered it (but quietly above the thick rich-colored pristine cigar in his clean steady hand), what he knew, divined of it. It would be evening, the ninth evening, he and the woman on either side of their host's empty place at the evening meal, he hearing the voices from without but not ceasing to eat, still chewing steadily, because it would be the same as though he were seeing them anyway—the two or three or four pirogues floating on the dark water beneath the platform on which the host stood, the voices gobbling and jabbering, incomprehensible and filled not with alarm and not exactly with rage or ever perhaps absolute surprise but rather just cacophony like those of disturbed marsh fowl, he (the convict) not ceasing to

chew but just looking up quietly and maybe without a great deal
of interrogation or surprise too as the Cajan burst in and stood before them, wild-faced, glaring, his blackened teeth gaped against
the inky orifice of his distended mouth, watching (the convict)
while the Cajan went through his violent pantomime of violent
evacuation, ejection, scooping something invisible into his arms
and hurling it out and downward and in the instant of completing
the gesture changing from instigator to victim of that which he
had set into pantomimic motion, clasping his head and, bowed
over and not otherwise moving, seeming to be swept on and away
before it, crying "Boom! Boom! Boom!", the convict watching him,
his jaw not chewing now, though for just that moment, thinking,
What? What is it he is trying to tell me? thinking (this a flash too,
since he could not have expressed this, and hence did not even
know that he had ever thought it) that though his life had been
cast here, circumscribed by this environment, accepted by this environment and accepting it in turn (and he had done well here—
this quietly, soberly indeed, if he had been able to phrase it, think
it instead of merely knowing it—better than he had ever done, who
had not even known until now how good work, making money,
could be) yet it was not his life, he still and would ever be no more
than the water bug upon the surface of the pond, the plumbless
and lurking depths of which he would never know, his only actual
contact with it being the instants when on lonely and glaring mud-
spits under the pitiless sun and amphitheatred by his motionless
and riveted semicircle of watching pirogues, he accepted the gambit which he had not elected, entered the lashing radius of the
armed tail and beat at the thrashing and hissing head with his
lightwood club, or this failing, embraced without hesitation the
armored body itself with the frail web of flesh and bone in which
he walked and lived and sought the raging life with an eight-inch
knife-blade.

So he and the woman merely watched the Cajan as he acted out
the whole charade of eviction—the little wiry man gesticulant and
wild, his hysterical shadow leaping and falling upon the rough wall
as he went through the pantomime of abandoning the cabin, gathering in pantomime his meagre belongings from the walls and corners—objects which no other man would want and only some
power or force like blind water or earthquake or fire would ever

dispossess him of, the woman watching too, her mouth slightly open upon a mass of chewed food, on her face an expression of placid astonishment, saying, "What? What's he saying?"

"I dont know," the convict said. "But I reckon if it's something we ought to know we will find it out when it's ready for us to." Because he was not alarmed, though by now he had read the other's meaning plainly enough. *He's fixing to leave,* he thought. *He's telling me to leave too*—this later, after they had quitted the table and the Cajan and the woman had gone to bed and the Cajan had risen from the pallet and approached the convict and once more went through the pantomime of abandoning the cabin, this time as one repeats a speech which may have been misunderstood, tediously, carefully repetitional as to a child, seeming to hold the convict with one hand while he gestured, talked, with the other, gesturing as though in single syllables, the convict (squatting, the knife open and the almost-finished paddle across his lap) watching, nodding his head, even speaking in English: "Yah; sure. You bet. I got you."—trimming again at the paddle but no faster, with no more haste than on any other night, serene in his belief that when the time came for him to know whatever it was, that would take care of itself, having already and without even knowing it, even before the possibility, the question, ever arose, declined, refused to accept even the thought of moving also, thinking about the hides, thinking, *If there was just some way he could tell me where to carry my share to get the money* but thinking this only for an instant between two delicate strokes of the blade because almost at once he thought, *I reckon as long as I can catch them I wont have no big trouble finding whoever it is that will buy them.*

So the next morning he helped the Cajan load his few belongings —the pitted rifle, a small bundle of clothing (again they traded, who could not even converse with one another, this time the few cooking vessels, a few rusty traps by definite allocation, and something embracing and abstractional which included the stove, the crude bunk, the house or its occupancy—something—in exchange for one alligator hide)—into the pirogue, then, squatting and as two children divide sticks they divided the hides, separating them into two piles, one-for-me-and-one-for-you, two-for-me-and-two-for-you, and the Cajan loaded his share and shoved away from the platform and paused again, though this time he only put the paddle down, gathered something invisibly into his two hands and flung it violently upward, crying "Boom? Boom?" on a rising inflection, nodding violently to the half-naked and savagely scoriated man on the platform who stared with a sort of grim equability back at him and said, "Sure. Boom. Boom." Then the Cajan went on. He did not look back. They watched him, already paddling rapidly, or the woman did; the convict had already turned.

"Maybe he was trying to tell us to leave too," she said.

"Yah," the convict said. "I thought of that last night. Hand me the paddle." She fetched it to him—the sapling, the one he had been trimming at nightly, not quite finished yet though one more evening would do it (he had been using a spare one of the Cajan's. The other had offered to let him keep it, to include it perhaps with the stove and the bunk and the cabin's freehold, but the convict had declined. Perhaps he had computed it by volume against so much alligator hide, this weighed against one more evening with the tedious and careful blade.) and he departed too with his knotted rope and mace, in the opposite direction, as though not only not content with refusing to quit the place he had been warned against, he must establish and affirm the irrevocable finality of his refusal by penetrating even further and deeper into it. And then and without warning the high fierce drowsing of his solitude gathered itself and struck at him.

He could not have told this if he had tried—this not yet mid-morning and he going on, alone for the first time, no pirogue emerging anywhere to fall in behind him, but he had not expected this anyway, he knew that the others would have departed too; it was not this, it was his very solitude, his desolation which was now his alone and in full since he had elected to remain; the sudden cessation of the paddle, the skiff shooting on for a moment yet while he thought, *What? What?* Then, *No. No. No,* as the silence and solitude and emptiness roared down upon him in a jeering bellow: and now reversed, the skiff spun violently on its heel, he the betrayed driving furiously back toward the platform where he knew it was already too late, that citadel where the very crux and dear breath of his life—the being allowed to work and earn money, that right and privilege which he believed he had earned to himself unaided, asking no favor of anyone or anything save the right to be let alone to pit his will and strength against the sauric protagonist of a land, a region, which he had not asked to be projected into—was being threatened, driving the home-made paddle in grim

fury, coming in sight of the platform at last and seeing the motor
launch lying alongside it with no surprise at all but actually with a
kind of pleasure as though at a visible justification of his outrage
and fear, the privilege of saying *I told you so* to his own affronting,
driving on toward it in a dreamlike state in which there seemed
to be no progress at all, in which, unimpeded and suffocating,
he strove dreamily with a weightless oar, with muscles without
strength or resiliency, at a medium without resistance, seeming to
watch the skiff creep infinitesimally across the sunny water and up
to the platform while a man in the launch (there were five of them
in all) gobbled at him in that same tongue he had been hearing
constantly now for ten days and still knew no word of, just as a
second man, followed by the woman carrying the baby and dressed
again for departure in the faded tunic and the sunbonnet, emerged
from the house, carrying (the man carried several other things but
the convict saw nothing else) the paper-wrapped bundle which the
convict had put behind the rafter ten days ago and no other hand
had touched since, he (the convict) on the platform too now, holding the skiff's painter in one hand and the bludgeonlike paddle in
the other, contriving to speak to the woman at last in a voice
dreamy and suffocating and incredibly calm: "Take it away from
him and carry it back into the house."

"So you can talk English, can you?" the man in the launch said.
"Why didn't you come out like they told you to last night?"

"Out?" the convict said. Again he even looked, glared, at the man
in the launch, contriving even again to control his voice: "I aint
got time to take trips. I'm busy," already turning to the woman
again, his mouth already open to repeat as the dreamy buzzing
voice of the man came to him and he turning once more, in a terrific and absolutely unbearable exasperation, crying, "Flood? What
flood? Hell a mile, it's done passed me twice months ago! It's gone!
What flood?" and then (he did not think this in actual words either
but he knew it, suffered that flashing insight into his own character
or destiny: how there was a peculiar quality of repetitiveness about
his present fate, how not only the almost seminal crises recurred
with a certain monotony, but the very physical circumstances followed a stupidly unimaginative pattern) the man in the launch
said, "Take him" and he was on his feet for a few minutes yet, lashing and striking in panting fury, then once more on his back on
hard unyielding planks while the four men swarmed over him in a

fierce wave of hard bones and panting curses and at last the thin dry vicious snapping of handcuffs.

"Damn it, are you mad?" the man in the launch said. "Cant you understand they are going to dynamite that levee at noon today?— Come on," he said to the others. "Get him aboard. Let's get out of here."

"I want my hides and boat," the convict said.

"Damn your hides," the man in the launch said. "If they dont get that levee blowed pretty soon you can hunt plenty more of them on the capitol steps at Baton Rouge. And this is all the boat you will need and you can say your prayers about it."

"I aint going without my boat," the convict said. He said it calmly and with complete finality, so calm, so final that for almost a minute nobody answered him, they just stood looking quietly down at him as he lay, half-naked, blistered and scarred, helpless and manacled hand and foot, on his back, delivering his ultimatum in a voice peaceful and quiet as that in which you talk to your bed-fellow before going to sleep. Then the man in the launch moved; he spat quietly over the side and said in a voice as calm and quiet as the convict's:

"All right. Bring his boat." They helped the woman, carrying the baby and the paper-wrapped parcel, into the launch. Then they helped the convict to his feet and into the launch too, the shackles on his wrists and ankles clashing. "I'd unlock you if you'd promise to behave yourself," the man said. The convict did not answer this at all.

"I want to hold the rope," he said.

"The rope?"

"Yes," the convict said. "The rope." So they lowered him into the stern and gave him the end of the painter after it had passed the towing cleat, and they went on. The convict did not look back. But then, he did not look forward either, he lay half sprawled, his shackled legs before him, the end of the skiff's painter in one shackled hand. The launch made two other stops; when the hazy wafer of the intolerable sun began to stand once more directly overhead there were fifteen people in the launch; and then the convict, sprawled and motionless, saw the flat brazen land begin to rise and become a greenish-black mass of swamp, bearded and convoluted, this in turn stopping short off and there spread before him an expanse of water embraced by a blue dissolution of shoreline and glittering thinly under the noon, larger than he had ever seen before, the sound of the launch's engine ceasing, the hull sliding on behind its fading bow-wave. "What are you doing?" the leader said.

"It's noon," the helmsman said. "I thought we might hear the dynamite." So they all listened, the launch lost of all forward motion, rocking slightly, the glitter-broken small waves slapping and whispering at the hull, but no sound, no tremble even, came anywhere under the fierce hazy sky; the long moment gathered itself and turned on and noon was past. "All right," the leader said. "Let's go." The engine started again, the hull began to gather speed. The leader came aft and stooped over the convict, key in hand. "I guess you'll have to behave now, whether you want to or not," he said, unlocking the manacles. "Wont you?"

"Yes," the convict said. They went on; after a time the shore vanished completely and a little sea got up. The convict was free now but he lay as before, the end of the skiff's painter in his hand, bent now with three or four turns about his wrist; he turned his head now and then to look back at the towing skiff as it slewed and bounced in the launch's wake; now and then he even looked out over the lake, the eyes alone moving, the face grave and expressionless, thinking, *This is a greater immensity of water, of waste and desolation, than I have ever seen before;* perhaps not; thinking three or four hours later, the shoreline raised again and broken into a clutter of sailing sloops and power cruisers, *These are more boats than I believed existed, a maritime race of which I also had no cognizance* or perhaps not thinking it but just watching as the launch opened the shored gut of the ship canal, the low smoke of the city beyond it, then a wharf, the launch slowing in; a quiet crowd of people watching with that same forlorn passivity he had seen before and whose race he did recognise even though he had not seen Vicksburg when he passed it—the brand, the unmistakable hallmark of the violently homeless, he more so than any, who would have permitted no man to call him one of them.

"All right," the leader said to him. "Here you are."

"The boat," the convict said.

"You've got it. What do you want me to do—give you a receipt for it?"

"No," the convict said. "I just want the boat."

"Take it. Only you ought to have a bookstrap or something to

carry it in." ("Carry it in?" the plump convict said. "Carry it where?
Where would you have to carry it?")

He (the tall one) told that: how he and the woman disembarked
and how one of the men helped him haul the skiff up out of the
water and how he stood there with the end of the painter wrapped
around his wrist and the man bustled up, saying, "All right. Next
load! Next load!" and how he told this man too about the boat and
the man cried, "Boat? Boat?" and how he (the convict) went with
them when they carried the skiff over and racked, berthed, it with
the others and how he lined himself up by a coca-cola sign and the
arch of a draw bridge so he could find the skiff again quick when
he returned, and how he and the woman (he carrying the paper-
wrapped parcel) were herded into a truck and after a while the
truck began to run in traffic, between close houses, then there was a
big building, an armory—

"Armory?" the plump one said. "You mean a jail."

"No. It was a kind of warehouse, with people with bundles laying on the floor." And how he thought maybe his partner might be
there and how he even looked about for the Cajan while waiting
for a chance to get back to the door again, where the soldier was
and how he got back to the door at last, the woman behind him
and his chest actually against the dropped rifle.

"Gwan, gwan," the soldier said. "Get back. They'll give you some
clothes in a minute. You cant walk around the streets that way. And
something to eat too. Maybe your kinfolks will come for you by
that time." And he told that too: how the woman said,

"Maybe if you told him you had some kinfolks here he would let
us out." And how he did not; he could not have expressed this
either, it too deep, too ingrained; he had never yet had to think it
into words through all the long generations of himself—his hillman's sober and jealous respect not for truth but for the power, the
strength, of lying—not to be niggard with lying but rather to use it
with respect and even care, delicate quick and strong, like a fine
and fatal blade. And how they fetched him clothes—a blue jumper
and overalls, and then food too (a brisk starched young woman
saying, "But the baby must be bathed, cleaned. It will die if you
dont" and the woman saying, "Yessum. He might holler some, he
aint never been bathed before. But he's a good baby.") and now it
was night, the unshaded bulbs harsh and savage and forlorn above

the snorers and he rising, gripping the woman awake, and then the window. He told that: how there were doors in plenty, leading he did not know where, but he had a hard time finding a window they could use but he found one at last, he carrying the parcel and the baby too while he climbed through first—"You ought to tore up a sheet and slid down it," the plump convict said. But he needed no sheet, there were cobbles under his feet now, in the rich darkness. The city was there too but he had not seen it yet and would not —the low constant glare; Bienville had stood there too, it had been the figment of an emasculate also calling himself Napoleon but no more, Andrew Jackson had found it one step from Pennsylvania Avenue. But the convict found it considerably further than one step back to the ship canal and the skiff, the coca-cola sign dim now, the draw bridge arching spidery against the jonquil sky at dawn: nor did he tell, any more than about the sixty-foot levee, how he got the skiff back into the water. The lake was behind him now; there was but one direction he could go. When he saw the River again he knew it at once. He should have; it was now ineradicably a part of his past, his life; it would be a part of what he would bequeath, if that were in store for him. But four weeks later it would look different from what it did now, and did: he (the Old Man) had recovered from his debauch, back in banks again, the Old Man, rippling placidly toward the sea, brown and rich as chocolate between levees whose inner faces were wrinkled as though in a frozen and aghast amazement, crowned with the rich green of summer in the willows; beyond them, sixty feet below, slick mules squatted against the broad pull of middle-busters in the richened soil which would not need to be planted, which would need only to be shown a cotton seed to sprout and make; there would be the symmetric miles of strong stalks by July, purple bloom in August, in September the black fields snowed over, spilled, the middles dragged smooth by the long sacks, the long black limber hands plucking, the hot air filled with the whine of gins, the September air then but now June air heavy with locust and (the towns) the smell of new paint and the sour smell of the paste which holds wall paper—the towns, the villages, the little lost wood landings on stilts on the inner face of the levee, the lower storeys bright and rank under the new paint and paper and even the marks on spile and post and tree of May's raging water-height fading beneath each bright silver gust of summer's loud and inconstant rain; there was a

store at the levee's lip, a few saddled and rope-bridled mules in the
sleepy dust, a few dogs, a handful of negroes sitting on the steps beneath the chewing tobacco and malaria medicine signs, and three
white men, one of them a deputy sheriff canvassing for votes to
beat his superior (who had given him his job) in the August primary, all pausing to watch the skiff emerge from the glitter-glare
of the afternoon water and approach and land, a woman carrying
a child stepping out, then a man, a tall man who, approaching,
proved to be dressed in a faded but recently washed and quite
clean suit of penitentiary clothing, stopping in the dust where the
mules dozed and watching with pale cold humorless eyes while
the deputy sheriff was still making toward his armpit that gesture
which everyone present realised was to have produced a pistol in
one flashing motion for a considerable time while still nothing came
of it. It was apparently enough for the newcomer, however.

"You a officer?" he said.

"You damn right I am," the deputy said. "Just let me get this
damn gun—"

"All right," the other said. "Yonder's your boat, and here's the
woman. But I never did find that bastard on the cottonhouse."

ONE OF THE GOVERNOR'S YOUNG MEN ARRIVED AT THE PENITENTIARY
the next morning. That is, he was fairly young (he would not see
thirty again though without doubt he did not want to, there being
that about him which indicated a character which never had and
never would want anything it did not, or was not about to, possess), a Phi Beta Kappa out of an Eastern university, a colonel on
the Governor's staff who did not buy it with a campaign contribu-
tion, who had stood in his negligent Eastern-cut clothes and his
arched nose and lazy contemptuous eyes on the galleries of any
number of little lost backwoods stores and told his stories and received the guffaws of his overalled and spitting hearers and with
the same look in his eyes fondled infants named in memory of the
last administration and in honor (or hope) of the next, and (it was
said of him and doubtless not true) by lazy accident the behinds
of some who were not infants any longer though still not old
enough to vote. He was in the Warden's office with a briefcase, and
presently the deputy warden of the levee was there too. He would
have been sent for presently though not yet, but he came anyhow,

without knocking, with his hat on, calling the Governor's young man loudly by a nickname and striking him with a flat hand on the back and lifted one thigh to the Warden's desk, almost between the Warden and the caller, the emissary. Or the vizier with the command, the knotted cord, as began to appear immediately.

"Well," the Governor's young man said, "you've played the devil, haven't you?" The Warden had a cigar. He had offered the caller one. It had been refused, though presently, while the Warden looked at the back of his neck with hard immobility even a little grim, the deputy leaned and reached back and opened the desk drawer and took one.

"Seems straight enough to me," the Warden said. "He got swept away against his will. He came back as soon as he could and surrendered."

"He even brought that damn boat back," the deputy said. "If he'd a throwed the boat away he could a walked back in three days. But no sir. He's got to bring the boat back. 'Here's your boat and here's the woman but I never found no bastard on no cottonhouse.'" He slapped his knee, guffawing. "Them convicts. A mule's got twice as much sense."

"A mule's got twice as much sense as anything except a rat," the emissary said in his pleasant voice. "But that's not the trouble."

"What is the trouble?" the Warden said.

"This man is dead."

"Hell fire, he aint dead," the deputy said. "He's up yonder in that bunkhouse right now, lying his head off probly. I'll take you up there and you can see him." The Warden was looking at the deputy.

"Look," he said. "Bledsoe was trying to tell me something about that Kate mule's leg. You better go up to the stable and—"

"I done tended to it," the deputy said. He didn't even look at the Warden. He was watching, talking to, the emissary. "No sir. He aint—"

"But he has received an official discharge as being dead. Not a pardon nor a parole either: a discharge. He's either dead, or free. In either case he doesn't belong here." Now both the Warden and the deputy looked at the emissary, the deputy's mouth open a little, the cigar poised in his hand to have its tip bitten off. The emissary spoke pleasantly, extremely distinctly: "On a report of death forwarded to the Governor by the Warden of the Penitentiary." The deputy closed his mouth, though otherwise he didn't move. "On the official evidence of the officer delegated at the time to the charge and returning of the body of the prisoner to the Penitentiary." Now the deputy put the cigar into his mouth and got slowly off the desk, the cigar rolling across his lip as he spoke:

"So that's it. I'm to be it, am I?" He laughed shortly, a stage laugh, two notes. "When I done been right three times running through three separate administrations? That's on a book somewhere too. Somebody in Jackson can find that too. And if they cant, I can show—"

"Three administrations?" the emissary said. "Well, well. That's pretty good."

"You damn right it's good," the deputy said. "The woods are full of folks that didn't." The Warden was again watching the back of the deputy's neck.

"Look," he said. "Why dont you step up to my house and get that bottle of whiskey out of the sideboard and bring it down here?"

"All right," the deputy said. "But I think we better settle this first. I'll tell you what we'll do—"

"We can settle it quicker with a drink or two," the Warden said. "You better step on up to your place and get a coat so the bottle—"

"That'll take too long," the deputy said. "I wont need no coat." He moved to the door, where he stopped and turned. "I'll tell you what to do. Just call twelve men in here and tell him it's a jury—he never seen but one before and he wont know no better—and try him over for robbing that train. Hamp can be the judge."

"You cant try a man twice for the same crime," the emissary said. "He might know that even if he doesn't know a jury when he sees one."

"Look," the Warden said.

"All right. Just call it a new train robbery. Tell him it happened yesterday, tell him he robbed another train while he was gone and just forgot it. He couldn't help himself. Besides, he wont care. He'd just as lief be here as out. He wouldn't have nowhere to go if he was out. None of them do. Turn one loose and be damned if he aint right back here by Christmas like it was a reunion or something, for doing the very same thing they caught him at before." He guffawed again. "Them convicts."

"Look," the Warden said. "While you're there, why dont you

open the bottle and see if the liquor's any good. Take a drink or two. Give yourself time to feel it. If it's not good, no use in bringing it."

"O. K.," the deputy said. He went out this time.

"Couldn't you lock the door?" the emissary said. The Warden squirmed faintly. That is, he shifted his position in his chair.

"After all, he's right," he said. "He's guessed right three times now. And he's kin to all the folks in Pittman County except the niggers."

"Maybe we can work fast then." The emissary opened the briefcase and took out a sheaf of papers. "So there you are," he said.

"There what are?"

"He escaped."

"But he came back voluntarily and surrendered."

"But he escaped."

"All right," the Warden said. "He escaped. Then what?" Now the emissary said look. That is, he said,

"Listen. I'm on per diem. That's tax-payers, votes. And if there's any possible chance for it to occur to anyone to hold an investigation about this, there'll be ten senators and twenty-five representatives here on a special train maybe. On per diem. And it will be mighty hard to keep some of them from going back to Jackson by way of Memphis or New Orleans—on per diem."

"All right," the Warden said. "What does he say to do?"

"This. The man left here in charge of one specific officer. But he was delivered back here by a different one."

"But he surren—" This time the Warden stopped of his own accord. He looked, stared almost, at the emissary. "All right. Go on."

"In specific charge of an appointed and delegated officer, who returned here and reported that the body of the prisoner was no longer in his possession; that, in fact, he did not know where the prisoner was. That's correct, isn't it?" The Warden said nothing. "Isn't that correct?" the emissary said, pleasantly, insistently.

"But you cant do that to him. I tell you he's kin to half the—"

"That's taken care of. The Chief has made a place for him on the highway patrol."

"Hell," the Warden said. "He cant ride a motorcycle. I dont even let him try to drive a truck."

"He wont have to. Surely an amazed and grateful State can supply the man who guessed right three times in succession in Mississippi general elections with a car to ride in and somebody to run it if necessary. He wont even have to stay in it all the time. Just so he's near enough so when an inspector sees the car and stops and blows the horn of it he can hear it and come out."

"I still dont like it," the Warden said.

"Neither do I. Your man could have saved all of this if he had just gone on and drowned himself, as he seems to have led everybody to believe he had. But he didn't. And the Chief says do. Can you think of anything better?" The Warden sighed.

"No," he said.

"All right." The emissary opened the papers and uncapped a pen and began to write. "Attempted escape from the Penitentiary, ten years' additional sentence," he said. "Deputy Warden Buckworth transferred to Highway Patrol. Call it for meritorious service even if you want to. It wont matter now. Done?"

"Done," the Warden said.

"Then suppose you send for him. Get it over with." So the Warden sent for the tall convict and he arrived presently, saturnine and grave, in his new bed-ticking, his jowls blue and close under the sunburn, his hair recently cut and neatly parted and smelling faintly of the prison barber's (the barber was in for life, for murdering his wife, still a barber) pomade. The Warden called him by name.

"You had bad luck, didn't you?" The convict said nothing. "They are going to have to add ten years to your time."

"All right," the convict said.

"It's hard luck. I'm sorry."

"All right," the convict said. "If that's the rule." So they gave him the ten years more and the Warden gave him the cigar and now he sat, jackknifed backward into the space between the upper and lower bunks, the unlighted cigar in his hand while the plump convict and four others listened to him. Or questioned him, that is, since it was all done, finished, now and he was safe again, so maybe it wasn't even worth talking about any more.

"All right," the plump one said. "So you come back into the River. Then what?"

"Nothing. I rowed."

"Wasn't it pretty hard rowing coming back?"

"The water was still high. It was running pretty hard still. I never made much speed for the first week or two. After that it got better."

Then, suddenly and quietly, something—the inarticulateness, the innate and inherited reluctance for speech, dissolved and he found himself, listened to himself, telling it quietly, the words coming not fast but easily to the tongue as he required them: How he paddled on (he found out by trying it that he could make better speed, if you could call it speed, next the bank—this after he had been carried suddenly and violently out to midstream before he could prevent it and found himself, the skiff, travelling back toward the region from which he had just escaped and he spent the better part of the morning getting back inshore and up to the canal again from which he had emerged at dawn) until night came and they tied up to the bank and ate some of the food he had secreted in his jumper before leaving the armory in New Orleans and the woman and the infant slept in the boat as usual and when daylight came they went on and tied up again that night too and the next day the food gave out and he came to a landing, a town, he didn't notice the name of it, and he got a job. It was a cane farm—

"Cane?" one of the other convicts said. "What does anybody want to raise cane for? You cut cane. You have to fight it where I come from. You burn it just to get shut of it."

"It was sorghum," the tall convict said.

"Sorghum?" another said. "A whole farm just raising sorghum? *Sorghum*? What did they do with it?" The tall one didn't know. He didn't ask, he just came up the levee and there was a truck waiting full of niggers and a white man said, "You there. Can you run a shovel plow?" and the convict said, "Yes," and the man said, "Jump in then," and the convict said, "Only I've got a—"

"Yes," the plump one said. "That's what I been aiming to ask. What did—" The tall convict's face was grave, his voice was calm, just a little short:

"They had tents for the folks to live in. They were behind." The plump one blinked at him.

"Did they think she was your wife?"

"I dont know. I reckon so." The plump one blinked at him.

"Wasn't she your wife? Just from time to time kind of, you might say?" The tall one didn't answer this at all. After a moment he raised the cigar and appeared to examine a loosening of the wrapper because after another moment he licked the cigar carefully near the end. "All right," the plump one said. "Then what?" So he worked there four days. He didn't like it. Maybe that was why: that he too could not quite put credence in that much of what he believed to be sorghum. So when they told him it was Saturday and paid him and the white man told him about somebody who was going to Baton Rouge the next day in a motor boat, he went to see the man and took the six dollars he had earned and bought food with it and tied the skiff behind the motor boat and went to Baton Rouge. It didn't take long and even after they left the motor boat at Baton Rouge and he was paddling again it seemed to the convict that the River was lower and the current not so fast, so hard, so they made fair speed, tying up to the bank at night among the willows, the woman and baby sleeping in the skiff as of old. Then the food gave out again. This time it was a wood landing, the wood stacked and waiting, a wagon and team being unladen of another load. The men with the wagon told him about the sawmill and helped him drag the skiff up the levee; they wanted to leave it there but he would not so they loaded it onto the wagon too and he and the woman got on the wagon too and they went to the sawmill. They gave them one room in a house to live in here. They paid two dollars a day and furnish. The work was hard. He liked it. He stayed there eight days.

"If you liked it so well, why did you quit?" the plump one said. The tall convict examined the cigar again, holding it up where the light fell upon the rich chocolate-colored flank.

"I got in trouble," he said.

"What trouble?"

"Woman. It was a fellow's wife."

"You mean you had been toting one piece up and down the country day and night for over a month, and now the first time you have a chance to stop and catch your breath almost you got to get in trouble over another one?" The tall convict had thought of that. He remembered it: how there were times, seconds, at first when if it had not been for the baby he might have, might have tried. But they were just seconds because in the next instant his whole being would seem to flee the very idea in a kind of savage and horrified revulsion; he would find himself looking from a distance at this millstone which the force and power of blind and risible Motion had fastened upon him, thinking, saying aloud actually, with harsh and savage outrage even though it had been two years since he had had a woman and that a nameless and not young negress, a casual, a straggler whom he had caught more or less by chance on one of

the fifth-Sunday visiting days, the man—husband or sweetheart—
whom she had come to see having been shot by a trusty a week or
so previous and she had not heard about it: "She aint even no good
to me for that."

"But you got this one, didn't you?" the plump convict said.

"Yah," the tall one said. The plump one blinked at him.

"Was it good?"

"It's all good," one of the others said. "Well? Go on. How many
more did you have on the way back? Sometimes when a fellow
starts getting it it looks like he just cant miss even if—" That was
all, the convict told them. They left the sawmill fast, he had no
time to buy food until they reached the next landing. There he
spent the whole sixteen dollars he had earned and they went on.
The River was lower now, there was no doubt of it, and sixteen dollars' worth looked like a lot of food and he thought ι..aybe it would
do, would be enough. But maybe there was more current in the
River still than it looked like. But this time it was Mississippi, it was
cotton; the plow handles felt right to his palms again, the strain
and squat of the slick buttocks against the middle buster's blade
was what he knew, even though they paid but a dollar a day here.
But that did it. He told it: they told him it was Saturday again and
paid him and he told about it—night, a smoked lantern in a disc of
worn and barren earth as smooth as silver, a circle of crouching
figures, the importunate murmurs and ejaculations, the meagre piles
of worn bills beneath the crouching knees, the dotted cubes clicking and scuttering in the dust; that did it. "How much did you
win?" the second convict said.

"Enough," the tall one said.

"But how much?"

"Enough," the tall one said. It was enough exactly; he gave it all
to the man who owned the second motor boat (he would not need
food now), he and the woman in the launch now and the skiff
towing behind, the woman with the baby and the paper-wrapped
parcel beneath his peaceful hand, on his lap; almost at once he
recognised, not Vicksburg because he had never seen Vicksburg, but
the trestle beneath which on his roaring wave of trees and houses
and dead animals he had shot, accompanied by thunder and lightning, a month and three weeks ago; he looked at it once without
heat, even without interest as the launch went on. But now he began
to watch the bank, the levee. He didn't know how he would know

but he knew he would, and then it was early afternoon and sure
enough the moment came and he said to the launch owner: "I reckon
this will do."

"Here?" the launch owner said. "This dont look like anywhere to
me."

"I reckon this is it," the convict said. So the launch put inshore,
the engine ceased, it drifted up and lay against the levee and the
owner cast the skiff loose.

"You better let me take you on until we come to something," he
said. "That was what I promised."

"I reckon this will do," the convict said. So they got out and
he stood with the grapevine painter in his hand while the launch
purred again and drew away, already curving; he did not watch
it. He laid the bundle down and made the painter fast to a willow
root and picked up the bundle and turned. He said no word, he
mounted the levee, passing the mark, the tide-line of the old raging, dry now and lined, traversed by shallow and empty cracks like
foolish and deprecatory senile grins, and entered a willow clump
and removed the overalls and shirt they had given him in New
Orleans and dropped them without even looking to see where they
fell and opened the parcel and took out the other, the known, the
desired, faded a little, stained and worn, but clean, recognisable,
and put them on and returned to the skiff and took up the paddle.
The woman was already in it.

The plump convict stood blinking at him. "So you come back,"
he said. "Well well." Now they all watched the tall convict as he bit
the end from the cigar neatly and with complete deliberation and
spat it out and licked the bite smooth and damp and took a match
from his pocket and examined the match for a moment as though
to be sure it was a good one, worthy of the cigar perhaps, and
raked it up his thigh with the same deliberation—a motion almost
too slow to set fire to it, it would seem—and held it until the
flame burned clear and free of sulphur, then put it to the cigar. The
plump one watched him, blinking rapidly and steadily. "And they
give you ten years more for running. That's bad. A fellow can get
used to what they give him at first, to start off with, I dont care
how much it is, even a hundred and ninety-nine years. But ten
more years. Ten years more, on top of that. When you never expected it. Ten more years to have to do without no society, no
female companionship—" He blinked steadily at the tall convict.

But he (the tall convict) had thought of that too. He had had a sweetheart. That is, he had gone to church singings and picnics with her—a girl a year or so younger than he, short-legged, with ripe breasts and a heavy mouth and dull eyes like ripe muscadines, who owned a baking-powder can almost full of ear-rings and brooches and rings bought (or presented at suggestion) from tencent stores. Presently he had divulged his plan to her, and there were times later when, musing, the thought occurred to him that possibly if it had not been for her he would not actually have attempted it—this a mere feeling, unworded, since he could not have phrased this either: that who to know what Capone's uncandled bridehood she might not have dreamed to be her destiny and fate, what fast car filled with authentic colored glass and machine guns, running traffic lights. But that was all past and done when the notion first occurred to him, and in the third month of his incarceration she came to see him. She wore ear-rings and a bracelet or so which he had never seen before and it never became quite clear how she had got that far from home, and she cried violently for the first three minutes though presently (and without his ever knowing either exactly how they had got separated or how she had made the acquaintance) he saw her in animated conversation with one of the guards. But she kissed him before she left that evening and said she would return the first chance she got, clinging to him, sweating a little, smelling of scent and soft young female flesh, slightly pneumatic. But she didn't come back though he continued to write to her, and seven months later he got an answer. It was a postcard, a colored lithograph of a Birmingham hotel, a childish X inked heavily across one window, the heavy writing on the reverse slanted and primer-like too: *This is where were honnymonning at. Your friend (Mrs) Vernon Waldrip*

The plump convict stood blinking at the tall one, rapidly and steadily. "Yes, sir," he said. "It's them ten more years that hurt. Ten more years to do without a woman, no woman a tall a fellow wants—" He blinked steadily and rapidly, watching the tall one. The other did not move, jackknifed backward between the two bunks, grave and clean, the cigar burning smoothly and richly in his clean steady hand, the smoke wreathing upward across his face saturnine, humorless, and calm. "Ten more years—"

"Women——!" the tall convict said.

Spotted Horses

– 1 –

A LITTLE WHILE BEFORE SUNDOWN THE MEN LOUNGING ABOUT THE gallery of the store saw, coming up the road from the south, a covered wagon drawn by mules and followed by a considerable string of obviously alive objects which in the levelling sun resembled vari-sized and -colored tatters torn at random from large billboards—circus posters, say—attached to the rear of the wagon and inherent with its own separate and collective motion, like the tail of a kite.

"What in the hell is that?" one said.

"It's a circus," Quick said. They began to rise, watching the wagon. Now they could see that the animals behind the wagon were horses. Two men rode in the wagon.

"Hell fire," the first man—his name was Freeman—said. "It's Flem Snopes." They were all standing when the wagon came up and stopped and Snopes got down and approached the steps. He might have departed only this morning. He wore the same cloth cap, the minute bow tie against the white shirt, the same gray trousers. He mounted the steps.

"Howdy, Flem," Quick said. The other looked briefly at all of them and none of them, mounting the steps. "Starting you a circus?"

"Gentlemen," he said. He crossed the gallery; they made way for him. Then they descended the steps and approached the wagon, at the tail of which the horses stood in a restive clump, larger than rabbits and gaudy as parrots and shackled to one another and to the wagon itself with sections of barbed wire. Calico-coated, small-bodied, with delicate legs and pink faces in which their mismatched eyes rolled wild and subdued, they huddled, gaudy motionless and alert, wild as deer, deadly as rattlesnakes, quiet as doves. The men stood at a respectful distance, looking at them. At that moment Jody Varner came through the group, shouldering himself to the front of it.

"Watch yourself, doc," a voice said from the rear. But it was al-

433

ready too late. The nearest animal rose on its hind legs with lightning rapidity and struck twice with its forefeet at Varner's face,
faster than a boxer, the movement of its surge against the wire
which held it travelling backward among the rest of the band in a
wave of thuds and lunges. "Hup, you broom-tailed hay-burning
sidewinders," the same voice said. This was the second man who
had arrived in the wagon. He was a stranger. He wore a heavy
densely black moustache, a wide pale hat. When he thrust himself
through and turned to herd them back from the horses they saw,
thrust into the hip pockets of his tight jeans pants, the butt of a
heavy pearl-handled pistol and a florid carton such as small cakes
come in. "Keep away from them, boys," he said. "They've got kind
of skittish, they aint been rode in so long."

"Since when have they been rode?" Quick said. The stranger
looked at Quick. He had a broad, quite cold, wind-gnawed face
and bleak cold eyes. His belly fitted neat and smooth as a peg into
the tight trousers.

"I reckon that was when they were rode on the ferry to get
across the Mississippi River," Varner said. The stranger looked at
him. "My name's Varner," Jody said.

"Hipps," the other said. "Call me Buck." Across the left side of
his head, obliterating the tip of that ear, was a savage and recent
gash gummed over with a blackish substance like axle-grease. They
looked at the scar. Then they watched him remove the carton from
his pocket and tilt a gingersnap into his hand and put the gingersnap into his mouth, beneath the moustache.

"You and Flem have some trouble back yonder?" Quick said. The
stranger ceased chewing. When he looked directly at anyone, his
eyes became like two pieces of flint turned suddenly up in dug
earth.

"Back where?" he said.

"Your nigh ear," Quick said.

"Oh," the other said. "That." He touched his ear. "That was my
mistake. I was absent-minded one night when I was staking them
out. Studying about something else and forgot how long the wire
was." He chewed. They looked at his ear. "Happen to any man
careless around a horse. Put a little axle-dope on it and you wont
notice it tomorrow though. They're pretty lively now, lazing along
all day doing nothing. It'll work out of them in a couple of days."
He put another gingersnap into his mouth, chewing, "Dont you be-

lieve they'll gentle?" No one answered. They looked at the ponies, grave and noncommittal. Jody turned and went back into the store. "Them's good, gentle ponies," the stranger said. "Watch now." He put the carton back into his pocket and approached the horses, his hand extended. The nearest one was standing on three legs now. It appeared to be asleep. Its eyelid drooped over the cerulean eye; its head was shaped like an ironing-board. Without even raising the eyelid it flicked its head, the yellow teeth cropped. For an instant it and the man appeared to be inextricable in one violence. Then they became motionless, the stranger's high heels dug into the earth, one hand gripping the animal's nostrils, holding the horse's head wrenched half around while it breathed in hoarse, smothered groans. "See?" the stranger said in a panting voice, the veins standing white and rigid in his neck and along his jaw. "See? All you got to do is handle them a little and work hell out of them for a couple of days. Now look out. Give me room back there." They gave back a little. The stranger gathered himself then sprang away. As he did so, a second horse slashed at his back, severing his vest from collar to hem down the back exactly as the trick swordsman severs a floating veil with one stroke.

"Sho now," Quick said. "But suppose a man dont happen to own a vest."

At that moment Jody Varner, followed by the blacksmith, thrust through them again. "All right, Buck," he said. "Better get them on into the lot. Eck here will help you." The stranger, the several halves of the vest swinging from either shoulder, mounted to the wagon seat, the blacksmith following.

"Get up, you transmogrified hallucinations of Job and Jezebel," the stranger said. The wagon moved on, the tethered ponies coming gaudily into motion behind it, behind which in turn the men followed at a respectful distance, on up the road and into the lane and so to the lot gate behind Mrs Littlejohn's. Eck got down and opened the gate. The wagon passed through but when the ponies saw the fence the herd surged backward against the wire which attached it to the wagon, standing on its collective hind legs and then trying to turn within itself, so that the wagon moved backward for a few feet until the Texan, cursing, managed to saw the mules about and so lock the wheels. The men following had already fallen rapidly back. "Here, Eck," the Texan said. "Get up here and take the reins." The blacksmith got back in the wagon and took the reins. Then they watched the Texan descend, carrying a looped-up blacksnake whip, and go around to the rear of the herd and drive it through the gate, the whip snaking about the harlequin rumps in methodical and pistol-like reports. Then the watchers hurried across Mrs Littlejohn's yard and mounted to the veranda, one end of which overlooked the lot.

"How you reckon he ever got them tied together?" Freeman said.

"I'd a heap rather watch how he aims to turn them loose," Quick said. The Texan had climbed back into the halted wagon. Presently he and Eck both appeared at the rear end of the open hood. The Texan grasped the wire and began to draw the first horse up to the wagon, the animal plunging and surging back against the wire as though trying to hang itself, the contagion passing back through the herd from animal to animal until they were rearing and plunging again against the wire.

"Come on, grab a holt," the Texan said. Eck grasped the wire also. The horses laid back against it, the pink faces tossing above the back-surging mass. "Pull him up, pull him up," the Texan said sharply. "They couldn't get up here in the wagon even if they wanted to." The wagon moved gradually backward until the head of the first horse was snubbed up to the tail-gate. The Texan took a turn of the wire quickly about one of the wagon stakes. "Keep the slack out of it," he said. He vanished and reappeared, almost in the same second, with a pair of heavy wire-cutters. "Hold them like that," he said, and leaped. He vanished, broad hat, flapping vest, wire-cutters and all, into a kaleidoscopic maelstrom of long teeth and wild eyes and slashing feet, from which presently the horses began to burst one by one like partridges flushing, each wearing a necklace of barbed wire. The first one crossed the lot at top speed, on a straight line. It galloped into the fence without any diminution whatever. The wire gave, recovered, and slammed the horse to earth where it lay for a moment, glaring, its legs still galloping in air. It scrambled up without having ceased to gallop and crossed the lot and galloped into the opposite fence and was slammed again to earth. The others were now freed. They whipped and whirled about the lot like dizzy fish in a bowl. It had seemed like a big lot until now, but now the very idea that all that fury and motion should be transpiring inside any one fence was something to be repudiated with contempt, like a mirror trick. From the ultimate dust the stranger, carrying the wire-cutters and his vest completely gone now, emerged. He was not running, he merely moved with a light-poised and watchful celerity, weaving among the calico rushes of the animals, feinting and dodging like a boxer until he reached the gate and crossed the yard and mounted to the veranda. One sleeve of his shirt hung only at one point from his shoulder. He ripped it off and wiped his face with it and threw it away and took out the paper carton and shook a gingersnap into his hand. He was breathing only a little heavily. "Pretty lively now," he said. "But it'll work out of them in a couple of days." The ponies still streaked back and forth through the growing dusk like hysterical fish, but not so violently now.

"What'll you give a man to reduce them odds a little for you?" Quick said. The Texan looked at him, the eyes bleak, pleasant and hard above the chewing jaw, the heavy moustache. "To take one of them off your hands?" Quick said.

At that moment the little periwinkle-eyed boy came along the veranda, saying, "Papa, papa; where's papa?"

"Who you looking for, sonny?" one said.

"It's Eck's boy," Quick said. "He's still out yonder in the wagon. Helping Mr Buck here." The boy went on to the end of the veranda, in diminutive overalls—a miniature replica of the men themselves.

"Papa," he said. "Papa." The blacksmith was still leaning from the rear of the wagon, still holding the end of the severed wire. The ponies, bunched for the moment, now slid past the wagon, flowing, stringing out again so that they appeared to have doubled in number, rushing on; the hard rapid light patter of unshod hooves came out of the dust. "Mamma says to come on to supper," the boy said.

The moon was almost full then. When supper was over and they had gathered again along the veranda, the alteration was hardly one of visibility even. It was merely a translation from the lapidary-dimensional of day to the treacherous and silver receptivity in which the horses huddled in mazy camouflage, or singly or in pairs rushed, fluid, phantom, and unceasing, to huddle again in mirage-like clumps from which came high abrupt squeals and the vicious thudding of hooves.

Ratliff was among them now. He had returned just before supper. He had not dared to take his team into the lot at all. They were now in Bookwright's stable a half mile from the store. "So Flem has come home again," he said. "Well, well, well. Will Varner

paid to get him to Texas, so I reckon it aint no more than fair for
you fellows to pay the freight on him back." From the lot there
came a high thin squeal. One of the animals emerged. It seemed
not to gallop but to flow, bodiless, without dimension. Yet there
was the rapid light beat of hard hooves on the packed earth.

"He aint said they was his yet," Quick said.

"He aint said they aint neither," Freeman said.

"I see," Ratliff said. "That's what you are holding back on. Until
he tells you whether they are his or not. Or maybe you can wait
until the auction's over and split up and some can follow Flem
and some can follow that Texas fellow and watch to see which
one spends the money. But then, when a man's done got trimmed,
I dont reckon he cares who's got the money."

"Maybe if Ratliff would leave here tonight, they wouldn't make
him buy one of them ponies tomorrow," a third said.

"That's a fact," Ratliff said. "A fellow can dodge a Snopes if he
just starts lively enough. In fact, I dont believe he would have to
pass more than two folks before he would have another victim
intervened betwixt them. You folks aint going to buy them things
sho enough, are you?" Nobody answered. They sat on the steps,
their backs against the veranda posts, or on the railing itself. Only
Ratliff and Quick sat in chairs, so that to them the others were
black silhouettes against the dreaming lambence of the moonlight
beyond the veranda. The pear tree across the road opposite was
now in full and frosty bloom, the twigs and branches springing not
outward from the limbs but standing motionless and perpendicular
above the horizontal boughs like the separate and upstreaming
hair of a drowned woman sleeping upon the uttermost floor of the
windless and tideless sea.

"Anse McCallum brought two of them horses back from Texas
once," one of the men on the steps said. He did not move to speak.
He was not speaking to anyone. "It was a good team. A little light.
He worked it for ten years. Light work, it was."

"I mind it," another said. "Anse claimed he traded fourteen rifle
cartridges for both of them, didn't he?"

"It was the rifle too, I heard," a third said.

"No, it was just the shells," the first said. "The fellow wanted to
swap him four more for the rifle too, but Anse said he never needed
them. Cost too much to get six of them back to Mississippi."

"Sho," the second said. "When a man dont have to invest so

much into a horse or a team, he dont need to expect so much from it." The three of them were not talking any louder, they were merely talking among themselves, to one another, as if they sat there alone. Ratliff, invisible in the shadow against the wall, made a sound, harsh, sardonic, not loud.

"Ratliff's laughing," a fourth said.

"Dont mind me," Ratliff said. The three speakers had not moved. They did not move now, yet there seemed to gather about the three silhouettes something stubborn, convinced, and passive, like children who have been chidden. A bird, a shadow, fleet and dark and swift, curved across the moonlight, upward into the pear tree and began to sing; a mockingbird.

"First one I've noticed this year," Freeman said.

"You can hear them along Whiteleaf every night," the first man said. "I heard one in February. In that snow. Singing in a gum."

"Gum is the first tree to put out," the third said. "That was why. It made it feel like singing, fixing to put out that way. That was why it taken a gum."

"Gum first to put out?" Quick said. "What about willow?"

"Willow aint a tree," Freeman said. "It's a weed."

"Well, I dont know what it is," the fourth said. "But it aint no weed. Because you can grub up a weed and you are done with it. I been grubbing up a clump of willows outen my spring pasture for fifteen years. They are the same size every year. Only difference is, it's just two or three more trees every time."

"And if I was you," Ratliff said, "that's just exactly where I would be come sunup tomorrow. Which of course you aint going to do. I reckon there aint nothing under the sun or in Frenchman's Bend neither that can keep you folks from giving Flem Snopes and that Texas man your money. But I'd sholy like to know just exactly who I was giving my money to. Seems like Eck here would tell you. Seems like he'd do that for his neighbors, dont it? Besides being Flem's cousin, him and that boy of his, Wallstreet, helped that Texas man tote water for them tonight and Eck's going to help him feed them in the morning too. Why, maybe Eck will be the one that will catch them and lead them up one at a time for you folks to bid on them. Aint that right, Eck?"

The other man sitting on the steps with his back against the post was the blacksmith. "I dont know," he said.

"Boys," Ratliff said, "Eck knows all about them horses. Flem's told him, how much they cost and how much him and that Texas man aim to get for them, make off of them. Come on, Eck. Tell us." The other did not move, sitting on the top step, not quite facing them, sitting there beneath the successive layers of their quiet and intent concentrated listening and waiting.

"I dont know," he said. Ratliff began to laugh. He sat in the chair, laughing while the others sat or lounged upon the steps and the railing, sitting beneath his laughing as Eck had sat beneath their listening and waiting. Ratliff ceased laughing. He rose. He yawned, quite loud.

"All right. You folks can buy them critters if you want to. But me, I'd just as soon buy a tiger or a rattlesnake. And if Flem Snopes offered me either one of them, I would be afraid to touch it for fear it would turn out to be a painted dog or a piece of garden hose when I went up to take possession of it. I bid you one and all goodnight." He entered the house. They did not look after him, though after a while they all shifted a little and looked down into the lot, upon the splotchy, sporadic surge and flow of the horses, from among which from time to time came an abrupt squeal, a thudding blow. In the pear tree the mockingbird's idiot reiteration pulsed and purled.

"Anse McCallum made a good team outen them two of hisn," the first man said. "They was a little light. That was all."

When the sun rose the next morning a wagon and three saddled mules stood in Mrs Littlejohn's lane and six men and Eck Snopes' son were already leaning on the fence, looking at the horses which huddled in a quiet clump before the barn door, watching the men in their turn. A second wagon came up the road and into the lane and stopped, and then there were eight men beside the boy standing at the fence, beyond which the horses stood, their blue-and-brown eyeballs rolling alertly in their gaudy faces. "So this here is the Snopes circus, is it?" one of the newcomers said. He glanced at the faces, then he went to the end of the row and stood beside the blacksmith and the little boy. "Are them Flem's horses?" he said to the blacksmith.

"Eck dont know who them horses belong to anymore than we do," one of the others said. "He knows that Flem come here on the same wagon with them, because he saw him. But that's all."

"And all he will know," a second said. "His own kin will be the

last man in the world to find out anything about Flem Snopes' business."

"No," the first said. "He wouldn't even be that. The first man
Flem would tell his business to would be the man that was left
after the last man died. Flem Snopes dont even tell himself what
he is up to. Not if he was laying in bed with himself in a empty
house in the dark of the moon."

"That's a fact," a third said. "Flem would trim Eck or any other
of his kin quick as he would us. Aint that right, Eck?"

"I dont know," Eck said. They were watching the horses, which
at that moment broke into a high-eared, stiff-kneed swirl and
flowed in a patchwork wave across the lot and brought up again,
facing the men along the fence, so they did not hear the Texan until he was among them. He wore a new shirt and another vest a little too small for him and he was just putting the paper carton back
into his hip pocket.

"Morning, morning," he said. "Come to get an early pick, have
you? Want to make me an offer for one or two before the bidding starts and runs the prices up?" They had not looked at the
stranger long. They were not looking at him now, but at the
horses in the lot, which had lowered their heads, snuffing into
the dust.

"I reckon we'll look a while first," one said.

"You are in time to look at them eating breakfast, anyhow," the
Texan said. "Which is more than they done without they staid
up all night." He opened the gate and entered it. At once the
horses jerked their heads up, watching him. "Here, Eck," the Texan
said over his shoulder, "two or three of you boys help me drive
them into the barn." After a moment Eck and two others approached the gate, the little boy at his father's heels, though the
other did not see him until he turned to shut the gate.

"You stay out of here," Eck said. "One of them things will snap
your head off same as a acorn before you even know it." He shut
the gate and went on after the others, whom the Texan had now
waved fanwise outward as he approached the horses which now
drew into a restive huddle, beginning to mill slightly, watching the
men. Mrs Littlejohn came out of the kitchen and crossed the yard
to the woodpile, watching the lot. She picked up two or three
sticks of wood and paused, watching the lot again. Now there were
two more men standing at the fence.

"Come on, come on," the Texan said. "They wont hurt you. They just aint never been in under a roof before."

"I just as lief let them stay out here, if that's what they want to do," Eck said.

"Get yourself a stick—there's a bunch of wagon stakes against the fence yonder—and when one of them tries to rush you, bust him over the head so he will understand what you mean." One of the men went to the fence and got three of the stakes and returned and distributed them. Mrs Littlejohn, her armful of wood complete now, paused again halfway back to the house, looking into the lot. The little boy was directly behind his father again, though this time the father had not discovered him yet. The men advanced toward the horses, the huddle of which began to break into gaudy units turning inward upon themselves. The Texan was cursing them in a loud steady cheerful voice. "Get in there, you banjo-faced jack rabbits. Dont hurry them, now. Let them take their time. Hi! Get in there. What do you think that barn is—a law court maybe? Or maybe a church and somebody is going to take up a collection on you?" The animals fell slowly back. Now and then one feinted to break from the huddle, the Texan driving it back each time with skillfully thrown bits of dirt. Then one at the rear saw the barn door just behind it but before the herd could break the Texan snatched the wagon stake from Eck and, followed by one of the other men, rushed at the horses and began to lay about the heads and shoulders, choosing by unerring instinct the point animal and striking it first square in the face then on the withers as it turned and then on the rump as it turned further, so that when the break came it was reversed and the entire herd rushed into the long open hallway and brought up against the further wall with a hollow, thunderous sound like that of a collapsing mine-shaft. "Seems to have held all right," the Texan said. He and the other man slammed the half-length doors and looked over them into the tunnel of the barn, at the far end of which the ponies were now a splotchy phantom moiling punctuated by crackings of wooden partitions and the dry reports of hooves which gradually died away. "Yep, it held all right," the Texan said. The other two came to the doors and looked over them. The little boy came up beside his father now, trying to see through a crack, and Eck saw him.

"Didn't I tell you to stay out of here?" Eck said. "Dont you know them things will kill you quicker than you can say scat? You go and get outside of that fence and stay there."

"Why dont you get your paw to buy you one of them, Wall?" one of the men said.

"Me buy one of them things?" Eck said. "When I can go to the river anytime and catch me a snapping turtle or a moccasin for nothing? You go on, now. Get out of here and stay out." The Texan had entered the barn. One of the men closed the doors after him and put the bar up again and over the top of the doors they watched the Texan go on down the hallway, toward the ponies which now huddled like gaudy phantoms in the gloom, quiet now and already beginning to snuff experimentally into the long lip-worn trough fastened against the rear wall. The little boy had merely gone around behind his father, to the other side, where he stood peering now through a knot-hole in a plank. The Texan opened a smaller door in the wall and entered it, though almost immediately he reappeared.

"I dont see nothing but shelled corn in here," he said. "Snopes said he would send some hay up here last night."

"Wont they eat corn either?" one of the men said.

"I dont know," the Texan said. "They aint never seen any that I know of. We'll find out in a minute though." He disappeared, though they could still hear him in the crib. Then he emerged once more, carrying a big double-ended feed-basket, and retreated into the gloom where the parti-colored rumps of the horses were now ranged quietly along the feeding-trough. Mrs Littlejohn appeared once more, on the veranda this time, carrying a big brass dinner bell. She raised it to make the first stroke. A small commotion set up among the ponies as the Texan approached but he began to speak to them at once, in a brisk loud unemphatic mixture of cursing and cajolery, disappearing among them. The men at the door heard the dry rattling of the corn-pellets into the trough, a sound broken by a single snort of amazed horror. A plank cracked with a loud report; before their eyes the depths of the hallway dissolved in loud fury, and while they stared over the doors, unable yet to begin to move, the entire interior exploded into mad tossing shapes like a downrush of flames.

"Hell fire," one of them said. "Jump!" he shouted. The three turned and ran frantically for the wagon, Eck last. Several voices from the fence were now shouting something but Eck did not even hear them until, in the act of scrambling madly at the tail-gate, he looked behind him and saw the little boy still leaning to the knot-hole in the door which in the next instant vanished into matchwood, the knot-hole itself exploding from his eye and leaving him, motionless in the diminutive overalls and still leaning forward a little until he vanished utterly beneath the towering parti-colored wave full of feet and glaring eyes and wild teeth which, overtopping, burst into scattering units, revealing at last the gaping orifice and the little boy still standing in it, unscratched, his eye still leaned to the vanished knot-hole.

"Wall!" Eck roared. The little boy turned and ran for the wagon. The horses were whipping back and forth across the lot, as if while in the barn they had once more doubled their number; two of them rushed up quattering and galloped all over the boy again without touching him as he ran, earnest and diminutive and seemingly without progress, though he reached the wagon at last, from which Eck, his sunburned skin now a sickly white, reached down and snatched the boy into the wagon by the straps of his overalls and slammed him face down across his knees and caught up a coiled hitching-rope from the bed of the wagon.

"Didn't I tell you to get out of here?" Eck said in a shaking voice. "Didn't I tell you?"

"If you're going to whip him, you better whip the rest of us too and then one of us can frail hell out of you," one of the others said.

"Or better still, take the rope and hang that durn fellow yonder," the second said. The Texan was now standing in the wrecked door of the barn, taking the gingersnap carton from his hip pocket. "Before he kills the rest of Frenchman's Bend too."

"You mean Flem Snopes," the first said. The Texan tilted the carton above his other open palm. The horses still rushed and swirled back and forth but they were beginning to slow now, trotting on high, stiff legs, although their eyes were still rolling whitely and various.

"I misdoubted that damn shell corn all along," the Texan said. "But at least they have seen what it looks like. They cant claim they aint got nothing out of this trip." He shook the carton over his open hand. Nothing came out of it. Mrs Littlejohn on the veranda made the first stroke with the dinner bell; at the sound the horses rushed again, the earth of the lot becoming vibrant with the light dry clatter of hooves. The Texan crumpled the carton and threw it aside. "Chuck wagon," he said. There were three more wagons in the lane now and there were twenty or more men at the fence when the Texan, followed by his three assistants and the little boy, passed through the gate. The bright cloudless early sun gleamed upon the pearl butt of the pistol in his hip pocket and upon the bell which Mrs Littlejohn still rang, peremptory, strong, and loud.

When the Texan, picking his teeth with a splintered kitchen match, emerged from the house twenty minutes later, the tethered wagons and riding horses and mules extended from the lot gate to Varner's store, and there were more than fifty men now standing along the fence beside the gate, watching him quietly, a little covertly, as he approached, rolling a little, slightly bowlegged, the high heels of his carved boots printing neatly into the dust. "Morning, gents," he said. "Here, Bud," he said to the little boy, who stood slightly behind him, looking at the protruding butt of the pistol. He took a coin from his pocket and gave it to the boy. "Run to the store and get me a box of gingersnaps." He looked about at the quiet faces, protuberant, sucking his teeth. He rolled the match from one side of his mouth to the other without touching it. "You boys done made your picks, have you? Ready to start her off, hah?" They did not answer. They were not looking at him now. That is, he began to have the feeling that each face had stopped looking at him the second before his gaze reached it. After a moment Freeman said:

"Aint you going to wait for Flem?"

"Why?" the Texan said. Then Freeman stopped looking at him too. There was nothing in Freeman's face either. There was nothing, no alteration, in the Texan's voice. "Eck, you done already picked out yours. So we can start her off when you are ready."

"I reckon not," Eck said. "I wouldn't buy nothing I was afraid to walk up and touch."

"Them little ponies?" the Texan said. "You helped water and feed them. I bet that boy of yours could walk up to any one of them."

"He better not let me catch him," Eck said. The Texan looked about at the quiet faces, his gaze at once abstract and alert, with an impenetrable surface quality like flint, as though the surface were impervious or perhaps there was nothing behind it.

"Them ponies is gentle as a dove, boys. The man that buys them

will get the best piece of horseflesh he ever forked or druv for the
money. Naturally they got spirit; I aint selling crowbait. Besides,
who'd want Texas crowbait anyway, with Mississippi full of it?"
His stare was still absent and unwinking; there was no mirth or
humor in his voice and there was neither mirth nor humor in the
single guffaw which came from the rear of the group. Two wagons
were now drawing out of the road at the same time, up to the
fence. The men got down from them and tied them to the fence
and approached. "Come up, boys," the Texan said. "You're just in
time to buy a good gentle horse cheap."

"How about that one that cut your vest off last night?" a voice
said. This time three or four guffawed. The Texan looked toward
the sound, bleak and unwinking.

"What about it?" he said. The laughter, if it had been laughter,
ceased. The Texan turned to the nearest gatepost and climbed to
the top of it, his alternate thighs delibrate and bulging in the
tight trousers, the butt of the pistol catching and losing the sun in
pearly gleams. Sitting on the post, he looked down at the faces
along the fence which were attentive, grave, reserved and not looking at him. "All right," he said. "Who's going to start her off with
a bid? Step right up; take your pick and make your bid, and when
the last one is sold, walk in that lot and put your rope on the best
piece of horseflesh you ever forked or druv for the money. There
aint a pony there that aint worth fifteen dollars. Young, sound,
good for saddle or work stock, guaranteed to outlast four ordinary
horses; you couldn't kill one of them with a axle-tree—" There was
a small violent commotion at the rear of the group. The little boy
appeared, burrowing among the motionless overalls. He approached the post, the new and unbroken paper carton lifted. The
Texan leaned down and took it and tore the end from it and shook
three or four of the cakes into the boy's hand, a hand as small and
almost as black as that of a coon. He held the carton in his hand
while he talked, pointing out the horses with it as he indicated
them. "Look at that one with the three stocking-feet and the frost-
bit ear; watch him now when they pass again. Look at that
shoulder-action; that horse is worth twenty dollars of any man's
money. Who'll make me a bid on him to start her off?" His voice
was harsh, ready, forensic. Along the fence below him the men
stood with, buttoned close in their overalls, the tobacco-sacks and
worn purses the sparse silver and frayed bills hoarded a coin at

a time in the cracks of chimneys or chinked into the logs of walls.
From time to time the horses broke and rushed with purposeless
violence and huddled again, watching the faces along the fence
with wild mismatched eyes. The lane was full of wagons now. As
the others arrived they would have to stop in the road beyond it
and the occupants came up the lane on foot. Mrs Littlejohn
came out of her kitchen. She crossed the yard, looking toward the
lot gate. There was a blackened wash pot set on four bricks in the
corner of the yard. She built a fire beneath the pot and came to
the fence and stood there for a time, her hands on her hips and the
smoke from the fire drifting blue and slow behind her. Then she
turned and went back into the house. "Come on boys," the Texan
said. "Who'll make me a bid?"

"Four bits," a voice said. The Texan did not even glance toward
it.

"Or, if he dont suit you, how about that fiddle-head horse without no mane to speak of? For a saddle pony, I'd rather have him
than that stocking-foot. I heard somebody say fifty cents just now.
I reckon he meant five dollars, didn't he? Do I hear five dollars?"

"Four bits for the lot," the same voice said. This time there were
no guffaws. It was the Texan who laughed, harshly, with only his
lower face, as if he were reciting a multiplication table.

"Fifty cents for the dried mud offen them, he means," he said.
"Who'll give a dollar more for the genuine Texas cockle-burrs?"
Mrs Littlejohn came out of the kitchen, carrying the sawn half of
a wooden hogshead which she set on a stump beside the smoking
pot, and stood with her hands on her hips, looking into the lot for
a while without coming to the fence this time. Then she went back
into the house. "What's the matter with you boys?" the Texan said.
"Here, Eck, you been helping me and you know them horses. How
about making me a bid on that wall-eyed one you picked out last
night? Here. Wait a minute." He thrust the paper carton into his
other hip pocket and swung his feet inward and dropped, cat-light,
into the lot. The ponies, huddled, watched him. Then they broke
before him and slid stiffly along the fence. He turned them and
they whirled and rushed back across the lot; whereupon, as though
he had been waiting his chance when they should have turned
their backs on him, the Texan began to run too, so that when they
reached the opposite side of the lot and turned, slowing to huddle
again, he was almost upon them. The earth became thunderous;

dust arose, out of which the animals began to burst like flushed
quail and into which, with that apparently unflagging faith in his
own invulnerability, the Texan rushed. For an instant the watchers
could see them in the dust—the pony backed into the angle of the
fence and the stable, the man facing it, reaching toward his hip.
Then the beast rushed at him in a sort of fatal and hopeless desperation and he struck it between the eyes with the pistol-butt and
felled it and leaped onto its prone head. The pony recovered almost at once and pawed itself to its knees and heaved at its pris-
oned head and fought itself up, dragging the man with it; for an
instant in the dust the watchers saw the man free of the earth
and in violent lateral motion like a rag attached to the horse's
head. Then the Texan's feet came back to earth and the dust blew
aside and revealed them, motionless, the Texan's sharp heels
braced into the ground, one hand gripping the pony's forelock
and the other its nostrils, the long evil muzzle wrung backward
over its scarred shoulder while it breathed in labored and hollow
groans. Mrs Littlejohn was in the yard again. No one had seen her
emerge this time. She carried an armful of clothing and a metal-
ridged washboard and she was standing motionless at the kitchen
steps, looking into the lot. Then she moved across the yard, still
looking into the lot, and dumped the garments into the tub, still
looking into the lot. "Look him over, boys," the Texan panted, turning his own suffused face and the protuberant glare of his eyes
toward the fence. "Look him over quick. Them shoulders and—"
He had relaxed for an instant apparently. The animal exploded
again; again for an instant the Texan was free of the earth, though
he was still talking: "—and legs you whoa I'll tear your face right
look him over quick boys worth fifteen dollars of let me get a holt
of who'll make me a bid whoa you blare-eyed jack rabbit, whoa!"
They were moving now—a kaleidoscope of inextricable and incredible violence on the periphery of which the metal clasps of the Texan's suspenders sun-glinted in ceaseless orbit, with terrific slowness
across the lot. Then the broad clay-colored hat soared deliberately
outward; an instant later the Texan followed it, though still on his
feet, and the pony shot free in mad, staglike bounds. The Texan
picked up the hat and struck the dust from it against his leg,
and returned to the fence and mounted the post again. He was
breathing heavily. Still the faces did not look at him as he took the
carton from his hip and shook a cake from it and put the cake into

his mouth, chewing, breathing harshly. Mrs Littlejohn turned away
and began to bail water from the pot into the tub, though after
each bucketful she turned her head and looked into the lot again.
"Now, boys," the Texan said. "Who says that pony aint worth fifteen dollars? You couldn't buy that much dynamite for just fifteen
dollars. There aint one of them cant do a mile in three minutes;
turn them into pasture and they will board themselves; work them
like hell all day and every time you think about it, lay them over
the head with a single-tree and after a couple of days every jack
rabbit one of them will be so tame you will have to put them out
of the house at night like a cat." He shook another cake from the
carton and ate it. "Come on, Eck," he said. "Start her off. How
about ten dollars for that horse, Eck?"

"What need I got for a horse I would need a bear-trap to catch?"
Eck said.

"Didn't you just see me catch him?"

"I seen you," Eck said. "And I don't want nothing as big as a
horse if I got to wrastle with it every time it finds me on the same
side of a fence it's on."

"All right," the Texan said. He was still breathing harshly, but
now there was nothing of fatigue or breathlessness in it. He shook
another cake into his palm and inserted it beneath his moustache.
"All right. I want to get this auction started. I aint come here to
live, no matter how good a country you folks claim you got. I'm going to give you that horse." For a moment there was no sound, not
even that of breathing except the Texan's.

"You going to give it to me?" Eck said.

"Yes. Provided you will start the bidding on the next one." Again
there was no sound save the Texan's breathing, and then the clash
of Mrs Littlejohn's pail against the rim of the pot.

"I just start the bidding," Eck said. "I dont have to buy it lessen
I aint over-topped." Another wagon had come up the lane. It was
battered and paintless. One wheel had been repaired by crossed
planks bound to the spokes with baling wire and the two underfed
mules wore a battered harness patched with bits of cotton rope;
the reins were ordinary cotton plow-lines, not new. It contained a
woman in a shapeless gray garment and a faded sunbonnet, and a
man in faded and patched though clean overalls. There was not
room for the wagon to draw out of the lane so the man left it standing where it was and got down and came forward—a thin man, not

large, with something about his eyes, something strained and washed-out, at once vague and intense, who shoved into the crowd at the rear, saying,

"What? What's that? Did he give him that horse?"

"All right," the Texan said. "That wall-eyed horse with the scarred neck belongs to you. Now. That one that looks like he's had his head in a flour barrel. What do you say? Ten dollars?"

"Did he give him that horse?" the newcomer said.

"A dollar," Eck said. The Texan's mouth was still open for speech; for an instant his face died so behind the hard eyes.

"A dollar?" he said. "One dollar? Did I actually hear that?"

"Durn it," Eck said. "Two dollars then. But I aint——"

"Wait," the newcomer said. "You, up there on the post." The Texan looked at him. When the others turned, they saw that the woman had left the wagon too, though they had not known she was there since they had not seen the wagon drive up. She came among them behind the man, gaunt in the gray shapeless garment and the sunbonnet, wearing stained canvas gymnasium shoes. She overtook the man but she did not touch him, standing just behind him, her hands rolled before her into the gray dress.

"Henry," she said in a flat voice. The man looked over his shoulder.

"Get back to that wagon," he said.

"Here, missus," the Texan said. "Henry's going to get the bargain of his life in about a minute. Here, boys, let the missus come up close where she can see. Henry's going to pick out that saddle-horse the missus has been wanting. Who says ten——"

"Henry," the woman said. She did not raise her voice. She had not once looked at the Texan. She touched the man's arm. He turned and struck her hand down.

"Get back to that wagon like I told you." The woman stood behind him, her hands rolled again into her dress. She was not looking at anything, speaking to anyone.

"He aint no more despair than to buy one of them things," she said. "And us not but five dollars away from the poorhouse, he aint no more despair." The man turned upon her with that curious air of leashed, of dreamlike fury. The others lounged along the fence in attitudes gravely inattentive, almost oblivious. Mrs Littlejohn had been washing for some time now, pumping rhythmically up and down above the washboard in the sud-foamed tub. She now stood erect again, her soap-raw hands on her hips, looking into the lot.

"Shut your mouth and get back in that wagon," the man said. "Do you want me to take a wagon stake to you?" He turned and looked up at the Texan. "Did you give him that horse?" he said. The Texan was looking at the woman. Then he looked at the man; still watching him, he tilted the paper carton over his open palm. A single cake came out of it.

"Yes," he said.

"Is the fellow that bids in this next horse going to get that first one too?"

"No," the Texan said.

"All right," the other said. "Are you going to give a horse to the man that makes the first bid on the next one?"

"No," the Texan said.

"Then if you were just starting the auction off by giving away a horse, why didn't you wait till we were all here?" The Texan stopped looking at the other. He raised the empty carton and squinted carefully into it, as if it might contain a precious jewel or perhaps a deadly insect. Then he crumpled it and dropped it carefully beside the post on which he sat.

"Eck bids two dollars," he said. "I believe he still thinks he's bidding on them scraps of bob-wire they come here in instead of on one of the horses. But I got to accept it. But are you boys——"

"So Eck's going to get two horses at a dollar a head," the newcomer said. "Three dollars." The woman touched him again. He flung her hand off without turning and she stood again, her hands rolled into her dress across her flat stomach, not looking at anything.

"Mister," she said, "we got chaps in the house that never had shoes last winter. We aint got corn to feed the stock. We got five dollars I earned weaving by firelight after dark. And he aint no more despair."

"Henry bids three dollars," the Texan said. "Raise him a dollar, Eck, and the horse is yours." Beyond the fence the horses rushed suddenly and for no reason and as suddenly stopped, staring at the faces along the fence.

"Henry," the woman said. The man was watching Eck. His

stained and broken teeth showed a little beneath his lip. His wrists
dangled into fists below the faded sleeves of his shirt too short from
many washings.

"Four dollars," Eck said.

"Five dollars!" the husband said, raising one clenched hand. He
shouldered himself forward toward the gatepost. The woman did
not follow him. She now looked at the Texan for the first time. Her
eyes were a washed gray also, as though they had faded too like
the dress and the sunbonnet.

"Mister," she said, "if you take that five dollars I earned my
chaps a-weaving for one of them things, it'll be a curse on you and
yours during all the time of man."

"Five dollars!" the husband shouted. He thrust himself up to the
post, his clenched hand on a level with the Texan's knees. He
opened it upon a wad of frayed banknotes and silver. "Five dollars!
And the man that raises it will have to beat my head off or I'll beat
hisn."

"All right," the Texan said. "Five dollars is bid. But dont you
shake your hand at me."

At five oclock that afternoon the Texan crumpled the third paper carton and dropped it to the earth beneath him. In the copper
slant of the leveling sun which fell also upon the line of limp garments in Mrs Littlejohn's backyard and which cast his shadow and
that of the post on which he sat long across the lot where now and
then the ponies still rushed in purposeless and tireless surges, the
Texan straightened his leg and thrust his hand into his pocket and
took out a coin and leaned down to the little boy. His voice was
now hoarse, spent. "Here, bud," he said. "Run to the store and get
me a box of gingersnaps." The men still stood along the fence,
tireless, in their overalls and faded shirts. Flem Snopes was there
now, appeared suddenly from nowhere, standing beside the fence
with a space the width of three or four men on either side of him,
standing there in his small yet definite isolation, chewing tobacco,
in the same gray trousers and minute bow tie in which he had departed last summer but in a new cap, gray too like the other, but
new, and overlaid with a bright golfer's plaid, looking also at the
horses in the lot. All of them save two had been sold for sums ranging from three dollars and a half to eleven and twelve dollars. The
purchasers, as they had bid them in, had gathered as though by
instinct into a separate group on the other side of the gate, where

they stood with their hands lying upon the top strand of the fence, watching with a still more sober intensity the animals which some of them had owned for seven and eight hours now but had not yet laid hands upon. The husband, Henry, stood beside the post on which the Texan sat. The wife had gone back to the wagon, where she sat gray in the gray garment; motionless, still looking at nothing, she might have been something inanimate which he had loaded into the wagon to move it somewhere, waiting now in the wagon until he should be ready to go on again, patient, insensate, timeless.

"I bought a horse and I paid cash for it," he said. His voice was harsh and spent too, the mad look in his eyes had a quality glazed now and even sightless. "And yet you expect me to stand around here till they are all sold before I can get my horse. Well, you can do all the expecting you want. I'm going to take my horse out of there and go home." The Texan looked down at him. The Texan's shirt was blotched with sweat. His big face was cold and still, his voice level.

"Take your horse then." After a moment Henry looked away. He stood with his head bent a little, swallowing from time to time.

"Aint you going to catch him for me?"

"It aint my horse," the Texan said in that flat still voice. After a while Henry raised his head. He did not look at the Texan.

"Who'll help me catch my horse?" he said. Nobody answered. They stood along the fence, looking quietly into the lot where the ponies huddled, already beginning to fade a little where the long shadow of the house lay upon them, deepening. From Mrs Little-john's kitchen the smell of frying ham came. A noisy cloud of sparrows swept across the lot and into a chinaberry tree beside the house, and in the high soft vague blue swallows stooped and whirled in erratic indecision, their cries like strings plucked at random. Without looking back, Henry raised his voice: "Bring that ere plow-line." After a time the wife moved. She got down from the wagon and took a coil of new cotton rope from it and approached. The husband took the rope from her and moved toward the gate. The Texan began to descend from the post, stiffly, as Henry put his hand on the latch. "Come on here," he said. The wife had stopped when he took the rope from her. She moved again, obediently, her hands rolled into the dress across her stomach, passing the Texan without looking at him.

"Dont go in there, missus," he said. She stopped, not looking at him, not looking at anything. The husband opened the gate and entered the lot and turned, holding the gate open but without raising his eyes.

"Come on here," he said.

"Dont you go in there, missus," the Texan said. The wife stood motionless between them, her face almost concealed by the sunbonnet, her hands folded across her stomach.

"I reckon I better," she said. The other men did not look at her at all, at her or Henry either. They stood along the fence, grave and quiet and inattentive, almost bemused. Then the wife passed through the gate; the husband shut it behind them and turned and began to move toward the huddled ponies, the wife following in the gray and shapeless garment within which she moved without inference of locomotion, like something on a moving platform, a float. The horses were watching them. They clotted and blended and shifted among themselves, on the point of breaking though not breaking yet. The husband shouted at them. He began to curse them, advancing, the wife following. Then the huddle broke, the animals moving with high, stiff knees, circling the two people who turned and followed again as the herd flowed and huddled again at the opposite side of the lot.

"There he is," the husband said "Get him into that corner." The herd divided; the horse which the husband had bought jolted on stiff legs. The wife shouted at it; it spun and poised, plunging, then the husband struck it across the face with the coiled rope and it whirled and slammed into the corner of the fence. "Keep him there now," the husband said. He shook out the rope, advancing. The horse watched him with wild, glaring eyes; it rushed again, straight toward the wife. She shouted at it and waved her arms but it soared past her in a long bound and rushed again into the huddle of its fellows. They followed and hemmed it again into another corner; again the wife failed to stop its rush for freedom and the husband turned and struck her with the coiled rope. "Why didn't you head him?" he said. "Why didn't you?" He struck her again; she did not move, not even to fend the rope with a raised arm. The men along the fence stood quietly, their faces lowered as though brooding upon the earth at their feet. Only Flem Snopes was still watching—if he ever had been looking into the lot at all, standing in his little island of isolation, chewing with his characteristic faint sidewise thrust beneath the new plaid cap.

The Texan said something, not loud, harsh and short. He entered the lot and went to the husband and jerked the uplifted rope from his hand. The husband whirled as though he were about to spring at the Texan, crouched slightly, his knees bent and his arms held slightly away from his sides, though his gaze never mounted higher than the Texan's carved and dusty boots. Then the Texan took the husband by the arm and led him back toward the gate, the wife following, and through the gate which he held open for the woman and then closed. He took a wad of banknotes from his trousers and removed a bill from it and put it into the woman's hand. "Get him into the wagon and get him on home," he said.

"What's that for?" Flem Snopes said. He had approached. He now stood beside the post on which the Texan had been sitting. The Texan did not look at him.

"Thinks he bought one of them ponies," the Texan said. He spoke in a flat still voice, like that of a man after a sharp run. "Get him on away, missus."

"Give him back that money," the husband said, in his lifeless, spent tone. "I bought that horse and I aim to have him if I got to shoot him before I can put a rope on him." The Texan did not even look at him.

"Get him on away from here, missus," he said.

"You take your money and I take my horse," the husband said. He was shaking slowly and steadily now, as though he were cold. His hands open and shut below the frayed cuffs of his shirt. "Give it back to him," he said.

"You dont own no horse of mine," the Texan said. "Get him on home, missus." The husband raised his spent face, his mad glazed eyes. He reached out his hand. The woman held the banknote in her folded hands across her stomach. For a while the husband's shaking hand merely fumbled at it. Then he drew the banknote free.

"It's my horse," he said. "I bought it. These fellows saw me. I paid for it. It's my horse. Here." He turned and extended the banknote toward Snopes. "You got something to do with these horses. I bought one. Here's the money for it. I bought one. Ask him." Snopes took the banknote. The others stood, gravely inattentive,

in relaxed attitudes along the fence. The sun had gone now; there
was nothing save violet shadow upon them and upon the lot
where once more and for no reason the ponies rushed and flowed.
At that moment the little boy came up, tireless and indefatigable
still, with the new paper carton. The Texan took it, though he did
not open it at once. He had dropped the rope and now the husband stooped for it, fumbling at it for sometime before he lifted it
from the ground. Then he stood with his head bent, his knuckles
whitening on the rope. The woman had not moved. Twilight was
coming fast now; there was a last mazy swirl of swallows against
the high and changing azure. Then the Texan tore the end from
the carton and tilted one of the cakes into his hand; he seemed to
be watching the hand as it shut slowly upon the cake until a fine
powder of snuff-colored dust began to rain from his fingers. He
rubbed the hand carefully on his thigh and raised his head and
glanced about until he saw the little boy and handed the carton
back to him.

"Here, bud," he said. Then he looked at the woman, his voice
flat, quiet again. "Mr Snopes will have your money for you tomorrow. Better get him in the wagon and get him on home. He dont
own no horse. You can get your money tomorrow from Mr Snopes."
The wife turned and went back to the wagon and got into it. No
one watched her, nor the husband who still stood, his head bent,
passing the rope from one hand to the other. They leaned along
the fence, grave and quiet, as though the fence were in another
land, another time.

"How many you got left?" Snopes said. The Texan roused; they
all seemed to rouse then, returning, listening again.

"Got three now," the Texan said. "Swap all three of them for a
buggy or a——"

"It's out in the road," Snopes said, a little shortly, a little quickly,
turning away. "Get your mules." He went on up the lane. They
watched the Texan enter the lot and cross it, the horses flowing before him but without the old irrational violence, as if they too
were spent, vitiated with the long day, and enter the barn and
then emerge, leading the two harnessed mules. The wagon had
been backed under the shed beside the barn. The Texan entered
this and came out a moment later, carrying a bedding-roll and his
coat, and led the mules back toward the gate, the ponies huddled
again and watching him with their various unmatching eyes, qui-

etly now, as if they too realised there was not only an armistice between them at last but that they would never look upon each other
again in both their lives. Someone opened the gate. The Texan led
the mules through it and they followed in a body, leaving the husband standing beside the closed gate, his head still bent and the
coiled rope in his hand. They passed the wagon in which the wife
sat, her gray garment fading into the dusk, almost the same color
and as still, looking at nothing; they passed the clothesline with
its limp and unwinded drying garments, walking through the hot
vivid smell of ham from Mrs Littlejohn's kitchen. When they
reached the end of the lane they could see the moon, almost full,
tremendous and pale and still lightless in the sky from which day
had not quite gone. Snopes was standing at the end of the lane beside an empty buggy. It was the one with the glittering wheels
and the fringed parasol top in which he and Will Varner had
used to drive. The Texan was motionless too, looking at it.

"Well well well," he said. "So this is it."

"If it dont suit you, you can ride one of the mules back to Texas,"
Snopes said.

"You bet," the Texan said. "Only I ought to have a powder puff or
at least a mandolin to ride it with." He backed the mules onto the
tongue and lifted the breast-yoke. Two of them came forward and
fastened the traces for him. Then they watched him get into the
buggy and raise the reins.

"Where you heading for?" one said. "Back to Texas?"

"In this?" the Texan said. "I wouldn't get past the first Texas saloon without starting the vigilance committee. Besides, I aint going
to waste all this here lace-trimmed top and these spindle wheels
just on Texas. Long as I am this far, I reckon I'll go on a day or
two and look-see them Northern towns. Washington and New York
and Baltimore. What's the short way to New York from here?"
They didn't know. But they told him how to reach Jefferson.

"You're already headed right," Freeman said. "Just keep right on
up the road past the schoolhouse."

"All right," the Texan said. "Well, remember about busting them
ponies over the head now and then until they get used to you. You
wont have any trouble with them then." He lifted the reins again.
As he did so Snopes stepped forward and got into the buggy.

"I'll ride as far as Varner's with you," he said.

"I didn't know I was going past Varner's," the Texan said.

"You can go to town that way," Snopes said. "Drive on." The Texan shook the reins. Then he said,

"Whoa." He straightened his leg and put his hand into his pocket. "Here, bud," he said to the little boy, "run to the store and— Never mind. I'll stop and get it myself, long as I am going back that way. Well, boys," he said. "Take care of yourselves." He swung the team around. The buggy went on. They looked after it.

"I reckon he aims to kind of come up on Jefferson from behind," Quick said.

"He'll be lighter when he gets there," Freeman said. "He can come up to it easy from any side he wants."

"Yes," Bookwright said. "His pockets wont rattle." They went back to the lot; they passed on through the narrow way between the two lines of patient and motionless wagons, which at the end was completely closed by the one in which the woman sat. The husband was still standing beside the gate with his coiled rope, and now night had completely come. The light itself had not changed so much; if anything, it was brighter but with that other-worldly quality of moonlight, so that when they stood once more looking into the lot, the splotchy bodies of the ponies had a distinctness, almost a brilliance, but without individual shape and without depth —no longer horses, no longer flesh and bone directed by a principle capable of calculated violence, no longer inherent with the capacity to hurt and harm.

"Well, what are we waiting for?" Freeman said. "For them to go to roost?"

"We better all get our ropes first," Quick said. "Get your ropes everybody." Some of them did not have ropes. When they left home that morning, they had not heard about the horses, the auction. They had merely happened through the village by chance and learned of it and stopped.

"Go to the store and get some then," Freeman said.

"The store will be closed now," Quick said.

"No it wont," Freeman said. "If it was closed, Lump Snopes would a been up here." So while the ones who had come prepared got their ropes from the wagons, the others went down to the store. The clerk was just closing it.

"You all aint started catching them yet, have you?" he said. "Good; I was afraid I wouldn't get there in time." He opened the door again and amid the old strong sunless smells of cheese and leather and molasses he measured and cut off sections of plow-line for them and in a body and the clerk in the center and still talking, voluble and unlistened to, they returned up the road. The pear tree before Mrs Littlejohn's was like drowned silver now in the moon. The mockingbird of last night, or another one, was already singing in it, and they now saw, tied to the fence, Ratliff's buckboard and team.

"I thought something was wrong all day," one said. "Ratliff wasn't there to give nobody advice." When they passed down the lane, Mrs Littlejohn was in her backyard, gathering the garments from the clothesline; they could still smell the ham. The others were waiting at the gate, beyond which the ponies, huddled again, were like phantom fish, suspended apparently without legs now in the brilliant treachery of the moon.

"I reckon the best way will be for us all to take and catch them one at a time," Freeman said.

"One at a time," the husband, Henry, said. Apparently he had not moved since the Texan had led his mules through the gate, save to lift his hands to the top of the gate, one of them still clutching the coiled rope. "One at a time," he said. He began to curse in a harsh, spent monotone. "After I've stood around here all day, waiting for that—" He cursed. He began to jerk at the gate, shaking it with spent violence until one of the others slid the latch back and it swung open and Henry entered it, the others following, the little boy pressing close behind his father until Eck became aware of him and turned.

"Here," he said. "Give me that rope. You stay out of here."

"Aw, paw," the boy said.

"No sir. Them things will kill you. They almost done it this morning. You stay out of here."

"But we got two to catch." For a moment Eck stood looking down at the boy.

"That's right," he said. "We got two. But you stay close to me now. And when I holler run, you run. You hear me?"

"Spread out, boys," Freeman said. "Keep them in front of us." They began to advance across the lot in a ragged crescent-shaped line, each one with his rope. The ponies were now at the far side of the lot. One of them snorted; the mass shifted within itself but without breaking. Freeman, glancing back, saw the little boy. "Get that boy out of here," he said.

"I reckon you better," Eck said to the boy. "You go and get in the wagon yonder. You can see us catch them from there." The little boy turned and trotted toward the shed beneath which the wagon stood. The line of men advanced, Henry a little in front.

"Watch them close now," Freeman said. "Maybe we better try to get them into the barn first—" At that moment the huddle broke. It parted and flowed in both directions along the fence. The men at the ends of the line began to run, waving their arms and shouting. "Head them," Freeman said tensely. "Turn them back." They turned them, driving them back upon themselves again; the animals merged and spun in short, huddling rushes, phantom and inextricable. "Hold them now," Freeman said. "Dont let them get by us." The line advanced again. Eck turned; he did not know why— whether a sound, what. The little boy was just behind him again.

"Didn't I tell you to get in that wagon and stay there?" Eck said.

"Watch out, paw!" the boy said. "There he is! There's ourn!" It was the one the Texan had given Eck. "Catch him, paw!"

"Get out of my way," Eck said. "Get back to that wagon." The line was still advancing. The ponies milled, clotting, forced gradually backward toward the open door of the barn. Henry was still slightly in front, crouched slightly, his thin figure, even in the mazy moonlight, emanating something of that spent fury. The splotchy huddle of animals seemed to be moving before the advancing line of men like a snowball which they might have been pushing before them by some invisible means, gradually nearer and nearer to the black yawn of the barn door. Later it was obvious that the ponies were so intent upon the men that they did not realise the barn was even behind them until they backed into the shadow of it. Then an indescribable sound, a movement desperate and despairing, arose among them; for an instant of static horror men and animals faced one another, then the men whirled and ran before a gaudy vomit of long wild faces and splotched chests which overtook and scattered them and flung them sprawling aside and completely obliterated from sight Henry and the little boy, neither of whom had moved though Henry had flung up both arms, still holding his coiled rope, the herd sweeping on across the lot, to crash through the gate which the last man through it had neglected to close, leaving it slightly ajar, carrying all of the gate save upright to which the hinges were nailed with them, and so among the teams and wagons which choked the lane, the teams springing and lunging too, snapping hitch-reins and tongues. Then the whole inextricable mass crashed among the wagons and eddied and divided about the one in which the woman sat, and rushed on down the lane and into the road, dividing, one half going one way and one half the other.

The men in the lot, except Henry, got to their feet and ran toward the gate. The little boy once more had not been touched, not even thrown off his feet; for a while his father held him clear of the ground in one hand, shaking him like a rag doll. "Didn't I tell you to stay in that wagon?" Eck cried. "Didn't I tell you?"

"Look out, paw!" the boy chattered out of the violent shaking, "there's ourn! There he goes!" It was the horse the Texan had given them again. It was as if they owned no other, the other one did not exist; as if by some absolute and instantaneous rapport of blood they had relegated to oblivion the one for which they had paid money. They ran to the gate and down the lane where the other men had disappeared. They saw the horse the Texan had given them whirl and dash back and rush through the gate into Mrs Littlejohn's yard and run up the front steps and crash once on the wooden veranda and vanish through the front door. Eck and the boy ran up onto the veranda. A lamp sat on a table just inside the door. In its mellow light they saw the horse fill the long hallway like a pinwheel, gaudy, furious and thunderous. A little further down the hall there was a varnished yellow melodeon. The horse crashed into it; it produced a single note, almost a chord, in bass, resonant and grave, of deep and sober astonishment; the horse with its monstrous and antic shadow whirled again and vanished through another door. It was a bedroom; Ratliff, in his underclothes and one sock and with the other sock in his hand and his back to the door, was leaning out the open window facing the lane, the lot. He looked back over his shoulder. For an instant he and the horse glared at one another. Then he sprang through the window as the horse backed out of the room and into the hall again and whirled and saw Eck and the little boy just entering the front door, Eck still carrying his rope. It whirled again and rushed on down the hall and onto the back porch just as Mrs Littlejohn, carrying an armful of clothes from the line and the washboard, mounted the steps.

"Get out of here, you son of a bitch," she said. She struck with the washboard; it divided neatly on the long mad face and the horse whirled and rushed back up the hall, where Eck and the boy now stood.

"Get to hell out of here, Wall!" Eck roared. He dropped to the floor, covering his head with his arms. The boy did not move, and for the third time the horse soared above the unwinking eyes and the unbowed and untouched head and onto the front veranda again just as Ratliff, still carrying the sock, ran around the corner of the house and up the steps. The horse whirled without breaking or pausing. It galloped to the end of the veranda and took the railing and soared outward, hobgoblin and floating, in the moon. It landed in the lot still running and crossed the lot and galloped through the wrecked gate and among the overturned wagons and the still intact one in which Henry's wife still sat, and on down the lane and into the road.

A quarter of a mile further on, the road gashed pallid and moony between the moony shadows of the bordering trees, the horse still galloping, galloping its shadow into the dust, the road descending now toward the creek and the bridge. It was of wood, just wide enough for a single vehicle. When the horse reached it, it was occupied by a wagon coming from the opposite direction and drawn by two mules already asleep in the harness and the soporific motion. On the seat was Tull and his wife, in splint chairs in the wagon behind them sat their four daughters, all returning belated from an all-day visit with some of Mrs Tull's kin. The horse neither checked nor swerved. It crashed once on the wooden bridge and rushed between the two mules which waked lunging in opposite directions in the traces, the horse now apparently scrambling along the wagon-tongue itself like a mad squirrel and scrabbling at the end-gate of the wagon with its forefeet as if it intended to climb into the wagon while Tull shouted at it and struck at its face with his whip. The mules were now trying to turn the wagon around in the middle of the bridge. It slewed and tilted, the bridge-rail cracked with a sharp report above the shrieks of the women; the horse scrambled at last across the back of one of the mules and Tull stood up in the wagon and kicked at its face. Then the front end of the wagon rose, flinging Tull, the reins now wrapped several times about his wrist, backward into the wagon bed among the overturned chairs and the exposed stockings and undergarments of his women. The pony scrambled free and crashed again on the wooden planking, galloping again. The wagon lurched again; the

mules had finally turned it on the bridge where there was not room
for it to turn and were now kicking themselves free of the traces.
When they came free, they snatched Tull bodily out of the wagon.
He struck the bridge on his face and was dragged for several feet
before the wrist-wrapped reins broke. Far up the road now, dis-
tancing the frantic mules, the pony faded on. While the five women
still shrieked above Tull's unconscious body, Eck and the little boy
came up, trotting, Eck still carrying his rope. He was panting.
"Which way'd he go?" he said.

In the now empty and moon-drenched lot, his wife and Mrs Littlejohn and Ratliff and Lump Snopes, the clerk, and three other
men raised Henry out of the trampled dust and carried him into
Mrs Littlejohn's back yard. His face was blanched and stony, his
eyes were closed, the weight of his head tautened his throat across
the protruding larynx; his teeth glinted dully beneath his lifted lip.
They carried him on toward the house, through the dappled shade
of the chinaberry trees. Across the dreaming and silver night a faint
sound like remote thunder came and ceased. "There's one of them
on the creek bridge," one of the men said.

"It's that one of Eck Snopes'," another said. "The one that was
in the house." Mrs Littlejohn had preceded them into the hall.
When they entered with Henry, she had already taken the lamp
from the table and she stood beside an open door, holding the
lamp high.

"Bring him in here," she said. She entered the room first and set
the lamp on the dresser. They followed with clumsy scufflings and
pantings and laid Henry on the bed and Mrs Littlejohn came to
the bed and stood looking down at Henry's peaceful and bloodless
face. "I'll declare," she said. "You men." They had drawn back a
little, clumped, shifting from one foot to another, not looking at
her nor at his wife either, who stood at the foot of the bed, motionless, her hands folded into her dress. "You all get out of here, V. K.,"
she said to Ratliff. "Go outside. See if you cant find something else
to play with that will kill some more of you."

"All right," Ratliff said. "Come on boys. Aint no more horses to
catch in here." They followed him toward the door, on tiptoe,
their shoes scuffling, their shadows monstrous on the wall.

"Go get Will Varner," Mrs Littlejohn said. "I reckon you can
tell him it's still a mule." They went out; they didn't look back.
They tiptoed up the hall and crossed the veranda and descended

into the moonlight. Now that they could pay attention to it, the silver air seemed to be filled with faint and sourceless sounds—shouts, thin and distant, again a brief thunder of hooves on a wooden bridge, more shouts faint and thin and earnest and clear as bells; once they even distinguished the words: "Whooey. Head him."

"He went through that house quick," Ratliff said. "He must have found another woman at home." Then Henry screamed in the house behind them. They looked back into the dark hall where a square of light fell through the bedroom door, listening while the scream sank into a harsh respiration: "Ah. Ah. Ah" on a rising note about to become screaming again. "Come on," Ratliff said. "We better get Varner." They went up the road in a body, treading the moon-blanched dust in the tremulous April night murmurous with the moving of sap and the wet bursting of burgeoning leaf and bud and constant with the thin and urgent cries and the brief and fading bursts of galloping hooves. Varner's house was dark, blank and without depth in the moonlight. They stood, clumped darkly in the silver yard and called up at the blank windows until suddenly someone was standing in one of them. It was Flem Snopes' wife. She was in a white garment; the heavy braided club of her hair looked almost black against it. She did not lean out, she merely stood there, full in the moon, apparently blank-eyed or certainly not looking downward at them—the heavy gold hair, the mask not tragic and perhaps not even doomed: just damned, the strong faint lift of breasts beneath marblelike fall of the garment; to those below what Brunhilde, what Rhinemaiden on what spurious river-rock of papier-mâché, what Helen returned to what topless and shoddy Argos, waiting for no one. "Evening, Mrs Snopes," Ratliff said. "We want Uncle Will. Henry Armstid is hurt at Mrs Littlejohn's." She vanished from the window. They waited in the moonlight, listening to the faint remote shouts and cries, until Varner emerged, sooner than they had actually expected, hunching into his coat and buttoning his trousers over the tail of his nightshirt, his suspenders still dangling in twin loops below the coat. He was carrying the battered bag which contained the plumber-like tools with which he drenched and wormed and blistered and floated or drew the teeth of horses and mules; he came down the steps, lean and loosejointed, his shrewd ruthless head cocked a little as he listened also to the faint bell-like cries and shouts with which the silver air was full.

"Are they still trying to catch them rabbits?" he said.

"All of them except Henry Armstid," Ratliff said. "He caught his."

"Hah," Varner said. "That you, V. K.? How many did you buy?"

"I was too late," Ratliff said. "I never got back in time."

"Hah," Varner said. They moved on to the gate and into the road again. "Well, it's a good bright cool night for running them." The moon was now high overhead, a pearled and mazy yawn in the soft sky, the ultimate ends of which rolled onward, whorl on whorl, beyond the pale stars and by pale stars surrounded. They walked in a close clump, tramping their shadows into the road's mild dust, blotting the shadows of the burgeoning trees which soared, trunk branch and twig against the pale sky, delicate and finely thinned. They passed the dark store. Then the pear tree came in sight. It rose in mazed and silver immobility like exploding snow; the mockingbird still sang in it. "Look at that tree," Varner said. "It ought to make this year, sho."

"Corn'll make this year too," one said.

"A moon like this is good for every growing thing outen earth," Varner said. "I mind when me and Mrs Varner was expecting Eula. Already had a mess of children and maybe we ought to quit then. But I wanted some more gals. Others had done married and moved away, and a passel of boys, soon as they get big enough to be worth anything, they aint got time to work. Got to set around store and talk. But a gal will stay home and work until she does get married. So there was a old woman told my mammy once that if a woman showed her belly to the full moon after she had done caught, it would be a gal. So Mrs Varner taken and laid every night with the moon on her nekid belly, until it fulled and after. I could lay my ear to her belly and hear Eula kicking and scrouging like all get-out, feeling the moon."

"You mean it actually worked sho enough, Uncle Will?" the other said.

"Hah," Varner said. "You might try it. You get enough women showing their nekid bellies to the moon or the sun either or even just to your hand fumbling around often enough and more than likely after a while there will be something in it you can lay your ear and listen to, provided something come up and you aint got away by that time. Hah, V. K.?" Someone guffawed.

"Dont ask me," Ratliff said. "I cant even get nowhere in time to buy a cheap horse." Two or three guffawed this time. Then they began to hear Henry's respirations from the house: "Ah. Ah. Ah." and they ceased abruptly, as if they had not been aware of their closeness to it. Varner walked on in front, lean, shambling, yet moving quite rapidly, though his head was still slanted with listening as the faint, urgent, indomitable cries murmured in the silver lambence, sourceless, at times almost musical, like fading bell-notes; again there was a brief rapid thunder of hooves on wooden planking.

"There's another one on the creek bridge," one said.

"They are going to come out even on them things, after all," Varner said. "They'll get the money back in exercise and relaxation. You take a man that aint got no other relaxation all year long except dodging mule-dung up and down a field furrow. And a night like this one, when a man aint old enough yet to lay still and sleep, and yet he aint young enough anymore to be tomcatting in and out of other folks' back windows, something like this is good for him. It'll make him sleep tomorrow night anyhow, provided he gets back home by then. If we had just knowed about this in time, we could have trained up a pack of horse-dogs. Then we could have held one of these field trials."

"That's one way to look at it, I reckon," Ratliff said. "In fact, it might be a considerable comfort to Bookwright and Quick and Freeman and Eck Snopes and them other new horse-owners if that side of it could be brought to their attention, because the chances are aint none of them thought to look at it in that light yet. Probably there aint a one of them that believes now there's any cure a tall for that Texas disease Flem Snopes and that Dead-eye Dick brought here."

"Hah," Varner said. He opened Mrs Littlejohn's gate. The dim light still fell outward across the hall from the bedroom door; beyond it, Armstid was saying "Ah. Ah. Ah" steadily. "There's a pill for every ill but the last one."

"Even if there was always time to take it," Ratliff said.

"Hah," Varner said again. He glanced back at Ratliff for an instant, pausing. But the little hard bright eyes were invisible now; it was only the bushy overhang of the brows which seemed to concentrate downward toward him in writhen immobility, not frowning but with a sort of fierce risibility. "Even if there was time to take it. Breathing is a sight-draft dated yesterday."

At nine oclock on the second morning after that, five men were sitting or squatting along the gallery of the store. The sixth was Ratliff. He was standing up, and talking: "Maybe there wasn't but one of them things in Mrs Littlejohn's house that night, like Eck says. But it was the biggest drove of just one horse I ever seen. It was in my rooms and it was on the front porch and I could hear Mrs Littlejohn hitting it over the head with that washboard in the back yard all at the same time. And still it was missing everybody everytime. I reckon that's what that Texas man meant by calling them bargains: that a man would need to be powerful unlucky to ever get close enough to one of them to get hurt." They laughed, all except Eck himself. He and the little boy were eating. When they mounted the steps, Eck had gone on into the store and emerged with a paper sack, from which he took a segment of cheese and with his pocket knife divided it carefully into two exact halves and gave one to the boy and took a handful of crackers from the sack and gave them to the boy, and now they squatted against the wall, side by side and, save for the difference in size, identical, eating.

"I wonder what that horse thought Ratliff was," one said. He held a spray of peach bloom between his teeth. It bore four blossoms like miniature ballet skirts of pink tulle. "Jumping out windows and running indoors in his shirt-tail? I wonder how many Ratliffs that horse thought he saw."

"I dont know," Ratliff said. "But if he saw just half as many of me as I saw of him, he was sholy surrounded. Everytime I turned my head, that thing was just running over me or just swirling to run back over that boy again. And that boy there, he stayed right under it one time to my certain knowledge for a full one-and-one-half minutes without ducking his head or even batting his eyes. Yes sir, when I looked around and seen that varmint in the door behind me blaring its eyes at me, I'd a made sho Flem Snopes had brought a tiger back from Texas except I knowed that couldn't no just one tiger completely fill a entire room." They laughed again, quietly. Lump Snopes, the clerk, sitting in the only chair tilted back against the door-facing and partly blocking the entrance, cackled suddenly.

"If Flem had knowed how quick you fellows was going to snap them horses up, he'd a probably brought some tigers," he said. "Monkeys too."

"So they was Flem's horses," Ratliff said. The laughter stopped.

The other three had open knives in their hands, with which they had been trimming idly at chips and slivers of wood. Now they sat apparently absorbed in the delicate and almost tedious movements of the knife-blades. The clerk had looked quickly up and found Ratliff watching him. His constant expression of incorrigible and mirthful disbelief had left him now; only the empty wrinkles of it remained about his mouth and eyes.

"Has Flem ever said they was?" he said. "But you town fellows are smarter than us country folks. Likely you done already read Flem's mind." But Ratliff was not looking at him now.

"And I reckon we'd a bought them," he said. He stood above them again, easy, intelligent, perhaps a little sombre but still perfectly impenetrable. "Eck here, for instance. With a wife and family to support. He owns two of them, though to be sho he never had to pay money for but one. I heard folks chasing them things up until midnight last night, but Eck and that boy aint been home a tall in two days." They laughed again, except Eck. He pared off a bit of cheese and speared it on the knife-point and put it into his mouth.

"Eck caught one of hisn," the second man said.

"That so?" Ratliff said. "Which one was it, Eck? The one he give you or the one you bought?"

"The one he give me," Eck said, chewing.

"Well, well," Ratliff said. "I hadn't heard about that. But Eck's still one horse short. And the one he had to pay money for. Which is pure proof enough that them horses wasn't Flem's because wouldn't no man even give his own blood kin something he couldn't even catch." They laughed again, but they stopped when the clerk spoke. There was no mirth in his voice at all.

"Listen," he said. "All right. We done all admitted you are too smart for anybody to get ahead of. You never bought no horse from Flem or nobody else, so maybe it aint none of your business and maybe you better just leave it at that."

"Sholy," Ratliff said. "It's done already been left at that two nights ago. The fellow that forgot to shut that lot gate done that. With the exception of Eck's horse. And we know that wasn't Flem's, because that horse was give to Eck for nothing."

"There's others besides Eck that aint got back home yet," the man with the peach spray said. "Bookwright and Quick are still chasing theirs. They was reported three miles west of Burtsboro

Old Town at eight oclock last night. They aint got close enough to it yet to tell which one it belongs to."

"Sholy," Ratliff said. "The only new horse-owner in this country that could a been found without bloodhounds since whoever it was left that gate open two nights ago, is Henry Armstid. He's laying right there in Mrs Littlejohn's bedroom where he can watch the lot so that any time the one he bought happens to run back into it, all he's got to do is to holler at his wife to run out with the rope and catch it—" He ceased, though he said, "Morning, Flem," so immediately afterward and with no change whatever in tone, that the pause was not even discernible. With the exception of the clerk, who sprang up, vacated the chair with a sort of servile alacrity, and Eck and the little boy who continued to eat, they watched above their stilled hands as Snopes in the gray trousers and the minute tie and the new cap with its bright overplaid mounted the steps. He was chewing; he already carried a piece of white pine board; he jerked his head at them, looking at nobody, and took the vacated chair and opened his knife and began to whittle. The clerk now leaned in the opposite side of the door, rubbing his back against the facing. The expression of merry and invincible disbelief had returned to his face, with a quality watchful and secret.

"You're just in time," he said. "Ratliff here seems to be in a considerable sweat about who actually owned them horses." Snopes drew his knife-blade neatly along the board, the neat, surgeon-like sliver curling before it. The others were whittling again, looking carefully at nothing, except Eck and the boy, who were still eating, and the clerk rubbing his back against the door-facing and watching Snopes with that secret and alert intensity. "Maybe you could put his mind at rest." Snopes turned his head slightly and spat, across the gallery and the steps and into the dust beyond them. He drew the knife back and began another curling sliver.

"He was there too," Snopes said. "He knows as much as anybody else." This time the clerk guffawed, chortling, his features gathering toward the center of his face as though plucked there by a hand. He slapped his leg, cackling.

"You might as well to quit," he said. "You cant beat him."

"I reckon not," Ratliff said. He stood above them, not looking at any of them, his gaze fixed apparently on the empty road beyond Mrs Littlejohn's house, impenetrable, brooding even. A hulking, half-grown boy in overalls too small for him appeared suddenly from nowhere in particular. He stood for a while in the road, just beyond spitting-range of the gallery, with the air of having come from nowhere in particular and of not knowing where he would go next when he should move again and of not being troubled by that fact. He was looking at nothing, certainly not toward the gallery, and no one on the gallery so much as looked at him except the little boy, who now watched the boy in the road, his periwinkle eyes grave and steady above the bitten cracker in his halted hand. The boy in the road moved on, thickly undulant in the tight overalls, and vanished beyond the corner of the store, the round head and the unwinking eyes of the little boy on the gallery turning steadily to watch him out of sight. Then the little boy bit the cracker again, chewing. "Of course there's Mrs Tull," Ratliff said. "But that's Eck she's going to sue for damaging Tull against that bridge. And as for Henry Armstid——"

"If a man aint got gumption enough to protect himself, it's his own look-out," the clerk said.

"Sholy," Ratliff said, still in that dreamy, abstracted tone, actually speaking over his shoulder even. "And Henry Armstid, that's all right because from what I hear of the conversation that taken place, Henry had already stopped owning that horse he thought was his before that Texas man left. And as for that broke leg, that wont put him out none because his wife can make his crop." The clerk had ceased to rub his back against the door. He watched the back of Ratliff's head, unwinking too, sober and intent; he glanced at Snopes who, chewing, was watching another sliver curl away from the advancing knife-blade, then he watched the back of Ratliff's head again.

"It wont be the first time she has made their crop," the man with the peach spray said. Ratliff glanced at him.

"You ought to know. This wont be the first time I ever saw you in their field, doing plowing Henry never got around to. How many days have you already given them this year?" The man with the peach spray removed it and spat carefully and put the spray back between his teeth.

"She can run a furrow straight as I can," the second said.

"They're unlucky," the third said. "When you are unlucky, it dont matter much what you do."

"Sholy," Ratliff said. "I've heard laziness called bad luck so much that maybe it is."

"He aint lazy," the third said. "When their mule died three or four years ago, him and her broke their land working time about in the traces with the other mule. They aint lazy."

"So that's all right," Ratliff said, gazing up the empty road again. "Likely she will begin right away to finish the plowing; that oldest gal is pretty near big enough to work with a mule, aint she? or at least to hold the plow stdeay while Mrs Armstid helps the mule?" He glanced again toward the man with the peach spray as though for an answer, but he was not looking at the other and he went on talking without any pause. The clerk stood with his rump and back pressed against the door-facing as if he had paused in the act of scratching, watching Ratliff quite hard now, unwinking. If Ratliff had looked at Flem Snopes, he would have seen nothing below the down-slanted peak of the cap save the steady motion of his jaws. Another sliver was curling with neat deliberation before the moving knife. "Plenty of time now because all she's got to do after she finishes washing Mrs Littlejohn's dishes and sweeping out the house to pay hers and Henry's board, is to go out home and milk and cook up enough vittles to last the children until tomorrow and feed them and get the littlest ones to sleep and wait outside the door until that biggest gal gets the bar up and gets into bed herself with the axe——"

"The axe?" the man with the peach spray said.

"She takes it to bed with her. She's just twelve, and what with this country still more or less full of them uncaught horses that never belonged to Flem Snopes, likely she feels maybe she cant swing a mere washboard like Mrs Littlejohn can—and then come back and wash up the supper dishes. And after that, not nothing to do until morning except to stay close enough where Henry can call her until it's light enough to chop the wood to cook breakfast and then help Mrs Littlejohn wash the dishes and make the beds and sweep while watching the road. Because likely any time now Flem Snopes will get back from wherever he has been since the auction, which of course is to town naturally to see about his cousin that's got into a little legal trouble, and so get that five dollars. 'Only maybe he wont give it back to me,' she says, and maybe that's what Mrs Littlejohn thought too, because she never said nothing. I could hear her——"

"And where did you happen to be during all this?" the clerk said.

"Listening," Ratliff said. He glanced back at the clerk, then he was looking away again, almost standing with his back to them. "—could hear her dumping the dishes into the pan like she was throwing them at it. 'Do you reckon he will give it back to me?' Mrs Armstid says. 'That Texas man give it to him and said he would. All the folks there saw him give Mr Snopes the money and heard him say I could get it from Mr Snopes tomorrow.' Mrs Little-john was washing the dishes now, washing them like a man would, like they was made out of iron. 'No,' she says. 'But asking him wont do no hurt.'—'If he wouldn't give it back, it aint no use to ask,' Mrs Armstid says.—'Suit yourself,' Mrs Littlejohn says. 'It's your money.' Then I couldn't hear nothing but the dishes for a while. 'Do you reckon he might give it back to me?' Mrs Armstid says. 'That Texas man said he would. They all heard him say it.'—'Then go and ask him for it,' Mrs Littlejohn says. Then I couldn't hear nothing but the dishes again. 'He wont give it back to me,' Mrs Armstid says.—'All right,' Mrs Littlejohn says. 'Dont ask him, then.' Then I just heard the dishes. They would have two pans, both washing. 'You dont reckon he would, do you?' Mrs Armstid says. Mrs Littlejohn never said nothing. It sounded like she was throw-ing the dishes at one another. 'Maybe I better go and talk to Henry,' Mrs Armstid says.—'I would,' Mrs Littlejohn says. And I be dog if it didn't sound exactly like she had two plates in her hands, beating them together like these here brass bucket-lids in a band. 'Then Henry can buy another five-dollar horse with it. Maybe he'll buy one next time that will out and out kill him. If I just thought he would, I'd give him back that money, myself.'—'I reckon I bet-ter talk to him first,' Mrs Armstid says. And then it sounded just like Mrs Littlejohn taken up the dishes and pans and all and throwed the whole business at the cookstove—" Ratliff ceased. Behind him the clerk was hissing "Psst! Psst! Flem. Flem!" Then he stopped, and all of them watched Mrs Armstid approach and mount the steps, gaunt in the shapeless gray garment, the stained tennis shoes hissing faintly on the boards. She came among them and stood, facing Snopes but not looking at anyone, her hands rolled into her apron.

"He said that day he wouldn't sell Henry that horse," she said in a flat toneless voice. "He said you had the money and I could get it from you." Snopes raised his head and turned it slightly again and spat neatly past the woman, across the gallery and into the road.

"He took all the money with him when he left," he said. Motionless, the gray garment hanging in rigid, almost formal folds like drapery in bronze, Mrs Armstid appeared to be watching something near Snopes' feet, as though she had not heard him, or as if she had quitted her body as soon as she finished speaking and although her body, hearing, had received the words, they would have no life nor meaning until she returned. The clerk was rubbing his back steadily against the door-facing again, watching her. The little boy was watching her too with his unwinking ineffable gaze, but nobody else was. The man with the peach spray removed it and spat and put the twig back into his mouth.

"He said Henry hadn't bought no horse," she said. "He said I could get the money from you."

"I reckon he forgot it," Snopes said. "He took all the money away with him when he left." He watched her a moment longer, then he trimmed again at the stick. The clerk rubbed his back gently against the door, watching her. After a time Mrs Armstid raised her head and looked up the road where it went on, mild with spring dust, past Mrs Littlejohn's, beginning to rise, on past the not-yet-bloomed (that would be in June) locust grove across the way, on past the schoolhouse, the weathered roof of which, rising beyond an orchard of peach and pear trees, resembled a hive swarmed about by a cloud of pink-and-white bees, ascending, mounting toward the crest of the hill where the church stood among its sparse gleam of marble headstones in the sombre cedar grove where during the long afternoons of summer the constant mourning doves called back and forth. She moved; once more the rubber soles hissed on the gnawed boards.

"I reckon it's about time to get dinner started," she said.

"How's Henry this morning, Mrs Armstid?" Ratliff said. She looked at him, pausing, the blank eyes waking for an instant.

"He's resting, I thank you kindly," she said. Then the eyes died again and she moved again. Snopes rose from the chair, closing his knife with his thumb and brushing a litter of minute shavings from his lap.

"Wait a minute," he said. Mrs Armstid paused again, half-turning, though still not looking at Snopes nor at any of them. *Because she cant possibly actually believe it,* Ratliff told himself, *Anymore than I do.* Snopes entered the store, the clerk, motionless again, his back and rump pressed against the door-facing as though waiting to start rubbing again, watched him enter, his head turning as the other passed him like the head of an owl, the little eyes blinking rapidly now. Jody Varner came up the road on his horse. He did not pass but instead turned in beside the store, toward the mulberry tree behind it where he was in the habit of hitching his horse. A wagon came up the road, creaking past. The man driving it lifted his hand; one or two of the men on the gallery lifted theirs in response. The wagon went on. Mrs Armstid looked after it. Snopes came out of the door, carrying a small striped paper bag and approached Mrs Armstid. "Here," he said. Her hand turned just enough to receive it. "A little sweetening for the chaps," he said. His other hand was already in his pocket, and as he turned back to the chair, he drew something from his pocket and handed it to the clerk, who took it. It was a five-cent piece. He sat down in the chair and tilted it back against the door again. He now had the knife in his hand again, already open. He turned his head slightly and spat again, neatly past the gray garment, into the road. The little boy was watching the sack in Mrs Armstid's hand. Then she seemed to discover it also, rousing.

"You're right kind," she said. She rolled the sack into the apron, the little boy's unwinking gaze fixed upon the lump her hands made beneath the cloth. She moved again. "I reckon I better get on and help with dinner," she said. She descended the steps, though as soon as she reached the level earth and began to retreat, the gray folds of the garment once more lost all inference and intimation of locomotion, so that she seemed to progress without motion like a figure on a retreating and diminishing float; a gray and blasted tree-trunk moving, somehow intact and upright, upon an unhurried flood. The clerk in the doorway cackled suddenly, explosively, chortling. He slapped his thigh.

"By God," he said, "you cant beat him."

Jody Varner, entering the store from the rear, paused in midstride like a pointing bird-dog. Then, on tiptoe, in complete silence and with astonishing speed, he darted behind the counter and sped up the gloomy tunnel, at the end of which a hulking, bear-shaped figure stooped, its entire head and shoulders wedged into the glass case which contained the needles and thread and snuff and tobacco and the stale gaudy candy. He snatched the boy savagely and viciously out; the boy gave a choked cry and struggled flabbily, cramming a final handful of something into his mouth, chewing.

But he ceased to struggle almost at once and became slack and inert save for his jaws. Varner dragged him around the counter as the clerk entered, seemed to bounce suddenly into the store with a sort of alert concern. "You, Saint Elmo!" he said.

"Aint I told you and told you to keep him out of here?" Varner demanded, shaking the boy. "He's damn near eaten that candy-case clean. Stand up!" The boy hung like a half-filled sack from Varner's hand, chewing with a kind of fatalistic desperation, the eyes shut tight in the vast flaccid colorless face, the ears moving steadily and faintly to the chewing. Save for the jaw and the ears, he appeared to have gone to sleep chewing.

"You, Saint Elmo!" the clerk said. "Stand up!" The boy assumed his own weight, though he did not open his eyes yet nor cease to chew. Varner released him. "Git on home," the clerk said. The boy turned obediently to re-enter the store. Varner jerked him about again.

"Not that way," he said. The boy crossed the gallery and descended the steps, the tight overalls undulant and reluctant across his flabby thighs. Before he reached the ground, his hand rose from his pocket to his mouth; again his ears moved faintly to the motion of chewing.

"He's worse than a rat, aint he?" the clerk said.

"Rat, hell," Varner said, breathing harshly. "He's worse than a goat. First thing I know, he'll graze on back and work through that lace leather and them hame-strings and lap-links and ring-bolts and eat me and you and him all three clean out the back door. And then be damned if I wuldn't be afraid to turn my back for fear he would cross the road and start in on the gin and the blacksmith shop. Now you mind what I say. If I catch him hanging around here one more time, I'm going to set a bear-trap for him." He went out onto the gallery, the clerk following. "Morning, gentlemen," he said.

"Who's that one, Jody?" Ratliff said. Save for the clerk in the background, they were the only two standing, and now, in juxtaposition, you could see the resemblance between them— a resemblance intangible, indefinite, not in figure, speech, dress, intelligence; certainly not in morals. Yet it was there, but with this bridgeless difference, this hallmark of his fate upon him: he would become an old man; Ratliff, too: but an old man who at about sixty-five would be caught and married by a creature not yet seventeen probably, who would for the rest of his life continue to take revenge upon him for her whole sex; Ratliff, never. The boy was moving without haste up the road. His hand rose again from his pocket to his mouth.

"That boy of I. O.'s," Varner said. "By God, I've done everything but put out poison for him."

"What?" Ratliff said. He glanced quickly about at the faces; for an instant there was in his own not only bewilderment but something almost like terror. "I thought—the other day you fellows told me—You said it was a woman, a young woman with a baby—Here now," he said. "Wait."

"This here's another one," Varner said. "I wish to hell he couldn't walk. Well, Eck, I hear you caught one of your horses."

"That's right," Eck said. He and the little boy had finished the crackers and cheese and he had sat for some time now, holding the empty bag.

"It was the one he give you, wasn't it?" Varner said.

"That's right," Eck said.

"Give the other one to me, paw," the little boy said.

"What happened?" Varner said.

"He broke his neck," Eck said.

"I know," Varner said. "But how?" Eck did not move. Watching him, they could almost see him visibly gathering and arranging words, speech. Varner, looking down at him, began to laugh steadily and harshly, sucking his teeth. "I'll tell you what happened. Eck and that boy finally run it into that blind lane of Freeman's, after a chase of about twenty-four hours. They figured it couldn't possibly climb them eight-foot fences of Freeman's so him and the boy tied their rope across the end of the lane, about three feet off the ground. And sho enough, soon as the horse come to the end of the lane and seen Freeman's barn, it whirled just like Eck figured it would and come helling back up that lane like a scared hen-hawk. It probably never even seen the rope at all. Mrs Freeman was watching from where she had run up onto the porch. She said that when it hit that rope, it looked just like one of these here great big Christmas pinwheels. But the one you bought got clean away, didn't it?"

"That's right," Eck said. "I never had time to see which way the other one went."

"Give him to me, paw," the little boy said.

"You wait till we catch him," Eck said. "We'll see about it then."

That afternoon Ratliff sat in the halted buckboard in front of Bookwright's gate. Bookwright stood in the road beside it. "You were wrong," Bookwright said. "He come back."

"He come back," Ratliff said. "I misjudged his . . . nerve aint the word I want, and sholy lack of it aint. But I wasn't wrong."

"Nonsense," Bookwright said. "He was gone all day yesterday. Nobody saw him going to town or coming back, but that's bound to be where he was at. Aint no man, I dont care if his name is Snopes, going to let his own blood kin rot in jail."

"He wont be in jail long. Court is next month, and after they send him to Parchman, he can stay outdoors again. He will even go back to farming, plowing. Of course it wont be his cotton, but then he never did make enough out of his own cotton to quite pay him for staying alive."

"Nonsense," Bookwright said. "I dont believe it. Flem aint going to let him go to the penitentiary."

"Yes," Ratliff said. "Because Flem Snopes has got to cancel all them loose-flying notes that turns up here and there every now and then. He's going to discharge at least some of the notes for good and all." They looked at one another—Ratliff grave and easy in the blue shirt, Bookwright sober too, black-browed, intent.

"I thought you said you and him burned them notes."

"I said we burned two notes that Mink Snopes gave me. Do you think that any Snopes is going to put all of anything on one piece of paper that can be destroyed by one match? Do you think there is any Snopes that dont know that?"

"Oh," Bookwright said. "Hah," he said, with no mirth. "I reckon you gave Henry Armstid back his five dollars too." Then Ratliff looked away. His face changed—something fleeting, quizzical, but not smiling, his eyes did not smile; it was gone.

"I could have," he said. "But I didn't. I might have if I could just been sho he would buy something this time that would sho enough kill him, like Mrs Littlejohn said. Besides, I wasn't protecting a Snopes from Snopeses; I wasn't even protecting a people from a Snopes. I was protecting something that wasn't even a people, that wasn't nothing but something that dont want nothing but to walk and feel the sun and wouldn't know how to hurt no man even if it would and wouldn't want to even if it could, just like I wouldn't stand by and see you steal a meat-bone from a dog. I never made

them Snopeses and I never made the folks that cant wait to bare
their backsides to them. I could do more, but I wont. I wont, I tell
you!"

"All right," Bookwright said. "Hook your drag up; it aint nothing
but a hill. I said it's all right."

– 2 –

The two actions of Armstid pl. vs. Snopes, and Tull pl. vs. Eck-
rum Snopes (and anyone else named Snopes or Varner either which
Tull's irate wife could contrive to involve, as the village well knew)
were accorded a change of venue by mutual agreement and arrangement among the litigants. Three of the parties did, that is,
because Flem Snopes flatly refused to recognise the existence of the
suit against himself, stating once and without heat and first turning
his head slightly aside to spit, "They wasn't none of my horses,"
then fell to whittling again while the baffled and helpless bailiff
stood before the tilted chair with the papers he was trying to serve.

"What a opportunity for that Snopes family lawyer this would a
been," Ratliff said when told about it. "What's his name? that quick-
fatherer, the Moses with his mouth full of mottoes and his coat-tail
full of them already halfgrown retroactive sons? I dont understand
yet how a man that has to spend as much time as I do being constantly reminded of them folks, still cant keep the names straight.
I. O. That he never had time to wait. This here would be probably
the one tried case in his whole legal existence where he wouldn't be
bothered with no narrow-ideaed client trying to make him stop
talking, and the squire presiding himself would be the only man in
company with authority to tell him to shut up."

So neither did the Varner surrey nor Ratliff's buckboard make
one among the wagons, the buggies, and the saddled horses and
mules which moved out of the village on that May Saturday morning, to converge upon Whiteleaf store eight miles away, coming not
only from Frenchman's Bend but from other directions too since by
that time, what Ratliff had called 'that Texas sickness,' that spotted
corruption of frantic and uncatchable horses, had spread as far as
twenty and thirty miles. So by the time the Frenchman's Bend people began to arrive, there were two dozen wagons, the teams reversed and eased of harness and tied to the rear wheels in order to
pass the day, and twice that many saddled animals already standing about the locust grove beside the store and the site of the hear-

ing had already been transferred from the store to an adjacent shed
where in the fall cotton would be stored. But by nine oclock it was
seen that even the shed would not hold them all, so the palladium
was moved again, from the shed to the grove itself. The horses
and mules and wagons were cleared from it; the single chair, the
gnawed table bearing a thick bible which had the appearance of
loving and constant use of a piece of old and perfectly-kept machinery and an almanac and a copy of Mississippi Reports dated
1881 and bearing along its opening edge a single thread-thin line of
soilure as if during all the time of his possession its owner (or
user) had opened it at only one page though that quite often, were
fetched from the shed to the grove; a wagon and four men were
dispatched and returned presently from the church a mile away
with four wooden pews for the litigants and their clansmen and
witnesses; behind these in turn the spectators stood—the men, the
women, the children, sober, attentive, and neat, not in their Sunday
clothes to be sure, but in the clean working garments donned that
morning for the Saturday's diversion of sitting about the country
stores or trips into the county seat, and in which they would return
to the field on Monday morning and would wear all that week until
Friday night came round again. The Justice of the Peace was a
neat, small, plump old man resembling a tender caricature of all
grandfathers who ever breathed, in a beautifully laundered though
collarless white shirt with immaculate starch-gleaming cuffs and
bosom, and steel-framed spectacles and neat, faintly curling white
hair. He sat behind the table and looked at them—at the gray
woman in the gray sunbonnet and dress, her clasped and motionless hands on her lap resembling a gnarl of pallid and drowned
roots from a drained swamp; at Tull in his faded but absolutely
clean shirt and the overalls which his womenfolks not only kept im-
maculately washed but starched and ironed also, and not creased
through the legs but flat across them from seam to seam, so that on
each Saturday morning they resembled the short pants of a small
boy, and the sedate and innocent blue of his eyes above the month-
old corn-silk beard which concealed most of his abraded face and
which gave him an air of incredible and paradoxical dissoluteness,
not as though at last and without warning he had appeared in the
sight of his fellowmen in his true character, but as if an old Italian
portrait of a child saint had been defaced by a vicious and idle
boy; at Mrs Tull, a strong, full-bosomed though slightly dumpy

woman with an expression of grim and seething outrage which the elapsed four weeks had apparently neither increased nor diminished but had merely set, an outrage which curiously and almost at once began to give the impression of being directed not at any Snopes or at any other man in particular but at all men, all males, and of which Tull himself was not at all the victim but the subject, who sat on one side of her husband while the biggest of the four daughters sat on the other as if they (or Mrs Tull at least) were not so much convinced that Tull might leap up and flee, as determined that he would not; and at Eck and the little boy, identical save for size, and Lump the clerk in a gray cap which someone actually recognised as being the one which Flem Snopes had worn when he went to Texas last year, who between spells of rapid blinking would sit staring at the Justice with the lidless intensity of a rat—and into the lens-distorted and irisless old-man's eyes of the Justice there grew an expression not only of amazement and bewilderment but, as in Ratliff's eyes while he stood on the store gallery four weeks ago, something very like terror.

"This—" he said. "I didn't expect—I didn't look to see—. I'm going to pray," he said. "I aint going to pray aloud. But I hope—" He looked at them. "I wish. . . . Maybe some of you all anyway had better do the same." He bowed his head. They watched him, quiet and grave, while he sat motionless behind the table, the light morning wind moving faintly in his thin hair and the shadow-stipple of windy leaves gliding and flowing across the starched bulge of bosom and the gleaming bone-buttoned cuffs, as rigid and almost as large as sections of six-inch stovepipe, at his joined hands. He raised his head. "Armstid against Snopes," he said. Mrs Armstid spoke. She did not move, she looked at nothing, her hands clasped in her lap, speaking in that flat, toneless and hopeless voice:

"That Texas man said——"

"Wait," the Justice said. He looked about at the faces, the blurred eyes fleeing behind the thick lenses. "Where is the defendant? I dont see him."

"He wouldn't come," the bailiff said.

"Wouldn't come?" the Justice said. "Didn't you serve the papers on him?"

"He wouldn't take them," the bailiff said. "He said——"

"Then he is in contempt!" the Justice cried.

"What for?" Lump Snopes said. "Aint nobody proved yet they was his horses." The Justice looked at him.

"Are you representing the defendant?" he said. Snopes blinked at him for a moment.

"What's that mean?" he said. "That you aim for me to pay whatever fine you think you can clap onto him?"

"So he refuses to defend himself," the Justice said. "Dont he know that I can find against him for that reason, even if pure justice and decency aint enough?"

"It'll be pure something," Snopes said. "It dont take no mind-reader to see how your mind is——"

"Shut up, Snopes," the bailiff said. "If you aint in this case, you keep out of it." He turned back to the Justice. "What you want me to do: go over to the Bend and fetch Snopes here anyway? I reckon I can do it."

"No," the Justice said. "Wait." He looked about at the sober faces again with that bafflement, that dread. "Does anybody here know for sho who them horses belonged to? Anybody?" They looked back at him, sober, attentive—at the neat immaculate old man sitting with his hands locked together on the table before him to still the trembling. "All right, Mrs Armstid," he said. "Tell the court what happened." She told it, unmoving, in the flat, inflectionless voice, looking at nothing, while they listened quietly, coming to the end and ceasing without even any fall of voice, as though the tale mattered nothing and came to nothing. The Justice was looking down at his hands. When she ceased, he looked up at her. "But you haven't showed yet that Snopes owned the horses. The one you want to sue is that Texas man. And he's gone. If you got a judgment against him, you couldn't collect the money. Dont you see?"

"Mr Snopes brought him here," Mrs Armstid said. "Likely that Texas man wouldn't have knowed where Frenchman's Bend was if Mr Snopes hadn't showed him."

"But it was the Texas man that sold the horses and collected the money for them." The Justice looked about again at the faces. "Is that right? You, Bookwright, is that what happened?"

"Yes," Bookwright said. The Justice looked at Mrs Armstid again, with that pity and grief. As the morning increased the wind had risen, so that from time to time gusts of it ran through the branches overhead, bringing a faint snow of petals, prematurely bloomed as the spring itself had condensed with spendthrift speed after the hard winter, and the heavy and drowsing scent of them, about the motionless heads.

"He give Mr Snopes Henry's money. He said Henry hadn't bought no horse. He said I could get the money from Mr Snopes tomorrow."

"And you have witnesses that saw and heard him?"

"Yes, sir. The other men that was there saw him give Mr Snopes the money and say that I could get it——"

"And you asked Snopes for the money?"

"Yes, sir. He said that Texas man taken it away with him when he left. But I would. . . ." She ceased again, perhaps looking down at her hands also. Certainly she was not looking at anyone.

"Yes?" the Justice said. "You would what?"

"I would know them five dollars. I earned them myself, weaving at night after Henry and the chaps was asleep. Some of the ladies in Jefferson would save up string and such and give it to me and I would weave things and sell them. I earned that money a little at a time and I would know it when I saw it because I would take the can outen the chimney and count it now and then while it was making up to enough to buy my chaps some shoes for next winter. I would know it if I was to see it again. If Mr Snopes would just let——"

"Suppose there was somebody seen Flem give that money back to that Texas fellow," Lump Snopes said suddenly.

"Did anybody here see that?" the Justice said.

"Yes," Snopes said, harshly and violently. "Eck here did." He looked at Eck. "Go on. Tell him." The Justice looked at Eck; the four Tull girls turned their heads as one head and looked at him, and Mrs Tull leaned forward to look past her husband, her face cold, furious, and contemptuous, and those standing shifted to look past one another's heads at Eck sitting motionless on the bench.

"Did you see Snopes give Armstid's money back to the Texas man, Eck?" the Justice said. Still Eck did not answer nor move, Lump Snopes made a gross violent sound through the side of his mouth.

"By God, I aint afraid to say it if Eck is. I seen him do it."

"Will you swear that as testimony?" Snopes looked at the Justice. He did not blink now.

"So you wont take my word," he said.

"I want the truth," the Justice said. "If I cant find that, I got to have sworn evidence of what I will have to accept as truth." He lifted the bible from the two other books.

"All right," the bailiff said. "Step up here." Snopes rose from the bench and approached. They watched him, though now there was no shifting nor craning, no movement at all among the faces, the still eyes. Snopes at the table looked back at them once, his gaze traversing swiftly the crescent-shaped rank; he looked at the Justice again. The bailiff grasped the bible; though the Justice did not release it yet.

"You are ready to swear you saw Snopes give that Texas man back the money he took from Henry Armstid for that horse?" he said.

"I said I was, didn't I?" Snopes said. The Justice released the bible.

"Swear him," he said.

"Put your left hand on the Book raise your right hand you solemnly swear and affirm—" the bailiff said rapidly. But Snopes had already done so, his left hand clapped onto the extended bible and the other hand raised and his head turned away as once more his gaze went rapidly along the circle of expressionless and intent faces, saying in that harsh and snarling voice:

"Yes. I saw Flem Snopes give back to that Texas man whatever money Henry Armstid or anybody else thinks Henry Armstid or anybody else paid Flem for any of them horses. Does that suit you?"

"Yes," the Justice said. Then there was no movement, no sound anywhere among them. The bailiff placed the bible quietly on the table beside the Justice's locked hands, and there was no movement save the flow and recover of the windy shadows and the drift of the locust petals. Then Mrs Armstid rose; she stood once more (or still) looking at nothing, her hands clasped across her middle.

"I reckon I can go now, cant I?" she said.

"Yes," the Justice said, rousing. "Unless you would like——"

"I better get started," she said. "It's a right far piece." She had not come in the wagon, but on one of the gaunt and underfed mules. One of the men followed her across the grove and untied the mule for her and led it up to a wagon, from one hub of which she mounted. Then they looked at the Justice again. He sat behind the table, his hands still joined before him, though his head was not

bowed now. Yet he did not move until the bailiff leaned and spoke
to him, when he roused, came suddenly awake without starting, as
an old man wakes from an old man's light sleep. He removed his
hands from the table and, looking down, he spoke exactly as if he
were reading from a paper:

"Tull against Snopes. Assault and——"

"Yes!" Mrs Tull said. "I'm going to say a word before you start."
She leaned, looking past Tull at Lump Snopes again. "If you think
you are going to lie and perjure Flem and Eck Snopes out of——"

"Now, mamma," Tull said. Now she spoke to Tull, without changing her position or her tone or even any break or pause in her
speech:

"Dont you say hush to me! You'll let Eck Snopes or Flem Snopes
or that whole Varner tribe snatch you out of the wagon and beat
you half to death against a wooden bridge. But when it comes to
suing them for your just rights and a punishment, oh no. Because
that wouldn't be neighborly. What's neighborly got to do with
you lying flat on your back in the middle of planting time while
we pick splinters out of your face?" By this time the bailiff was
shouting,

"Order! Order! This here's a law court!" Mrs Tull ceased. She
sat back, breathing hard, staring at the Justice, who sat and spoke
again as if he were reading aloud:

"—assault and battery on the person of Vernon Tull, through the
agency and instrument of one horse, unnamed, belonging to Eck-
rum Snopes. Evidence of physical detriment and suffering, defendant himself. Witnesses, Mrs Tull and daughters——"

"Eck Snopes saw it too," Mrs Tull said, though with less violence
now. "He was there. He got there in plenty of time to see it. Let
him deny it. Let him look me in the face and deny it if he——"

"If you please, ma'am," the Justice said. He said it so quietly that
Mrs Tull hushed and became quite calm, almost a rational and
composed being. "The injury to your husband aint disputed. And
the agency of the horse aint disputed. The law says that when a
man owns a creature which he knows to be dangerous and if that
creature is restrained and restricted from the public commons by a
pen or enclosure capable of restraining and restricting it, if a man
enter that pen or enclosure, whether he knows the creature in it is
dangerous or not dangerous, then that man has committed trespass
and the owner of that creature is not liable. But if that creature

known to him to be dangerous ceases to be restrained by that suitable pen or enclosure, either by accident or design and either with or without the owner's knowledge, then that owner is liable. That's the law. All necessary now is to establish first, the ownership of the horse, and second, that the horse was a dangerous creature within the definition of the law as provided."

"Hah," Mrs Tull said. She said it exactly as Bookwright would have. "Dangerous. Ask Vernon Tull. Ask Henry Armstid if them things was pets."

"If you please, ma'am," the Justice said. He was looking at Eck. "What is the defendant's position? Denial of ownership?"

"What?" Eck said.

"Was that your horse that ran over Mr Tull?"

"Yes," Eck said. "It was mine. How much do I have to p——"

"Hah," Mrs Tull said again. "Denial of ownership. When there were at least forty men—fools too, or they wouldn't have been there. But even a fool's word is good about what he saw and heard —at least forty men heard that Texas murderer give that horse to Eck Snopes. Not sell it to him, mind; give it to him."

"What?" the Justice said. "Gave it to him?"

"Yes," Eck said. "He give it to me. I'm sorry Tull happened to be using that bridge too at the same time. How much do I——"

"Wait," the Justice said. "What did you give him? a note? a swap of some kind?"

"No," Eck said. "He just pointed to it in the lot and told me it belonged to me."

"And he didn't give you a bill of sale or a deed or anything in writing?"

"I reckon he never had time," Eck said. "And after Lon Quick forgot and left that gate open, never nobody had time to do no writing even if we had a thought of it."

"What's all this?" Mrs Tull said. "Eck Snopes has just told you he owned that horse. And if you wont take his word, there were forty men standing at that gate all day long doing nothing, that heard that murdering card-playing whiskey-drinking antichrist—" This time the Justice raised one hand, in its enormous pristine cuff, toward her. He did not look at her.

"Wait," he said. "Then what did he do?" he said to Eck. "Just lead the horse up and put the rope in your hand?"

"No," Eck said. "Him nor nobody else never got no ropes on none of them. He just pointed to the horse in the lot and said it was mine and auctioned off the rest of them and got into the buggy and said good-bye and druv off. And we got our ropes and went into the lot, only Lon Quick forgot to shut the gate. I'm sorry it made Tull's mules snatch him outen the wagon. How much do I owe him?" Then he stopped, because the Justice was no longer looking at him and, as he realised a moment later, no longer listening either. Instead, he was sitting back in the chair, actually leaning back in it for the first time, his head bent slightly and his hands resting on the table before him, the fingers lightly overlapped. They watched him quietly for almost a half-minute before anyone realised that he was looking quietly and steadily at Mrs Tull.

"Well, Mrs Tull," he said, "by your own testimony, Eck never owned that horse."

"What?" Mrs Tull said. It was not loud at all. "What did you say?"

"In the law, ownership cant be conferred or invested by word-of-mouth. It must be established either by recorded or authentic document, or by possession or occupation. By your testimony and his both, he never gave that Texan anything in exchange for that horse, and by his testimony the Texas man never gave him any paper to prove he owned it, and by his testimony and by what I know myself from these last four weeks, nobody yet has ever laid hand or rope either on any one of them. So that horse never came into Eck's possession at all. That Texas man could have given that same horse to a dozen other men standing around that gate that day, without even needing to tell Eck he had done it; and Eck himself could have transferred all his title and equity in it to Mr Tull right there while Mr Tull was lying unconscious on that bridge just by thinking it to himself, and Mr Tull's title would be just as legal as Eck's."

"So I get nothing," Mrs Tull said. Her voice was still calm, quiet, though probably no one but Tull realised that it was too calm and quiet. "My team is made to run away by a wild spotted mad dog, my wagon is wrecked; my husband is jerked out of it and knocked unconscious and unable to work for a whole week with less than half of our seed in the ground, and I get nothing."

"Wait," the Justice said. "The law——"

"The law," Mrs Tull said. She stood suddenly up—a short, broad, strong woman, balanced on the balls of her planted feet.

"Now, mamma," Tull said.

"Yes, ma'am," the Justice said. "Your damages are fixed by statute. The law says that when a suit for damages is brought against the owner of an animal which has committed damage or injury, if the owner of the animal either cant or wont assume liability, the injured or damaged party shall find recompense in the body of the animal. And since Eck Snopes never owned that horse at all, and since you just heard a case here this morning that failed to prove that Flem Snopes had any equity in any of them, that horse still belongs to that Texas man. Or did belong. Because now that horse that made your team run away and snatch your husband out of the wagon, belongs to you and Mr Tull."

"Now, mamma!" Tull said. He rose quickly. But Mrs Tull was still quiet, only quite rigid and breathing hard, until Tull spoke. Then she turned on him, not screaming: shouting; presently the bailiff was banging the table-top with his hand-polished hickory cane and roaring "Order! Order!" while the neat old man, thrust backward in his chair as though about to dodge and trembling with an old man's palsy, looked on with amazed unbelief.

"The horse!" Mrs Tull shouted. "We see it for five seconds, while it is climbing into the wagon with us and then out again. Then it's gone, God dont know where and thank the Lord He dont! And the mules gone with it and the wagon wrecked and you laying there on the bridge with your face full of kindling-wood and bleeding like a hog and dead for all we knew. And he gives us the horse! Dont hush me! Get on to that wagon, fool that would sit there behind a pair of young mules with the reins tied around his wrist! Get on to that wagon, all of you!"

"I cant stand no more!" the old Justice cried. "I wont! This court's adjourned! Adjourned!"

A Rose for Emily

a note on paper of an archaic shape, in a thin, flowing calligraphy in faded ink, to the effect that she no longer went out at all. The tax notice was also enclosed, without comment.

They called a special meeting of the Board of Aldermen. A deputation waited upon her, knocked at the door through which no

– 1 –

WHEN MISS EMILY GRIERSON DIED, OUR WHOLE TOWN WENT TO HER funeral: the men through a sort of respectful affection for a fallen monument, the women mostly out of curiosity to see the inside of her house, which no one save an old manservant—a combined gardener and cook—had seen in at least ten years.

It was a big, squarish frame house that had once been white, decorated with cupolas and spires and scrolled balconies in the heavily lightsome style of the seventies, set on what had once been our most select street. But garages and cotton gins had encroached and obliterated even the august names of that neighborhood; only Miss Emily's house was left, lifting its stubborn and coquettish decay above the cotton wagons and the gasoline pumps—an eyesore among eyesores. And now Miss Emily had gone to join the representatives of those august names where they lay in the cedarbemused cemetery among the ranked and anonymous graves of Union and Confederate soldiers who fell at the battle of Jefferson.

Alive, Miss Emily had been a tradition, a duty, and a care; a sort of hereditary obligation upon the town, dating from that day in 1894 when Colonel Sartoris, the mayor—he who fathered the edict that no Negro woman should appear on the streets without an apron—remitted her taxes, the dispensation dating from the death of her father on into perpetuity. Not that Miss Emily would have accepted charity. Colonel Sartoris invented an involved tale to the effect that Miss Emily's father had loaned money to the town, which the town, as a matter of business, preferred this way of repaying. Only a man of Colonel Sartoris' generation and thought could have invented it, and only a woman could have believed it.

When the next generation, with its more modern ideas, became mayors and aldermen, this arrangement created some little dissatisfaction. On the first of the year they mailed her a tax notice. February came, and there was no reply. They wrote her a formal letter, asking her to call at the sheriff's office at her convenience. A week later the mayor wrote her himself, offering to call or to send his car for her, and received in reply a note on paper of an archaic shape, in a thin, flowing calligraphy in faded ink, to the effect that she no longer went out at all. The tax notice was also enclosed, without comment.

They called a special meeting of the Board of Aldermen. A deputation waited upon her, knocked at the door through which no visitor had passed since she ceased giving china-painting lessons eight or ten years earlier. They were admitted by the old Negro into a dim hall from which a stairway mounted into still more shadow. It smelled of dust and disuse—a close, dank smell. The Negro led them into the parlor. It was furnished in heavy, leather-covered furniture. When the Negro opened the blinds of one window, they could see that the leather was cracked; and when they sat down, a faint dust rose sluggishly about their thighs, spinning with slow motes in the single sun-ray. On a tarnished gilt easel before the fireplace stood a crayon portrait of Miss Emily's father.

They rose when she entered—a small, fat woman in black, with a thin gold chain descending to her waist and vanishing into her belt, leaning on an ebony cane with a tarnished gold head. Her skeleton was small and spare; perhaps that was why what would have been merely plumpness in another was obesity in her. She looked bloated, like a body long submerged in motionless water, and of that pallid hue. Her eyes, lost in the fatty ridges of her face, looked like two small pieces of coal pressed into a lump of dough as they moved from one face to another while the visitors stated their errand.

She did not ask them to sit. She just stood in the door and listened quietly until the spokesman came to a stumbling halt. Then they could hear the invisible watch ticking at the end of the gold chain.

Her voice was dry and cold. "I have no taxes in Jefferson. Colonel Sartoris explained it to me. Perhaps one of you can gain access to the city records and satisfy yourselves."

"But we have. We are the city authorities, Miss Emily. Didn't you get a notice from the sheriff, signed by him?"

"I received a paper, yes," Miss Emily said. "Perhaps he considers himself the sheriff . . . I have no taxes in Jefferson."

"But there is nothing on the books to show that, you see. We must go by the—"

"See Colonel Sartoris. I have no taxes in Jefferson."

"But, Miss Emily—"

"See Colonel Sartoris." (Colonel Sartoris had been dead almost ten years.) "I have no taxes in Jefferson. Tobe!" The Negro appeared. "Show these gentlemen out."

– 2 –

So she vanquished them, horse and foot, just as she had vanquished their fathers thirty years before about the smell. That was two years after her father's death and a short time after her sweetheart—the one we believed would marry her—had deserted her. After her father's death she went out very little; after her sweetheart went away, people hardly saw her at all. A few of the ladies had the temerity to call, but were not received, and the only sign of life about the place was the Negro man—a young man then—going in and out with a market basket.

"Just as if a man—any man—could keep a kitchen properly," the ladies said; so they were not surprised when the smell developed. It was another link between the gross, teeming world and the high and mighty Griersons.

A neighbor, a woman, complained to the mayor, Judge Stevens, eighty years old.

"But what will you have me do about it, madam?" he said.

"Why, send her word to stop it," the woman said. "Isn't there a law?"

"I'm sure that won't be necessary," Judge Stevens said. "It's probably just a snake or a rat that nigger of hers killed in the yard. I'll speak to him about it."

The next day he received two more complaints, one from a man who came in diffident deprecation. "We really must do something about it, Judge. I'd be the last one in the world to bother Miss Emily, but we've got to do something." That night the Board of Aldermen met—three graybeards and one younger man, a member of the rising generation.

"It's simple enough," he said. "Send her word to have her place cleaned up. Give her a certain time to do it in, and if she don't . . ."

"Dammit, sir," Judge Stevens said, "will you accuse a lady to her face of smelling bad?"

So the next night, after midnight, four men crossed Miss Emily's lawn and slunk about the house like burglars, sniffing along the base of the brickwork and at the cellar openings while one of them performed a regular sowing motion with his hand out of a sack slung from his shoulder. They broke open the cellar door and sprinkled lime there, and in all the outbuildings. As they recrossed the lawn, a window that had been dark was lighted and Miss Emily sat in it, the light behind her, and her upright torso motionless as that of an idol. They crept quietly across the lawn and into the shadow of the locusts that lined the street. After a week or two the smell went away.

That was when people had begun to feel really sorry for her. People in our town, remembering how old lady Wyatt, her greataunt, had gone completely crazy at last, believed that the Griersons held themselves a little too high for what they really were. None of the young men were quite good enough for Miss Emily and such. We had long thought of them as a tableau, Miss Emily a slender figure in white in the background, her father a spraddled silhouette in the foreground, his back to her and clutching a horsewhip, the two of them framed by the back-flung front door. So when she got to be thirty and was still single, we were not pleased exactly, but vindicated; even with insanity in the family she wouldn't have turned down all of her chances if they had really materialized.

When her father died, it got about that the house was all that was left to her; and in a way, people were glad. At last they could pity Miss Emily. Being left alone, and a pauper, she had become humanized. Now she too would know the old thrill and the old despair of a penny more or less.

The day after his death all the ladies prepared to call at the house and offer condolence and aid, as is our custom. Miss Emily met them at the door, dressed as usual and with no trace of grief on her face. She told them that her father was not dead. She did that for three days, with the ministers calling on her, and the doctors, trying to persuade her to let them dispose of the body. Just as they were about to resort to law and force, she broke down, and they buried her father quickly.

We did not say she was crazy then. We believed she had to do that. We remembered all the young men her father had driven away, and we knew that with nothing left, she would have to cling to that which had robbed her, as people will.

had begun to say "Poor Emily," and while the two female cousins were visiting her.

– 3 –

She was sick for a long time. When we saw her again, her hair was cut short, making her look like a girl, with a vague resemblance to those angels in colored church windows—sort of tragic and serene.

The town had just let the contracts for paving the sidewalks, and in the summer after her father's death they began the work. The construction company came with niggers and mules and machinery, and a foreman named Homer Barron, a Yankee—a big, dark, ready man, with a big voice and eyes lighter than his face. The little boys would follow in groups to hear him cuss the niggers, and the niggers singing in time to the rise and fall of picks. Pretty soon he knew everybody in town. Whenever you heard a lot of laughing anywhere about the square, Homer Barron would be in the center of the group. Presently we began to see him and Miss Emily on Sunday afternoons driving in the yellow-wheeled buggy and the matched team of bays from the livery stable.

At first we were glad that Miss Emily would have an interest, because the ladies all said, "Of course a Grierson would not think seriously of a Northerner, a day laborer." But there were still others, older people, who said that even grief could not cause a real lady to forget *noblesse oblige*—without calling it *noblesse obige*. They just said, "Poor Emily. Her kinsfolk should come to her." She had some kin in Alabama; but years ago her father had fallen out with them over the estate of old lady Wyatt, the crazy woman, and there was no communication between the two families. They had not even been represented at the funeral.

And as soon as the old people said, "Poor Emily," the whispering began. "Do you suppose it's really so?" they said to one another. "Of course it is. What else could . . ." This behind their hands; rustling of craned silk and satin behind jalousies closed upon the sun of Sunday afternoon as the thin, swift clop-clop-clop of the matched team passed: "Poor Emily."

She carried her head high enough—even when we believed that she was fallen. It was as if she demanded more than ever the recognition of her dignity as the last Grierson; as if it had wanted that touch of earthiness to reaffirm her imperviousness. Like when she bought the rat poison, the arsenic. That was over a year after they had begun to say "Poor Emily," and while the two female cousins were visiting her.

"I want some poison," she said to the druggist. She was over thirty then, still a slight woman, though thinner than usual, with cold, haughty black eyes in a face the flesh of which was strained across the temples and about the eye-sockets as you imagine a lighthouse-keeper's face ought to look. "I want some poison," she said.

"Yes, Miss Emily. What kind? For rats and such? I'd recom—"

"I want the best you have. I don't care what kind."

The druggist named several. "They'll kill anything up to an elephant. But what you want is—"

"Arsenic," Miss Emily said. "Is that a good one?"

"Is . . . arsenic? Yes, ma'am. But what you want—"

"I want arsenic."

The druggist looked down at her. She looked back at him, erect, her face like a strained flag. "Why, of course," the druggist said. "If that's what you want. But the law requires you to tell what you are going to use it for."

Miss Emily just stared at him, her head tilted back in order to look him eye for eye, until he looked away and went and got the arsenic and wrapped it up. The Negro delivery boy brought her the package; the druggist didn't come back. When she opened the package at home there was written on the box, under the skull and bones: "For rats."

– 4 –

So the next day we all said, "She will kill herself"; and we said it would be the best thing. When she had first begun to be seen with Homer Barron, we had said, "She will marry him." Then we said, "She will persuade him yet," because Homer himself had remarked —he liked men, and it was known that he drank with the younger men in the Elks' Club—that he was not a marrying man. Later we said, "Poor Emily" behind the jalousies as they passed on Sunday afternoon in the glittering buggy, Miss Emily with her head high and Homer Barron with his hat cocked and a cigar in his teeth, reins and whip in a yellow glove.

Then some of the ladies began to say that it was a disgrace to the town and a bad example to the young people. The men did not want to interfere, but at last the ladies forced the Baptist minister —Miss Emily's people were Episcopal—to call upon her. He would never divulge what happened during that interview, but he refused to go back again. The next Sunday they again drove about the streets, and the following day the minister's wife wrote to Miss Emily's relations in Alabama.

So she had blood-kin under her roof again and we sat back to watch developments. At first nothing happened. Then we were sure that they were to be married. We learned that Miss Emily had been to the jeweler's and ordered a man's toilet set in silver, with the letters H. B. on each piece. Two days later we learned that she had bought a complete outfit of men's clothing, including a nightshirt, and we said, "They are married." We were really glad. We were glad because the two female cousins were even more Grierson than Miss Emily had ever been.

So we were not surprised when Homer Barron—the streets had been finished some time since—was gone. We were a little disappointed that there was not a public blowing-off, but we believed that he had gone on to prepare for Miss Emily's coming, or to give her a chance to get rid of the cousins. (By that time it was a cabal, and we were all Miss Emily's allies to help circumvent the cousins.) Sure enough, after another week they departed. And, as we had expected all along, within three days Homer Barron was back in town. A neighbor saw the Negro man admit him at the kitchen door at dusk one evening.

And that was the last we saw of Homer Barron. And of Miss Emily for some time. The Negro man went in and out with the market basket, but the front door remained closed. Now and then we would see her at a window for a moment, as the men did that night when they sprinkled the lime, but for almost six months she did not appear on the streets. Then we knew that this was to be expected too; as if that quality of her father which had thwarted her woman's life so many times had been too virulent and too furious to die.

When we next saw Miss Emily, she had grown fat and her hair was turning gray. During the next few years it grew grayer and grayer until it attained an even pepper-and-salt iron-gray, when it ceased turning. Up to the day of her death at seventy-four it was still that vigorous iron-gray, like the hair of an active man.

From that time on her front door remained closed, save for a period of six or seven years, when she was about forty, during which she gave lessons in china-painting. She fitted up a studio

in one of the downstairs rooms, where the daughters and grand-
daughters of Colonel Sartoris' contemporaries were sent to her with
the same regularity and in the same spirit that they were sent to
church on Sundays with a twenty-five-cent piece for the collection
plate. Meanwhile her taxes had been remitted.

Then the newer generation became the backbone and the spirit
of the town, and the painting pupils grew up and fell away and did
not send their children to her with boxes of color and tedious
brushes and pictures cut from the ladies' magazines. The front door
closed upon the last one and remained closed for good. When the
town got free postal delivery, Miss Emily alone refused to let them
fasten the metal numbers above her door and attach a mailbox to
it. She would not listen to them.

Daily, monthly, yearly we watched the Negro grow grayer and
more stooped, going in and out with the market basket. Each
December we sent her a tax notice, which would be returned by
the post office a week later, unclaimed. Now and then we would
see her in one of the downstairs windows—she had evidently shut
up the top floor of the house—like the carven torso of an idol in a
niche, looking or not looking at us, we could never tell which. Thus
she passed from generation to generation—dear, inescapable, impervious, tranquil, and perverse.

And so she died. Fell ill in the house filled with dust and shadows, with only a doddering Negro man to wait on her. We did not
even know she was sick; we had long since given up trying to get
any information from the Negro. He talked to no one, probably
not even to her, for his voice had grown harsh and rusty, as if from
disuse.

She died in one of the downstairs rooms, in a heavy walnut bed
with a curtain, her gray head propped on a pillow yellow and
moldy with age and lack of sunlight.

–5–

The Negro met the first of the ladies at the front door and let
them in, with their hushed, sibilant voices and their quick, curious
glances, and then he disappeared. He walked right through the
house and out the back and was not seen again.

The two female cousins came at once. They held the funeral on
the second day, with the town coming to look at Miss Emily beneath a mass of bought flowers, with the crayon face of her father

musing profoundly above the bier and the ladies sibilant and macabre; and the very old men—some in their brushed Confederate uniforms—on the porch and the lawn, talking of Miss Emily as if she had been a contemporary of theirs, believing that they had danced with her and courted her perhaps, confusing time with its mathematical progression, as the old do, to whom all the past is not a diminishing road but, instead, a huge meadow which no winter ever quite touches, divided from them now by the narrow bottleneck of the most recent decade of years.

Already we knew that there was one room in that region above stairs which no one had seen in forty years, and which would have to be forced. They waited until Miss Emily was decently in the ground before they opened it.

The violence of breaking down the door seemed to fill this room with pervading dust. A thin, acrid pall as of the tomb seemed to lie everywhere upon this room decked and furnished as for a bridal: upon the valance curtains of faded rose color, upon the rose-shaded lights, upon the dressing table, upon the delicate array of crystal and the man's toilet things backed with tarnished silver, silver so tarnished that the monogram was obscured. Among them lay a collar and tie, as if they had just been removed, which, lifted, left upon the surface a pale crescent in the dust. Upon a chair hung the suit, carefully folded; beneath it the two mute shoes and the discarded socks.

The man himself lay in the bed.

For a long while we just stood there, looking down at the profound and fleshless grin. The body had apparently once lain in the attitude of an embrace, but now the long sleep that outlasts love, that conquers even the grimace of love, had cuckolded him. What was left of him, rotted beneath what was left of the nightshirt, had become inextricable from the bed in which he lay; and upon him and upon the pillow beside him lay that even coating of the patient and biding dust.

Then we noticed that in the second pillow was the indentation of a head. One of us lifted something from it, and leaning forward, that faint and invisible dust dry and acrid in the nostrils, we saw a long strand of iron-gray hair.

Barn Burning

THE STORE IN WHICH THE JUSTICE OF THE PEACE'S COURT WAS SITTING smelled of cheese. The boy, crouched on his nail keg at the back of the crowded room, knew he smelled cheese, and more: from where he sat he could see the ranked shelves close-packed with the solid, squat, dynamic shapes of tin cans whose labels his stomach read, not from the lettering which meant nothing to his mind but from the scarlet devils and the silver curve of fish—this, the cheese which he knew he smelled and the hermetic meat which his intestines believed he smelled coming in intermittent gusts momentary and brief between the other constant one, the smell and sense just a little of fear because mostly of despair and grief, the old fierce pull of blood. He could not see the table where the Justice sat and before which his father and his father's enemy (*our enemy* he thought in that despair; *ourn! mine and hisn both! He's my father!*) stood, but he could hear them, the two of them that is, because his father had said no word yet:

"But what proof have you, Mr. Harris?"

"I told you. The hog got into my corn. I caught it up and sent it back to him. He had no fence that would hold it. I told him so, warned him. The next time I put the hog in my pen. When he came to get it I gave him enough wire to patch up his pen. The next time I put the hog up and kept it. I rode down to his house and saw the wire I gave him still rolled on to the spool in his yard. I told him he could have the hog when he paid me a dollar pound fee. That evening a nigger came with the dollar and got the hog. He was a strange nigger. He said, 'He say to tell you wood and hay kin burn.' I said, 'What?' 'That whut he say to tell you,' the nigger said. 'Wood and hay kin burn.' That night my barn burned. I got the stock out but I lost the barn."

"Where is the nigger? Have you got him?"

"He was a strange nigger, I tell you. I don't know what became of him."

"But that's not proof. Don't you see that's not proof?"

"Get that boy up here. He knows." For a moment the boy

499

thought too that the man meant his older brother until Harris said,
"Not him. The little one. The boy," and, crouching, small for his
age, small and wiry like his father, in patched and faded jeans even
too small for him, with straight, uncombed, brown hair and eyes
gray and wild as storm scud, he saw the men between himself and
the table part and become a lane of grim faces, at the end of which
he saw the Justice, a shabby, collarless, graying man in spectacles,
beckoning him. He felt no floor under his bare feet; he seemed to
walk beneath the palpable weight of the grim turning faces. His
father, stiff in his black Sunday coat donned not for the trial but
for the moving, did not even look at him. *He aims for me to lie,*
he thought, again with that frantic grief and despair. *And I will
have to do hit.*

"What's your name, boy?" the Justice said.

"Colonel Sartoris Snopes," the boy whispered.

"Hey?" the Justice said. "Talk louder. Colonel Sartoris? I reckon
anybody named for Colonel Sartoris in this country can't help but
tell the truth, can they?" The boy said nothing. *Enemy! Enemy!* he
thought; for a moment he could not even see, could not see that
the Justice's face was kindly nor discern that his voice was troubled
when he spoke to the man named Harris: "Do you want me to
question this boy?" But he could hear, and during those subsequent
long seconds while there was absolutely no sound in the crowded
little room save that of quiet and intent breathing it was as if he
had swung outward at the end of a grape vine, over a ravine, and
at the top of the swing had been caught in a prolonged instant of
mesmerized gravity, weightless in time.

"No!" Harris said violently, explosively. "Damnation! Send him
out of here!" Now time, the fluid world, rushed beneath him again,
the voices coming to him again through the smell of cheese and
sealed meat, the fear and despair and the old grief of blood:

"This case is closed. I can't find against you, Snopes, but I can
give you advice. Leave this country and don't come back to it."

His father spoke for the first time, his voice cold and harsh, level,
without emphasis: "I aim to. I don't figure to stay in a country
among people who . . ." he said something unprintable and vile,
addressed to no one.

"That'll do," the Justice said. "Take your wagon and get out of
this country before dark. Case dismissed."

His father turned, and he followed the stiff black coat, the wiry figure walking a little stiffly from where a Confederate provost's man's musket ball had taken him in the heel on a stolen horse thirty years ago, followed the two backs now, since his older brother had appeared from somewhere in the crowd, no taller than the father but thicker, chewing tobacco steadily, between the two lines of grim-faced men and out of the store and across the worn gallery and down the sagging steps and among the dogs and half-grown boys in the mild May dust, where as he passed a voice hissed:

"Barn burner!"

Again he could not see, whirling; there was a face in a red haze, moonlike, bigger than the full moon, the owner of it half again his size, he leaping in the red haze toward the face, feeling no blow, feeling no shock when his head struck the earth, scrabbling up and leaping again, feeling no blow this time either and tasting no blood, scrabbling up to see the other boy in full flight and himself already leaping into pursuit as his father's hand jerked him back, the harsh, cold voice speaking above him: "Go get in the wagon."

It stood in a grove of locusts and mulberries across the road. His two hulking sisters in their Sunday dresses and his mother and her sister in calico and sunbonnets were already in it, sitting on and among the sorry residue of the dozen and more movings which even the boy could remember—the battered stove, the broken beds and chairs, the clock inlaid with mother-of-pearl, which would not run, stopped at some fourteen minutes past two o'clock of a dead and forgotten day and time, which had been his mother's dowry. She was crying, though when she saw him she drew her sleeve across her face and began to descend from the wagon. "Get back," the father said.

"He's hurt. I got to get some water and wash his . . ."

"Get back in the wagon," his father said. He got in too, over the tail-gate. His father mounted to the seat where the older brother already sat and struck the gaunt mules two savage blows with the peeled willow, but without heat. It was not even sadistic; it was exactly that same quality which in later years would cause his descendants to over-run the engine before putting a motor car into motion, striking and reining back in the same movement. The wagon went on, the store with its quiet crowd of grimly watching men dropped behind; a curve in the road hid it. *Forever* he thought. *Maybe he's done satisfied now, now that he has* . . . stopping himself, not to say it aloud even to himself. His mother's hand touched his shoulder.

"Does hit hurt?" she said.

"Naw," he said. "Hit don't hurt. Lemme be."

"Can't you wipe some of the blood off before hit dries?"

"I'll wash to-night," he said. "Lemme be, I tell you."

The wagon went on. He did not know where they were going. None of them ever did or ever asked, because it was always somewhere, always a house of sorts waiting for them a day or two days or even three days away. Likely his father had already arranged to make a crop on another farm before he . . . Again he had to stop himself. He (the father) always did. There was something about his wolflike independence and even courage when the advantage was at least neutral which impressed strangers, as if they got from his latent ravening ferocity not so much a sense of dependability as a feeling that his ferocious conviction in the rightness of his own actions would be of advantage to all whose interest lay with his.

That night they camped, in a grove of oaks and beeches where a spring ran. The nights were still cool and they had a fire against it, of a rail lifted from a nearby fence and cut into lengths—a small fire, neat, niggard almost, a shrewd fire; such fires were his father's habit and custom always, even in freezing weather. Older, the boy might have remarked this and wondered why not a big one; why should not a man who had not only seen the waste and extravagance of war, but who had in his blood an inherent voracious prodigality with material not his own, have burned everything in sight? Then he might have gone a step farther and thought that that was the reason: that niggard blaze was the living fruit of nights passed during those four years in the woods hiding from all men, blue or gray, with his strings of horses (captured horses, he called them). And older still, he might have divined the true reason: that the element of fire spoke to some deep mainspring of his father's being, as the element of steel or of powder spoke to other men, as the one weapon for the preservation of integrity, else breath were not worth the breathing, and hence to be regarded with respect and used with discretion.

But he did not think this now and he had seen those same niggard blazes all his life. He merely ate his supper beside it and was already half asleep over his iron plate when his father called him, and once more he followed the stiff back, the stiff and ruthless limp, up the slope and on to the starlit road where, turning, he could see his father against the stars but without face or depth— a shape black, flat, and bloodless as though cut from tin in the iron folds of the frockcoat which had not been made for him, the voice harsh like tin and without heat like tin:

"You were fixing to tell them. You would have told him." He didn't answer. His father struck him with the flat of his hand on the side of the head, hard but without heat, exactly as he had struck the two mules at the store, exactly as he would strike either of them with any stick in order to kill a horse fly, his voice still without heat or anger: "You're getting to be a man. You got to learn. You got to learn to stick to your own blood or you ain't going to have any blood to stick to you. Do you think either of them, any man there this morning, would? Don't you know all they wanted was a chance to get at me because they knew I had them beat? Eh?" Later, twenty years later, he was to tell himself, "If I had said they wanted only truth, justice, he would have hit me again." But now he said nothing. He was not crying. He just stood there. "Answer me," his father said.

"Yes," he whispered. His father turned.

"Get on to bed. We'll be there tomorrow."

Tomorrow they were there. In the early afternoon the wagon stopped before a paintless two-room house identical almost with the dozen others it had stopped before even in the boy's ten years, and again, as on the other dozen occasions, his mother and aunt got down and began to unload the wagon, although his two sisters and his father and brother had not moved.

"Likely hit ain't fitten for hawgs," one of the sisters said.

"Nevertheless, fit it will and you'll hog it and like it," his father said. "Get out of them chairs and help your Ma unload."

The two sisters got down, big, bovine, in a flutter of cheap ribbons; one of them drew from the jumbled wagon bed a battered lantern, the other a worn broom. His father handed the reins to the older son and began to climb stiffly over the wheel. "When they get unloaded, take the team to the barn and feed them." Then he said, and at first the boy thought he was still speaking to his brother: "Come with me."

"Me?" he said.

"Yes," his father said. "You."

"Abner," his mother said. His father paused and looked back—the harsh level stare beneath the shaggy, graying, irascible brows.

"I reckon I'll have a word with the man that aims to begin tomorrow owning me body and soul for the next eight months."

They went back up the road. A week ago—or before last night, that is—he would have asked where they were going, but not now. His father had struck him before last night but never before had he paused afterward to explain why; it was as if the blow and the following calm, outrageous voice still rang, repercussed, divulging nothing to him save the terrible handicap of being young, the light weight of his few years, just heavy enough to prevent his soaring free of the world as it seemed to be ordered but not heavy enough to keep him footed solid in it, to resist it and try to change the course of its events.

Presently he could see the grove of oaks and cedars and the other flowering trees and shrubs where the house would be, though not the house yet. They walked beside a fence massed with honeysuckle and Cherokee roses and came to a gate swinging open between two brick pillars, and now, beyond a sweep of drive, he saw the house for the first time and at that instant he forgot his father and the terror and despair both, and even when he remembered his father again (who had not stopped) the terror and despair did not return. Because, for all the twelve movings, they had sojourned until now in a poor country, a land of small farms and fields and houses, and he had never seen a house like this before. *Hit's big as a courthouse* he thought quietly, with a surge of peace and joy whose reason he could not have thought into words, being too young for that: *They are safe from him. People whose lives are a part of this peace and dignity are beyond his touch, he no more to them than a buzzing wasp: capable of stinging for a little moment but that's all; the spell of this peace and dignity rendering even the barns and stable and cribs which belong to it impervious to the puny flames he might contrive* . . . this, the peace and joy, ebbing for an instant as he looked again at the stiff black back, the stiff and implacable limp of the figure which was not dwarfed by the house, for the reason that it had never looked big anywhere and which now, against the serene columned backdrop, had more than ever that impervious quality of something cut ruthlessly from tin, depthless, as though, sidewise to the sun, it would cast no shadow. Watching him, the boy remarked the absolutely undeviating course

which his father held and saw the stiff foot come squarely down in
a pile of fresh droppings where a horse had stood in the drive and
which his father could have avoided by a simple change of stride.
But it ebbed only for a moment, though he could not have thought
this into words either, walking on in the spell of the house, which
he could even want but without envy, without sorrow, certainly
never with that ravening and jealous rage which unknown to him
walked in the ironlike black coat before him: *Maybe he will feel it
too. Maybe it will even change him now from what maybe he
couldn't help but be.*

They crossed the portico. Now he could hear his father's stiff
foot as it came down on the boards with clocklike finality, a sound
out of all proportion to the displacement of the body it bore and
which was not dwarfed either by the white door before it, as
though it had attained to a sort of vicious and ravening minimum
not to be dwarfed by anything—the flat, wide, black hat, the formal coat of broadcloth which had once been black but which had
now that friction-glazed greenish cast of the bodies of old house
flies, the lifted sleeve which was too large, the lifted hand like a
curled claw. The door opened so promptly that the boy knew the
Negro must have been watching them all the time, an old man with
neat grizzled hair, in a linen jacket, who stood barring the door
with his body, saying, "Wipe yo foots, white man, fo you come in
here. Major ain't home nohow."

"Get out of my way, nigger," his father said, without heat too,
flinging the door back and the Negro also and entering, his hat
still on his head. And now the boy saw the prints of the stiff foot
on the doorjamb and saw them appear on the pale rug behind
the machinelike deliberation of the foot which seemed to bear (or
transmit) twice the weight which the body compassed. The Negro
was shouting "Miss Lula! Miss Lula!" somewhere behind them, then
the boy, deluged as though by a warm wave by a suave turn of car-
peted stair and a pendant glitter of chandeliers and a mute gleam
of gold frames, heard the swift feet and saw her too, a lady—perhaps he had never seen her like before either—in a gray, smooth
gown with lace at the throat and an apron tied at the waist and
the sleeves turned back, wiping cake or biscuit dough from her
hands with a towel as she came up the hall, looking not at his father at all but at the tracks on the blond rug with an expression of
incredulous amazement.

"I tried," the Negro cried. "I tole him to . . ."

"Will you please go away?" she said in a shaking voice. "Major de Spain is not at home. Will you please go away?"

His father had not spoken again. He did not speak again. He did not even look at her. He just stood stiff in the center of the rug, in his hat, the shaggy iron-gray brows twitching slightly above the pebble-colored eyes as he appeared to examine the house with brief deliberation. Then with the same deliberation he turned; the boy watched him pivot on the good leg and saw the stiff foot drag round the arc of the turning, leaving a final long and fading smear. His father never looked at it, he never once looked down at the rug. The Negro held the door. It closed behind them, upon the hysteric and indistinguishable woman-wail. His father stopped at the top of the steps and scraped his boot clean on the edge of it. At the gate he stopped again. He stood for a moment, planted stiffly on the stiff foot, looking back at the house. "Pretty and white, ain't it?" he said. "That's sweat. Nigger sweat. Maybe it ain't white enough yet to suit him. Maybe he wants to mix some white sweat with it."

Two hours later the boy was chopping wood behind the house within which his mother and aunt and the two sisters (the mother and aunt, not the two girls, he knew that; even at this distance and muffled by walls the flat loud voices of the two girls emanated an incorrigible idle inertia) were setting up the stove to prepare a meal, when he heard the hooves and saw the linen-clad man on a fine sorrel mare, whom he recognized even before he saw the rolled rug in front of the Negro youth following on a fat bay carriage horse—a suffused, angry face vanishing, still at full gallop, beyond the corner of the house where his father and brother were sitting in the two tilted chairs; and a moment later, almost before he could have put the axe down, he heard the hooves again and watched the sorrel mare go back out of the yard, already galloping again. Then his father began to shout one of the sisters' names, who presently emerged backward from the kitchen door dragging the rolled rug along the ground by one end while the other sister walked behind it.

"If you ain't going to tote, go on and set up the wash pot," the first said.

"You, Sarty!" the second shouted. "Set up the wash pot!" His father appeared at the door, framed against that shabbiness, as he had been against that other bland perfection, impervious to either, the mother's anxious face at his shoulder.

"Go on," the father said. "Pick it up." The two sisters stooped, broad, lethargic; stooping, they presented an incredible expanse of pale cloth and a flutter of tawdry ribbons.

"If I thought enough of a rug to have to git hit all the way from France I wouldn't keep hit where folks coming in would have to tromp on hit," the first said. They raised the rug.

"Abner," the mother said. "Let me do it."

"You go back and git dinner," his father said. "I'll tend to this."

From the woodpile through the rest of the afternoon the boy watched them, the rug spread flat in the dust beside the bubbling wash-pot, the two sisters stooping over it with that profound and lethargic reluctance, while the father stood over them in turn, implacable and grim, driving them though never raising his voice again. He could smell the harsh homemade lye they were using; he saw his mother come to the door once and look toward them with an expression not anxious now but very like despair; he saw his father turn, and he fell to with the axe and saw from the corner of his eye his father raise from the ground a flattish fragment of field stone and examine it and return to the pot, and this time his mother actually spoke: "Abner. Abner. Please don't. Please, Abner."

Then he was done too. It was dusk; the whippoorwills had already begun. He could smell coffee from the room where they would presently eat the cold food remaining from the mid-afternoon meal, though when he entered the house he realized they were having coffee again probably because there was a fire on the hearth, before which the rug now lay spread over the backs of the two chairs. The tracks of his father's foot were gone. Where they had been were now long, water-cloudy scoriations resembling the sporadic course of a lilliputian mowing machine.

It still hung there while they ate the cold food and then went to bed, scattered without order or claim up and down the two rooms, his mother in one bed, where his father would later lie, the older brother in the other, himself, the aunt, and the two sisters on pallets on the floor. But his father was not in bed yet. The last thing the boy remembered was the depthless, harsh silhouette of the hat and coat bending over the rug and it seemed to him that he had not even closed his eyes when the silhouette was standing over him, the fire almost dead behind it, the stiff foot prodding him awake. "Catch up the mule," his father said.

When he returned with the mule his father was standing in the black door, the rolled rug over his shoulder. "Ain't you going to ride?" he said.

"No. Give me your foot."

He bent his knee into his father's hand, the wiry, surprising power flowed smoothly, rising, he rising with it, on to the mule's bare back (they had owned a saddle once; the boy could remember it though not when or where) and with the same effortlessness his father swung the rug up in front of him. Now in the starlight they retraced the afternoon's path, up the dusty road rife with honeysuckle, through the gate and up the black tunnel of the drive to the lightless house, where he sat on the mule and felt the rough warp of the rug drag across his thighs and vanish.

"Don't you want me to help?" he whispered. His father did not answer and now he heard again that stiff foot striking the hollow portico with that wooden and clocklike deliberation, that outrageous overstatement of the weight it carried. The rug, hunched, not flung (the boy could tell that even in the darkness) from his father's shoulder struck the angle of wall and floor with a sound unbelievably loud, thunderous, then the foot again, unhurried and enormous; a light came on in the house and the boy sat, tense, breathing steadily and quietly and just a little fast, though the foot itself did not increase its beat at all, descending the steps now; now the boy could see him.

"Don't you want to ride now?" he whispered. "We kin both ride now," the light within the house altering now, flaring up and sinking. *He's coming down the stairs now,* he thought. He had already ridden the mule up beside the horse block; presently his father was up behind him and he doubled the reins over and slashed the mule across the neck, but before the animal could begin to trot the hard, thin arm came round him, the hard, knotted hand jerking the mule back to a walk.

In the first red rays of the sun they were in the lot, putting plow gear on the mules. This time the sorrel mare was in the lot before he heard it at all, the rider collarless and even bareheaded, trembling, speaking in a shaking voice as the woman in the house had done, his father merely looking up once before stooping again to the hame he was buckling, so that the man on the mare spoke to his stooping back:

"You must realize you have ruined that rug. Wasn't there anybody here, any of your women . . ." he ceased, shaking, the boy watching him, the older brother leaning now in the stable door, chewing, blinking slowly and steadily at nothing apparently. "It cost a hundred dollars. But you never had a hundred dollars. You never will. So I'm going to charge you twenty bushels of corn against your crop. I'll add it in your contract and when you come to the commissary you can sign it. That won't keep Mrs. de Spain quiet but maybe it will teach you to wipe your feet off before you enter her house again."

Then he was gone. The boy looked at his father, who still had not spoken or even looked up again, who was now adjusting the logger-head in the hame.

"Pap," he said. His father looked at him—the inscrutable face, the shaggy brows beneath which the gray eyes glinted coldly. Suddenly the boy went toward him, fast, stopping as suddenly. "You done the best you could!" he cried. "If he wanted hit done different why didn't he wait and tell you how? He won't git no twenty bushels! He won't git none! We'll gether hit and hide hit! I kin watch . . ."

"Did you put the cutter back in that straight stock like I told you?"

"No, sir," he said.

"Then go do it."

That was Wednesday. During the rest of that week he worked steadily, at what was within his scope and some which was beyond it, with an industry that did not need to be driven nor even commanded twice; he had this from his mother, with the difference that some at least of what he did he liked to do, such as splitting wood with the half-size axe which his mother and aunt had earned, or saved money somehow, to present him with at Christmas. In company with the two older women (and on one afternoon, even one of the sisters), he built pens for the shoat and the cow which were a part of his father's contract with the landlord, and one afternoon, his father being absent, gone somewhere on one of the mules, he went to the field.

They were running a middle buster now, his brother holding the plow straight while he handled the reins, and walking beside the straining mule, the rich black soil shearing cool and damp against his bare ankles, he thought *Maybe this is the end of it. Maybe even that twenty bushels that seems hard to have to pay for just a rug will be a cheap price for him to stop forever and always from being what he used to be;* thinking, dreaming now, so that his brother had to speak sharply to him to mind the mule: *Maybe he even won't collect the twenty bushels. Maybe it will all add up and balance and vanish—corn, rug, fire; the terror and grief, the being pulled two ways like between two teams of horses—gone, done with for ever and ever.*

Then it was Saturday; he looked up from beneath the mule he was harnessing and saw his father in the black coat and hat. "Not that," his father said. "The wagon gear." And then, two hours later, sitting in the wagon bed behind his father and brother on the seat, the wagon accomplished a final curve, and he saw the weathered paintless store with its tattered tobacco- and patent-medicine posters and the tethered wagons and saddle animals below the gallery. He mounted the gnawed steps behind his father and brother, and there again was the lane of quiet, watching faces for the three of them to walk through. He saw the man in spectacles sitting at the plank table and he did not need to be told this was a Justice of the Peace; he sent one glare of fierce, exultant, partisan defiance at the man in collar and cravat now, whom he had seen but twice before in his life, and that on a galloping horse, who now wore on his face an expression not of rage but of amazed unbelief which the boy could not have known was at the incredible circumstance of being sued by one of his own tenants, and came and stood against his father and cried at the Justice: "He ain't done it! He ain't burnt . . ."

"Go back to the wagon," his father said.

"Burnt?" the Justice said. "Do I understand this rug was burned too?"

"Does anybody here claim it was?" his father said. "Go back to the wagon." But he did not, he merely retreated to the rear of the room, crowded as that other had been, but not to sit down this time, instead, to stand pressing among the motionless bodies, listening to the voices:

"And you claim twenty bushels of corn is too high for the damage you did to the rug?"

"He brought the rug to me and said he wanted the tracks washed out of it. I washed the tracks out and took the rug back to him."

"But you didn't carry the rug back to him in the same condition it was in before you made the tracks on it."

His father did not answer, and now for perhaps half a minute there was no sound at all save that of breathing, the faint, steady suspiration of complete and intent listening.

"You decline to answer that, Mr. Snopes?" Again his father did not answer. "I'm going to find against you, Mr. Snopes. I'm going to find that you were responsible for the injury to Major de Spain's rug and hold you liable for it. But twenty bushels of corn seems a little high for a man in your circumstances to have to pay. Major de Spain claims it cost a hundred dollars. October corn will be worth about fifty cents. I figure that if Major de Spain can stand a ninety-five dollar loss on something he paid cash for, you can stand a five-dollar loss you haven't earned yet. I hold you in damages to Major de Spain to the amount of ten bushels of corn over and above your contract with him, to be paid to him out of your crop at gathering time. Court adjourned."

It had taken no time hardly, the morning was but half begun. He thought they would return home and perhaps back to the field, since they were late, far behind all other farmers. But instead his father passed on behind the wagon, merely indicating with his hand for the older brother to follow with it, and crossed the road toward the blacksmith shop opposite, pressing on after his father, overtaking him, speaking, whispering up at the harsh, calm face beneath the weathered hat: "He won't git no ten bushels neither. He won't git one. We'll . . ." until his father glanced for an instant down at him, the face absolutely calm, the grizzled eyebrows tangled above the cold eyes, the voice almost pleasant, almost gentle: "You think so? Well, we'll wait till October anyway."

The matter of the wagon—the setting of a spoke or two and the tightening of the tires—did not take long either, the business of the tires accomplished by driving the wagon into the spring branch behind the shop and letting it stand there, the mules nuzzling into the water from time to time, and the boy on the seat with the idle reins, looking up the slope and through the sooty tunnel of the shed where the slow hammer rang and where his father sat on an upended cypress bolt, easily, either talking or listening, still sitting there when the boy brought the dripping wagon up out of the branch and halted it before the door.

"Take them on to the shade and hitch," his father said. He did so and returned. His father and the smith and a third man squatting on his heels inside the door were talking, about crops and animals; the boy, squatting too in the ammoniac dust and hoofparings and scales of rust, heard his father tell a long and unhurried story out of the time before the birth of the older brother even when he had been a professional horsetrader. And then his father came up beside him where he stood before a tattered last year's circus poster on the other side of the store, gazing rapt and quiet at the scarlet horses, the incredible poisings and convolutions of tulle and tights and the painted leers of comedians, and said, "It's time to eat."

But not at home. Squatting beside his brother against the front wall, he watched his father emerge from the store and produce from a paper sack a segment of cheese and divide it carefully and deliberately into three with his pocket knife and produce crackers from the same sack. They all three squatted on the gallery and ate, slowly, without talking; then in the store again, they drank from a tin dipper tepid water smelling of the cedar bucket and of living beech trees. And still they did not go home. It was a horse lot this time, a tall rail fence upon and along which men stood and sat and out of which one by one horses were led, to be walked and trotted and then cantered back and forth along the road while the slow swapping and buying went on and the sun began to slant westward, they—the three of them—watching and listening, the older brother with his muddy eyes and his steady, inevitable tobacco, the father commenting now and then on certain of the animals, to no one in particular.

It was after sundown when they reached home. They ate supper by lamplight, then, sitting on the doorstep, the boy watched the night fully accomplish, listening to the whippoorwills and the frogs, when he heard his mother's voice: "Abner! No! No! Oh, God. Oh, God. Abner!" and he rose, whirled, and saw the altered light through the door where a candle stub now burned in a bottle neck on the table and his father, still in the hat and coat, at once formal and burlesque as though dressed carefully for some shabby and ceremonial violence, emptying the reservoir of the lamp back into the five-gallon kerosene can from which it had been filled, while the mother tugged at his arm until he shifted the lamp to the other hand and flung her back, not savagely or viciously, just hard, into the wall, her hands flung out against the wall for balance, her mouth open and in her face the same quality of hopeless despair as had been in her voice. Then his father saw him standing in the door.

"Go to the barn and get that can of oil we were oiling the wagon with," he said. The boy did not move. Then he could speak.

"What . . ." he cried. "What are you . . ."

"Go get that oil," his father said. "Go."

Then he was moving, running, outside the house, toward the stable: this the old habit, the old blood which he had not been permitted to choose for himself, which had been bequeathed him willy nilly and which had run for so long (and who knew where, battening on what of outrage and savagery and lust) before it came to him. *I could keep on,* he thought. *I could run on and on and never look back, never need to see his face again. Only I can't. I can't,* the rusted can in his hand now, the liquid sploshing in it as he ran back to the house and into it, into the sound of his mother's weeping in the next room, and handed the can to his father.

"Ain't you going to even send a nigger?" he cried. "At least you sent a nigger before!"

This time his father didn't strike him. The hand came even faster than the blow had, the same hand which had set the can on the table with almost excruciating care flashing from the can toward him too quick for him to follow it, gripping him by the back of his shirt and on to tiptoe before he had seen it quit the can, the face stooping at him in breathless and frozen ferocity, the cold, dead voice speaking over him to the older brother who leaned against the table, chewing with that steady, curious, sidewise motion of cows:

"Empty the can into the big one and go on. I'll catch up with you."

"Better tie him up to the bedpost," the brother said.

"Do like I told you," the father said. Then the boy was moving, his bunched shirt and the hard, bony hand between his shoulder-blades, his toes just touching the floor, across the room and into the other one, past the sisters sitting with spread heavy thighs in the two chairs over the cold hearth, and to where his mother and aunt sat side by side on the bed, the aunt's arms about his mother's shoulders.

"Hold him," the father said. The aunt made a startled movement. "Not you," the father said. "Lennie. Take hold of him. I want to see you do it." His mother took him by the wrist. "You'll hold him better than that. If he gets loose don't you know what he is going to do? He will go up yonder." He jerked his head toward the road. "Maybe I'd better tie him."

"I'll hold him," his mother whispered.

"See you do then." Then his father was gone, the stiff foot heavy and measured upon the boards, ceasing at last.

Then he began to struggle. His mother caught him in both arms, he jerking and wrenching at them. He would be stronger in the end, he knew that. But he had no time to wait for it. "Lemme go!" he cried. "I don't want to have to hit you!"

"Let him go!" the aunt said. "If he don't go, before God, I am going up there myself!"

"Don't you see I can't?" his mother cried. "Sarty! Sarty! No! No! Help me, Lizzie!"

Then he was free. His aunt grasped at him but it was too late. He whirled, running, his mother stumbled forward on to her knees behind him, crying to the nearer sister: "Catch him, Net! Catch him!" But that was too late too, the sister (the sisters were twins, born at the same time, yet either of them now gave the impression of being, encompassing as much living meat and volume and weight as any other two of the family) not yet having begun to rise from the chair, her head, face, alone merely turned, presenting to him in the flying instant an astonishing expanse of young female features untroubled by any surprise even, wearing only an expression of bovine interest. Then he was out of the room, out of the house, in the mild dust of the starlit road and the heavy rifeness of honeysuckle, the pale ribbon unspooling with terrific slowness under his running feet, reaching the gate at last and turning in, running, his heart and lungs drumming, on up the drive toward the lighted house, the lighted door. He did not knock, he burst in, sobbing for breath, incapable for the moment of speech; he saw the astonished face of the Negro in the linen jacket without knowing when the Negro had appeared.

"De Spain!" he cried, panted. "Where's . . ." then he saw the white man too emerging from a white door down the hall. "Barn!" he cried. "Barn!"

"What?" the white man said. "Barn?"

"Yes!" the boy cried. "Barn!"

"Catch him!" the white man shouted.

But it was too late this time too. The Negro grasped his shirt, but the entire sleeve, rotten with washing, carried away, and he was out that door too and in the drive again, and had actually never ceased to run even while he was screaming into the white man's face.

Behind him the white man was shouting, "My horse! Fetch my horse!" and he thought for an instant of cutting across the park and climbing the fence into the road, but he did not know the park nor how high the vine-massed fence might be and he dared not risk it. So he ran on down the drive, blood and breath roaring; presently he was in the road again though he could not see it. He could not hear either: the galloping mare was almost upon him before he heard her, and even then he held his course, as if the very urgency of his wild grief and need must in a moment more find him wings, waiting until the ultimate instant to hurl himself aside and into the weed-choked roadside ditch as the horse thundered past and on, for an instant in furious silhouette against the stars, the tranquil early summer night sky which, even before the shape of the horse and rider vanished, stained abruptly and violently upward: a long, swirling roar incredible and soundless, blotting the stars, and he springing up and into the road again, running again, knowing it was too late yet still running even after he heard the shot and, an instant later, two shots, pausing now without knowing he had ceased to run, crying "Pap! Pap!", running again before he knew he had begun to run, stumbling, tripping over something and scrabbling up again without ceasing to run, looking backward over his shoulder at the glare as he got up, running on among the invisible trees, panting, sobbing, "Father! Father!"

At midnight he was sitting on the crest of a hill. He did not know it was midnight and he did not know how far he had come. But there was no glare behind him now and he sat now, his back toward what he had called home for four days anyhow, his face toward the dark woods which he would enter when breath was strong again, small, shaking steadily in the chill darkness, hugging himself into the remainder of his thin, rotten shirt, the grief and despair now no longer terror and fear but just grief and despair. *Father. My father,* he thought. "He was brave!" he cried suddenly, aloud but not loud, no more than a whisper: "He was! He was in the war! He was in Colonel Sartoris' cav'ry!" not knowing that his father had gone to that war a private in the fine old European sense, wearing no uniform, admitting the authority of and giving fidelity to no man or army or flag, going to war as Malbrouck himself did: for booty—it meant nothing and less than nothing to him if it were enemy booty or his own.

The slow constellations wheeled on. It would be dawn and then sun-up after a while and he would be hungry. But that would be tomorrow and now he was only cold, and walking would cure that. His breathing was easier now and he decided to get up and go on, and then he found that he had been asleep because he knew it was almost dawn, the night almost over. He could tell that from the whippoorwills. They were everywhere now among the dark trees below him, constant and inflectioned and ceaseless, so that, as the instant for giving over to the day birds drew nearer and nearer, there was no interval at all between them. He got up. He was a little stiff, but walking would cure that too as it would the cold, and soon there would be the sun. He went on down the hill, toward the dark woods within which the liquid silver voices of the birds called unceasing—the rapid and urgent beating of the urgent and quiring heart of the late spring night. He did not look back.

Dry September

THROUGH THE BLOODY SEPTEMBER TWILIGHT, AFTERMATH OF SIXTY-
two rainless days, it had gone like a fire in dry grass—the rumor,
the story, whatever it was. Something about Miss Minnie Cooper
and a Negro. Attacked, insulted, frightened: none of them, gathered in the barber shop on that Saturday evening where the ceiling
fan stirred, without freshening it, the vitiated air, sending back
upon them, in recurrent surges of stale pomade and lotion, their
own stale breath and odors, knew exactly what had happened.

"Except it wasn't Will Mayes," a barber said. He was a man of
middle age; a thin, sand-colored man with a mild face, who was
shaving a client. "I know Will Mayes. He's a good nigger. And I
know Miss Minnie Cooper, too."

"What do you know about her?" a second barber said.

"Who is she?" the client said. "A young girl?"

"No," the barber said. "She's about forty, I reckon. She aint married. That's why I dont believe—"

"Believe, hell!" a hulking youth in a sweat-stained silk shirt said.
"Wont you take a white woman's word before a nigger's?"

"I dont believe Will Mayes did it," the barber said. "I know Will
Mayes."

"Maybe you know who did it, then. Maybe you already got him
out of town, you damn niggerlover."

"I dont believe anybody did anything. I dont believe anything
happened. I leave it to you fellows if them ladies that get old without getting married dont have notions that a man cant—"

"Then you are a hell of a white man," the client said. He moved
under the cloth. The youth had sprung to his feet.

"You dont?" he said. "Do you accuse a white woman of lying?"

The barber held the razor poised above the half-risen client. He
did not look around.

"It's this durn weather," another said. "It's enough to make a
man do anything. Even to her."

Nobody laughed. The barber said in his mild, stubborn tone: "I aint accusing nobody of nothing. I just know and you fellows know how a woman that never—"

"You damn niggerlover!" the youth said.

"Shut up, Butch," another said. "We'll get the facts in plenty of time to act."

"Who is? Who's getting them?" the youth said. "Facts, hell! I—"

"You're a fine white man," the client said. "Aint you?" In his frothy beard he looked like a desert rat in the moving pictures. "You tell them, Jack," he said to the youth. "If there aint any white men in this town, you can count on me, even if I aint only a drummer and a stranger."

"That's right, boys," the barber said. "Find out the truth first. I know Will Mayes."

"Well, by God!" the youth shouted. "To think that a white man in this town—"

"Shut up, Butch," the second speaker said. "We got plenty of time."

The client sat up. He looked at the speaker. "Do you claim that anything excuses a nigger attacking a white woman? Do you mean to tell me you are a white man and you'll stand for it? You better go back North where you came from. The South dont want your kind here."

"North what?" the second said. "I was born and raised in this town."

"Well, by God!" the youth said. He looked about with a strained, baffled gaze, as if he was trying to remember what it was he wanted to say or to do. He drew his sleeve across his sweating face. "Damn if I'm going to let a white woman—"

"You tell them, Jack," the drummer said. "By God, if they—"

The screen door crashed open. A man stood in the floor, his feet apart and his heavy-set body poised easily. His white shirt was open at the throat; he wore a felt hat. His hot, bold glance swept the group. His name was McLendon. He had commanded troops at the front in France and had been decorated for valor.

"Well," he said, "are you going to sit there and let a black son rape a white woman on the streets of Jefferson?"

Butch sprang up again. The silk of his shirt clung flat to his heavy shoulders. At each armpit was a dark halfmoon. "That's what I been telling them! That's what I—"

"Did it really happen?" a third said. "This aint the first man scare she ever had, like Hawkshaw says. Wasn't there something about a man on the kitchen roof, watching her undress, about a year ago?"

"What?" the client said. "What's that?" The barber had been slowly forcing him back into the chair; he arrested himself reclining, his head lifted, the barber still pressing him down.

McLendon whirled on the third speaker. "Happen? What the hell difference does it make? Are you going to let the black sons get away with it until one really does it?"

"That's what I'm telling them!" Butch shouted. He cursed, long and steady, pointless.

"Here, here," a fourth said. "Not so loud. Dont talk so loud."

"Sure," McLendon said; "no talking necessary at all. I've done my talking. Who's with me?" He poised on the balls of his feet, roving his gaze.

The barber held the drummer's face down, the razor poised. "Find out the facts first, boys. I know Willy Mayes. It wasn't him. Let's get the sheriff and do this thing right."

McLendon whirled upon him his furious, rigid face. The barber did not look away. They looked like men of different races. The other barbers had ceased also above their prone clients. "You mean to tell me," McLendon said, "that you'd take a nigger's word before a white woman's? Why, you damn niggerloving—"

The third speaker rose and grasped McLendon's arm; he too had been a soldier. "Now, now. Let's figure this thing out. Who knows anything about what really happened?"

"Figure out hell!" McLendon jerked his arm free. "All that're with me get up from there. The ones that aint—" He roved his gaze, dragging his sleeve across his face.

Three men rose. The drummer in the chair sat up. "Here," he said, jerking at the cloth about his neck; "get this rag off me. I'm with him. I dont live here, but by God, if our mothers and wives and sisters—" He smeared the cloth over his face and flung it to the floor. McLendon stood in the floor and cursed the others. Another rose and moved toward him. The remainder sat uncomfortable, not looking at one another, then one by one they rose and joined him.

The barber picked the cloth from the floor. He began to fold it neatly. "Boys, dont do that. Will Mayes never done it. I know."

"Come on," McLendon said. He whirled. From his hip pocket

protruded the butt of a heavy automatic pistol. They went out. The screen door crashed behind them reverberant in the dead air.

The barber wiped the razor carefully and swiftly, and put it away, and ran to the rear, and took his hat from the wall. "I'll be back as soon as I can," he said to the other barbers. "I cant let—" He went out, running. The two other barbers followed him to the door and caught it on the rebound, leaning out and looking up the street after him. The air was flat and dead. It had a metallic taste at the base of the tongue.

"What can he do?" the first said. The second one was saying "Jees Christ, Jees Christ" under his breath. "I'd just as lief be Will Mayes as Hawk, if he gets McLendon riled."

"Jees Christ, Jees Christ," the second whispered.

"You reckon he really done it to her?" the first said.

– 2 –

She was thirty-eight or thirty-nine. She lived in a small frame house with her invalid mother and a thin, sallow, unflagging aunt, where each morning between ten and eleven she would appear on the porch in a lace-trimmed boudoir cap, to sit swinging in the porch swing until noon. After dinner she lay down for a while, until the afternoon began to cool. Then, in one of the three or four new voile dresses which she had each summer, she would go downtown to spend the afternoon in the stores with the other ladies, where they would handle the goods and haggle over the prices in cold, immediate voices, without any intention of buying.

She was of comfortable people—not the best in Jefferson, but good people enough—and she was still on the slender side of ordinary looking, with a bright, faintly haggard manner and dress. When she was young she had had a slender, nervous body and a sort of hard vivacity which had enabled her for a time to ride upon the crest of the town's social life as exemplified by the high school party and church social period of her contemporaries while still children enough to be unclassconscious.

She was the last to realize that she was losing ground; that those among whom she had been a little brighter and louder flame than any other were beginning to learn the pleasure of snobbery—male —and retaliation—female. That was when her face began to wear that bright, haggard look. She still carried it to parties on shadowy porticoes and summer lawns, like a mask or a flag, with that bafflement of furious repudiation of truth in her eyes. One evening at a party she heard a boy and two girls, all schoolmates, talking. She never accepted another invitation.

She watched the girls with whom she had grown up as they married and got homes and children, but no man ever called on her steadily until the children of the other girls had been calling her "aunty" for several years, the while their mothers told them in bright voices about how popular Aunt Minnie had been as a girl. Then the town began to see her driving on Sunday afternoons with the cashier in the bank. He was a widower of about forty—a high-colored man, smelling always faintly of the barber shop or of whisky. He owned the first automobile in town, a red runabout; Minnie had the first motoring bonnet and veil the town ever saw. Then the town began to say: "Poor Minnie." "But she is old enough to take care of herself,' others said. That was when she began to ask her old schoolmates that their children call her "cousin" instead of "aunty."

It was twelve years now since she had been relegated into adultery by public opinion, and eight years since the cashier had gone to a Memphis bank, returning for one day each Christmas, which he spent at an annual bachelors' party at a hunting club on the river. From behind their curtains the neighbors would see the party pass, and during the over-the-way Christmas day visiting they would tell her about him, about how well he looked, and how they heard that he was prospering in the city, watching with bright, secret eyes her haggard, bright face. Usually by that hour there would be the scent of whisky on her breath. It was supplied her by a youth, a clerk at the soda fountain: "Sure; I buy it for the old gal. I reckon she's entitled to a little fun."

Her mother kept to her room altogether now; the gaunt aunt ran the house. Against that background Minnie's bright dresses, her idle and empty days, had a quality of furious unreality. She went out in the evenings only with women now, neighbors, to the moving pictures. Each afternoon she dressed in one of the new dresses and went downtown alone, where her young "cousins" were already strolling in the late afternoons with their delicate, silken heads and thin, awkward arms and conscious hips, clinging to one another or shrieking and giggling with paired boys in the soda fountain when she passed and went on along the serried store fronts, in the doors of which the sitting and lounging men did not even follow her with their eyes any more.

– 3 –

The barber went swiftly up the street where the sparse lights, insect-swirled, glared in rigid and violent suspension in the lifeless air. The day had died in a pall of dust; above the darkened square, shrouded by the spent dust, the sky was as clear as the inside of a brass bell. Below the east was a rumor of the twice-waxed moon.

When he overtook them McLendon and three others were getting into a car parked in an alley. McLendon stooped his thick head, peering out beneath the top. "Changed your mind, did you?" he said. "Damn good thing; by God, tomorrow when this town hears about how you talked tonight—"

"Now, now," the other ex-soldier said. "Hawkshaw's all right. Come on, Hawk; jump in."

"Will Mayes never done it, boys," the barber said. "If anybody done it. Why, you all know well as I do there aint any town where they got better niggers than us. And you know how a lady will kind of think things about men when there aint any reason to, and Miss Minnie anyway—"

"Sure, sure," the soldier said. "We're just going to talk to him a little; that's all."

"Talk hell!" Butch said. "When we're through with the—"

"Shut up, for God's sake!" the soldier said. "Do you want everybody in town—"

"Tell them, by God!" McLendon said. "Tell every one of the sons that'll let a white woman—"

"Let's go; let's go: here's the other car." The second car slid squealing out of a cloud of dust at the alley mouth. McLendon started his car and took the lead. Dust lay like fog in the street. The street lights hung nimbused as in water. They drove on out of town.

A rutted lane turned at right angles. Dust hung above it too, and above all the land. The dark bulk of the ice plant, where the Negro Mayes was night watchman, rose against the sky. "Better stop here, hadn't we?" the soldier said. McLendon did not reply. He hurled the car up and slammed to a stop, the headlights glaring on the blank wall.

"Listen here, boys," the barber said; "if he's here, dont that prove he never done it? Dont it? If it was him, he would run. Dont you see he would?" The second car came up and stopped. McLendon got down; Butch sprang down beside him. "Listen, boys," the barber said.

"Cut the lights off!" McLendon said. The breathless dark rushed down. There was no sound in it save their lungs as they sought air in the parched dust in which for two months they had lived; then the diminishing crunch of McLendon's and Butch's feet, and a moment later McLendon's voice:

"Will! . . . Will!"

Below the east the wan hemorrhage of the moon increased. It heaved above the ridge, silvering the air, the dust, so that they seemed to breathe, live, in a bowl of molten lead. There was no sound of nightbird nor insect, no sound save their breathing and a faint ticking of contracting metal about the cars. Where their bodies touched one another they seemed to sweat dryly, for no more moisture came. "Christ!" a voice said; "let's get out of here."

But they didn't move until vague noises began to grow out of the darkness ahead; then they got out and waited tensely in the breathless dark. There was another sound: a blow, a hissing expulsion of breath and McLendon cursing in undertone. They stood a moment longer, then they ran forward. They ran in a stumbling clump, as though they were fleeing something. "Kill him, kill the son," a voice whispered. McLendon flung them back.

"Not here," he said. "Get him into the car." "Kill him, kill the black son!" the voice murmured. They dragged the Negro to the car. The barber had waited beside the car. He could feel himself sweating and he knew he was going to be sick at the stomach.

"What is it, captains?" the Negro said. "I aint done nothing. 'Fore God, Mr John." Someone produced handcuffs. They worked busily about the Negro as though he were a post, quiet, intent, getting in one another's way. He submitted to the handcuffs, looking swiftly and constantly from dim face to dim face. "Who's here, captains?" he said, leaning to peer into the faces until they could feel his breath and smell his sweaty reek. He spoke a name or two. "What you all say I done, Mr John?"

McLendon jerked the car door open. "Get in!" he said.

The Negro did not move. "What you all going to do with me,

Mr John? I aint done nothing. White folks, captains, I aint done nothing: I swear 'fore God." He called another name.

"Get in!" McLendon said. He struck the Negro. The others expelled their breath in a dry hissing and struck him with random blows and he whirled and cursed them, and swept his manacled hands across their faces and slashed the barber upon the mouth, and the barber struck him also. "Get him in there," McLendon said. They pushed at him. He ceased struggling and got in and sat quietly as the others took their places. He sat between the barber and the soldier, drawing his limbs in so as not to touch them, his eyes going swiftly and constantly from face to face. Butch clung to the running board. The car moved on. The barber nursed his mouth with his handkerchief.

"What's the matter, Hawk?" the soldier said.

"Nothing," the barber said. They regained the highroad and turned away from town. The second car dropped back out of the dust. They went on, gaining speed; the final fringe of houses dropped behind.

"Goddamn, he stinks!" the soldier said.

"We'll fix that," the drummer in front beside McLendon said. On the running board Butch cursed into the hot rush of air. The barber leaned suddenly forward and touched McLendon's arm.

"Let me out, John," he said.

"Jump out, niggerlover," McLendon said without turning his head. He drove swiftly. Behind them the sourceless lights of the second car glared in the dust. Presently McLendon turned into a narrow road. It was rutted with disuse. It led back to an abandoned brick kiln—a series of reddish mounds and weed- and vine-choked vats without bottom. It had been used for pasture once, until one day the owner missed one of his mules. Although he prodded carefully in the vats with a long pole, he could not even find the bottom of them.

"John," the barber said.

"Jump out, then," McLendon said, hurling the car along the ruts. Beside the barber the Negro spoke:

"Mr Henry."

The barber sat forward. The narrow tunnel of the road rushed up and past. Their motion was like an extinct furnace blast: cooler, but utterly dead. The car bounded from rut to rut.

"Mr Henry," the Negro said.

The barber began to tug furiously at the door. "Look out, there!" the soldier said, but the barber had already kicked the door open and swung onto the running board. The soldier leaned across the Negro and grasped at him, but he had already jumped. The car went on without checking speed.

The impetus hurled him crashing through dust-sheathed weeds, into the ditch. Dust puffed about him, and in a thin, vicious crackling of sapless stems he lay choking and retching until the second car passed and died away. Then he rose and limped on until he reached the highroad and turned toward town, brushing at his clothes with his hands. The moon was higher, riding high and clear of the dust at last, and after a while the town began to glare beneath the dust. He went on, limping. Presently he heard cars and the glow of them grew in the dust behind him and he left the road and crouched again in the weeds until they passed. McLendon's car came last now. There were four people in it and Butch was not on the running board.

They went on; the dust swallowed them; the glare and the sound died away. The dust of them hung for a while, but soon the eternal dust absorbed it again. The barber climbed back onto the road and limped on toward town.

– 4 –

As she dressed for supper on that Saturday evening, her own flesh felt like fever. Her hands trembled among the hooks and eyes, and her eyes had a feverish look, and her hair swirled crisp and crackling under the comb. While she was still dressing the friends called for her and sat while she donned her sheerest underthings and stockings and a new voile dress. "Do you feel strong enough to go out?" they said, their eyes bright too, with a dark glitter. "When you have had time to get over the shock, you must tell us what happened. What he said and did; everything."

In the leafed darkness, as they walked toward the square, she began to breathe deeply, something like a swimmer preparing to dive, until she ceased trembling, the four of them walking slowly because of the terrible heat and out of solicitude for her. But as they neared the square she began to tremble again, walking with her head up, her hands clenched at her sides, their voices about her murmurous, also with that feverish, glittering quality of their eyes.

They entered the square, she in the center of the group, fragile in her fresh dress. She was trembling worse. She walked slower and slower, as children eat ice cream, her head up and her eyes bright in the haggard banner of her face, passing the hotel and the coatless drummers in chairs along the curb looking around at her: "That's the one: see? The one in pink in the middle." "Is that her? What did they do with the nigger? Did they—?" "Sure. He's all right." "All right, is he?" "Sure. He went on a little trip." Then the drug store, where even the young men lounging in the doorway tipped their hats and followed with their eyes the motion of her hips and legs when she passed.

They went on, passing the lifted hats of the gentlemen, the suddenly ceased voices, deferent, protective. "Do you see?" the friends said. Their voices sounded like long, hovering sighs of hissing exultation. "There's not a Negro on the square. Not one."

They reached the picture show. It was like a miniature fairyland with its lighted lobby and colored lithographs of life caught in its terrible and beautiful mutations. Her lips began to tingle. In the dark, when the picture began, it would be all right; she could hold back the laughing so it would not waste away so fast and so soon. So she hurried on before the turning faces, the undertones of low astonishment, and they took their accustomed places where she could see the aisle against the silver glare and the young men and girls coming in two and two against it.

The lights flicked away; the screen glowed silver, and soon life began to unfold, beautiful and passionate and sad, while still the young men and girls entered, scented and sibilant in the half dark, their paired backs in silhouette delicate and sleek, their slim, quick bodies awkward, divinely young, while beyond them the silver dream accumulated, inevitably on and on. She began to laugh. In trying to suppress it, it made more noise than ever; heads began to turn. Still laughing, her friends raised her and led her out, and she stood at the curb, laughing on a high, sustained note, until the taxi came up and they helped her in.

They removed the pink voile and the sheer underthings and the stockings, and put her to bed, and cracked ice for her temples, and sent for the doctor. He was hard to locate, so they ministered to her with hushed ejaculations, renewing the ice and fanning her. While the ice was fresh and cold she stopped laughing and lay still for a time, moaning only a little. But soon the laughing welled again and her voice rose screaming.

"Shhhhhhhhhhh! Shhhhhhhhhhhhhhh!" they said, freshening the
icepack, smoothing her hair, examining it for gray; "poor girl!"
Then to one another: "Do you suppose anything really happened?"
their eyes darkly aglitter, secret and passionate. "Shhhhhhhhhh!
Poor girl! Poor Minnie!"

–5–

It was midnight when McLendon drove up to his neat new
house. It was trim and fresh as a birdcage and almost as small, with
its clean, green-and-white paint. He locked the car and mounted the
porch and entered. His wife rose from a chair beside the reading
lamp. McLendon stopped in the floor and stared at her until she
looked down.

"Look at that clock," he said, lifting his arm, pointing. She stood
before him, her face lowered, a magazine in her hands. Her face
was pale, strained, and weary-looking. "Haven't I told you about
sitting up like this, waiting to see when I come in?"

"John," she said. She laid the magazine down. Poised on the balls
of his feet, he glared at her with his hot eyes, his sweating face.

"Didn't I tell you?" He went toward her. She looked up then. He
caught her shoulder. She stood passive, looking at him.

"Don't, John. I couldn't sleep . . . The heat; something. Please,
John. You're hurting me."

"Didn't I tell you?" He released her and half struck, half flung her
across the chair, and she lay there and watched him quietly as he
left the room.

He went on through the house, ripping off his shirt, and on the
dark, screened porch at the rear he stood and mopped his head and
shoulders with the shirt and flung it away. He took the pistol from
his hip and laid it on the table beside the bed, and sat on the bed
and removed his shoes, and rose and slipped his trousers off. He
was sweating again already, and he stooped and hunted furiously
for the shirt. At last he found it and wiped his body again, and,
with his body pressed against the dusty screen, he stood panting.
There was no movement, no sound, not even an insect. The dark
world seemed to lie stricken beneath the cold moon and the lidless
stars.

That Evening Sun

MONDAY IS NO DIFFERENT FROM ANY OTHER WEEKDAY IN JEFFERSON now. The streets are paved now, and the telephone and electric companies are cutting down more and more of the shade trees—the water oaks, the maples and locusts and elms—to make room for iron poles bearing clusters of bloated and ghostly and bloodless grapes, and we have a city laundry which makes the rounds on Monday morning, gathering the bundles of clothes into bright-colored, specially-made motor cars: the soiled wearing of a whole week now flees apparitionlike behind alert and irritable electric horns, with a long diminishing noise of rubber and asphalt like tearing silk, and even the Negro women who still take in white people's washing after the old custom, fetch and deliver it in automobiles.

But fifteen years ago, on Monday morning the quiet, dusty, shady streets would be full of Negro women with, balanced on their steady, turbaned heads, bundles of clothes tied up in sheets, almost as large as cotton bales, carried so without touch of hand between the kitchen door of the white house and the blackened washpot beside a cabin door in Negro Hollow.

Nancy would set her bundle on the top of her head, then upon the bundle in turn she would set the black straw sailor hat which she wore winter and summer. She was tall, with a high, sad face sunken a little where her teeth were missing. Sometimes we would go a part of the way down the lane and across the pasture with her, to watch the balanced bundle and the hat that never bobbed nor wavered, even when she walked down into the ditch and up the other side and stooped through the fence. She would go down on her hands and knees and crawl through the gap, her head rigid, up-tilted, the bundle steady as a rock or a balloon, and rise to her feet again and go on.

Sometimes the husbands of the washing women would fetch and deliver the clothes, but Jesus never did that for Nancy, even before father told him to stay away from our house, even when Dilsey was sick and Nancy would come to cook for us.

And then about half the time we'd have to go down the lane to Nancy's cabin and tell her to come on and cook breakfast. We would stop at the ditch, because father told us to not have anything to do with Jesus—he was a short black man, with a razor scar down his face—and we would throw rocks at Nancy's house until she came to the door, leaning her head around it without any clothes on.

"What yawl mean, chunking my house?" Nancy said. "What you little devils mean?"

"Father says for you to come on and get breakfast," Caddy said. "Father says it's over a half an hour now, and you've got to come this minute."

"I aint studying no breakfast," Nancy said. "I going to get my sleep out."

"I bet you're drunk," Jason said. "Father says you're drunk. Are you drunk, Nancy?"

"Who says I is?" Nancy said. "I got to get my sleep out. I aint studying no breakfast."

So after a while we quit chunking the cabin and went back home. When she finally came, it was too late for me to go to school. So we thought it was whisky until that day they arrested her again and they were taking her to jail and they passed Mr Stovall. He was the cashier in the bank and a deacon in the Baptist church, and Nancy began to say:

"When you going to pay me, white man? When you going to pay me, white man? It's been three times now since you paid me a cent—" Mr Stovall knocked her down, but she kept on saying, "When you going to pay me, white man? It's been three times now since—" until Mr Stovall kicked her in the mouth with his heel and the marshal caught Mr Stovall back, and Nancy lying in the street, laughing. She turned her head and spat out some blood and teeth and said, "It's been three times now since he paid me a cent."

That was how she lost her teeth, and all that day they told about Nancy and Mr Stovall, and all that night the ones that passed the jail could hear Nancy singing and yelling. They could see her hands holding to the window bars, and a lot of them stopped along the fence, listening to her and to the jailer trying to make her stop. She didn't shut up until almost daylight, when the jailer began to hear a bumping and scraping upstairs and he went up there and found Nancy hanging from the window bar. He said that it was cocaine and not whisky, because no nigger would try to commit suicide unless he was full of cocaine, because a nigger full of cocaine wasn't a nigger any longer.

The jailer cut her down and revived her; then he beat her, whipped her. She had hung herself with her dress. She had fixed it all right, but when they arrested her she didn't have on anything except a dress and so she didn't have anything to tie her hands with and she couldn't make her hands let go of the window ledge. So the jailer heard the noise and ran up there and found Nancy hanging from the window, stark naked, her belly already swelling out a little, like a little balloon.

When Dilsey was sick in her cabin and Nancy was cooking for us, we could see her apron swelling out; that was before father told Jesus to stay away from the house. Jesus was in the kitchen, sitting behind the stove, with his razor scar on his black face like a piece of dirty string. He said it was a watermelon that Nancy had under her dress.

"It never come off of your vine, though," Nancy said.

"Off of what vine?" Caddy said.

"I can cut down the vine it did come off of," Jesus said.

"What makes you want to talk like that before these chillen?" Nancy said. "Whyn't you go on to work? You done et. You want Mr Jason to catch you hanging around his kitchen, talking that way before these chillen?"

"Talking what way?" Caddy said. "What vine?"

"I cant hang around white man's kitchen," Jesus said. "But white man can hang around mine. White man can come in my house, but I cant stop him. When white man want to come in my house, I aint got no house. I cant stop him, but he cant kick me outen it. He cant do that."

Dilsey was still sick in her cabin. Father told Jesus to stay off our place. Dilsey was still sick. It was a long time. We were in the library after supper.

"Isn't Nancy through in the kitchen yet?" mother said. "It seems to me that she has had plenty of time to have finished the dishes."

"Let Quentin go and see," father said. "Go and see if Nancy is through, Quentin. Tell her she can go on home."

I went to the kitchen. Nancy was through. The dishes were put away and the fire was out. Nancy was sitting in a chair, close to the cold stove. She looked at me.

"Mother wants to know if you are through," I said.

"Yes," Nancy said. She looked at me. "I done finished." She looked at me.

"What is it?" I said. "What is it?"

"I aint nothing but a nigger," Nancy said. "It aint none of my fault."

She looked at me, sitting in the chair before the cold stove, the sailor hat on her head. I went back to the library. It was the cold stove and all, when you think of a kitchen being warm and busy and cheerful. And with a cold stove and the dishes all put away, and nobody wanting to eat at that hour.

"Is she through?" mother said.

"Yessum," I said.

"What is she doing?" mother said.

"She's not doing anything. She's through."

"I'll go and see," father said.

"Maybe she's waiting for Jesus to come and take her home," Caddy said.

"Jesus is gone," I said. Nancy told us how one morning she woke up and Jesus was gone.

"He quit me," Nancy said. "Done gone to Memphis, I reckon. Dodging them city *po*-lice for a while, I reckon."

"And a good riddance," father said. "I hope he stays there."

"Nancy's scaired of the dark," Jason said.

"So are you," Caddy said.

"I'm not," Jason said.

"Scairy cat," Caddy said.

"I'm not," Jason said.

"You, Candace!" mother said. Father came back.

"I am going to walk down the lane with Nancy," he said. "She says that Jesus is back."

"Has she seen him?" mother said.

"No. Some Negro sent her word that he was back in town. I wont be long."

"You'll leave me alone, to take Nancy home?" mother said. "Is her safety more precious to you than mine?"

"I wont be long," father said.

"You'll leave these children unprotected, with that Negro about?"

"I'm going too," Caddy said. "Let me go, Father."

"What would he do with them, if he were unfortunate enough to have them?" father said.

"I want to go, too," Jason said.

"Jason!" mother said. She was speaking to father. You could tell that by the way she said the name. Like she believed that all day father had been trying to think of doing the thing she wouldn't like the most, and that she knew all the time that after a while he would think of it. I stayed quiet, because father and I both knew that mother would want him to make me stay with her if she just thought of it in time. So father didn't look at me. I was the oldest. I was nine and Caddy was seven and Jason was five.

"Nonsense," father said. "We wont be long."

Nancy had her hat on. We came to the lane. "Jesus always been good to me," Nancy said. "Whenever he had two dollars, one of them was mine." We walked in the lane. "If I can just get through the lane," Nancy said, "I be all right then."

The lane was always dark. "This is where Jason got scaired on Hallowe'en," Caddy said.

"I didn't," Jason said.

"Cant Aunt Rachel do anything with him?" father said. Aunt Rachel was old. She lived in a cabin beyond Nancy's, by herself. She had white hair and she smoked a pipe in the door, all day long; she didn't work any more. They said she was Jesus' mother. Sometimes she said she was and sometimes she said she wasn't any kin to Jesus.

"Yes, you did," Caddy said. "You were scairder than Frony. You were scairder than T. P. even. Scairder than niggers."

"Cant nobody do nothing with him," Nancy said. "He say I done woke up the devil in him and aint but one thing going to lay it down again."

"Well, he's gone now," father said. "There's nothing for you to be afraid of now. And if you'd just let white men alone."

"Let what white men alone?" Caddy said. "How let them alone?"

"He aint gone nowhere," Nancy said. "I can feel him. I can feel him now, in this lane. He hearing us talk, every word, hid somewhere, waiting. I aint seen him, and I aint going to see him again but once more, with that razor in his mouth. That razor on that string down his back, inside his shirt. And then I aint going to be even surprised."

"I wasn't scaired," Jason said.

"If you'd behave yourself, you'd have kept out of this," father said. "But it's all right now. He's probably in St. Louis now. Probably got another wife by now and forgot all about you."

"If he has, I better not find out about it," Nancy said. "I'd stand there right over them, and every time he wropped her, I'd cut that arm off. I'd cut his head off and I'd slit her belly and I'd shove—"

"Hush," father said.

"Slit whose belly, Nancy?" Caddy said.

"I wasn't scaired," Jason said. "I'd walk right down this lane by myself."

"Yah," Caddy said. "You wouldn't dare to put your foot down in it if we were not here too."

— 2 —

Dilsey was still sick, so we took Nancy home every night until mother said, "How much longer is this going on? I to be left alone in this big house while you take home a frightened Negro?"

We fixed a pallet in the kitchen for Nancy. One night we waked up, hearing the sound. It was not singing and it was not crying, coming up the dark stairs. There was a light in mother's room and we heard father going down the hall, down the back stairs, and Caddy and I went into the hall. The floor was cold. Our toes curled away from it while we listened to the sound. It was like singing and it wasn't like singing, like the sounds that Negroes make.

Then it stopped and we heard father going down the back stairs, and we went to the head of the stairs. Then the sound began again, in the stairway, not loud, and we could see Nancy's eyes halfway up the stairs, against the wall. They looked like cat's eyes do, like a big cat against the wall, watching us. When we came down the steps to where she was, she quit making the sound again, and we stood there until father came back up from the kitchen, with his pistol in his hand. He went back down with Nancy and they came back with Nancy's pallet.

We spread the pallet in our room. After the light in mother's room went off, we could see Nancy's eyes again. "Nancy," Caddy whispered, "are you asleep, Nancy?"

Nancy whispered something. It was oh or no, I dont know which. Like nobody had made it, like it came from nowhere and went nowhere, until it was like Nancy was not there at all; that I had looked so hard at her eyes on the stairs that they had got printed on my eyeballs, like the sun does when you have closed your eyes and there is no sun. "Jesus," Nancy whispered. "Jesus."

"Was it Jesus?" Caddy said. "Did he try to come into the kitchen?"

"Jesus," Nancy said. Like this: Jeeeeeeeeeeeeeeeesus, until the sound went out, like a match or a candle does.

"It's the other Jesus she means," I said.

"Can you see us, Nancy?" Caddy whispered. "Can you see our eyes too?"

"I aint nothing but a nigger," Nancy said. "God knows. God knows."

"What did you see down there in the kitchen?" Caddy whispered. "What tried to get in?"

"God knows," Nancy said. We could see her eyes. "God knows."

Dilsey got well. She cooked dinner. "You'd better stay in bed a day or two longer," father said.

"What for?" Dilsey said. "If I had been a day later, this place would be to rack and ruin. Get on out of here now, and let me get my kitchen straight again."

Dilsey cooked supper too. And that night, just before dark, Nancy came into the kitchen.

"How do you know he's back?" Dilsey said. "You aint seen him."

"Jesus is a nigger," Jason said.

"I can feel him," Nancy said. "I can feel him laying yonder in the ditch."

"Tonight?" Dilsey said. "Is he there tonight?"

"Dilsey's a nigger too," Jason said.

"You try to eat something," Dilsey said.

"I dont want nothing," Nancy said.

"I aint a nigger," Jason said.

"Drink some coffee," Dilsey said. She poured a cup of coffee for Nancy. "Do you know he's out there tonight? How come you know it's tonight?"

"I know," Nancy said. "He's there, waiting. I know. I done lived with him too long. I know what he is fixing to do fore he know it himself."

"Drink some coffee," Dilsey said. Nancy held the cup to her

mouth and blew into the cup. Her mouth pursed out like a spreading adder's, like a rubber mouth, like she had blown all the color out of her lips with blowing the coffee.

"I aint a nigger," Jason said. "Are you a nigger, Nancy?"

"I hellborn, child," Nancy said. "I wont be nothing soon. I going back where I come from soon."

– 3 –

She began to drink the coffee. While she was drinking, holding the cup in both hands, she began to make the sound again. She made the sound into the cup and the coffee sploshed out onto her hands and her dress. Her eyes looked at us and she sat there, her elbows on her knees, holding the cup in both hands, looking at us across the wet cup, making the sound. "Look at Nancy," Jason said. "Nancy cant cook for us now. Dilsey's got well now."

"You hush up," Dilsey said. Nancy held the cup in both hands, looking at us, making the sound, like there were two of them: one looking at us and the other making the sound. "Whyn't you let Mr Jason telefoam the marshal?" Dilsey said. Nancy stopped then, holding the cup in her long brown hands. She tried to drink some coffee again, but it sploshed out of the cup, onto her hands and her dress, and she put the cup down. Jason watched her.

"I cant swallow it," Nancy said. "I swallows but it wont go down me."

"You go down to the cabin," Dilsey said. "Frony will fix you a pallet and I'll be there soon."

"Wont no nigger stop him," Nancy said.

"I aint a nigger," Jason said. "Am I, Dilsey?"

"I reckon not," Dilsey said. She looked at Nancy. "I dont reckon so. What you going to do, then?"

Nancy looked at us. Her eyes went fast, like she was afraid there wasn't time to look, without hardly moving at all. She looked at us, at all three of us at one time. "You member that night I stayed in yawls' room?" she said. She told about how we waked up early the next morning, and played. We had to play quiet, on her pallet, until father woke up and it was time to get breakfast. "Go and ask your maw to let me stay here tonight," Nancy said. "I wont need no pallet. We can play some more."

Caddy asked mother. Jason went too. "I cant have Negroes sleeping in the bedrooms," mother said. Jason cried. He cried until mother said he couldn't have any dessert for three days if he didn't stop. Then Jason said he would stop if Dilsey would make a chocolate cake. Father was there.

"Why dont you do something about it?" mother said. "What do we have officers for?"

"Why is Nancy afraid of Jesus?" Caddy said. "Are you afraid of father, mother?"

"What could the officers do?" father said. "If Nancy hasn't seen him, how could the officers find him?"

"Then why is she afraid?" mother said.

"She says he is there. She says she knows he is there tonight."

"Yet we pay taxes," mother said. "I must wait here alone in this big house while you take a Negro woman home."

"You know that I am not lying outside with a razor," father said.

"I'll stop if Dilsey will make a chocolate cake," Jason said. Mother told us to go out and father said he didn't know if Jason would get a chocolate cake or not, but he knew what Jason was going to get in about a minute. We went back to the kitchen and told Nancy.

"Father said for you to go home and lock the door, and you'll be all right," Caddy said. "All right from what, Nancy? Is Jesus mad at you?" Nancy was holding the coffee cup in her hands again, her elbows on her knees and her hands holding the cup between her knees. She was looking into the cup. "What have you done that made Jesus mad?" Caddy said. Nancy let the cup go. It didn't break on the floor, but the coffee spilled out, and Nancy sat there with her hands still making the shape of the cup. She began to make the sound again, not loud. Not singing and not unsinging. We watched her.

"Here," Dilsey said. "You quit that, now. You get aholt of yourself. You wait here. I going to get Versh to walk home with you." Dilsey went out.

We looked at Nancy. Her shoulders kept shaking, but she quit making the sound. We watched her. "What's Jesus going to do to you?" Caddy said. "He went away."

Nancy looked at us. "We had fun that night I stayed in yawls' room, didn't we?"

"I didn't," Jason said. "I didn't have any fun."

"You were asleep in mother's room," Caddy said. "You were not there."

"Let's go down to my house and have some more fun," Nancy said.

"Mother wont let us," I said. "It's too late now."

"Dont bother her," Nancy said. "We can tell her in the morning. She wont mind."

"She wouldn't let us," I said.

"Dont ask her now," Nancy said. "Dont bother her now."

"She didn't say we couldn't go," Caddy said.

"We didn't ask," I said.

"If you go, I'll tell," Jason said.

"We'll have fun," Nancy said. "They wont mind, just to my house. I been working for yawl a long time. They wont mind."

"I'm not afraid to go," Caddy said. "Jason is the one that's afraid. He'll tell."

"I'm not," Jason said.

"Yes, you are," Caddy said. "You'll tell."

"I wont tell," Jason said. "I'm not afraid."

"Jason aint afraid to go with me," Nancy said. "Is you, Jason?"

"Jason is going to tell," Caddy said. The lane was dark. We passed the pasture gate. "I bet if something was to jump out from behind that gate, Jason would holler."

"I wouldn't," Jason said. We walked down the lane. Nancy was talking loud.

"What are you talking so loud for, Nancy?" Caddy said.

"Who; me?" Nancy said. "Listen at Quentin and Caddy and Jason saying I'm talking loud."

"You talk like there was five of us here," Caddy said. "You talk like father was here too."

"Who; me talking loud, Mr Jason?" Nancy said.

"Nancy called Jason 'Mister,' " Caddy said.

"Listen how Caddy and Quentin and Jason talk," Nancy said.

"We're not talking loud," Caddy said. "You're the one that's talking like father—"

"Hush," Nancy said; "hush, Mr Jason."

"Nancy called Jason 'Mister' aguh—"

"Hush," Nancy said. She was talking loud when we crossed the ditch and stooped through the fence where she used to stoop through with the clothes on her head. Then we came to her house. We were going fast then. She opened the door. The smell of the house was like the lamp and the smell of Nancy was like the wick, like they were waiting for one another to begin to smell. She lit the lamp and closed the door and put the bar up. Then she quit talking loud, looking at us.

"What're we going to do?" Caddy said.

"What do yawl want to do?" Nancy said.

"You said we would have some fun," Caddy said.

There was something about Nancy's house; something you could smell besides Nancy and the house. Jason smelled it, even. 'I dont want to stay here," he said. "I want to go home."

"Go home, then," Caddy said.

"I dont want to go by myself," Jason said.

"We're going to have some fun," Nancy said.

"How?" Caddy said.

Nancy stood by the door. She was looking at us, only it was like she had emptied her eyes, like she had quit using them. "What do you want to do?" she said.

"Tell us a story," Caddy said. "Can you tell a story?"

"Yes," Nancy said.

"Tell it," Caddy said. We looked at Nancy. "You dont know any stories."

"Yes," Nancy said. "Yes, I do."

She came and sat in a chair before the hearth. There was a little fire there. Nancy built it up, when it was already hot inside. She built a good blaze. She told a story. She talked like her eyes looked, like her eyes watching us and her voice talking to us did not belong to her. Like she was living somewhere else, waiting somewhere else. She was outside the cabin. Her voice was inside and the shape of her, the Nancy that could stoop under a barbed wire fence with a bundle of clothes balanced on her head as though without weight, like a balloon, was there. But that was all. "And so this here queen come walking up to the ditch, where that bad man was hiding. She was walking up to the ditch, and she say, 'If I can just get past this here ditch,' was what she say . . ."

"What ditch?" Caddy said. "A ditch like that one out there? Why did a queen want to go into a ditch?"

"To get to her house," Nancy said. She looked at us. "She had to cross the ditch to get into her house quick and bar the door."

"Why did she want to go home and bar the door?" Caddy said.

– 4 –

Nancy looked at us. She quit talking. She looked at us. Jason's legs stuck straight out of his pants where he sat on Nancy's lap. "I dont think that's a good story," he said. "I want to go home."

"Maybe we had better," Caddy said. She got up from the floor. "I bet they are looking for us right now." She went toward the door.

"No," Nancy said. "Dont open it." She got up quick and passed Caddy. She didn't touch the door, the wooden bar.

"Why not?" Caddy said.

"Come back to the lamp," Nancy said. "We'll have fun. You dont have to go."

"We ought to go," Caddy said. "Unless we have a lot of fun." She and Nancy came back to the fire, the lamp.

"I want to go home," Jason said. "I'm going to tell."

"I know another story," Nancy said. She stood close to the lamp. She looked at Caddy, like when your eyes look up at a stick balanced on your nose. She had to look down to see Caddy, but her eyes looked like that, like when you are balancing a stick.

"I wont listen to it," Jason said. "I'll bang on the floor."

"It's a good one," Nancy said. "It's better than the other one."

"What's it about?" Caddy said. Nancy was standing by the lamp. Her hand was on the lamp, against the light, long and brown.

"Your hand is on that hot globe," Caddy said. "Dont it feel hot to your hand?"

Nancy looked at her hand on the lamp chimney. She took her hand away, slow. She stood there, looking at Caddy, wringing her long hand as though it were tied to her wrist with a string.

"Let's do something else," Caddy said.

"I want to go home," Jason said.

"I got some popcorn," Nancy said. She looked at Caddy and then at Jason and then at me and then at Caddy again. "I got some popcorn."

"I dont like popcorn," Jason said. "I'd rather have candy."

Nancy looked at Jason. "You can hold the popper." She was still wringing her hand; it was long and limp and brown.

"All right," Jason said. "I'll stay a while if I can do that. Caddy cant hold it. I'll want to go home again if Caddy holds the popper."

Nancy built up the fire. "Look at Nancy putting her hands in the fire," Caddy said. "What's the matter with you, Nancy?"

"I got popcorn," Nancy said. "I got some." She took the popper from under the bed. It was broken. Jason began to cry.

"Now we cant have any popcorn," he said.

"We ought to go home, anyway," Caddy said. "Come on, Quentin."

"Wait," Nancy said; "wait. I can fix it. Dont you want to help me fix it?"

"I dont think I want any," Caddy said. "It's too late now."

"You help me, Jason," Nancy said. "Dont you want to help me?"

"No," Jason said. "I want to go home."

"Hush," Nancy said; "hush. Watch. Watch me. I can fix it so Jason can hold it and pop the corn." She got a piece of wire and fixed the popper.

"It wont hold good," Caddy said.

"Yes, it will," Nancy said. "Yawl watch. Yawl help me shell some corn."

The popcorn was under the bed too. We shelled it into the popper and Nancy helped Jason hold the popper over the fire.

"It's not popping," Jason said. "I want to go home."

"You wait," Nancy said. "It'll begin to pop. We'll have fun then." She was sitting close to the fire. The lamp was turned up so high it was beginning to smoke.

"Why dont you turn it down some?" I said

"It's all right," Nancy said. "I'll clean it. Yawl wait. The popcorn will start in a minute."

"I don't believe it's going to start," Caddy said. "We ought to start home, anyway. They'll be worried."

"No," Nancy said. "It's going to pop. Dilsey will tell um yawl with me. I been working for yawl long time. They wont mind if yawl at my house. You wait, now. It'll start popping any minute now."

Then Jason got some smoke in his eyes and he began to cry. He dropped the popper into the fire. Nancy got a wet rag and wiped Jason's face, but he didn't stop crying.

"Hush," she said. "Hush." But he didn't hush. Caddy took the popper out of the fire.

"It's burned up," she said. "You'll have to get some more popcorn, Nancy."

"Did you put all of it in?" Nancy said.

"Yes," Caddy said. Nancy looked at Caddy. Then she took the popper and opened it and poured the cinders into her apron and began to sort the grains, her hands long and brown, and we watching her.

"Haven't you got any more?" Caddy said.

"Yes," Nancy said; "yes. Look. This here aint burnt. All we need to do is—"

"I want to go home," Jason said. "I'm going to tell."

"Hush," Caddy said. We all listened. Nancy's head was already turned toward the barred door, her eyes filled with red lamplight. "Somebody is coming," Caddy said.

Then Nancy began to make that sound again, not loud, sitting there above the fire, her long hands dangling between her knees; all of a sudden water began to come out on her face in big drops, running down her face, carrying in each one a little turning ball of firelight like a spark until it dropped off her chin. "She's not crying," I said.

"I aint crying," Nancy said. Her eyes were closed. "I aint crying. Who is it?"

"I dont know," Caddy said. She went to the door and looked out. "We've got to go now," she said. "Here comes father."

"I'm going to tell," Jason said. "Yawl made me come."

The water still ran down Nancy's face. She turned in her chair. "Listen. Tell him. Tell him we going to have fun. Tell him I take good care of yawl until in the morning. Tell him to let me come home with yawl and sleep on the floor. Tell him I wont need no pallet. We'll have fun. You member last time how we had so much fun?"

"I didn't have fun," Jason said. "You hurt me. You put smoke in my eyes. I'm going to tell."

– 5 –

Father came in. He looked at us. Nancy did not get up.

"Tell him," she said.

"Caddy made us come down here," Jason said. "I didn't want to."

Father came to the fire. Nancy looked up at him. "Cant you go to Aunt Rachel's and stay?" he said. Nancy looked up at father, her hands between her knees. "He's not here," father said. "I would have seen him. There's not a soul in sight."

"He in the ditch," Nancy said. "He waiting in the ditch yonder."

"Nonsense," father said. He looked at Nancy. "Do you know he's there?"

"I got the sign," Nancy said.

"What sign?"

"I got it. It was on the table when I come in. It was a hogbone, with blood meat still on it, laying by the lamp. He's out there. When yawl walk out that door, I gone."

"Gone where, Nancy?" Caddy said.

"I'm not a tattletale," Jason said.

"Nonsense," father said.

"He out there," Nancy said. "He looking through that window this minute, waiting for yawl to go. Then I gone."

"Nonsense," father said. "Lock up your house and we'll take you on to Aunt Rachel's."

" 'Twont do no good," Nancy said. She didn't look at father now, but he looked down at her, at her long, limp, moving hands. "Putting it off wont do no good."

"Then what do you want to do?" father said.

"I dont know," Nancy said. "I cant do nothing. Just put it off. And that dont do no good. I reckon it belong to me. I reckon what I going to get aint no more than mine."

"Get what?" Caddy said. "What's yours?"

"Nothing," father said. "You all must get to bed."

"Caddy made me come," Jason said.

"Go on to Aunt Rachel's," father said.

"It wont do no good," Nancy said. She sat before the fire, her elbows on her knees, her long hands between her knees. "When even your own kitchen wouldn't do no good. When even if I was sleeping on the floor in the room with your chillen, and the next morning there I am, and blood—"

"Hush," father said. "Lock the door and put out the lamp and go to bed."

"I scaired of the dark," Nancy said. "I scaired for it to happen in the dark."

"You mean you're going to sit right here with the lamp lighted?" father said. Then Nancy began to make the sound again, sitting before the fire, her long hands between her knees. "Ah, damnation," father said. "Come along, chillen. It's past bedtime."

"When yawl go home, I gone," Nancy said. She talked quieter

now, and her face looked quiet, like her hands. "Anyway, I got my coffin money saved up with Mr. Lovelady." Mr. Lovelady was a short, dirty man who collected the Negro insurance, coming around to the cabins or the kitchens every Saturday morning, to collect fifteen cents. He and his wife lived at the hotel. One morning his wife committed suicide. They had a child, a little girl. He and the child went away. After a week or two he came back alone. We would see him going along the lanes and the back streets on Saturday mornings.

"Nonsense," father said. "You'll be the first thing I'll see in the kitchen tomorrow morning."

"You'll see what you'll see, I reckon," Nancy said. "But it will take the Lord to say what that will be."

– 6 –

We left her sitting before the fire.

"Come and put the bar up," father said. But she didn't move. She didn't look at us again, sitting quietly there between the lamp and the fire. From some distance down the lane we could look back and see her through the open door.

"What, Father?" Caddy said. "What's going to happen?"

"Nothing," father said. Jason was on father's back, so Jason was the tallest of all of us. We went down into the ditch. I looked at it, quiet. I couldn't see much where the moonlight and the shadows tangled.

"If Jesus is hid here, he can see us, cant he?" Caddy said.

"He's not there," father said. "He went away a long time ago."

"You made me come," Jason said, high; against the sky it looked like father had two heads, a little one and a big one. "I didn't want to."

We went up out of the ditch. We could still see Nancy's house and the open door, but we couldn't see Nancy now, sitting before the fire with the door open, because she was tired. "I just done got tired," she said. "I just a nigger. It aint no fault of mine."

But we could hear her, because she began just after we came up out of the ditch, the sound that was not singing and not unsinging. "Who will do our washing now, Father?" I said.

"I'm not a nigger," Jason said, high and close above father's head.

"You're worse," Caddy said, "you are a tattletale. If something was to jump out, you'd be scairder than a nigger."

"I wouldn't," Jason said.

"You'd cry," Caddy said.

"Caddy," father said.

"I wouldn't!" Jason said.

"Scairy cat," Caddy said.

"Candace!" father said.

Turnabout

The American—the older one—wore no pink Bedfords. His breeches were of plain whipcord, like the tunic. And the tunic had no long London-cut skirts, so that below the Sam Browne the tail of it stuck straight out like the tunic of a military policeman beneath his holster belt. And he wore simple puttees and the easy shoes of a man of middle age, instead of Savile Row boots, and the shoes and the puttees did not match in shade, and the ordnance belt did not match either of them, and the pilot's wings on his breast were just wings. But the ribbon beneath them was a good ribbon, and the insigne on his shoulders were the twin bars of a captain. He was not tall. His face was thin, a little aquiline; the eyes intelligent and a little tired. He was past twenty-five; looking at him, one thought, not Phi Beta Kappa exactly, but Skull and Bones perhaps, or possibly a Rhodes scholarship.

One of the men who faced him probably could not see him at all. He was being held on his feet by an American military policeman. He was quite drunk, and in contrast with the heavy-jawed policeman who held him erect on his long, slim, boneless legs, he looked like a masquerading girl. He was possibly eighteen, tall, with a pink-and-white face and blue eyes, and a mouth like a girl's mouth. He wore a pea-coat, buttoned awry and stained with recent mud, and upon his blond head, at that unmistakable and rakish swagger which no other people can ever approach or imitate, the cap of a Royal Naval Officer.

"What's this, corporal?" the American captain said. "What's the trouble? He's an Englishman. You'd better let their M. P.'s take care of him."

"I know he is," the policeman said. He spoke heavily, breathing heavily, in the voice of a man under physical strain; for all his girlish delicacy of limb, the English boy was heavier—or more helpless—than he looked. "Stand up!" the policeman said. "They're officers!"

The English boy made an effort then. He pulled himself together, focusing his eyes. He swayed, throwing his arms about the police-

547

man's neck, and with the other hand he saluted, his hand flicking, fingers curled a little, to his right ear, already swaying again and catching himself again. "Cheer-o, sir," he said. "Name's not Beatty, I hope."

"No," the captain said.

"Ah," the English boy said. "Hoped not. My mistake. No offense, what?"

"No offense," the captain said quietly. But he was looking at the policeman. The second American spoke. He was a lieutenant, also a pilot. But he was not twenty-five and he wore the pink breeches, the London boots, and his tunic might have been a British tunic save for the collar.

"It's one of those navy eggs," he said. "They pick them out of the gutters here all night long. You don't come to town often enough."

"Oh," the captain said. "I've heard about them. I remember now." He also remarked now that, though the street was a busy one—it was just outside a popular café—and there were many passers, soldier, civilian, women, yet none of them so much as paused, as though it were a familiar sight. He was looking at the policeman. "Can't you take him to his ship?"

"I thought of that before the captain did," the policeman said. "He says he can't go aboard his ship after dark because he puts the ship away at sundown."

"Puts it away?"

"Stand up, sailor!" the policeman said savagely, jerking at his lax burden. "Maybe the captain can make sense out of it. Damned if I can. He says they keep the boat under the wharf. Run it under the wharf at night, and that they can't get it out again until the tide goes out tomorrow."

"Under the wharf? A boat? What is this?" He was now speaking to the lieutenant. "Do they operate some kind of aquatic motor-cycles?"

"Something like that," the lieutenant said. "You've seen them—the boats. Launches, camouflaged and all. Dashing up and down the harbor. You've seen them. They do that all day and sleep in the gutters here all night."

"Oh," the captain said. "I thought those boats were ship commanders' launches. You mean to tell me they use officers just to—"

"I don't know," the lieutenant said. "Maybe they use them to

fetch hot water from one ship to another. Or buns. Or maybe to
go back and forth fast when they forget napkins or something."

"Nonsense," the captain said. He looked at the English boy
again.

"That's what they do," the lieutenant said. "Town's lousy with
them all night long. Gutters full, and their M. P.'s carting them
away in batches, like nursemaids in a park. Maybe the French give
them the launches to get them out of the gutters during the day."

"Oh," the captain said, "I see." But it was clear that he didn't see,
wasn't listening, didn't believe what he did hear. He looked at the
English boy. "Well, you can't leave him here in that shape," he
said.

Again the English boy tried to pull himself together. "Quite
all right, 'sure you," he said glassily, his voice pleasant, cheerful
almost, quite courteous. "Used to it. Confounded rough *pavé*,
though. Should force French do something about it. Visiting lads
jolly well deserve decent field to play on, what?"

"And he was jolly well using all of it too," the policeman said
savagely. "He must think he's a one-man team, maybe."

At that moment a fifth man came up. He was a British military
policeman. "Nah then," he said. "What's this? What's this?" Then he
saw the Americans' shoulder bars. He saluted. At the sound of his
voice the English boy turned, swaying, peering.

"Oh, hullo, Albert," he said.

"Nah then, Mr. Hope," the British policeman said. He said to the
American policeman, over his shoulder: "What is it this time?"

"Likely nothing," the American said. "The way you guys run a
war. But I'm a stranger here. Here. Take him."

"What is this, corporal?" the captain said. "What was he doing?"

"He won't call it nothing," the American policeman said, jerking
his head at the British policeman. "He'll just call it a thrush or a
robin or something. I turn into this street about three blocks back
a while ago, and I find it blocked with a line of trucks going up
from the docks, and the drivers all hollering ahead what the hell
the trouble is. So I come on, and I find it is about three blocks of
them, blocking the cross streets too; and I come on to the head of
it where the trouble is, and I find about a dozen of the drivers out
in front, holding a caucus or something in the middle of the street,
and I come up and I say, 'What's going on here?' and they leave me
through and I find this egg here laying—"

"Yer talking about one of His Majesty's officers, my man," the British policeman said.

"Watch yourself, corporal," the captain said. "And you found this officer—"

"He had done gone to bed in the middle of the street, with an empty basket for a pillow. Laying there with his hands under his head and his knees crossed, arguing with them about whether he ought to get up and move or not. He said that the trucks could turn back and go around by another street, but that he couldn't use any other street, because this street was his."

"His street?"

The English boy had listened, interested, pleasant. "Billet, you see," he said. "Must have order, even in war emergency. Billet by lot. This street mine; no poaching, eh? Next street Jamie Wuther-spoon's. But trucks can go by that street because Jamie not using it yet. Not in bed yet. Insomnia. Knew so. Told them. Trucks go that way. See now?"

"Was that it, corporal?" the captain said.

"He told you. He wouldn't get up. He just laid there, arguing with them. He was telling one of them to go somewhere and bring back a copy of their articles of war—"

"King's Regulations; yes," the captain said.

"—and see if the book said whether he had the right of way, or the trucks. And then I got him up, and then the captain come along. And that's all. And with the captain's permission I'll now hand him over to His Majesty's wet nur—"

"That'll do, corporal," the captain said. "You can go. I'll see to this." The policeman saluted and went on. The British policeman was now supporting the English boy. "Can't you take him?" the captain said. "Where are their quarters?"

"I don't rightly know, sir, if they have quarters or not. We—I usually see them about the pubs until daylight. They don't seem to use quarters."

"You mean, they really aren't off of ships?"

"Well, sir, they might be ships, in a manner of speaking. But a man would have to be a bit sleepier than him to sleep in one of them."

"I see," the captain said. He looked at the policeman. "What kind of boats are they?"

This time the policeman's voice was immediate, final and completely inflectionless. It was like a closed door. "I don't rightly know, sir."

"Oh," the captain said. "Quite. Well, he's in no shape to stay about pubs until daylight this time."

"Perhaps I can find him a bit of a pub with a back table, where he can sleep," the policeman said. But the captain was not listening. He was looking across the street, where the lights of another café fell across the pavement. The English boy yawned terrifically, like a child does, his mouth pink and frankly gaped as a child's.

The captain turned to the policeman:

"Would you mind stepping across there and asking for Captain Bogard's driver? I'll take care of Mr. Hope."

The policeman departed. The captain now supported the English boy, his hand beneath the other's arm. Again the boy yawned like a weary child. "Steady," the captain said. "The car will be here in a minute."

"Right," the English boy said through the yawn.

– 2 –

Once in the car, he went to sleep immediately with the peaceful suddenness of babies, sitting between the two Americans. But though the aerodrome was only thirty minutes away, he was awake when they arrived, apparently quite fresh, and asking for whisky. When they entered the mess he appeared quite sober, only blinking a little in the lighted room, in his raked cap and his awry-buttoned pea-jacket and a soiled silk muffler, embroidered with a club insignia which Bogard recognized to have come from a famous preparatory school, twisted about his throat.

"Ah," he said, his voice fresh, clear now, not blurred, quite cheerful, quite loud, so that the others in the room turned and looked at him. "Jolly. Whisky, what?" He went straight as a bird dog to the bar in the corner, the lieutenant following. Bogard had turned and gone on to the other end of the room, where five men sat about a card table.

"What's he admiral of?" one said.

"Of the whole Scotch navy, when I found him," Bogard said.

Another looked up. "Oh, I thought I'd seen him in town." He looked at the guest. "Maybe it's because he was on his feet that I didn't recognize him when he came in. You usually see them lying down in the gutter."

"Oh," the first said. He, too, looked around. "Is he one of those guys?"

"Sure. You've seen them. Sitting on the curb, you know, with a couple of limey M. P.'s hauling at their arms."

"Yes. I've seen them," the other said. They all looked at the English boy. He stood at the bar, talking, his voice loud, cheerful. "They all look like him too," the speaker said. "About seventeen or eighteen. They run those little boats that are always dashing in and out."

"Is that what they do?" a third said. "You mean, there's a male marine auxiliary to the Waacs? Good Lord, I sure made a mistake when I enlisted. But this war never was advertised right."

"I don't know," Bogard said. "I guess they do more than just ride around."

But they were not listening to him. They were looking at the guest. "They run by clock," the first said. "You can see the condition of one of them after sunset and almost tell what time it is. But what I don't see is, how a man that's in that shape at one o'clock every morning can even see a battleship the next day."

"Maybe when they have a message to send out to a ship," another said, "they just make duplicates and line the launches up and point them toward the ship and give each one a duplicate of the message and let them go. And the ones that miss the ship just cruise around the harbor until they hit a dock somewhere."

"It must be more than that," Bogard said.

He was about to say something else, but at that moment the guest turned from the bar and approached, carrying a glass. He walked steadily enough, but his color was high and his eyes were bright, and he was talking, loud, cheerful, as he came up.

"I say. Won't you chaps join—" He ceased. He seemed to remark something; he was looking at their breasts. "Oh, I say. You fly. All of you. Oh, good gad! Find it jolly, eh?"

"Yes," somebody said. "Jolly."

"But dangerous, what?"

"A little faster than tennis," another said. The guest looked at him, bright, affable, intent.

Another said quickly, "Bogard says you command a vessel."

"Hardly a vessel. Thanks, though. And not command. Ronnie does that. Ranks me a bit. Age."

"Ronnie?"

"Yes. Nice. Good egg. Old, though. Stickler."

"Stickler?"

"Frightful. You'd not believe it. Whenever we sight smoke and I have the glass, he sheers away. Keeps the ship hull down all the while. No beaver then. Had me two down a fortnight yesterday."

The Americans glanced at one another. "No beaver?"

"We play it. With basket masts, you see. See a basket mast. Beaver! One up. The Ergenstrasse doesn't count any more, though."

The men about the table looked at one another. Bogard spoke. "I see. When you or Ronnie see a ship with basket masts, you get a beaver on the other. I see. What is the Ergenstrasse?"

"She's German. Interned. Tramp steamer. Foremast rigged so it looks something like a basket mast. Booms, cables, I dare say. I didn't think it looked very much like a basket mast, myself. But Ronnie said yes. Called it one day. Then one day they shifted her across the basin and I called her on Ronnie. So we decided to not count her any more. See now, eh?"

"Oh," the one who had made the tennis remark said, "I see. You and Ronnie run about in the launch, playing beaver. H'm'm. That's nice. Did you ever pl—"

"Jerry," Bogard said. The guest had not moved. He looked down at the speaker, still smiling, his eyes quite wide.

The speaker still looked at the guest. "Has yours and Ronnie's boat got a yellow stern?"

"A yellow stern?" the English boy said. He had quit smiling, but his face was still pleasant.

"I thought that maybe when the boats had two captains, they might paint the sterns yellow or something."

"Oh," the guest said. "Burt and Reeves aren't officers."

"Burt and Reeves," the other said, in a musing tone. "So they go, too. Do they play beaver too?"

"Jerry," Bogard said. The other looked at him. Bogard jerked his head a little. "Come over here." The other rose. They went aside. "Lay off of him," Bogard said. "I mean it, now. He's just a kid. When you were that age, how much sense did you have? Just about enough to get to chapel on time."

"My country hadn't been at war going on four years, though," Jerry said. "Here we are, spending our money and getting shot at by the clock, and it's not even our fight, and these limeys that would have been goose-stepping twelve months now if it hadn't been—"

"Shut it," Bogard said. "You sound like a Liberty Loan."

"—taking it like it was a fair or something. 'Jolly.'" His voice was now falsetto, lilting. "'But dangerous, what?'"

"Sh-h-h-h," Bogard said.

"I'd like to catch him and his Ronnie out in the harbor, just once. Any harbor. London's. I wouldn't want anything but a Jenny, either. Jenny? Hell, I'd take a bicycle and a pair of water wings! I'll show him some war."

"Well, you lay off him now. He'll be gone soon."

"What are you going to do with him?"

"I'm going to take him along this morning. Let him have Harper's place out front. He says he can handle a Lewis. Says they have one on the boat. Something he was telling me—about how he once shot out a channel-marker light at seven hundred yards."

"Well, that's your business. Maybe he can beat you."

"Beat me?"

"Playing beaver. And then you can take on Ronnie."

"I'll show him some war, anyway," Bogard said. He looked at the guest. "His people have been in it three years now, and he seems to take it like a sophomore in town for the big game." He looked at Jerry again. "But you lay off him now."

As they approached the table, the guest's voice was loud and cheerful: ". . . if he got the glasses first, he would go in close and look, but when I got them first, he'd sheer off where I couldn't see anything but the smoke. Frightful stickler. Frightful. But Ergenstrasse not counting any more. And if you make a mistake and call her, you lose two beaver from your score. If Ronnie were only to forget and call her we'd be even."

– 3 –

At two o'clock the English boy was still talking, his voice bright, innocent and cheerful. He was telling them how Switzerland had been spoiled by 1914, and instead of the vacation which his father had promised him for his sixteenth birthday, when that birthday came he and his tutor had had to do with Wales. But that he and the tutor had got pretty high and that he dared to say—with all due respect to any present who might have had the advantage of Switzerland, of course—that one could see probably as far from Wales as from Switzerland. "Perspire as much and breathe as hard, anyway," he added. And about him the Americans sat, a little hard-bitten, a little sober, somewhat older, listening to him with a kind of cold astonishment. They had been getting up for some time now and going out and returning in flying clothes, carrying helmets and goggles. An orderly entered with a tray of coffee cups, and the guest realized that for some time now he had been hearing engines in the darkness outside.

At last Bogard rose. "Come along," he said. "We'll get your togs." When they emerged from the mess, the sound of the engines was quite loud—an idling thunder. In alignment along the invisible tarmac was a vague rank of short banks of flickering blue-green fire suspended apparently in mid-air. They crossed the aerodrome to Bogard's quarters, where the lieutenant, McGinnis, sat on a cot fastening his flying boots. Bogard reached down a Sidcott suit and threw it across the cot. "Put this on," he said.

"Will I need all this?" the guest said. "Shall we be gone that long?"

"Probably," Bogard said. "Better use it. Cold upstairs."

The guest picked up the suit. "I say," he said. "I say, Ronnie and I have a do ourselves, tomor—today. Do you think Ronnie won't mind if I am a bit late? Might not wait for me."

"We'll be back before teatime," McGinnis said. He seemed quite busy with his boot. "Promise you." The English boy looked at him.

"What time should you be back?" Bogard said.

"Oh, well," the English boy said, "I dare say it will be all right. They let Ronnie say when to go, anyway. He'll wait for me if I should be a bit late."

"He'll wait," Bogard said. "Get your suit on."

"Right," the other said. They helped him into the suit. "Never been up before," he said, chattily, pleasantly. "Dare say you can see farther than from mountains, eh?"

"See more, anyway," McGinnis said. "You'll like it."

"Oh, rather. If Ronnie only waits for me. Lark. But dangerous, isn't it?"

"Go on," McGinnis said. "You're kidding me."

"Shut your trap, Mac," Bogard said. "Come along. Want some more coffee?" He looked at the guest, but McGinnis answered:

"No. Got something better than coffee. Coffee makes such a confounded stain on the wings."

"On the wings?" the English boy said. "Why coffee on the
wings."

"Stow it, I said, Mac," Bogard said. "Come along."

They recrossed the aerodrome, approaching the muttering banks
of flame. When they drew near, the guest began to discern the
shape, the outlines, of the Handley-Page. It looked like a Pullman
coach run upslanted aground into the skeleton of the first floor of
an incomplete skyscraper. The guest looked at it quietly.

"It's larger than a cruiser," he said in his bright, interested voice.
"I say, you know. This doesn't fly in one lump. You can't pull my
leg. Seen them before. It comes in two parts: Captain Bogard and
me in one; Mac and 'nother chap in other. What?"

"No," McGinnis said. Bogard had vanished. "It all goes up in one
lump. Big lark, eh? Buzzard, what?"

"Buzzard?" the guest murmured. "Oh, I say. A cruiser. Flying. I
say, now."

"And listen," McGinnis said. His hand came forth; something
cold fumbled against the hand of the English boy—a bottle. "When
you feel yourself getting sick, see? Take a pull at it."

"Oh, shall I get sick?"

"Sure. We all do. Part of flying. This will stop it. But if it doesn't.
See?"

"What? Quite. What?"

"Not overside. Don't spew it overside."

"Not overside?"

"It'll blow back in Bogy's and my face. Can't see. Bingo. Finished. See?"

"Oh, quite. What shall I do with it?" Their voices were quiet,
brief, grave as conspirators.

"Just duck your head and let her go."

"Oh, quite."

Bogard returned. "Show him how to get into the front pit, will
you?" he said. McGinnis led the way through the trap. Forward,
rising to the slant of the fuselage, the passage narrowed; a man
would need to crawl.

"Crawl in there and keep going," McGinnis said.

"It looks like a dog kennel," the guest said.

"Doesn't it, though?" McGinnis agreed cheerfully. "Cut along with you." Stooping, he could hear the other scuttling forward. "You'll find a Lewis gun up there, like as not," he said into the tunnel.

The voice of the guest came back: "Found it."

"The gunnery sergeant will be along in a minute and show you if it is loaded."

"It's loaded," the guest said; almost on the heels of his words the gun fired, a brief staccato burst. There were shouts, the loudest from the ground beneath the nose of the aeroplane. "It's quite all right," the English boy's voice said. "I pointed it west before I let it off. Nothing back there but Marine office and your brigade headquarters. Ronnie and I always do this before we go anywhere. Sorry if I was too soon. Oh, by the way," he added, "my name's Claude. Don't think I mentioned it."

On the ground, Bogard and two other officers stood. They had come up running. "Fired it west," one said. "How in hell does he know which way is west?"

"He's a sailor," the other said. "You forgot that."

"He seems to be a machine gunner too," Bogard said.

"Let's hope he doesn't forget that," the first said.

– 4 –

Nevertheless, Bogard kept an eye on the silhouetted head rising from the round gunpit in the nose ten feet ahead of him. "He did work that gun, though," he said to McGinnis beside him. "He even put the drum on himself, didn't he?"

"Yes," McGinnis said. "If he just doesn't forget and think that that gun is him and his tutor looking around from a Welsh alp."

"Maybe I should not have brought him," Bogard said. McGinnis didn't answer. Bogard jockeyed the wheel a little. Ahead, in the gunner's pit, the guest's head moved this way and that continuously, looking. "We'll get there and unload and haul air for home," Bogard said. "Maybe in the dark—Confound it, it would be a shame for his country to be in this mess for four years and him not even to see a gun pointed in his direction."

"He'll see one tonight if he don't keep his head in," McGinnis said.

But the boy did not do that. Not even when they had reached the objective and McGinnis had crawled down to the bomb toggles. And even when the searchlights found them and Bogard signaled to the other machines and dived, the two engines snarling full speed into and through the bursting shells, he could see the boy's face in the searchlight's glare, leaned far overside, coming sharply out as a spotlighted face on a stage, with an expression upon it of childlike interest and delight. "But he's firing that Lewis," Bogard thought. "Straight too"; nosing the machine farther down, watching the pinpoint swing into the sights, his right hand lifted, waiting to drop into McGinnis' sight. He dropped his hand; above the noise of the engines he seemed to hear the click and whistle of the released bombs as the machine, freed of the weight, shot zooming in a long upward bounce that carried it for an instant out of the light. Then he was pretty busy for a time, coming into and through the shells again, shooting athwart another beam that caught and held long enough for him to see the English boy lean- ing far over the side, looking back and down past the right wing, the undercarriage. "Maybe he's read about it somewhere," Bogard thought, turning, looking back to pick up the rest of the flight.

Then it was all over, the darkness cool and empty and peaceful and almost quiet, with only the steady sound of the engines. McGinnis climbed back into the office, and standing up in his seat, he fired the colored pistol this time and stood for a moment longer, looking backward toward where the searchlights still probed and sabered. He sat down again.

"O.K.," he said. "I counted all four of them. Let's haul air." Then he looked forward. "What's become of the King's Own? You didn't hang him onto a bomb release, did you?" Bogard looked. The for- ward pit was empty. It was in dim silhouette again now, against the stars, but there was nothing there now save the gun. "No," McGinnis said: "there he is. See? Leaning overside. Dammit, I told him not to spew it! There he comes back." The guest's head came into view again. But again it sank out of sight.

"He's coming back," Bogard said. "Stop him. Tell him we're go- ing to have every squadron in the Hun Channel group on top of us in thirty minutes."

McGinnis swung himself down and stooped at the entrance to the passage. "Get back!" he shouted. The other was almost out; they squatted so, face to face like two dogs, shouting at one an- other above the noise of the still-unthrottled engines on either side of the fabric walls. The English boy's voice was thin and high.

"Bomb!" he shrieked.

"Yes," McGinnis shouted, "they were bombs! We gave them hell! Get back, I tell you! Have every Hun in France on us in ten minutes! Get back to your gun!"

Again the boy's voice came, high, faint above the noise: "Bomb! All right?"

"Yes! Yes! All right. Back to your gun, damn you!"

McGinnis climbed back into the office. "He went back. Want me to take her awhile?"

"All right," Bogard said. He passed McGinnis the wheel. "Ease her back some. I'd just as soon it was daylight when they come down on us."

"Right," McGinnis said. He moved the wheel suddenly. "What's the matter with that right wing?" he said. "Watch it. . . . See? I'm flying on the right aileron and a little rudder. Feel it."

Bogard took the wheel a moment. "I didn't notice that. Wire somewhere, I guess. I didn't think any of those shells were that close. Watch her, though."

"Right," McGinnis said. "And so you are going with him on his boat tomorrow—today."

"Yes. I promised him. Confound it, you can't hurt a kid, you know."

"Why don't you take Collier along, with his mandolin? Then you could sail around and sing."

"I promised him," Bogard said. "Get that wing up a little."

"Right," McGinnis said.

Thirty minutes later it was beginning to be dawn; the sky was gray. Presently McGinnis said: "Well, here they come. Look at them! They look like mosquitoes in September. I hope he don't get worked up now and think he's playing beaver. If he does he'll just be one down to Ronnie, provided the devil has a beard. . . . Want the wheel?"

– 5 –

At eight o'clock the beach, the Channel, was beneath them. Throttled back, the machine drifted down as Bogard ruddered it gently into the Channel wind. His face was strained, a little tired.

McGinnis looked tired, too, and he needed a shave.

"What do you guess he is looking at now?" he said. For again the English boy was leaning over the right side of the cockpit, looking backward and downward past the right wing.

"I don't know," Bogard said. "Maybe bullet holes." He blasted the port engine. "Must have the riggers—"

"He could see some closer than that," McGinnis said. "I'll swear I saw tracer going into his back at one time. Or maybe it's the ocean he's looking at. But he must have seen that when he came over from England." Then Bogard leveled off; the nose rose sharply, the sand, the curling tide edge fled alongside. Yet still the English boy hung far overside, looking backward and downward at something beneath the right wing, his face rapt, with utter and childlike interest. Until the machine was completely stopped he continued to do so. Then he ducked down, and in the abrupt silence of the engines they could hear him crawling in the passage. He emerged just as the two pilots climbed stiffly down from the office, his face bright, eager; his voice high, excited.

"Oh, I say! Oh, good gad! What a chap. What a judge of distance! If Ronnie could only have seen! Oh, good gad! Or maybe they aren't like ours—don't load themselves as soon as the air strikes them."

The Americans looked at him. "What don't what?" McGinnis said. "The bomb. It was magnificent; I say, I shan't forget it. Oh, I say, you know! It was splendid!"

After a while McGinnis said, "The bomb?" in a fainting voice. Then the two pilots glared at each other; they said in unison: "That right wing!" Then as one they clawed down through the trap and, with the guest at their heels, they ran around the machine and looked beneath the right wing. The bomb, suspended by its tail, hung straight down like a plumb bob beside the right wheel, its tip just touching the sand. And parallel with the wheel track was the long delicate line in the sand where its ultimate tip had dragged. Behind them the English boy's voice was high, clear, childlike:

"Frightened, myself. Tried to tell you. But realized you knew your business better than I. Skill. Marvelous. Oh, I say, I shan't forget it."

– 6 –

A marine with a bayoneted rifle passed Bogard onto the wharf and directed him to the boat. The wharf was empty, and he didn't even see the boat until he approached the edge of the wharf and looked directly down into it and upon the backs of two stooping men in greasy dungarees, who rose and glanced briefly at him and stooped again.

It was about thirty feet long and about three feet wide. It was painted with gray-green camouflage. It was quarter-decked forward, with two blunt, raked exhaust stacks. "Good Lord," Bogard thought, "if all that deck is engine—" Just aft the deck was the control seat; he saw a big wheel, an instrument panel. Rising to a height of about a foot above the free-board, and running from the stern forward to where the deck began, and continuing on across the after edge of the deck and thence back down the other gunwale to the stern, was a solid screen, also camouflaged, which inclosed the boat save for the width of the stern, which was open. Facing the steersman's seat like an eye was a hole in the screen about eight inches in diameter. And looking down into the long, narrow, still, vicious shape, he saw a machine gun swiveled at the stern, and he looked at the low screen—including which the whole vessel did not sit much more than a yard above water level—with its single empty forward-staring eye, and he thought quietly: "It's steel. It's made of steel." And his face was quite sober, quite thoughtful, and he drew his trench coat about him and buttoned it, as though he were getting cold.

He heard steps behind him and turned. But it was only an orderly from the aerodrome, accompanied by the marine with the rifle. The orderly was carrying a largish bundle wrapped in paper.

"From Lieutenant McGinnis to the captain," the orderly said.

Bogard took the bundle. The orderly and the marine retreated. He opened the bundle. It contained some objects and a scrawled note. The objects were a new yellow silk sofa cushion and a Japanese parasol, obviously borrowed, and a comb and a roll of toilet paper. The note said:

Couldn't find a camera anywhere and Collier wouldn't let me have his mandolin. But maybe Ronnie can play on the comb.

MAC.

Bogard looked at the objects. But his face was still quite thoughtful, quite grave. He rewrapped the things and carried the bundle on up the wharf and dropped it quietly into the water.

As he returned toward the invisible boat he saw two men approaching. He recognized the boy at once—tall, slender, already talking, voluble, his head bent a little toward his shorter companion, who plodded along beside him, hands in pockets, smoking a pipe. The boy still wore the pea-coat beneath a flapping oilskin, but in place of the rakish and casual cap he now wore an infantryman's soiled Balaclava helmet, with, floating behind him as though upon the sound of his voice, a curtainlike piece of cloth almost as long as a burnous.

"Hullo, there!" he cried, still a hundred yards away.

But it was the second man that Bogard was watching, thinking to himself that he had never in his life seen a more curious figure. There was something stolid about the very shape of his hunched shoulders, his slightly down-looking face. He was a head shorter than the other. His face was ruddy, too, but its mold was of a profound gravity that was almost dour. It was the face of a man of twenty who has been for a year trying, even while asleep, to look twenty-one. He wore a high-necked sweater and dungaree slacks; above this a leather jacket; and above this a soiled naval officer's warmer that reached almost to his heels and which had one shoulder strap missing and not one remaining button at all. On his head was a plaid fore-and-aft deer stalker's cap, tied on by a narrow scarf brought across and down, hiding his ears, and then wrapped once about his throat and knotted with a hangman's noose beneath his left ear. It was unbelievably soiled, and with his hands elbow-deep in his pockets and his hunched shoulders and his bent head, he looked like someone's grandmother hung, say, for a witch. Clamped upside down between his teeth was a short brier pipe.

"Here he is!" the boy cried. "This is Ronnie. Captain Bogard."

"How are you?" Bogard said. He extended his hand. The other said no word, but his hand came forth, limp. It was quite cold, but it was hard, calloused. But he said no word; he just glanced briefly at Bogard and then away. But in that instant Bogard caught something in the look, something strange—a flicker; a kind of covert and curious respect, something like a boy of fifteen looking at a circus trapezist.

But he said no word. He ducked on; Bogard watched him drop from sight over the wharf edge as though he had jumped feet first into the sea. He remarked now that the engines in the invisible boat were running.

"We might get aboard too," the boy said. He started toward the

boat, then he stopped. He touched Bogard's arm. "Yonder!" he
hissed. "See?" His voice was thin with excitement.

"What?" Bogard also whispered; automatically he looked backward and upward, after old habit. The other was gripping his arm
and pointing across the harbor.

"There! Over there. The Ergenstrasse. They have shifted her
again." Across the harbor lay an ancient, rusting, sway-backed
hulk. It was small and nondescript, and, remembering, Bogard saw
that the foremast was a strange mess of cables and booms, resembling—allowing for a great deal of license or looseness of imagery
—a basket mast. Beside him the boy was almost chortling. "Do
you think that Ronnie noticed?" he hissed. "Do you?"

"I don't know," Bogard said.

"Oh, good gad! If he should glance up and call her before he no-
tices, we'll be even. Oh, good gad! But come along." He went on;
he was still chortling. "Careful," he said. "Frightful ladder."

He descended first, the two men in the boat rising and saluting.
Ronnie had disappeared, save for his backside, which now filled
a small hatch leading forward beneath the deck. Bogard descended
gingerly.

"Good Lord," he said. "Do you have to climb up and down this
every day?"

"Frightful, isn't it?" the other said, in his happy voice. "But you
know yourself. Try to run a war with makeshifts, then wonder why
it takes so long." The narrow hull slid and surged, even with
Bogard's added weight. "Sits right on top, you see," the boy said.
"Would float on a lawn, in a heavy dew. Goes right over them like
a bit of paper."

"It does?" Bogard said.

"Oh, absolutely. That's why, you see." Bogard didn't see, but he
was too busy letting himself gingerly down to a sitting posture.
There were no thwarts; no seats save a long, thick, cylindrical
ridge which ran along the bottom of the boat from the driver's seat
to the stern. Ronnie had backed into sight. He now sat behind the
wheel, bent over the instrument panel. But when he glanced back
over his shoulder he did not speak. His face was merely interrogatory. Across his face there was now a long smudge of grease. The
boy's face was empty, too, now.

"Right," he said. He looked forward, where one of the seamen
had gone. "Ready forward?" he said.

"Aye, sir," the seaman said.

The other seaman was at the stern line. "Ready aft?"

"Aye, sir."

"Cast off." The boat sheered away, purring, a boiling of water under the stern. The boy looked down at Bogard. "Silly business. Do it shipshape, though. Can't tell when silly fourstriper—" His face changed again, immediate, solicitous. "I say. Will you be warm? I never thought to fetch—"

"I'll be all right," Bogard said. But the other was already taking off his oilskin. "No, no," Bogard said. "I won't take it."

"You'll tell me if you get cold?"

"Yes. Sure." He was looking down at the cylinder on which he sat. It was a half cylinder—that is, like the hot-water tank to some Gargantuan stove, sliced down the middle and bolted, open side down, to the floor plates. It was twenty feet long and more than two feet thick. Its top rose as high as the gunwales and between it and the hull on either side was just room enough for a man to place his feet to walk.

"That's Muriel," the boy said.

"Muriel?"

"Yes. The one before that was Agatha. After my aunt. The first one Ronnie and I had was Alice in Wonderland. Ronnie and I were the White Rabbit. Jolly, eh?"

"Oh, you and Ronnie have had three, have you?"

"Oh, yes," the boy said. He leaned down. "He didn't notice," he whispered. His face was again bright, gleeful. "When we come back," he said. "You watch."

"Oh," Bogard said. "The Ergenstrasse." He looked astern, and then he thought: "Good Lord! We must be going—traveling." He looked out now, broadside, and saw the harbor line fleeing past, and he thought to himself that the boat was well-nigh moving at the speed at which the Handley-Page flew, left the ground. They were beginning to bound now, even in the sheltered water, from one wave crest to the next with a distinct shock. His hand still rested on the cylinder on which he sat. He looked down at it again, following it from where it seemed to emerge beneath Ronnie's seat, to where it beveled into the stern. "It's the air in her, I suppose," he said.

"The what?" the boy said.

"The air. Stored up in her. That makes the boat ride high."

"Oh, yes. I dare say. Very likely. I hadn't thought about it." He came forward, his burnous whipping in the wind, and sat down beside Bogard. Their heads were below the top of the screen.

Astern the harbor fled, diminishing, sinking into the sea. The boat had begun to lift now, swooping forward and down, shocking almost stationary for a moment, then lifting and swooping again; a gout of spray came aboard over the bows like a flung shovelful of shot. "I wish you'd take this coat," the boy said.

Bogard didn't answer. He looked around at the bright face. "We're outside, aren't we?" he said quietly.

"Yes. . . . Do take it, won't you?"

"Thanks, no. I'll be all right. We won't be long, anyway, I guess."

"No. We'll turn soon. It won't be so bad then."

"Yes. I'll be all right when we turn." Then they did turn. The motion became easier. That is, the boat didn't bang head-on, shuddering, into the swells. They came up beneath now, and the boat fled with increased speed, with a long, sickening, yawing motion, first to one side and then the other. But it fled on, and Bogard looked astern with that same soberness with which he had first looked down into the boat. "We're going east now," he said.

"With just a spot of north," the boy said. "Makes her ride a bit better, what?"

"Yes," Bogard said. Astern there was nothing now save empty sea and the delicate needlelike cant of the machine gun against the boiling and slewing wake, and the two seamen crouching quietly in the stern. "Yes. It's easier." Then he said: "How far do we go?"

The boy leaned closer. He moved closer. His voice was happy, confidential, proud, though lowered a little: "It's Ronnie's show. He thought of it. Not that I wouldn't have, in time. Gratitude and all that. But he's the older, you see. Thinks fast. Courtesy, *noblesse oblige*—all that. Thought of it soon as I told him this morning. I said, 'Oh, I say. I've been there. I've seen it'; and he said, 'Not flying'; and I said, 'Strewth'; and he said 'How far? No lying now'; and I said, 'Oh, far. Tremendous. Gone all night'; and he said, 'Flying all night. That must have been to Berlin'; and I said, 'I don't know. I dare say'; and he thought. I could see him thinking. Because he is the older, you see. More experience in courtesy, right thing. And he said, 'Berlin. No fun to that chap, dashing out and back with us.'

And he thought and I waited, and I said, 'But we can't take him to Berlin. Too far. Don't know the way, either'; and he said—fast, like a shot—said, 'But there's Kiel'; and I knew—"

"What?" Bogard said. Without moving, his whole body sprang. "Kiel? In this?"

"Absolutely. Ronnie thought of it. Smart, even if he is a stickler. Said at once, 'Zeebrugge no show at all for that chap. Must do best we can for him. Berlin,' Ronnie said. 'My Gad! Berlin.'"

"Listen," Bogard said. He had turned now, facing the other, his face quite grave. "What is this boat for?"

"For?"

"What does it do?" Then, knowing beforehand the answer to his own question, he said, putting his hand on the cylinder: "What is this in here? A torpedo, isn't it?"

"I thought you knew," the boy said.

"No," Bogard said. "I didn't know." His voice seemed to reach him from a distance, dry, cricketlike: "How do you fire it?"

"Fire it?"

"How do you get it out of the boat? When that hatch was open a while ago I could see the engines. They were right in front of the end of this tube."

"Oh," the boy said. "You pull a gadget there and the torpedo drops out astern. As soon as the screw touches the water it begins to turn, and then the torpedo is ready, loaded. Then all you have to do is turn the boat quickly and the torpedo goes on."

"You mean—" Bogard said. After a moment his voice obeyed him again. "You mean you aim the torpedo with the boat and release it and it starts moving, and you turn the boat out of the way and the torpedo passes through the same water that the boat just vacated?"

"Knew you'd catch on," the boy said. "Told Ronnie so. Airman. Tamer than yours, though. But can't be helped. Best we can do, just on water. But knew you'd catch on."

"Listen," Bogard said. His voice sounded to him quite calm. The boat fled on, yawing over the swells. He sat quite motionless. It seemed to him that he could hear himself talking to himself: "Go on. Ask him. Ask him what? Ask him how close to the ship do you have to be before you fire. . . . Listen," he said, in that calm voice. "Now, you tell Ronnie, you see. You just tell him—just say—" He could feel his voice ratting off on him again, so he stopped it. He sat quite motionless, waiting for it to come back; the boy leaning now, looking at his face. Again the boy's voice was solicitous:

"I say. You're not feeling well. These confounded shallow boats."

"It's not that," Bogard said. "I just— Do your orders say Kiel?"

"Oh, no. They let Ronnie say. Just so we bring the boat back. This is for you. Gratitude. Ronnie's idea. Tame, after flying. But if you'd rather, eh?"

"Yes, some place closer. You see, I—"

"Quite. I see. No vacations in wartime. I'll tell Ronnie." He went forward. Bogard did not move. The boat fled in long, slewing swoops. Bogard looked quietly astern, at the scudding sea, the sky.

"My God!" he thought. "Can you beat it? Can you beat it?"

The boy came back; Bogard turned to him a face the color of dirty paper. "All right now," the boy said. "Not Kiel. Nearer place, hunting probably just as good. Ronnie says he knows you will understand." He was tugging at his pocket. He brought out a bottle. "Here. Haven't forgot last night. Do the same for you. Good for the stomach, eh?"

Bogard drank, gulping—a big one. He extended the bottle, but the boy refused. "Never touch it on duty," he said. "Not like you chaps. Tame here."

The boat fled on. The sun was already down the west. But Bogard had lost all count of time, of distance. Ahead he could see white seas through the round eye opposite Ronnie's face, and Ronnie's hand on the wheel and the granitelike jut of his profiled jaw and the dead upside-down pipe. The boat fled on.

Then the boy leaned and touched his shoulder. He half rose. The boy was pointing. The sun was reddish; against it, outside them and about two miles away, a vessel—a trawler, it looked like—at anchor swung a tall mast.

"Lightship!" the boy shouted. "Theirs." Ahead Bogard could see a low, flat mole—the entrance to a harbor. "Channel!" the boy shouted. He swept his arm in both directions. "Mines!" His voice swept back on the wind. "Place filthy with them. All sides. Beneath us too. Lark, eh?"

– 7 –

Against the mole a fair surf was beating. Running before the seas now, the boat seemed to leap from one roller to the next; in the intervals while the screw was in the air the engine seemed to be trying to tear itself out by the roots. But it did not slow; when it passed the end of the mole the boat seemed to be standing almost erect on its rudder, like a sailfish. The mole was a mile away. From the end of it little faint lights began to flicker like fireflies. The boy leaned. "Down," he said. "Machine guns. Might stop a stray."

"What do I do?" Bogard shouted. "What can I do?"

"Stout fellow! Give them hell, what? Knew you'd like it!"

Crouching, Bogard looked up at the boy, his face wild. "I can handle the machine gun!"

"No need," the boy shouted back. "Give them first innings. Sporting. Visitors, eh?" He was looking forward. "There she is. See?" They were in the harbor now, the basin opening before them. Anchored in the channel was a big freighter. Painted midships of the hull was a huge Argentine flag. "Must get back to stations!" the boy shouted down to him. Then at that moment Ronnie spoke for the first time. The boat was hurtling along now in smoother water. Its speed did not slacken and Ronnie did not turn his head when he spoke. He just swung his jutting jaw and the clamped cold pipe a little, and said from the side of his mouth a single word:

"Beaver."

The boy, stooped over what he had called his gadget, jerked up, his expression astonished and outraged. Bogard also looked forward and saw Ronnie's arm pointing to starboard. It was a light cruiser at anchor a mile away. She had basket masts, and as he looked a gun flashed from her after turret. "Oh, damn!" the boy cried. "Oh, you putt! Oh, confound you, Ronnie! Now I'm three down!" But he had already stooped again over his gadget, his face bright and empty and alert again; not sober; just calm, waiting. Again Bogard looked forward and felt the boat pivot on its rudder and head directly for the freighter at terrific speed, Ronnie now with one hand on the wheel and the other lifted and extended at the height of his head.

But it seemed to Bogard that the hand would never drop. He crouched, not sitting, watching with a kind of quiet horror the painted flag increase like a moving picture of a locomotive taken from between the rails. Again the gun crashed from the cruiser behind them, and the freighter fired point-blank at them from its poop. Bogard heard neither shot.

"Man, man!" he shouted. "For God's sake!"

Ronnie's hand dropped. Again the boat spun on its rudder. Bogard saw the bow rise, pivoting; he expected the hull to slam broadside on into the ship. But it didn't. It shot off on a long tangent. He was waiting for it to make a wide sweep, heading seaward, putting the freighter astern, and he thought of the cruiser again. "Get a broadside, this time, once we clear the freighter," he thought. Then he remembered the freighter, the torpedo, and he looked back toward the freighter to watch the torpedo strike, and saw to his horror that the boat was now bearing down on the freighter again, in a skidding turn. Like a man in a dream, he watched himself rush down upon the ship and shoot past under her counter, still skidding, close enough to see the faces on her decks. "They missed and they are going to run down the torpedo and catch it and shoot it again," he thought idiotically.

So the boy had to touch his shoulder before he knew he was behind him. The boy's voice was quite calm: "Under Ronnie's seat there. A bit of a crank handle. If you'll just hand it to me—"

He found the crank. He passed it back; he was thinking dreamily: "Mac would say they had a telephone on board." But he didn't look at once to see what the boy was doing with it, for in that still and peaceful horror he was watching Ronnie, the cold pipe rigid in his jaw, hurling the boat at top speed round and round the freighter, so near that he could see the rivets in the plates. Then he looked aft, his face wild, importunate, and he saw what the boy was doing with the crank. He had fitted it into what was obviously a small windlass low on one flank of the tube near the head. He glanced up and saw Bogard's face. "Didn't go that time!" he shouted cheerfully.

"Go?" Bogard shouted. "It didn't— The torpedo—"

The boy and one of the seamen were quite busy, stooping over the windlass and the tube. "No. Clumsy. Always happening. Should think clever chaps like engineers— Happens, though. Draw her in and try her again."

"But the nose, the cap!" Bogard shouted. "It's still in the tube, isn't it? It's all right, isn't it?"

"Absolutely. But it's working now. Loaded. Screw's started turning. Get it back and drop it clear. If we should stop or slow up it would overtake us. Drive back into the tube. Bingo! What?"

Bogard was on his feet now, turned, braced to the terrific merry-go-round of the boat. High above them the freighter seemed to be spinning on her heel like a trick picture in the movies. "Let me have that winch!" he cried.

"Steady!" the boy said. "Mustn't draw her back too fast. Jam her into the head of the tube ourselves. Same bingo! Best let us. Every cobbler to his last, what?"

"Oh, quite," Bogard said. "Oh, absolutely." It was like someone else was using his mouth. He leaned, braced, his hands on the cold tube, beside the others. He was hot inside, but his outside was cold. He could feel all his flesh jerking with cold as he watched the blunt, grained hand of the seaman turning the windlass in short, easy, inch-long arcs, while at the head of the tube the boy bent, tapping the cylinder with a spanner, lightly, his head turned with listening delicate and deliberate as a watchmaker. The boat rushed on in those furious, slewing turns. Bogard saw a long, drooping thread loop down from somebody's mouth, between his hands, and he found that the thread came from his own mouth.

He didn't hear the boy speak, nor notice when he stood up. He just felt the boat straighten out, flinging him to his knees beside the tube. The seaman had gone back to the stern and the boy stooped again over his gadget. Bogard knelt now, quite sick. He did not feel the boat when it swung again, nor hear the gun from the cruiser which had not dared to fire and the freighter which had not been able to fire, firing again. He did not feel anything at all when he saw the huge, painted flag directly ahead and increasing with locomotive speed, and Ronnie's lifted hand drop. But this time he knew that the torpedo was gone; in pivoting and spinning this time the whole boat seemed to leave the water; he saw the bow of the boat shoot skyward like the nose of a pursuit ship going into a wingover. Then his outraged stomach denied him. He saw neither the geyser nor heard the detonation as he sprawled over the tube. He felt only a hand grasp him by the slack of his coat, and the voice of one of the seamen: "Steady all, sir. I've got you."

– 8 –

A voice roused him, a hand. He was half sitting in the narrow starboard runway, half lying across the tube. He had been there for quite a while; quite a while ago he had felt someone spread a garment over him. But he had not raised his head. "I'm all right," he had said. "You keep it."

"Don't need it," the boy said. "Going home now."

"I'm sorry I—" Bogard said.

"Quite. Confounded shallow boats. Turn any stomach until you get used to them. Ronnie and I both, at first. Each time. You wouldn't believe it. Believe human stomach hold so much. Here." It was the bottle. "Good drink. Take enormous one. Good for stomach."

Bogard drank. Soon he did feel better, warmer. When the hand touched him later, he found that he had been asleep.

It was the boy again. The pea-coat was too small for him; shrunken, perhaps. Below the cuffs his long, slender, girl's wrists were blue with cold. Then Bogard realized what the garment was that had been laid over him. But before Bogard could speak, the boy leaned down, whispering; his face was gleeful: "He didn't notice!"

"What?"

"Ergenstrasse! He didn't notice that they had shifted her. Gad, I'd be just one down, then." He watched Bogard's face with bright, eager eyes. "Beaver, you know. I say. Feeling better, eh?"

"Yes," Bogard said, "I am."

"He didn't notice at all. Oh, gad! Oh, Jove!"

Bogard rose and sat on the tube. The entrance to the harbor was just ahead; the boat had slowed a little. It was just dusk. He said quietly: "Does this often happen?" The boy looked at him. Bogard touched the tube. "This. Failing to go out."

"Oh, yes. Why they put the windlass on them. That was later. Made first boat; whole thing blew up one day. So put on windlass."

"But it happens sometimes, even now? I mean, sometimes they blow up, even with the windlass?"

"Well, can't say, of course. Boats go out. Not come back. Possible. Not ever know, of course. Not heard of one captured yet, though. Possible. Not to us, though. Not yet."

"Yes," Bogard said. "Yes." They entered the harbor, the boat moving still fast, but throttled now and smooth, across the dusk-filled basin. Again the boy leaned down, his voice gleeful.

"Not a word, now!" he hissed. "Steady all!" He stood up; he raised his voice: "I say, Ronnie." Ronnie did not turn his head, but Bogard could tell that he was listening. "That Argentine ship was amusing, eh? In there. How do you suppose it got past us here? Might have stopped here as well. French would buy the wheat." He paused, diabolical—Machiavelli with the face of a strayed angel. "I say. How long has it been since we had a strange ship in here? Been months, eh?" Again he leaned, hissing. "Watch, now!" But Bogard could not see Ronnie's head move at all. "He's looking, though!" the boy whispered, breathed. And Ronnie was looking, though his head had not moved at all. Then there came into view, in silhouette against the dusk-filled sky, the vague, basket-like shape of the interned vessel's foremast. At once Ronnie's arm rose, pointing; again he spoke without turning his head, out of the side of his mouth, past the cold, clamped pipe, a single word:

"Beaver."

The boy moved like a released spring, like a heeled dog freed. "Oh, damn you!" he cried. "Oh, you putt! It's the Ergenstrasse! Oh, confound you! I'm just one down now!" He had stepped in one stride completely over Bogard, and he now leaned down over Ronnie. "What?" The boat was slowing in toward the wharf, the engine idle. "Aren't I, Ronnie? Just one down now?"

The boat drifted in; the seaman had again crawled forward onto the deck. Ronnie spoke for the third and last time. "Right," he said.

– 9 –

"I want," Bogard said, "a case of Scotch. The best we've got. And fix it up good. It's to go to town. And I want a responsible man to deliver it." The responsible man came. "This is for a child," Bogard said, indicating the package. "You'll find him in the Street of the Twelve Hours, somewhere near the Café Twelve Hours. He'll be in the gutter. You'll know him. A child about six feet long. Any English M. P. will show him to you. If he is asleep, don't wake him. Just sit there and wait until he wakes up. Then give him this. Tell him it is from Captain Bogard."

– 10 –

About a month later a copy of the English Gazette which had strayed onto an American aerodrome carried the following item in the casualty lists:

Missing: Torpedo Boat XOOI. Midshipmen R. Boyce Smith and L. C. W. Hope, R. N. R., Boatswain's Mate Burt and Able Seaman Reeves. Channel Fleet, Light Torpedo Division. Failed to return from coast patrol duty.

Shortly after that the American Air Service headquarters also issued a bulletin:

For extraordinary valor over and beyond the routine of duty, Captain H. S. Bogard, with his crew, composed of Second Lieutenant Darrel McGinnis and Aviation Gunners Watts and Harper, on a daylight raid and without scout protection, destroyed with bombs an ammunition depot several miles behind the enemy's lines. From here, beset by enemy aircraft in superior numbers, these men proceeded with what bombs remained to the enemy's corps headquarters at Blank and partially demolished this château, and then returned safely without loss of a man.

And regarding which exploit, it might have added, had it failed and had Captain Bogard come out of it alive, he would have been immediately and thoroughly court-martialed.

Carrying his remaining two bombs, he had dived the Handley-Page at the château where the generals sat at lunch, until McGinnis, at the toggles below him, began to shout at him, before he ever signaled. He didn't signal until he could discern separately the slate tiles of the roof. Then his hand dropped and he zoomed, and he held the aeroplane so, in its wild snarl, his lips parted, his breath hissing, thinking: "God! God! If they were all there—all the generals, the admirals, the presidents and the kings—theirs, ours—all of them."

Shingles for the Lord

Pap got up a good hour before daylight and caught the mule and rid down to Killegrews' to borrow the froe and maul. He ought to been back with it in forty minutes. But the sun had rose and I had done milked and fed and was eating my breakfast when he got back, with the mule not only in a lather but right on the edge of the thumps too.

"Fox hunting," he said. "Fox hunting. A seventy-year-old man, with both feet and one knee, too, already in the grave, squatting all night on a hill and calling himself listening to a fox race that he couldn't even hear unless they had come right up onto the same log he was setting on and bayed into his ear trumpet. Give me my breakfast," he told maw. "Whitfield is standing there right this minute, straddle of that board tree with his watch in his hand."

And he was. We rid on past the church, and there was not only Solon Quick's school-bus truck but Reverend Whitfield's old mare too. We tied the mule to a sapling and hung our dinner bucket on a limb, and with pap toting Killegrew's froe and maul and the wedges and me toting our ax, we went on to the board tree where Solon and Homer Bookwright, with their froes and mauls and axes and wedges, was setting on two upended cuts, and Whitfield was standing jest like pap said, in his boiled shirt and his black hat and pants and necktie, holding his watch in his hand. It was gold and in the morning sunlight it looked big as a full-growed squash.

"You're late," he said.

So pap told again about how Old Man Killegrew had been off fox hunting all night, and nobody at home to lend him the froe but Mrs. Killegrew and the cook. And naturally, the cook wasn't going to lend none of Killegrew's tools out, and Mrs. Killegrew was worser deaf than even Killegrew. If you was to run in and tell her the house was afire, she would jest keep on rocking and say she thought so, too, unless she began to holler back to the cook to turn the dogs loose before you could even open your mouth.

"You could have gone yesterday and borrowed the froe," Whitfield said. "You have known for a month now that you had promised this one day out of a whole summer toward putting a roof on the house of God."

"We aint but two hours late," pap said. "I reckon the Lord will forgive it. He ain't interested in time, nohow. He's interested in salvation."

Whitfield never even waited for pap to finish. It looked to me like he even got taller, thundering down at pap like a cloudburst. "He ain't interested in neither! Why should He be, when He owns them both? And why He should turn around for the poor, mizzling souls of men that can't even borrow tools in time to replace the shingles on His church, I don't know either. Maybe it's just because He made them. Maybe He just said to Himself: 'I made them; I don't know why. But since I did, I Godfrey, I'll roll My sleeves up and drag them into glory whether they will or no!'"

But that wasn't here nor there either now, and I reckon he knowed it, jest like he knowed there wasn't going to be nothing atall here as long as he stayed. So he put the watch back into his pocket and motioned Solon and Homer up, and we all taken off our hats except him while he stood there with his face raised into the sun and his eyes shut and his eyebrows looking like a big iron-gray caterpillar lying along the edge of a cliff. "Lord," he said, "make them good straight shingles to lay smooth, and let them split out easy; they're for You," and opened his eyes and looked at us again, mostly at pap, and went and untied his mare and clumb up slow and stiff, like old men do, and rid away.

Pap put down the froe and maul and laid the three wedges in a neat row on the ground and taken up the ax.

"Well, men," he said, "let's get started. We're already late."

"Me and Homer ain't," Solon said. "We was here." This time him and Homer didn't set on the cuts. They squatted on their heels. Then I seen that Homer was whittling on a stick. I hadn't noticed it before. "I make it two hours and a little over," Solon said. "More or less."

Pap was still about half stooped over, holding the ax. "It's nigher one," he said. "But call it two for the sake of the argument. What about it?"

"What argument?" Homer said.

"All right," pap said. "Two hours then. What about it?"

"Which is three man-hour units a hour, multiplied by two hours," Solon said. "Or a total of six work units." When the WPA first come to Yoknapatawpha County and started to giving out jobs and grub and mattresses, Solon went in to Jefferson to get on it. He would drive his school-bus truck the twenty-two miles in to town every morning and come back that night. He done that for almost a week before he found out he would not only have to sign his farm off into somebody else's name, he couldn't even own and run the school bus that he had built himself. So he come back that night and never went back no more, and since then hadn't nobody better mention WPA to him unless they aimed to fight, too, though every now and then he would turn up with something all figured down into work units like he done now. "Six units short."

"Four of which you and Homer could have already worked out while you was setting here waiting on me," pap said.

"Except that we didn't," Solon said. "We promised Whitfield two units of twelve three-unit hours toward getting some new shingles on the church roof. We been here ever since sunup, waiting for the third unit to show up, so we could start. You don't seem to kept up with these modern ideas about work that's been flooding and uplifting the country in the last few years."

"What modren ideas?" pap said. "I didn't know there was but one idea about work—until it is done, it ain't done, and when it is done, it is."

Homer made another long, steady whittle on the stick. His knife was sharp as a razor.

Solon taken out his snuffbox and filled the top and tilted the snuff into his lip and offered the box to Homer, and Homer shaken his head, and Solon put the top back on the box and put the box back into his pocket.

"So," pap said, "jest because I had to wait two hours for a old seventy-year man to get back from fox hunting that never had no more business setting out in the woods all night than he would 'a' had setting all night in a highway juke joint, we all three have got to come back here tomorrow to finish them two hours that you and Homer——"

"I ain't," Solon said. "I don't know about Homer. I promised Whitfield one day. I was here at sunup to start it. When the sun goes down, I will consider I have done finished it."

"I see," pap said. "I see. It's me that's got to come back. By myself. I got to break into a full morning to make up them two hours that you and Homer spent resting. I got to spend two hours of the next day making up for the two hours of the day before that you and Homer never even worked."

"It's going to more than jest break into a morning," Solon said. "It's going to wreck it. There's six units left over. Six one-man-hour units. Maybe you can work twice as fast as me and Homer put together and finish them in four hours, but I don't believe you can work three times as fast and finish in two."

Pap was standing up now. He was breathing hard. We could hear him. "So," he said. "So." He swung the ax and druv the blade into one of the cuts and snatched it up onto its flat end, ready to split. "So I'm to be penalized a half a day of my own time, from my own work that's waiting for me at home right this minute, to do six hours more work than the work you fellers lacked two hours of even doing atall, purely and simply because I am jest a average hard-working farmer trying to do the best he can, instead of a durn froe-owning millionaire named Quick or Bookwright."

They went to work then, splitting the cuts into bolts and riving the bolts into shingles for Tull and Snopes and the others that had promised for tomorrow to start nailing onto the church roof when they finished pulling the old shingles off. They set flat on the ground in a kind of circle, with their legs spraddled out on either side of the propped-up bolt, Solon and Homer working light and easy and steady as two clocks ticking, but pap making every lick of hisn like he was killing a moccasin. If he had jest swung the maul half as fast as he swung it hard, he would have rove as many shingles as Solon and Homer together, swinging the maul up over his head and holding it there for what looked like a whole minute sometimes and then swinging it down onto the blade of the froe, and not only a shingle flying off every lick but the froe going on into the ground clean up to the helve eye, and pap setting there wrenching at it slow and steady and hard, like he jest wished it would try to hang on a root or a rock and stay there.

"Here, here," Solon said. "If you don't watch out you won't have nothing to do neither during them six extra units tomorrow morning but rest."

Pap never even looked up. "Get out of the way," he said. And Solon done it. If he hadn't moved the water bucket, pap would have split it, too, right on top of the bolt, and this time the whole shingle went whirling past Solon's shin jest like a scythe blade.

"What you ought to do is to hire somebody to work out them extra overtime units," Solon said.

"With what?" pap said. "I ain't had no WPA experience in dickering over labor. Get out of the way."

But Solon had already moved this time. Pap would have had to change his whole position or else made this one curve. So this one missed Solon, too, and pap set there wrenching the froe, slow and hard and steady, back out of the ground.

"Maybe there's something else besides cash you might be able to trade with," Solon said. "You might use that dog."

That was when pap actually stopped. I didn't know it myself then either, but I found it out a good long time before Solon did. Pap set there with the maul up over his head and the blade of the froe set against the block for the next lick, looking up at Solon. "The dog?" he said.

It was a kind of mixed hound, with a little bird dog and some collie and maybe a considerable of almost anything else, but it would ease through the woods without no more noise than a hant and pick up a squirrel's trail on the ground and bark jest once, unless it knowed you was where you could see it, and then tiptoe that trail out jest like a man and never make another sound until it treed, and only then when it knowed you hadn't kept in sight of it. It belonged to pap and Vernon Tull together. Will Varner give it to Tull as a puppy, and pap raised it for a half interest; me and him trained it and it slept in my bed with me until it got so big maw finally run it out of the house, and for the last six months Solon had been trying to buy it. Him and Tull had agreed on two dollars for Tull's half of it, but Solon and pap was still six dollars apart on ourn, because pap said it was worth ten dollars of anybody's money and if Tull wasn't going to collect his full half of that, he was going to collect it for him.

"So that's it," pap said. "Them things wasn't work units atall. They was dog units."

"Jest a suggestion," Solon said. "Jest a friendly offer to keep them runaway shingles from breaking up your private business for six hours tomorrow morning. You sell me your half of that trick overgrown fyce and I'll finish these shingles for you."

"Naturally including them six extra units of one dollars," pap said.

"No, no," Solon said. "I'll pay you the same two dollars for your half of that dog that me and Tull agreed on for his half of it. You meet me here tomorrow morning with the dog and you can go on back home or wherever them urgent private affairs are located, and forget about that church roof."

For about ten seconds more, pap set there with the maul up over his head, looking at Solon. Then for about three seconds he wasn't looking at Solon or at nothing else. Then he was looking at Solon again. It was jest exactly like after about two and nine-tenths seconds he found out he wasn't looking at Solon, so he looked back at him as quick as he could. "Hah," he said. Then he began to laugh. It was laughing all right, because his mouth was open and that's what it sounded like. But it never went no further back than his teeth and it never come nowhere near reaching as high up as his eyes. And he never said "Look out" this time neither. He jest shifted fast on his hips and swung the maul down, the froe done already druv through the bolt and into the ground while the shingle was still whirling off to slap Solon across the shin.

Then they went back at it again. Up to this time I could tell pap's licks from Solon's and Homer's, even with my back turned, not because they was louder or steadier, because Solon and Homer worked steady, too, and the froe never made no especial noise jest going into the ground, but because they was so infrequent; you would hear five or six of Solon's and Homer's little polite chipping licks before you would hear pap's froe go "chug!" and know that another shingle had went whirling off somewhere. But from now on pap's sounded jest as light and quick and polite as Solon's or Homer's either, and, if anything, even a little faster, with the shingles piling up steadier than I could stack them, almost; until now there was going to be more than a plenty of them for Tull and the others to shingle with tomorrow, right on up to noon, when we heard Armstid's farm bell, and Solon laid his froe and maul down and looked at his watch too. And I wasn't so far away neither, but by the time I caught up with pap he had untied the mule from the sapling and was already on it. And maybe Solon and Homer thought they had pap, and maybe for a minute I did, too, but I jest wish they could have seen his face then. He reached our dinner bucket down from the limb and handed it to me.

"Go on and eat," he said. "Don't wait for me. Him and his work units. If he wants to know where I went, tell him I forgot something and went home to get it. Tell him I had to go back home to get two spoons for us to eat our dinner with. No, don't tell him that. If he hears I went somewhere to get something I needed to use, even if it's jest a tool to eat with, he will refuse to believe I jest went home, for the reason that I don't own anything there that even I would borrow." He hauled the mule around and heeled him in the flank. Then he pulled up again. "And when I come back, no matter what I say, don't pay no attention to it. No matter what happens, don't you say nothing. Don't open your mouth a-tall, you hear?"

Then he went on, and I went back to where Solon and Homer was setting on the running board of Solon's school-bus truck, eating, and sho enough Solon said jest exactly what pap said he was going to.

"I admire his optimism, but he's mistaken. If it's something he needs that he can't use his natural hands and feet for, he's going somewhere else than jest his own house."

We had jest went back to the shingles when pap rid up and got down and tied the mule back to the sapling and come and taken up the ax and snicked the blade into the next cut.

"Well, men," he said, "I been thinking about it. I still don't think it's right, but I still ain't thought of anything to do about it. But somebody's got to make up for them two hours nobody worked this morning, and since you fellers are two to one against me, it looks like it's going to be me that makes them up. But I got work waiting at home for me tomorrow. I got corn that's crying out loud for me right now. Or maybe that's jest a lie too. Maybe the whole thing is, I don't mind admitting here in private that I been outfigured, but I be dog if I'm going to set here by myself tomorrow morning admitting it in public. Anyway, I ain't. So I'm going to trade with you, Solon. You can have the dog."

Solon looked at pap. "I don't know as I want to trade now," he said.

"I see," pap said. The ax was still stuck in the cut. He began to pump it up and down to back it out.

"Wait," Solon said. "Put that durn ax down." But pap held the ax raised for the lick, looking at Solon and waiting. "You're swapping me half a dog for a half a day's work," Solon said.

"Your half of the dog for that half a day's work you still owe on these shingles."

"And the two dollars," pap said. "That you and Tull agreed on. I sell you half the dog for two dollars, and you come back here to-morrow and finish the shingles. You give me the two dollars now, and I'll meet you here in the morning with the dog, and you can show me the receipt from Tull for his half then."

"Me and Tull have already agreed," Solon said.

"All right," pap said. "Then you can pay Tull his two dollars and bring his receipt with you without no trouble."

"Tull will be at the church tomorrow morning, pulling off them old shingles," Solon said.

"All right," pap said. "Then it won't be no trouble at all for you to get a receipt from him. You can stop at the church when you pass. Tull ain't named Grier. He won't need to be off somewhere borrowing a crowbar."

So Solon taken out his purse and paid pap the two dollars and they went back to work. And now it looked like they really was try-ing to finish that afternoon, not jest Solon, but even Homer, that didn't seem to be concerned in it nohow, and pap, that had already swapped a half a dog to get rid of whatever work Solon claimed would be left over. I quit trying to stay up with them; I jest stacked shingles.

Then Solon laid his froe and maul down. "Well, men," he said, "I don't know what you fellers think, but I consider this a day."

"All right," pap said. "You are the one to decide when to quit, since whatever elbow units you consider are going to be shy to-morrow will be yourn."

"That's a fact," Solon said. "And since I am giving a day and a half to the church instead of jest a day, like I started out doing, I reckon I better get on home and tend to a little of my own work." He picked up his froe and maul and ax, and went to his truck and stood waiting for Homer to come and get in.

"I'll be here in the morning with the dog," pap said.

"Sholy," Solon said. It sounded like he had forgot about the dog, or that it wasn't no longer any importance. But he stood there again and looked hard and quiet at pap for about a second. "And a bill of sale from Tull for his half of it. As you say, it won't be no trouble a-tall to get that from him." Him and Homer got into the truck and he started the engine. You couldn't say jest what it was. It was almost like Solon was hurrying himself, so pap wouldn't have to make any excuse or pretense toward doing or not doing anything. "I have always understood the fact that lightning don't have to hit twice is one of the reasons why they named it lightning. So getting lightning-struck is a mistake that might happen to any man. The mistake I seem to made is, I never realized in time that what I was looking at was a cloud. I'll see you in the morning."

"With the dog," pap said.

"Certainly," Solon said, again like it had slipped his mind completely. "With the dog."

Then him and Homer drove off. Then pap got up.

"What?" I said. "What? You swapped him your half of Tull's dog for that half a day's work tomorrow. Now what?"

"Yes," pap said. "Only before that I had already swapped Tull a half a day's work pulling off them old shingles tomorrow, for Tull's half of that dog. Only we ain't going to wait until tomorrow. We're going to pull them shingles off tonight, and without no more racket about it than is necessary. I don't aim to have nothing on my mind tomorrow but watching Mr. Solon Work-Unit Quick trying to get a bill of sale for two dollars or ten dollars either on the other half of that dog. And we'll do it tonight. I don't want him jest to find out at sunup tomorrow that he is too late. I want him to find out then that even when he laid down to sleep he was already too late."

So we went back home and I fed and milked while pap went down to Killegrews' to carry the froe and maul back and to borrow a crowbar. But of all places in the world and doing what under the sun with it, Old Man Killegrew had went and lost his crowbar out of a boat into forty feet of water. And pap said how he come within a inch of going to Solon's and borrowing his crowbar out of pure poetic justice, only Solon might have smelled the rat jest from the idea of the crowbar. So pap went to Armstid's and borrowed hisn and come back and we et supper and cleaned and filled the lantern while maw still tried to find out what we was up to that couldn't wait till morning.

We left her still talking, even as far as the front gate, and come on back to the church, walking this time, with the rope and crowbar and a hammer for me, and the lantern still dark. Whitfield and Snopes was unloading a ladder from Snopes' wagon when we passed the church on the way home before dark, so all we had to do was to set the ladder up against the church. Then pap clumb up onto the roof with the lantern and pulled off shingles until he could hang the lantern inside behind the decking, where it could shine

out through the cracks in the planks, but you couldn't see it unless
you was passing in the road, and by that time anybody would 'a'
already heard us. Then I clumb up with the rope, and pap reached
it through the decking and around a rafter and back and tied the
ends around our waists, and we started. And we went at it. We had
them old shingles jest raining down, me using the claw hammer and
pap using the crowbar, working the bar under a whole patch of
shingles at one time and then laying back on the bar like in one
more lick or if the crowbar ever happened for one second to get a
solid holt, he would tilt up that whole roof at one time like a
hinged box lid.

That's exactly what he finally done. He laid back on the bar and
this time it got a holt. It wasn't jest a patch of shingles, it was a
whole section of decking, so that when he lunged back he snatched
that whole section of roof from around the lantern like you would
shuck a corn nubbin. The lantern was hanging on a nail. He never
even moved the nail, he jest pulled the board off of it, so that it
looked like for a whole minute I watched the lantern, and the crowbar, too, setting there in the empty air in a little mess of floating
shingles, with the empty nail still sticking through the bail of the
lantern, before the whole thing started down into the church. It
hit the floor and bounced once. Then it hit the floor again, and this
time the whole church jest blowed up into a pit of yellow jumping
fire, with me and pap hanging over the edge of it on two ropes.

I don't know what become of the rope nor how we got out of it.
I don't remember climbing down. Jest pap yelling behind me and
pushing me about halfway down the ladder and then throwing me
the rest of the way by a handful of my overhalls, and then we was
both on the ground, running for the water barrel. It set under the
gutter spout at the side, and Armstid was there then; he had happened to go out to his lot about a hour back and seen the lantern
on the church roof, and it stayed on his mind until finally he come
up to see what was going on, and got there jest in time to stand
yelling back and forth with pap across the water barrel. And I
believe we still would have put it out. Pap turned and squatted
against the barrel and got a holt of it over his shoulder and stood
up with that barrel that was almost full and run around the corner
and up the steps of the church and hooked his toe on the top step
and come down with the barrel busting on top of him and knocking him cold out as a wedge.

So we had to drag him back first, and maw was there then, and Mrs. Armstid about the same time, and me and Armstid run with the two fire buckets to the spring, and when we got back there was a plenty there, Whitfield, too, with more buckets, and we done what we could, but the spring was two hundred yards away and ten buckets emptied it and it taken five minutes to fill again, and so finally we all jest stood around where pap had come to again with a big cut on his head and watched it go. It was a old church, long dried out, and full of old colored-picture charts that Whitfield had accumulated for more than fifty years, that the lantern had lit right in the middle of when it finally exploded. There was a special nail where he would keep a old long nightshirt he would wear to baptize in. I would use to watch it all the time during church and Sunday school, and me and the other boys would go past the church sometimes jest to peep in at it, because to a boy of ten it wasn't jest a cloth garment or even a iron armor; it was the old strong Archangel Michael his self, that had fit and strove and conquered sin for so long that it finally had the same contempt for the human beings that returned always to sin as hogs and dogs done that the old strong archangel his self must have had.

For a long time it never burned, even after everything else inside had. We could watch it, hanging there among the fire, not like it had knowed in its time too much water to burn easy, but like it had strove and fit with the devil and all the hosts of hell too long to burn in jest a fire that Res Grier started, trying to beat Solon Quick out of half a dog. But at last it went, too, not in a hurry still, but jest all at once, kind of roaring right on up and out against the stars and the far dark spaces. And then there wasn't nothing but jest pap, drenched and groggy-looking, on the ground, with the rest of us around him, and Whitfield like always in his boiled shirt and his black hat and pants, standing there with his hat on, too, like he had strove too long to save what hadn't ought to been created in the first place, from the damnation it didn't even want to escape, to bother to need to take his hat off in any presence. He looked around at us from under it; we was all there now, all that belonged to that church and used it to be born and marry and die from—us and the Armstids and Tulls, and Bookwright and Quick and Snopes.

"I was wrong," Whitfield said. "I told you we would meet here tomorrow to roof a church. We'll meet here in the morning to raise one."

"Of course we got to have a church," pap said. "We're going to have one. And we're going to have it soon. But there's some of us done already give a day or so this week, at the cost of our own work. Which is right and just, and we're going to give more, and glad to. But I don't believe that the Lord——"

Whitfield let him finish. He never moved. He jest stood there until pap finally run down of his own accord and hushed and set there on the ground mostly not looking at maw, before Whitfield opened his mouth.

"Not you," Whitfield said. "Arsonist."

"Arsonist?" pap said.

"Yes," Whitfield said. "If there is any pursuit in which you can engage without carrying flood and fire and destruction and death behind you, do it. But not one hand shall you lay to this new house until you have proved to us that you are to be trusted again with the powers and capacities of a man." He looked about at us again. "Tull and Snopes and Armstid have already promised for tomorrow. I understand that Quick had another half day he intended——"

"I can give another day," Solon said.

"I can give the rest of the week," Homer said.

"I ain't rushed neither," Snopes said.

"That will be enough to start with, then," Whitfield said. "It's late now. Let us all go home."

He went first. He didn't look back once, at the church or at us. He went to the old mare and clumb up slow and stiff and powerful, and was gone, and we went too, scattering. But I looked back at it. It was jest a shell now, with a red and fading core, and I had hated it at times and feared it at others, and I should have been glad. But there was something that even that fire hadn't even touched. Maybe that's all it was—jest indestructibility, endurability—that old man that could plan to build it back while its walls was still fire-fierce and then calmly turn his back and go away because he knowed that the men that never had nothing to give toward the new one but their work would be there at sunup tomorrow, and the day after that, and the day after that, too, as long as it was needed, to give that work to build it back again. So it hadn't gone a-tall; it didn't no more care for that little fire and flood than Whitfield's old baptizing gown had done. Then we was home. Maw had left so fast the lamp was still lit, and we could see pap now, still leaving a puddle where he stood, with a cut across the back of his head where the barrel had busted and the blood-streaked water soaking him to the waist.

"Get them wet clothes off," maw said.

"I don't know as I will or not," pap said. "I been publicly notified that I ain't fitten to associate with white folks, so I publicly notify them same white folks and Methodists, too, not to try to associate with me, or the devil can have the hindmost."

But maw hadn't even listened. When she come back with a pan of water and a towel and the liniment bottle, pap was already in his nightshirt.

"I don't want none of that neither," he said. "If my head wasn't worth busting, it ain't worth patching." But she never paid no mind to that neither. She washed his head off and dried it and put the bandage on and went out again, and pap went and got into bed.

"Hand me my snuff; then you get out of here and stay out too," he said.

But before I could do that maw come back. She had a glass of hot toddy, and she went to the bed and stood there with it, and pap turned his head and looked at it.

"What's that?" he said.

But maw never answered, and then he set up in bed and drawed a long, shuddering breath—we could hear it—and after a minute he put out his hand for the toddy and set there holding it and drawing his breath, and then he taken a sip of it.

"I Godfrey, if him and all of them put together think they can keep me from working on my own church like ary other man, he better be a good man to try it." He taken another sip of the toddy. Then he taken a long one. "Arsonist," he said. "Work units. Dog units. And now arsonist. I Godfrey, what a day!"

A Justice

-1-

UNTIL GRANDFATHER DIED, WE WOULD GO OUT TO THE FARM EVERY Saturday afternoon. We would leave home right after dinner in the surrey, I in front with Roskus, and Grandfather and Caddy and Jason in the back. Grandfather and Roskus would talk, with the horses going fast, because it was the best team in the county. They would carry the surrey fast along the levels and up some of the hills even. But this was in north Mississippi, and on some of the hills Roskus and I could smell Grandfather's cigar.

The farm was four miles away. There was a long, low house in the grove, not painted but kept whole and sound by a clever car-penter from the quarters named Sam Fathers, and behind it the barns and smokehouses, and further still, the quarters themselves, also kept whole and sound by Sam Fathers. He did nothing else, and they said he was almost a hundred years old. He lived with the Negroes and they—the white people; the Negroes called him a blue-gum—called him a Negro. But he wasn't a Negro. That's what I'm going to tell about.

When we got there, Mr. Stokes, the manager, would send a Ne-gro boy with Caddy and Jason to the creek to fish, because Caddy was a girl and Jason was too little, but I wouldn't go with them. I would go to Sam Fathers' shop, where he would be making breast-yokes or wagon wheels, and I would always bring him some to-bacco. Then he would stop working and he would fill his pipe—he made them himself, out of creek clay with a reed stem—and he would tell me about the old days. He talked like a nigger—that is, he said his words like niggers do, but he didn't say the same words —and his hair was nigger hair. But his skin wasn't quite the color of a light nigger and his nose and his mouth and chin were not nig-ger nose and mouth and chin. And his shape was not like the shape of a nigger when he gets old. He was straight in the back, not tall, a li le broad, and his face was still all the time, like he might be somewhere else all the while he was working or when people, even white people, talked to him, or while he talked to me. It was just the same all the time, like he might be away up on a roof by himself, driving nails. Sometimes he would quit work with something half-finished on the bench, and sit down and smoke. And he wouldn't jump up and go back to work when Mr. Stokes or even Grandfather came along.

So I would give him the tobacco and he would stop work and sit down and fill his pipe and talk to me.

"These niggers," he said. "They call me Uncle Blue-Gum. And the white folks, they call me Sam Fathers."

"Isn't that your name?" I said.

"No. Not in the old days. I remember. I remember how I never saw but one white man until I was a boy big as you are; a whisky trader that came every summer to the Plantation. It was the Man himself that named me. He didn't name me Sam Fathers, though."

"The Man?" I said.

"He owned the Plantation, the Negroes, my mammy too. He owned all the land that I knew of until I was grown. He was a Choctaw chief. He sold my mammy to your great-grandpappy. He said I didn't have to go unless I wanted to, because I was a warrior too then. He was the one who named me Had-Two-Fathers."

"Had-Two-Fathers?" I said. "That's not a name. That's not anything."

"It was my name once. Listen."

– 2 –

This is how Herman Basket told it when I was big enough to hear talk. He said that when Doom came back from New Orleans, he brought this woman with him. He brought six black people, though Herman Basket said they already had more black people in the Plantation than they could find use for. Sometimes they would run the black men with dogs, like you would a fox or a cat or a coon. And then Doom brought six more when he came home from New Orleans. He said he won them on the steamboat, and so he had to take them. He got off the steamboat with the six black people, Herman Basket said, and a big box in which something was alive, and the gold box of New Orleans salt about the size of a gold watch. And Herman Basket told how Doom took a puppy out of the box in which something was alive, and how he made a bullet of bread and a pinch of the salt in the gold box, and put the bullet into the puppy and the puppy died.

That was the kind of a man that Doom was, Herman Basket said. He told how, when Doom got off the steamboat that night, he wore a coat with gold all over it, and he had three gold watches, but Herman Basket said that even after seven years, Doom's eyes had not changed. He said that Doom's eyes were just the same as before he went away, before his name was Doom, and he and Herman Basket and my pappy were sleeping on the same pallet and talking at night, as boys will.

Doom's name was Ikkemotubbe then, and he was not born to be the Man, because Doom's mother's brother was the Man, and the Man had a son of his own, as well as a brother. But even then, and Doom no bigger than you are, Herman Basket said that sometimes the Man would look at Doom and he would say: "O Sister's Son, your eye is a bad eye, like the eye of a bad horse."

So the Man was not sorry when Doom got to be a young man and said that he would go to New Orleans, Herman Basket said. The Man was getting old then. He used to like to play mumble-peg and to pitch horseshoes both, but now he just liked mumble-peg. So he was not sorry when Doom went away, though he didn't forget about Doom. Herman Basket said that each summer when the whisky-trader came, the Man would ask him about Doom. "He calls himself David Callicoat now," the Man would say. "But his name is Ikkemotubbe. You haven't heard maybe of a David Callicoat getting drowned in the Big River, or killed in the white man's fight at New Orleans?"

But Herman Basket said they didn't hear from Doom at all until he had been gone seven years. Then one day Herman Basket and my pappy got a written stick from Doom to meet him at the Big River. Because the steamboat didn't come up our river any more then. The steamboat was still in our river, but it didn't go anywhere any more. Herman Basket told how one day during the high water, about three years after Doom went away, the steamboat came and crawled up on a sand-bar and died.

That was how Doom got his second name, the one before Doom. Herman Basket told how four times a year the steamboat would come up our river, and how the People would go to the river and camp and wait to see the steamboat pass, and he said that the white man who told the steamboat where to swim was named David Callicoat. So when Doom told Herman Basket and pappy that he was going to New Orleans, he said, "And I'll tell you something else.

From now on, my name is not Ikkemotubbe. It's David Callicoat. And some day I'm going to own a steamboat, too." That was the kind of man that Doom was, Herman Basket said.

So after seven years he sent them the written stick and Herman Basket and pappy took the wagon and went to meet Doom at the Big River, and Doom got off the steamboat with the six black people. " I won them on the steamboat," Doom said. "You and Craw-ford (my pappy's name was Crawfish-ford, but usually it was Craw-ford) can divide them."

"I don't want them," Herman Basket said that pappy said.

"Then Herman can have them all," Doom said.

"I don't want them either," Herman Basket said.

"All right," Doom said. Then Herman Basket said he asked Doom if his name was still David Callicoat, but instead of answering, Doom told one of the black people something in the white man's talk, and the black man lit a pine knot. Then Herman Basket said they were watching Doom take the puppy from the box and make the bullet of bread and the New Orleans salt which Doom had in the little gold box, when he said that pappy said:

"I believe you said that Herman and I were to divide these black people."

Then Herman Basket said he saw that one of the black people was a woman.

"You and Herman don't want them," Doom said.

"I wasn't thinking when I said that," pappy said. "I will take the lot with the woman in it. Herman can have the other three."

"I don't want them," Herman Basket said.

"You can have four, then," pappy said. "I will take the woman and one other."

"I don't want them," Herman Basket said.

"I will take only the woman," pappy said. "You can have the other five."

"I don't want them," Herman Basket said.

"You don't want them, either," Doom said to pappy. "You said so yourself."

Then Herman Basket said that the puppy was dead. "You didn't tell us your new name," he said to Doom.

"My name is Doom now," Doom said. "It was given me by a French chief in New Orleans. In French talking, Doo-um; in our talking, Doom."

"What does it mean?" Herman Basket said.

He said how Doom looked at him for a while. "It means the Man," Doom said.

Herman Basket told how they thought about that. He said they stood there in the dark, with the other puppies in the box, the ones that Doom hadn't used, whimpering and scuffing, and the light of the pine knot shining on the eyeballs of the black people and on Doom's gold coat and on the puppy that had died.

"You cannot be the Man," Herman Basket said. "You are only on the sister's side. And the Man has a brother and a son."

"That's right," Doom said. "But if I were the Man, I would give Craw-ford those black people. I would give Herman something, too. For every black man I gave Craw-ford, I would give Herman a horse, if I were the Man."

"Craw-ford only wants this woman," Herman Basket said.

"I would give Herman six horses, anyway," Doom said. "But maybe the Man has already given Herman a horse."

"No," Herman Basket said. "My ghost is still walking."

It took them three days to reach the Plantation. They camped on the road at night. Herman Basket said that they did not talk.

They reached the Plantation on the third day. He said that the Man was not very glad to see Doom, even though Doom brought a present of candy for the Man's son. Doom had something for all his kinsfolk, even for the Man's brother. The Man's brother lived by himself in a cabin by the creek. His name was Sometimes-Wakeup. Sometimes the People took him food. The rest of the time they didn't see him. Herman Basket told how he and pappy went with Doom to visit Sometimes-Wakeup in his cabin. It was at night, and Doom told Herman Basket to close the door. Then Doom took the puppy from pappy and set it on the floor and made a bullet of bread and the New Orleans salt for Sometimes-Wakeup to see how it worked. When they left, Herman Basket said how Sometimes-Wakeup burned a stick and covered his head with the blanket.

That was the first night that Doom was at home. On the next day Herman Basket told how the Man began to act strange at his food, and died before the doctor could get there and burn sticks. When the Willow-Bearer went to fetch the Man's son to be the Man, they found that he had acted strange and then died too.

"Now Sometimes-Wakeup will have to be the Man," pappy said.

So the Willow-Bearer went to fetch Sometimes-Wakeup to come and be the Man. The Willow-Bearer came back soon. "Sometimes-Wakeup does not want to be the Man," the Willow-Bearer said. "He is sitting in his cabin with his head in his blanket."

"Then Ikkemotubbe will have to be the Man," pappy said.

So Doom was the Man. But Herman Basket said that pappy's ghost would not be easy. Herman Basket said he told pappy to give Doom a little time. "I am still walking," Herman Basket said.

"But this is a serious matter with me," pappy said.

He said that at last pappy went to Doom, before the Man and his son had entered the earth, before the eating and the horse-racing were over. "What woman?" Doom said.

"You said that when you were the Man," pappy said. Herman Basket said that Doom looked at pappy but that pappy was not looking at Doom.

"I think you don't trust me," Doom said. Herman Basket said how pappy did not look at Doom. "I think you still believe that that puppy was sick," Doom said. "Think about it."

Herman Basket said that pappy thought.

"What do you think now?" Doom said.

But Herman Basket said that pappy still did not look at Doom. "I think it was a well dog," pappy said.

– 3 –

At last the eating and the horse-racing were over and the Man and his son had entered the earth. Then Doom said, "Tomorrow we will go and fetch the steamboat." Herman Basket told how Doom had been talking about the steamboat ever since he became the Man, and about how the House was not big enough. So that evening Doom said, "Tomorrow we will go and fetch the steamboat that died in the river."

Herman Basket said how the steamboat was twelve miles away, and that it could not even swim in the water. So the next morning there was no one in the Plantation except Doom and the black people. He told how it took Doom all that day to find the People. Doom used the dogs, and he found some of the People in hollow logs in the creek bottom. That night he made all the men sleep in the House. He kept the dogs in the House, too.

Herman Basket told how he heard Doom and pappy talking in the dark. "I don't think you trust me," Doom said.

"I trust you," pappy said.

"That is what I would advise," Doom said.

"I wish you could advise that to my ghost," pappy said.

The next morning they went to the steamboat. The women and the black people walked. The men rode in the wagons, with Doom following behind with the dogs.

The steamboat was lying on its side on the sand-bar. When they came to it, there were three white men on it. "Now we can go back home," pappy said.

But Doom talked to the white men. "Does this steamboat belong to you?" Doom said.

"It does not belong to you," the white men said. And though they had guns, Herman Basket said they did not look like men who would own a boat.

"Shall we kill them?" he said to Doom. But he said that Doom was still talking to the men on the steamboat.

"What will you take for it?" Doom said.

"What will you give for it?" the white men said.

"It is dead," Doom said. "It's not worth much."

"Will you give ten black people?" the white men said.

"All right," Doom said. "Let the black people who came with me from the Big River come forward." They came forward, the five men and the woman. "Let four more black people come forward." Four more came forward. "You are now to eat of the corn of those white men yonder," Doom said. "May it nourish you." The white men went away, the ten black people following them. "Now," Doom said, "let us make the steamboat get up and walk."

Herman Basket said that he and pappy did not go into the river with the others, because pappy said to go aside and talk. They went aside. Pappy talked, but Herman Basket said that he said he did not think it was right to kill white men, but pappy said how they could fill the white men with rocks and sink them in the river and nobody would find them. So Herman Basket said they overtook the three white men and the ten black people, then they turned back toward the boat. Just before they came to the steamboat, pappy said to the black men: "Go on to the Man. Go and help make the steamboat get up and walk. I will take this woman on home."

"This woman is my wife," one of the black men said. "I want her to stay with me."

"Do you want to be arranged in the river with rocks in your inside too?" pappy said to the black man.

"Do you want to be arranged in the river yourself?" the black man said to pappy. "There are two of you, and nine of us."

Herman Basket said that pappy thought. Then pappy said, "Let us go to the steamboat and help the Man."

They went to the steamboat. But Herman Basket said that Doom did not notice the ten black people until it was time to return to the Plantation. Herman Basket told how Doom looked at the black people, then looked at pappy. "It seems that the white men did not want these black people," Doom said.

"So it seems," pappy said.

"The white men went away, did they?" Doom said.

"So it seems," pappy said.

Herman Basket told how every night Doom would make all the men sleep in the House, with the dogs in the House too, and how each morning they would return to the steamboat in the wagons. The wagons would not hold everybody, so after the second day the women stayed at home. But it was three days before Doom noticed that pappy was staying at home too. Herman Basket said that the woman's husband may have told Doom. "Craw-ford hurt his back lifting the steamboat," Herman Basket said he told Doom. "He said he would stay at the Plantation and sit with his feet in the Hot Spring so that the sickness in his back could return to the earth."

"That is a good idea," Doom said. "He has been doing this for three days, has he? Then the sickness should be down in his legs by now."

When they returned to the Plantation that night, Doom sent for pappy. He asked pappy if the sickness had moved. Pappy said how the sickness moved very slow. "You must sit in the Spring more," Doom said.

"That is what I think," pappy said.

"Suppose you sit in the Spring at night too," Doom said.

"The night air will make it worse," pappy said.

"Not with a fire there," Doom said. "I will send one of the black people with you to keep the fire burning."

"Which one of the black people?" pappy said.

"The husband of the woman which I won on the steamboat," Doom said.

"I think my back is better," pappy said.

"Let us try it," Doom said.

"I know my back is better," pappy said.

"Let us try it, anyway," Doom said. Just before dark Doom sent four of the People to fix pappy and the black man at the Spring. Herman Basket said the People returned quickly. He said that as they entered the House, pappy entered also.

"The sickness began to move suddenly," pappy said. "It has reached my feet since noon today."

"Do you think it will be gone by morning?" Doom said.

"I think so," pappy said.

"Perhaps you had better sit in the Spring tonight and make sure," Doom said.

"I know it will be gone by morning," pappy said.

– 4 –

When it got to be summer, Herman Basket said that the steamboat was out of the river bottom. It had taken them five months to get it out of the bottom, because they had to cut down the trees to make a path for it. But now he said the steamboat could walk faster on the logs. He told how pappy helped. Pappy had a certain place on one of the ropes near the steamboat that nobody was allowed to take, Herman Basket said. It was just under the front porch of the steamboat where Doom sat in his chair, with a boy with a branch to shade him and another boy with a branch to drive away the flying beasts. The dogs rode on the boat too.

In the summer, while the steamboat was still walking, Herman Basket told how the husband of the woman came to Doom again. "I have done what I could for you," Doom said. "Why don't you go to Craw-ford and adjust this matter yourself?"

The black man said that he had done that. He said that pappy said to adjust it by a cock-fight, pappy's cock against the black man's, the winner to have the woman, the one who refused to fight to lose by default. The black man said he told pappy he did not have a cock, and that pappy said that in that case the black man lost by default and that the woman belonged to pappy. "And what am I to do?" the black man said.

Doom thought. Then Herman Basket said that Doom called to him and asked him which was pappy's best cock and Herman Basket told Doom that pappy had only one. "That black one?" Doom

said. Herman Basket said he told Doom that was the one. "Ah,"
Doom said. Herman Basket told how Doom sat in his chair on the
porch of the steamboat while it walked, looking down at the People and the black men pulling the ropes, making the steamboat
walk. "Go and tell Craw-ford you have a cock," Doom said to the
black man. "Just tell him you will have a cock in the pit. Let it be
tomorrow morning. We will let the steamboat sit down and rest."
The black man went away. Then Herman Basket said that Doom
was looking at him, and that he did not look at Doom. Because
he said there was but one better cock in the Plantation than pappy's, and that one belonged to Doom. "I think that that puppy was
not sick," Doom said. "What do you think?"

Herman Basket said that he did not look at Doom. "That is what
I think," he said.

"That is what I would advise," Doom said.

Herman Basket told how the next day the steamboat sat and
rested. The pit was in the stable. The People and the black people
were there. Pappy had his cock in the pit. Then the black man put
his cock into the pit. Herman Basket said that pappy looked at the
black man's cock.

"This cock belongs to Ikkemotubbe," pappy said.

"It is his," the People told pappy. "Ikkemotubbe gave it to him
with all to witness."

Herman Basket said that pappy had already picked up his cock.
"This is not right," pappy said. "We ought not to let him risk his
wife on a cock-fight."

"Then you withdraw?" the black man said.

"Let me think," pappy said. He thought. The People watched.
The black man reminded pappy of what he had said about de-
faulting. Pappy said he did not mean to say that and that he
withdrew it. The People told him that he could only withdraw by
forfeiting the match. Herman Basket said that pappy thought again.
The People watched. "All right," pappy said. "But I am being taken
advantage of."

The cocks fought. Pappy's cock fell. Pappy took it up quickly.
Herman Basket said it was like pappy had been waiting for his
cock to fall so he could pick it quickly up. "Wait," he said. He
looked at the People. "Now they have fought. Isn't that true?" The
People said that it was true. "So that settles what I said about forfeiting."

Herman Basket said that pappy began to get out of the pit.

"Aren't you going to fight?" the black man said.

"I don't think this will settle anything," pappy said. "Do you?"

Herman Basket told how the black man looked at pappy. Then he quit looking at pappy. He was squatting. Herman Basket said the People looked at the black man looking at the earth between his feet. They watched him take up a clod of dirt, and then they watched the dust come out between the black man's fingers. "Do you think that this will settle anything?" pappy said.

"No," the black man said. Herman Basket said that the People could not hear him very good. But he said that pappy could hear him.

"Neither do I," pappy said. "It would not be right to risk your wife on a cock-fight."

Herman Basket told how the black man looked up, with the dry dust about the fingers of his hand. He said the black man's eyes looked red in the dark pit, like the eyes of a fox. "Will you let the cocks fight again?" the black man said.

"Do you agree that it doesn't settle anything?" pappy said.

"Yes," the black man said.

Pappy put his cock back into the ring. Herman Basket said that pappy's cock was dead before it had time to act strange, even. The black man's cock stood upon it and started to crow, but the black man struck the live cock away and he jumped up and down on the dead cock until it did not look like a cock at all, Herman Basket said.

Then it was fall, and Herman Basket told how the steamboat came to the Plantation and stopped beside the House and died again. He said that for two months they had been in sight of the Plantation, making the steamboat walk on the logs, but now the steamboat was beside the House and the House was big enough to please Doom. He gave an eating. It lasted a week. When it was over, Herman Basket told how the black man came to Doom a third time. Herman Basket said that the black man's eyes were red again, like those of a fox, and that they could hear his breathing in the room. "Come to my cabin," he said to Doom. "I have something to show you."

"I thought it was about that time," Doom said. He looked about the room, but Herman Basket told Doom that pappy had just stepped out. "Tell him to come also," Doom said. When they came to the black man's cabin, Doom sent two of the People to fetch pappy. Then they entered the cabin. What the black man wanted to show Doom was a new man.

"Look," the black man said. "You are the Man. You are to see justice done."

"What is wrong with this man?" Doom said.

"Look at the color of him," the black man said. He began to look around the cabin. Herman Basket said that his eyes went red and then brown and then red, like those of a fox. He said they could hear the black man's breathing. "Do I get justice?" the black man said. "You are the Man."

"You should be proud of a fine yellow man like this," Doom said. He looked at the new man. "I don't see that justice can darken him any," Doom said. He looked about the cabin also. "Come forward, Craw-ford," he said. "This is a man, not a copper snake; he will not harm you." But Herman Basket said that pappy would not come forward. He said the black man's eyes went red and then brown and then red when he breathed. "Yao," Doom said, "this is not right. Any man is entitled to have his melon patch protected from these wild bucks of the woods. But first let us name this man." Doom thought. Herman Basket said the black man's eyes went quieter now, and his breath went quieter too. "We will call him Had-Two-Fathers," Doom said.

– 5 –

Sam Fathers lit his pipe again. He did it deliberately, rising and lifting between thumb and forefinger from his forge a coal of fire. Then he came back and sat down. It was getting late. Caddy and Jason had come back from the creek, and I could see Grandfather and Mr. Stokes talking beside the carriage, and at that moment, as though he had felt my gaze, Grandfather turned and called my name.

"What did your pappy do then?" I said.

"He and Herman Basket built the fence," Sam Fathers said. "Herman Basket told how Doom made them set two posts into the ground, with a sapling across the top of them. The nigger and pappy were there. Doom had not told them about the fence then. Herman Basket said it was just like when he and pappy and Doom were boys, sleeping on the same pallet, and Doom would wake them at night and make them get up and go hunting with him, or when he would make them stand up with him and fight with their fists, just for fun, until Herman Basket and pappy would hide from Doom.

"They fixed the sapling across the two posts and Doom said to the nigger: 'This is a fence. Can you climb it?'

"Herman Basket said the nigger put his hand on the sapling and sailed over it like a bird.

"Then Doom said to pappy: 'Climb this fence.'

" 'This fence is too high to climb,' pappy said.

" 'Climb this fence, and I will give you the woman,' Doom said.

"Herman Basket said pappy looked at the fence a while. 'Let me go under this fence,' he said.

" 'No,' Doom said.

"Herman Basket told me how pappy began to sit down on the ground. 'It's not that I don't trust you,' pappy said.

" 'We will build the fence this high,' Doom said.

" 'What fence?' Herman Basket said.

" 'The fence around the cabin of this black man,' Doom said.

" 'I can't build a fence I couldn't climb,' pappy said.

" 'Herman will help you,' Doom said.

"Herman Basket said it was just like when Doom used to wake them and make them go hunting. He said the dogs found him and pappy about noon the next day, and that they began the fence that afternoon. He told me how they had to cut the saplings in the creek bottom and drag them in by hand, because Doom would not let them use the wagon. So sometimes one post would take them three or four days. 'Never mind,' Doom said. 'You have plenty of time. And the exercise will make Craw-ford sleep at night.'

"He told me how they worked on the fence all that winter and all the next summer, until after the whisky trader had come and gone. Then it was finished. He said that on the day they set the last post, the nigger came out of the cabin and put his hand on the top of a post (it was a palisade fence, the posts set upright in the ground) and flew out like a bird. 'This is a good fence,' the nigger said. 'Wait,' he said. 'I have something to show you.' Herman Basket said he flew back over the fence again and went into the cabin and came back. Herman Basket said that he was carrying a new man and that he held the new man up so they could see it above the fence. 'What do you think about this for color?' he said."

Grandfather called me again. This time I got up. The sun was already down beyond the peach orchard. I was just twelve then, and to me the story did not seem to have got anywhere, to have had point or end. Yet I obeyed Grandfather's voice, not that I was tired of Sam Fathers' talking, but with that immediacy of children with which they flee temporarily something which they do not quite understand; that, and the instinctive promptness with which we all obeyed Grandfather, not from concern of impatience or reprimand, but because we all believed that he did fine things, that his waking life passed from one fine (if faintly grandiose) picture to another.

They were in the surrey, waiting for me. I got in; the horses moved at once, impatient too for the stable. Caddy had one fish, about the size of a chip, and she was wet to the waist. We drove on, the team already trotting. When we passed Mr. Stokes' kitchen we could smell ham cooking. The smell followed us on to the gate. When we turned onto the road home it was almost sundown. Then we couldn't smell the cooking ham any more. "What were you and Sam talking about?" Grandfather said.

We went on, in that strange, faintly sinister suspension of twilight in which I believed that I could still see Sam Fathers back there, sitting on his wooden block, definite, immobile, and complete, like something looked upon after a long time in a preservative bath in a museum. That was it. I was just twelve then, and I would have to wait until I had passed on and through and beyond the suspension of twilight. Then I knew that I would know. But then Sam Fathers would be dead.

"Nothing, sir," I said. "We were just talking."

Wash

Sutpen stood above the pallet bed on which the mother and child lay. Between the shrunken planking of the wall the early sunlight fell in long pencil strokes, breaking upon his straddled legs and upon the riding whip in his hand, and lay across the still shape of the mother, who lay looking up at him from still, inscrutable, sullen eyes, the child at her side wrapped in a piece of dingy though clean cloth. Behind them an old Negro woman squatted beside the rough hearth where a meager fire smoldered.

"Well, Milly," Sutpen said, "too bad you're not a mare. Then I could give you a decent stall in the stable."

Still the girl on the pallet did not move. She merely continued to look up at him without expression, with a young, sullen, inscrutable face still pale from recent travail. Sutpen moved, bringing into the splintered pencils of sunlight the face of a man of sixty. He said quietly to the squatting Negress, "Griselda foaled this morning."

"Horse or mare?" the Negress said.

"A horse. A damned fine colt. . . . What's this?" He indicated the pallet with the hand which held the whip.

"That un's a mare, I reckon."

"Hah," Sutpen said. "A damned fine colt. Going to be the spit and image of old Rob Roy when I rode him North in '61. Do you remember?"

"Yes, Marster."

"Hah." He glanced back towards the pallet. None could have said if the girl still watched him or not. Again his whip hand indicated the pallet. "Do whatever they need with whatever we've got to do it with." He went out, passing out the crazy doorway and stepping down into the rank weeds (there yet leaned rusting against the corner of the porch the scythe which Wash had borrowed from him three months ago to cut them with) where his horse waited, where Wash stood holding the reins.

When Colonel Sutpen rode away to fight the Yankees, Wash did not go. "I'm looking after the Kernel's place and niggers," he would tell all who asked him and some who had not asked—a gaunt, malaria-ridden man with pale, questioning eyes, who looked about thirty-five, thought it was known that he had not only a daughter but an eight-year-old granddaughter as well. This was a lie, as most of them—the few remaining men between eighteen and fifty —to whom he told it, knew, though there were some who believed that he himself really believed it, though even these believed that he had better sense than to put it to the test with Mrs. Sutpen or the Sutpen slaves. Knew better or was just too lazy and shiftless to try it, they said, knowing that his sole connection with the Sutpen plantation lay in the fact that for years now Colonel Sutpen had allowed him to squat in a crazy shack on a slough in the river bottom on the Sutpen place, which Sutpen had built for a fishing lodge in his bachelor days and which had since fallen in dilapidation from disuse, so that now it looked like an aged or sick wild beast crawled terrifically there to drink in the act of dying.

The Sutpen slaves themselves heard of his statement. They laughed. It was not the first time they had laughed at him, calling him white trash behind his back. They began to ask him themselves, in groups, meeting him in the faint road which led up from the slough and the old fish camp, "Why ain't you at de war, white man?"

Pausing, he would look about the ring of black faces and white eyes and teeth behind which derision lurked. "Because I got a daughter and family to keep," he said. "Git out of my road, niggers."

"Niggers?" they repeated; "niggers?" laughing now. "Who him, calling us niggers?"

"Yes," he said. "I ain't got no niggers to look after my folks if I was gone."

"Nor nothing else but dat shack down yon dat Cunnel wouldn't *let* none of us live in."

Now he cursed them; sometimes he rushed at them, snatching up a stick from the ground while they scattered before him, yet seeming to surround him still with that black laughing, derisive, evasive, inescapable, leaving him panting and impotent and raging. Once it happened in the very back yard of the big house itself. This was after bitter news had come down from the Tennessee mountains and from Vicksburg, and Sherman had passed through the plantation, and most of the Negroes had followed him. Almost everything else had gone with the Federal troops, and Mrs. Sutpen had sent word to Wash that he could have the scuppernongs ripening in the arbor in the back yard. This time it was a house servant, one of the few Negroes who remained; this time the Negress had to retreat up the kitchen steps, where she turned. "Stop right dar, white man. Stop right whar you is. You ain't never crossed dese steps whilst Cunnel here, and you ain't ghy' do hit now."

This was true. But there was this of a kind of pride: he had never tried to enter the big house, even though he believed that if he had, Sutpen would have received him, permitted him. "But I ain't going to give no black nigger the chance to tell me I can't go nowhere," he said to himself. "I ain't even going to give Kernel the chance to have to cuss a nigger on my account." This, though he and Sutpen had spent more than one afternoon together on those rare Sundays when there would be no company in the house. Perhaps his mind knew that it was because Sutpen had nothing else to do, being a man who could not bear his own company. Yet the fact remained that the two of them would spend whole afternoons in the scuppernong arbor, Sutpen in the hammock and Wash squatting against a post, a pail of cistern water between them, taking drink for drink from the same demijohn. Meanwhile on weekdays he would see the fine figure of the man—they were the same age almost to a day, though neither of them (perhaps because Wash had a grandchild while Sutpen's son was a youth in school) ever thought of himself as being so—on the fine figure of the black stallion, galloping about the plantation. For that moment his heart would be quiet and proud. It would seem to him that that world in which Negroes, whom the Bible told him had been created and cursed by God to be brute and vassal to all men of white skin, were better found and housed and even clothed than he and his; that world in which he sensed always about him mocking echoes of black laughter was but a dream and an illusion, and that the actual world was this one across which his own lonely apotheosis seemed to gallop on the black thoroughbred, thinking how the Book said also that all men were created in the image of God and hence all men made the same image in God's eyes at least; so that he could say, as though speaking of himself, "A fine proud man. If

God Himself was to come down and ride the natural earth, that's what He would aim to look like."

Sutpen returned in 1865, on the black stallion. He seemed to have aged ten years. His son had been killed in action the same winter in which his wife had died. He returned with his citation for gallantry from the hand of General Lee to a ruined plantation, where for a year now his daughter had subsisted partially on the meager bounty of the man to whom fifteen years ago he had granted permission to live in that tumbledown fishing camp whose very existence he had at the time forgotten. Wash was there to meet him, unchanged: still gaunt, still ageless, with his pale, questioning gaze, his air diffident, a little servile, a little familiar. "Well, Kernel," Wash said, "they kilt us but they ain't whupped us yit, air they?"

That was the tenor of their conversation for the next five years. It was inferior whisky which they drank now together from a stoneware jug, and it was not in the scuppernong arbor. It was in the rear of the little store which Sutpen managed to set up on the highroad: a frame shelved room where, with Wash for clerk and porter, he dispensed kerosene and staple foodstuffs and stale gaudy candy and cheap beads and ribbons to Negroes or poor whites of Wash's own kind, who came afoot or on gaunt mules to haggle tediously for dimes and quarters with a man who at one time could gallop (the black stallion was still alive; the stable in which his jealous get lived was in better repair than the house where the master himself lived) for ten miles across his own fertile land and who had led troops gallantly in battle; until Sutpen in fury would empty the store, close and lock the doors from the inside. Then he and Wash would repair to the rear and the jug. But the talk would not be quiet now, as when Sutpen lay in the hammock, delivering an arrogant monologue while Wash squatted guffawing against his post. They both sat now, though Sutpen had the single chair while Wash used whatever box or keg was handy, and even this for just a little while, because soon Sutpen would reach that stage of impotent and furious undefeat in which he would rise, swaying and plunging, and declare again that he would take his pistol and the black stallion and ride single-handed into Washington and kill Lincoln, dead now, and Sherman, now a private citizen. "Kill them!" he would shout. "Shoot them down like the dogs they are—"

"Sho, Kernel; sho, Kernel," Wash would say, catching Sutpen as he fell. Then he would commandeer the first passing wagon or, lacking that, he would walk the mile to the nearest neighbor and borrow one and return and carry Sutpen home. He entered the house now. He had been doing so for a long time, taking Sutpen home in whatever borrowed wagon might be, talking him into locomotion with cajoling murmurs as though he were a horse, a stallion himself. The daughter would meet them and hold open the door without a word. He would carry his burden through the once white formal entrance, surmounted by a fanlight imported piece by piece from Europe and with a board now nailed over a missing pane, across a velvet carpet from which all nap was now gone, and up a formal stairs, now but a fading ghost of bare boards between two strips of fading paint, and into the bedroom. It would be dusk by now, and he would let his burden sprawl onto the bed and undress it and then he would sit quietly in a chair beside. After a time the daughter would come to the door. "We're all right now," he would tell her. "Don't you worry none, Miss Judith."

Then it would become dark, and after a while he would lie down on the floor beside the bed, though not to sleep, because after a time—sometimes before midnight—the man on the bed would stir and groan and then speak. "Wash?"

"Hyer I am, Kernel. You go back to sleep. We ain't whupped yit, air we? Me and you kin do hit."

Even then he had already seen the ribbon about his granddaughter's waist. She was now fifteen, already mature, after the early way of her kind. He knew where the ribbon came from; he had been seeing it and its kind daily for three years, even if she had lied about where she got it, which she did not, at once bold, sullen, and fearful. "Sho now," he said "Ef Kernel wants to give hit to you, I hope you minded to thank him."

His heart was quiet, even when he saw the dress, watching her secret, defiant, frightened face when she told him that Miss Judith, the daughter, had helped her to make it. But he was quite grave when he approached Sutpen after they closed the store that afternoon, following the other to the rear.

"Get the jug," Sutpen directed.

"Wait," Wash said. "Not yit for a minute."

Neither did Sutpen deny the dress. "What about it?" he said.

But Wash met his arrogant stare; he spoke quietly. "I've knowed you for going on twenty years. I ain't never yit denied to do what you told me to do. And I'm a man nigh sixty. And she ain't nothing but a fifteen-year-old gal."

"Meaning that I'd harm a girl? I, a man as old as you are?"

"If you was ara other man, I'd say you was as old as me. And old or no old, I wouldn't let her keep that dress nor nothing else that come from your hand. But you are different."

"How different?" But Wash merely looked at him with his pale, questioning, sober eyes. "So that's why you are afraid of me?"

Now Wash's gaze no longer questioned. It was tranquil, serene. "I ain't afraid. Because you air brave. It ain't that you were a brave man at one minute or day of your life and got a paper to show hit from General Lee. But you air brave, the same as you air alive and breathing. That's where hit's different. Hit don't need no ticket from nobody to tell me that. And I know that whatever you handle or tech, whether hit's a regiment of men or a ignorant gal or just a hound dog, that you will make hit right."

Now it was Sutpen who looked away, turning suddenly, brusquely. "Get the jug," he said sharply.

"Sho, Kernel," Wash said.

So on that Sunday dawn two years later, having watched the Negro midwife, which he had walked three miles to fetch, enter the crazy door beyond which his granddaughter lay wailing, his heart was still quiet though concerned. He knew what they had been saying—the Negroes in cabins about the land, the white men who loafed all day long about the store, watching quietly the three of them: Sutpen, himself, his granddaughter with her air of brazen and shrinking defiance as her condition became daily more and more obvious, like three actors that came and went upon a stage. "I know what they say to one another," he thought. "I can almost hyear them: *Wash Jones has fixed old Sutpen at last. Hit taken him twenty years, but he has done hit at last.*"

It would be dawn after a while, though not yet. From the house, where the lamp shone dim beyond the warped doorframe, his granddaughter's voice came steadily as though run by a clock, while thinking went slowly and terrifically, fumbling, involved somehow with a sound of galloping hooves, until there broke suddenly free in mid-gallop the fine proud figure of the man on the fine proud stallion, galloping; and then that at which thinking fumbled, broke free too and quite clear, not in justification nor even explanation, but as the apotheosis, lonely, explicable, beyond all fouling by human touch: "He is bigger than all them Yankees that kilt his son and his wife and taken his niggers and ruined his land, bigger than this hyer durn country that he fit for and that has denied him into keeping a little country store; bigger than the denial which hit helt to his lips like the bitter cup in the Book. And how could I have lived this nigh to him for twenty years without being teched and changed by him? Maybe I ain't as big as him and maybe I ain't done none of the galloping. But at least I done been drug along. Me and him kin do hit, if so be he will show me what he aims for me to do."

Then it was dawn. Suddenly he could see the house, and the old Negress in the door looking at him. Then he realized that his granddaughter's voice had ceased. "It's a girl," the Negress said. "You can go tell him if you want to." She reëntered the house.

"A girl," he repeated; "a girl"; in astonishment, hearing the galloping hooves, seeing the proud galloping figure emerge again. He seemed to watch it pass, galloping through avatars which marked the accumulation of years, time, to the climax where it galloped beneath a brandished saber and a shot-torn flag rushing down a sky in color like thunderous sulphur, thinking for the first time in his life that perhaps Sutpen was an old man like himself. "Gittin a gal," he thought in that astonishment; then he thought with the pleased surprise of a child: "Yes, sir. Be dawg if I ain't lived to be a great-grandpaw after all."

He entered the house. He moved clumsily, on tiptoe, as if he no longer lived there, as if the infant which had just drawn breath and cried in light had dispossessed him, be it of his own blood too though it might. But even above the pallet he could see little save the blur of his granddaughter's exhausted face. Then the Negress squatting at the hearth spoke, "You better gawn tell him if you going to. Hit's daylight now."

But this was not necessary. He had no more than turned the corner of the porch where the scythe leaned which he had borrowed three months ago to clear away the weeds through which he walked, when Sutpen himself rode up on the old stallion. He did not wonder how Sutpen had got the word. He took it for granted that this was what had brought the other out at this hour on Sunday morning, and he stood while the other dismounted, and he took the reins from Sutpen's hand, an expression on his gaunt face almost imbecile with a kind of weary triumph, saying, "Hit's a gal, Kernel. I be dawg if you ain't as old as I am—" until Sutpen passed him and entered the house. He stood there with the reins in his hand and heard Sutpen cross the floor to the pallet. He heard what Sutpen said, and something seemed to stop dead in him before going on.

The sun was now up, the swift sun of Mississippi latitudes, and it seemed to him that he stood beneath a strange sky, in a strange scene, familiar only as things are familiar in dreams, like the dreams of falling to one who has never climbed. "I kain't have heard what I thought I heard," he thought quietly. "I know I kain't." Yet the voice, the familiar voice which had said the words was still speaking, talking now to the old Negress about a colt foaled that morning. "That's why he was up so early," he thought. "That was hit. Hit ain't me and mine. Hit ain't even hisn that got him outen bed."

Sutpen emerged. He descended into the weeds, moving with that heavy deliberation which would have been haste when he was younger. He had not yet looked full at Wash. He said, "Dicey will stay and tend to her. You better—" Then he seemed to see Wash facing him and paused. "What?" he said.

"You said—" To his own ears Wash's voice sounded flat and ducklike, like a deaf man's. "You said if she was a mare, you could give her a good stall in the stable."

"Well?" Sutpen said. His eyes widened and narrowed, almost like a man's fists flexing and shutting, as Wash began to advance towards him, stooping a little. Very astonishment kept Sutpen still for the moment, watching that man whom in twenty years he had no more known to make any motion save at command than he had the horse which he rode. Again his eyes narrowed and widened; without moving he seemed to rear suddenly upright. "Stand back," he said suddenly and sharply. "Don't you touch me."

"I'm going to tech you, Kernel," Wash said in that flat, quiet, almost soft voice, advancing.

Sutpen raised the hand which held the riding whip; the old Negress peered around the crazy door with her black gargoyle face of a worn gnome. "Stand back, Wash," Sutpen said. Then he struck. The old Negress leaped down into the weeds with the agility of a goat and fled. Sutpen slashed Wash again across the face with the whip, striking him to his knees. When Wash rose and advanced once more he held in his hands the scythe which he had borrowed from Sutpen three months ago and which Sutpen would never need again.

When he reëntered the house his granddaughter stirred on the pallet bed and called his name fretfully. "What was that?" she said.

"What was what, honey?"

"That ere racket out there."

" 'Twarn't nothing," he said gently. He knelt and touched her hot forehead clumsily. "Do you want ara thing?"

"I want a sup of water," she said querulously. "I been laying here wanting a sup of water a long time, but don't nobody care enough to pay me no mind."

"Sho now," he said soothingly. He rose stiffly and fetched the dipper of water and raised her head to drink and laid her back and watched her turn to the child with an absolutely stonelike face. But a moment later he saw that she was crying quietly. "Now, now," he said, "I wouldn't do that. Old Dicey says hit's a right fine gal. Hit's all right now. Hit's all over now. Hit ain't no need to cry now."

But she continued to cry quietly, almost sullenly, and he rose again and stood uncomfortably above the pallet for a time, thinking as he had thought when his own wife lay so and then his daughter in turn: "Women. Hit's a mystry to me. They seem to want em, and yit when they git em they cry about hit. Hit's a mystry to me. To ara man." Then he moved away and drew a chair up to the window and sat down.

Through all that long, bright, sunny forenoon he sat at the window, waiting. Now and then he rose and tiptoed to the pallet. But his granddaughter slept now, her face sullen and calm and weary, the child in the crook of her arm. Then he returned to the chair and sat again, waiting, wondering why it took them so long, until he remembered that it was Sunday. He was sitting there at mid-afternoon when a half-grown white boy came around the corner of the house upon the body and gave a choked cry and looked up and glared for a mesmerized instant at Wash in the window before he turned and fled. Then Wash rose and tiptoed again to the pallet.

The granddaughter was awake now, wakened perhaps by the boy's cry without hearing it. "Milly," he said, "air you hungry?" She didn't answer, turning her face away. He built up the fire on the hearth and cooked the food which he had brought home the day

before: fatback it was, and cold corn pone; he poured water into
the stale coffee pot and heated it. But she would not eat when he
carried the plate to her, so he ate himself, quietly, alone, and left
the dishes as they were and returned to the window.

Now he seemed to sense, feel, the men who would be gathering
with horses and guns and dogs—the curious, and the vengeful:
men of Sutpen's own kind, who had made the company about Sutpen's table in the time when Wash himself had yet to approach
nearer to the house than the scuppernong arbor—men who had
also shown the lesser ones how to fight in battle, who maybe also
had signed papers from the generals saying that they were among
the first of the brave; who had also galloped in the old days arrogant and proud on the fine horses across the fine plantations—
symbols also of admiration and hope; instruments too of despair
and grief.

That was whom they would expect him to run from. It seemed to
him that he had no more to run from than he had to run to. If he
ran, he would merely be fleeing one set of bragging and evil shadows for another just like them, since they were all of a kind
throughout all the earth which he knew, and he was old, too old to
flee far even if he were to flee. He could never escape them, no matter how much or how far he ran: a man going on sixty could not
run that far. Not far enough to escape beyond the boundaries of
earth where such men lived, set the order and the rule of living. It
seemed to him that he now saw for the first time, after five years,
how it was that Yankees or any other living armies had managed
to whip them: the gallant, the proud, the brave; the acknowledged
and chosen best among them all to carry courage and honor and
pride. Maybe if he had gone to the war with them he would have
discovered them sooner. But if he had discovered them sooner,
what would he have done with his life since? How could he have
borne to remember for five years what his life had been before?

Now it was getting toward sunset. The child had been crying;
when he went to the pallet he saw his granddaughter nursing it,
her face still bemused, sullen, inscrutable. "Air you hungry yit?" he
said.

"I don't want nothing."

"You ought to eat."

This time she did not answer at all, looking down at the child.
He returned to his chair and found that the sun had set. "Hit kain't

be much longer," he thought. He could feel them quite near now, the curious and the vengeful. He could even seem to hear what they were saying about him, the undercurrent of believing beyond the immediate fury: *Old Wash Jones he come a tumble at last. He thought he had Sutpen, but Sutpen fooled him. He thought he had Kernel where he would have to marry the gal or pay up. And Kernel refused.* "But I never expected that, Kernel!" he cried aloud, catching himself at the sound of his own voice, glancing quickly back to find his granddaughter watching him.

"Who you talking to now?" she said.

"Hit ain't nothing. I was just thinking and talked out before I knowed hit."

Her face was becoming indistinct again, again a sullen blur in the twilight. "I reckon so. I reckon you'll have to holler louder than that before he'll hear you, up yonder at that house. And I reckon you'll need to do more than holler before you get him down here too."

"Sho now," he said. "Don't you worry none." But already thinking was going smoothly on: "You know I never. You know how I ain't never expected or asked nothing from ara living man but what I expected from you. And I never asked that. I didn't think hit would need. I said, *I don't need to. What need has a fellow like Wash Jones to question or doubt the man that General Lee himself says in a handwrote ticket that he was brave?* Brave," he thought. "Better if nara one of them had never rid back home in '65"; thinking *Better if his kind and mine too had never drawn the breath of life on this earth. Better that all who remain of us be blasted from the face of earth than that another Wash Jones should see his whole life shredded from him and shrivel away like a dried shuck thrown onto the fire.*

He ceased, became still. He heard the horses, suddenly and plainly; presently he saw the lantern and the movement of men, the glint of gun barrels, in its moving light. Yet he did not stir. It was quite dark now, and he listened to the voices and the sounds of underbrush as they surrounded the house. The lantern itself came on; its light fell upon the quiet body in the weeds and stopped, the horses tall and shadowy. A man descended and stooped in the lantern light, above the body. He held a pistol; he rose and faced the house. "Jones," he said.

"I'm here," Wash said quietly from the window. "That you, Major?"

"Come out."

"Sho," he said quietly. "I just want to see to my granddaughter."

"We'll see to her. Come on out."

"Sho, Major. Just a minute."

"Show a light. Light your lamp."

"Sho. In just a minute." They could hear his voice retreat into the house, though they could not see him as he went swiftly to the crack in the chimney where he kept the butcher knife: the one thing in his slovenly life and house in which he took pride, since it was razor sharp. He approached the pallet, his granddaughter's voice:

"Who is it? Light the lamp, Grandpaw."

"Hit won't need no light, honey. Hit won't take but a minute," he said, kneeling, fumbling toward her voice, whispering now. "Where air you?"

"Right here," she said fretfully. "Where would I be? What is . . ." His hand touched her face. "What is . . . Grandpaw! Grand. . . ."

"Jones!" the sheriff said. "Come out of there!"

"In just a minute, Major," he said. Now he rose and moved swiftly. He knew where in the dark the can of kerosene was, just as he knew that it was full, since it was not two days ago that he had filled it at the store and held it there until he got a ride home with it, since the five gallons were heavy. There were still coals on the hearth; besides, the crazy building itself was like tinder: the coals, the hearth, the walls exploding in a single blue glare. Against it the waiting men saw him in a wild instant springing toward them with the lifted scythe before the horses reared and whirled. They checked the horses and turned them back toward the glare, yet still in wild relief against it the gaunt figure ran toward them with the lifted scythe.

"Jones!" the sheriff shouted; "stop! Stop, or I'll shoot. Jones! *Jones!*" Yet still the gaunt, furious figure came on against the glare and roar of the flames. With the scythe lifted, it bore down upon them, upon the wild glaring eyes of the horses and the swinging glints of gun barrels, without any cry, any sound.

An Odor of Verbena

—1—

IT WAS JUST AFTER SUPPER. I HAD JUST OPENED MY *Coke* ON THE
table beneath the lamp; I heard Professor Wilkins' feet in the hall
and then the instant of silence as he put his hand to the door knob,
and I should have known. People talk glibly of presentiment, but I
had none. I heard his feet on the stairs and then in the hall approaching and there was nothing in the feet because although
I had lived in his house for three college years now and although
both he and Mrs. Wilkins called me Bayard in the house, he would
no more have entered my room without knocking than I would
have entered his—or hers. Then he flung the door violently inward
against the doorstop with one of those gestures with or by which
an almost painfully unflagging preceptory of youth ultimately aber-
rates, and stood there saying, "Bayard. Bayard, my son, my dear
son."

I should have known; I should have been prepared. Or maybe I
was prepared because I remember how I closed the book carefully,
even marking the place, before I rose. He (Professor Wilkins) was
doing something, bustling at something; it was my hat and cloak
which he handed me and which I took although I would not need
the cloak, unless even then I was thinking (although it was October, the equinox had not occurred) that the rains and the cool
weather would arrive before I should see this room again and so I
would need the cloak anyway to return to it if I returned, thinking
'God, if he had only done this last night, flung that door crashing
and bouncing against the stop last night without knocking so I
could have gotten there before it happened, been there when it did,
beside him on whatever spot, wherever it was that he would have
to fall and lie in the dust and dirt.'

"Your boy is downstairs in the kitchen," he said. It was not until years later that he told me (someone did; it must have been Judge Wilkins) how Ringo had apparently flung the cook aside and come on into the house and into the library where he and Mrs. Wilkins were sitting and said without preamble and already turning to withdraw: "They shot Colonel Sartoris this morning. Tell him I be waiting in the kitchen" and was gone before either of them could move. "He has ridden forty miles yet he refuses to eat anything." We were moving toward the door now—the door on my side of which I had lived for three years now with what I knew, what I knew now I must have believed and expected, yet beyond which I had heard the approaching feet yet heard nothing in the feet. "If there was just anything I could do."

"Yes, sir," I said. "A fresh horse for my boy. He will want to go back with me."

"By all means take mine—Mrs. Wilkins'," he cried. His tone was no different yet he did cry it and I suppose that at the same moment we both realised that was funny—a short-legged deep-barreled mare who looked exactly like a spinster music teacher, which Mrs. Wilkins drove to a basket phaeton—which was good for me, like being doused with a pail of cold water would have been good for me.

"Thank you, sir," I said. "We won't need it. I will get a fresh horse for him at the livery stable when I get my mare." Good for me, because even before I finished speaking I knew that would not be necessary either, that Ringo would have stopped at the livery stable before he came out to the college and attended to that and that the fresh horse for him and my mare both would be saddled and waiting now at the side fence and we would not have to go through Oxford at all. Loosh would not have thought of that if he had come for me, he would have come straight to the college, to Professor Wilkins', and told his news and then sat down and let me take charge from then on. But not Ringo.

He followed me from the room. From now until Ringo and I rode away into the hot thick dusty darkness quick and strained for the overdue equinox like a laboring delayed woman, he would be somewhere either just beside me or just behind me and I never to know exactly nor care which. He was trying to find the words with which to offer me his pistol too. I could almost hear him: "Ah, this unhappy land, not ten years recovered from the fever yet still men must kill one another, still we must pay Cain's price in his own coin." But he did not actually say it. He just followed me, somewhere beside or behind me as we descended the stairs toward where Mrs. Wilkins waited in the hall beneath the chandelier—a thin gray woman who reminded me of Granny, not that she looked like Granny probably but because she had known Granny—a lifted anxious still face which was thinking *Who lives by the sword shall die by it* just as Granny would have thought, toward which I walked, had to walk not because I was Granny's grandson and had lived in her house for three college years and was about the age of her son when he was killed in almost the last battle nine years ago, but because I was now The Sartoris. (The Sartoris: that had been one of the concomitant flashes, along with the *at last it has happened* when Professor Wilkins opened my door.) She didn't offer me a horse and pistol, not because she liked me any less than Professor Wilkins but because she was a woman and so wiser than any man, else the men would not have gone on with the War for two years after they knew they were whipped. She just put her hands (a small woman, no bigger than Granny had been) on my shoulders and said, "Give my love to Drusilla and your Aunt Jenny. And come back when you can."

"Only I don't know when that will be," I said. "I don't know how many things I will have to attend to." Yes, I lied even to her; it had not been but a minute yet since he had flung that door bouncing into the stop yet already I was beginning to realise, to become aware of that which I still had no yardstick to measure save that one consisting of what, despite myself, despite my raising and background (or maybe because of them) I had for some time known I was becoming and had feared the test of it; I remember how I thought while her hands still rested on my shoulders: *At least this will be my chance to find out if I am what I think I am or if I just hope; if I am going to do what I have taught myself is right or if I am just going to wish I were.*

We went on to the kitchen, Professor Wilkins still somewhere beside or behind me and still offering me the pistol and horse in a dozen different ways. Ringo was waiting; I remember how I thought then that no matter what might happen to either of us, I would never be The Sartoris to him. He was twenty-four too, but in a way he had changed even less than I had since that day when we had nailed Grumby's body to the door of the old compress.

Maybe it was because he had outgrown me, had changed so much that summer while he and Granny traded mules with the Yankees that since then I had had to do most of the changing just to catch up with him. He was sitting quietly in a chair beside the cold stove, spent-looking too who had ridden forty miles (at one time, either in Jefferson or when he was alone at last on the road somewhere, he had cried; dust was now caked and dried in the tear-channels on his face) and would ride forty more yet would not eat, looking up at me a little red-eyed with weariness (or maybe it was more than just weariness and so I would never catch up with him) then rising without a word and going on toward the door and I following and Professor Wilkins still offering the horse and the pistol without speaking the words and still thinking (I could feel that too) *Dies by the sword. Dies by the sword.*

Ringo had the two horses saddled at the side gate, as I had known he would—the fresh one for himself and my mare father had given me three years ago, that could do a mile under two minutes any day and a mile every eight minutes all day long. He was already mounted when I realised that what Professor Wilkins wanted was to shake my hand. We shook hands; I knew he believed he was touching flesh which might not be alive tomorrow night and I thought for a second how if I told him what I was going to do, since we had talked about it, about how if there was anything at all in the Book, anything of hope and peace for His blind and bewildered spawn which He had chosen above all others to offer immortality, *Thou shalt not kill* must be it, since maybe he even believed that he had taught it to me except that he had not, nobody had, not even myself since it went further than just having been learned. But I did not tell him. He was too old to be forced so, to condone even in principle such a decision; he was too old to have to stick to principle in the face of blood and raising and background, to be faced without warning and made to deliver like by a highwayman out of the dark: only the young could do that—one still young enough to have his youth supplied him gratis as a reason (not an excuse) for cowardice.

So I said nothing. I just shook his hand and mounted too, and Ringo and I rode on. We would not have to pass through Oxford now and so soon (there was a thin sickle of moon like the heel print of a boot in wet sand) the road to Jefferson lay before us, the road which I had travelled for the first time three years ago with Father and travelled twice at Christmas time and then in June and September and twice at Christmas time again and then June and September again each college term since alone on the mare, not even knowing that this was peace; and now this time and maybe last time who would not die (I knew that) but who maybe forever after could never again hold up his head. The horses took the gait which they would hold for forty miles. My mare knew the long road ahead and Ringo had a good beast too, had talked Hilliard at the livery stable out of a good horse too. Maybe it was the tears, the channels of dried mud across which his strain-reddened eyes had looked at me, but I rather think it was that same quality which used to enable him to replenish his and Granny's supply of United States Army letterheads during that time—some outrageous assurance gained from too long and too close association with white people: the one whom he called Granny, the other with whom he had slept from the time we were born until Father rebuilt the house. We spoke one time, then no more:

"We could bushwhack him," he said. "Like we done Grumby that day. But I reckon that wouldn't suit that white skin you walks around in."

"No," I said. We rode on; it was October; there was plenty of time still for verbena although I would have to reach home before I would realise there was a need for it; plenty of time for verbena yet from the garden where Aunt Jenny puttered beside old Joby, in a pair of Father's old cavalry gauntlets, among the coaxed and ordered beds, the quaint and odorous old names, for though it was October no rain had come yet and hence no frost to bring (or leave behind) the first half-warm half-chill nights of Indian Summer— the drowsing air cool and empty for geese yet languid still with the old hot dusty smell of fox grape and sassafras—the nights when before I became a man and went to college to learn law Ringo and I, with lantern and axe and crokersack and six dogs (one to follow the trail and five more just for the tonguing, the music) would hunt possum in the pasture where, hidden, we had seen our first Yankee that afternoon on the bright horse, where for the last year now you could hear the whistling of the trains which had no longer belonged to Mr. Redmond for a long while now and which at some instant, some second during the morning Father too had relinquished along with the pipe which Ringo said he was smoking, which slipped from his hand as he fell. We rode on, toward the house where he would be lying in the parlor now, in his regimentals (sabre too) and where Drusilla would be waiting for me beneath all the festive glitter of the chandeliers, in the yellow ball gown and the sprig of verbena in her hair, holding the two loaded pistols (I could see that too, who had had no presentiment; I could see her, in the formal brilliant room arranged formally for obsequy, not tall, not slender as a woman is but as a youth, a boy, is motionless, in yellow, the face calm, almost bemused, the head simple and severe, the balancing sprig of verbena above each ear, the two arms bent at the elbows, the two hands shoulder high, the two identical duelling pistols lying upon, not clutched in, one to each: the Greek amphora priestess of a succinct and formal violence).

–2–

Drusilla said that he had a dream. I was twenty then and she and I would walk in the garden in the summer twilight while we waited for Father to ride in from the railroad. I was just twenty then: that summer before I entered the University to take the law degree which Father decided I should have and four years after the one, the day, the evening when Father and Drusilla had kept old Cash Benbow from becoming United States Marshal and returned home still unmarried and Mrs. Habersham herded them into her carriage and drove them back to town and dug her husband out of his little dim hole in the new bank and made him sign Father's peace bond for killing the two carpet baggers, and took Father and Drusilla to the minister herself and saw that they were married. And Father had rebuilt the house too, on the same blackened spot, over the same cellar, where the other had burned, only larger, much larger: Drusilla said that the house was the aura of Father's dream just as a bride's trousseau and veil is the aura of hers. And Aunt Jenny had come to live with us now so we had the garden (Drusilla would no more have bothered with flowers than Father himself would have, who even now, even four years after it was over, still seemed to exist, breathe, in that last year of it while she had ridden in man's clothes and with her hair cut short like any other member of Father's troop, across Georgia and both Carolinas in front of Sherman's army) for her to gather sprigs of verbena from to wear in her hair because she said verbena was the only scent you could smell above the smell of horses and courage and so it was the only one that was worth the wearing. The railroad was hardly begun then and Father and Mr. Redmond were not only still partners, they were still friends, which as George Wyatt said was easily a record for Father, and he would leave the house at daybreak on Jupiter, riding up and down the unfinished line with two saddle-bags of gold coins borrowed on Friday to pay the men on Saturday, keeping just two cross-ties ahead of the sheriff as Aunt Jenny said. So we walked in the dusk, slowly between Aunt Jenny's flower beds while Drusilla (in a dress now, who still would have worn pants all the time if Father had let her) leaned lightly on my arm and I smelled the verbena in her hair as I had smelled the rain in it and in Father's beard that night four years ago when he and Drusilla and Uncle Buck McCaslin found Grumby and then came home and found Ringo and me more than just asleep: escaped into that oblivion which God or Nature or whoever it was had supplied us with for the time being, who had had to perform more than should be required of children because there should be some limit to the age, the youth at least below which one should not have to kill. This was just after the Saturday night when he returned and I watched him clean the derringer and reload it and we learned that the dead man was almost a neighbor, a hill man who had been in the first infantry regiment when it voted Father out of command: and we never to know if the man actually intended to rob Father or not because Father had shot too quick, but only that he had a wife and several children in a dirt-floored cabin in the hills, to whom Father the next day sent some money and she (the wife) walked into the house two days later while we were sitting at the dinner table and flung the money at Father's face.

"But nobody could have more of a dream than Colonel Sutpen," I said. He had been Father's second-in-command in the first regiment and had been elected colonel when the regiment deposed Father after Second Manassas, and it was Sutpen and not the regiment whom Father never forgave. He was underbred, a cold ruthless man who had come into the country about thirty years before the War, nobody knew from where except Father said you could look at him and know he would not dare to tell. He had got some land and nobody knew how he did that either, and he got money from somewhere—Father said they all believed he robbed steamboats, either as a card sharper or as an out-and-out highwayman—and built a big house and married and set up as a gentleman. Then he lost everything in the War like everybody else, all hope of

descendants too (his son killed his daughter's fiancé on the eve of
the wedding and vanished) yet he came back home and set out
singlehanded to rebuild his plantation. He had no friends to borrow from and he had nobody to leave it to and he was past sixty
years old, yet he set out to rebuild his place like it used to be; they
told how he was too busy to bother with politics or anything; how
when Father and the other men organised the nightriders to keep
the carpet baggers from organising the Negroes into an insurrection,
he refused to have anything to do with it. Father stopped hating
him long enough to ride out to see Sutpen himself and he (Sutpen)
came to the door with a lamp and did not even invite them to
come in and discuss it; Father said, "Are you with us or against
us?" and he said, "I'm for my land. If every man of you would re-
habilitate his own land, the country will take care of itself" and
Father challenged him to bring the lamp out and set it on a stump
where they could both see to shoot and Sutpen would not. "Nobody could have more of a dream than that."

"Yes. But his dream is just Sutpen. John's is not. He is thinking of
this whole country which he is trying to raise by its bootstraps, so
that all the people in it, not just his kind nor his old regiment, but
all the people, black and white, the women and children back in
the hills who don't even own shoes—Don't you see?"

"But how can they get any good from what he wants to do for
them if they are—after he has———"

"Killed some of them? I suppose you include those two carpet
baggers he had to kill to hold that first election, don't you?"

"They were men. Human beings."

"They were Northerners, foreigners who had no business here.
They were pirates." We walked on, her weight hardly discernible
on my arm, her head just reaching my shoulder. I had always been
a little taller than she, even on that night at Hawkhurst while we
listened to the niggers passing in the road, and she had changed
but little since—the same boy-hard body, the close implacable head
with its savagely cropped hair which I had watched from the
wagon above the tide of crazed singing niggers as we went down
into the river—the body not slender as women are but as boys are
slender. "A dream is not a very safe thing to be near, Bayard. I
know; I had one once. It's like a loaded pistol with a hair trigger:
if it stays alive long enough, somebody is going to be hurt. But if
it's a good dream, it's worth it. There are not many dreams in the

world, but there are a lot of human lives. And one human life or two dozen——"

"Are not worth anything?"

"No. Not anything.—Listen. I hear Jupiter. I'll beat you to the house." She was already running, the skirts she did not like to wear lifted almost to her knees, her legs beneath it running as boys run just as she rode like men ride.

I was twenty then. But the next time I was twenty-four; I had been three years at the University and in another two weeks I would ride back to Oxford for the final year and my degree. It was just last summer, last August, and Father had just beat Redmond for the State legislature. The railroad was finished now and the partnership between Father and Redmond had been dissolved so long ago that most people would have forgotten they were ever partners if it hadn't been for the enmity between them. There had been a third partner but nobody hardly remembered his name now; he and his name both had vanished in the fury of the conflict which set up between Father and Redmond almost before they began to lay the rails, between Father's violent and ruthless dictatorialness and will to dominate (the idea was his; he did think of the railroad first and then took Redmond in) and that quality in Redmond (as George Wyatt said, he was not a coward or Father would never have teamed with him) which permitted him to stand as much as he did from Father, to bear and bear and bear until something (not his will nor his courage) broke in him. During the War Redmond had not been a soldier, he had had something to do with cotton for the Government; he could have made money himself out of it but he had not and everybody knew he had not, Father knew it, yet Father would even taunt him with not having smelled powder. He was wrong; he knew he was when it was too late for him to stop just as a drunkard reaches a point where it is too late for him to stop, where he promises himself that he will and maybe believes he will or can but it is too late. Finally they reached the point (they had both put everything they could mortgage or borrow into it for Father to ride up and down the line, paying the workmen and the waybills on the rails at the last possible instant) where even Father realised that one of them would have to get out. So (they were not speaking then; it was arranged by Judge Benbow) they met and agreed to buy or sell, naming a price which, in reference to what they had put into it, was ridiculously low but which each

believed the other could not raise—at least Father claimed that
Redmond did not believe he could raise it. So Redmond accepted
the price, and found out that Father had the money. And according to Father, that's what started it, although Uncle Buck McCaslin
said Father could not have owned a half interest in even one hog,
let alone a railroad, and not dissolve the business either sworn enemy or death-pledged friend to his recent partner. So they parted
and Father finished the road. By that time, seeing that he was going to finish it, some Northern people sold him a locomotive on
credit which he named for Aunt Jenny, with a silver oil can in the
cab with her name engraved on it; and last summer the first train
ran into Jefferson, the engine decorated with flowers and Father in
the cab blowing blast after blast on the whistle when he passed
Redmond's house; and there were speeches at the station, with
more flowers and a Confederate flag and girls in white dresses and
red sashes and a band, and Father stood on the pilot of the engine
and made a direct and absolutely needless allusion to Mr. Redmond. That was it. He wouldn't let him alone. George Wyatt came
to me right afterward and told me. "Right or wrong," he said, "us
boys and most of the other folks in this county know John's right.
But he ought to let Redmond alone. I know what's wrong: he's had
to kill too many folks, and that's bad for a man. We all know Colonel's brave as a lion, but Redmond ain't no coward either and there
ain't any use in making a brave man that made one mistake eat
crow all the time. Can't you talk to him?"

"I don't know," I said. "I'll try." But I had no chance. That is, I
could have talked to him and he would have listened, but he could
not have heard me because he had stepped straight from the pilot
of that engine into the race for the Legislature. Maybe he knew
that Redmond would have to oppose him to save his face even
though he (Redmond) must have known that, after that train ran
into Jefferson, he had no chance against Father, or maybe Redmond had already announced his candidacy and Father entered
the race just because of that, I don't remember. Anyway they ran, a
bitter contest in which Father continued to badger Redmond without reason or need, since they both knew it would be a landslide
for Father. And it was, and we thought he was satisfied. Maybe he
thought so himself, as the drunkard believes that he is done with
drink; and it was that afternoon and Drusilla and I walked in the
garden in the twilight and I said something about what George

Wyatt had told me and she released my arm and turned me to face her and said, "This from you? You? Have you forgotten Grumby?"

"No," I said. "I never will forget him."

"You never will. I wouldn't let you. There are worse things than killing men, Bayard. There are worse things than being killed. Sometimes I think the finest thing that can happen to a man is to love something, a woman preferably, well, hard hard hard, then to die young because he believed what he could not help but believe and was what he could not (could not? would not) help but be." Now she was looking at me in a way she never had before. I did not know what it meant then and was not to know until tonight since neither of us knew then that two months later Father would be dead. I just knew that she was looking at me as she never had before and that the scent of the verbena in her hair seemed to have increased a hundred times, to have got a hundred times stronger, to be everywhere in the dusk in which something was about to happen which I had never dreamed of. Then she spoke. "Kiss me, Bayard."

"No. You are Father's wife."

"And eight years older than you are. And your fourth cousin too. And I have black hair. Kiss me, Bayard."

"No."

"Kiss me, Bayard." So I leaned my face down to her. But she didn't move, standing so, bent lightly back from me from the waist, looking at me; now it was she who said, "No." So I put my arms around her. Then she came to me, melted as women will and can, the arms with the wrist- and elbow-power to control horses about my shoulders, using the wrists to hold my face to hers until there was no longer need for the wrists; I thought then of the woman of thirty, the symbol of the ancient and eternal Snake and of the men who have written of her, and I realised then the immitigable chasm between all life and all print—that those who can, do, those who cannot and suffer enough because they can't, write about it. Then I was free, I could see her again, I saw her still watching me with that dark inscrutable look, looking up at me now across her down-slanted face; I watched her arms rise with almost the exact gesture with which she had put them around me as if she were repeating the empty and formal gesture of all promise so that I should never forget it, the elbows angling outward as she put her hands to the sprig of verbena in her hair, I standing straight and rigid facing

the slightly bent head, the short jagged hair, the rigid curiously
formal angle of the bare arms gleaming faintly in the last of light
as she removed the verbena sprig and put it into my lapel, and I
thought how the War had tried to stamp all the women of her generation and class in the South into a type and how it had failed—
the suffering, the identical experience (hers and Aunt Jenny's had
been almost the same except that Aunt Jenny had spent a few
nights with her husband before they brought him back home in an
ammunition wagon while Gavin Breckbridge was just Drusilla's
fiancé) was there in the eyes, yet beyond that was the incorrigibly
individual woman: not like so many men who return from wars to
live on Government reservations like so many steers, emasculate
and empty of all save an identical experience which they cannot
forget and dare not, else they would cease to live at that moment,
almost interchangeable save for the old habit of answering to a
given name.

"Now I must tell Father," I said.

"Yes," she said. "You must tell him. Kiss me." So again it was like
it had been before. No. Twice, a thousand times and never like—
the eternal and symbolical thirty to a young man, a youth, each
time both cumulative and retroactive, immitigably unrepetitive,
each wherein remembering excludes experience, each wherein experience antedates remembering; the skill without weariness, the
knowledge virginal to surfeit, the cunning secret muscles to guide
and control just as within the wrists and elbows lay slumbering the
mastery of horses: she stood back, already turning, not looking at
me when she spoke, never having looked at me, already moving
swiftly on in the dusk: "Tell John. Tell him tonight."

I intended to. I went to the house and into the office at once; I
went to the center of the rug before the cold hearth, I don't know
why, and stood there rigid like soldiers stand, looking at eye level
straight across the room and above his head and said "Father" and
then stopped. Because he did not even hear me. He said, "Yes, Bayard?" but he did not hear me although he was sitting behind the
desk doing nothing, immobile, as still as I was rigid, one hand on
the desk with a dead cigar in it, a bottle of brandy and a filled and
untasted glass beside his hand, clothed quiet and bemused in whatever triumph it was he felt since the last overwhelming return of
votes had come in late in the afternoon. So I waited until after sup-

per. We went to the diningroom and stood side by side until Aunt
Jenny entered and then Drusilla, in the yellow ball gown, who
walked straight to me and gave me one fierce inscrutable look then
went to her place and waited for me to draw her chair while Father
drew Aunt Jenny's. He had roused by then, not to talk himself but
rather to sit at the head of the table and reply to Drusilla as she
talked with a sort of feverish and glittering volubility—to reply
now and then to her with that courteous intolerant pride which
had lately become a little forensic, as if merely being in a political
contest filled with fierce and empty oratory had retroactively made
a lawyer of him who was anything and everything except a lawyer.
Then Drusilla and Aunt Jenny rose and left us and he said, "Wait"
to me who had made no move to follow and directed Joby to bring
one of the bottles of wine which he had fetched back from New
Orleans when he went there last to borrow money to liquidate his
first private railroad bonds. Then I stood again like soldiers stand,
gazing at eye level above his head while he sat half-turned from the
table, a little paunchy now though not much, a little grizzled too in
the hair though his beard was as strong as ever, with that spurious
forensic air of lawyers and the intolerant eyes which in the last two
years had acquired that transparent film which the eyes of carnivo-
rous animals have and from behind which they look at a world
which no ruminant ever sees, perhaps dares to see, which I have
seen before on the eyes of men who have killed too much, who
have killed so much that never again as long as they live will they
ever be alone. I said again, "Father," then I told him.

"Hah?" he said. "Sit down." I sat down, I looked at him, watched
him fill both glasses and this time I knew it was worse with him
than not hearing: it didn't even matter. "You are doing well in the
law, Judge Wilkins tells me. I am pleased to hear that. I have not
needed you in my affairs so far, but from now on I shall. I have
now accomplished the active portion of my aims in which you
could not have helped me; I acted as the land and the time demanded and you were too young for that, I wished to shield you.
But now the land and the time too are changing; what will follow
will be a matter of consolidation, of pettifogging and doubtless
chicanery in which I would be a babe in arms but in which you,
trained in the law, can hold your own—our own. Yes, I have accomplished my aim, and now I shall do a little moral house-clean-

ing. I am tired of killing men, no matter what the necessity nor the end. Tomorrow, when I go to town and meet Ben Redmond, I shall be unarmed."

– 3 –

We reached home just before midnight; we didn't have to pass through Jefferson either. Before we turned in the gates I could see the lights, the chandeliers—hall, parlor, and what Aunt Jenny (without any effort or perhaps even design on her part) had taught even Ringo to call the drawing room, the light falling outward across the portico, past the columns. Then I saw the horses, the faint shine of leather and buckle-glints on the black silhouettes and then the men too—Wyatt and others of Father's old troop—and I had forgot that they would be there. I had forgot that they would be there; I remember how I thought, since I was tired and spent with strain, *Now it will have to begin tonight. I won't even have until tomorrow in which to begin to resist.* They had a watchman, a picquet out, I suppose, because they seemed to know at once that we were in the drive. Wyatt met me, I halted the mare, I could look down at him and at the others gathered a few yards behind him with that curious vulture-like formality which Southern men assume in such situations.

"Well, boy," George said.

"Was it—" I said. "Was he——"

"It was all right. It was in front. Redmond ain't no coward. John had the derringer inside his cuff like always, but he never touched it, never made a move toward it." I have seen him do it, he showed me once: the pistol (it was not four inches long) held flat inside his left wrist by a clip he made himself of wire and an old clock spring; he would raise both hands at the same time, cross them, fire the pistol from beneath his left hand almost as if he were hiding from his own vision what he was doing; when he killed one of the men he shot a hole through his own coat sleeve. "But you want to get on to the house," Wyatt said. He began to stand aside, then he spoke again: "We'll take this off your hands, any of us. Me." I hadn't moved the mare yet and I had made no move to speak, yet he continued quickly, as if he had already rehearsed all this, his speech and mine, and knew what I would say and only spoke himself as he would have removed his hat on entering a house or used 'sir' in conversing with a stranger: "You're young, just a boy, you

ain't had any experience in this kind of thing. Besides, you got them
two ladies in the house to think about. He would understand, all
right."

"I reckon I can attend to it," I said.

"Sure," he said; there was no surprise, nothing at all, in his voice
because he had already rehearsed this: "I reckon we all knew that's
what you would say." He stepped back then; almost it was as
though he and not I bade the mare to move on. But they all followed, still with that unctuous and voracious formality. Then I saw
Drusilla standing at the top of the front steps, in the light from the
open door and the windows like a theatre scene, in the yellow ball
gown and even from here I believed that I could smell the verbena
in her hair, standing there motionless yet emanating something
louder than the two shots must have been—something voracious
too and passionate. Then, although I had dismounted and someone
had taken the mare, I seemed to be still in the saddle and to watch
myself enter that scene which she had postulated like another actor
while in the background for chorus Wyatt and the others stood
with the unctuous formality which the Southern man shows in the
presence of death—that Roman holiday engendered by mist-born
Protestantism grafted onto this land of violent sun, of violent alteration from snow to heat-stroke which has produced a race impervious to both. I mounted the steps toward the figure straight and
yellow and immobile as a candle which moved only to extend one
hand; we stood together and looked down at them where they
stood clumped, the horses too gathered in a tight group beyond
them at the rim of light from the brilliant door and windows. One
of them stamped and blew his breath and jangled his gear.

"Thank you, gentlemen," I said. "My aunt and my—Drusilla
thank you. There's no need for you to stay. Goodnight." They murmured, turning. George Wyatt paused, looking back at me.

"Tomorrow?" he said.

"Tomorrow." Then they went on, carrying their hats and tiptoe-
ing, even on the ground, the quiet and resilient earth, as though
anyone in that house awake would try to sleep, anyone already
asleep in it whom they could have wakened. Then they were gone
and Drusilla and I turned and crossed the portico, her hand lying
light on my wrist yet discharging into me with a shock like electricity that dark and passionate voracity, the face at my shoulder
—the jagged hair with a verbena sprig above each ear, the eyes

staring at me with that fierce exaltation. We entered the hall and
crossed it, her hand guiding me without pressure, and entered the
parlor. Then for the first time I realised it—the alteration which is
death—not that he was now just clay but that he was lying down.
But I didn't look at him yet because I knew that when I did I
would begin to pant; I went to Aunt Jenny who had just risen from
a chair behind which Louvinia stood. She was Father's sister, taller
than Drusilla but no older, whose husband had been killed at the
very beginning of the War, by a shell from a Federal frigate at Fort
Moultrie, come to us from Carolina six years ago. Ringo and I went
to Tennessee Junction in the wagon to meet her. It was January,
cold and clear and with ice in the ruts; we returned just before dark
with Aunt Jenny on the seat beside me holding a lace parasol and
Ringo in the wagon bed nursing a hamper basket containing two
bottles of old sherry and the two jasmine cuttings which were
bushes in the garden now, and the panes of colored glass which
she had salvaged from the Carolina house where she and Father
and Uncle Bayard were born and which Father had set in a fanlight about one of the drawing room windows for her—who came
up the drive and Father (home now from the railroad) went down
the steps and lifted her from the wagon and said, "Well, Jenny,"
and she said, "Well, Johnny," and began to cry. She stood too, looking at me as I approached—the same hair, the same high nose, the
same eyes as Father's except that they were intent and very wise
instead of intolerant. She said nothing at all, she just kissed me, her
hands light on my shoulders. Then Drusilla spoke, as if she had
been waiting with a sort of dreadful patience for the empty ceremony to be done, in a voice like a bell: clear, unsentient, on a
single pitch, silvery and triumphant: "Come, Bayard."

"Hadn't you better go to bed now?" Aunt Jenny said.

"Yes," Drusilla said in that silvery ecstatic voice, "Oh yes. There
will be plenty of time for sleep." I followed her, her hand again
guiding me without pressure; now I looked at him. It was just as I
had imagined it—sabre, plumes, and all—but with that alteration,
that irrevocable difference which I had known to expect yet had
not realised, as you can put food into your stomach which for a
while the stomach declines to assimilate—the illimitable grief and
regret as I looked down at the face which I knew—the nose, the
hair, the eyelids closed over the intolerance—the face which I realised I now saw in repose for the first time in my life; the empty

hands still now beneath the invisible stain of what had been (once, surely) needless blood, the hands now appearing clumsy in their very inertness, too clumsy to have performed the fatal actions which forever afterward he must have waked and slept with and maybe was glad to lay down at last—those curious appendages clumsily conceived to begin with yet with which man has taught himself to do so much, so much more than they were intended to do or could be forgiven for doing, which had now surrendered that life to which his intolerant heart had fiercely held; and then I knew that in a minute I would begin to pant. So Drusilla must have spoken twice before I heard her and turned and saw in the instant Aunt Jenny and Louvinia watching us, hearing Drusilla now, the unsentient bell quality gone now, her voice whispering into that quiet death-filled room with a passionate and dying fall: "Bayard." She faced me, she was quite near; again the scent of the verbena in her hair seemed to have increased a hundred times as she stood holding out to me, one in either hand, the two duelling pistols. "Take them, Bayard," she said, in the same tone in which she had said "Kiss me" last summer, already pressing them into my hands, watching me with that passionate and voracious exaltation, speaking in a voice fainting and passionate with promise: "Take them. I have kept them for you. I give them to you. Oh you will thank me, you will remember me who put into your hands what they say is an attribute only of God's, who took what belongs to heaven and gave it to you. Do you feel them? the long true barrels true as justice, the triggers (you have fired them) quick as retribution, the two of them slender and invincible and fatal as the physical shape of love?" Again I watched her arms angle out and upward as she removed the two verbena sprigs from her hair in two motions faster than the eye could follow, already putting one of them into my lapel and crushing the other in her other hand while she still spoke in that rapid passionate voice not much louder than a whisper: "There. One I give to you to wear tomorrow (it will not fade), the other I cast away, like this—" dropping the crushed bloom at her feet. "I abjure it. I abjure verbena forever more; I have smelled it above the odor of courage; that was all I wanted. Now let me look at you." She stood back, staring at me—the face tearless and exalted, the feverish eyes brilliant and voracious. "How beautiful you are: do you know it? How beautiful: young, to be permitted to kill, to be permitted vengeance, to take into your bare hands the fire of

heaven that cast down Lucifer. No; I. I gave it to you; I put it into
your hands; Oh you will thank me, you will remember me when I
am dead and you are an old man saying to himself, 'I have tasted
all things.'—It will be the right hand, won't it?" She moved; she
had taken my right hand which still held one of the pistols before I
knew what she was about to do; she had bent and kissed it before
I comprehended why she took it. Then she stopped dead still, still
stooping in that attitude of fierce exultant humility, her hot lips
and her hot hands still touching my flesh, light on my flesh as dead
leaves yet communicating to it that battery charge dark, passionate
and damned forever of all peace. Because they are wise, women are
—a touch, lips or fingers, and the knowledge, even clairvoyance,
goes straight to the heart without bothering the laggard brain at
all. She stood erect now, staring at me with intolerable and amazed
incredulity which occupied her face alone for a whole minute while
her eyes were completely empty; it seemed to me that I stood
there for a full minute while Aunt Jenny and Louvinia watched us,
waiting for her eyes to fill. There was no blood in her face at
all, her mouth open a little and pale as one of those rubber rings
women seal fruit jars with. Then her eyes filled with an expression
of bitter and passionate betrayal. "Why, he's not—" she said. "He's
not—And I kissed his hand," she said in an aghast whisper; "*I
kissed his hand!*" beginning to laugh, the laughter, rising, becoming
a scream yet still remaining laughter, screaming with laughter, trying herself to deaden the sound by putting her hand over her
mouth, the laughter spilling between her fingers like vomit, the incredulous betrayed eyes still watching me across the hand.

"Louvinia!" Aunt Jenny said. They both came to her. Louvinia
touched and held her and Drusilla turned her face to Louvinia.

"I kissed his hand, Louvinia!" she cried. "Did you see it? *I kissed
his hand!*" the laughter rising again, becoming the scream again yet
still remaining laughter, she still trying to hold it back with her
hand like a small child who has filled its mouth too full.

"Take her upstairs," Aunt Jenny said. But they were already moving toward the door, Louvinia half-carrying Drusilla, the laughter
diminishing as they neared the door as though it waited for the
larger space of the empty and brilliant hall to rise again. Then it
was gone; Aunt Jenny and I stood there and I knew soon that I
would begin to pant. I could feel it beginning like you feel regurgi-
tation beginning, as though there were not enough air in the room,

the house, not enough air anywhere under the heavy hot low sky
where the equinox couldn't seem to accomplish, nothing in the air
for breathing, for the lungs. Now it was Aunt Jenny who said "Bayard" twice before I heard her. "You are not going to try to kill him.
All right."

"All right?" I said.

"Yes. All right. Don't let it be Drusilla, a poor hysterical young
woman. And don't let it be him, Bayard, because he's dead now.
And don't let it be George Wyatt and those others who will be waiting for you tomorrow morning. I know you are not afraid."

"But what good will that do?" I said. "What good will that do?"
It almost began then; I stopped it just in time. "I must live with myself, you see."

"Then it's not just Drusilla? Not just him? Not just George Wyatt
and Jefferson?"

"No," I said.

"Will you promise to let me see you before you go to town tomorrow?" I looked at her; we looked at one another for a moment.
Then she put her hands on my shoulders and kissed me and released me, all in one motion. "Goodnight, son," she said. Then she
was gone too and now it could begin. I knew that in a minute I
would look at him and it would begin and I did look at him, feeling the long-held breath, the hiatus before it started, thinking how
maybe I should have said, "Goodbye, Father" but did not. Instead
I crossed to the piano and laid the pistols carefully on it, still keeping the panting from getting too loud too soon. Then I was outside
on the porch and (I don't know how long it had been) I looked in
the window and saw Simon squatting on a stool beside him. Simon
had been his body servant during the War and when they came
home Simon had a uniform too—a Confederate private's coat with
a Yankee brigadier's star on it and he had put it on now too, like
they had dressed Father, squatting on the stool beside him, not crying, not weeping the facile tears which are the white man's futile
trait and which Negroes know nothing about but just sitting there,
motionless, his lower lip slacked down a little; he raised his hand
and touched the coffin, the black hand rigid and fragile-looking as
a clutch of dead twigs, then dropped the hand; once he turned his
head and I saw his eyes roll red and unwinking in his skull like
those of a cornered fox. It had begun by that time; I panted, standing there, and this was it—the regret and grief, the despair out of

which the tragic mute insensitive bones stand up that can bear anything, anything.

– 4 –

After a while the whippoorwills stopped and I heard the first day
bird, a mockingbird. It had sung all night too but now it was the
day song, no longer the drowsy moony fluting. Then they all began—the sparrows from the stable, the thrush that lived in Aunt
Jenny's garden, and I heard a quail too from the pasture and now
there was light in the room. But I didn't move at once. I still lay on
the bed (I hadn't undressed) with my hands under my head and
the scent of Drusilla's verbena faint from where my coat lay on a
chair, watching the light grow, watching it turn rosy with the sun.
After a while I heard Louvinia come up across the back yard and
go into the kitchen; I heard the door and then the long crash of her
armful of stovewood into the box. Soon they would begin to arrive—the carriages and buggies in the drive—but not for a while
yet because they too would wait first to see what I was going to do.
So the house was quiet when I went down to the diningroom, no
sound in it except Simon snoring in the parlor, probably still sitting
on the stool though I didn't look in to see. Instead I stood at the
diningroom window and drank the coffee which Louvinia brought
me, then I went to the stable; I saw Joby watching me from the
kitchen door as I crossed the yard and in the stable Loosh looked
up at me across Betsy's head, a curry comb in his hand, though
Ringo didn't look at me at all. We curried Jupiter then. I didn't
know if we would be able to without trouble or not, since always
Father would come in first and touch him and tell him to stand
and he would stand like a marble horse (or pale bronze rather)
while Loosh curried him. But he stood for me too, a little restive
but he stood, then that was done and now it was almost nine
o'clock and soon they would begin to arrive and I told Ringo to
bring Betsy on to the house.

I went on to the house and into the hall. I had not had to pant
in some time now but it was there, waiting, a part of the alteration,
as though by being dead and no longer needing air he had taken
all of it, all that he had compassed and claimed and postulated between the walls which he had built, along with him. Aunt Jenny
must have been waiting; she came out of the diningroom at once,
without a sound, dressed, the hair that was like Father's combed

and smooth above the eyes that were different from Father's eyes because they were not intolerant but just intent and grave and (she was wise too) without pity. "Are you going now?" she said.

"Yes." I looked at her. Yes, thank God, without pity. "You see, I want to be thought well of."

"I do," she said. "Even if you spend the day hidden in the stable loft, I still do."

"Maybe if she knew that I was going. Was going to town anyway."

"No," she said. "No, Bayard." We looked at one another. Then she said quietly, "All right. She's awake." So I mounted the stairs. I mounted steadily, not fast because if I had gone fast the panting would have started again or I might have had to slow for a second at the turn or at the top and I would not have gone on. So I went slowly and steadily, across the hall to her door and knocked and opened it. She was sitting at the window, in something soft and loose for morning in her bedroom only she never did look like morning in a bedroom because here was no hair to fall about her shoulders. She looked up, she sat there looking at me with her feverish brilliant eyes and I remembered I still had the verbena sprig in my lapel and suddenly she began to laugh again. It seemed to come not from her mouth but to burst out all over her face like sweat does and with a dreadful and painful convulsion as when you have vomited until it hurts you yet still you must vomit again —burst out all over her face except her eyes, the brilliant incredulous eyes looking at me out of the laughter as if they belonged to somebody else, as if they were two inert fragments of tar or coal lying on the bottom of a receptacle filled with turmoil: "I kissed his hand! *I kissed his hand!*" Louvinia entered, Aunt Jenny must have sent her directly after me; again I walked slowly and steadily so it would not start yet, down the stairs where Aunt Jenny stood beneath the chandelier in the hall as Mrs. Wilkins had stood yesterday at the University. She had my hat in her hand. "Even if you hid all day in the stable, Bayard," she said. I took the hat; she said quietly, pleasantly, as if she were talking to a stranger, a guest: "I used to see a lot of blockade runners in Charleston. They were heroes in a way, you see—not heroes because they were helping to prolong the Confederacy but heroes in the sense that David Crockett or John Sevier would have been to small boys or fool young women. There was one of them, an Englishman. He had no business there; it was the money of course, as with all of them. But he was the Davy Crockett to us because by that time we had all forgot what money was, what you could do with it. He must have been a gentleman once or associated with gentlemen before he changed his name, and he had a vocabulary of seven words, though I must admit he got along quite well with them. The first four were, 'I'll have rum, thanks,' and then, when he had the rum, he would use the other three—across the champagne, to whatever ruffled bosom or low gown: 'No bloody moon.' No bloody moon, Bayard."

Ringo was waiting with Betsy at the front steps. Again he did not look at me, his face sullen, downcast even while he handed me the reins. But he said nothing, nor did I look back. And sure enough I was just in time; I passed the Compson carriage at the gates, General Compson lifted his hat as I did mine as we passed. It was four miles to town but I had not gone two of them when I heard the horse coming up behind me and I did not look back because I knew it was Ringo. I did not look back; he came up on one of the carriage horses, he rode up beside me and looked me full in the face for one moment, the sullen determined face, the eyes rolling at me defiant and momentary and red; we rode on. Now we were in town—the long shady street leading to the square, the new courthouse at the end of it; it was eleven o'clock now: long past breakfast and not yet noon so there were only women on the street, not to recognise me perhaps or at least not the walking stopped sudden and dead in midwalking as if the legs contained the sudden eyes, the caught breath, that not to begin until we reached the square and I thinking *If I could only be invisible until I reach the stairs to his office and begin to mount.* But I could not, I was not; we rode up to the Holston House and I saw the row of feet along the gallery rail come suddenly and quietly down and I did not look at them, I stopped Betsy and waited until Ringo was down then I dismounted and gave him the reins. "Wait for me here," I said.

"I'm going with you," he said, not loud; we stood there under the still circumspect eyes and spoke quietly to one another like two conspirators. Then I saw the pistol, the outline of it inside his shirt, probably the one we had taken from Grumby that day we killed him.

"No you ain't," I said.

"Yes I am."

"No you ain't." So I walked on, along the street in the hot sun. It was almost noon now and I could smell nothing except the verbena in my coat, as if it had gathered all the sun, all the suspended fierce heat in which the equinox could not seem to occur and were distilling it so that I moved in a cloud of verbena as I might have moved in a cloud of smoke from a cigar. Then George Wyatt was beside me (I don't know where he came from) and five or six others of Father's old troop a few yards behind, George's hand on my arm, drawing me into a doorway out of the avid eyes like caught breaths.

"Have you got that derringer?" George said.

"No," I said.

"Good," George said. "They are tricky things to fool with. Couldn't nobody but Colonel ever handle one right; I never could. So you take this. I tried it this morning and I know it's right. Here." He was already fumbling the pistol into my pocket, then the same thing seemed to happen to him that happened to Drusilla last night when she kissed my hand—something communicated by touch straight to the simple code by which he lived, without going through the brain at all: so that he too stood suddenly back, the pistol in his hand, staring at me with his pale outraged eyes and speaking in a whisper thin with fury: "Who are you? Is your name Sartoris? By God, if you don't kill him, I'm going to." Now it was not panting, it was a terrible desire to laugh, to laugh as Drusilla had, and say, "That's what Drusilla said." But I didn't. I said,

"I'm tending to this. You stay out of it. I don't need any help." Then his fierce eyes faded gradually, exactly as you turn a lamp down.

"Well," he said, putting the pistol back into his pocket. "You'll have to excuse me, son. I should have knowed you wouldn't do anything that would keep John from laying quiet. We'll follow you and wait at the foot of the steps. And remember: he's a brave man, but he's been sitting in that office by himself since yesterday morning waiting for you and his nerves are on edge."

"I'll remember," I said. "I don't need any help." I had started on when suddenly I said it without having any warning that I was going to: "No bloody moon."

"What?" he said. I didn't answer. I went on across the square itself now, in the hot sun, they following though not close so that I never saw them again until afterward, surrounded by the remote still eyes not following me yet either, just stopped where they were before the stores and about the door to the courthouse, waiting. I walked steadily on enclosed in the now fierce odor of the verbena sprig. Then shadow fell upon me; I did not pause, I looked once at the small faded sign nailed to the brick *B. J. Redmond. Atty at Law* and began to mount the stairs, the wooden steps scuffed by the heavy bewildered boots of countrymen approaching litigation and stained by tobacco spit, on down the dim corridor to the door which bore the name again, *B. J. Redmond* and knocked once and opened it. He sat behind the desk, not much taller than Father but thicker as a man gets who spends most of his time sitting and listening to people, freshly shaven and with fresh linen; a lawyer yet it was not a lawyer's face—a face much thinner than the body would indicate, strained (and yes, tragic; I know that now) and exhausted beneath the neat recent steady strokes of the razor, holding a pistol flat on the desk before him, loose beneath his hand and aimed at nothing. There was no smell of drink, not even of tobacco in the neat clean dingy room although I knew he smoked. I didn't pause. I walked steadily toward him. It was not twenty feet from door to desk yet I seemed to walk in a dreamlike state in which there was neither time nor distance, as though the mere act of walking was no more intended to encompass space than was his sitting. We didn't speak. It was as if we both knew what the passage of words would be and the futility of it; how he might have said, "Go out, Bayard. Go away, boy" and then, "Draw then. I will allow you to draw" and it would have been the same as if he had never said it. So we did not speak; I just walked steadily toward him as the pistol rose from the desk. I watched it, I could see the foreshortened slant of the barrel and I knew it would miss me though his hand did not tremble. I walked toward him, toward the pistol in the rocklike hand, I heard no bullet. Maybe I didn't even hear the explosion though I remember the sudden orange bloom and smoke as they appeared against his white shirt as they had appeared against Grumby's greasy Confederate coat; I still watched that foreshortened slant of barrel which I knew was not aimed at me and saw the second orange flash and smoke and heard no bullet that time either. Then I stopped; it was done then. I watched the pistol descend to the desk in short jerks; I saw him release it and sit back, both hands on the desk, I looked at his face and I knew too what it was to want air when there was nothing in the circumambience for the lungs. He rose, shoved the chair back with a convulsive motion and rose, with a queer ducking motion of his head; with his head still ducked aside and one arm extended as though he couldn't see and the other hand resting on the desk as if he couldn't stand alone, he turned and crossed to the wall and took his hat from the rack and with his head still ducked aside and one hand extended he blundered along the wall and passed me and reached the door and went through it. He was brave; no one denied that. He walked down those stairs and out onto the street where George Wyatt and the other six of Father's old troop waited and where the other men had begun to run now; he walked through the middle of them with his hat on and his head up (they told me how someone shouted at him: "Have you killed that boy too?"), saying no word, staring straight ahead and with his back to them, on to the station where the south-bound train was just in and got on it with no baggage, nothing, and went away from Jefferson and from Mississippi and never came back.

I heard their feet on the stairs then in the corridor then in the room, but for a while yet (it wasn't that long, of course) I still sat behind the desk as he had sat, the flat of the pistol still warm under my hand, my hand growing slowly numb between the pistol and my forehead. Then I raised my head; the little room was full of men. "My God!" George Wyatt cried. "You took the pistol away from him and then missed him, missed him *twice*?" Then he answered himself—that same rapport for violence which Drusilla had and which in George's case was actual character judgment: "No; wait. You walked in here without even a pocket knife and let him miss you twice. My God in heaven." He turned, shouting: "Get to hell out of here! You, White, ride out to Sartoris and tell his folks it's all over and he's all right. Ride!" So they departed, went away; presently only George was left, watching me with that pale bleak stare which was speculative yet not at all ratiocinative. "Well by God," he said. "—Do you want a drink?"

"No," I said. "I'm hungry. I didn't eat any breakfast."

"I reckon not, if you got up this morning aiming to do what you did. Come on. We'll go to the Holston House."

"No," I said. "No. Not there."

"Why not? You ain't done anything to be ashamed of. I wouldn't have done it that way, myself. I'd a shot at him once, anyway. But that's your way or you wouldn't have done it."

"Yes," I said. "I would do it again."

"Be damned if I would.—You want to come home with me? We'll have time to eat and then ride out there in time for the——" But I couldn't do that either.

"No," I said. "I'm not hungry after all. I think I'll go home."

"Don't you want to wait and ride out with me?"

"No. I'll go on."

"You don't want to stay here, anyway." He looked around the room again, where the smell of powder smoke still lingered a little, still lay somewhere on the hot dead air though invisible now, blinking a little with his fierce pale unintroverted eyes. "Well by God," he said again. "Maybe you're right, maybe there has been enough killing in your family without—Come on." We left the office. I waited at the foot of the stairs and soon Ringo came up with the horses. We crossed the square again. There were no feet on the Holston House railing now (it was twelve o'clock) but a group of men stood before the door who raised their hats and I raised mine and Ringo and I rode on.

We did not go fast. Soon it was one, maybe after; the carriages and buggies would begin to leave the square soon, so I turned from the road at the end of the pasture and I sat the mare, trying to open the gate without dismounting, until Ringo dismounted and opened it. We crossed the pasture in the hard fierce sun; I could have seen the house now but I didn't look. Then we were in the shade, the close thick airless shade of the creek bottom; the old rails still lay in the undergrowth where we had built the pen to hide the Yankee mules. Presently I heard the water, then I could see the sunny glints. We dismounted. I lay on my back, I thought *Now it can begin again if it wants to.* But it did not. I went to sleep. I went to sleep almost before I had stopped thinking. I slept for almost five hours and I didn't dream anything at all yet I waked myself up crying, crying too hard to stop it. Ringo was squatting beside me and the sun was gone though there was a bird of some sort still singing somewhere and the whistle of the north-bound evening train sounded and the short broken puffs of starting where it had evidently stopped at our flag station. After a while I began to stop and Ringo brought his hat full of water from the creek but instead I went down to the water myself and bathed my face.

There was still a good deal of light in the pasture, though the whippoorwills had begun, and when we reached the house there was a mockingbird singing in the magnolia, the night song now, the drowsy moony one, and again the moon like the rim print of a heel in wet sand. There was just one light in the hall now and so it was all over though I could still smell the flowers even above the verbena in my coat. I had not looked at him again. I had started to before I left the house but I did not, I did not see him again and all the pictures we had of him were bad ones because a picture could no more have held him dead than the house could have kept his body. But I didn't need to see him again because he was there, he would always be there; maybe what Drusilla meant by his dream was not something which he possessed but something which he had bequeathed us which we could never forget, which would even assume the corporeal shape of him whenever any of us, black or white, closed our eyes. I went into the house. There was no light in the drawing room except the last of the afterglow which came through the western window where Aunt Jenny's colored glass was; I was about to go on upstairs when I saw her sitting there beside the window. She didn't call me and I didn't speak Drusilla's name, I just went to the door and stood there. "She's gone," Aunt Jenny said. "She took the evening train. She has gone to Montgomery, to Dennison." Denny had been married about a year now; he was living in Montgomery, reading law.

"I see," I said. "Then she didn't——" But there wasn't any use in that either; Jed White must have got there before one o'clock and told them. And besides, Aunt Jenny didn't answer. She could have lied to me but she didn't, she said,

"Come here." I went to her chair. "Kneel down. I can't see you."

"Don't you want the lamp?"

"No. Kneel down." So I knelt beside the chair. "So you had a perfectly splendid Saturday afternoon, didn't you? Tell me about it." Then she put her hands on my shoulders. I watched them come up as though she were trying to stop them; I felt them on my shoulders as if they had a separate life of their own and were trying to do something which for my sake she was trying to restrain, prevent. Then she gave up or she was not strong enough because they came up and took my face between them, hard, and suddenly the tears sprang and streamed down her face like Drusilla's laughing had. "Oh, damn you Sartorises!" she said. "Damn you! Damn you!"

As I passed down the hall the light came up in the diningroom and I could hear Louvinia laying the table for supper. So the stairs were lighted quite well. But the upper hall was dark. I saw her open door (that unmistakable way in which an open door stands open when nobody lives in the room any more) and I realised I had not believed that she was really gone. So I didn't look into the room. I went on to mine and entered. And then for a long moment I thought it was the verbena in my lapel which I still smelled. I thought that until I had crossed the room and looked down at the pillow on which it lay—the single sprig of it (without looking she would pinch off a half dozen of them and they would be all of a size, almost all of a shape, as if a machine had stamped them out) filling the room, the dusk, the evening with that odor which she said you could smell alone above the smell of horses.

Percy Grimm

I<small>N THE TOWN ON THAT DAY LIVED A YOUNG MAN NAMED</small> P<small>ERCY</small> Grimm. He was about twentyfive and a captain in the State national guard. He had been born in the town and had lived there all his life save for the periods of the summer encampments. He was too young to have been in the European War, though it was not until 1921 or '22 that he realised that he would never forgive his parents for that fact. His father, a hardware merchant, did not understand this. He thought that the boy was just lazy and in a fair way to become perfectly worthless, when in reality the boy was suffering the terrible tragedy of having been born not alone too late but not late enough to have escaped first hand knowledge of the lost time when he should have been a man instead of a child. And now, with the hysteria passed away and the ones who had been loudest in the hysteria and even the ones, the heroes who had suffered and served, beginning to look at one another a little askance, he had no one to tell it, to open his heart to. In fact, his first serious fight was with an exsoldier who made some remark to the effect that if he had to do it again, he would fight this time on the German side and against France. At once Grimm took him up. "Against America too?" he said.

"If America's fool enough to help France out again," the soldier said. Grimm struck him at once; he was smaller than the soldier, still in his teens. The result was foregone; even Grimm doubtless knew that. But he took his punishment until even the soldier begged the bystanders to hold the boy back. And he wore the scars of that battle as proudly as he was later to wear the uniform itself for which he had blindly fought.

It was the new civilian-military act which saved him. He was like a man who had been for a long time in a swamp, in the dark. It was as though he not only could see no path ahead of him, he knew that there was none. Then suddenly his life opened definite and clear. The wasted years in which he had shown no ability in school, in which he had been known as lazy, recalcitrant, without ambition, were behind him, forgotten. He could now see his life

643

opening before him, uncomplex and inescapable as a barren corridor, completely freed now of ever again having to think or decide, the burden which he now assumed and carried as bright and weightless and martial as his insignatory brass: a sublime and implicit faith in physical courage and blind obedience, and a belief that the white race is superior to any and all other races and that the American is superior to all other white races and that the American uniform is superior to all men, and that all that would ever be required of him in payment for this belief, this privilege, would be his own life. On each national holiday that had any martial flavor whatever he dressed in his captain's uniform and came downtown. And those who saw him remembered him again on the day of the fight with the exsoldier as, glittering, with his marksman's badge (he was a fine shot) and his bars, grave, erect, he walked among the civilians with about him an air half belligerent and half the selfconscious pride of a boy.

He was not a member of the American Legion, but that was his parents' fault and not his. But when Christmas was fetched back from Mottstown on that Saturday afternoon, he had already been to the commander of the local Post. His idea, his words, were quite simple and direct. "We got to preserve order," he said. "We must let the law take its course. The law, the nation. It is the right of no civilian to sentence a man to death. And we, the soldiers in Jefferson, are the ones to see to that."

"How do you know that anybody is planning anything different?" the legion commander said. "Have you heard any talk?"

"I dont know. I haven't listened." He didn't lie. It was as though he did not attach enough importance to what might or might not have been said by the civilian citizens to lie about it. "That's not the question. It's whether or not we, as soldiers, that have worn the uniform, are going to be the first to state where we stand. To show these people right off just where the government of the country stands on such things. That there wont be any need for them even to talk." His plan was quite simple. It was to form the legion Post into a platoon, with himself in command vide his active commission. "But if they dont want me to command, that's all right too. I'll be second, if they say. Or a sergeant or a corporal." And he meant it. It was not vainglory that he wanted. He was too sincere. So sincere, so humorless, that the legion commander withheld the flippant refusal he was about to make.

"I still dont think that there is any need of it. And if there was, we would all have to act as civilians. I couldn't use the Post like that. After all, we are not soldiers now. I dont think I would, if I could."

Grimm looked at him, without anger, but rather as if he were some kind of bug. "Yet you wore the uniform once," he said, with a kind of patience. He said: "I suppose you wont use your authority to keep me from talking to them, will you? As individuals?"

"No. I haven't any authority to do that, anyway. But just as individuals, mind. You mustn't use my name at all."

Then Grimm gave him a shot on his own account. "I am not likely to do that," he said. Then he was gone. That was Saturday, about four o'clock. For the rest of that afternoon he circulated about the stores and offices where the legion members worked, so that by nightfall he had enough of them also worked up to his own pitch to compose a fair platoon. He was indefatigable, restrained yet forceful; there was something about him irresistible and prophetlike. Yet the recruits were with the commander in one thing: the official designation of the legion must be kept out of it—whereupon and without deliberate intent, he had gained his original end: he was now in command. He got them all together just before suppertime and divided them into squads and appointed officers and a staff; the younger ones, the ones who had not gone to France, taking proper fire by now. He addressed them, briefly, coldly: ". . . order . . . course of justice . . . let the people see that we have worn the uniform of the United States . . . And one thing more." For the moment now he had descended to familiarity: the regimental commander who knows his men by their first names. "I'll leave this to you fellows. I'll do what you say. I thought it might be a good thing if I wear my uniform until this business is settled. So they can see that Uncle Sam is present in more than spirit."

"But he's not," one said quickly, immediately; he was of the same cut as the commander, who by the way was not present. "This is not government trouble yet. Kennedy might not like it. This is Jefferson's trouble, not Washington's."

"Make him like it," Grimm said. "What does your legion stand for, if not for the protection of America and Americans?"

"No," the other said. "I reckon we better not make a parade out of this. We can do what we want without that. Better. Aint that right, boys?"

"All right," Grimm said. "I'll do as you say. But every man will want a pistol. We'll have a small arms' inspection here in one hour. Every man will report here."

"What's Kennedy going to say about pistols?" one said.

"I'll see to that," Grimm said. "Report here in one hour exactly, with side arms." He dismissed them. He crossed the quiet square to the sheriff's office. The sheriff was at home, they told him. "At home?" he repeated. "Now? What's he doing at home now?"

"Eating, I reckon. A man as big as him has got to eat several times a day."

"At home," Grimm repeated. He did not glare; it was again that cold and detached expression with which he had looked at the legion commander. "Eating," he said. He went out, already walking fast. He recrossed the empty square, the quiet square empty of people peacefully at suppertables about that peaceful town and that peaceful country. He went to the sheriff's home. The sheriff said No at once.

"Fifteen or twenty folks milling around the square with pistols in their pants? No, no. That wont do. I cant have that. That wont do. You let me run this."

For a moment longer Grimm looked at the sheriff. Then he turned, already walking fast again. "All right," he said. "If that's the way you want it. I dont interfere with you and you dont interfere with me, then." It didn't sound like a threat. It was too flat, too final, too without heat. He went on, rapidly. The sheriff watched him; then he called. Grimm turned.

"You leave yours at home, too," the sheriff said. "You hear me?" Grimm didn't answer. He went on. The sheriff watched him out of sight, frowning.

That evening after supper the sheriff went back downtown— something he had not done for years save when urgent and inescapable business called. He found a picket of Grimm's men at the jail, and another in the courthouse, and a third patrolling the square and the adjacent streets. The others, the relief, they told the sheriff, were in the cotton office where Grimm was employed, which they were using for an orderly room, a P.C. The sheriff met Grimm on the street, making a round of inspection. "Come here, boy," the sheriff said. Grimm halted. He did not approach; the sheriff went to him. He patted Grimm's hip with a fat hand. "I told you to leave that at home," he said. Grimm said nothing. He watched the sheriff levelly. The sheriff sighed. "Well, if you wont, I reckon I'll have to make you a special deputy. But you aint to even show that gun unless I tell you to. You hear me?"

"Certainly not," Grimm said. "You certainly wouldn't want me to draw it if I didn't see any need to."

"I mean, not till I tell you to."

"Certainly," Grimm said, without heat, patiently, immediately. "That's what we both said. Dont you worry. I'll be there."

Later, as the town quieted for the night, as the picture show emptied and the drug stores closed one by one, Grimm's platoon began to drop off too. He did not protest, watching them coldly; they became a little sheepish, defensive. Again without knowing it he had played a trump card. Because of the fact that they felt sheepish, feeling that somehow they had fallen short of his own cold ardor, they would return tomorrow if just to show him. A few remained; it was Saturday night anyhow, and someone got more chairs from somewhere and they started a poker game. It ran all night, though from time to time Grimm (he was not in the game; neither would he permit his second in command, the only other there who held the equivalent of commissioned rank, to engage) sent a squad out to make a patrol of the square. By this time the night marshal was one of them, though he too did not take a hand in the game.

Sunday was quiet. The poker game ran quietly through that day, broken by the periodical patrols, while the quiet church bells rang and the congregations gathered in decorous clumps of summer colors. About the square it was already known that the special Grand Jury would meet tomorrow. Somehow the very sound of the two words with their evocation secret and irrevocable and something of a hidden and unsleeping and omnipotent eye watching the doings of men, began to reassure Grimm's men in their own makebelieve. So quickly is man unwittingly and unpredictably moved that without knowing that they were thinking it, the town had suddenly accepted Grimm with respect and perhaps a little awe and a deal of actual faith and confidence, as though somehow his vision and patriotism and pride in the town, the occasion, had been quicker and truer than theirs. His men anyway assumed and accepted this; after the sleepless night, the tenseness, the holiday, the suttee of volition's surrender, they were almost at the pitch where they might die for him, if occasion rose. They now moved in a grave and slightly aweinspiring reflected light which was almost as palpable as the khaki would have been which Grimm wished them to wear, wished that they wore, as though each time they returned to the orderly room they dressed themselves anew in suave and austerely splendid scraps of his dream.

This lasted through Sunday night. The poker game ran. The caution, the surreptitiousness, which had clothed it was now gone. There was something about it too assured and serenely confident to the braggadocio; tonight when they heard the marshal's feet on the stairs, one said, "Ware M.P.'s," and for an instant they glanced at one another with hard, bright, daredevil eyes; then one said, quite loud: "Throw the son of a bitch out," and another through pursed lips made the immemorial sound. And so the next morning, Monday, when the first country cars and wagons began to gather, the platoon was again intact. And they now wore uniforms. It was their faces. Most of them were of an age, a generation, an experience. But it was more than that. They now had a profound and bleak gravity as they stood where crowds milled, grave, austere, detached, looking with blank, bleak eyes at the slow throngs who, feeling, sensing without knowing, drifted before them, slowing, staring, so that they would be ringed with faces rapt and empty and immobile as the faces of cows, approaching and drifting on, to be replaced. And all morning the voices came and went, in quiet question and answer: "There he goes. That young fellow with the automatic pistol. He's the captain of them. Special officer sent by the governor. He's the head of the whole thing. Sheriff ain' got no say in it today."

Later, when it was too late, Grimm told the sheriff: "If you had just listened to me. Let me bring him out of that cell in a squad of men, instead of sending him across the square with one deputy and not even handcuffed to him, in all that crowd where that damned Buford didn't dare shoot, even if he could hit a barn door."

"How did I know he aimed to break, would think of trying it right then and there?" the sheriff said. "When Stevens had done told me he would plead guilty and take a life sentence."

But it was too late then. It was all over then. It happened in the middle of the square, halfway between the sidewalk and the courthouse, in the midst of a throng of people thick as on Fair Day, though the first that Grimm knew of it was when he heard the deputy's pistol twice, fired into the air. He knew at once what had happened, though he was at the time inside the courthouse. His reaction was definite and immediate. He was already running toward the shots when he shouted back over his shoulder at the man who had tagged him now for almost fortyeight hours as half aide and half orderly: "Turn in the fire alarm!"

"The fire alarm?" the aide said. "What—"

"Turn in the fire alarm!" Grimm shouted back. "It dont matter what folks think, just so they know that something . . ." He did not finish; he was gone.

He ran among running people, overtaking and passing them, since he had an objective and they did not; they were just running, the black, blunt, huge automatic opening a way for him like a plow. They looked at his tense, hard, young face with faces blanched and gaped, with round, toothed orifices; they made one long sound like a murmuring sigh: "There . . . went that way . . ." But already Grimm had seen the deputy, running, his pistol aloft in his hand. Grimm glanced once about and sprang forward again; in the throng which had evidently been pacing the deputy and the prisoner across the square was the inevitable hulking youth in the uniform of the Western Union, leading his bicycle by the horns like a docile cow. Grimm rammed the pistol back into the holster and flung the boy aside and sprang onto the bicycle, with never a break in motion.

The bicycle possessed neither horn nor bell. Yet they sensed him somehow and made way; in this too he seemed to be served by certitude, the blind and untroubled faith in the rightness and infallibility of his actions. When he overtook the running deputy he slowed the bicycle. The deputy turned upon him a face sweating, gaped with shouting and running. "He turned," the deputy screamed. "Into that alley by—"

"I know," Grimm said. "Was he handcuffed?"

"Yes!" the deputy said. The bicycle leaped on.

'Then he cant run very fast,' Grimm thought. 'He'll have to hole up soon. Get out of the open, anyway.' He turned into the alley, fast. It ran back between two houses, with a board fence on one side. At that moment the fire siren sounded for the first time, beginning and mounting to a slow and sustained scream that seemed at last to pass beyond the realm of hearing, into that of sense, like soundless vibration. Grimm wheeled on, thinking swiftly, logically, with a kind of fierce and constrained joy. 'The first thing he will want is to get out of sight,' he thought, looking about. On one hand the lane was open, on the other stood the board fence six feet high. At the end it was cut short off by a wooden gate, beyond which was a pasture and then a deep ditch which was a town landmark. The tops of tall trees which grew in it just showed above the rim; a regiment could hide and deploy in it. "Ah," he said, aloud. Without stopping or slowing he swept the bicycle around and pedalled back down the lane toward the street which he had just quitted. The wail of the siren was dying now, descending back into hearing again, and as he slewed the bicycle into the street he saw briefly the running people and a car bearing down upon him. For all his pedalling the car overtook him; its occupants leaned shouting toward his set, forwardlooking face. "Get in here!" they shouted. "In here!" He did not answer. He did not look at them. The car had overshot him, slowing; now he passed it at his swift, silent, steady pace; again the car speeded up and passed him, the men leaning out and looking ahead. He was going fast too, silent, with the delicate swiftness of an apparition, the implacable undeviation of Juggernaut or Fate. Behind him the siren began again its rising wail. When next the men in the car looked back for him, he had vanished completely.

He had turned full speed into another lane. His face was rocklike, calm, still bright with that expression of fulfillment, of grave and reckless joy. This lane was more rutted than the other, and deeper. It came out at last upon a barren knoll where, springing to earth while the bicycle shot on, falling, he could see the full span of the ravine along the edge of town, his view of it broken by two or three Negro cabins which lined the edge of it. He was quite motionless, still, alone, fateful, like a landmark almost. Again from the town behind him the scream of the siren began to fall.

Then he saw Christmas. He saw the man, small with distance, appear up out of the ditch, his hands close together. As Grimm watched he saw the fugitive's hands glint once like the flash of a heliograph as the sun struck the handcuffs, and it seemed to him that even from here he could hear the panting and desperate breath of the man who even now was not free. Then the tiny figure ran again and vanished beyond the nearest Negro cabin.

Grimm ran too now. He ran swiftly, yet there was no haste about him, no effort. There was nothing vengeful about him either, no fury, no outrage. Christmas saw that, himself. Because for an instant they looked at one another almost face to face. That was when Grimm, running, was in the act of passing beyond the corner of the cabin. At that instant Christmas leaped from the rear window of it, with an effect as of magic, his manacled hands high and now glinting as if they were on fire. For an instant they glared at one another, the one stopped in the act of crouching from the leap, the other in midstride of running, before Grimm's momentum carried him past the corner. In that instant he saw that Christmas now carried a heavy nickelplated pistol. Grimm whirled and turned and sprang back past the corner, drawing the automatic.

He was thinking swiftly, calmly, with that quiet joy: 'He can do two things. He can try for the ditch again, or he can dodge around the house until one of us gets a shot. And the ditch is on his side of the house.' He reacted immediately. He ran at full speed around the corner which he had just turned. He did it as though under the protection of a magic or a providence, or as if he knew that Christmas would not be waiting there with the pistol. He ran on past the next corner without pausing.

He was beside the ditch now. He stopped, motionless in midstride. Above the blunt, cold rake of the automatic his face had that serene, unearthly luminousness of angels in church windows. He was moving again almost before he had stopped, with that lean, swift, blind obedience to whatever Player moved him on the Board. He ran to the ditch. But in the beginning of his plunge downward into the brush that choked the steep descent he turned, clawing. He saw now that the cabin sat some two feet above the earth. He had not noticed it before, in his haste. He knew now that he had lost a point. That Christmas had been watching his legs all the time beneath the house. He said, "Good man."

His plunge carried him some distance before he could stop himself and climb back out. He seemed indefatigable, not flesh and blood, as if the Player who moved him for pawn likewise found him breath. Without a pause, in the same surge that carried him up out of the ditch again, he was running again. He ran around the cabin in time to see Christmas fling himself over a fence three hundred yards away. He did not fire, because Christmas was now running through a small garden and straight toward a house. Running, he saw Christmas leap up the back steps and enter the house. "Hah," Grimm said. "The preacher's house. Hightower's house."

He did not slow, though he swerved and ran around the house and to the street. The car which had passed him and lost him and then returned was just where it should have been, just where the Player had desired it to be. It stopped without signal from him and three men got out. Without a word Grimm turned and ran across the yard and into the house where the old disgraced minister lived alone, and the three men followed, rushing into the hall, pausing, bringing with them into its stale and cloistral dimness something of the savage summer sunlight which they had just left.

It was upon them, of them: its shameless savageness. Out of it their faces seemed to glare with bodiless suspension as though from haloes as they stooped and raised Hightower, his face bleeding, from the floor where Christmas, running up the hall, his raised and armed and manacled hands full of glare and glitter like lightning bolts, so that he resembled a vengeful and furious god pronouncing a doom, had struck him down. They held the old man on his feet.

"Which room?" Grimm said, shaking him. "Which room, old man?"

"Gentlemen!" Hightower said. Then he said: "Men! Men!"

"Which room, old man?" Grimm shouted.

They held Hightower on his feet; in the gloomy hall, after the sunlight, he too with his bald head and his big pale face streaked with blood, was terrible. "Men!" he cried. "Listen to me. He was here that night. He was with me the night of the murder. I swear to God—"

"Jesus Christ!" Grimm cried, his young voice clear and outraged like that of a young priest. "Has every preacher and old maid in Jefferson taken their pants down to the yellowbellied son of a bitch?" He flung the old man aside and ran on.

It was as though he had been merely waiting for the Player to move him again, because with that unfailing certitude he ran straight to the kitchen and into the doorway, already firing, almost before he could have seen the table overturned and standing on its edge across the corner of the room, and the bright and glittering hands of the man who crouched behind it, resting upon the upper edge. Grimm emptied the automatic's magazine into the table; later someone covered all five shots with a folded handkerchief.

But the Player was not done yet. When the others reached the kitchen they saw the table flung aside now and Grimm stooping over the body. When they approached to see what he was about, they saw that the man was not dead yet, and when they saw what Grimm was doing one of the men gave a choked cry and stumbled back into the wall and began to vomit. Then Grimm too sprang back, flinging behind him the bloody butcher knife. "Now you'll let white women alone, even in hell," he said. But the man on the floor had not moved. He just lay there, with his eyes open and empty of everything save consciousness, and with something, a shadow, about his mouth. For a long moment he looked up at them with peaceful and unfathomable and unbearable eyes. Then his face, body, all, seemed to collapse, to fall in upon itself, and from out the slashed garments about his hips and loins the pent black blood seemed to rush like a released breath. It seemed to rush out of his pale body like the rush of sparks from a rising rocket; upon that black blast the man seemed to rise soaring into their memories forever and ever. They are not to lose it, in whatever peaceful valleys, beside whatever placid and reassuring streams of old age, in the mirroring faces of whatever children they will contemplate old disasters and newer hopes. It will be there, musing, quiet, steadfast, not fading and not particularly threatful, but of itself alone serene, of itself alone triumphant. Again from the town, deadened a little by the walls, the scream of the siren mounted toward its unbelievable crescendo, passing out of the realm of hearing.

The Courthouse

(*A Name for the City*)

THE COURTHOUSE IS LESS OLD THAN THE TOWN, WHICH BEGAN SOME-where under the turn of the century as a Chickasaw Agency trading-post and so continued for almost thirty years before it discovered, not that it lacked a depository for its records and certainly not that it needed one, but that only by creating or anyway decreeing one, could it cope with a situation which otherwise was going to cost somebody money;

The settlement had the records; even the simple dispossession of Indians begot in time a minuscule of archive, let alone the normal litter of man's ramshackle confederation against environment—that time and that wilderness—in this case, a meagre, fading, dogeared, uncorrelated, at times illiterate sheaf of land grants and patents and transfers and deeds, and tax- and militia-rolls, and bills of sale for slaves, and counting-house lists of spurious currency and exchange rates, and liens and mortgages, and listed rewards for escaped or stolen Negroes and other livestock, and diary-like annotations of births and marriages and deaths and public hangings and land-auctions, accumulating slowly for those three decades in a sort of iron pirate's chest in the back room of the postoffice-tradingpost-store, until that day thirty years later when, because of a jailbreak compounded by an ancient monster iron padlock transported a thousand miles by horseback from Carolina, the box was removed to a small new lean-to room like a wood- or tool-shed built two days ago against one outside wall of the morticed-log mud-chinked shake-down jail; and thus was born the Yoknapatawpha County courthouse: by simple fortuity, not only less old than even the jail, but come into existence at all by chance and accident: the box containing the documents not moved from any place, but simply to one; removed from the trading-post back room not for any reason inherent in either the back room or the box, but on the contrary: which—the box—was not only in nobody's way in the back room, it was even missed when gone since it had served as another seat or

655

stool among the powder- and whiskey-kegs and firkins of salt and lard about the stove on winter nights; and was moved at all for the simple reason that suddenly the settlement (overnight it would become a town without having been a village; one day in about a hundred years it would wake frantically from its communal slumber into a rash of Rotary and Lion Clubs and Chambers of Commerce and City Beautifuls: a furious beating of hollow drums toward nowhere, but merely to sound louder than the next little human clotting to its north or south or east or west, dubbing itself city as Napoleon dubbed himself emperor and defending the expedient by padding its census rolls—a fever, a delirium in which it would confound forever seething with motion and motion with progress. But that was a hundred years away yet; now it was frontier, the men and women pioneers, tough, simple, and durable, seeking money or adventure or freedom or simple escape, and not too particular how they did it.) discovered itself faced not so much with a problem which had to be solved, as a Damocles sword of dilemma from which it had to save itself;

Even the jailbreak was fortuity: a gang—three or four—of Natchez Trace bandits (twenty-five years later legend would begin to affirm, and a hundred years later would still be at it, that two of the bandits were the Harpes themselves, Big Harpe anyway, since the circumstances, the method of the breakout left behind like a smell, an odor, a kind of gargantuan and bizarre playfulness at once humorous and terrifying, as if the settlement had fallen, blundered, into the notice or range of an idle and whimsical giant. Which— that they were the Harpes—was impossible, since the Harpes and even the last of Mason's ruffians were dead or scattered by this time, and the robbers would have had to belong to John Murrel's organization—if they needed to belong to any at all other than the simple fraternity of rapine.) captured by chance by an incidental band of civilian more-or-less militia and brought in to the Jefferson jail because it was the nearest one, the militia band being part of a general muster at Jefferson two days before for a Fourth-of-July barbecue, which by the second day had been refined by hardy elimination into one drunken brawling which rendered even the hardiest survivors vulnerable enough to be ejected from the settlement by the civilian residents, the band which was to make the capture having been carried, still comatose, in one of the evicting

wagons to a swamp four miles from Jefferson known as Hurricane
Bottoms, where they made camp to regain their strength or at least
their legs, and where that night the four—or three—bandits, on the
way across country to their hideout from their last exploit on the
Trace, stumbled onto the campfire. And here report divided; some
said that the sergeant in command of the militia recognised one of
the bandits as a deserter from his corps, others said that one of the
bandits recognised in the sergeant a former follower of his, the
bandit's, trade. Anyway, on the fourth morning all of them, captors
and prisoners, returned to Jefferson in a group, some said in confederation now seeking more drink, others said that the captors
brought their prizes back to the settlement in revenge for having
been evicted from it. Because these were frontier, pioneer times,
when personal liberty and freedom were almost a physical condition
like fire or flood, and no community was going to interfere with
anyone's morals as long as the amoralist practised somewhere else,
and so Jefferson, being neither on the Trace nor the River but lying
about midway between, naturally wanted no part of the underworld
of either;

But they had some of it now, taken as it were by surprise, unawares,
without warning to prepare and fend off. They put the bandits into
the log-and-mudchinking jail, which until now had had no lock at
all since its clients so far had been amateurs—local brawlers and
drunkards and runaway slaves—for whom a single heavy wooden
beam in slots across the outside of the door like on a corncrib, had
sufficed. But they had now what might be four—three—Dillingers
or Jesse Jameses of the time, with rewards on their heads. So they
locked the jail; they bored an auger hole through the door and
another through the jamb and passed a length of heavy chain
through the holes and sent a messenger on the run across to the
postoffice-store to fetch the ancient Carolina lock from the last
Nashville mail-pouch—the iron monster weighing almost fifteen
pounds, with a key almost as long as a bayonet, not just the only
lock in that part of the country, but the oldest lock in that cranny
of the United States, brought there by one of the three men who
were what was to be Yoknapatawpha County's coeval pioneers and
settlers, leaving in it the three oldest names—Alexander Holston,
who came as half groom and half bodyguard to Doctor Samuel
Habersham, and half nurse and half tutor to the doctor's eight-year-

old motherless son, the three of them riding horseback across Tennessee from the Cumberland Gap along with Louis Grenier, the Huguenot younger son who brought the first slaves into the country and was granted the first big land patent and so became the first cotton planter; while Doctor Habersham, with his worn black bag of pills and knives and his brawny taciturn bodyguard and his half orphan child, became the settlement itself (for a time, before it was named, the settlement was known as Doctor Habersham's, then Habersham's, then simply Habersham; a hundred years later, during a schism between two ladies' clubs over the naming of the streets in order to get free mail delivery, a movement was started, first, to change the name back to Habersham; then, failing that, to divide the town in two and call one half of it Habersham after the old pioneer doctor and founder)—friend of old Issetibbeha, the Chickasaw chief (the motherless Habersham boy, now a man of twenty-five, married one of Issetibbeha's grand-daughters and in the thirties emigrated to Oklahoma with his wife's dispossessed people), first unofficial, then official Chickasaw agent until he resigned in a letter of furious denunciation addressed to the President of the United States himself; and—his charge and pupil a man now—Alexander Holston became the settlement's first publican, establishing the tavern still known as the Holston House, the original log walls and puncheon floors and hand-morticed joints of which are still buried somewhere beneath the modern pressed glass and brick veneer and neon tubes. The lock was his;

Fifteen pounds of useless iron lugged a thousand miles through a desert of precipice and swamp, of flood and drouth and wild beasts and wild Indians and wilder white men, displacing that fifteen pounds better given to food or seed to plant food or even powder to defend with, to become a fixture, a kind of landmark, in the bar of a wilderness ordinary, locking and securing nothing, because there was nothing behind the heavy bars and shutters needing further locking and securing; not even a paper weight because the only papers in the Holston House were the twisted spills in an old powder horn above the mantel for lighting tobacco; always a little in the way, since it had constantly to be moved: from bar to shelf to mantel then back to bar again until they finally thought about putting it on the bi-monthly mail-pouch; familiar, known, presently the oldest unchanged thing in the settlement, older than the people since Issetibbeha and Doctor Habersham were dead, and Alexander Holston was an old man crippled with arthritis, and Louis Grenier had a settlement of his own on his vast plantation, half of which was not even in Yoknapatawpha County, and the settlement rarely saw him; older than the town, since there were new names in it now even when the old blood ran in them—Sartoris and Stevens, Compson and McCaslin and Sutpen and Coldfield—and you no longer shot a bear or deer or wild turkey simply by standing for a while in your kitchen door, not to mention the pouch of mail— letters and even newspapers—which came from Nashville every two weeks by a special rider who did nothing else and was paid a salary for it by the Federal Government; and that was the second phase of the monster Carolina lock's transubstantiation into the Yoknapatawpha County courthouse;

The pouch didn't always reach the settlement every two weeks, nor even always every month. But sooner or later it did, and everybody knew it would, because it—the cowhide saddlebag not even large enough to hold a full change of clothing, containing three or four letters and half that many badly-printed one- and two-sheet newspapers already three or four months out of date and usually half and sometimes wholly misinformed or incorrect to begin with —was the United States, the power and the will to liberty, owning liegence to no man, bringing even into that still almost pathless wilderness the thin peremptory voice of the nation which had wrenched its freedom from one of the most powerful peoples on earth and then again within the same lifespan successfully defended it; so peremptory and audible that the man who carried the pouch on the galloping horse didn't even carry any arms except a tin horn, traversing month after month, blatantly, flagrantly, almost contemptuously, a region where for no more than the boots on his feet, men would murder a traveller and gut him like a bear or deer or fish and fill the cavity with rocks and sink the evidence in the nearest water; not even deigning to pass quietly where other men, even though armed and in parties, tried to move secretly or at least without uproar, but instead announcing his solitary advent as far ahead of himself as the ring of the horn would carry. So it was not long before Alexander Holston's lock had moved to the mail-pouch. Not that the pouch needed one, having come already the three hundred miles from Nashville without a lock. (It had been projected at first that the lock remain on the pouch constantly. That is, not just while the pouch was in the settlement, but while it was on the horse between Nashville and the settlement too. The rider refused, succinctly, in three words, one of which was printable. His reason was the lock's weight. They pointed out to him that this would not hold water, since not only—the rider was a frail irascible little man weighing less than a hundred pounds—would the fifteen pounds of lock even then fail to bring his weight up to that of a normal adult male, the added weight of the lock would merely match that of the pistols which his employer, the United States Government, believed he carried and even paid him for having done so, the rider's reply to this being succinct too though not so glib: that the lock weighed fifteen pounds either at the back door of the store in the settlement, or at that of the postoffice in Nashville. But since Nashville and the settlement were three hundred miles apart, by the time the horse had carried it from one to the other, the lock weighed fifteen pounds to the mile times three hundred miles, or forty-five hundred pounds. Which was manifest nonsense, a physical impossibility either in lock or horse. Yet indubitably fifteen pounds times three hundred miles was forty-five hundred something, either pounds or miles—especially as while they were still trying to unravel it, the rider repeated his first three succinct—two unprintable—words.) So less than ever would the pouch need a lock in the back room of the trading-post, surrounded and enclosed once more by civilization, where its very intactness, its presence to receive a lock, proved its lack of that need during the three hundred miles of rapine-haunted Trace; needing a lock as little as it was equipped to receive one, since it had been necessary to slit the leather with a knife just under each jaw of the opening and insert the lock's iron mandible through the two slits and clash it home, so that any other hand with a similar knife could have cut the whole lock from the pouch as easily as it had been clasped onto it. So the old lock was not even a symbol of security: it was a gesture of salutation, of free men to free men, of civilization to civilization across not just the three hundred miles of wilderness to Nashville, but the fifteen hundred to Washington: of respect without servility, allegiance without abasement to the government which they had helped to found and had accepted with pride but still as free men, still free to withdraw from it at any moment when the two of them found themselves no longer compatible, the old lock meeting the pouch each time on its arrival, to clasp it in iron and inviolable symbolism, while old Alec Holston, childless bachelor, grew a little older and grayer, a little more arthritic in flesh and temper too, a little stiffer and more rigid in bone and pride too, since the lock was still his, he had merely lent it, and so in a sense he was the grandfather in the settlement of the inviolability not just of government mail, but of a free government of free men too, so long as the government remembered to let men live free, not under it but beside it;

That was the lock; they put it on the jail. They did it quickly, not even waiting until a messenger could have got back from the Holston House with old Alec's permission to remove it from the mail-pouch or use it for the new purpose. Not that he would have objected on principle nor refused his permission except by simple instinct; that is, he would probably have been the first to suggest the lock if he had known in time or thought of it first, but he would have refused at once if he thought the thing was contemplated without consulting him. Which everybody in the settlement knew, though this was not at all why they didn't wait for the messenger. In fact, no messenger had ever been sent to old Alec; they didn't have time to send one, let alone wait until he got back; they didn't want the lock to keep the bandits in, since (as was later proved) the old lock would have been no more obstacle for the bandits to pass than the customary wooden bar; they didn't need the lock to protect the settlement from the bandits, but to protect the bandits from the settlement. Because the prisoners had barely reached the settlement when it developed that there was a faction bent on lynching them at once, out of hand, without preliminary—a small but determined gang which tried to wrest the prisoners from their captors while the militia was still trying to find someone to surrender them to, and would have succeeded except for a man named Compson, who had come to the settlement a few years ago with a race-horse, which he swapped to Ikkemotubbe, Issetibbeha's successor in the chiefship, for a square mile of what was to be the most valuable land in the future town of Jefferson, who, legend said, drew a pistol and held the ravishers at bay until the bandits could be got into the jail and the auger holes bored and someone sent to fetch old Alec Holston's lock. Because there were indeed new names and faces too in the settlement now—faces so new as to have (to the older residents) no discernible antecedents other than mamma-

linity, nor past other than the simple years which had scored them;
and names so new as to have no discernible (nor discoverable
either) antecedents or past at all, as though they had been invented
yesterday, report dividing again: to the effect that there were more
people in the settlement that day than the militia sergeant whom
one or all of the bandits might recognise;

So Compson locked the jail, and a courier with the two best horses
in the settlement—one to ride and one to lead—cut through the
woods to the Trace to ride the hundred-odd miles to Natchez with
news of the capture and authority to dicker for the reward; and
that evening in the Holston House kitchen was held the settlement's
first municipal meeting, prototype not only of the town council after
the settlement would be a town, but of the Chamber of Commerce
when it would begin to proclaim itself a city, with Compson presiding, not old Alec, who was quite old now, grim, taciturn, sitting
even on a hot July night before a smoldering log in his vast chimney, his back even turned to the table (he was not interested in
the deliberation; the prisoners were his already since his lock held
them; whatever the conference decided would have to be submitted
to him for ratification anyway before anyone could touch his lock to
open it) around which the progenitors of the Jefferson city fathers
sat in what was almost a council of war, not only discussing the
collecting of the reward, but the keeping and defending it. Because
there were two factions of opposition now: not only the lynching
party, but the militia band too, who now claimed that as prizes the
prisoners still belonged to their original captors; that they—the
militia—had merely surrendered the prisoners' custody but had
relinquished nothing of any reward: on the prospect of which, the
militia band had got more whiskey from the trading-post store and
had built a tremendous bonfire in front of the jail, around which
they and the lynching party had now confederated in a wassail or
conference of their own. Or so they thought. Because the truth was
that Compson, in the name of a crisis in the public peace and
welfare, had made a formal demand on the professional bag of
Doctor Peabody, old Doctor Habersham's successor, and the three
of them—Compson, Peabody, and the post trader (his name was
Ratcliffe; a hundred years later it would still exist in the county, but
by that time it had passed through two inheritors who had dispensed with the eye in the transmission of words, using only the

ear, so that by the time the fourth one had been compelled by simple necessity to learn to write it again, it had lost the 'c' and the final 'fe' too) added the laudanum to the keg of whiskey and sent it as a gift from the settlement to the astonished militia sergeant, and returned to the Holston House kitchen to wait until the last of the uproar died; then the law-and-order party made a rapid sortie and gathered up all the comatose opposition, lynchers and captors too, and dumped them all into the jail with the prisoners and locked the door again and went home to bed—until the next morning, when the first arrivals were met by a scene resembling an outdoor stage setting: which was how the legend of the mad Harpes started: a thing not just fantastical but incomprehensible, not just whimsical but a little terrifying (though at least it was bloodless, which would have contented neither Harpe): not just the lock gone from the door nor even just the door gone from the jail, but the entire wall gone, the mud-chinked axe-morticed logs unjointed neatly and quietly in the darkness and stacked as neatly to one side, leaving the jail open to the world like a stage on which the late insurgents still lay sprawled and various in deathlike slumber, the whole settlement gathered now to watch Compson trying to kick at least one of them awake, until one of the Holston slaves—the cook's husband, the waiter-groom-hostler—ran into the crowd shouting, 'Whar de lock, whar de lock, ole Boss say whar de lock.'

It was gone (as were three horses belonging to three of the lynching faction). They couldn't even find the heavy door and the chain, and at first they were almost betrayed into believing that the bandits had had to take the door in order to steal the chain and lock, catching themselves back from the very brink of this wanton accusation of rationality. But the lock was gone; nor did it take the settlement long to realise that it was not the escaped bandits and the aborted reward, but the lock, and not a simple situation which faced them, but a problem which threatened, the slave departing back to the Holston House at a dead run and then reappearing at the dead run almost before the door, the walls, had had time to hide him, engulf and then eject him again, darting through the crowd and up to Compson himself now, saying, 'Ole Boss say fetch de lock'—not send the lock, but bring the lock. So Compson and his lieutenants (and this was where the mail rider began to appear, or rather, to emerge

—the fragile wisp of a man ageless, hairless and toothless, who looked too frail even to approach a horse, let alone ride one six hundred miles every two weeks, yet who did so, and not only that but had wind enough left not only to announce and precede but even follow his passing with the jeering musical triumph of the horn:—a contempt for possible—probable—despoilers matched only by that for the official dross of which he might be despoiled, and which agreed to remain in civilised bounds only so long as the despoilers had the taste to refrain)—repaired to the kitchen where old Alec still sat before his smoldering log, his back still to the room, and still not turning it this time either. And that was all. He ordered the immediate return of his lock. It was not even an ultimatum, it was a simple instruction, a decree, impersonal, the mail rider now well into the fringe of the group, saying nothing and missing nothing, like a weightless desiccated or fossil bird, not a vulture of course nor even quite a hawk, but say a pterodactyl chick arrested just out of the egg ten glaciers ago and so old in simple infancy as to be the worn and weary ancestor of all subsequent life. They pointed out to old Alec that the only reason the lock could be missing was that the bandits had not had time or been able to cut it out of the door, and that even three fleeing madmen on stolen horses would not carry a six-foot oak door very far, and that a party of Ikkemotubbe's young men were even now trailing the horses westward toward the River and that without doubt the lock would be found at any moment, probably under the first bush at the edge of the settlement: knowing better, knowing that there was no limit to the fantastic and the terrifying and the bizarre, of which the men were capable who already, just to escape from a log jail, had quietly removed one entire wall and stacked it in neat piecemeal at the roadside, and that they nor old Alec neither would ever see his lock again;

Nor did they; the rest of that afternoon and all the next day too, while old Alec still smoked his pipe in front of his smoldering log, the settlement's sheepish and raging elders hunted for it, with (by now: the next afternoon) Ikkemotubbe's Chickasaws helping too, or anyway present, watching: the wild men, the wilderness's tameless evictant children looking only the more wild and homeless for the white man's denim and butternut and felt and straw which they wore, standing or squatting or following, grave, attentive and inter-

ested, while the white men sweated and cursed among the bordering thickets of their punily-clawed foothold; and always the rider,
Pettigrew, ubiquitous, everywhere, not helping search himself and
never in anyone's way, but always present, inscrutable, saturnine,
missing nothing: until at last toward sundown Compson crashed
savagely out of the last bramble-brake and flung the sweat from
his face with a full-armed sweep sufficient to repudiate a throne,
and said,

'All right, god damn it, we'll pay him for it.' Because they had
already considered that last gambit; they had already realised its
seriousness from the very fact that Peabody had tried to make a
joke about it which everyone knew that even Peabody did not think
humorous:

'Yes—and quick too, before he has time to advise with Pettigrew
and price it by the pound.'

'By the pound?' Compson said.

'Pettigrew just weighed it by the three hundred miles from Nashville. Old Alec might start from Carolina. That's fifteen thousand
pounds.'

'Oh,' Compson said. So he blew in his men by means of a foxhorn
which one of the Indians wore on a thong around his neck, though
even then they paused for one last quick conference; again it was
Peabody who stopped them.

'Who'll pay for it?' he said. 'It would be just like him to want a
dollar a pound for it, even if by Pettigrew's scale he had found it
in the ashes of his fireplace.' They—Compson anyway—had probably already thought of that; that, as much as Pettigrew's presence,
was probably why he was trying to rush them into old Alec's presence with the offer so quickly that none would have the face to
renege on a pro-rata share. But Peabody had torn it now. Compson
looked about at them, sweating, grimly enraged.

'That means Peabody will probably pay one dollar,' he said. 'Who
pays the other fourteen? Me?' Then Ratcliffe, the trader, the store's
proprietor, solved it—a solution so simple, so limitless in retroact,
that they didn't even wonder why nobody had thought of it before;
which not only solved the problem but abolished it; and not just
that one, but all problems, from now on into perpetuity, opening
to their vision like the rending of a veil, like a glorious prophecy,
the vast splendid limitless panorama of America: that land of
boundless opportunity, that bourne, created not by nor of the peo-

ple, but for the people, as was the heavenly manna of old, with no
return demand on man save the chewing and swallowing since out
of its own matchless Allgood it would create produce train support
and perpetuate a race of laborers dedicated to the single purpose
of picking the manna up and putting it into his lax hand or even
between his jaws—illimitable, vast, without beginning or end, not
even a trade or a craft but a beneficence as are sunlight and rain
and air, inalienable and immutable.

'Put it on the Book,' Ratcliffe said—the Book: not a ledger, but
the ledger, since it was probably the only thing of its kind between
Nashville and Natchez, unless there might happen to be a similar
one a few miles south at the first Choctaw agency at Yalo Busha—
a ruled, paper-backed copybook such as might have come out of a
schoolroom, in which accrued, with the United States as debtor, in
Mohataha's name (the Chickasaw matriarch, Ikkemotubbe's mother
and old Issetibbeha's sister, who—she could write her name, or anyway make something with a pen or pencil which was agreed to be,
or at least accepted to be, a valid signature—signed all the con-
veyances as her son's kingdom passed to the white people, regular-
ising it in law anyway) the crawling tedious list of calico and gun-
powder, whiskey and salt and snuff and denim pants and osseous
candy drawn from Ratcliffe's shelves by her descendants and sub-
jects and Negro slaves. That was all the settlement had to do: add
the lock to the list, the account. It wouldn't even matter at what
price they entered it. They could have priced it on Pettigrew's scale
of fifteen pounds times the distance not just to Carolina but to
Washington itself, and nobody would ever notice it probably; they
could have charged the United States with seventeen thousand five
hundred dollars' worth of the fossilised and indestructible candy,
and none would ever read the entry. So it was solved, done, finished, ended. They didn't even have to discuss it. They didn't even
think about it any more, unless perhaps here and there to marvel
(a little speculatively probably) at their own moderation, since they
wanted nothing—least of all, to escape any just blame—but a fair
and decent adjustment of the lock. They went back to where old
Alec still sat with his pipe in front of his dim hearth. Only they had
overestimated him; he didn't want any money at all, he wanted his
lock. Whereupon what little remained of Compson's patience went
too.

'Your lock's gone,' he told old Alec harshly. 'You'll take fifteen dollars for it,' he said, his voice already fading, because even that rage could recognise impasse when it saw it. Nevertheless, the rage, the impotence, the sweating, the *too much*—whatever it was— forced the voice on for one word more: 'Or—' before it stopped for good and allowed Peabody to fill the gap:

'Or else?' Peabody said, and not to old Alec, but to Compson. 'Or else what?' Then Ratcliffe saved that too.

'Wait,' he said. 'Uncle Alec's going to take fifty dollars for his lock. A guarantee of fifty dollars. He'll give us the name of the blacksmith back in Cal'lina that made it for him, and we'll send back there and have a new one made. Going and coming and all'll cost about fifty dollars. We'll give Uncle Alec the fifty dollars to hold as a guarantee. Then when the new lock comes, he'll give us back the money. All right, Uncle Alec?' And that could have been all of it. It probably would have been, except for Pettigrew. It was not that they had forgotten him, nor even assimilated him. They had simply sealed—healed him off (so they thought)—him into their civic crisis as the desperate and defenseless oyster immobilises its atom of inevictable grit. Nobody had seen him move yet he now stood in the center of them where Compson and Ratcliffe and Peabody faced old Alec in the chair. You might have said that he had oozed there, except for that adamantine quality which might (in emergency) become invisible but never insubstantial and never in this world fluid; he spoke in a voice bland, reasonable and impersonal, then stood there being looked at, frail and child-sized, impermeable as diamond and manifest with portent, bringing into that backwoods room a thousand miles deep in pathless wilderness, the whole vast incalculable weight of federality, not just representing the government nor even himself just the government; for that moment at least, he was the United States.

'Uncle Alec hasn't lost any lock,' he said. 'That was Uncle Sam.'

After a moment someone said, 'What?'

'That's right,' Pettigrew said. 'Whoever put that lock of Holston's on that mail bag either made a voluntary gift to the United States, and the same law covers the United States Government that covers minor children: you can give something to them, but you can't take it back, or he or they done something else.'

They looked at him. Again after a while somebody said something; it was Ratcliffe. 'What else?' Ratcliffe said. Pettigrew answered, still bland, impersonal, heatless and glib: 'Committed a violation of act of Congress as especially made and provided for the defacement of government property, penalty of five thousand dollars or not less than one year in a Federal jail or both. For whoever cut them two slits in the bag to put the lock in, act of Congress as especially made and provided for the injury or destruction of government property, penalty of ten thousand dollars or not less than five years in a Federal jail or both.' He did not move even yet; he simply spoke directly to old Alec: 'I reckon you're going to have supper here same as usual sooner or later or more or less.'

'Wait,' Ratcliffe said. He turned to Compson. 'Is that true?'

'What the hell difference does it make whether it's true or not?' Compson said. 'What do you think he's going to do as soon as he gets to Nashville?' He said violently to Pettigrew: 'You were supposed to leave for Nashville yesterday. What were you hanging around here for?'

'Nothing to go to Nashville for,' Pettigrew said. 'You dont want any mail. You aint got anything to lock it up with.'

'So we aint,' Ratcliffe said. 'So we'll let the United States find the United States' lock.' This time Pettigrew looked at no one. He wasn't even speaking to anyone, any more than old Alec had been when he decreed the return of his lock:

'Act of Congress as made and provided for the unauthorised removal and or use or willful or felonious use or misuse or loss of government property, penalty the value of the article plus five hundred to ten thousand dollars or thirty days to twenty years in a Federal jail or both. They may even make a new one when they read where you have charged a postoffice department lock to the Bureau of Indian Affairs.' He moved; now he was speaking to old Alec again: 'I'm going out to my horse. When this meeting is over and you get back to cooking, you can send your nigger for me.'

Then he was gone. After a while Ratcliffe said, 'What do you reckon he aims to get out of this? A reward?' But that was wrong; they all knew better than that.

'He's already getting what he wants,' Compson said, and cursed again. 'Confusion. Just damned confusion.' But that was wrong too; they all knew that too, though it was Peabody who said it:

'No. Not confusion. A man who will ride six hundred miles through this country every two weeks, with nothing for protection but a foxhorn, aint really interested in confusion any more than he is in money.' So they didn't know yet what was in Pettigrew's mind.

But they knew what he would do. That is, they knew that they did not know at all, either what he would do, or how, or when, and that there was nothing whatever that they could do about it until they discovered why. And they saw now that they had no possible means to discover that; they realised now that they had known him for three years now, during which, fragile and inviolable and undeviable and preceded for a mile or more by the strong sweet ringing of the horn, on his strong and tireless horse he would complete the bi-monthly trip from Nashville to the settlement and for the next three or four days would live among them, yet that they knew nothing whatever about him, and even now knew only that they dared not, simply dared not, take any chance, sitting for a while longer in the darkening room while old Alec still smoked, his back still squarely turned to them and their quandary too; then dispersing to their own cabins for the evening meal—with what appetite they could bring to it, since presently they had drifted back through the summer darkness when by ordinary they would have been already in bed, to the back room of Ratcliffe's store now, to sit again while Ratcliffe recapitulated in his mixture of bewilderment and alarm (and something else which they recognised was respect as they realised that he—Ratcliffe—was unshakably convinced that Pettigrew's aim was money; that Pettigrew had invented or evolved a scheme so richly rewarding that he—Ratcliffe—had not only been unable to forestall him and do it first, he—Ratcliffe—couldn't even guess what it was after he had been given a hint) until Compson interrupted him.

'Hell,' Compson said. 'Everybody knows what's wrong with him. It's ethics. He's a damned moralist.'

'Ethics?' Peabody said. He sounded almost startled. He said quickly: 'That's bad. How can we corrupt an ethical man?'

'Who wants to corrupt him?' Compson said. 'All we want him to do is stay on that damned horse and blow whatever extra wind he's got into that damned horn.'

But Peabody was not even listening. He said, 'Ethics,' almost dreamily. He said, 'Wait.' They watched him. He said suddenly to Ratcliffe: 'I've heard it somewhere. If anybody here knows it, it'll be you. What's his name?'

'His name?' Ratcliffe said. 'Pettigrew's? Oh. His christian name.' Ratcliffe told him. 'Why?'

'Nothing,' Peabody said. 'I'm going home. Anybody else coming?'

He spoke directly to nobody and said and would say no more, but
that was enough: a straw perhaps, but at least a straw; enough anyway for the others to watch and say nothing either as Compson got
up to and said to Ratcliffe:

'You coming?' and the three of them walked away together, beyond earshot then beyond sight too. Then Compson said, 'All right.
What?'

'It may not work,' Peabody said. 'But you two will have to back
me up. When I speak for the whole settlement, you and Ratcliffe
will have to make it stick. Will you?'

Compson cursed. 'But at least tell us a little of what we're going
to guarantee.' So Peabody told them, some of it, and the next morning entered the stall in the Holston House stable where Pettigrew
was grooming his ugly hammer-headed ironmuscled horse.

'We decided not to charge that lock to old Mohataha, after all,'
Peabody said.

'That so?' Pettigrew said. 'Nobody in Washington would ever
catch it. Certainly not the ones that can read.'

'We're going to pay for it ourselves,' Peabody said. 'In fact, we're
going to do a little more. We've got to repair that jail wall anyhow;
we've got to build one wall anyway. So by building three more, we
will have another room. We got to build one anyway, so that dont
count. So by building an extra three-wall room, we will have another four-wall house. That will be the courthouse.' Pettigrew had
been hissing gently between his teeth at each stroke of the brush,
like a professional Irish groom. Now he stopped, the brush and his
hand arrested in midstroke, and turned his head a little.

'Courthouse?'

'We're going to have a town,' Peabody said. 'We already got a
church—that's Whitfield's cabin. And we're going to build a school
too soon as we get around to it. But we're going to build the courthouse today; we've already got something to put in it to make it a
courthouse: that iron box that's been in Ratcliffe's way in the store
for the last ten years. Then we'll have a town. We've already even
named her.'

Now Pettigrew stood up, very slowly. They looked at one another.
After a moment Pettigrew said, 'So?'

'Ratcliffe says your name's Jefferson,' Peabody said.

'That's right,' Pettigrew said. 'Thomas Jefferson Pettigrew. I'm
from old Ferginny.'

'Any kin?' Peabody said.

'No,' Pettigrew said. 'My ma named me for him, so I would have some of his luck.'

'Luck?' Peabody said.

Pettigrew didn't smile. 'That's right. She didn't mean luck. She never had any schooling. She didn't know the word she wanted to say.'

'Have you had it?' Peabody said. Nor did Pettigrew smile now. 'I'm sorry,' Peabody said. 'Try to forget it.' He said: 'We decided to name her Jefferson.' Now Pettigrew didn't seem to breathe even. He just stood there, small, frail, less than boysize, childless and bachelor, incorrigibly kinless and tieless, looking at Peabody. Then he breathed, and raising the brush, he turned back to the horse and for an instant Peabody thought he was going back to the grooming. But instead of making the stroke, he laid the hand and the brush against the horse's flank and stood for a moment, his face turned away and his head bent a little. Then he raised his head and turned his face back toward Peabody.

'You could call that lock 'axle grease' on that Indian account,' he said.

'Fifty dollars' worth of axle grease?' Peabody said.

'To grease the wagons for Oklahoma,' Pettigrew said.

'So we could,' Peabody said. 'Only her name's Jefferson now. We cant ever forget that any more now.' And that was the courthouse—the courthouse which it had taken them almost thirty years not only to realise they didn't have, but to discover that they hadn't even needed, missed, lacked; and which, before they had owned it six months, they discovered was nowhere near enough. Because somewhere between the dark of that first day and the dawn of the next, something happened to them. They began that same day; they restored the jail wall and cut new logs and split out shakes and raised the little floorless lean-to against it and moved the iron chest from Ratcliffe's back room; it took only the two days and cost nothing but the labor and not much of that per capita since the whole settlement was involved to a man, not to mention the settlement's two slaves—Holston's man and the one belonging to the German blacksmith—; Ratcliffe too, all he had to do was put up the bar across the inside of his back door, since his entire patronage was countable in one glance sweating and cursing among the logs and shakes of the half dismantled jail across the way opposite—including Ikke-

motubbe's Chickasaw, though these were neither sweating nor cursing: the grave dark men dressed in their Sunday clothes except for
the trousers, pants, which they carried rolled neatly under their
arms or perhaps tied by the two legs around their necks like capes
or rather hussars' dolmans where they had forded the creek, squatting or lounging along the shade, courteous, interested, and reposed
(even old Mohataha herself, the matriarch, barefoot in a purple silk
gown and a plumed hat, sitting in a gilt brocade empire chair in a
wagon behind two mules, under a silver-handled Paris parasol held
by a female slave child)—because they (the other white men, his
confreres, or—during this first day—his co-victims) had not yet remarked the thing—quality—something—esoteric, eccentric, in Ratcliffe's manner, attitude,—not an obstruction nor even an impedi-
ment, not even when on the second day they discovered what it
was, because he was among them, busy too, sweating and cursing
too, but rather like a single chip, infinitesimal, on an otherwise
broken flood or tide, a single body or substance, alien and unrecon-
ciled, a single thin almost unheard voice crying thinly out of the
roar of a mob: 'Wait, look here, listen—'

Because they were too busy raging and sweating among the dismantled logs and felling the new ones in the adjacent woods and
trimming and notching and dragging them out and mixing the tenu-
ous clay mud to chink them together with; it was not until the second day that they learned what was troubling Ratcliffe, because
now they had time, the work going no slower, no lessening of sweat
but on the contrary, if anything the work going even a little faster
because now there was a lightness in the speed and all that was
abated was the rage and the outrage, because somewhere between
the dark and the dawn of the first and the second day, something had
happened to them—the men who had spent that first long hot endless July day sweating and raging about the wrecked jail, flinging
indiscriminately and savagely aside the dismantled logs and the
log-like laudanum-smitten inmates in order to rebuild the one, cursing old Holston and the lock and the four—three—bandits and the
eleven militiamen who had arrested them, and Compson and Pettigrew and Peabody and the United States of America—the same
men met at the project before sunrise on the next day which was
already promising to be hot and endless too, but with the rage and
the fury absent now, quiet, not grave so much as sobered, a little

amazed, diffident, blinking a little perhaps, looking a little aside
from one another, a little unfamiliar even to one another in the new
jonquil-colored light, looking about them at the meagre huddle of
crude cabins set without order and every one a little awry to every
other and all dwarfed to doll-houses by the vast loom of the woods
which enclosed them—the tiny clearing clawed punily not even
into the flank of pathless wilderness but into the loin, the groin, the
secret parts, which was the irrevocable cast die of their lives, fates,
pasts and futures—not even speaking for a while yet since each one
probably believed (a little shamefaced too) that the thought was
solitarily his, until at last one spoke for all and then it was all right
since it had taken one conjoined breath to shape that sound, the
speaker speaking not loud, diffidently, tentatively, as you insert the
first light tentative push of wind into the mouthpiece of a strange
untried foxhorn: 'By God. Jefferson.'

'Jefferson, Mississippi,' a second added.

'Jefferson, Yoknapatawpha County, Mississippi,' a third corrected;
who, which one, didn't matter this time either since it was still one
conjoined breathing, one compound dream-state, mused and static,
well capable of lasting on past sunrise too, though they probably
knew better too since Compson was still there: the gnat, the thorn,
the catalyst.

'It aint until we finish the goddamned thing,' Compson said.
'Come on. Let's get at it.' So they finished it that day, working rapidly now, with speed and lightness too, concentrated yet inattentive,
to get it done and that quickly, not to finish it but to get it out of
the way, behind them; not to finish it quickly in order to own, possess it sooner, but to be able to obliterate, efface, it the sooner, as
if they had also known in that first yellow light that it would not be
near enough, would not even be the beginning; that the little lean-to
room they were building would not even be a pattern and could not
even be called practice, working on until noon, the hour to stop and
eat, by which time Louis Grenier had arrived from Frenchman's
Bend (his plantation: his manor, his kitchens and stables and kennels and slave quarters and gardens and promenades and fields
which a hundred years later will have vanished, his name and his
blood too, leaving nothing but the name of his plantation and his
own fading corrupted legend like a thin layer of the native ephemeral yet inevictable dust on a section of country surrounding a little lost paintless crossroads store) twenty miles away behind a slave

coachman and footman in his imported English carriage and what was said to be the finest matched team outside of Natchez or Nashville, and Compson said, 'I reckon that'll do'—all knowing what he meant: not abandonment: to complete it, of course, but so little remained now that the two slaves could finish it. The four in fact, since, although as soon as it was assumed that the two Grenier Negroes would lend the two local ones a hand, Compson demurred on the grounds that who would dare violate the rigid protocol of bondage by ordering a stable-servant, let alone a house-servant, to do manual labor, not to mention having the temerity to approach old Louis Grenier with the suggestion, Peabody nipped that at once.

'One of them can use my shadow,' he said. 'It never blenched out there with a white doctor standing in it,' and even offered to be emissary to old Grenier, except that Grenier himself forestalled them. So they ate Holston's noon ordinary, while the Chickasaws, squatting unmoving still where the creep of shade had left them in the full fierce glare of July noon about the wagon where old Mohataha still sat under her slave-borne Paris parasol, ate their lunches too which (Mohataha's and her personal retinue's came out of a woven whiteoak withe fishbasket in the wagonbed) they appeared to have carried in from what, patterning the white people, they called their plantation too, under their arms inside the rolled-up trousers. Then they moved back to the front gallery and —not the settlement any more now: the town; it had been a town for thirty-one hours now—watched the four slaves put up the final log and pin down the final shake on the roof and hang the door, and then, Ratcliffe leading something like the court chamberlain across a castle courtyard, cross back to the store and enter and emerge carrying the iron chest, the grave Chickasaws watching too the white man's slaves sweating the white man's ponderable dense inscrutable medicine into its new shrine. And now they had time to find out what was bothering Ratcliffe.

'That lock,' Ratcliffe said.

'What?' somebody said.

'That Indian axle-grease,' Ratcliffe said.

'What?' they said again. But they knew, understood, now. It was neither lock nor axle-grease; it was the fifteen dollars which could have been charged to the Indian Department on Ratcliffe's books and nobody would have ever found it, noticed it, missed it. It was not greed on Ratcliffe's part, and least of all was he advocating corruption. The idea was not even new to him; it did not need any casual man on a horse riding in to the settlement once every two or three weeks, to reveal to him that possibility; he had thought of that the first time he had charged the first sack of peppermint candy to the first one of old Mohataha's forty-year-old grandchildren and had refrained from adding two zeroes to the ten or fifteen cents for ten years now, wondering each time why he did refrain, amazed at his own virtue or at least his strength of will. It was a matter of principle. It was he—they: the settlement (town now)—who had thought of charging the lock to the United States as a provable lock, a communal risk, a concrete ineradicable object, win lose or draw, let the chips fall where they may, on that dim day when some Federal inspector might, just barely might, audit the Chickasaw affairs; it was the United States itself which had voluntarily offered to show them how to transmute the inevictable lock into proofless and ephemeral axle grease—the little scrawny childsized man, solitary unarmed impregnable and unalarmed, not even defying them, not even advocate and representative of the United States, but *the* United States, as though the United States had said, 'Please accept a gift of fifteen dollars,' (the town had actually paid old Alec fifteen dollars for the lock; he would accept no more) and they had not even declined it but simply abolished it since, as soon as Pettigrew breathed it into sound, the United States had already forever lost it; as though Pettigrew had put the actual ponderable fifteen gold coins into—say, Compson's or Peabody's—hands and they had dropped them down a rathole or a well, doing no man any good, neither restoration to the ravaged nor emolument to the ravager, leaving in fact the whole race of man, as long as it endured, forever and irrevocably fifteen dollars deficit, fifteen dollars in the red;

That was Ratcliffe's trouble. But they didn't even listen. They heard him out of course, but they didn't even listen. Or perhaps they didn't even hear him either, sitting along the shade on Holston's gallery, looking, seeing, already a year away; it was barely the tenth of July; there was the long summer, the bright soft dry fall until the November rains, but they would require not two days this time but two years and maybe more, with a winter of planning and preparation before hand. They even had an instrument available and waiting, like providence almost: a man named Sutpen who had come into the settlement that same spring—a big gaunt friendless

passion-worn untalkative man who walked in a fading aura of anonymity and violence like a man just entered a warm room or at least
a shelter, out of a blizzard, bringing with him thirty-odd men slaves
even wilder and more equivocal than the native wild men, the
Chickasaws, to whom the settlement had become accustomed, who
(the new Negroes) spoke no English but instead what Compson,
who had visited New Orleans, said was the Carib-Spanish-French
of the Sugar Islands, and who (Sutpen) had bought or proved on
or anyway acquired a tract of land in the opposite direction and
was apparently bent on establishing a place on an even more am-
bitious and grandiose scale than Grenier's; he had even brought with
him a tame Parisian architect—or captive rather, since it was said
in Ratcliffe's back room that the man slept at night in a kind of pit
at the site of the chateau he was planning, tied wrist to wrist with
one of his captor's Carib slaves; indeed, the settlement had only to
see him once to know that he was no dociler than his captor, any
more than the weasel or rattlesnake is no less untame than the wolf
or bear before which it gives way until completely and hopelessly
cornered:—a man no larger than Pettigrew, with humorous sardonic
undefeated eyes which had seen everything and believed none of it,
in the broad expensive hat and brocaded waistcoat and ruffled
wrists of a half-artist half-boulevardier; and they—Compson perhaps, Peabody certainly—could imagine him in his mudstained
brierslashed brocade and lace standing in a trackless wilderness
dreaming colonnades and porticoes and fountains and promenades
in the style of David, with just behind each elbow an identical
giant half-naked Negro not even watching him, only breathing,
moving each time he took a step or shifted like his shadow repeated in two and blown to gigantic size;

So they even had an architect. He listened to them for perhaps a
minute in Ratcliffe's back room. Then he made an indescribable
gesture and said, 'Bah. You do not need advice. You are too poor.
You have only your hands, and clay to make good brick. You dont
have any money. You dont even have anything to copy: how can
you go wrong?' But he taught them how to mold the brick; he
designed and built the kiln to bake the brick in, plenty of them
since they had probably known from that first yellow morning too
that one edifice was not going to be enough. But although both
were conceived in the same instant and planned simultaneously

during the same winter and built in continuation during the next
three years, the courthouse of course came first, and in March, with
stakes and hanks of fishline, the architect laid out in a grove of oaks
opposite the tavern and the store, the square and simple founda-
tions, the irrevocable design not only of the courthouse but of the
town too, telling them as much: 'In fifty years you will be trying to
change it in the name of what you will call progress. But you will
fail; but you will never be able to get away from it.' But they had
already seen that, standing thigh-deep in wilderness also but with
more than a vision to look at since they had at least the fishline and
the stakes, perhaps less than fifty years, perhaps—who knew?—less
than twenty-five even: a Square, the courthouse in its grove the
center; quadrangular around it, the stores, two-storey, the offices of
the lawyers and doctors and dentists, the lodge-rooms and audi-
toriums, above them; school and church and tavern and bank and
jail each in its ordered place; the four broad diverging avenues
straight as plumb-lines in the four directions, becoming the network
of roads and by-roads until the whole county would be covered with
it: the hands, the prehensile fingers clawing dragging lightward out
of the disappearing wilderness year by year as up from the bottom
of the receding sea, the broad rich fecund burgeoning fields, pushing thrusting each year further and further back the wilderness and
its denizens—the wild bear and deer and turkey, and the wild men
(or not so wild any more, familiar now, harmless now, just obsolete:
anachronism out of an old dead time and a dead age; regrettable
of course, even actually regretted by the old men, fiercely as old Doctor Habersham did, and with less fire but still as irreconcilable and
stubborn as old Alec Holston and a few others were still doing,
until in a few more years the last of them would have passed and
vanished in their turn too, obsolescent too: because this was a white
man's land; that was its fate, or not even fate but destiny, its high
destiny in the roster of the earth)—the veins, arteries, life- and
pulse-stream along which would flow the aggrandisement of harvest:
the gold: the cotton and the grain;

But above all, the courthouse: the center, the focus, the hub; sitting
looming in the center of the county's circumference like a single
cloud in its ring of horizon, laying its vast shadow to the uttermost
rim of horizon; musing, brooding, symbolic and ponderable, tall as
cloud, solid as rock, dominating all: protector of the weak, judiciate

and curb of the passions and lusts, repository and guardian of the
aspirations and the hopes; rising course by brick course during that
first summer, simply square, simplest Georgian colonial (this, by the
Paris architect who was creating at Sutpen's Hundred something
like a wing of Versailles glimpsed in a Lilliput's gothic nightmare—
in revenge, Gavin Stevens would say a hundred years later, when
Sutpen's own legend in the county would include the anecdote of
the time the architect broke somehow out of his dungeon and tried
to flee and Sutpen and his Negro head man and hunter ran him
down with dogs in the swamp and brought him back) since, as the
architect had told them, they had no money to buy bad taste with
nor even anything from which to copy what bad taste might still
have been within their compass; this one too still costing nothing
but the labor and—the second year now—most of that was slave
since there were still more slave owners in the settlement which
had been a town and named for going on two years now, already a
town and already named when the first ones waked up on that
yellow morning two years back:—men other than Holston and the
blacksmith (Compson was one now) who owned one or two or
three Negroes, besides Grenier and Sutpen who had set up camps
beside the creek in Compson's pasture for the two gangs of their
Negroes to live in until the two buildings—the courthouse and the
jail—should be completed. But not altogether slave, the boundmen,
the unfree, because there were still the white men too, the same
ones who on that hot July morning two and now three years ago
had gathered in a kind of outraged unbelief to fling, hurl up in
raging sweating impotent fury the little three-walled lean-to—the
same men (with affairs of their own they might have been attending
to or work of their own or for which they were being hired, paid,
that they should have been doing) standing or lounging about the
scaffolding and the stacks of brick and puddles of clay mortar for an
hour or two hours or half a day, then putting aside one of the
Negroes and taking his place with trowel or saw or adze, unbidden
or unreproved either since there was none present with the right
to order or deny; a stranger might have said probably for that
reason, simply because now they didn't have to, except that it was
more than that, working peacefully now that there was no outrage
and fury, and twice as fast because there was no urgency since this
was no more to be hurried by man or men than the burgeoning of a
crop, working (this paradox too to anyone except men like Grenier

and Compson and Peabody who had grown from infancy among
slaves, breathed the same air and even suckled the same breast with
the sons of Ham: black and white, free and unfree, shoulder to
shoulder in the same tireless lift and rhythm as if they had the same
aim and hope, which they did have as far as the Negro was capable,
as even Ratcliffe, son of a long pure line of Anglo-Saxon mountain
people and—destined—father of an equally long and pure line of
white trash tenant farmers who never owned a slave and never
would since each had and would imbibe with his mother's milk a
personal violent antipathy not at all to slavery but to black skins,
could have explained: the slave's simple child's mind had fired at
once with the thought that he was helping to build not only the
biggest edifice in the country, but probably the biggest he had ever
seen; this was all but this was enough) as one because it was theirs,
bigger than any because it was the sum of all and, being the sum
of all, it must raise all of their hopes and aspirations level with its
own aspirant and soaring cupola, so that, sweating and tireless and
unflagging, they would look about at one another a little shyly, a
little amazed, with something like humility too, as if they were
realising, or were for a moment at least capable of believing, that
men, all men, including themselves, were a little better, purer
maybe even, than they had thought, expected, or even needed to be.
Though they were still having a little trouble with Ratcliffe: the
money, the Holston lock-Chickasaw axle grease fifteen dollars; not
trouble really because it had never been an obstruction even three
years ago when it was new, and now after three years even the light
impedeless chip was worn by familiarity and custom to less than a
toothpick: merely present, merely visible, or that is, audible: and
no trouble *with* Ratcliffe because he made one too contraposed the
toothpick; more: he was its chief victim, sufferer, since where with
the others was mostly inattention, a little humor, now and then a
little fading annoyance and impatience, with him was shame, bafflement, a little of anguish and despair like a man struggling with a
congenital vice, hopeless, indomitable, already defeated. It was not
even the money any more now, the fifteen dollars. It was the fact
that they had refused it and, refusing it, had maybe committed a
fatal and irremediable error. He would try to explain it: 'It's like
Old Moster and the rest of them up there that run the luck, would
look down at us and say, Well well, looks like them durn pecker-
woods down there dont want them fifteen dollars we was going to

give them free-gratis-for-nothing. So maybe they dont want nothing from us. So maybe we better do like they seem to want, and let them sweat and swivet and scrabble through the best they can by themselves.'

Which they—the town—did, though even then the courthouse was not finished for another six years. Not but that they thought it was: complete: simple and square, floored and roofed and windowed, with a central hallway and the four offices—sheriff and tax assessor and circuit- and chancery-clerk (which—the chancery-clerk's office —would contain the ballot boxes and booths for voting)—below, and the courtroom and jury-room and the judge's chambers above —even to the pigeons and English sparrows, migrants too but not pioneers, inevictably urban in fact, come all the way from the Atlantic coast as soon as the town became a town with a name, taking possession of the gutters and eave-boxes almost before the final hammer was withdrawn, uxorious and interminable the one, garrulous and myriad the other. Then in the sixth year old Alec Holston died and bequeathed back to the town the fifteen dollars it had paid him for the lock; two years before, Louis Grenier had died and his heirs still held in trust on demand the fifteen hundred dollars his will had devised it, and now there was another newcomer in the county, a man named John Sartoris, with slaves and gear and money too like Grenier and Sutpen, but who was an even better stalemate to Sutpen than Grenier had been because it was apparent at once that he, Sartoris, was the sort of man who could even cope with Sutpen in the sense that a man with a sabre or even a small sword and heart enough for it could cope with one with an axe; and that summer (Sutpen's Paris architect had long since gone back to whatever place he came from and to which he had made his one abortive midnight try to return, but his trickle, flow of bricks had never even faltered: his molds and kilns had finished the jail and were now raising the walls of two churches and by the half-century would have completed what would be known through all north Mississippi and east Tennessee as *the* Academy, *the* Female Institute) there was a committee: Compson and Sartoris and Peabody (and *in absentia* Sutpen: nor would the town ever know exactly how much of the additional cost Sutpen and Sartoris made up): and the next year the eight disjointed marble columns were landed from an Italian ship at New Orleans, into a steamboat up the Mississippi to

Vicksburg, and into a smaller steamboat up the Yazoo and Sun-flower and Tallahatchie, to Ikkemotubbe's old landing which Sutpen now owned, and thence the twelve miles by oxen into Jefferson: the two identical four-column porticoes, one on the north and one on the south, each with its balcony of wroughtiron New Orleans grillwork, on one of which—the south one—in 1861 Sartoris would stand in the first Confederate uniform the town had ever seen, while in the Square below the Richmond mustering officers en-rolled and swore in the regiment which Sartoris as its colonel would take to Virginia as a part of Bee, to be Jackson's extreme left in front of the Henry house at First Manassas, and from both of which each May and November for a hundred years, bailiffs in their orderly appointive almost hereditary succession would cry without inflection or punctuation either 'oyes oyes honorable circuit court of Yoknapatawpha County come all and ye shall be heard' and beneath which for that same length of time too except for the seven years between '63 and '70 which didn't really count a century afterward except to a few irreconcilable old ladies, the white male citizens of the county would pass to vote for county and state offices, because when in '63 a United States military force burned the Square and the business district, the courthouse survived. It didn't escape: it simply survived: harder than axes, tougher than fire, more fixed than dynamite; encircled by the tumbled and blackened ruins of lesser walls, it still stood, even the topless smoke-stained columns, gutted of course and roofless, but immune, not one hair even out of the Paris architect's almost forgotten plumb, so that all they had to do (it took nine years to build; they needed twenty-five to restore it) was put in new floors for the two storeys and a new roof, and this time with a cupola with a four-faced clock and a bell to strike the hours and ring alarms; by this time the Square, the banks and the stores and the lawyers' and doctors' and dentists' offices, had been restored, and the English sparrows were back too which had never really deserted—the garrulous noisy independent swarms which, as though concomitant with, inextricable from regularised and roted human quarreling, had appeared in possession of cornices and gutter-boxes almost before the last nail was driven—and now the pigeons also, interminably murmurous, nesting in, already usurp-ing, the belfry even though they couldn't seem to get used to the bell, bursting out of the cupola at each stroke of the hour in frantic clouds, to sink and burst and whirl again at each succeeding stroke, until the last one: then vanishing back through the slatted louvers until nothing remained but the frantic and murmurous cooing like the fading echoes of the bell itself, the source of the alarm never recognised and even the alarm itself unremembered, as the actual stroke of the bell is no longer remembered by the vibration-fading air. Because they—the sparrows and the pigeons—endured, durable, a hundred years, the oldest things there except the courthouse centennial and serene above the town most of whose people now no longer even knew who Doctor Habersham and old Alec Holston and Louis Grenier were, had been; centennial and serene above the change: the electricity and gasoline, the neon and the crowded cacophonous air; even Negroes passing in beneath the balconies and into the chancery clerk's office to cast ballots too, voting for the same white-skinned rascals and demagogues and white supremacy champions that the white ones did—durable: every few years the county fathers, dreaming of bakshish, would instigate a movement to tear it down and erect a new modern one, but someone would at the last moment defeat them; they will try it again of course and be defeated perhaps once again or even maybe twice again, but no more than that. Because its fate is to stand in the hinterland of America: its doom is its longevity; like a man, its simple age is its own reproach, and after the hundred years, will become unbearable. But not for a little while yet; for a little while yet the sparrows and the pigeons: garrulous myriad and independent the one, the other uxorious and interminable, at once frantic and tranquil—until the clock strikes again which even after a hundred years, they still seem unable to get used to, bursting in one swirling explosion out of the belfry as though, the hour, instead of merely adding one puny infinitesimal more to the long weary increment since Genesis, had shattered the virgin pristine air with the first loud dingdong of time and doom.